ID0295196

MONTY'S FIGHT FOR VICTORY

MONTY'S FIGHT FOR VICTORY

Leo Kessler

This first world edition published in Great Britain 2006 by
SEVERN HOUSE PUBLISHERS LTD of
9–15 High Street, Sutton, Surrey SM1 1DF.
This first world edition published in the USA 2006 by
SEVERN HOUSE PUBLISHERS INC of
595 Madison Avenue, New York, N.Y. 10022.

Copyright © 2006 by Leo Kessler.

All rights reserved.
The moral right of the author has been asserted.

British Library Cataloguing in Publication Data

Kessler, Leo, 1926-
  Monty's fight for victory
  1. Montgomery of Alamein, Bernard Law Montgomery,
     Viscount, 1887-1976 - Fiction
  2. World War, 1939-1945 - Campaigns - Germany - Fiction
  3. War stories
  I. Title
  823.9'14 [F]

  ISBN-13: 978-0-7278-6416-1
  ISBN-10: 0-7278-6416-5

Except where actual historical events and characters are being
described for the storyline of this novel, all situations in this
publication are fictitious and any resemblance to living persons
is purely coincidental.

All Severn House titles are printed on acid-free paper.

Typeset by Palimpsest Book Production Ltd.,
Grangemouth, Stirlingshire, Scotland.
Printed and bound in Great Britain by
MPG Books Ltd., Bodmin, Cornwall.

To my darling Gill, whose constant help and support during a very difficult time made this possible.

'I don't know if we could have done it without Monty. It was his sort of battle. Whatever they say about him, he got us there.'

General Bedell-Smith
Eisenhower's Chief-of-Staff

'A beaten army not long ago master of Europe retreats before its pursuers. The goal is not long to be denied to those who have come so far and fought so well under proud and faithful leadership. Forward all on wings of flame to final victory.'

Churchill to his Troops on the Rhine, Germany,
March 1945

Book One
DEFEAT

One

The supreme commander shivered. The former French technical college in Rheims, which was now his head-quarters, had steam heat. Still on this grey March day it seemed damned cold to him. He told himself that perhaps the overwhelming problem he faced this day might have something to do with it. Now he had been working on it ever since the cables had landed on his desk at quarter to eight that morning. Still he had not come up with a solution.

He rose from his desk in what the GIs called 'Ike's little red schoolhouse' and lit another of the sixty Camels he smoked a day. A vein started to twitch nervously at the side of his right temple. He didn't seem to notice it. Outside at the station opposite, ancient French locomotives chugged back and forth. Down below, the Red Ball Express trucks, manned by Blacks, roared in a steady, never-ending column heading for the front in Germany. But the balding, middle-aged Supreme Commander with the nervous twitch heard neither the locomotives nor the trucks. His mind was concentrated totally on the two top secret cables that lay on his desk next to the furled 'Stars and Stripes' banner. Those damned cables demanded a decision from him, an over-whelming one, perhaps the most important he would ever make in all these months as commander of the great Anglo-American army.

The first cabled message to arrive had been from his boss in Washington, General Marshall. Marshall, who had made him what he was, had demanded to know what his

3

intentions were now that Germany was virtually defeated. Did he, General Eisenhower, not think he should direct his armies towards the Bavarian-Austrian Alps where Hitler had his home on a mountain at Berchtesgaden? Intelligence was reporting that the Nazis were organizing a last-ditch defence there with their most fanatical and elite troops. In the high snow-capped mountains the Germans might hold out for years; and America was sick of the war in Europe. The US press was demanding the 'boys' should be brought home some time before the summer of 1945.

The second cable was from his most senior commander, the 'Victor of El Alamein.' He'd not spoken to the pesky little Britisher Field Marshal Montgomery for six weeks now; he had been so angry with his subordinate. Now 'Monty' had had the audacity to signal not a *query*, but a *demand*. He wanted to drive with his own armies and the attached US Ninth Army straight from the Rhine and head right for the German capital, Berlin.

Gloomily, Eisenhower slumped back at his desk, which only a month before had belonged to some obscure French teacher, his head wreathed in cigarette smoke, wondering what he should do.

Over the last two years since he had first been sent to London a green and newly promoted one-star general, he had taken many tough decisions. Week in, week out, month after month, he had taken them. They had matured him, steeled him against the carping criticism of the envious, the impotent, the inferior, especially the British, who had now become the junior partner in the great Anglo-American coalition. But as he set there, smoking moodily this chilly late March day, he knew full well that the decision he would soon have to make would bring down on him the worst criticism he had ever been subjected to hitherto, especially if he adopted the 'Marshall' suggestion. The British, led by Montgomery and Premier Churchill, would fall on him like a ton of bricks.

Eisenhower told himself that there were only sufficient

supplies and men for one major push. Therefore it had to be either Bavaria or Berlin. If he gave Monty his head and allowed him to go hell-for-leather for Berlin, the Britisher would gain the kudos of final victory in Germany; how the little bastard would gloat.

The Supreme Commander actually shivered at the thought. Naturally that decision would infuriate his American commanders, Patton, Bradley and the like. They would be in charge of any drive on Bavaria. Take that away from them in favour of the Berlin deal and there'd be a near mutiny in the American Army camp. Patton especially would blow his top. But if he gave Patton and Bradley the go-ahead, all hell would break loose in London. The British press was actively anti-American as it was. They'd have a field day. Churchill would be forced to attack; and Churchill, the half-American,[*] was a formidable opponent when roused.

Eisenhower breathed out hard and wondered yet again why he had ever accepted the post of supreme commander. Hell, in 1941 as a lowly lieutenant colonel he would have been glad to accept the job of battalion commander. Now he was a five-star general, the only one on regular duty in the whole of the US Army. But was he happy? Was he hell! He lit yet another Camel from the one still glowing in the overflowing ashtray. He looked at his first draft yet once more, but he didn't get far with it. For there was a polite knock on his office door and, without waiting for an answer, Lieutenant Kay Summersby came in bearing his morning cup of coffee on a tray.

'Your java, sir,' she announced and winked.

He forced himself to wink back. After all, here he was a balding old boy, who was very much married, being idolized by a former model with green eyes and a mass of red hair, who was half his age.

'Thanks, Kay,' he said, forcing that ear-to-ear smile of his which had become famous throughout the Free World,

---

[*] Churchill's mother was an American.

as she moved across the room with the sexy grace of a former model, and put the steaming mug of coffee on his desk.

She smiled her beautiful smile and using the old GI phrase said, 'Nothing too good for the boys in the service, sir.'

'Cut out the "sir", Kay,' he said, his smile vanishing.

She looked at his worn, lined face, with the worry lines creasing his high bald forehead. 'Tough morning, Ike?' she asked, obviously concerned about the man who had already promised her he would divorce his 'Mamie', his nagging wife, back in the States, and marry her when the opportunity arose.

'Yeah,' he agreed, taking a careful sip of the hot coffee. 'A regular sonovabitch, if you'll pardon my French, Kay.'

She touched his nicotine-stained hand briefly. 'Anything you can tell me about, Ike?'

'Hell, Kay, you know I have no secrets from you. Over the years you've gotten to know more top secrets than most of my brass.' He tapped the cable from Montgomery marked in the damned Englishman's own hand: For Ike's Eyes Only, and told her his dilemma. 'So you see, Kay, this day I've got to make a decision that's gonna hurt somebody at the top, whatever I do.' He shook his head. 'Kay, I've got to tell you – it's one helluva mess.'

There was silence in the cold office for a few moments, as each of them pondered the problem. Outside the roar of the Red Ball Express trucks had ceased. Perhaps there had been an accident. Everyone knew that the 'darkies', as Eisenhower called his black soldiers, were lousy drivers. In the corridor, a peevish voice was complaining, 'I don't know what gets into those GI clerks of ours. I mean to say, what does a goddam private first class need a French maid for? Shoot, it's bad enough for officers like us.'

Someone else laughed. 'Grow up, Captain. The GIs don't need no French maid to clean out their billets, that's for sure.'

6

Eisenhower frowned. The little interchange outside in the corridor reminded him of his exposed position here in this new French HQ. Here there was an enormous staff of over 5,000 soldiers, more than a couple of regiments of infantry. All of them were living on the gravy train from GI to general, billeted in the fancy chateaux of the local Rheims champagne barons and the like. If the press ever found out how his HQ staff lived with their French mistresses, fancy French chow, even their goddam poodles, while the GIs slogged it out at the front on cold C-rations, there'd be one hell to pay. Marshall in Washington, puritan that he was, would see that heads rolled – and one of those heads might well be that of Dwight D. Eisenhower.

Kay, sitting on the edge of his desk, swinging her shapely nylon-clad legs back and forth, broke the silence with, 'Look Ike, you're an American, aren't you?'

He nodded.

'Well, if you're an American, you have to make a decision that will be acceptable to your fellow Americans. Besides, Ike, when we've won this war, you know, you'll be eligible for the highest office in the land.'

Eisenhower jerked up his head, suddenly very alert. 'What d'you mean, Kay?'

'Politics – the Presidency.'

He looked at the pretty Irish woman, as if she had suddenly gone crazy.

'*Politics . . . the Presidency,*' he echoed stupidly.

'Come off it, Ike! You should know better than me. After every successful war that the USA has fought, the leading American generals have always been proposed as candidates for the highest office. Look at Washington . . . Look at Grant.'

Eisenhower was flattered, but at the same time hesitant. 'Well, I don't know about that, Kay,' he began hesitantly.

She leaned over – he caught an enticing glimpse of smooth white thigh above the nylons – and squeezed his hand. 'Ike, I'm firmly convinced that one day you're going to be President of the United States. For that reason, you've got to play this business here this morning very carefully.'

'How, Kay?'

'Like this. Your personal priority now is not winning the war against Germany. We've already crossed the Rhine and it's only a matter of weeks, perhaps even days, before the Krauts throw in the towel. Now, Ike, you've got to look out for yourself. You've got to make yourself as popular as you can back in the States, now while you're in the public eye. Once the war's over, the average John Doe stateside will have other things on his mind than the war in Europe —'

'I understand that, Kay,' he broke in. Outside the trucks of the Red Ball Express were moving again and the sound reminded him that he had to make that urgent overwhelming decision this day. 'But how does this affect my – er – political career, Kay?'

'Like this. You must make sure, especially to the people in the States, that it was their own *American* boys who won the final victory over the Jerries. After all, the USA is fielding three soldiers to every one that the British have in Europe under your command. Who cares about Churchill, Montgomery and all the rest of those snooty British back in London? The British have had their day. Sooner or later they'll lose their Empire and then they'll be nobodies, just a little island off the coast of Europe.' She paused momentarily for breath, her pretty face a little flushed with so much urgent talk.

He waited, running over what she had just said in his head. She was right of course, but naturally things weren't as easy as she imagined. Still, she was making her point and it might make the decision ahead of him easier.

'Let's face it, Ike,' she continued. 'You don't like Montgomery, do you?'

He nodded cautiously.

'It's nearly two years ago now since he won the Battle of El Alamein. Since then, what has he done?' She shrugged eloquently. '*Nothing*, but try to upstage you, darling, and make your life miserable.' Her green eyes flashed and her jaw hardened. Ike told himself that Kay Summersby, his one time driver who today was perhaps the most important woman in the whole of SHAEF',* was a tough cookie. 'You owe him nothing. So why do you bother with his wishes? The only decision you can make this day, Ike, is give their heads to your American commanders. Let Patton drive to Bavaria and forget Berlin.'

'But what am I going to do with Montgomery then? He's got nearly a million men under his command, after all, Kay.'

'Let him play soldier elsewhere. You know how slow Montgomery moves. By the time he thinks your decision through, the war will be over.'

'But Berlin, Kay—'

'Forget Berlin,' she cut him off sharply. 'It's only a bloody place name on the map. Let the Russians have it if they want it. They'll take it before Montgomery gets started anyway. Signal Patton to get moving towards Bavaria. You know what Ole Blood an' Guts is like. He'll probably be champing at the bit already. Once you give him the go-ahead, Ike, he'll be off like a shot. And you can rely on him to carry out the mission successfully. That way he and the US Army – and more importantly, *you* – will grab the headlines you'll need for your future career in politics.' She spread out her hands, the nails bright red with varnish, as if they had been dipped in blood. 'Imagine the headline, Ike. "*Ike the conqueror of Nazi Germany!*" Hell, that alone is worth a couple of million votes when the time comes.'

*Supreme Allied Command.

9

'You think so, Kay,' Eisenhower said, a little over-whelmed by it all.

'I damn well *know* so, Ike.'

Again she leaned over his desk and revealed more of that delightful naked thigh. She thrust his yellow writing pad towards him. She ordered the man who was in charge of the destinies, the life or death, of five million young men, 'Come on, let's not waste any more time. Get to it.'

'Get to what?'

She grinned at him maliciously. 'Get to drafting that signal to that little fart Monty, as Patton calls him, telling him he's out. He's not going to Berlin this year or any other year for that matter.'

Suddenly Ike's face lit up and he shared her malicious grin. 'Of course, you're right, Kay.'

'I always am – or nearly always am.'

Ike seized his pen and started writing:

As soon as you have joined hands with Bradley[*] the Ninth US Army will revert to Bradley's command. Bradley will be responsible for mopping up.

Leaning over Eisenhower's shoulder now, Kay Summersby said enthusiastically as the former continued writing, 'That's the way, Ike darling . . . Now give Montgomery the Berlin bit . . . make him squirm. Think of the way he's treated you in the past, Ike.'

'Yeah,' Ike agreed, not looking up from the yellow scratch pad. 'The first time I met him in the desert as a new brigadier general he told me to stop smoking in his august presence as if I was some goddam shave-tail second lieutenant.'

She nodded and said almost as if to herself, 'As my old

[*]General Bradley, Commander of the US 12th Army Group and Montgomery's equivalent.

biddy of an Irish grandmother would have said, "and bad cess to the devil . . ." He bloody well deserves all that's coming his way this day.'

Outside, the trucks of the Red Ball Express continued to rumble their way to the front in Germany with their cargoes of sudden death.

Two

All was chaos, noise and bloody horror. Cherry-red flame stabbed the pre-dawn darkness, penetrating the brown drifting smoke of the battle raging in the medieval German village. Obscenely, mortars belched. A heavy machine gun chattered like an angry woodpecker. Tracer, white, green, red, zipped urgently into the burning sky. For a moment or two the men's uplifted faces were coloured an unreal, garish hue. On both sides the plaintive cries of the wounded, British and German, rose above the angry snap-and-crack of the surprise small-arms battle, lamenting, cursing, pleading for help, '*Sanitäter* . . .? Stretcher-bearers . . .?' and in sheer panicked fear, 'God, someone give's a hand, mates, *I'm blind*!'

Major Savage cursed. For a week now he and his elite of the British Sixth Airborne Reconnaissance Regiment had been advancing from their drop zone on the enemy bank of the Rhine, with hardly any trouble, save from some suicidal kid in the uniform of the Hitler Youth. He could have counted his company's casualties on the fingers of both hands. As Sergeant Meek, driving the armoured jeep next to him, had commented, 'Christ, Major, after Normandy this is roses, roses all the frigging way!'

Now they had walked right into a trap. Two companies of German officer cadets, all veterans of six months on the *Wehrmacht*'s Eastern Front: fanatical Nazis the bunch of them, tougher, better and more determined than the *Waffen SS* themselves. Again Savage cursed. It was all his fault.

12

His men were dying up front because he hadn't recce'd the village properly. He'd just bashed on regardless, believing the village would be a walkover.

Savage ducked as a burst of slugs ripped the length of the wall next to the jeep. Behind him his gunner pressed the trigger of his twin Brownings. Tracer hissed across the street in a lethal morse. A shrill scream. A German hurtled from an upper window of the half-timbered house opposite. He slammed into the pavement like a sack of wet cement. 'Good show, Corporal Hawkins,' Savage began.

He didn't finish. A stick grenade whipped through the smoke. Next to him, Meek, face lathered in sweat despite the morning cold, swung the wheel to the right madly. Just in time. Only feet away the German grenade exploded in red fury. Glowing razor-sharp shrapnel flew everywhere. Up front Savage and Meek ducked, as the deadly shards howled off the side of the jeep. Behind them the corporal slumped over his twin Brownings, his shattered face slipping down like molten red wax.

Savage had had enough. He rose to his feet. He cupped his dirty hands about his mouth. 'Sunray to all,' he yelled above the murderous racket, punctuated by the screams, yells and cries of agony of the paras and the German cadets, fighting and dying in the burning German village. 'Bren gunners fire all out . . . Take alternative side of the street . . . We're pulling back . . . Pulling back . . . Don't leave the wounded . . . *PULL BACK!*'

Veterans of Normandy, the Battle of the Bulge and the Rhine drop as they were, the paras knew when they were beaten and they respected the CO for knowing that, too. If he had been some young hotshot straight from Blighty, he would have them battling it out with the Jerries until there was nothing left of the company. Not scarfaced, battle-wise Major Savage. Young as he was, the 'Old Man', as they called him, knew it was time to run away and fight another day.

Already the bren gunners were beginning to belt away. They blasted the German-held houses to their front, spraying them with magazine after magazine of ammunition, trying to force the officer cadets to keep their heads down, while their comrades pulled back, dragging their wounded, groaning comrades with them.

Savage's jeep was hit. One of the cadets had sneaked up behind the burning shop, bearing the legend '*Rosenblum-Pferdeschlachter*' and the old warning '*Juden Unerwünscht**', and fired his rocket launcher, the *Panzerfaust*, straight at the little vehicle. The front tyres exploded. Smoke started to pour from the ruptured engine. Behind, the Browning gunner slumped dead over his machine guns, arms outstretched, a pattern of blood around his head like some latterday Christ on the Cross

Savage shook his head in despair. Meek looked up at him as they scrambled out of the smoking jeep which could explode at any moment. 'Don't take on sir . . . It's just one o' them things.'

Savage bit his bottom lip. 'It shouldn't have happened . . . What a bloody mess, Sergeant. I—' He never finished. Meek, dazed as he was from the explosion of the rocket, had spotted the cadet sneaking up on them before he could fire his machine pistol. Meek beat him to it. With his hand tucked in close to his right hip, he snapped off a sharp vicious burst from his own weapon. At that range he couldn't miss. The German flung up his arms in a wild gesture of despair. A sudden line of bloody buttonholes appeared across his chest. He felt into a shell hole, the bullets from his Schmeisser ripping purposelessly into the air above him.

Then the officer and the NCO were pulling back, firing to left and right, urging the wounded to ever greater haste

---

*Horse-Butcher. Jews not wished for.

as a roar went up from the cadets, spotting that the Tommies were quitting the village.

'*Alles für Deutschland. Heil Hitler . . . Alles für Deutschland.*' Ignoring the fire from the brengunners covering the paras' retreat, they surged forward, yelling their battlecry.

The rickety bridge, which two hours before Savage's men had crossed so confidently, loomed up out of the fog of war. A heap of dead bodies, German and British lay there, killed in hand-to-hand fighting, like passionate lovers who had succumbed in some final embrace. Savage looked away. He had been the cause of their death. For a moment he wished he could lie there too, atoning for his carelessness and over-optimism. Then he pulled himself together. 'We'll cover the line of the canal . . . I'll whistle up the gunners . . . Give us covering fire, Sergeant.'

'Sir,' Meek answered. He could see the Old Man was suffering.

Together they crossed the piled-up bodies, their faces contorted at the thought that they were crunching over the corpses of their comrades; young men in the prime of life who had joked and laughed as they had drunk their canteens of char and wolfed down their wads of corned beef and plum jam before they had started, joking, 'It'll be as easy as falling off a log, mates.' Now they were dead.

Behind them, one of the cadets yelling '*Alles für Deutschland*', as if he were drunk or drugged, or perhaps both, came racing over the bridge. Meek snapped off a burst from the hip without appearing to aim. The German staggered on a few paces, as if seen in slow motion. His legs started to give away. The stick grenade dropped from his suddenly nerveless fingers. He stopped abruptly and held on to the bridge. He watched the grenade spluttering at his feet without moving, not attempting to escape before it was too late. The grenade exploded; the cadet hadn't a chance at such close range. The blast took him over the parapet. With dramatic slowness, like some expert high diver preparing to do a double sommersault at an exhibition, he went straight down into the canal. He didn't come up.

The last jeep came racing up. It zig-zagged from left to right wildly, trying to dodge the angry German fire. The wounded packed into it moaned and cried out in panic.

'Christ,' Meek yelled above the noise, 'the jeep's covered in red crosses!'

Savage didn't respond. This was total war. The Jerries no longer respected such things; neither did the paras for that matter.

'Keep going, Sims,' he yelled at the driver, blood pouring down from beneath his red beret. 'Get the poor bastards out, while you can.' He forgot the wounded. He had to try to save the rest. 'Spread out men!' he cried as the Germans started moving forward again, convinced they'd got the Tommies on the run.

The paras needed no urging, now they'd got the canal between them and the Germans. They knew what the Old Man was going to do. He did so. Hastily, savage grabbed the mike and started yelling for artillery support.

Savage got it, almost immediately. And no one could match Montgomery's artillery. With a banshee-like howl, the twenty-five pounders, some half a mile away, opened up. In an instant the world turned crazy. Flight after flight of shells flew overhead. The paras, or so they said later, could actually feel the missiles flying over them.

The attacking Germans hesitated. Not for long. Suddenly, as great smoking brown shell holes appeared like the work of gigantic moles in front of them, they went to ground. Veterans that they were, they knew what was coming. The Tommies were ranging in. First they'd fire a salvo to the attackers' front, then to the rear. The third salvo, however, would be dead on target. Madly, hugging the ground like frenzied passionate lovers, the German officer cadets

scraped away the damp March soil, trying to bury themselves before the full fury of the English artillery hit them.

On the other side of the canal, Savage breathed out hard
and relaxed a little. The pressure was off. They were saved
for the time being. The Royal Artillery of 12th Corps would
give them the cover they needed, at least until the German
artillery started to return counter-fire on the English gunners'
positions. By then he would have commenced his final
retreat – for that's what it really was. He had failed to take
his objective. Now there was no other word for it: they
were retreating, bloody well running away.

Savage wiped the sweat and the grime from his forehead
beneath his ragged old para red beret with its tarnished
silver wing. 'Meek,' he said, raising his voice above the
racket the British guns were making. 'What do the casualties look like?'

Meek, who was well over six feet and broad with it,
certainly didn't live up to his name, especially now as he
waited for any German officer cadet who was foolish enough
to show himself. His tough face was flushed with anger as
he replied, 'Bloody, sir . . . very bloody . . .' His look
changed to one of concern when he saw Savage actually
flinch at his words. 'It looks as if A Company's about had
it, sir. But, 'he added hastily, 'some of our blokes might
just be Jerry prisoners. The Jerries took us by surprise at
the beginning . . .' His voice trailed away to nothing. Savage
was no longer listening; he was too shocked by the news
that his cherished A, to which he had belonged ever since
he had been a raw subaltern in North Africa back in 1943,
had suffered such a grievous loss: a loss for which he blamed
himself.

'It just shouldn't have happened, Sergeant,' he faltered
in the same instant that on the other side of the canal, the
first German 88mm cannon opened up. There was a shrill,
high-pitched sound like a great piece of canvas being ripped
apart. A second later, the feared German gun's shell hissed

over their heads and slammed into the British artillery lines half a mile behind where they lay.

Meek, with a weak attempt to break the tension, folded his big paws together and intoned in the manner of the battalion padre, 'For what we are about to receive let the Good Lord make us thankful . . .'

Savage shook his head like a man trying hard to wake up from a bad dream. Then he was himself again, the veteran paratroop commander who had won his first Military Cross at the age of 19, 'All right, Sergeant Meek, let's get the lads back. Those who are still unwounded will cover the retreat of the wounded . . . I'm in charge here.'

Meek hesitated.

Savage didn't give him a chance to object, he snapped above the racket made by the feared 88 as another joined in the counter-fire, 'Move it, Sergeant . . . At the double now!'

Sergeant Meek 'moved it' . . .

Brigadier Poett was waiting for the survivors as they came staggering in, past his HQ, heading for the Casualty Clearing Station, where the MO and his medical orderlies were already waiting for them in their blood-stained aprons. Tall and skinny, his face under the rimless para helmet looking like some Crusader knight, he showed no emotion at the sight of the wounded. Some tried to salute; others were too badly hit to even attempt a salute, supported as they were by their battle-weary comrades. A few, shocked by what had amounted to a massacre, groped their way to the medics, one arm extended as if they were blind, mumbling meaningless phrases to themselves.

Brigadier Poett frowned. He had seen types like that before. They were not a pleasant sight. They were broken men, wounded not in the body, but in their minds. They were no further use to him or the Parachute Regiment of which they had once been so proud. They were finished. He dismissed them and turned his attention to young Savage who was coming up with the rearguard, the handful of unwounded men of A Company who had covered the withdrawal. Savage looked weary and miserable. Poett could guess why and with most other officers under his command he would not have particularly bothered; he would have let them get over their shock, the humiliation of defeat, in their own time. Not Savage. He was too valuable an officer. After all, how many officers in the Sixth Airborne Reconnaissance Regiment had won the Military Cross twice over before they were twenty-one? Officers like that had to be nurtured.

Savage came to attention and gave him a weary salute, his handsome if scarred face crestfallen. Poett didn't even let him report. He said straight off, 'Rotten luck, John. I'd forgotten how bloody-minded old Jerry is when he can field his really first-class troops.'

'A Company shouldn't have been allowed to walk into a trap like that, sir. I was a bloody fool not to realize it was going to be a bad show. I deserve to be court-martialled for it. A Company is a write-off.'

Poett pretended not to hear. He said, 'See to your chaps first, John. Then come and have a scotch with me. You look as if you need it, old chap. I've got something to say to you.' Poett saw the changed look on Savage's face and added hastily, 'No, John, nothing like that. I've got a posting for you and the rest of your fit chaps. You're going to the rear.'

'Not the *rear*, sir!' the younger officer blurted out, while close by Sergeant Meek listening discreetly to the conversation between the two of them, said, his mind racing, 'Bugger that for a tale of soldiers. I'm not going to any sodding RHU!'*

---

*Reinforcement Holding Unit. A unit where soldiers went to wait for a posting. It was a place dreaded by soldiers who had once belonged to a field unit. There they were alone without comrades, upon whom their lives depended in an active fighting outfit.

Poett forced himself to laugh, though the wounded every-where and the young blinded para wailing in the nearby ditch didn't give him much encouragement to do so. 'Don't worry, John. You're not going to a RHU or some pencil-pushing job on the staff. In fact, you might well, for all I know, be going up in the world for a lowly major.'

'Sir?'

'Yes. You're being sent to Second Army HQ at my recom-mendation.'

'Second Army HQ, sir?' Savage echoed a little foolishly.

'Yes to see the Master personally.'

Poett saw the look of bewilderment on Savage's young face grow even more. 'Yes, that's right, the *Master* . . . No less a person than Field Marshal Sir Bernard Law Montgomery personally.'

Nearby Meek whistled softly through his missing front teeth. 'Christ Almighty,' he said in his broad Yorkshire accent. 'Well, I'll go to our frigging house!'

Three

The little field marshal had been walking back to his caravan, looted from an Italian general back in the desert years before, carrying his glass of warm milk, when the signals officer came out from the main HQ, calling, 'Sir, sir, urgent message from the supreme commander.'

Montgomery frowned. He didn't like to be disturbed after dinner in the mess with his young allied officers, his 'eyes and ears', as he called them, for every morning they sallied forth to the fighting fronts to discover and report to him personally what was *really* going on. At this time of the night, he wanted to retire to his caravan, drink his milk, say his prayers, take a pee in his chamber pot and then drop off into an untroubled sleep. Great commander that he was, he knew that he needed all the sleep he could get to face the manifold problems of the next day.

He signed for the signal while the fearful signals officer explained, 'Top priority, sir . . . For your eyes only.' The young major knew, too, that the Master, as his officers called Montgomery, hated having his routine disturbed. It was said that even during the ten day crucial battle of El Alamein, he had always retired to his bunk at ten and had promptly fallen asleep; he had never changed his personal timetable by as much as a minute.

Montgomery snapped, 'Stand by outside the caravan in case I need you, Major.' He then retired to the privacy of his Italian caravan. There he finished off the rest of his milk before it got cold and then, propping his army-issue

21

spectacles at the end of his beaky nose, he opened the 'eyes only' signal from Eisenhower.

Swiftly he ran through the opening paragraphs. Like most Yanks, Eisenhower liked to waffle, he told himself. Good commanders, he believed, should be succinct and straight to the point, just as Churchill was with his one line memos. *Bradley will be responsible for mopping up . . . and with minimum delay*, he read, *will deliver the main thrust on the axis Erfurt-Leipzig-Dresden to join hands with the Russians.*

He paused and asked himself what possible strategic value would an attack in that direction have? Then he spotted the real reason for this 'eyes only' signal to him: *The place – Berlin – has become, so far as I am concerned, nothing but a geographical location and I have never been interested in these. My purpose is to destroy the enemy's force and his power to resist!*

Berlin – a geographical location! Montgomery almost dropped Eisenhower's message with shock. Berlin was the capital of Germany: the symbol of Nazi power, the head of the whole Hitler beast. Amputate that head with one swift cutting stroke and the beast would collapse and die. With Berlin gone, there would be no need to fight on; the German armies all over Europe would surrender. Montgomery had been in no doubt about that.

Sitting there on the edge of the little wooden, army-issue chair with the camp outside settling down for the night, staring at the single photograph, that of German Field Marshal Model, who had replaced Rommel as his chief opponent now, the little field marshal breathed, 'For what? Why the Erfurt-Leipzig-Dresden axis? And what was to be the role of his own armies? If they were not to march on Berlin, as he had always believed in these last months under Eisenhower's command, what was to be their objective? It could only be some kind of side-show. Had this been what he had been fighting for for nearly six years? Had all the effort, the bloody sacrifice of his young men's lives over two continents, Africa and Europe, and a dozen different European countries, been for *this*?' In despair, the little field marshal, alone in his caravan, sucked his teeth, hands clutching the signal from the supreme commander.

But even as he sat there, digesting the impact of the signal in those first few minutes after reading it, Montgomery had known the answer to his as yet unspoken questions. The new strategy had been created, now that the war in Germany was virtually won, in order to heighten the prestige of the US Army and sway public opinion back in the United States. The world must know that it had been the US Army which had won the war in Europe as it would undoubtedly do against Japan, too. The rest of the war here in Germany would be fought, *not* for strategic or political purposes, but for the sake of American prestige.

His skinny face twisted as if he were in actual physical pain, the little field marshal slammed his puny fist down on the table in front of him so that it trembled. What fools the Yanks were! Didn't they realize that war was a kind of continuation of politics and that young men's liveas shouldn't be thrown away in battle if there was no political advantage in the future to justify their supreme sacrifice. 'What absolute, bloody simple-minded fools, they are!' he moaned, looking up at the roof of his little caravan that night, as if he were pleading with God himself to do something.

God didn't!

Montgomery's normal precise, logical mind ran riot that night. If Berlin wasn't taken and left to the Russians, as Eisenhower evidently thought it should, the Soviet Red Army under the dictator Marshal Stalin, whom Eisenhower was blind enough to call 'Uncle Joe', as if he were some kindly elderly uncle, would do what it liked with central Germany. What could a war-weary Britain, a weak and corrupt France and a beaten, disarmed and divided Germany do to stop him, especially as the Yanks would pull out as soon as possible, as they had done after the First World War? The further Eisenhower allowed the Russians to penetrate into Germany after taking Berlin, the sooner they'd reach the Channel coast one day. Then it might well be the summer of 1940, Dunkirk, and the British being kicked out of the continent all over again. The whole war, as far as Britain was concerned, might well have been fought for nothing.

How long he sat there, considering the grave, even overwhelming problem raised by Eisenhower's surprise signal, Montgomery could never remember later. But by the time he had calmed down and had started to reason an alternative, the camp had settled down for the night. All was silent. The only sounds were the distant rumble of the heavy barrage up at the front, the steady slow crunch of the sentry's boots as he crunched up and down the gravel path leading up to the Italian caravan, and the occasional stiffled cough of the signals' major as he still waited for any message that the Master might care to send.

Still sunk in gloom, Montgomery considered the Russian problem. He had already dismissed the drive on Berlin. Realist that he was, he knew the Yanks would have their way. They'd head purposelessly for Czechoslovakia and the Austro-Bavarian Alps. Berlin was out. So now, with Germany virtually defeated, he'd have to tackle the new enemy, their ally, the Russians.

From London and his own intelligence sources, in particular from Ultra[*] Montgomery already knew that Russia was landing para-agents far behind the German lines in the north of Germany. Indeed there had been some vague and as yet unconfirmed reports that the Red Army had dropped agents as far north as Denmark, still occupied by a German army, over a half a million strong. Here, so it was said, they were

[*] The war-winning British decoding operation at Bletchley Park in the Home Counties.

24

trying to co-ordinate the efforts of the very strong and anti-German Danish communist party. What that meant, Montgomery felt, was easy to guess; you didn't need a crystal ball for that.

After they had captured Berlin, the Russians wouldn't stop at the River Elbe further to the west. They would cross before the Western Allies could do and head for the coast of the Baltic Sea.

Then there'd be no stopping the Red Army. In their present state, the Germans, although deadly scared of the Russians who were already raping and pillaging their way across the almost beaten Reich, would be only capable of putting up token resistance. The Russians would break through them, push through the Schleswig-Holstein peninsula, right into neighbouring Denmark. Once there, they would control the exit from the Baltic into the North Sea. People might say that they would withdraw under pressure; Montgomery didn't believe it. In every other country they had occupied in the last few months, the Russians had set up a 'popular fraternal government', backed by Red Army bayonets, and those governments had been simply tools of Kremlin imperialist policies. In short, the Baltic would become a Soviet lake and a direct threat to the British homeland on the other side of the North Sea.

'So what am I going to do about it?' Montgomery asked himself aloud, forgetting that the sentry and the signals major might hear him. He frowned. He didn't want them telling tales that the Master was going to his dotage and was 'beginning to talk to himself'. Great commanders should never show signs of weakness to their subordinates. He stared at the cynical face of Model on the wall opposite. Model stared back at him through his monocle quizzically, almost as if he could feel for his opponent at this moment. Model was heading for a defeat in a short few weeks. Perhaps he, Montgomery, was heading the same way.

Montgomery dismissed Model hastily. The German commander-in-chief was almost a man of the past. He had to think of the future, not only of this country, but his own. After years of defeat after defeat, he had given Britain its first real victory at El Alamein and a few months later had driven the Hun out of Africa. Now he was Britain's most celebrated hero. Was he, who had contributed so much to the Hun's defeat and the military glory of his native country, now to sink into the obscurity from which he had come in 1940?

A lot of people back home disliked him. The King did, for one. Churchill would support him as long as he produced victories. But there were many in the military establishment in London, whom he had crossed over the last years, who would revel in his downfall. Up to the crossing of the Rhine in this last week of March 1945, he had been a military hero in Britain. What would happen now to his reputation if he sat on his thumbs, impotently, doing nothing, while the Yanks gained the kudos of final victory in Europe? His skinny face hardened. He had to produce something out of the hat – and soon.

'By God yes!' Again he spoke the words aloud, not caring now whether anyone heard him or not. Sudden resolution flushed his face. Tired as he was usually at this time of the night, he felt the adrenalin and fresh energy surging through his lean body. Even now there was still a chance to gain something for his country – and naturally for himself, too – while Eisenhower made a balls of things over Berlin. He rose to his feet and walked hurriedly to the big map of North Germany, criss-crossed with the red and blue chinagraph marks which indicated the progress of his own and enemy divisions.

For what seemed a considerable while, he peered at it carefully, glasses perched at the end of his beaky nose, his bright blue eyes sparkling with new determination. Then he had it. It was something that he did not need anyone's approval to carry out. Churchill would approve politically; he hated the Reds. As for Eisenhower and Supreme Headquarters in France, they'd be only too glad to believe that for once he was carrying out orders and was reconciled to the side-show that the supreme commander had dreamed up for him. He pulled off his glasses hurriedly and went to the door.

The signals officer leaned against the camouflaged netting that helped to conceal the little forward headquarters. Now he was tired; he would have dearly loved to have turned in. But he daren't risk it. He didn't want the Master sending him off to the front to have his head blown off by some stupid Jerry at this stage of the war. So he kept himself awake – and warm – with the thoughts of the nice little Belgie whore he'd met behind the *Bon Marché* the last time he'd had a forty-eight hour leave in Brussels. He had thought, as she stood in the blacked-out doorway, flashing her torch on the lower half of her body so that he'd know she was on the game, that he might be offered a quick 'knee-trembler' in that same doorway for a handful of greasy Belgie france. But gosh how he had been mistaken. She had given him the works. Knickers off, French kiss, a bit of perverted sex that would have had him in jail in England if he'd been caught doing it. It had been one hundred percent better – and cheaper – than what those part-time lady whores offered on London's Shaftesbury Avenue.

'Major!' Montgomery's voice cut sharply into his sexual reverie. He straightened up as if he had just been shot and dropped the cigarette he had been smoking to the grass.

'Sorry, sir,' he commenced. 'I wouldn't have smoked if I'd known—'

'Never mind, my boy,' Montgomery chortled in his good humour now that he had made his decision. 'When you've taken down this message and encoded it for me, I am personally going to give you one of Mr Churchill's own cigars. He left them behind when he came to view the crossing of the Rhine a few days ago. And you know,' he added with a chuckle, 'I do not touch the noxious weed.'

'Yessir, I know sir,' the major stuttered. He knew it well. Everyone at HQ was in deadly fear of being caught smoking by the rabid anti-cigarette field marshal. He'd even told the King himself off for smoking during one of his briefings.

'Now then . . . in you come and let's get cracking. There's no time to waste. Urgent signal to General F. Browning, Deputy-Commander, 18th Allied Airborne Corps . . .'

Four

'Get them knees up . . . Let's have a bit o' movement there . . . Now then, you bunch o' pregnant ducks, by the right – quick march!' the drill sergeant's voice rose to a hysterical crescendo as he thrust his pacing stick under his right arm and set off briskly, blanco powder rising everywhere as the prisoners slapped their sides and moved off with him. 'Left . . . right, left . . . come on now, me lucky lads, remember who you are, bags o' swank now!'

Heavy ammunition boots crashing up and down on the old Belgian parade ground, they crossed the square under the eagle eye of the sergeant major standing just behind the commandant and Major Savage.

'They come here as military criminals,' the military prison's commandant said, a weak-faced captain, who kept touching his trim Ronald Coleman moustache as if to reassure himself that it was still there. 'And leave it, soldiers.'

Behind him the sergeant major, who had the look of an old sweat, whispered out of the side of his mouth to Sergeant Meek, 'Loves hissen, he docs with his frigging tash. All bullshit of course.'

'Drill, drill and more drill, that's our motto here,' the commandant said. 'That makes real soldiers of 'em, you know, Major.'

Savage didn't comment. He was observing the prisoners too carefully. He saw that they came from all the British Army's regiments. They wore the glengarry of the Scottish infantry, the black berets of the Tank Corps, there were

29

even a few stiff pre-war caps of the Guards. But he was looking for the red beret of the Parachute Regiment.

That's why 'Boy' Browning, the handsome ex-Guards officer who was in charge of Britain's airborne forces, had sent him here. 'Before you see Monty, Savage,' he had said straight off, as soon as he, Savage, had reported to the Airborne Corps HQ, 'I want you to find bodies. Monty's a stickler for having the minute details solved before he discusses a problem. The fine details as far as you and I are concerned are these. We need bodies.' Browning had stared out of the window of his office as if he expected to find those 'bodies' outside. But there were none save for a few wan paras, limping about in gym shoes and obviously doing 'light duties', carrying out some easy fatigue or other. Further away there were several in the blue uniform of a military hospital, one without a foot supporting himself on crutches. Obviously, at headquarters at least, the Airborne Corps was running out of those celebrated bodies.

'Our losses in parachute troops have been very high, Savage,' Browning had continued. 'As you know, virtually the whole of the First Airborne Division was virtually wiped out at Arnhem last September. Thousands alone went into the Hun bag. And during the Rhine crossing, your own division, the Sixth Airborne, lost about a third of its effectives.' Browning had shaken his handsome head. 'It's a bad show, Savage, a really bad show.'

Savage had felt a sigh of relief that he had not been singled out as an officer who had caused some of those losses, which resulted in the lack of bodies. He had nodded his head, but had said nothing. He knew general officers. They always did the talking and the deciding. He had waited to find out what Browning had decided. When his decision had come, it had surprised him. For he had always thought of Browning as a typical guards officer, not too bright, not too imaginative, believing that his soldiers had only one thought, which was to be smart, never ask questions of an officer and to die bravely, never asking why they should die.

'There must be some of our chaps tucked away behind the lines,' he had announced. 'Now with Monty breathing down our necks, we can go turfing 'em out of every office or cookhouse or the like. We've got to concentrate on the spots where, with a bit of luck, we might find the most of them, bad boys that they may be – the command military prisons.'

'The glasshouse!' Savage had heard himself exclaim with surprise. 'Exactly,' Browning had smiled and swept back his moustache as if pleased with himself. 'You start immediately at the one we've got just outside Brussels on the road from the Belgie capital to Louvain . . .'

One of the prisoners, a puny fellow with the insignia of the Pay Corps stumbled and sprawled full length on the wet concrete. The drill sergeant was on to him like a shot. He ran to him, while the others halted and automatically started marking time. He poked the fallen pay clerk with the brass-shod point of his pacing stick and yelled at the top of his voice, as if the clerk was miles away instead of at his feet, 'Get up at once you 'orrible, idle man!'

The commandant gave Savage a self-satisfied smile and stroked that silly moustache of his again. 'We don't believe in mollycoddling here,' he said.

'Yes, I can see,' Savage said ironically, as the drill sergeant poked the fallen man hard once again: something forbidden by King's Regulations. But irony was wasted on the commandant with his Ronald Coleman moustache. 'Captain,' he added, 'I'm not much interested in theories about military re-education. I'm after bodies, ones who will fight, and I'm in a damned hurry.'

The commandant wasn't flustered. 'Sent a draft of fifty to the Northumberland Fusiliers last week, right to the front. None of them, or so the Fusiliers' CO had reported, have deserted yet.'

Savage didn't comment on that 'yet' and the commandant went on to add, 'Naturally I don't send people the old lags. They're here to learn a thorough lesson.' He licked his fleshy deep-red lips, the sure sign of a sensualist and sadist. 'They'd be no good at the front. They'd be back within the week. No guts, lack of moral fibre, you know, Major.'

Savage knew the time had come to shock the self-satisfied bastard and stop his waffle. 'I don't care who they are, as long as they belong to the Parachute Regiment. Men with the worst records as far as I'm concerned. Men who have struck their officers, deserted under fire, murderers even.' He fixed the other officer with a hard look from his bright blue eyes. 'You have got murderers among your – er – students, haven't you, Captain?'

The commandant looked at him aghast, his self-assurance destroyed by that question. 'Yes . . . yes,' he stuttered, 'I suppose so. But I'm afraid the type which has got nothing to lose doesn't take to camp discipline easily. They—'

'You mean they say "fuck you". What can you do to me, Captain?' Savage interrupted harshly. 'All right, where have you got your bad boys, Captain. I want to see them now, especially if they belonged to my regiment.'

'It's a bit difficult, Major,' the commandant said miserably. 'They simply won't listen to reason—'

'*Now!*'

The commandant with the Ronald Coleman moustache excused himself – urgent business elsewhere. But the big sergeant major with the face that seemed to have been hewn from the granite of his native Aberdeen, told Meek that he'd go along with him and his officer. 'They're tame enough, ye ken,' he said. 'They dinna want to rock the boat – they're safe enough here. But –' his dark Celtic face turned grim suddenly – 'it's yon Scouse, he's one of your paratroopers. When he gets the mood on him, there could be fireworks. Bad bugger, a canny bolshy rabble-rouser that one.'

Now they approached the old one-storey barracks that housed the glasshouse's 'bad boys'. At both ends someone had had a wooden elevated watchtower erected. In each sat one of the 'staffs', as the guards were called, each armed with a telephone and, more significantly, a twelve-bore shotgun.

Savage saw the gun at once and, turning to the sergeant major said, 'Going a bit far, isn't it, Sarnt Major?'

'Perhaps, sir. But wait till ye see you fellers.'

A few moments later Savage did and noted immediately that a lot of them wore the beret and the silver wings of the Parachute Regiment. But despite the fact that they were slumped on straw mattresses, wore dirty old uniforms and were mostly unshaven, all of those in the regiment had polished their winged para badges. The sight gave him some hope. It seemed to signify that they were still proud of the regiment to which they had once belonged. Perhaps he could find his 'bodies' here after all.

Next moment his hopes were dashed somewhat when the Scottish sergeant major commanded, 'All right you lot, on your feet. Officer, on yer feet!'

Not a soldier moved. They continued to lie there, staring into nothing or playing cards for matchsticks.

Meek, who at times belied his name radically, cursed under his breath and clicked back the triggers to both barrels of the twelve-bore shot gun. 'Let's be having you,' he said softly, raising the weapon, which would have been deadly at such close quarters.

No one moved as before, but a small man huddled in the dirty straw which smelled of animal urine, raised himself carelessly from his cards and said, 'Fuck off.' His voice was low. But the menace in it was very clear.

Meek moved forward a pace threateningly, face suddenly flushed with anger.

Savage stopped him with a sharp look. This had to be Scouse, he told himself to judge from the man's accent. He waited, considering what to do next. He knew the type: good men in a scrap, some bar-room brawl, but lousy soldiers who didn't take to discipline. They made the best 'barrack-room lawyers', who could always put forward a slick case for their bolshy attitude – hence the name.

Slowly, while the prisoners watched, he unbuckled his pistol belt. Wordlessly he handed the belt to the shocked sergeant major. The latter gasped. 'But sir, there's nigh on fifty o' yon criminals.'

Savage ignored the protest. Slowly he walked down the crowded barrack room to where Scouse lay, watching calmly, though Savage suspected the Liverpudlian barrack-room lawyer was as surprised as the rest. He stopped in front of the man, taking in his battered face with its ugly pockmarks, 'You're Scouse, aren't you?'

'Yer, what of it?' He looked up, challenging Savage.

'They say you're the ringleader of this mob.'

Scouse said nothing. At the end of the room, Meek curled his finger tighter round the triggers of the twelve-bore. He wouldn't hesitate to kill the cocky bastard and the rest for that matter, if necessary. They wore the proud badge and wings of his regiment, but they wouldn't fight like the men of A Company who were now resting in makeshift graves in German-held territory. What good were the cowardly bastards?

'You may think you're someone who gives the orders,' Savage continued, not taking his gaze off the prisoner for an instant, 'but you don't, and you *don't* tell an officer to fuck off. Not this particular officer anyway.'

Still Scouse didn't seem impressed. 'Our officers fucked off at Arnhem when it got too hot for them and left us to fish for ourselves. Why should I respect frigging officers?'

'Because of this.' Savage bent and slapped the Scouse's face lightly, almost in play.

There was a gasp from the others. Someone at the back of the room, and Savage told himself he was glad the speaker wasn't a paratrooper, said, 'Don't let him get away with that, Scouse. We'll back you up.'

'But he's one of our blokes,' another prisoner objected. 'Fifth Brigade . . . Brigadier Poett's lot.'

Savage waited, keeping his cold blue eyes fixed on Scouse before he said finally, breaking the sudden silence. 'Well, what's it going to be, Scouse? I'm unarmed and I've just broken King's Regulations by striking a subordinate. The bigshots could court-martial me for that.' He forced a dry little laugh. 'I could end up here with you shower of shit if I was unlucky.'

Someone laughed.

It seemed to break the tension. Scouse cursed under his breath. He dropped his cards angrily, but that was about it. He turned on his belly in the straws and stared at the wall in silence.

At the door, the sergeant major whispered to Meek, still holding the shotgun levelled, although the danger seemed to have passed, 'Yon major o' yourn is a canny one, that he is . . . All the same, I'd watch that Liverpudlian bastard. Ay, that I would.'

Savage turned away from the sulky soldier lying in the straw and faced up to the others. He smiled at them. 'I'm recruiting,' he announced, 'for the old regiment. We've had bad losses in Germany and there are no reinforcements coming through the pipeline from the UK. We – I – need you. You're all trained paras, mature men with battlefield experience.' He forced a winning tone into his voice, 'What about it, lads? It'll be a chance to get back to the old regiment.'

'But what's in it for us, sir?' Savage noted that 'sir' and thought immediately that it was a good sign.

'For you. Well you might make a handsome corpse,' he joked. Then he added hastily, 'Your freedom. If you volunteer to join the Sixth, I have the authority to have your crime sheets destroyed. You'll be able to make a completely fresh start, and when you're finally demobbed, you'll have a clean sheet to go into civvie street.'

'Come off it, sir –' again that 'sir' – 'we're not just off the boat, Major. How do we know that you'll tear up our crime sheets?'

Savage didn't answer straightaway. Instead he turned to the sergeant-major

'Sarnt-Major.' He indicated the sulky Liverpudlian. 'His.'

'*His*, sir?' the NCO echoed a little increduously.

Savage nodded.

Seemingly reluctantly, the sergeant major drew the list of the Scouse's crimes and charges out of his pouch and handed it to the officer.

Savage held it up for all the prisoners to see. 'Eight crimes going back to Dunkirk in 1940,' he explained. 'Desertion in the face of the enemy. He could have been shot for that.' He let his words sink in and then with a sudden, violent gesture that surprised them, he ripped the sheet in two and then in two again.

There was a dramatic gasp from the prisoners. Slowly Savage let the pieces of paper drift down to the dirty straw-covered floor. 'Does that convince you, soldier?' he asked the man who had asked the question.

'Cor ferk a duck, sir,' the man breathed, as if he didn't believe the evidence of his own eyes. 'If you can tear up his nibs' crime sheet,' he indicated the still sulky Scouse, 'then . . .' He broke off, as if there was no need for any further explanation.

Now Savage was firm and determined and in a hurry, as if there was no further time to be wasted. 'All right, all those of you from the Parachute Regiment who are prepared to come with me – remember when you join me your record will be clean, as pure as driven slush,' he laughed. They did too. 'All of you, fall in outside. The three tonners are already waiting for you. You'll be kitted out, new smocks, new battledress, in particular new wings and badges.'

They liked that and Savage could see that they still had some pride in their old formation, the Parachute Regiment. After all, they had once belonged to the elite formation, swaggering round town with their silver cap badge and, more importantly, the blue wings on their shoulder indicating that they had risked death by jumping out of an aeroplane eight times. How they had impressed the girls!

Now he waited as first one and then the next rose slowly to his feet, not daring to look at his mates as he collected his bits and pieces together, brushing the straw off his dirty uniform, adjusting his faded red beret, as if he were going on parade back in the old days when they had been good soldiers.

Standing at the back of the room, Meek lowered his shotgun. There were already a score or so of the prisoners on their feet. The sergeant felt Savage was in control of the situation. The old Scottish sergeant major, the old sweat well used to the funny ways of the British Tommy, was not so sure. Scouse, face still sullen, rose to his feet and with a scowl on his pock-marked face reluctantly started to stuff his pathetic possessions into a bag.

The sergeant major said to Meek, 'Watch him, chum. He's a real bad *egg*, yon Scouse. See yer officer never turns his back on him.' He shook his greying head. 'Ye never can ken what a bastard like that 'un might do . . .'

Five

The next twenty-four hours passed speedily. Under Savage's and Meek's direction, aided by the handful of survivors from the major's decimated A Company, the former prisoners prepared themselves for combat once again. But first Savage knew he had to restore some of their old pride in their membership of the Parachute Regiment. Swiftly they were kitted out in new battledress, camouflaged airborne smocks and the like. But when the consignment of the blue cloth parachute wings arrived, he didn't allow the men to sew them themselves as they had done with the other bits and pieces that signified they were paras. Instead, Meek came into the ex-prisoners' Nissen hut, smart too in a well-pressed new battledress, his boots polished to a high gloss as if he were back in the parachute depot, his silver parachute wings on the new beret, burnished and sparkling-silver. He announced, 'All right, you lot. Get fell in outside. The CO's gonna award you yer wings. And woe betide anyone who lets me down with a bad turn out.'

In the corner, Scouse, as sullen as ever, looked up and sneered, 'So it's back to bullshit agen, is it? If it moves, salute it; if it don't, whitewash it.' He hawked and spat deliberately on the concrete floor.

Meek wasn't going to accept the challenge this day; it could wait. Instead he threatened, 'If you don't clean up that gob o' spit before you go on parade, mate, I'm gonna ram this,' he indicated his new swagger stick which he had acquired somewhere or other, 'right up yer ass, so far up

38

it, that yer frigging eyeballs will pop out.' And with that he marched out, leaving the others smiling at Scouse's discomfort; smiles which grew even broader when Scouse knelt down and with a piece of army form blank* began to clean up his spittle from the floor.

It was a fine April morning, clear and fresh after the night's rain, with a fresh breeze sweeping in from the south to clear away the usual smog over Brussels. Savage felt good as he marched on to the little square, followed by a well-turned out corporal from the original A Company bearing a tray holding the coveted blue wings that signified that a man had fallen out of an aeroplane eight times and risked death.

He waited till Meek had called the men to attention before announcing, 'I shall call out your names in alphabetical order. Each man will step forward and receive his wings. Later Sergeant Meek will enter the receipt of wings into the man's paybook. Now, I'll just add this, once at Ringway, and the like, you first received your wings and were very proud of them.' He glanced hard at the three ranks drawn up in front of him, their appearance transformed since they had left the glasshouse – even Scouse seemed smarter – and hoped he was getting through to them. 'Now you will receive them for a second time and again I hope you will wear them with the same pride as before. This is your second chance to be good soldiers. You won't get another. I shall see to that if you fail me.' His frown vanished. 'All right, Private Able . . .'

One after another they marched to where the officer and corporal were waiting. They saluted smartly, received the precious wings, saluted once more, their salute being returned by Savage with full military ceremony. Even Scouse seemed to have become tamer. He marched up, swinging his arms shoulder-height as if he were some eager

*ie lavatory paper.

young recruit at the depot, saluted smartly and received his wings, but when he turned, Sergeant Meek watching him carefully, could see his face was as dark and evil as ever. To himself, he said, I've got my eye on you, you Liverpudlian bastard. One wrong move, Scouse, and you're for the frigging chop.

But Savage was facing other problems. He had been too long at the front to know what wires to pull in Brussels in order to get the weapons and vehicles he needed. For he knew that the Sixth Airborne up in the line wouldn't be able to supply him; they were advancing on foot – the most modern force in the British Army – or using captured German transport, even pulling their own supplies in hand-carts, as if they belonged to a medieval army on the move. Supply officers, it seemed, here in the fleshpots of the Belgian capital were sitting on what they had, trying to justify their existence here. 'Sorry, old boy,' they'd say to Savage, 'love to help. But can't get so-and-so for love nor money. Nothing coming through Antwerp from the UK.'

In vain Savage pleaded he was working directly for the Airborne's deputy commander and was in urgent need of brens, gammon bombs and, in particular, of jeeps for a new mission in Germany. '*Jeeps!*' they'd exclaim as if he were asking for the British Royal Family's crown jewels. 'We haven't seen an intact jeep since the Ardennes show last January! Why, the Belgies are offering a fortune for them on the black market, even bits and pieces of wrecked ones.'

But on the day he was scheduled to see Montgomery at his Brussels main HQ, Meek who knew the problem, said, whispering out of the side of his mouth, 'Don't worry, sir. With your permission I'm going to give them old lags of ours a twelve hour leave in Brussels. They've done well so far and I think, before we go back to Germany, they ought to get a bit o' dirty water off'n their chests.' He winked knowingly.

Savage knew what the big NCO meant. He'd let them

have a got at the whores, who were present in their thousands in the centre of the Belgian capital. Still, he was surprised at Meek's sudden generosity. Meek must have been able to read his mind, for he added, with another wink, 'Yes I know, sir, I'm a real old softy. All heart. But you see I'm also out for number one. I hope that the lads will be so grateful to their old sarge that they might be bringing me a present back from the big city – and I don't mean a stick o' rock'. And with that cryptic statement, Major Savage had to be satisfied.

Montgomery was kindness itself. He was well known for his harshness with his senior officers. He'd sack them at a snap of his finger and thumb. He reasoned they were very experienced and shouldn't make mistakes. If they did, it often resulted in the death of brave young men in the firing line. They, however, would presumably live to die of old age in their beds. Young fighting soldiers might never enjoy that privilege. Hence, young infantry and tank officers, whose survival rate lasted only weeks, had to be spoiled, cherished.

Thus, although he knew that Major Savage had lost most of a company only a few days before because of his haste, he didn't take him to task on that score – after all he had already won two military crosses before he had been twenty-one. He offered Savage tea and biscuits in his office in the Brussels HQ – a place he hated; he much preferred his simple caravan – and said when Savage settled down, 'You see Savage, I am faced with a very complex military – and political – situation. It's due, in part to our American friends – who simply do not understand the reasons for war.'

'I see, sir,' Savage replied dutifully, though in reality he didn't see at all.

'As far as you must understand the situation, this is what I need to know. For the want of troops, now that I don't have any American troops at my disposal, I will be forced to stop on a line between the Elbe and Weser, roughly between Hamburg and Bremen, the big German ports. For it looks as if the Boche are going to defend that particular line. If they do, they bar my progress up to the Baltic through Schleswig-Holstein and on to Denmark.'

Montgomery let Savage have a sip of his too weak tea. As with all liquids the Master preferred them weak and watery. 'But undoubtedly, in the end, I shall be able to break through that line with what I've got. That is the military side of it, Savage,' He smiled at the younger officer and the latter wondered why the devil was a British field marball and a famous one to boot, discussing such high-level matters with him, a lowly major.

'But the Elbe–Weser line is not my major problem,' Monty continued. 'No, my major problem is that of our ally, the Russians, namely the Red Army at this moment advancing rapidly westwards towards us.' He turned his piercing blue eyes on Savage abruptly, as though searching for something in the younger man's face, known only to him.

Savage tensed. It was clear that this was going to be a task that Montgomery was soon to hand him which would be important – why all this help and top-level briefings – but very complex. And not a little dangerous, too, my lad, a little inner voice warned him. He put down his cup and, craning his head forward, listened more intently.

'General Eisenhower, in all his wisdom, has decided our allied armies will not stop at the River Elbe but turn eastwards and march on Berlin. No one, however has told the Russians where *they* are supposed to stop. Our information is that they won't. While we mark time or try to break through into Schleswig-Holstein, they'll keep on westwards. The result? The mouth of the Baltic Sea will be in Russian hands. That, I cannot allow to happen. Do I make myself clear, Major?'

'Yessir,' Savage, caught off guard, stuttered hastily.

'So the upshot of all this is the following, Major. You will get the chaps who will do a recce for one, finding the best way across the Elbe without a major engagement, with your objective the Baltic, somewhere in the general area of Lubeck. Succeed in that and you'll stop the Russians from controlling the whole sea, especially when you've got your own Sixth Airborne Division coming up right behind you to take over a large stretch of the coastline in that area. It is my guess that the Russians won't risk a confrontation with us and the Americans at this stage of the game. But if they beat us to the Baltic and are in place there, it would be the devil's own job, Major Savage, to winkle them out again.'

Suddenly Montgomery's serious mood vanished. He looked at the young officer with an abrupt twinkle in his eye. 'I have a shrewd idea that *if* and *when* we seal off the Schleswig-Holstein peninsula, it will produce some surprising results, Savage.'

Monty paused and seemed to be waiting for an answer or a reaction, so Savage, confused by the way things were going, asked, 'In what way, sir?'

Montgomery looked like the proverbial cat that has just swallowed the cream. He said, 'The Boche knows that he's lost the game. We've about knocked him for six. That's exceedingly clear. So why does he continue fighting up north and naturally over to the east where the Russians are?' Monty answered his own question, 'I shall tell you. Because he wants to gain as much time as possible to rescue his chaps, civilian and military, fleeing from the Red Army in the east. They say there's a million or so on the eastern bank of the River Elbe desperately trying to get to their own lines on the the other side. The Boche know, after what they did in Russia, what the Russians will do to them if they are captured by the Russians, especially the German womenfolk. Already we've heard some terrible stories of mass rape and the like and it is not German propaganda, I can assure you.'

Savage nodded, but didn't comment. One didn't voluntarily interrupt field marshals, especially one like Montgomery.

'The result is then that the Boche is running and fighting to save his own precious neck, and we're bearing the brunt of that Boche stubborn defence on our front. But once we block the Russian advance from the east, and there's no more chance of saving those German soldiers and civilians in the east, what will those in authority on our front do, Savage, eh?' Montgomery cocked his head to one side and looked quizzically at Savage like some cheeky city sparrow.

This time Savage answered what was really a rhetorical question. 'The Jerries' will pack up, sir. What would be the point of continuing the fight, losing more men and destroying more of their towns and villages?'

'Exactly, Savage. With all authority here in the north in the hands of the military, who are usually realistic and sensible, not like that mad man Hitler, it could mean that there would be a tremendous mass surrender of all German troops in Northern Germany, Denmark and also Norway, too. According to our intelligence there are one and a half million of them and more are pouring in from the east every day. Now . . .'

But Savage was no longer listening. Suddenly it dawned on Savage what the little field marshal was saying. Montgomery was not only concerned about the military situation, he was also intent on furthering his military reputation. Vain and headstrong as he was, the little field marshal wanted the kudos of final victory for himself. If he couldn't conquer Berlin and conclude his decade-long fighting career on that supreme, high note, then he would have what was left of the whole German army north of the River Elbe surrender to him personally.

'You see what I mean, Savage,' Monty said, confirming what the latter was thinking. 'If they surrender up there, it would be a really first-class achievement. Good egg, you know. The surrender of the Greater German *Wehrmacht* as the Boche call it, what.'

Savage returned his smile. Whatever the faults of the cocky, conceited little British commander were, he seemed to be the only senior British officer who realized that now Britain's real interests were not solely the conquest of what was left of Nazi Germany, but the preservation of her Empire and her status as a world power. Britain, in the final analysis, had to be seen as playing a major part in winning the war in the west, not just as merely a minor participant, aiding the victorious Yanks in some sort of unimportant side-show.

Five minutes later they parted, with Montgomery solemnly shaking Savage's hand and wishing him the best of luck adding, as the latter returned to his jeep, 'Remember, Savage, you may feel at this moment that you are merely a minor cog in the wheel, but you aren't. You and those who follow in your lead are striking a blow for the future of our country . . . perhaps even for that of our whole Empire. It is a solemn thought, especially at your age, young man.'

It was. As he left, Savage pondered what he had just heard. Here, he was, Savage told himself grimly, leading a company of paras, half of whom had been in jail only a day or so before, in an attempt to find a route through a whole German army, to be followed by a decimated airborne division that had no heavy armament or transport. It was going to be a tough assignment, a very tough one.

But when he got to the company, Major Savage, still worried whether he would be able to tackle the assignment successfully, got a surprise. Standing in the middle of the little square, surrounded by a crowd of curious paras, there was a brand new jeep, painted in the olive drab of the US Army. In the driving seat was that same para from the detention camp who had challenged Savage with: 'What's in it for us?'

Now he was grinning all over his rogue's face and telling

his tale yet once again. 'Damn easy it was, mates. I lifted the Belgie cop's pistol right behind his back in the tram and as I was wondering where I might flog it on the black market, up drove this black Yank in a jeep leading a little convoy. Black as the ace of spades he was, but all the same he was some kind of officer.' The speaker cast a furtive look at Major Savage, but the latter said nothing so he continued, 'Funny that way, the Yanks. Won't let the blacks eat with them in the same mess, but then they make them officers . . .'

'Get on with it, Charlie,' his listeners urged impatiently.

'Well, then it came to me, mates. We needed another jeep and here's this black Yank sitting in a brand new one. So I decided he ought – the Yank I mean – to make a swap. The jeep for Rommel's own pistol.'

'Rommel's own pistol, Charlie,' they echoed. 'You pulling our pisser, Charlie?'

'Honest, no mates. He jumped at it. Gonna write to his folks back home.' Here Charlie attempted to imitate an American accent and failed lamentably. 'Tell 'em he'd captured Rommel personal like and taken his shooter off 'n him – Yanks'll believe anything.' He gave them a big knowing wink. 'That's how we got the jeep.' He looked directly at Savage as if he wondered what the major was going to do now.

Charlie need not have worried. Savage had noted that 'we' instead of 'I'. Charlie could well have flogged the stolen pistol on the Belgie black market and 'got his leg over', as he would have phrased it. Instead, he had contributed to the company's meagre supply of transport. At that moment, worried as he was by the magnitude of his assignment, Savage told himself that it might be a good sign. Perhaps his old lags were rallying to the cause after all.

They left twelve hours later, just before the dawn. Down below in the Belgian capital there was now a dimout instead of the full blackout, but it was dark enough and

Savage hoped that it would cover the departure of his little convoy. Savage was wrong. The fat Belgian major with the well-fed, brick-red face that indicated very high blood pressure was on duty, as always working for his new masters now that the Germans had finally departed from his native country. From his position, he viewed the little convoy heading north through the capital and then on towards the frontier with Germany where the war was. He noted the red berets through his night glasses, and the twin Brownings mounted in the four jeeps and at the back of the fifteen-hundred-weight trucks. He nodded his head, He could guess where these 'Red Devils', as the English called them, were going. It was worth reporting to the other side. His new masters seemed to want every un-important scrap of information of what the English were up to in Northern Germany.

The fat Belgian major sat back as the little convoy dis-appeared into the pre-dawn gloom. He had a new mistress. Previously she had belonged to a German general on von Stupnagel's staff here in Brussels and she had expensive tastes. He needed all the money he could make. With a grunt, he crossed over to the cupboard where he had his radio transmitter hidden. With fingers like hairy pork sausages, the sweat running down his brick-red face, he started to tap out the Morse . . .

They cleared Brussels just as the sun started to rise on the horizon like a blood-red ball. It was going to be a fine spring day and Savage's worries began to disappear. At the wheel, Charlie, who had tricked the black Yank with 'Rommel's pistol', whistled happily as they headed for Bourg-Leopold and then Germany. Savage's good mood increased even more.

'Well, Meek,' he said airily, 'what think you? They seem to be shaping up all right, don't they?' He meant the former prisoners.

Meek gave a little shrug as if he weren't totally convinced.

'I suppose so, sir,' he agreed. 'The proof of the pudding'll be when we get them in the line. Another day and we'll be in Indian country and then we'll see.'

'Indian country?' Savage enquired idly, enjoying the fine spring morning.

'You know, sir, them cowboy pictures before the war when the good 'uns in the white hats are tackled by the Redskins.'

Savage laughed. 'Don't think we'll meet many Redskins where we're going, Meek.'

'Well, something like that, sir. Anyhow we've got to watch our front,' he paused significantly, 'and our back.' He indicated the Bedford truck behind them where in the seat next to driver, Scouse was sharpening his trench knife to a razor-sharp cutting edge as if his very life depended upon it.

Book Two
INTO INDIAN COUNTRY

One

An uneasy stillness lay over the shattered land. To Savage, who had experienced it before – the strange loneliness of the front – it was the premonition of impending danger.

Savage sniffed the dawn air. There was a strange smell too. It was a kind of raunchy stench that he remembered vaguely from his boyhood when his parents had taken him to Whipsnade Zoo: the pungent smell of the monkey house.

He stood up in the stationary jeep and focussed his glasses on his front sweeping them round in a 180-degree arc. Nothing much. The trees were beginning to sprout and the grip of winter had loosened its hold on the land. It could have been to the untutored eye a scene of peace and new promise. But Savage, the veteran, knew that could not be. The world was still at war. There was danger and death lurking out there somewhere, his every instinct told him that.

He bent down and touched Charlie on the shoulder. 'All right, move up that rise to the right – slowly,' he commanded. 'Meek, stand by the Brownings.' He turned round and held up his hand, palm outwards, to indicate to the rest of the little convoy to stay where they were. After his A Company's debacle on the canal, he wasn't going to run into an ambush yet again.

At a snail's pace the jeep began to move up the rise. Behind the driver, Meek positioned himself at the twin Browning machine guns. Suddenly the April morning lost its beauty. Now there was tension in the very air. All of them, veterans that they were, knew that they might well be dead in the next few minutes if anything went wrong. What did beauty mean to men like themselves?

They neared the top of the hill now. The smell grew stronger. Suddenly Meek gripped the trigger of his machine guns. Something was moving on the other side. 'Stand fast!' Savage commanded harshly. 'Don't fire till I tell you.' He too knew that there was something moving there. Could be it a German? Slowly, not taking his gaze off the hilltop for an instant, he loosened the flap of the .38 revolver holster.

And then there it was, looking perhaps more piteous than a human being might in such a situation. A horse, a poor skinny-ribbed thing, was dragging itself over the top, hopping forward the best it could on three legs, dark red patches of congealed blood spread across its flanks, foam bubbling at its distended nostrils.

Charlie at the wheel gasped, 'A poor old bloody nag!' Despite the carnage that he and the rest of the men in the jeep had seen, they were appalled at the sight of the dying animal. Savage was tempted there and then to draw his revolver and put the poor creature out of its misery. He resisted the temptation. He knew it would be foolish to do so. So they continued their progress past the horse lying on the ground now panting hard, as if it had come to the end of a long race, fixing them with its great liquid eyes. Savage looked away in the same instant that he saw the great tragedy beyond and Charlie hit the brakes with a 'Holy shit . . . What a fucking mess!'

In front there was what was obviously a German farmer in his black peaked cap and heavy boots. He had been propped against a tree shattered by machine gun fire as if deliberately. Savage thought he had a typical farmer's face, heavy and muscular, with that peasant stubborn cunning-ness common to his kind. Now the top plate of his false teeth hung out of his mouth in a kind of mocking defiance, which said, 'No, no, you won't catch me out!' But he had been wrong. A burst of machine gun fire *had* caught him out. Now his chest was shattered, his rib cage a gleaming white against the red gore of his upper body.

Beyond the dead farmer there were dead bodies of humans and animals everywhere, scattered among wrecked farm-carts, with stove pipes protruding from them, the fleeing refugees' pathetic bits and pieces scattered everywhere, one-time household treasures perhaps now torn and trampled underfoot by the hooves of many horses.

'Bloody brylcreem cream boys!' Charlie swore, re-covering from his shock at the sight of what was a massacre of defenceless civilians.

'Not the RAF,' Savage corrected the driver. 'This is what the Jerry calls a trek, a group of refugees from the east trying to make it to their people in the north. But it wasn't the fighter-bomber boys who caught them. They don't fly horses.'

'How do you mean, sir?' Meek asked, taking his gaze off a dead old woman, her skirts thrown up to reveal her open legs clad in faded blue bloomers in the kind of obscene sexual invitation that she had probably never offered in real life.

'Look at those marks of horses' hooves where they have trampled on the poor sods,' Savage explained. His voice rose. 'And look over there, next to that poor dead kid with the rag doll in her arms. Got it?'

'Sir,' the other two said in unison.

'That's a sabre next to the poor devil and pilots don't wear sabres.'

'Well, what do *you* make of it, sir?' Charlie asked.

Savage frowned and hesitated for a moment or two. 'Well, my guess is that these Jerries were caught by cavalry and the only cavalry that could do that – get over the Elbe and vanish again – are the Cossacks. It couldn't be the Jerries – they wouldn't want to kill their own kinsfolk and we don't have cavalry. So it has to Russian Cossacks.'

The other two stared at the handsome scarred officer dumfounded. 'But the Russians are our allies, sir,' they protested.

'I know,' Savage responded a little helplessly. He told himself that he wasn't going to tell them what Monty had told him. He'd let them remain puzzled. He'd bumped into Monty's Russians sooner than he had expected. Now if the Russians, in the form of the Cossacks, went on like this, he'd soon be fighting not only the Germans, but the Russians as well.

But Savage knew he had no time to dwell on the matter; he'd deal with that problem if and when it occurred. Now he said, 'We haven't time to bury the poor devils. Besides, the locals, wherever they are, will come out to loot what they can find and probably bury them.'

Out of the corner of his eye Savage noted how Scouse's pock-marked wolfish face lit up at the mention of loot. He saw too that the Scots from his original A Company looked relieved. Scots didn't like the business of burying the dead, especially the cutting off of the identity discs and stuffing one in the mouth of the corpse and closing the poor devil's jaw firmly to stop it from dropping out.* Now they were only too pleased when Savage gave the signal to start up once again and leave that scene of death.

It had been relatively easy for Savage to slip such a small body of men through the German front which was very fluid as the enemy continued to retreat. Behind him, some ten or fiften miles or so, the bulk of the Sixth Airborne

*The plastic identity discs came in two parts, hanging round the soldier's neck by means of a piece of string. One was taken away for records' purposes; the other remained with the buried corpse for whenever the body was retrieved and buried in a military cemetery.

Division was finding it more difficult, especially as they didn't have the motorized transport to keep them moving fast down the roads, which were naturally held to the last by the Germans.

Now as they bumped down country roads and over ploughed fields to reach their next objective – a small bridge across a river they had to use unless they wanted to make a long detour – Savage was concerned with trying to take the bridge by surprise. He had lost one company in such an operation; he didn't want to lose another.

But as they approached the bridge, there seemed no sign of life about it, though the terrain was ideally suited for defence. There were small fir woods to both sides of the opposite end of the bridge, and beyond a small rise from which any enemy gun position could dominate the bridge area. He dropped his glasses and, turning to Sergeant Meek, asked, 'What do you make of it, Meek?'

'Too good to be true, sir, in my opinion. If the Jerries were going to defend anything that'd be the place to do it.'

'Agreed.' Savage thought for a few moments, the only sound that of the twittering of the birds in the woods and the steady beat of the jeep's engine. 'Well, there's no other way for it, Meek. That's the route – the only one – and we've got to follow it.' He frowned. 'Get the chaps to deploy and give cover. I'm going to check that bridge.'

Meek looked worried. 'Bloody hell, sir,' he snorted. 'You want to win the Victoria Cross or sommat?'

Savage forced a grin. 'I'm the only officer in this mob, Meek, you may remember. Without an officer to record any deed of daring-do, there's no VC . . . All right snap to it.'

Meek snapped to it. Minutes later, Savage, carrying pliers in one hand and his revolver in the other hand, advanced on the silent and now somewhat sinister bridge. For the birds had suddenly stopped twittering and behind him the drivers had switched off their engines. Suddenly he felt all alone in the world.

The bridge was the usual type of country one, with the usual legend posted at its entrance: *Nur für land-wirkschaftlichen Betrieb* – only for agricultural use. That cheered him up somewhat. Perhaps, because of that, the retreating Jerries had neglected to mine the bridge and defend it from those now ominiously silent woods to both sides of it. He licked his suddenly dry lips and stepped on to the bridge itself. Below a medium-sized stream tumbled and gurgled, filled with melted snow waters from the higher hills beyond. Savage leaned over the little steel parapet. He looked for the tell-tale signs of explosives – red wire and the like. Nothing. He crossed to the other side and peered down. Still nothing, save for the shadows of trout fleeing away from the sudden disturbance. He turned and then signalled with raised thumb that things were going alright.

Now, not so cautiously as before, he crossed to the other side of the bridge – and stopped short. To his immediate front, the earth had been disturbed recently. There was a series of little hillocks of brown earth looking like the work of a platoon of Jerry moles. He recognized them immediately. Teller mines, he told himself. Ten or so pounds of high explosive in large round steel plates, hence the name[*], aimed at blowing up any vehicle that ventured unwittingly across them.

He cursed. Yet at the same time was relieved. If that was all that the enemy was prepared to use to stop their advance, he could cope with it, though it might be time-consuming. He turned again and held his fingers outstretched on the top of his battered beret. It was the infantry signal for 'rally on me'.

The drivers started up immediately. It was as if inactivity scared them more than moving forward into enemy territory and the unknown. Swiftly they crossed the bridge and lined behind where Savage was standing. He rapped out

[*]Teller – German for plate.

56

his orders, 'All right, chaps, we're gonna lift the buggers broad enough for the vehicles to get through. You all know the drill. But don't get complacent. The Jerries, as you know, are cunning buggers with their mines. Take your time and don't lift until you're sure they're not booby trapped.'

The front rank went to work. With their little pig-sticker bayonets and, in some cases, with screwdrivers from the vehicles' tool kit, they started to iron the the earth until they found the outlines of the big ugly anti-tank mines. Hastily with their fingers they then dug into the spoil until the surface of the exposed mine was revealed. Thereafter it took only seconds to unscrew the Teller mine detonator located on the top of the devilish killer device. But experienced as they were, they didnt lift the now apparently harmless mine. The Germans usually didn't make their mines as easy to lift as that. With sensitive fingers, the sweat standing out in opaque beads on their foreheads, they felt around the edge of the mine. So far nobody had found any device attaching the mine to another concealed and yet unlifted device which would blow them to hell. Still the clearance was not completed. Now came the final and most dangerous stage of the whole nasty business. Sweating ever more profusely, the para slightly tilted the mine and groped – and probably prayed while he did so – for the last dirty trick the Jerry sappers might play – a matchbox detonator concealed beneath the Teller mine. If the mine were lifted while it was still concealed in place, it would explode the whole ten pounds or so of high explosive in the lifter's face and one very dead para would be the result.

Doing his best to encourage his men, advancing with them, scanning the ground ahead for the tell-tale mound of new brown earth which would indicate a mine, Savage sweated as well and prayed that they'd soon be through the minefield. Every minute they spent here in the open, presented to any enemy as if on a silver tablet, increased the danger.

They were at what Savage took to be the end of the mine-field when it happened. In the same instant that he gasped with shock at the realization that there were anti-personnel *schu* mines, the deadly 'deballockers', as the men called them*, mixed with the Teller mines, the Spandau opened up with a vicious burst, the tracer zipping angrily towards the paras bent over the mines. '*DOWN!*' Savage yelled frantically.

They need no urging. They dropped their tools and fell face downwards over their tasks. Just in time. The bullets hissed above their heads and as Savage woke up to what was happening, he realized that they had again walked into a trap. If they tried to move back across the bridge, the unseen gunner would get them. If they pushed on forward, they'd run straight into the deadly anti-personnel mines. 'Christ almighty,' he moaned to himself, 'what in heaven's name am I going to do?'

* Due to the fact that the *schu* mine rose to about waist height and if a man were unlucky, the metal balls it contained might well emasculate him.

Two

'Here the Cossacks come now, Comrade Marshal,' the chief of staff announced as the handsome army commander in his elegant uniform pressed the breast of his plump mistress in the back of the looted German army Mercedes. The chief of staff took his gaze away as Marshal Rokossovsky played idly with the Russian woman's nipple trying to get it erect through the tight fabric of her silken blouse. He didn't like the sight. The common soldiers shouldn't see their commanders enjoying themselves like this, especially these beaten Cossacks.

Most of them had lost their horses. They stumbled forward on foot. Most were wounded. Some suffered bravely in the true Cossack fashion. Others came on, glassy-eyed and stumbling like men escaping from some terrible nightmare. One or two appeared to have gone mad. They mumbled insane gibberish, eyes rolling wildly in their demented fantasy.

Rokossovsky was not perturbed. He had suffered enough himself in Stalin's gulags and seen enough of battlefield misery. It had become part and parcel of his life ever since the start of the Great Fatherland War. He took his hand off his mistress's plump breast and said, 'What men are these, Comrade General?'

Before the chief of staff could answer, there was the clip-clop of hooves and a huge man on a fine, but mud-splattered horse rode up to the car. With his fur hat tilted to one side in the true bold Cossack fashion, his face proud and challenging he raised his curved sabre in salute and said, 'Hetman Dmitrov, commander Ninth Cossack Cavalry, Comrade Marshal. Gulag rats like yourself – *once.*'

The chief of staff opened his mouth, face suddenly flushed red with anger at such impertinence from the damned Cossack. Rokossovsky held up his hand to stop him. The bold Cossack amused him. There were few of his junior leaders who dared to speak to him in that fashion.

'What did you say?' he demanded and lit yet another of the paper-tube *pappiroki* he preferred to the handrolled, often in newspaper, cigarettes the soldiers were issued with.

The Cossack wasn't afraid; perhaps he had been through too much to be afraid any more. In his deep bass, he said, 'We are the gulag rats. According to the authorities we are traitors, reactionaries, turncoats – the scum of our Soviet fatherland. It is our task, Comrade Marshal, to murder, burn, rape and frighten the Fritz till he fills his pants, for our Soviet fatherland.' There was no mistaking the contempt in his voice, as he paused for breath, reined in his nervous horse and winked at the marshal's mistress, who was eyeing this bold giant of a Cossack with some interest. 'And this, comrade is our reward.' He indicated the pathetic survivors of his regiment filing by behind him.

The chief of staff dabbed his brow with his handkerchief soaked in cheap scent. At the front there was no time to wash and he knew he stank. Now he was stinking more at the crazy cheek of this Cossack gulag rat.

Hetman Dmitrov seemed to notice nothing of all this. If anything, his gaze was concentrated, together with his mind, on the soft breasts of the marshal's mistress. What luxury it would be for a weary warrior to sink his head between them like between two silken pillows. Why, her body would naturally be all over as silky as any pillow. What pleasure she could give to a man, even one as tired from fighting and riding as he was.

The marshal seemed to notice his interest in the woman.

He said sharply, for he, too, fancied himself as a ladies' man, who had always been successful with women even before he had achieved such high rank, 'Comrade Hetman, let me ask you a couple of questions.'

'I am at your disposal, Comrade Marshal,' the hetman replied in the old fashioned Imperial Russian Army fashion. He swept his sabre upwards again in a silver-flashing salute.

Rokossovsky told himself, Yes, you are, you cheeky bastard – totally at my disposal, to let live and to make die. But he didn't say that aloud. Instead he asked, 'What of the immediate front? What are the Fritzes up to between here and the River Elbe?'

'Up to?' the Cossack leader guffawed, showing his fine set of steel false teeth. 'They're running, Comrade Marshal, running with their hindlegs in their hands and their pants full of shit.'

'So how is it your Cossacks suffered so badly, eh?'

By way of an answer, Hetman Dmitrov indicated the wrecked German tank lying on its side in the nearby ditch, its crew scattered among the trees, the bits and pieces of their wrecked bodies dangling from the branches like some monstrous gory-red human fruit. 'We ran up against some Fritz tanks on our way back, Comrade, and even we Cossacks can't kill tanks with our sabres, though we tried.'

'Well said, Hetman,' the marshal answered. 'And how far did you get on your reconnaissance? To the Elbe?'

'To the Elbe!' the Cossack leader spat contemptuously into the dust at his horse's hooves. 'That far. *Nyet*. Way beyond the Fritz river.'

'*Boshe moi.*' Rokossovsky cursed in admiration and indicated that his adjutant up front should give him his bottle of pepper Vodka which he always drank on these long drives to the fighting front. 'We shall drink to that, Hetman.'

The Cossack smiled, once again revealing those gleaming polished metal teeth of his. 'You are kindness itself, your honour.' He licked his thick sensual lips in anticipation.

The marshal shook his head at the Cossack's boldness – or was it stupidity – at using the old formality of the Czarist days. He handed the rider the bottle of choice vodka. The Hetman's eyes gleamed. Carefully he wiped the neck with the trailing sleeve of his Cossack coat, as if it was a very precious thing, then lifting it to his lips and tilting back his head took a tremendous swig before gasping, '*Nastrovyanpan . . . spasive!*'

'Now then,' Rokossovskg asked when he had returned the precious bottle, 'any sign of the English on the other side of the river if, as you say, you got that far in your reconnaissance?'

'Not altogether,' he replied warily.

'What's that supposed to mean, Hetman?'

'I knew I was not supposed to come into contact with the English. We are allies with them and the Americans after all.'

'Get on with it,' the marshal snapped. 'What's that "not altogether" supposed to mean?'

'Well, Marshal, it was like this. We were about at the end of our patrol. The men were getting tired, and the horses too. We'd had some women,' he smiled winningly at the mistress, who actually blushed, 'and some firewater, too, that we took off the Fritzes. So we thought we'd just about done enough when we heard the sound of motors.' He shrugged. 'Then we had to make a decision. Motors could mean Fritz troops and not civilians. Had we the strength to tackle regular army Fritzes? Should we go to ground and see if they were soldiers or civilians?'

'And they were English?' the marshal cut him short. He was getting tired of the way the former gulag rat was making a play for his mistress, the whore, right in front of his eyes. He had sent colonels like the Cossack to punishment battalions from which there was no return for far less than making eyes at his whore.

'Well, I think so, Comrade Marshal,' the Cossack agreed,

seemingly not noticing the marshal's sudden temper. 'We let them go by because they weren't Fritzes and afterwards one of my boys picked up this.' He reached inside his long black coat where he kept that precious leather bag of his native earth and with his big paw, marked with the slashes of sabre-fighting of the old days, thrust something at the marshal.

Reluctantly Marshal Rokossovsky took it in his delicate, well-manicured hand. He knew the Cossacks wiped their arses on tufts of grass and didn't wash much in general. God only knew what one might catch from them, even their colonels. While the Cossack continued to ogle his whore unashamedly, he looked at what the former had offered him. It was a beret, old and faded, so that the red colour of the material had almost vanished, adorned by a tarnished silver badge denoting a stylized wing. Despite its condition, he knew what it was. It was the cap of an English paratrooper. In the newsreels of the abortive English airborne drop at Arnhem in Holland the previous year he had seen such badges.

Rokossovsky frowned. He even forgot the way that the Cossack was making up to his whore. In his position there were plenty of other pretty women who were only too eager to sleep with a marshal of the Soviet Union. He made up his mind. 'Get someone to look after your mount,' he snapped very businesslike now. 'You're coming with me, Hetman.'

The Cossack beamed. 'I have lice, Comade Marshal. In the warmth of your fine car, the little darlings will come to life. Maybe they might start to wander about—'

'Get in,' Rokossovksy ordered.

The Cossack didn't need a second invitation. Minutes later he was squeezed in the back of the captured Mercedes, his leg pressing hard against the plump thigh of the not unwilling marshal's whore . . .

* * *

With the practised ease of the veteran tactician that he was, the marshal swept his pale, delicate hand over the big map on the table of his headquarters. Outside, well-dressed staff officers with neat uniforms and clean faces came and went in their quiet orderly fashion. Indeed, in the large German castle which served as Rokossovsky's HQ in East Germany, the war seemed a long way away and the Cossack Hetman in his battered Cossack coat, fingering his leather bag of earth a little nervously, totally out of place.

'Those blue crayon marks,' the Marshal explained as if he were talking to an idiot, 'are our positions here in Mecklenburg, Colonel.' He pointed to the red crayon marks. 'Those are the Fritz positions – or at least they were as of this morning.'

Outside, the green-hatted NKVD troops patrolled at their steady pace and even the elegant staff officers got out of the way of the feared secret police. The hetman, who was not as stupid as the Marshal thought he was, told himself that even marshals of the Soviet Union came under the supervision of Old Leather Face's[*] secret police. The realization did his heart good. As important as these big shots were, they all caved in in fear when it came to dealing with the Soviet dictator in the Kremlin.

The hetman forgot the NKVD police and the marshal too for that matter. He concentrated on the mistress sitting opposite and her shapely knees clad in sheer black silk. God, he'd like to be between them now before whatever the marshal had planned for him – and this order to come to Rokossovsky's HQ meant there was something in the wind – took him back to the front.

Only the previous day, after they had shot up the Fritz *trek*, he had raped three German women: two 14-year olds and the usual granny. He had taken the *babushka*, not on

[*] Nickname for the pock-marked, tanned head of the Soviet Union, Josef Stalin.

account of her withered charms – she'd had long hairs sprouting from her chin – but because every Cossack knew that sex with an old woman always meant luck; and he had the feeling he was soon going to need all the luck possible.

Inwardly he chuckled at the memory of the old dear dancing the mattress polka with him on the top of the kitchen table the Fritzes had brought with them, with his men whistling and cheering him on, while she threshed and twist as he had given it to her. Now he thought the old *babushka* had been the lucky one; she'd liked it . . .

But that had been more than twenty-four hours ago. The hetman could feel his loins stirring at the sight of those black-clad women's knees, especially as the marshal's whore had opened them slightly and was revealing more than perhaps she should.

Marshal Rokossovsky tapped his knuckles a little angrily on the map. He knew the Cossack bastard wasn't really listening to him. His mind was elsewhere, probably trying to look at the whore's knickers the way she kept her legs open like that in her shameless fashion. He raised his voice. 'Now then, Hetman, this is what I want you to do. I am going to give you another Cossack battalion, fully mounted and armed, fresh to the front from their native Kuban. In fact they are already here on my sector of the line.'

'And Comrade Marshal?'

'You are to advance on a line Schwerin, Wismar, which is the coast, and beat the English there. It is the order of Marshal Stalin that we shall take as much of the Baltic coast as we can before the English do so and the Fritzes collapse completely.'

The Cossack took his eyes off the mistress's shapely black-clad knees. 'But the English are our allies, Comrade Marshal,' he objected.

'*Were!*' Rokossovksy said simply. 'Our beloved leader in Moscow knows no allies in this Great Patriotic War of ours.' Whether the Cossack noticed the sneer in the marshal's voice didn't matter; Rokossovsky, the former gulag rat himself, knew the bastard wouldn't survive what was to come.

'And what am I to do if the English object?' the Cossack said. 'Even my bunch of rogues and gulag rats do not betray comrades who have fought beside them in battle.' He couldn't contain himself. 'We leave the stab in the back to higher echelons.'

Marshal Rokossovsky allowed himself a wintry smile. He knew only too well what the damned Cossack meant, but it wasn't wise to allow such thoughts to be expressed aloud. 'I know nothing of that, Hetman. What are you to do?' He answered his own question with a gesture. It was that of someone drawing a sharp knife across the throat of someone else. '*Poneneyo?*'

The hetman nodded his head somberly. He knew well what the Marshal meant. For some reason he clutched the bag of his native earth underneath his black coat. It was the earth of his native Volga, for in true Cossack fashion he intended to be buried in the good soil of his homeland wherever death overtook him. Even if it was the hated Germany where he had to die, a handful of the earth from the leather bag would ensure it would always be that of his native Volga.

'Now,' Rokossovsky said in way of dismisal, his mind already full of his continued offensive against the crumbling German front in the north, 'the day is yours. You take over the Kuban Cossacks tomorrow and then you start westwards. In the meantime,' he added, looking pointedly at his whore, 'there are enough whores about the place for you to take your pick.' Surprisingly for such a fastidious man, he made an obscene gesture with the circle of his forefinger and thumb and the middle finger of his other hand. 'There'll be plenty of polka dancing for you, if you wish it, and vodka too. That'll be all.'

The Cossack touched his two fingers almost to his fur

cap in salute. He knew that he was being dismissed in this crude fashion because the marshal was jealous of the way he had got on with his woman. The thought made him feel good. He would have liked to have the mistress, but he couldn't. What did it matter? A woman was a woman, pretty or ugly, eighteen or eighty. They were all the same in the dark.

So he swaggered out of the HQ, ignoring even the hard suspicious looks of the 'greencaps'. He'd get drunk, he'd whore and undoubtedly in due course, he would be killed in battle. What did it all matter? Life was too short and dangerous to worry about such matters – at least for a Cossack. 'March or croak', that was his motto. A happy man, without apparently a single care in the world, the hetman went on his way, whistling as he did so . . .

Three

The Typhon fell out of sky as if by magic. One moment it was just a vague sound in the distance the next it was zooming in at tree-top height, its prop wash sending the tall grass around the stream whipping back and forth. Although they had not managed to put out any recognition panels, pinned-down by the machine-gunner on the hillock as they were, the Typhoon pilot saw their problem at once. As the heavy plane roared overhead, Savage caught a glimpse of the pilot in the cockpit as he raised his thumb to signal he had spotted them and was coming in for another sortie.

Savage's heart beat faster. 'Thank God,' he said hoarsely as he lay there waiting for the unknown enemy machine gunner's next burst of fire.

It didn't come. For now the Typhoon fell out of the afternoon sky once more and this time he was coming for the kill. Almost touching the ground in order to make his fire accurate and not strike the men lying full length on their bellies just beyond the minefield, he roared in at nearly 400 miles an hour, four 20mm cannon spitting angry fire. Like angry hornets the red bursts of fire hurried towards the gunner, trailing ziz-zags of brown smoke behind them. A mine was struck behind the prostrate men. It showered them with clods of earth and pebbles. They didn't mind. They knew the Typhoon would get them out of the deadly trap in which they found themselves.

Now the pilot upped his fire. The 20mm shells started

to eject the earth in front of them in angry violent spurts. The shells climbed the hillside. Up there the unknown gunner tried to raise his machine gun to meet the new challenge. Too late. Now the shells were ripping the hillside apart. No one could survive that terrible maelstrom of fire. The gunner broke for the first time. He abandoned the gun. Savage could see him vaguely through the white smoke of the exploding shells. Even as the gunner attempted to make his escape, Savage told himself he was a poor soldier. He was trying to run uphill. He might have escaped if he had attempted to do so *downhill*; he would have gained more speed that way and the fire was climbing, not falling. But he didn't. Naturally the gunner didn't stand a chance. He stopped in mid-stride, one foot raised in the air, as if considering whether to continue or not. The next moment he fell flat to the ground, dead before he reached it, and the Typhoon was roaring high into the sky, twisting in the barrel roll of victory. A few moments later the plane was marely a black dot in the spring sky.

Suddenly there was a heavy echoing silence. For a few moments nobody moved. Then like silent ghosts rising from the grave, the men began to lever themselves from the earth. Someone farted hard. It broke the tension. Someone said, 'Dirty pig. It int enough that the Jerries shit on us . . .'

Savage was not listening. Carefully he surveyed their front – just in case. But nothing moved ahead. The pilot had done his work well. The dead gunner had been the sole opposition. He frowned and wondered what had been the point of it all, the mines, without troops to cover them, save for the lone gunner. He didn't know what to make of it. He turned and commanded, 'Sergeant Meek, you come with me . . . The rest of you, lads, start bringing your vehicles across. Looks OK now.'

Together he and the big sergeant started to plod up the hill to the burned patch of charred grass and soil. The air stank of acrid fumes. They didn't notice. Both of them experienced battlefield veterans as they were, were wondering why the enemy had left behind a single soldier to cover the crossing site after so much preparation, or so it seemed, to equip the trap. It seemed totally unlike the professional German soldier, who knew all the tricks of their murderous trade to waste time like that.

They skirted the still smoking mound of earth littered with the bits and pieces of the Spandau machine gun which the Typhoon pilot's cannon had shredded like thin paper. They moved up the hill a little to where the dead gunner lay on his back, red buttonholes stitched by the pilot running its length. They stopped and stared at the body. It was covered by the usual camouflaged cape worn by German snipers, a black peaked cap obscuring the face a little. It smelled like all German military did. Yet there was something unmilitary about the corpse. For a moment Savage was puzzled, then two things struck him about the body. The corpse wore neither the jackboots nor the newer gaiters and boots of the *Wehrmacht*. Instead it wore civilian shoes and very small ones at that. They were dainty even with a slight high heel. He frowned and bent down to look at the dead man's face. The movement must have dislodged the peaked cap. It rolled to one side, as if suddenly it had a life of its own, to reveal long hair – even for a German – and an unmistakeable female face with plucked eyebrows.

'Cor, ferk a duck!' Sergeant Meek exclaimed. 'It's a frigging judy.'

'A judy, it is, 'Savage agreed slowly, face set in a puzzled frown. 'What the devil is a woman – no, a girl – doing defending an important position like this with a Spandau?'

'And all on her lonesome at that,' Meek agreed. 'Christ sir, she can't be more than fourteen or fifteen.' With the toe of his boot he had turned the corpse fully over so that they could get a better view of her. 'Why, she ain't got no tits to speak of, like, sir.'

Savage nodded his head in agreement. 'I know that the Jerries are scraping the barrel, calling up anybody who can hold and fire a rifle. But this is going too far. She's a mere kid and why is she, *was she*,' he corrected himself, 'defending a position like this?'

Meek shook his head, equally bewildered. 'Search me, sir.'

As they walked back to the vehicle, which was clouding the air with the fumes of petrol as the drivers gunned their engines eager to get away from this strange place, the old NCO said, 'That's the second bloody mystery this day, sir.'

Deep in thought, Savage nodded absently. 'First that civvie trek massacred, perhaps by the Russians – and what the Russkis are doing over here, God only knows. They're supposed to be miles away over the other side of the River Elbe. And now this young tart covering the well-laid mine-field like that. Just one tart. All very strange.' He shook his head again like a sorely troubled man.

'Very strange indeed, Meek,' Savage said as he got back into the jeep, next to Charlie who, obviously awed by the place, was gunning his engine impatiently too. 'One thing is clear, however.'

'And what's that, sir?

'Well, if the Jerries are pulling back using the main roads, defending them till the pressure from our side gets too much and they retreat, we ought to be OK on the side and country roads. Well, that's what I thought when we set out. But obviously that's not the case, is it? We've had two bloody examples of that this day.'

'Yessir. And?'

'The general –' he meant the commander of the Sixth Airborne – 'wants us to get our finger out of the orifice and move at all possible speed.' At that moment Savage thought it not wise to tell Meek the business with the Russians; a lot of the older men were quite left-wing these days and he had enough problems on his hands with the old lags as it was. 'So, if we're going to have problems on these side roads, then we use the main ones.'

'But the Jerries are using them, 'Meek objected.

'Yes, I know. But we're going to take a chance. We'll mingle with their columns – we did it before during the breakout from Normandy, we're using the same camouflaged smocks as their SS and they're using our jeeps and the like.'

Meek whistled softly and said, 'Risky, sir?'

'I know, Sergeant. But life's like that. As the chaps would say, "roll on death and let's have a fuck at the angels".'

'If you say so, sir.' And with that they moved off.

All that late April afternoon, with the permanent barrage rumbling in the distance indicating the battle was still continuing, they rolled north. Occasionally allied fighters buzzed them, coming down low to check them. But now they had their recognition panels draped across the bonnets of their vehicles and with a swift waggle of their wings and a wave from the pilot, the allied fighters, looking for targets of opportunity, would speed away northwards, looking for their 'kills'. Now and again the little convoy of paratroopers passed through tumbledown hamlets and medieval villages. But the half-timbered, white-painted houses were tightly shuttered, with not an inhabitant in sight, though the paras, fingers on the triggers of their weapons, knew that there were fearful civilians pressed tightly behind the doors and shuttering, waiting for the sound of their passing to end. Twice they ran through farming communities adorned with the white of surrender: sheets, towels, old longjohns, anything that indicated there'd be no trouble here. In both cases, the streets were packed with drunken DPs[*], slave labourers from half a dozen German occupied countries, enjoying their freedom and cheering wildly at the smiling paras as they went on their way.

[*] Displaced Persons.

In the Bedford truck, a sour-faced Scouse grunted to his neighbour, one of the original A Company, 'Lucky foreign buggers. Get pissed like that – and women too. I bet they'll fuck their way home tonight, going at it like a sodding fiddler's elbow. And us? We're still liable to get our bleeding heads shot off.' He spat angrily out of the back of the little truck.

The A Company soldier, who like most of his comrades had no time for Scouse and his kind, said, 'Ah, but that lot might get a social disease from being naughty, Scouse, start pissing in ten different directions. You wouldn't like that, mate, would you. Besides, when this little lot is over, His Majesty will award you a nice big putty medal.' He grinned at Scouse's discomforture. 'Now what do you say to that, Scouse?'

By way of a rejoinder, Scouse held up a dirty middle finger.

The old A company man laughed. 'Fraid I can't, Scouse. Cos I've got a double-decker bus up there already, mate.'

So they rolled on, with Savage in the lead jeep studying his map carefully while Meek, who wasn't letting his guard down for a moment (though the flat dull countryside seemed empty now as if they were the last men left alive in the world) poised behind his twin Brownings, ready to open fire at the first sign of trouble.

Savage was heading for Celle, the first major town ahead and the centre of a road network, leading north-west to the great port of Bremen and from there ever northwards to Denmark. To the northeast, the route he had chosen, and which, God willing, wouldn't be the one the German army's main force would select if it was heading for Denmark, led to Hamburg and to the north-east Lubeck and the Baltic coast.

According to the maps and the briefing he had received from the Sixth Airborne's divisional intelligence officer before he had set out on his mission, after Celle he would enter a huge swampy forest area which ran for miles. Before the war it had been the favourite weekend holiday target for Hamburg's citizens. There were villages enough in the forest, but few roads, which ran dead-straight for the great port and the River Elbe. As the divisional intelligence officer had commented, 'Tight little places closed in by the tress and swamps on both sides. Could be held by a couple of likely lads of the Hitler Youth, armed with one of those damned rocket-launchers of theirs – the *Panzerfaust*. Not to worry, dear boy,' he had added in the foppish manner he had adopted when briefing combat officers, whom he knew never took him seriously anyway. Intelligence officers were always regarded as nervous nellies, ready to fill their breeches at any moment. 'Your main problem is getting across the Elbe at here,' he had stabbed the map with his well-manicured forefinger, 'between Dannenberg and a place called Geesthacht.'

'Why?' Savage had asked.

'No bridge,' the intelligence officer had answered laconically.

Savage had grinned, even though he had been a little shocked. How was he going to carry out the mission that Monty had given him to lead the division as swiftly as possible to the Baltic coast, if there wasn't a bridge available?

The divisional expert had taken it lightly. 'Oh, well,' he had said airily. 'Not to worry. You frontline chaps always come up with a solution, don't you, what?'

Now, as the shadows lengthened, Savage pushed the problem of the River Elbe to the back of his mind. The way things were going, he told himself, he'd have to play this thing bit by bit. First things, first. Soon he'd have to give the men a break. They definitely needed a brew-up and something warm to eat. After all, he told himself, the British soldier seemed to live on his 'char'. Without it, he couldn't apparently function; and he couldn't allow his paras to brew up after dark. In this 'Indian country', as Meek had called it, a fire would be a dead giveaway. He looked at his watch. It was nearly six. At seven it would be dark. The time had come to find a suitable spot to stop. Thereafter he'd decide what to do next.

'I think we'll pull in over there, Sergeant Meek,' he ordered, indicating a small clearing in the pine forest to the right of the little cobbled road. 'Time for a brew up.'

'Right-o, sir,' Meek agreed. He licked his dry lips. 'I'm fair parched myself.'

Five minutes later while Savage posted sentries, the men busied themselves with lighting their Tommy cookers, or if they didn't possess the petrol stoves which were highly dangerous because they were inclined to explode if the petrol jets were not perfectly clean, filling tins with earth, dousing the earth with petrol and using them as heaters. Others were opening the cases of compo rations, pulling out the tins, throwing the ones they hated, such as soyalink sausages and pilchards to one side, grabbing the fruit salad which contained the sugar they all craved, and with the usual wag cracking the usual joke by asking, 'Which can has got the cunt in it, corp?'

Five minutes later, they were wolfing down great slabs of corned beef between iron-hard biscuits, produced by Spillers, who before the war had produced the same biscuits for pet-dogs, or spooning greasy chunks of meat from the tins of 'Meat and Vegetables', washing down the whole lot with steaming mugs of char.

Watching them with Meek, Savage told himself the old lags seemed to be soldiering once again. 'They're settling in, Sergeant Meek,' he commented savouring the first of his seven ration cigarettes which were also part of the ration box. 'The old lags, I mean.'

Meek wasn't totally convinced. Shifting the boiled sweet he was sucking from one side of his mouth to the other, the big Yorkshireman looked at the men squatting in the grass, savouring the simple food and enjoying this time out of the action. He said slowly, 'Ay for the most part. But yon Scouse, I don't know, sir.'

'Oh, come on, Sergeant Meek, where in devil's name is he going to run to, out here in the middle of nowhere, if that's what you're thinking. Besides, he'd stand a fair chance of being shot if he ran into any Jerries doing so, remember that now.'

Still Meek wasn't convinced and Savage didn't think the matter was important enough to pursue. So he changed the subject. 'Let's give 'em another five minutes and then be on our way. We'll travel with our convoy lights on. I know it's risky, Meek, but I'm banking on the fact that if we meet the Old Hun he'll take us for one of their own units travelling with our convoy lights on.'

'Good idea, sir. But why the hurry. I would have thought first light would have been a better time to start. The men could kip till then.'

'Meek, that would be the best on any other occasion. Just before dawn, most men are half asleep, both ours and theirs. But I'm hoping we can get through before it gets light . . .' He broke off suddenly and smelled the air, nostrils twitching like those of some predatory wild animal. 'Funny pong,' he concluded. 'Can't make it out.'

Meek followed suit. He shook his greying head. 'I can't smell nothing,' he said. 'You was saying, sir – get through what?'

Savage dismissed the sickly sweet pungent smell and answered, 'Celle. After that, God willing, it'll be a plain run to the Elbe . . .'

But Savage was mistaken. There was not going to be a plain run for his little force this night.

Four

The doctor's personal *Kapo* could see his chief was nervous as he packed what *Herr Stabsarz** Kunz called playfully his 'little souvenirs of my camp life' into the packing case that would be off to the university, where the collections of such little souvenirs were kept until *Obergruppen-führer* Himmler of the SS built the museum he had planned for all the deposits from the camps.

Naturally the *Kapo*, the former Hamburg communist leader who was biding his time until he and his comrades started shooting the bastards who had beaten and tortured them for so long, knew his nervousness was part fear and part elation. Kunz, bespectacled and weak-chinned, not at all what one would expect from a long-time member of the SS, was scared shitless that the allies would get him before he made his escape into this new role that that bastard Himmler had selected for him. At the same time Kunz was excited at the propsect. Already he had changed from the flashy black SS uniform he had worn in the camp, complete with his sole decoration, the Sport Medal, Third Class, into that of the *Wehrmacht* with the silver runes of the Fighting SS on its collar.

Now as he swaggered into the room in his new uniform, buckling on the heavy pistol belt, complete with spare magazines, and with even a stick grenade tucked down the side of his boot in the style of a real hairy-arsed front swine, he said, 'How do I look, Bruno, you red swine?'

---

* Staff Doctor.

Bruno remembered the times when that 'red swine' had been accompanied by a slash from the dog whip that Kunz had habitually used on the poor swine of the camp. Now it meant nothing. Perhaps just a master and servant thing. All the same he clicked to attention, hands rigid at the sides of his filthy pyjama suit. 'Beg to report everything running according to plan, *Oberstabsarzt*'. He told himself that you could never be sure of how these SS buggers would react. It was better to flatter them; hence the use of *Oberstabsarzt*,*

Despite his preoccupation with his new role as a fighting man, Kunz was flattered by the elevated rank. 'Good,' he said. 'Have you packed the tit yet?'

'*Jawohl, Oberstabsarzt*,' Bruno bellowed, as if he were some raw recruit on the parade answering his drill sergeant. 'Packed especially well, sir.'

Kunz tightened the pistol belt about his skinny waist and threw an admiring glance at himself in the full length mirror in the corner next to the pile of prepared and carefully labelled skulls which had been his first project in 1941 when he had been posted from the east to this small auxiliary camp to Belsen further up the road on the other side of Celle.

'Good, Bruno, I am especially proud of that tit. Pity it has to go to the *Reichsführer*. I'd like it for my own private collection. The tit is always good for a long chat at the dinner table.'

'Yessir . . . understood, sir,' Bruno, still standing to attention, barked in the military fashion that he always adopted with the camp doctor, more especially now that he was to take up some sort of combat soldier function. Under his breath, he whispered, 'Pig. Hope one day somebody does the same to your shit tits.'

He and Kunz had come across the tit back in 1943. Apparently it had come from some Polack. The wench must have possessed an enormous bosom, for even when the

*Senior staff doctor.

mass of flesh had been shrunk and skinned, the 'tit' had been twice the size of a pair of normal, woman's tits. But that hadn't been the reason Kunz had seized it from the mad Polack. It had been the fact that the tit had been tattoed with an obscene sex act, which had occasioned Kunz to comment (rather prissily for him, who routinely took twelve- and thirteen-year-old girls to his bed in order to deflower them), 'Only your inferior Slavs could think of that sort of piggery, Bruno.'

It had long been Kunz's wish to have the tit turned into a tobacco pouch. As he often said rather ruefilly to his servant, 'What a conversation it would make at an evening *stammtisch*.' He meant the table reserved for cronies at the local inn. 'I could take it and make a show of filling my pipe with tobacco from it – I'll have to learn to smoke a pipe, of course – and they'd look and I'd say, casually naturally, "Oh yes, quite an interesting history this tabacco pouch. Made from a Warsaw whore's tit by the way . . .".'

Now as he set the *Wehrmacht* cap on his bald head at what he thought was a typically bold, arrogant SS officer's angle, he snapped, 'Going to have a last look at the old place. Fond memories and all that, Bruno. We Germans are a sentimental race, aren't we just.'

'*Jawohl, Obarstabsarzt,*' Bruno bellowed as Kunz swaggered out, his pistol belt sagging, just as his breeches were, too. 'Arsa with ears,' Bruno swore, relaxing. Then he got on with the packing of the SS doctor's 'priceless collection', as Kunz called it, maintaining that 'their like won't be seen for another thousand years, I'll be bound,' a sentiment with which the ex-communist docker agreed wholeheartedly

The Belsen auxiliary camp looked like all the camps that Doctor Kunz had served in ever since he had been first appointed to Dachau back in the late thirties: a half a dozen hectares of hard-packed naked farmland shaped in the form of a great hexagon by the high triple wire that ran round it.

Inside the wire patrolled by fierce German shepherd dogs, trained to go for any would-be escapee's genitals, there was the usual collection of dreary dark-brown wooden huts. They were grouped around an earthen square dominated by the crooked cross flag, hanging limply from its pole, and that ironic sign: '*WORK MAKES FREE*'.

Not that the emaciated wretched prisoners in their striped uniforms and wooden clogs, assembling under the machine guns of the watchtowers, would ever be free

As he swaggered through the camp, with the prisoners cringing and bowing as he passed, he told himself they wouldn't be allowed to survive. They knew too much about this auxiliary camp and the Belsen one on the other side of Celle. 'Dead men tell no tales,' he muttered under his breath as he walked deliberately over a corpse lying in the dirt. Next moment he regretted doing so. The body gave off what sounded like a long wet fart and the spring air was flooded with that cloying sickly smell of human gas that even after all these years he couldn't get used to. Hastily he took out the silver cigarette case decorated with the skull and crossbones of the SS and lit a cigarette. It was Turkish and perfumed but it could hide the stench of that awful odour. He went hurriedly, already forgetting this little 'sentimental journey' into a life that he would soon be leaving.

There'd be no more experiments of a kind that he had not dared dream of as an ambitious medical student; no more cringing frightened prisoners, one-time professors, politicians and the like, who were completely at his mercy, whose lives had depended upon his mood of the moment, his every idle whim; and, above all, no more 'green fruit', as he called them: those tender little virgins, with their brown smudges of pubic hair and faint, pink-tipped breasts that always made his heart beat frantically when he toyed with them till that final sadistic plunge into their unused vagina and their spines arching like a taut bow.

He tossed away the cigarette at the thought, already noting the prisoners' dull eyes light up as they spotted the still glowing cigarette end, waiting till he had passed on so that they could fight for it in the mud. In the old days he often took pleasure in shooting the one who managed to seize the prized cigarette end. Not now. He patted his pistol holster as if he were already leading his new killers in battle. Now in his new role, he would find worthier human targets to shoot and kill than these sub-humans that surrounded him at the moment.

Mindful of the new mission, he strode to the gate. The young SS sentries, all cripples from the Eastern Front or old men pressed into service in this 'eleventh hour', clicked to attention. He returned the salute casually. 'Keep up your guard, men,' he warned them. 'We still have a duty to perform for our Führer.'

'But I've got my old woman back home in bed in Nienburg, sick as a dog,' one of the old greybeards quavered, the snot dribbling from his red nose. 'I ought to be with her.'

Kunz looked at the sway-backed old man with his World War One medal ribbons contemptuously. 'How can you think of such personal matters, *Sturmann* in Germany's hour of need? What do our personal affairs concern our beloved Führer? Our duty is to obey and sacrifice our lives willingly, if we are called upon to do so. *Sturmann*, you ought to be ashamed of yourself – 'He broke off suddenly. A van with the legend '*Wolfert & Sohne, Spedition, Celle*' came chugging towards the camp, the gas balloon on its roof which supplied it with its fuel wobbling and trembling like a live thing.

Kunz forgot the old greybeard. It was the van, part of the transport which the organization had been assembling for the last few months ever since the Battle of the Ardennes when the German army had commenced its retreat into the Reich and the organization had come into its own.

It had been around then that he and the rest of the future adult leaders had been summoned to Berlin to hear from no less a person than *Reichsführer SS Heinrich Himmler* what their surprising new task was to be.

The future leaders had come from all branches of the services and civilian life: wounded veterans, no longer of any use to the official fighting force; people like himself whose jobs in the slave camps would no longer be needed; state officials in key positions, which the enemy would need if they wanted to keep Germany running if they managed to conquer what was left of the battered Reich. And surprisingly enough in this dark hour of Germany's greatest need, all of them, like Kunz, were amazingly optimistic. As Kunz's neighbour at the Himmler briefing, a former *Luftwaffe* pilot, whose face was so hideously burned that he kept it hidden behind a silken mask, had said in his strange guttural voice, the product of some clever surgeon's skill, 'They will never conquer us, *Stabsarzt*. The Führer has promised us a Reich that will last a thousand years and *we* will see that it does, come what may.'

Himmler had obviously shared the terrible mutilated pilot's confidence. Swiftly he sketched the new secret organization. 'It will consist of some five thousand odd of our best girls and boys, all volunteers from the Hitler Youth organizations and all with para-military training and armed from the secret arms caches which we have been hiding all over the country since the Jewish-Bolsheviks have had the audacity to cross our frontiers.' Himmler had shown his ugly teeth in a parody of a smile. 'And who will suspect such apparently harmless youths and maidens of attempting to do any harm, what, comrades?'

There had been a murmur of agreement from his audience, who were too intrigued by what they were going to hear here to waste time on applause.

'Now comrades,' Himmler had continued, peering at them through his pince-nez which made him look like some small-town high school teacher, 'what, you may ask, have you, all established men and women, to do with a bunch of young people in short trousers? I shall tell you.

'These boys and girls are to use the arms and supplies which have been secreted for them from the Reich's frontier, through the Eifel and well into the Rhineland and beyond, not only to deal with –' he drew his finger across his skinny, hen-neck threat significantly – 'these allied invaders in their twos and threes, wherever they are in small numbers, but also to ensure that none of the local German populace stray from the path of our holy National Socialism.' He had looked grim and here and there members of the audience muttered 'swine', 'defeatist bastards', 'traitor' and the like.

'Yes, indeed,' Himmler had agreed sadly with the comments, 'there are unfortunately such people among our ranks. After all the sacrifices our dear Führer Adolf Hitler has made for the German people, there are those who will undoubtedly offer succour and assistance to the enemy when they arrive.' There was something akin to a sob in his voice and at that moment Doctor Kunz's heart had gone out to the *Reichsführer*. He asked himself what kind of a swine could cause such a noble man to suffer such grief and pain.

'But they must not survive to enjoy the fruits of their treachery, folk-comrades. They must be liquidated.' His voice had grown hard and determined once more.' *Wiped off the face of this earth!*'

'*Hoch, hoch*,' they had cried, thrusting out their right arms in the German greeting and crying almost hysterically, '*Heil Hitler . . . heil Hitler!*' as their eyes glowed with fanatical loyalty.

Himmler had smiled with pleasure and then said, 'And who shall carry out that liquidation? I shall tell you. Those brave boys and girls in their short trousers – and they shall do so, folk-comrades, under your guidance. Yes,' his voice had risen and he had lifted his right finger to emphasize his point, 'under your leadership. You will lead this new secret organization, which will put fear and trembling into those Reds and Jews who have the temerity to *attempt* to invade our homeland.'

He paused and his skinny chest had heaved to and fro with the effort of so much talk. Finally he had caught his breath. 'Folk-comrades, I welcome you to *Operation Werewolf!*'

That had been a month before. In the meantime Dr Kunz had prepared for his new role as Werewolf Leader. He rather fancied himself as a dashing figure in field uniform which might well win the Iron Cross before the war was over. Besides, the role he was to play in this secret organization, composed of young people half his age, would be comparatively safe. After all, when everything was established and running he would take up the post of a small town GP and leave the dirty work to the youth. With his new identity already provided by the Berlin Main Office of the SS, what he had done in the camps (though personally he could see nothing wrong in it; after all it had all been done in the name of science) would be obliterated. Dr Kunz would be forgotten, killed in action in the confused last days of the fighting. Middle-aged Dr Med Havelmann, a humble small town practitioner, bombed out from his native Hamburg would be a totally different proposition altogether.

To some extent, however, his plans had been upset by his first meeting with Otto Grube, the Werewolf's contact, a local farmer's son to judge by his accent and manners. Two days before, he had driven up in the gas-power removal van with which he covered the area, accompanied by two of his local 'hunting commandos', as the Werewolf cells called themselves.

The kids, a girl and a boy both about sixteen, looked the part. They were bronzed, keen-looking and hard. To Kunz they fitted ideally the motto of modern German youth: tough as leather, as fast as a greyhound and as hard as Krupp steel. Otto Grube never even came close to that standard. He had rolled out of the truck's driving seat, a great mass of sweating blubber, his head tilted permanently to one side like some village idiot and, waddling up to Dr Kunz, said, 'Name – Grube. I'm in charge.' He offered a pudgy hand that glistened with sweat too, the fingernails encrusted with dirt so much so that Kunz had hesitated to take it. In the end he had, wondering how such a gross misshapen creature could have been chosen for the role he was to play in the Werewolf Organization. His type would have been given a lethal injection by the 'angel-makers' of the SS back in the good old days and quickly seen off. But Kunz reasoned that perhaps his appearance, as grotesque as it was, gave him the cover he needed if the enemy authorities ever came to suspect him.

Now this day, his last at the camp, he was to receive final details of the local military situation from Grube. Not something he looked forward to as the van slowed down at the gate and Grube honked his horn impatiently when the greybeard sentries were too slow opening it for him.

He was eating as usual. Where he got the food from, Kunz didn't know, but he was stuffing a salami sandwich down his throat, the butter from the sandwich dripping down his hairless chin. In his usual crude manner he didn't deign to get down to greet Kunz. Instead he rolled down the window and said, 'We're on full, alert, Kunz. Those wet-tails of the *Wehrmacht* had mined the bridge at Hannebach. But as soon as the Tommies appeared they did a bunk and left one of our people trying to hold up the enemy. Naturally she failed.' He swallowed the rest of his sandwich in one gulp, wiped the dripping butter from his chin with the back of his hand and belched. He looked as Kunz, who was obviously overwhelmed at so much military information. 'I'm just telling you this, Kunz, for your information. I'll take care of the Tommies. Your job is to get on to HQ and see if they can help us in any way.'

Kunz opened his mouth to protest he was a doctor, a member of Reichsführer Himmler's inner circle and an SS officer, not a damned messenger boy. Then he thought better of it. Only recently he had heard the rumour that Grube had personally nailed a village priest to his own church like some latter day Jesus on the Cross because the priest had preached a speedy end to the war. Numbly he nodded his understanding and Grube smiled, if one could call his lopsided grimace a smile. 'Don't bother taking any of your green fruit with you, Konz. I can provide you with plenty of teenagers and willing Hitler Maidens ready to sacrifice their all for the cause.'

And with that he was gone, leaving a perplexed Kunz wondering how the ugly bastard knew about his teenage girls . . .

Book Three
SLAUGHTER AT CELLE

One

B oth senior commanders, American and British, seemed satisfied with the progress of their various strageies that second week of April 1945. While Patton streaked off to meet the Russians in Czechoslovakia – hoping to capture Prague, the capital, before the Red Army – and secretly prepared to fight the erstwhile ally for that prize, two of Eisenhower's armies had surrounded the German army Group B in what was called the Ruhr Pocket. As he boasted to Lieutenant Kay Summersby at the time, 'Gee, Kay what a victory it's going to be when the Krauts surrender there.' Eisenhower had given her that famous ear-to-ear smile of his. 'Twice the number of Krauts who surrendered to us in North African back in 1943.'

'Think of the headlines stateside,' had been her response.

In a way Montgomery, the British commander, was pleased that Eisenhower had carried out what he regarded as the American's 'worthless effort' in the Ruhr. The strategy ensured that Model's army group could not turn about and drive into his right flank as his under-manncd and under-supplied army drove ever northwards. All the same, he could have used American troops, especially airborne ones to bolster up his attack. Then, although the surrounded German troops in the Ruhr did prevent the Russian armies west of Berlin attacking through them just in case they came into conflict with the Americans, there was still Rokossovksy's army doing what it liked in East Germany. And Montgomery, who had mct the Russian army commander once, had the greatest respect for the elegant former gulag rat. Indeed, when the latter had asked him how he had spent his time when not in action, 'did he drink' or 'did he keep a mistress' like he, the Russian did, right up front in his tactical headquarters, Montgomery had to reply, that 'I drink my milk and go to bed early'. As Monty had confessed to his favourite aide Major John Poston, 'Cheeky bugger, what, John! Nobody has ever asked me that kind of question before.' He had shaken his head and added, 'But the man's got style – and he's dangerous.'

Now, with that in mind, Montgomery was worried with the progress of his Sixth Airborne Division which, lacking men and motor transport, was moving more slowly than he had anticipated. Thus it was that on the same day that Major Savage far north in Germany prepared to make his move on Celle, he had Boy Browning, the deputy commander of the Airborne Corps, fly to his headquarters for an urgent conference. He didn't particularly like the ex-Guards officer – in fact he didn't like most Guards officers. Besides, the man was a notorious womanizer, who bathed in the fame of his celebrity wife the novelist Daphne du Maurier.

So, he commenced the conference with the tetchy query, 'I need paratroopers. Where do I get them, General?

Browning, the urbane ex-Guards officer, was not used to such direct questions. The Guards Brigade didn't go in for that sort of thing. But, he told himself, as he fumbled for answers, Montgomery had come from some provincial infantry regiment, the kind which spent all their service in India, or some such god forsaken place. 'The Guards never serve anywhere east of Suez' had always been the brigade's motto.

'Well, sir, bodies are awfully short,' he managed to answer.

'The Yanks?'

He shook his head. 'My commander, who you know, sir, is an American, is not inclined to let us have American paratroopers, sir.'

Montgomery looked at him hard. 'Come on, Browning,' he rasped, very direct, almost threatening now, 'there must be bodies somewhere now, perhaps in the UK. You're an old soldier. You know how the squaddies are always trying to find some way of getting back home and trying to swing the lead there while other chaps do the fighting overseas.' He had a sudden thought. 'What about the First Airborne Division? They have been refitting ever since Arnhem?'

Browning experienced a moment of *Schadenfreude*. After all, it had been Montgomery's fault that the division had suffered such grievous casualties. Hadn't he personally warned the army commander about trying to capture the bridge across the Rhine at Arnhem, telling Montgomery, 'I think, sir you're going a bridge too far.'

Monty seemed to sense what the tall airborne soldier in his elegant uniform was thinking, for he said, 'Well, surely they will have trained some parachutists by now. I need bodies and I have a plan.'

Reluctantly, Browning answered, 'Of course, sir, they have. But remember most of the volunteers for airborne training with the First are barely eighteen. And you know that regulation will not allow a boy under eighteen and a half to be sent to a fighting front.'

Monty had dismissed the objection with a wave of his hand. 'Rubblish! Boys like fighting, especially volunteers. In the last war we had youths of fourteen and fifteen in the trenches. Come on, General, time is of the essence. What have you got to offer?'

Browning thought fast. He wasn't particular concerned with individual soldiers. Working classes were there to fight and die, if necessary. But he was concerned in keeping large scale fighting formations intact. If a commander was going to amount to anything he needed to have men to command; and at this moment he was not going to reduce the strength of the First Airborne back to the skeleton formation it had been after Arnhem. 'Well, sir, there are two companies of recent recruits in training at Ringway. I think they're halfway through their parachute—'

'They'll do,' Monty interrupted him, patience exhausted. He knew Browning's game. As far as he was concerned, Browning wouldn't be going much further in any post-war British Army. 'Put them on immediate alert to come to the Continent. Fly them out, say, here, to Brussels. I need them for a drop.'

Browning looked at Montgomery aghast. 'But they're very raw, sir and only half-trained. I just said they're—'

But Field Marshal Montgomery was no longer listening. Browning had disappointed him; he had been too negative. Why should he explain to such an officer what his plans were to help Major Savage and his ex-lags from the glasshouse? Browning was dismissed . . .

'I don't want to fratenize with frawliens,' Scouse sneered, digging the dirt from beneath his big toe with his pigstriker bayonet, as they sat crosslegged in the barn waiting for the order to move out. 'I want to fuck the Jerry tarts!'

'But it's forbidden, Scouse,' Charlie, Savage's driver said. 'General Eisenhower said we've not got nothing to do with the Jerries. You're not supposed to talk even to their kids over eight. They'll pit yer back in the glasshouse if they caught yer doing out with a Jerry bint.'

Scouse laughed in Charlie's face although, these days Charlie was the only one of the ex-Brussels lags who seemed to want to have anything to do with him. 'Well if I fuck 'em, I can say the judy's under the age of eight, mate.'

Charlie pulled a face. 'You're bloody disgusting, Scouse, you know that.'

Scouse was unmoved. 'I know I am. But who cares? The way things are going, mate, we could all be dead by tomorrow. Besides, can you see that Yank, General frigging Eisenhower come up here to see what I'm up? Not sodding likely! Generals never come up this far. Too bloody dangerous and they know it. They send up silly sods like us to get our sodding heads blown off.'

Sergeant Meek, who had just come in from the latrine – the pigsty outside – where, as was his morning wont, he had rubbed black Cherry Blossom boot polish into his thinning locks to hide the grey, snapped, 'And if you don't shut up, Scouse, you'll get my size-ten boot up yer arse if you don't stop rabbiting on. Now, get yersen sorted out. It won't be long now.'

Five minutes later he yelled, 'All right get fell in and get yersens outside and look a bloody bit regimental, will yer. At the moment you all look like a shower o' shit.'

Savage caught the sergeant's words as they filed out into the dawn gloom and grinned despite what was to come. 'You sound very regimental this morning, Sergeant Meek,' he said.

'Just getting 'em ready for some real peacetime soldiering, sir' Meek said. 'They've had it too good so far, sir.'

Savage's amused grin vanished when he remembered what lay ahead for his small force of lightly armed paras. All the same, he knew they were all experienced combat soldiers. Even his old lags had lost their prison pallor by now. A few days in the open air had worked wonders. Now they looked tough and rugged, their faces red and weathered by being constantly out of doors, eating solid plain food, sleeping on earth or in barns such as last night's resting place, with no cover save a groundsheet or a gas cape thrown over a hastily dug hole in the ground. If anybody could get through Celle and whatever defences the place possessed, it would be his veterans of the old A Company and the old lags from the glasshouse.

'All right men,' he said huskily, 'I won't kid you. What we're going to do won't be any cakewalk—'

'They never are,' Scouse intoned. But no one was listening to the barrack-room lawyer now.

'We're going to get through a fair-sized German town,

which lies on an important crossroads so there should be German troops about. We're to avoid them, if we can. Therefore I require strict fire discipline. Of course, if you're fired on and can't dodge away, you fire back. Otherwise you wait for orders from me or Sergeant Meek. Understood?'

There was a hoarse murmur of agreement from the assembled paras. To their right a fire fight had broken out. Flares hissed into the sky, colouring it a garish green hue. They could hear the high-pitched hysterical burr of German spandaus, followed by the slow tick-tick of British bren guns like the work of some irate woodpecker. Savage told himself it might be one of the lead elements of the Sixth Airborne which he had been told were now only a couple of miles behind him. He hoped so. With the handful of men at his disposal he couldn't manage any serious opposition. But he had been promised 'a bit of help out of the sky'. As the follow-up weren't using code, they had been forced to radio in clear and so he thought the message could be taken in two ways: one, they were promising an airdrop of supplies, perhaps even more jeeps parachuted in; or two, reinforcements. But he thought that was hardly likely. The Sixth Airborne was running out of men as it was and they had left their parachuting equipment on the Rhine after that murderous daytime drop which had caused them a terrible thirty percent casualties.

So he dismissed the sounds of the skirmish and concentrated on the briefing. 'I have located the main crossroads on my map. Once there, we shall take the left fork leading in the general direction of a place called Luneburg and then on to the port of Hamburg. Once we're a mile up that branch road we'll be in a forest that should provide us with the cover we need. Now, I know you're asking how we're going to get through that crossroads if it's guarded? I'll tell you. We're going to pretend we're a small Jerry convoy.'

Even Sergeant Meek, the imperturbable one, was taken

aback by that. 'But sir,' he protested, 'not one of us speaks a word of German.'

'I do,' Scouse, seizing the chance, broke in. 'I can say, "Du schlafen mit me, Frawlein".'

Again the Liverpudlian was ignored and, murming a curse under his breath, felt silent.

'Any questions, chaps?'

There were none. Questions seemed superfluous. The decisions were made; they had to obey. It was the way of the common soldier in combat. He was asked, but in reality he had no control over his own future. Only the God of war could do that. So they stood by their vehicles, waiting for the order to mount up, now that they had put on their camouflage smocks and rimless helmets, which they didn't wear normally, but which, with the smocks, would make them look in the darkness more like German soldiers. Some urinated while they waited, a sure sign of nerves. Others licked their lips constantly as if they were very thirsty. A few prayed. But not many.

Now there was hardly any sound, save the faint hiss of the night wind in the spring trees and the dying chatter of the fire fight to their south. Under his breath Savage counted off the seconds to the start, eyes fixed on the green glowing dial of his wristwatch. He had done this so many times before, but you never got used to it, Savage told himself. There was always that nervous tingling in the flesh, the strange sense of unreality, as if this couldn't be happening to you; the knowledge that one moment you were a full, strong, male human being and that the next you could be an instant cripple writhing in agony on the ground, yelling for the stretcher-bearers, a part of your life finished, inexorably over. Or worse – dead!

'Eight . . . nine . . . TEN . . .'

He finished the countdown and was glad to do so. The tension was over. Now Fate would decide. 'All chaps,' he sang out, 'mount up!'

95

To their rear there came now, instead of the sounds of the fire fight between the Sixth Airborne's point and the German defenders, the steady roar of aeroplane engines. But with the noise of the convoy's motors being started up, the little group of paras didn't hear. They were on their way . . .

Back in his caravan headquarters, Monty awoke from an untroubled sleep. He took his false teeth from the water-glass at the side of his bunk bed a little hastily for he could hear the careful tread of his batman on the gravel path outside bringing his morning tea. After the tea, and if he were lucky, a nice digestive biscuit as a treat, he read the most important signals of the day. Normally he didn't get too excited about such things. Even the more drastic had lost their impact over the years. Still, the one he was waiting for would please him if it signalled success. It would feed his personal vanity. It would show Ike that the British army didn't need the Yanks to solve their problems. Scraping the barrel as Britain was for manpower, she still could provide the men to carry out vital tasks.

For a moment or two Montgomery, not a man given to introspection, allowed his mind to wander over the last six last years of war.

He remembered on that terrible last day of Dunkirk, how his future boss, another field marshal, had wept on his shoulder at the ignominy of defeat and the fact that the Boche were chasing a British army out of Europe, something they hadn't been able to do in the four terrible years of the 'last show'. He remembered too how the army establishment, all those hearty-looking red-faced generals, had hated him in 1941 for his radical revolutionary methods. How he had fired them by the dozen if they didn't live up to his standards of fitness and mental alertness. Generals and full colonels, who had done nothing more strenuous than lift a whisky-and-soda or a fat cigar, he had ordered to go out for a dawn run or else . . .

Then, before he had gone to Africa, presumably as the establishment thought to be sacked speedily like all those other Eighth Army commanders before him – and good riddance too – he had ordered the poor weak stuttering King George VI not to smoke in his presence and ordered Churchill himself not to interfere in military affairs. In Africa, after years of defeat and defeat, he had not produced another failure. Instead he had given the British nation its first real victory at the Battle of El Alamein. By 1943 he had become Britain's first real wartime hero. When he had returned home a year later, people had touched him like they might have done some god to see if he were real. That summer, whatever the Yanks might say to the contrary, he had masterminded and won the battle of the Normandy landings.

Now as he waited for the signal, he felt another idea begin to unfurl in his fertile brain like some snake preparing to strike. For a moment the magnitude of that thought took his breath away and made him gasp. He had already planned to upstage Ike and force the surrender of all German troops in the north after stopping the Russian drive to the mouth of the Baltic (something which for the time being would have to remain secret for obvious reasons). That particular triumph would gain him no kudos until finally the wartime allies fell out, as they surely would, and Russia would replace Nazi Germany as the main enemy of the West; though at the moment, concerned as he was with the prestige of the US Army, Eisenhower did not seem to have a vague idea of the future danger presented by Russia – why, he even called the cruel Russian dictator, Josef Stalin, 'Uncle Joe', as if he were some kindly avuncular figure, loved by his people.

But what if he, Monty, took the future surrender of the German army in the north a stage further? What if he forced the German commanders' hand and would only accept their surrender if it were allied to an even greater surrender?

Montgomery never thought that exciting thought to its logical conclusion that early morning. For he could suddenly hear someone running down the gravel path outside the caravan, crying to the batman bearing his morning tea mug, 'Cut of the way, old chap! Got an urgent message for the Master. Christ, sorry, you've spilled his char . . .' It was the signal.

Two

There was no mistaking the old familiar sound of the Dakotas. Savage, and Sergeant Meek manning the Brownings behind him in the lead jeep, recognized it immediately. Both of them seemed to have spent a lot of their time jumping out of the old American paratroop workhorse in recent years. Meek shoved his helmet to the back of his head and stared up at the velvet sky, still patched here and there by silver stars. He caught sight of the familiar silhouette. First one, then another, and a third. Excitedly he cried above the roar of aircraft coming down low to make a drop, 'It's them all right, sir! Our lads!'

Savage didn't waste time. He pulled out his flashlight and hoped its beam would reach that high. Hastily he flashed his recognition signal. Breath bated, he waited to see if the navigator in the lead plane had caught it. He had. But the plane was almost passed when he did. He flashed back the Sixth Airborne signal, red upon green and then red again.

Savage didn't wait for him to finish as behind him Meek counted off the number of planes and concluded. 'Nine, sir. Could be at least a company up there if they're carrying bodies.' That was exactly what Savage was now attempting to find out: bodies or supplies. Naturally he could use both. Yet at the moment, live paras were of more importance.

But he was not fated to receive an answer to his query. For the noise of the low-flying aircraft had alerted the defences of Celle, perhaps a mile away from the where they had stopped in the middle of a sugarbeet field, which seemed to be the local crop. Suddenly, startlingly, searchlights clicked on to north and south of the town. Ice-cold fingers of light probed the sky for the first sight of the airborne invaders. Without waiting to sight them, the youthful gunners, many of them under-age volunteers from the Hitler Youth and Hitler Maidens opened up with their flak cannon. A white wall of brilliant white rushed into the sky, while on the ground signal flares exploded to alert others to the impending danger.

'Poor sods,' Charlie, the driver said and spat over the side of the jeep. 'I hope they make it.'

'So do I,' Savage agreed. He'd seen such scenes far too often in the past. Often enough they resulted in mass slaughter as had been the case on the recent Rhine drop. Sometimes, however, the paras were lucky, jumping at a death-defying low height from their planes and thus avoiding the inevitable. He prayed the men up there, heading for the north of the town before the searchlights coned them, were expert enough to be able to jump at such low altitudes and save themselves. But at the moment, he told himself, there was little he could do but join up with them and provide them with the ground defence they needed when they were at their most vulnerable collecting themselves and their battle gear on the ground. 'All right, Charlie,' he snapped, 'Move it.'

Charlie 'moved it'. Behind, the rest of the little convoy followed, the sound of their engines starting up, drowned by the hammering of the flak and the first of the heavy guns taking up the challenge around Celle. Although he dare not express the thought, Savage was grateful in a way. The poor sods in the planes, now coming down even lower to drop the paras, were diverting the enemy's attention from his own little band. But although Savage might have thought that, he was wrong. He was already being watched, as they bumped and jolted across the ploughedfield, heading for the cobbled road leading to the outskirts of Celle beyond . . .

Surprisingly enough Dr Kunz, as ineffectual as he might be miltarily, had managed to alert the *Luftwaffe* at the fighter base between Celle and Luneburg. For days the Allied fighters which dominated the north German airspace had ranged far and wide trying to find the base of the feared German jet fighter, the twin-engined Messerschmitt 262. Now the fanatical young pilots who guessed they weren't going to survive the war took the opportunity of taking their revenge for the merciless bombing of their shattered homeland by the Anglo-Americans. In the absence of Allied fighters, they roared into the now evening sky to wreak havoc on the lumbering Dakotas flying at almost stalling speed as they prepared to drop their teenage, half-trained paratroopers.

At almost 600 mph, a hundred miles faster than the fastest Allied fighter, they came streaking in, seeking out their prey. They didn't have long to look. The interior lights of the transport planes flashing off and on, as they signalled their cargoes that it was time to go, gave them away almost immediately. Teeth bared in merciless grins, eyes hard and unfeeling behind their goggles, the German jet pilots homed in on their targets immediately. Even as the paras lined up at the Dakotas' doors, packed tightly behind each other, waiting for the jumpmaster to order them out, the jets' cannon started to wink their lethal white lights. Twenty-millimetre shells zipped through the air in a lethal morse. They tore great metal lumps off the Dakotas' fuselage. Screaming and yelling the paras fell out of the planes without orders. Some of them were already dead as soon as they left the door. Others crumbled in their chutes, as the shells tore them apart. Others fell shrieking to the fields below, their chutes failed and useless, to smash in a bone-smashing mess below.

Down there Dr Kunz, watching the slaughter, told himself that this wasn't war; it was a ruthless massacre. Still, it was what these Jewish Anglo-American plutocrats who had dared to desecrate the holy soil of Germany deserved. His face lit up with a crazy pleasure as he tried to count the number of dead parachutists hanging in their shrouds. But the first burst of enemy fire soon put an end to that. Swiftly he retreated to the safety of the shelters just outside the guardhouse of the main camp, Bergen-Belsen itself. Let that fat, impertinent swine Grube carry on now . . .

But Grube had other things on his mind that dawn. He had planned everything. He had settled his Werewolf hunting commando in an ideal position to deal with the Tommies coming across the fields. As for the unexpected airborne invasion that Kunz, the fool, had reported, the *Luftwaffe* seemed to be dealing with it. Besides there were plenty of guards at Bergen-Belsen to tackle those who might survive, though he didn't expect there would be many. It was Giselle who functioned as his 'assistant', though the sixteen-year-old Hitler Maiden Führerin hadn't the slightest idea what kind of assistance he expected from her.

Now, together in the underground bunker which he had picked for his secure HQ, safe from what the Allies might throw at Celle when they got that far, he was already having to restrain his great white paws, with the fingers like hairy pork sausages, from touching her nubile teenage body. For he sensed her sexuality every time she moved, all jiggling little tits under her artifical silk blouse and tight little buttocks in the black Hitler Maiden skirt. Every time she bent down and exposed her prim white cotton knickers encasing those delightful twin globes, he felt an excited stirring in his loins.

Of course, she didn't want his ugly misshapen body. Probably she dreamed of those handsome young pilots above in their chic leather jackets with the knight's Cross of the Iron Cross dangling from their throat and their caps, battered and punched into shape, set at a dashing, jaunty angle. But whether she wanted him or not, he was determined he was going to have her this day with the world all around appearing to fall apart. For Grube, as fanatical as he was to a certain extent – based on a hatred of nearly every one due to the way he had been treated on account of his appearance – was not committed to the National Socialist cause to the bitter end. He had realized right at the beginning when the Party had needed him that he had been lucky to have escaped their euthanasia programme. In the first years of the war, if he'd have been unlucky they might well have got rid of him with a lethal injection in the dirty cellar of some so-called 'nursing home'. Just up the road at Bergen-Belsen he had seen enough of what those fancy doctors in their flash SS officer uniforms could get up to. He was not going to go down with the sinking Nazi ship now. He was going to gratify his sexual pleasures, enjoy the power he possessed over the Nazi fools, from *Herr Doktor* Kunz downwards, and when it was all over, he'd take a dive, marry some fat local girl, and live off his memories, happy with the knowledge that, despite his ugly mug and misshapen body, he had fucked more women than those prim, middle-class arseholes had, who would be ruling Germany once again by then.

The bunker rocked as a salvo of shells exploded close by. It woke him from his sexual reverie. Loose bits of plaster drifted down from the ceiling like snowflakes. The girl started and instinctively grabbed hold of him, eyes full of fear. His big soft hands did the same. But his approach was not instinctive, but calculating. He reached out for her breasts. He grunted with pleasure as he felt them beneath the thin material of her blouse. For a moment or two she didn't seem to realize what he was about. Then, when he tried to push his hands underneath her blouse and fumble with her nipples, which were erect and exciting (for him) already, she tried to push him away. With a gasp, almost submerged in his fat bulk as she was, she said, 'No, please . . . Get off. I'm a virgin . . .'

'Come on,' he said, pushing upwards and seizing her

103

breasts. He squeezed them cruelly. She yelped with pain. 'What does it matter? Yer'll have to have it up yer one day. Why shouldn't I be the first?

'But I don't want to, Herr Grube,' she pleaded. 'I'm frightened enough as—'

He lost patience with her. Freeing one pudgy big hand, he hauled it back and slapped her hard across the mouth. Her lip split and blood trickled from the wounded lip. 'Do as you're told. I'm your superior officer, remember.' Next moment he had ripped off the Hitler Maiden skirt and there she was in her simple white knickers, the dark fuzz of her pubic hair showing through the thin material.

His heart started to pound almost painfully. He felt his penis rise. There was no going back now. With his free hand, still holding her tight to his big sweaty body with the other, he ripped open his flies.

'*No!*' she shrieked as she saw his erection, ugly, engorged with blood. 'No . . . *Please* . . .'

'Shut up,' he said thickly. '*Halt die Schnauze, Mensch!*' Then he seemed unable to speak any more; his breath was coming at such a furious rate. It was as if he were choking. Blindly he ripped off her knickers.

In vain she tried to keep her legs pressed tightly together and then, as she felt his monstrous thing pushing at her abdomen, wriggle to left and right in frantic panic. To no avail. He brought all his strength to bear. He penetrated her.

She screamed. It was like some animal of the forest being caught in a trap. She ripped her nails across the back of his bullike neck. He didn't seem even to notice. Grunting in piglike satisfaction, he forced her back against the bunker's little table. Easily he thrust her spread legs higher into the air so that he could get the utmost pleasure from her child's body. Then he ploughed into her, gasping with the effort, the sweat pouring down his brick-red ugly face in rivulets, grunting with satisfaction. Until at last everything had exploded inside him and he flopped over her poor battered little body as if he might well be unconscious or even dead, leaving her to sob in silent misery, until finally she was able to slide from beneath his inert bulk, bleeding like a stuck pig on her father's farm at sausage-making time, knowing implicitly now that if the Tommies somewhere on the ground above didn't kill Grube, the bastard, she would . . .

Above, the young parachutists tumbling from the damaged, dying Dakotas, some with their chutes ablaze, others hurtling down in a 'roman candle* were now no longer a cohesive battle formation able to concern themselves with killing people like Grube or anyone else for that matter; they were instead totally concernd with saving themselves.

Spread over a mile or so of countryside, the survivors found themselves alone or in small groups of frightened young men, unable to orientate themselves without the aid of the handful of battle-experienced NCOs who had jumped with them to guide them but who, too, had vanished in the slaughter of the Dakotas. Some showed the usual initiative of the Parachute Regiment, as young as they were. They followed the unwritten motto of the regiment and headed for the sound of firing. 'If yer lost, soldier,' their NCOs had lectured back during training, 'head for the battle. If yer can't do anything else, you can make a bloody handsome corpse.' The exhortation had usually ended in a laugh. But now those few who followed that advice were ending up as a corpse – and not a very handsome one at that.

For that terrible dawn seemed to threaten violent death at every fresh bend in the road or wooded trail for those who found themselves in the thick woods of the area, miles away from the appointed dropping zone. It came in forms

---

* When the para's chute didn't open and he plunged straight to his death.

that they had never anticipated when they had boarded the Dakotas so confidently back in England: short-panted, long-haired boys with bicycles, who appeared from nowhere and blasted them into eternity with stovepipe-like rocket launchers; old greybeards, who looked older than their grandads back home, but who were still capable of firing their rifles and then, as the young para lay on the ground writhing in his fatal agony, plunging their bayonets into the helpless youngster mercilessly until he no longer moved; and worst of all, strange men, hollow-faced with shaven heads, who might well have been sleep-walking zombies, for they appeared to be wearing pyjamas, who babbled in languages that couldn't be German.

There were gangs of them, stuffing themselves with raw potatoes and carrots from the fields as they advanced in grim shuffling determination, armed with sticks, iron rods, sickles they had looted from the terrified local farmers. Escaping as they were from that great camp of terror, they were out for revenge. They didn't recognize these lonely British soldiers as liberators. They were soldiers, who wore the same clothing, in part, as the SS, who had tortured and murdered them for so long. So the newly freed members of Bergen-Belsen Concentration Camp slaughtered the boys mercilessly, beating them to the ground, slashing and hacking at them with all the fury that their starved bodies could muster, urinating upon them to show their contempt as the bloody, almost unrecognizible youths accepted the benison of death; then looting the bodies, fighting each for the emergency ration chocolate bar in the dead para's upper pocket before staggering away in that uncanny frightening gait of theirs to find yet another victim . . .

'God Almighty!' Sergeant Meek cursed as the dawn broke very slowly, as if some god up on high was reluctant to reveal this crazy wartorn world below, 'It's crackers!' He took a swig of the looted German gin and felt the liquid flood his parched mouth with its fiery warmth. 'The bloody world's gone absolutely crackers!' He shook his greying head, for already the boot polish had melted in the heat of battle and run down his face in black streaks. Now, however, he didn't care what people thought of him. Indeed at that particular moment he would have dearly loved to have been some white-haired grandpa, sitting by the fire, smoking his pipe and staring at the glowing coals, far, far away from this terrible slaughter.

Savage, appalled at the slaughter of the young men sent to help him, horrified as he had never been before in the course of a battle, though he could see it at a distance and guess the true mangintute of the horror on the other side of the fields, sniffed the air suddenly. There was the cloying sickly smell of petrol suddenly, as if someone had left a couple of jerricans open among the vehicles. Next moment he dismissed the thought. His men knew only too well that their ability to survive might well depend upon their ability to move fast; and without petrol they would not be able to do that. He forgot the petrol, and the horror of the slaughter of their reinforcements.

'All right, Sergeant Meek,' he snapped very businesslike now. 'Let's get the hell out of here while everything seems so confused.' He ducked automatically as a plane raced by overhead. He flashed a look upwards. It was a Tiffie. The flyboys were coming in to meet the challange of the jerry jets. It was an encouraging sign. For a while, it seemed to him that his handful of paras had been fighting the war up here all by themselves. Now the Typhoons were buzzing in at tree top height, strafing the ground ahead of them with cannonfire. He felt so completely out on a limb. Hastily he whirled his right arm round to the others. It was the sign for 'move it – quickly'.

His drivers needed no urging. They, too, wanted to get out of this place of death at speed. Now as they re-started, the stench of petrol grew ever stronger. It was then that Meek tumbled to it. He pressed down hard on the ground next to the lead jeep. It was strangely soggy. It gave easily under his feet, although it hadn't rained for a week and the earth should have been harder, and that stink of petrol grew almost overpowering. Meek knocked Charlie's hands off the jeep's steering wheel. 'Hey, Sarge,' the driver protested, 'what the frig's going on?'

Meek didn't answer. He hadn't the time. He swung round at Savage who was staring at the top of the slight rise to their front. Up there a series of angry blue sparks was running down to meet them like jumping crackers on some peacetime Guy Fawkes night. 'Sir . . . sir,' he cried frantically, 'the petrol . . . They're going to set us alight.'

'*What* . . . who is going to . . .' But Savage never finished. Ten yards or so beneath the top of the rise, the sparks suddenly ignited on the petrol-soaked earth and like a horrifying gigantic blowtorch a great burst of searing started to hiss furiously in their direction.

Three

As the great mass of fiery red rushed towards them, Savage almost panicked and yelled above the roar of the holocaust, 'Forget the vehicles . . . Run for it!' The men were already running. They didn't know where. But running they were, arms working like pistons. To their right, the deer, alerted by the initial smoke before the petrol-soaked meadow had gone up in flames, came streaming from the forest, streaming to the rear in wild panic, jostling and fighting each other to escape the roaring wall of red.

Savage took a wild guess. 'Follow the deer, lads, if you can. They'll know a way out . . . Follow the deer!' Even as he shouted the command, he knew it was absurd. He knew his men hadn't a hope in hell of keeping up with the deer, who were making great bounds forward. But behind there were their newly born fawns. They could not keep up the adults' pace and he had the feeling that their mothers might lag behind and not abandon them. Now and then Meek turned and started to race behind the fleeing animals.

Now the flames swept round the first of the abandoned jeeps. Like some angry feral cats, they felt their way silently, seeking for some gap in the jeep's defence. They found it. A muffled crump. Next instant the jeep's petrol tank exploded. The jeep rose feet off the ground. A moment later it slammed down again, its tyres bursting like shells, flames leaping up everywhere. The wall of killer fire raced on to the nearest of the paras' vehicles.

Ahead the deer had almost vanished, save for a few fawns

Leo Kessler

and their mothers, for as Savage had guessed, their mother
instinct had been too strong, even in this moment of mortal
danger for them to abandon their newly born offspring. And
Savage spotted at once that they were heading in a different
direction from the others. They had turned to the right where
the land suddenly sloped steeply.

He gave a crazy gasp of relief. 'Water . . . Meek . . . the
deer . . . they . . . have found water . . .' Now in the clear
light of the spring dawn, reflecting the light of the fire, he
could see the silver ribbon of a brook of the kind common
to this boggy area. 'Come on . . . keep up.' He grabbed
Meek's arm and tugged hard, realizing just for the first time
how old the sergeant was. His face was lathered with sweat
and his eyes bulging from his head like those of a madman.
He was at the end of his physical strength. 'Leave me . . .'
he attempted to gasp, his lungs sounding like a pair of
cracked leather bellows.

'Shut up,' Savage cried brutally. He tugged even harder
at the NCO's arm. 'Keep going . . .'

Behind them the fifteen-cwt Belford, which carried most
of their additional ammunition, went up in a tremendous
roar. Tracer – white, green, red – zigzagged crazily into
the morning sky. Slugs howled away at crazy angles. To
their right rear, a trooper yelled out in absolute agony. He
stopped. He clawed the air, as if he were attempting to
climb the rungs of an invisible ladder. He never made it.
The flames caught up with him. He groaned and crum-
pled. Savage caught one last horrifying glimpse of the para
being consumed by the fiery wall, shrivelling up almost
immediately into a charred pygmy. Then tugging hard at
a sobbing, heaving-chested Meek, he was running again
for his life . . .

Grube climbed up the ladder from the underground bunker.
He had wanted the girl he had just raped again to go up
the ladder ahead of him so that he could look up her skirt

110

and see her taut nakedness beneath; he had felt the sight might arouse him once more. She had refused because she had been in a sulk. He had given way easily, telling her as he slapped her across her tear-stained face, 'Don't worry, my girl. You'll be begging for it soon.' Besides, he would have her sooner or later, there was no doubt about that, whether she liked it or not.

Now he climbed awkwardly up the right shaft and carefully peered out. The heat hit him across the face like a blow from a hot flabby fist. He gasped with the shock. The wall of fire was still sweeping downhill, though it was getting weaker by the instant, as the petrol evaporated. Still, he told himself, it had done the trick. He and his handful of Hitler Youth and Maidens had pulled it off. He blinked to clear his vision. Everything came into clearer vision. The Tommies had fled save for the two charred skeletons, the bones projecting through the blackened flesh like polished ivory. They had not be able to outrun the fire. Their vehicles, too, had not escaped. They were all wrecks, the rubber tyres still burning.

Grube nodded his satisfaction. They had stopped the Tommy advance on Celle more efficiently and more cheaply than the *Wehrmacht* could have done, that is if the *Wehrmacht* had been prepared to fight for the place; and Grube knew that any sensible regimental officer wouldn't have. By this time army units in the area must have known what would happen if the enemy caught them in the same place that housed North Germany's largest concentration camp; they would be shot out of hand.

Already the Allies were making a lot of stupid fuss whenever they discovered such places. Why, God knew! After all, it was said that the English had invented the concentration camp in one of their old wars in Africa a long time before. Still as he viewed that scene of death and destruction below, Grube knew the English would want to exact their revenge and it would be an even more brutal revenge when they discovered the camp. They might kill everyone in sight, and *he* aimed to survive this war.

For a moment or two he considered what he ought to do. Naturally he would take the girl again. It would be one of the memories upon which he could warm himself in years to come when he was married to some comfortable sexless fat *Hausfrau* whose life consisted of dusting and cleaning and cooking heavy meals of potatoes and meat, which she would gorge and make herself even fatter. When the Allies came he had thought of building up a collection of sexual objects from his conquests – knickers, naked pictures, pubic hair, things like that – to remind him of the good times. In the end he had dismissed the idea. A little thing like that might just well give him away if the enemy came looking for him. No, he had decided reluctantly, he'd have to appear from now onwards to have spent the war as a fat misshapen farmer's son not wanted by the 'Greater German Army'.

One last fling in a few moments and Otto Grube (which wasn't his real name) and his furniture removal van would disappear for good. His leadership of the *Werwolfkommando* would pass on to that fool Dr Kunz and he would ensure in one way or another that Kunz would soon be located by the enemy's secret service despite the new idenity that *Reichsführer SS* Himmler provided for him. He grinned his ugly smile at the thought. How safe they all thought they were, these supposed officers in their fancy uniforms with their new names and new papers. In reality they were only too vunerable.

His grin vanished. It was about time he made himself scarce. The Allies would be soon attacking once more. They wouldn't let the Germans get away with the defeat at Celle. Already he could hear the phone below jingling. That meant that Ilse in Kamen was calling, or perhaps Ingrid in Bielefeld closer by was calling their latest information about Allied troop movements. *Kluge Schweinehund*, Grube said to himself as he started to fight his bulk back down the tight shaft which led up to the underground bunker. The enemy hadn't yet cottoned on to the fact that some of the German telephonic exchanges were still working despite the Allied bombardments and artillery shelling. That meant brave operatives, always female, could still telephone up the line to the next exchange, passing on details of what kind of enemy troops and transport was passing through their immediate neighbourhood to the front. It was an ideal intelligence ploy which Grube had used several times.*

Now as the Hitler Maiden cowered in the corner fearfully, he listened to the faint voice of the operator as she passed on the information she had already gleaned this early morning. 'Heavy guns,' she said again . . . 'I counted them . . . ten at least . . . those tanks which throw flames . . .' She meant enemy flame-thrower tanks, terribly feared by the German soldier. 'Rocket batteries . . .'

Click! The phone went dead suddenly. He rapped the base of his own phone. Nothing. Stubborn silence. He tried again. Still nothing. He gave up. It had happened to him before in the middle of a conversation just like now. The enemy soldier had come across the operator hidden somewhere in the ruins of her exchange and had tumbled to what she was up to immediately. Her ashen face and trembling hands would reveal everything. Then they'd show no mercy. The poor woman would be dragged screaming outside, propped or bound to the nearest telegraph pole she'd be shot out of hand. In this cruel world of total war this April, no trial was needed and justice was very definitely blind.

Grube shook his head. The woman would be dead by now. He had spoken to her before. Perhaps it was better she was dead. She might have been able to recognize his voice? It was safer – for him – this way. Even as he put

*This actually happened in the campaign in the north, but the Allied forces were mostly unaware of the spies in their midst.

the dead phone down, he told himself that that click signified the end of his short career with Operation Werewolf.
He turned back to the cowering girl and with a ugly grin
on his face, he said, undoing his flies, 'One last time and
then you're free to go.' He unleashed his already erect penis
from the confines of his trousers. It sprang out and stood
there, trembling slightly like a policeman's truncheon.

The girl tried to squeeze deeper into the corner. *'Nein,
bitte nicht, Herr Grube ... Habe erbarmen mit mir, Herr
Grube. Ich bin nur fünfzehn –'* Her plea ended in a sudden
yelp of pain, as he grabbed her by the hair and dragged her
face closer to his loins.

He didn't seem to hear. 'Just one last time . . . Something
special to remember you by, *Schatz*,' he said, his voice thick
with passion and the thought of what he was going to make
her do in a moment. He dragged her ever closer.

'Bitte nein . . .' Her voice was smothered in the same
instant that that heavy artillery which Montgomery had
ordered forward to break the deadlock at Celle started to
fire . . .

Normally Monty didn't interfere in the activities of his
subordinate officers under the rank of brigadier general. He
thought that it wasn't right to do so for a full field marshal.
Besides the young officers needed to make decisions without
outside influence. As he was often fond of quoting Marshal
Foch, 'It's takes sixteen thousand dead to train a divisional
commander,' adding to that cynical statement (for Monty
didn't like wasting his soldiers' lives unnecessarily; he had
seen too much of that sort of thing in the trenches in the
'first show'), 'but it's a bit cheaper in the British Army'.
Thus it was with surprise that Brigadier Poett was informed
that same morning that the Master was on his way to Fifth
Brigade's HQ, and he wasn't coming to inspect the troops,
but on urgent business which might have 'far-reaching
consequences'.

Poett didn't flap like many another brigadier before him. He knew he was doing his job well and the only fault, he knew, that Monty might find with him was due to his lack of men and wheeled transport; he was lagging behind in his race for the Baltic.

As was customary, Monty opened his neat hamper of sandwiches and flask of tea and ate them quietly as Poett briefed him on the latest situation which wasn't good. But the Field Marshal took it in his stride and due to his false teeth took his time with his sandwiches. It was midday, wasn't it, he seemed to say, time to eat for a normal person. Poett's staff, however, continued to stare at the little officer in wonder. Why sandwiches when he could have something perfectly good, perhaps even better than normal, from their own mess. But that was Montgomery's way; he wasn't changing it for anyone.

Finally he spoke. 'Another setback, Poett. But please, I don't blame you. You are running your operation on a shoe-string thanks to the Yanks who are not aiding us in the slightest. No matter. We shall cope.' He gave a throaty little cough and took a cautious sip of his weak milky tea. 'I'm afraid we have to. Now, what is the state of Major Savage's reconnaissance company?'

Poett pointed to the big map of the area around Celle. 'His casualties have been surprisingly light under the circumstances. But of course he's now totally without transport.'

Montgomery nodded sagely. 'And due to this recent debacle with the chaps from the First Airborne we have no further Dakotas to air-supply him with new jeeps and so forth!'

Brigadier Poett looked glum.

Montgomery caught the look. Quickly he said, 'Don't despair, old chap. We're still going to knock the Hun for six. We have to, don't we?'

'Yessir. Of course, sir,' the tall brigadier replied smartly, though he had not the slightest idea what Montgomery was going on about 'knocking the Hun for six' in that awful sporting imagery the field marshal was inclined to use as if battle were a game of cricket or a horserace.

Outside they were bringing in more casualties in the ambulance jeeps, the moaning wounded strapped to both sides of the little vehicles and in some cases, with a couple of stretchers across the bonnet as well. Hastily the stretcher bearers and the orderlies rushed out to take them inside the triage tent where the medical officers would sort them out into rough sets of three: those who would die; others who would take longer to recover from their wounds; and the most important group: the lightly wounded who could be sent back into battle soon again.

Monty winced. Once in the First War he had nearly been a victim of that cruel, heartless system himself. He had been so badly wounded in the lungs that he had been left to die outside the triage tent for hours until some medical officer realizing that the tough little major in the unfashionable infantry regiment wasn't 'going to peg it', as he put it crudely, had brought him inside and tended his wounds, saving the future field marshal from death at an early age. In the years since then many soldiers, German mainly, but also a few senior British ones, had wished that unknown MO had not bothered.

Monty always concerned about the lives of his soldiers, dismissed the wounded from his mind. The situation was too earnest. He turned back to Poett and his staff. 'Two points,' he snapped in that precise manner of his. 'First.'

'Sir?'

Outside they were bringing in a young soldier, his face swathed in bandages, through which he cried in absolute panic, 'Don't tell me I'm blind. For God's sake don't tell me *that*, sir!'

Poett said a quick prayer that they'd get the poor bugger inside and out of earshot. He knew that he should have better control of himself and not let himself be rattled by such matters. But the strain of this all-important dash to the German coast with the limited resources available to him was beginning to tell.

Monty noted the brigadier's look and said quickly, 'The news I bring is good news, Poett. So point one. Aerial reconnaissance has discovered that all the bridges over the Elbe on our section of the front are down – *save one.*' Monty allowed himself a little chirpy grin. 'To be exact, that in your line of march, Poet.' He leaned forward and pointed at the map. 'Here on the Elbe up from Boizenberg at a place called Geetschacht. It's a railway bridge, I believe. Obviously the Hun hasn't yet blown it because the main line train from Hamburg to Berlin runs across it. They'll keep it open as long as possible to bring back their troops in the east and their civvies who are fleeing with them.'

'But they'll blow it eventually, sir,' Poett objected, 'once we close on the place.'

Monty responded at once. 'Of course, they'll try. But I've already alerted TAC Air Force. As soon as you get close, Air is going to run round-the-clock patrols on the area. Any attempt made by the Huns to blow the structure, will meet the full force of our Tiffys and the like.' He beamed at Poett like a conjuror at a kids' party who had just successfully pulled a rabbit out of a top hat and amazed his youthful audience.

'And point two, sir? After all Savage's got to get to the bridge first – and without transport . . .' He shrugged and left the rest of his sentence unfinished.

'Again good news, Poett. Point two. I have arranged for a section of brand-new Wasps to be rushed up to Savage, or as far as the RASC* can get them, and so give the major the transport and the firepower he has lacked so far.'

---

*Royal Army Service Corps, the Army's transport service at that time.

Poett looked impressed. Monty was delivering to them the feared weapon in the armoury of the British Infantry. The very thought of that terrible device sent a cold shiver down his spine. As always when the device was mentioned, he remembered his father's old batman coming to visit them between the wars. He'd been a mere kid then, not even at prep school. With the naive innocence of his tender years he had asked the old soldier why he wore what looked like a black bandage under his cap. The old man had looked at him like no one else had at that time, even his father at his most fearsome, and said, 'Are yer sure you want to know young master?'

He said he did. For many years and a good few nightmares afterwards, Poett had fervently wished he had never said those words. For the old ex-batman had then started to unwind the black bandage. He had taken his time, while he, the little boy, had watched fascinated, wondering what the old man would reveal. Then he had done so, and he had gasped with shock, his baby face suddenly ashen. First there had come a stretch of wrinkled flesh, with what appeared to be two holes, leaking what looked like yellow wax from them. Later he learned from his father that this was where the batman's ears had once been. That had been followed by a hairless pate flecked by red patches where no skin or flesh had grown since the Great War. Poett had promptly been sick.

Now as Monty wound up his flying visit and his orderly packed together his luncheon hamper, Poett remembered that poor old man and the terrible damage which the flame thrower had wrought upon him – a handful of seconds of murderous, all consuming flame and he had been ruined for life. Poett pulled himself together. 'Thank you, sir for your help,' he said, mind agigated by the thought of the terrible weapon that Monty had just offered his division, and, in particular, Savage.

'If the Wasp doesn't do the trick, Poett,' the field marshal said, rising to his feet and pulling at the old civilian corduroy trousers he wore instead of the khaki uniform ones, 'God knows what will. But I shall say this. Another seven days and I want your chaps to be over the Elbe and on their way to the Baltic coast.' His face was suddenly cold and hard and Poett knew instantly what the field marshal meant. The Wasp was forgotten now.

'I shall do my utomost, sir,' he said, drawing himself up to his full height and saluting.

Montgomery didn't respond.

He left, leaving Poett thinking hard, knowing that Monty's last remark had not just been an order; it had been a warning. If he, Poett, didn't make, it, he, Monty, would be out of a job . . .

Book Four
DEATH BY FIRE

One

Confused, angry, breathless, the two young paras of the First Airborne easily left the pyjama-clad mob, braying like a pack of hunting dogs, behind them. The concentration camp inmates in their striped uniforms were too emaciated and weak to keep up the chase for long. Their cry of 'Soldiers – kill them' died away as they turned to the left and began to burn a farmhouse and loot whatever they could find.

Now the two paras relaxed a little. The bigger of the two with a cockney accent said, 'Ferk this for a tale of soldiers, Bert, we're ferking well lost and far from home.' He shrugged his big shoulders. 'And the lads have had it as well, poor sods.'

Bert, small, tough looking, spat dryly on to the cobbled country road. 'You can say that again, mucker.' Again he spat. 'But what we gonna do, 'arry?'

Harry the smart cockney had his answer ready. 'We gotta go to ground mate. Till our lads catch up with us. The rest of the blokes can't be far behind.'

'But where are they, mate' his comrade asked.

Harry looked around. He could see that there was trouble everywhere. All around Celle there was fighting. If he had been an imaginative man he would have said the German town looked like the end of the world. Clouds of black smoke flecked with cherry red flames were rising on all sides. Somewhere a gasometer had blown. Now it was burning away fiercely, every now and again spitting

123

frightening angry jets of violent blue flame. Over where the concentration camp was, with its strange frightening pyjama-clad skeletons, there were flames too. But there was also the noise of herds of squealing pigs having their throats cut as if the starving prisoners were indulging in mass slaughter in their overwhelming hunger.

Harry guessed that not only were the newly released prisoners killing the pigs, but also their SS guards. 'O, lad,' he said after a few moments of consideration, 'I think the best thing for us is to go to ground where we are, the further we wander around this bloody place, the more likely we will bump into more trouble than the two of us with these 'ere pop guns' – he indicated his sten gun – 'can handle.'

Thus it was that Dr Kunz, the new commander of the Werewolf Resistance Organization, met his end. In his arrogant yet stupid manner, he could not realize that the past and his part in it as the important camp doctor, and officer of the SS, with his power of life and death over the hapless prisoners, was over. He felt that by merely destroying his uniform he could shrug off the past and his former life like one might take off a smelly suit of clothes. Now he thought his life would continue as a middle class well-off doctor who had an important part to play in his new community. He didn't realize that the Germany which he had served so well as an educated criminal would now stink to high heaven in the nostrils of the civilized world well into the end of the twentieth century.

Consequently, when a heavy nailed boot wielded by Harry crashed down the door which the Werewolf Organization had provided for Kunz's cover, the former SS officer didn't realize that he was no longer of any importance whatsoever. Nor did he realize that he was faced by two desperate young paratroopers who were determined to save their lives at any cost. Now clad in civilian trousers and a vest, for he had no time to put on a civilian shirt, he started for the smashed door angrily.

'Heaven, ass and cloudburst,' he cried angrily when he saw the paratroopers. 'What in three devils name is going on here?' He stopped dead when he realized the dirty unshaven soldiers facing him were not German. Still, as he recognized almost immediately that they were British, he had not yet lost his SS arrogance. Summing up what he could remember of his schoolboy English, he snapped, 'What you do Tommy? This is civilian house forbidden, you understand?' He repeated the word, wagging his finger to make his point clear, 'Forboden, FORBIDDEN.'

It was a fatal mistake. In that same instance, Dr Kunz, former head of Bergen-Belsen concentration camp, revealed his inner arm. On the pale flesh there was tattooed a series of numbers which indicated his blood group. For, as all SS men from simple private to general, he had had the number tattooed upon his induction into the SS. The number in case he was wounded, would have made it easy for any SS medical officer to treat him.

Even the two young paratroopers who had never been in action before, knew all about the SS blood group markings. The survivors of their division which the SS had decimated at the Battle of Arnhem, had told the young recruits often enough all about the SS.

Harry gasped, as he recognized that the man facing them was a former SS man dressed in civilian clothes. His comrade didn't hesitate. Almost automatically he pressed the trigger of his sten gun. The cheap little machine pistol quivered at his side. Empty cartridge cases clattered to the tiled entrance floor. Dr Kunz gave a strange unearthly groan as the slugs tore his chest apart. 'Sickened . . . ' he commenced. He never ended the sentence. He fell on his knees to the floor. Blood spouted in a bright red arc from the holes stitched across his chest. 'Mein Gott!' Next moment he fell face forward, dead before he hit the tiles.

The para's chest was heaving as if he had just run a great race. He stared down in sudden silence, while the echo of that sudden burst of deadly fire died away. They would live not knowing that they had played a minor role in the history of the Nazi Resistance Movement in World War Two. They had put an end to this movement in the Celle area of Lower Saxony. In a way they were a kind of hero, but who would ever know?

Two miles away the young RASC second lieutenant wiped the sweat off his brow, remembered he had to salute a senior officer and did so, saying, 'Sorry, sir, but it's been a bloody long trip. At times we didn't think we were going to get through to you. There were bloody Jerries everywhere.' He indicated the line of trucks. Some of them with their canvas tops ripped as if by shell fire and bullets.

Savage nodded his understanding. 'Well, young chap, you did it, that's the main thing. Come on over here and we'll give you a shot of quartermaster's rum.' Around him Savage's paratroopers looked at the monsters half concealed in the back of the Bedford trucks. Their eyes were suddenly filled with fear. Savage pretended not to notice. He said, 'Sergeant Meek, get the officer a cup of tea and rum. He needs it, and you men get the digit out of the orifice and help the RASC wallers to unload those trucks in double quick time'.

Sergeant Meek, the old sweat, didn't like what he saw either, but old regular soldier that he was, he never questioned orders. Within ten minutes the trucks were unloaded and the RASC drivers were preparing a quick 'brew up'. But it was clear that even they were not enjoying their char, they were only too eager to get out of the front line and away from the monsters they had brought up to help the paratroopers at Field Marshal Montgomery's express command. But the paratroopers who were now going to use these deadly little track devices knew they couldn't dodge, as they put it, 'the frigging column'. They were lumbered with them and they didn't like that knowledge one little bit.

Savage ignored the looks on their faces. 'I think you all know the wasp,' he said. 'An adapted bren gun carrier for the infantry, what you might call a handy pocket size flame thrower. It's going to replace the jeeps and the other equipment we lost yesterday.' He paused. His tone was subdued and he kept his gaze fairly low. For already he could hear the mumblings and protests and grumblings from the rear rank of his men. 'No Jerry infantry-man is going to hang around when he sees one of our wasps spurting flames of 30 or 40 yards.'

'And what about us, sir?' It was Scouse's voice. Naturally he would be the first to protest. Savage could guess why. He was in one of his bolshy moods and Savage had a feeling this time he had the support of some of the old lads from the Brussels glasshouse.

'Well, what about us?' Savage decided to humour the Liverpudlian for the time being. He didn't need trouble at this juncture for it seemed that everyone from Monty downwards was breathing down his neck to get a move on.

'Do you think the bloody Jerries are going to stand about waiting till we get close enough to flame them?' Scouse sneered, and this time he deliberately forgot to say sir. 'Not bloody likely, they are going to bang away at the wasp with everything they have bloody well got. And when they hit one of those little sods over, there won't be much left of the wasp or us neither. We'll be a heap of frigging coke, that's what we'll be.'

There was a murmur of agreement from some of the old lags. A flushed and angry Savage could see he had a problem on his hands, a serious one. Before he started his final drive to the river Elbe he was running into trouble in his own backyard. Automatically his hand fell to his pistol holster and Sergeant Meek standing next to him backed off a pace for a better feel of fire, just in case. Slowly he raised his sten gun and cocked it.

'Alright, we have heard your complaints, Scouse,'

Sergeant Meek said, 'now frigging well get on with it, and you others, we want to be out of here toot sweet.' He half turned as if to go back to the trucks but Scouse's sneering voice stopped him in his tracks.

The barrack-room lawyer said angrily, 'Who the fuck do you think you are, talking to us like that just 'cos you've got a couple of stripes on your shoulder, and you too sir with your pips.'

Swiftly Savage turned back, his weary unshaven face flushed even more. 'What did you say?' he thundered. Meek raised his sten gun higher. There was going to be real trouble, he knew that. Scouse the loudmouth Liverpudlian had been waiting for this opportunity to reassert his authority among the paras all along. Now he appeared to have some of the old gang backing him up again.

Scouse stood his ground He knew the ordinary foot sloggers horror of the flame thrower. He knew too that if a wasp was hit none of its crew would survive the conflagration. The mix which fuelled the flame thrower would go up immediately, perhaps even explode – and that would be that. 'I don't want to fry just so you get another gong, Savage.' He turned to the others. 'None of us do lads, do we?' A smirk passed his ugly pockmarked face. He knew he was winning the others over to his way of thinking.

Savage had been in such situations before. Out in the North African desert some of the old sweats had served for two to three years without a home leave. Naturally they had grown bolshy especially as the Jerries had bombarded them with pornographic leaflets detailing just what a good time their wives and girlfriends were having with the rich Yanks back in Blighty. Why, there had even been a large scale mutiny out there which the brass had hushed up. But there was no reason for allowing soldiers to refuse to obey orders, especially when those soldiers were in the line. Monty, he knew, did not believe in the kind of executions carried out in the trenches in the Great War. All the same, the Master would not have tolerated this kind of thing when so much was at stake. Neither could he.

Savage controlled his temper. What he might have to do in a moment was very grave. He didn't want to have to do it but if the worse came to the worst he could. He looked directly at Scouse. 'I'm not asking you to get on with it, I am ordering you to do so. If you don't, Scouse, you'll take the consequences.'

Scouse sneered, 'You and who's army?' Always in his young years he had come through by threats, the brutality of Liverpool's slum back streets and his overconfident swagger; and in the toughest of situations he had always landed on his feet.

Not this time. Savage pulled out his revolver, deliberately he uncocked the weapon and pointed it directly at Scouse. The other paras who had been Scouse's supporters, lost heart immediately, they scattered swiftly. They could see from the look on Savage's face that he meant business. In a minute Scouse might well be dead. Scouse for his part was too full of himself to see what was about to happen. Savage raised his pistol higher and said, 'I am going to count to three and then I'm going to kill you, one, two . . .' Scouse saw his danger too late, he flung up his hands as if to protect the soft flesh to ward off the hard steel of a bullet. Still he could not bring himself to quite give in. Then it was too late. Quite deliberately, hand steady as a rock, Savage fired a single round. Scouse staggered a pace, his evil face was suffused with pain and a look of utter disbelief that it was happening to him. The next moment he pitched forward dead.

Half an hour later, the little convoy of wasps was heading north once more, the RASC men had already left heading at top speed for the safety of the rear area. They had done their job. Let the paras earn the extra two bob a day to do the fighting. Behind they left a solitary grave. Hurriedly and carelessly dug; a heap of fresh brown earth surmounted by a rough cross made of a couple of sticks of pine from which hung a battered paratrooper helmet. Meek had hastily taken the bayonet, heated the point and burnt the letters of the cross which meant eternity. KIA – Killed in Action. His only comment had been, 'Lucky bugger, I could have put barrack-room lawyer and frigging deserter . . .'

Two

The little boy in the short pants and black peaked cap started at the sound of the little convoy approaching. Suddenly he dropped the bundle of sticks he had been collecting at the edge of the cobbled road leading north to the River Elbe. He straightened to attention, his right arm shot out in the Nazi salute. But the customary 'Heil Hitler' died on his lips as he saw he was mistaken. These weren't German troops, they were the soldiers of Jewish Capitalist invaders, as he had been taught to call them at school by Herr Lehrer Kuehlhans. In the next moment he forgot his firewood and fled back into the forest.

Meek gave a cynical chuckle. 'Cheeky little bugger,' he explained to Savage as they stood watching the road ahead and the forest of pines to the other sides, an ideal place for an ambush. 'Thought we was Jerries,' he said. Savage's face remained serious. 'That's what they've been trained to do all their lives, even the kids,' he commented. 'Part of their way of life'. He wiped the dust from his face with his dirty khaki handkerchief. They'd been going through the Luneburg Forest all day now, getting steadily north-wards. Everything had gone smoothly. The enemy seemed in full flight everywhere. Behind them they had left the wreckage of a defeated army, tanks tilted in the ditches, their fuel run out; wrecked artillery pieces, their barrels destroyed and peeled back like metal banana skins where some conscientious gunner had thrown a grenade down it and destroyed the piece; and three groups of tough wooden crosses with German helmets hanging from them, the work of some flying allied fighter bomber.

Still Savage, his nerves tense, body apprehensive and taut ready for the first surprising impact of bullets against the paper-thin steel of the Wasp's chassis, was not relaxing his guard for one moment. Surely there were some fanatics out there; SS men, eager officer cadets still prepared to die for 'Folk, Fatherland and Führer'. At this stage of the game he was not prepared to take the slightest risk. He had a job to do and he had men, good hard fighting men who he wanted to bring through safely on this last battle of the long war. He said to Meek, 'Keep your eyes peeled.' Cheerfully the loyal NCO with the boot-polished hair answered, 'Like the proverbial tinned tomato, sir.'

They rattled on to the armoured convoy, spread out like some latter-day pioneer American wagon trail advancing ever deeper in, like 'Injun country'. All the same the men were relaxed and happy. They had used Wasp radios to tune to BBC Radio London and the Forces Radio, singing their own ribald version of 'Colonel Bogey' being played as a Guard band. 'Bollocks, and the same to you . . . Where was the engine driver when the boiler bust . . . They found his bollocks . . .' It was their time out of war, enjoying the simple pleasure of a sing-along, remembering that somewhere out there was another peaceful world which knew nothing of the terror and sudden violent death they lived twenty-four hours a day, day after day, week after week until they 'caught it', as they called death with callous realism, and with death, as all of the men knew, there was only one way out of the infantry – feet first.

They turned a slight bend in the cobbled forest road, the trees dripping with a thin bitter rain that had now commenced falling. Those who could, huddled low in their gas capes, the raindrops dripping from the helmets and running down their faces in opaque pears. Savage, for his part, disdained such protection, he needed freedom of movement. For ahead through the rain he had caught a glimpse of one of the red-brick, half-timbered houses surrounded by gothic steepled churches, typical of the country.

Savage tugged at his binoculars. He focussed them quickly. The lenses blurred almost immediately. Not before, however, he caught a glimpse of the boy who had been collecting firewood talking urgently to a skinny youth, also wearing a black peaked cap, not much older than the firewood boy. 'Bugger it,' he cursed, lowering useless binoculars.

'What is it? asked Meek.

'That kid,' said Savage. 'I'll bet my bottom dollar he's letting on that he's just spotted us.'

'Not to worry sir,' Meek said easily, 'they're probably filling their pants at the sight of us. Bet you, sir, they'll be running for their sodding mamas in haf a mo'.'

But the old sweat was wrong for once. Next instant there was a burst of violet light next to the church. A clump of explosives. A brilliant white glowing anti-tank shell came hurtling towards the little convoy like a 'bat out of hell'.

'Look out,' Savage shrieked with all his strength, 'the place is defended.'

His paras needed no warning. Veterans that they were, they reacted instinctively. Charlie, Savage's driver, swung the Wasp's wheel violently to the right, others did the same. Just in the nick of time. As Charlie stalled the engine in his haste and the Wasp shuddered to a stop just short of the ditch to the right, the solid shell slammed on to the cobbled road just a yard away. His men in the leading carrier, nostrils filled with the awful stench of the shell, were shocked into momentary silence. Then both Meek and Savage started yelling out orders, as the long barrelled seventy-five millimetre anti-tank gun next to the steeple swung round for another. Meek reacted first, before Savage yelled his own orders for the attack. He pulled out a smoke grenade and flung it with all his strength. It landed in the village street between the leading Wasp and the anti-tank gun. A sharp plop. Next moment it exploded. Almost immediately thick brown smoke started to rise from the little steel egg. In a flash it had formed an effective smoke screen between the convoy and the German defenders of the hamlet. Savage knew it wouldn't last long. Time was of the essence. As a burst of ragged small arms fire erupted from the half-timbered houses to the front of the hamlet, he cupped his hands and cried above the angry snap-and-crack of the smaller arms fire, 'Number Two – ready to flame, at the double now . . . for Christ's sake.'

The number two Wasp crew reacted frantically. They knew too their smoke cover wouldn't last much longer. Already the silhouette of the anti-tank gun was beginning to appear. In a matter of seconds, its crew would open fire again. Stalled as they were, they'd be sitting ducks, stuck out there in the middle of the dead straight road that led into the hamlet.

'Ready to flame, sir,' the gunner of the second Wasp yelled furiously, ignoring the slugs bouncing off the carrier's thin steeled sides like heavy tropical rain on a tin-roofed shack.

'*Flame 'Em*,' Savage yelled back urgently. The gunner fired. There was a great hiss. It was like that of some primeval monster drawing in air before it struck, an urgent sucking noise. In an instant the air all around seemed burning hot this cold April day. A terrifying rod of blue, pink-tinged flame shot forward some fifty yards or more. Savage upfront felt the very air dragged from his lungs by that tremendous flame. He choked and gasped for breath like a man being strangled.

In the first house, the flame turned the vegetation and trees into charred matchsticks. The grass blackened. Next second it withered. For an instant, Savage thought of what that flame would do to any human being in its way.

Number three fired now. Its flame curled and twisted

around the shop next to where the German anti-tank gun was positioned. Like some feral cat, it twisted and snarled and curled about the shop. The glass window cracked and shattered. A second later the paint on the walls started to bubble and spit. The shop front disappeared momentarily. A black pile of mushroom smoke rose into the grey morning sky. A charred bag of bones, which had been a human being, tumbled from the shop door and lay on the cobbles burning fiercely, shrinking visibly under that intense heat.

Savage wiped the sweat from his brick-red face. 'Excellent,' he yelled as if he was congratulating some gun crew on a practise range. But his heart wasn't in it. He knew he was slaughtering his fellow human beings in the most terrible, fiendish way. No man, even the German enemy, should die like this. But he knew too there was no time for such considerations now. The anti-tank gun crew had not broken and run as he thought they might do. They were prepared to fight to the terrible end. 'Troop will advance,' he cried above the crackle of the flames consuming the shop. 'Sergeant Meek, get that bloody gun.' Number three Wasp gunner swept past the first two carriers, tense and ready behind his terrible weapon. He knew that if his driver stalled the Wasp engine of the vehicle and it went through a track, which it might well do as they zig-zagged crazily from side to side, they'd be dead ducks. At that range the Jerry anti-tank gun couldn't miss. Still they charged boldly forward, igniting the bullet's piping of the Wasp's sides.

The men of number three carrier could see the crew of the German unit as they taxied behind its shield. They'd fire any moment. Just next to the armour rocket a gunner's assistant knelt ready, the great seventy-five millimetre shell cradled in his arms ready in an instant to feed the shell into the gun's breech. But the man never got a chance to do so. Number three gunner fired. At that range he couldn't miss. He fired. Again that terrible rod of flame slipped out. It engulfed the gun and its crew. They screamed hideously as it did so. Evan at that distance, Savage could feel that terrible, flesh-eating haze in his nostrils assailed by the cloying stench of burning flesh. He clutched the side of the Wasp in white-knuckled horror at what they were doing. How could men subject their fellow men to such terror? Where was their Christian God and His supposed mercy this grey damp morning?

Then it was over. They rattled through the hamlet. They passed houses burning brightly. A handful of human torches stumbled blindly out of them. They screamed and shrieked as the terrible flame continued to consume their soft vulnerable glare. Savage wanted to avert his gaze. He couldn't. He had to see his handiwork. How could he face his God one day – perhaps soon – if he didn't? He caught one horrifying glimpse of the Germans' pearly white bones gleaming like polished ivory and then the Wasps were crunching over their writhing bodies turning them into a blackened scarlet pulp paste as they went through. Monty's 'gift' had proved its worth, but at what cost . . .

'*Slava krasnaya armyee . . . Davoi*,' echoed the Cossack battlecry in a deep bass voice as they urged their excited nervous horses into the shallows. The battle had commenced . . .

'*Urrah*,' the Cossacks on the flanks cried as they came splashing out of the River Elbe on both flanks. Geese fled their approach squawking in protest. Dogs barked hysterically. Wild stabs of scarlet flame cut the velvet darkness. In an instant all was confused chaos.

The hetman's horse skidded to a stop on the cobbles. Blood jetted a bright red from a great wound in its flank. As it went down, the hetman cursed as the poor beast sank to its knees, 'Boshe moi.' Effortlessly he sprang from the saddle. He grabbed a tommy gun from a dead Cossack. He dashed forward, firing short bursts from left to right.

'*Davoi* you Gulag rats,' he urged his Cossacks. '*Davoi* . . . *davoi*!' He urged frantically as a fat German, clad only in his underwear and jackboots, loomed up out of the darkness. Instinctively he pressed the trigger of his sub-machine gun. The Fritz screamed, his hands clutching frantically at his ripped open stomach. 'Save you bothering about stomach powder anymore, Fritz!' the hetman roared heartlessly as he pelted by.

A German leaned out of an upstairs window, rifle clutched in his fat hands. A gulag rat fired. The German yelped and fell out of the window. He hit the ground like a sack of wet cement. A machine-gun burred in high-pitched hysteria. Tracer, red and white, zipped through the darkness like a swarm of angry hornets. Behind the hetman half a dozen gulag rats skidded to a stop, dropped their weapons and hit the cobbles in a mess of twitching limbs.

The hetman didn't hesitate. He grabbed the grenade tucked down the side of his boot and flung it towards the pit. It exploded with a flash of blinding white light. The hetman ducked and heard the shrapnel pattering down on his helmet like heavy summer rain on a tin roof. A head rolled to a stop at his feet like a football abandoned by some careless child. It bore a Hitler-type moustache. 'Heil Hitler!' he cried and ran on. A knife hissed through the air. Behind the hetman a man yelped and went down, clutching his shoulder with fingers through which the blood jetted in bright scarlet spurts. Then they were in the cottages, slaughtering the Fritzes. An officer rushed at the hetman, dressed only in his underwear, his teeth bared in anger, hands clutching at the Russian's throat. The hetman launched a kick at his guts – and missed. The Fritz's sausage fingers fastened on his neck. The hetman tried in vain to break his grip, red and white stars exploding in front of his eyes. The officer's garlic-laden breath assailed his nostrils as the hetman writhed back and forth, choking for air, attempting frantically to free himself, clawing at the

Fritz's shoulders, ripping skin and cotton from them in his frenzy.

His ears started to pop. The blackness, charged with bright scarlet, threatened to overcome him. Instinctively his hands felt down below the Fritz's gut and found his genitals, soft, heavy and yielding. He didn't hesitate. He would be out in another moment. He twisted with the last of his remaining strength. The Fritz screamed high and shrill. The grip on the hetman's neck relaxed. He did not wait for a second invitation. His right elbow slammed into the Fritz's gasping mouth. The officer's false teeth plopped obscenely out of his mouth in the same instant that a gulag rat's bayonet sank deep between his shoulder. The Fritz's officer cap dropped to the ground.

The hetman lay on the cobbles next to him while his men raced forward to the foremost cottages and the church, firing from the hip as they ran, shooting down those of the battalion who attempted to surrender. Then they began their looting. This was the only reward that the gulag rats expected for daily risking their miserable lives for a Russia that had once sentenced them to the camps and a slow death. Pannenburg was theirs.

Book Five

ONE MORE RIVER TO CROSS

One

Hurriedly General von Rammsau fingered the Knight's Cross of the Iron Cross which hung from his scrawny neck, as if to assure himself that the high decoration that the Führer himself had awarded him still hung there. But as his batman Heinz pointed urgently to the telephone and mouthed, 'Field Marshal Keitel,' he forgot the medal. He grabbed his wig and slipped it on his bald, wrinkled pate; in his haste putting it on the wrong way. He knew what a bastard the arrogant most senior officer in the German Army was, who also had the Führer's ear. So when he took the phone, he said as calmly as he could, trying to control his breathing, 'Von Rammsau . . .'

Keitel in Berlin didn't waste any time. 'Hier Keitel,' he snapped. 'Rammsau, you are to be taken off the Führer's Reserve List of General Officers.' Keitel, being Keitel, couldn't refrain naturally from one of his little poisoned barbs. 'Bout time too, you've had a good war up there in the fleshpots of Hamburg.'

'Danke, sir,' the aged general heard himself saying automatically, though his head was already spinning at the surprise announcement. 'My command?'

'This,' Keitel responded. 'Within the next twelve hours you are to take over command of a section of the Hamburg front along the Elbe.'

Von Rammsau was tempted to ask 'What Hamburg front?' for although he had his quarters in the great port city, he had never heard of such a battle front. But he stopped himself just in time. Instead he said, trying to convey some enthusiasm as if this was the best news he had heard in a long time, '*Vielen Dank*, Herr General Field Marshal. What section, sir?

'That between Lauenburg with the route five leading to Berlin and along the same roadway heading for Bergdorf and on to Hamburg itself.'

Again Rammsau heard himself mutter, 'Thank you' as if he were grateful for the great honour that Keitel had bestowed upon him. 'And my forces, sir?'

At the other end of the line, he heard Keitel snort as if he could not be bothered with such trivia; after all he was Germany's most senior soldier. Still, it seemed he was prepared to honour this aged general who hadn't seen action for nearly half a decade.

'You'll have the police division from Hamburg, a battle group of officer cadets from Schwerin and whatever stragglers you can collect retreating from the other side of the Elbe, the cowardly swines. Don't desitate to shoot some of them as an example to the others, if they appear reluctant to do their duty to the Fatherland.'

'Naturally, sir,' he said promptly, as if he was accustomed to shooting and stringing up reluctant heroes every day that dawned.

'Good, Rammsau. Now these are your specific orders, given to me personally by the Führer himself.'

The old general thought he might cry 'Heil Hitler' at this moment in an excess of patriotic zeal, but then thought better of it. Instead he asked, very military now, 'My specific orders, sir?'

'To defend the line of the Elbe. Your primary concern will be to stop the Tommies crossing the railway bridge at Lauenburg before we finally destroy the structure. If the enemy sieze that bridge intact and start crossing in strength and with armour, there is little we have to stop them 'till they reach the Baltic coast.'

'I understand, sir.'

Keitel paused significantly and an expectant, tense Rammsau wondered what was coming next. When it did, it shocked him so much that he nearly dropped the phone. 'And let me add this, Rammsau,' Keitel said, his voice suddenly full of dire menace. 'If that bridge does fall into the Tommies' hands intact, you must realize that your head will be forfeited. General and simple soldier, the Führer in his infinite wisdom has decreed that all must pay the penalty for failure and that penalty is death, understood?'

'Understood, sir,' von Rammsau answered, all faked enthusiasm vanished from his reedy, old man's voice.

'*Ende,*' Keitel snapped.

Next moment the phone went dead in the old General's hand. But von Rammsau didn't put it down. Instead he gazed at it aghast. *An active command . . . no failure . . . head at stake . . .* The words hammered at his brain like threats.

Heaven, arse and cloudburst, he cursed to himself. Was Keitel out of his mind? The war was lost. Any damn fool knew that. In due course the Tommies could cross this so-called 'Elbe Line', defended by a collection of lightly armed, middle-aged Hamburg cops and if he were unlucky, he might well end up dangling from the nearest lampost with the cruel chicken wire they used in such barbaric executions cutting into his skinny neck.

He swallowed hard and handed the phone back to his waiting batman. 'Bad news, sir?' the latter asked.

He forced himself to conceal his dire sense of doom. He said, 'Not really, Heinz. Better get my field uniform out, it's in mothballs somewhere or other in the big wardrobe.'

'Field uniform, sir?

Von Rammsau was too shocked to notice the sudden look of alarm in his batman's eyes. '*Jawohl*, I've been given an active command, we're going back to war once more.'

'Congratulatons, sir,' Heinz said. Under his breath he told

himself, Without yours truly, old friend, you're not going with me.

'My loyal Heinz,' the general said, as he was wont to call his batman who had brought him home from many a drunken Hamburg society dinner in these last years. There and then his 'loyal Heinz' decided to go 'on the trot' before the day was over.

General Kuno von Rammsau had enjoyed a good war, though he had thought at the beginning he had been damned unlucky. The wound he had suffered in 1940 had been damned painful and he had been relegated because of it from temporary major general to his pre-war rank of full colonel; then he had thought his military career was over and promotion was out. After all, every regular officer knew that it was only war that brought rapid promotion.

But he had been wrong. Successfully helping the then unknown Rommel to force a crossing on the River Meuse into France and being wounded in doing so had made him a minor hero riding on the coat-tails of Rommel's later fame in France when he had reached the French coast in double quick time and forced the surrender of a whole British division in the process.

The Führer had visited him personally in Berlin's La Charite hospital where his wounded was being treated. Here, while the newsreel cameras had swirled and reporters' flash bulbs had exploded, the leader had draped the Knight's Cross around his neck. Unfortunately he had only been wounded in his right buttock so that doctors had hastily rigged up a sling around his right arm so that the ceremony looked more dramatic for the 'poison dwarf's' tabloids.

Thereafter, the new major general, and a hero in battle too awarded Germany's highest decoration for bravery, had been given a routine office job in Hamburg. There he had been invited to all the major functions of the rich and great. A Knight's Cross holder routinely dined with them as a welcome adornment in the Hotel Atlantik and the even posher Hotel Vier Jahreszeiten. Here his only problem seemed to be, rough old soldier that he had been up to 1940, was how to eat caviar (for Hamburg did itself proud in such matters) and kiss a lady's hand correctly: 'bend and do not touch the skin, that's not *knigge*, Herr General.'

It was a good life, a very good one indeed. The state and the Hamburg government provided him with everything he needed. His quarters were paid for, even his well-tailored uniforms – the port's fashionable tailors were only too eager to assist him in return for a picture of his heroic self in their windows. Indeed the only thing that General Kuno von Rammsau did pay for was the curious services of the delightfully wanton Jutta von Hansen, who was half his age and who provided the kind of sex he had never experienced in a lifetime of army brothels and certainly not in his own marital bed.

Blonde and pale like some porcelain doll, she had taken him completely by surprise when she had given him that china-blue-eyed look of hers and had uttered that first cruel command of hers after a drunken party when he had drunk far too much French champagne in Senator Larsen's waterfront mansion.

There he had been struck by her curious boots which reached right up to the tight silk shirt she had worn. But not only the boots intrigued him. His interest became more intense when she had crossed her shapely booted legs to reveal she was not wearing any knickers. She had caught his look and had grated in a harsh domineering voice, totally unlike the sound of it up until that moment. 'You dirty swine. Stop looking up my skirt, or by God, it'll be the worse for you, I swear. I'll make you pay for it, by God I will.' And she had given him a hard threatening look which had frightened him more than the French had done on the Meuse.

Despite the fact that he had long regarded himself as impotent, he had immediately felt a strong sexual attraction to the much younger woman, especially as she began to 'bully' him and 'put him in his place' (as he called it) almost at once. That attraction increased tenfold when in a drunken moment she had wrenched a blacking brush from Heinz's surprised grip when he had been polishing the general's boots in the kitchen of his quarters, given them to von Rammsau and had barked, flourishing the little dog whip she had found somewhere or other, 'Get cleaning, you swine and if I find a speck of dirt on them, you'll be for it. I'll thrash you to within an inch of your worthless life, you won't be able to sit down again for at least a week.' She had cracked the whip and then brought it down smartly across the general's skinny rump. He had felt the pain – but also a kind of sexual pleasure. Then he had begun to polish the old boots for all he was worth, sensing the growing tumescence between his limbs. It was then they had become lovers – if it could have been called that. Naturally she required a reward – many of them – for servicing the 'randy old bugger' as she referred to the general behind his back to her other, much younger lovers. 'To get him aroused is like trying to raise the *Titanic*, sometimes I get muscular spasms, I take so long using my whip on his skinny old arse.' There was French underwear, made from expensive lace, cigarettes by the hundred for her lovers who smoked and always as much precious black market petrol for her illegal little Opel Wanderer run-around.

But the General always paid and indeed was eager to do so. For he had never been happier in his whole life. Now as he waited for Heinz to bring his field uniform, Kuno von Rammsau stared miserably across Hamburg's inner lake, the Alster, telling himself that his whole life had fallen apart. Never again would Jutta tempt and torture him till she deigned to whip his bottom for some imagined crime or other. That was over now, together with the grand dinners at Hamburg's Rathaus; the French champagne and caviar; the lazy afternoons at the country home of Hamburg's rich merchants out in Reinbek and Aumuhle – and the generous bribes they offered for any army contracts he could put their way. Now von Rammsau told himself in the depths of despair, it was death at the front or behind it, hanging from a noose.

He roused himself. He had to tell her before it was too late and he was off to his new command – and his death. Even as he picked up the phone to do so, he felt the bitter tears of self-pity rolling down his wrinkled cheeks. Poor Jutta, what would she do without him? God, he hoped she wouldn't starve without his help.

In the event, Jutta von Hansen would always land on her feet, or to put it more correctly, on her back; the position she had adopted now as her telephone started to ring. She lay naked on the fur rug she had draped across the silken sheets of the bed, staring at her own naked image in the ceiling mirror, gently stroking between her spread legs, savouring the feel of her lover who had just left. It was a good feeling and she had needed no dog whip to arouse the sexual passion of the young paratroop lieutenant, who had pleasured her twice in a matter of minutes, or so it seemed.

The ringing of the phone brought her back to reality. She stopped that pleasurable stroking and picked up the receiver. Miserably Kuno von Rammsau told her of Keitel's message and the bombshell which had exploded so dramatically and, as he put it in a broken voice, 'Destroyed our lives together, my little darling.'

'Silly old fart,' was her tart response. 'You deserve a damn good whipping for that kind of silly talk.' For Jutta's sharp mind was already working at top speed. She needed Kuno von Rammsau, as ancient as he was. She had worked out that there would be a future in a defeated Germany for years to come and she had no intention of whoring for British soldiers once the inevitable defeat came. She'd heard that Tommies drank tea all the time, had lousy teeth and

147

no money. That wasn't for her. She needed to get out of Germany before she might be forced to service that kind of individual. But to do so she needed money, plenty of it, and in this very instant as von Rammsau continued to bewail his fate, it came to her that her aged lover was just the person to provide that money. For he was to be in charge of a sector of the front which contained the richest of Hamburg's suburbs, with power of life and death over those fat merchants – and their possessions – resident out there.

'Kuno,' she ordered, 'you are not going to die if you do as I order.'

The old general caught his breath. He knew just how smart Jutta was. Could she really help him? She could and she would. Kuno von Rammsau was not fated to die at the front. Instead the general would die of old age in a fancy Spanish nursing home in Andalusia. Admittedly he would be long ga-ga by that time, but he would be happy with it. While Jutta dallied with the teenage Spanish gitanos – all pearly white teeth and flashing dark eyes – she fancied, he would lie in his bed drinking sangria all day and scotch (the real thing, not the Spanish rotgut) far into the night. That April in 1945 when he was given his new command, would turn out to be the best thing that had ever happened to him. The 'Elbe Front' might exist for a day or two before the Tommies sauntered through it, but by then he and Jutta would be on their way to a new life . . .

Two

They had skirted the last major German town, Lauenburg before they reached the River Elbe, ploughing through the muddy fields to avoid being spotted. As they churned their way through the wet lands, Savage in the leading Wasp remembered how his school history book had stated that the royal family had originated from that same small provincial town before becoming the Duke of Hanover and finally succeeding to the British throne and changing themselves to the House of Windsor in the First World War. How strange that was. Now he had sworn an oath to fight for their descendants. It seemed to make a mockery of the whole business.

Now the little group of paras were camped out in a tight spinney which Savage hoped would conceal them and their deadly little vehicles from the road running to the Elbe and the bridge at Lauenburg. Naturally being British soldiers and having the British soldier's terrible thirst for tea when there was nothing stronger in the form of 'wallop' (a composite form of tea, sugar and milk mixed together) available, the men had got down to make an immediate 'brew-up'. They had half filled old cans with soil, saturated the earth with petrol and ignited the makeshift stove. The compo tea now bubbled merrily and the great culinary delicacy Spam spluttered ready to be wolfed down greedily. Despite the fact that the American pork meat was eaten with rock-hard army biscuits, made by the dog food manufacturer Spillers, the sandwich was regarded as a great treat.

Idly Savage and Sergeant Meek ate their Spam sandwiches and listened to the chatter of their men. It was the usual stuff that frontline soldiers talk about: women, wallop and the war (in that order). But the two of them could not ignore the thunder of the guns to their right. It was the permanent barrage put up by the artillery of General Horrocks' XXX Corps. The guns were pouring their fire ceaselessly on the port of Bremen, still under siege by the tall British general's infantry. Horrocks wanted Bremen without a fight – it was too late in the war to suffer a large number of casualties. Still, he needed to capture the port, for there was a large fleet of the latest German U-boats which could sail halfway round the world without surfacing, and there was no knowing what the fanatical U-boat commanders might do even if the rest of the Third Reich surrendered.

To the two men's right, there was more firing. But it was different. Savage couldn't identity it. It was closer and lighter.

'Penny for them, sir.' Meek broke his silent reverie.

'It's that firing near the Elbe, Meek.'

Meek nodded. 'It is funny sir, I must admit. I can't make out the weapons being used. There's Jerry spandaus out there but the other stuff . . .' He shrugged and left the rest of his sentence unsaid.

'Russian perhaps.'

'Perhaps, but what are the Reds doing on the Elbe, sir. Even on this side of the river? They would be trouble, even if they are supposed to be our allies.'

Savage swallowed the rest of the iron-hard biscuit with difficulty and promised he'd never make his poor dog swallow another dog biscuit. 'You're right there, Meek. If the Jerries defending the Elbe panicked at the Russians, they could well blow up the bridge at Lauenburg and then we're in trouble, real trouble. How we're gonna get the follow up armour across without a bridge? It'll take at least a day to get a Bailey bridge across a river of that size.'

'The sappers'll do it, sir,' Meek answered stoutly. 'They always do.'

In the darkness under the star-filled velvet sky, Savage smiled to himself. One couldn't fault old sweats like Sergeant Meek. They might moan and bitch at times, but they could always be relied upon to rally to the cause when things looked black and the chips were down. He dismissed the Russians, if it were the Russians who were firing to his right and said, 'Get the men kipped out for the night, Meek, and post sentries. An hour on stag and an hour off. Reveille's gonna be first light.'

Charlie, standing close by started to sing softly, 'Kiss me good night, Sergeant Major, tuck me in my little wooden bed . . . we all love you Sergeant Major.'

The old song came to an abrupt end as Meek snapped, 'Private Tusker, you'll be on a frigging fizzer toot-sweet if you don't turn that howling off.'

'Yes, Sergeant Meek, sir,' their driver said politely in no way worried by the threat. 'But don't forget my blanket.'

Savage laughed. The men were in good heart obviously, although they knew the morrow might well bring sudden death. For then they'd be in the Elbe facing a dug-in enemy and risking all sorts of dangers. Meek, for his part, knowing that the men would be only too glad to curl into their blankets and grab an hour's sleep turned back to Savage. 'The drill, sir?'

'A mug of char and a dog biscuit. Time for a crap and a weapon check and we move out at convoy distance by dawn. We'll be in the first Wasp, half a mile or so in front of the others – just in case.'

Meek nodded sagely. He knew what that meant. If the balloon went up and the Jerries spotted them, they'd get the job, but the men behind them would have a chance to escape, if they were lucky.

Savage yawned and realized just how tired he was. Lazily

he finished with, 'Keep your fingers crossed, Meek, we're off into the unknown at dawn and for chrissake let's hope we don't meet the Russians. I don't think Monty would be too happy if we started a third world war.' He yawned and stretched his arms aloft. 'Now, I'm going to hit the hay, sarge.' And with that he vanished into the darkness, to find his own blanket roll.

Meek watched him go and told himself yet again what a fine officer Savage was. He hoped he'd get through the end of this show. He deserved to. But the old regular had his doubts. Officers like Savage who led from the front rarely did, especially if they were in the infantry. Then he forgot the officer and started his final round of the little camp among the firs, like a good regular NCO should . . .

Some two or three miles from the great river, the Cossack hetman was not concerned with such details. In true Cossack fashion, the scar-faced horseman believed what would happen, would and there was nothing he could do about it. Cossacks were supposed to die young in battle. Why bother with the trivia of army life? Cossacks lived for the day, perhaps even for the hour when in battle. One moment you were alive, the next dead. If that was to be, and he believed firmly that was the nature of war, you should treat each day as if it were your last one. Vodka and women, plump fat women with breasts like melons and bellies like silken pillows to rest your head on. What more could a fighting Cossack expect?

Now as his command approached the little township of Dannenburg situated on the Elbe just below the bridge at Lauenburg, he neglected all reconnaissance, the way a conventional commander would do it. Already the German defenders had turned a searchlight on the fast-flowing river and were firing along its silver beam whenever they spotted the Cossack riders in the shallows. They knew the Russians were there all right.

Still all the same, the hetman was not going to allow his command to be wiped out and defeated. He had a rough and ready plan which entailed sacrificing some of his men but which would fool the Fritzes and win the day for them. He knew his rivers. Just like the Volga in winter, the flooded Elbe would have concealed inlet 'dead ground' that the German fire couldn't reach. There were even sand banks for those he had already condemned to death for the sake of his plan. Most of the riders of that squadron would reach it before the Fritzes slaughtered them. By then with the enemy fully occupied with this soft target, his riders concealed in the inlets to left and right, would have crossed and – god willing – have begun turning the enemy flank – and he knew the Fritzes of old. Once they spotted a Cossack, who they knew didn't take prisoners, charging full out at them, swinging his frightening sabre above his furcapped head, they'd fill their pants and run for it.

Now he wasted no more time. He struck his fingers in his mouth and whistled shrilly at his waiting rider. Raising his stirrups, he whirled his sabre, '*Krasnaya armyee. Davoi.*'

Three

This last Tuesday in April 1945, the western world changed irrevocably. Not that anyone seemed to notice at the time. In the surrounded Führer's bunker in Berlin, Hitler's SS flunkies prepared to burn the Führer's body and that of his new wife Eva Braun. The rest of his entourage trapped in the fetid underground chambers paid no attention to the event. They drank and whored taking turns to use the chair of the dead Führer's dentist to heighten their sexual pleasure. Drunkenly they planned their escape; they never did.

The so-called 'thousand year Reich' Hitler had often boasted about, had lasted exactly twelve years and four months. The Third Reich was in ruins. Chaos reigned.

Perhaps old 'leather-face' as the pockmarked Soviet dictator Stalin was known behind his back, did have some inkling that the world was changing. That day he addressed his general staff, the Stavka in the Kremlin. He said, 'We are finished with the Fritzes. Now Berlin and the other central European capitals, Warsaw, Vienna etc are ours. Churchill may hate it. The Yankies are so naive that they don't know what power lies in our hands. We are *the* power in central Europe.'

The benign look which made the Americans call him Uncle Joe, vanished from his dark Georgian face. 'When the Americans leave Europe there is no stopping us from conquering the rest of the continent.' He pointed his curved pipe at his generals almost threateningly. 'We Russians

154

deserve the fruits of victory. Ensure that we do so even if it means a confrontation with the English. Comrade Generals, this is going to be the Soviets' century.'

The German Prominenz who had survived clearly knew nothing of the Kossack hetman who was most likely to start the incident which might cause a drastic breakdown with the erstwhile American allies. If anyone were to stop the Russians, it would be Major Savage and his paras. Great powerful men that they were, Stalin, Eisenhower and the like, knew nothing of these humble men who might disrupt any long-range plans they had.

For a while, at least, perhaps even a matter of days, the future of Germany would be in the hands of these obscure men, a perverted ancient German general, a wild Cossack leader who seemed to be possessed of a death wish, and a stolid British major intent on doing his duty to the King Emperor and at the same time trying to save the lives of his young soldiers.

The moon was ice-cold. It hung at a slant in the black velvet of the wintry sky. Like silver the frost glittered on the skeletal branches of the trees, quivering slightly in the icy wind. All was tense brooding expectation. There was no sound save the muted rumble of the permanent barrage on another front.

Hidden in their foxholes, the assault troops waited. Two hours ago they had been issued with a hundred grammes of vodka. But that was long gone. Now they were sober and cold – and afraid. The Fritzes would undoubtedly be waiting for them on the other side of the river. They would be mown down like cattle. But there was no alternative. Behind them the green-caped swines of the NKVD (Soviet Secret Police) were dug in; they would not hesitate to open fire on anyone who attempted to desert the line. As always they were between the devil and the deep blue sea.

A sudden crack! They jumped. A hush. To their right the first flare hissed into the dark night. It burst in a shower of red. Instantly all their upturned faces were coloured a blood-red, eerie hue. Another flare whooshed into the sky – and another. It was the signal.

Colonel Hetman Dmitrov, Commander of the Ninth Cossack Battalion, sprang to his feet, sabre already drawn, glittering silver in that glowing unnatural light. 'Come on, you rats, do you wish to live for ever? *Davai!*'

'*Davai! Davai!*' His officers and NCOs took up the command all along the line, urging their men forward, kicking and striking the more reluctant ones, drawing their pistols to make their meaning quite clear.

The men stumbled towards the river in a ragged line, following their giant of a colonel, fur hat set at a rakish angle at the side of his shaven skull, waving his sword and laughing uproariously like a crazy man.

The German machine-gunners opened up at once. Tracer, white, glowing and lethal, started to hiss across the surface of the river. With a roar the Russian artillery joined in. Shells started to explode on the far bank, the near-misses plunging into the water, sending up great spouts of writhing, wild white water. In an instant, all was earsplitting noise and confusion as the soldiers of the Black Cossack Battalion went down everywhere in the slippery mud, to be trampled ever deeper by the boots of their frenzied comrades.

The hetman strode into the water, still waving his sword and laughing. Bullets cut the surface all around him as the Germans intensified their fire, but the hetman did not seem to notice. He waded steadily towards the other side, sword flashing in the flames of the fires that had broken out on the bank.

Now, carried away by a fevered blood lust, more and more of his men were wading in after the big colonel, scrambling and slipping through the mud and jellied, bloody gore of their dead and dying comrades. Screaming inhumanly, their teeth bared wolfishly, their eyes wide and wild, they splashed into the water to meet the slaughter on the other side.

The hetman, still laughing madly, swung his sabre. The blade cleaved through the German's arm. It fell to the mud at his feet. He stared at it as if bewildered. But only for an instant. Next moment he swung his terrible, blood-red weapon again. The Fritz went down screaming horribly, his face almost split in two.

'*Davai!* . . . *Davai!*' the hetman cried at his men still struggling through the water, now running a bright crimson and littered with the floating bodies of the dead.

'The colonel's got a hole in his arse! . . . Follow the colonel! . . . The colonel's got a hole in his arse!' they bellowed. '*Follow the Colonel!*'

Already the terrified Germans were beginning to surrender. Dropping their weapons and raising their hands, eyes bulging with fear, they begged for mercy, '*Kamerad . . . Kamerad . . . Nicht, schiessen, bitte*. NICHT SCHIESSEN!'

But the hetman's ex-convicts had no mercy. Carried away by the frenzied blood-lust of battle, they stabbed, slashed, sliced, chopped, cutting the Germans down where they stood. Teeth gleaming white against their blackened faces, eyes glittering like those of the demented, they flung themselves at the hated enemy and massacred them.

Now there was no stopping Colonel Dmitrov's men. They ran straight at the remaining enemy machine guns. Men fell screaming and howling in their lonely misery, writhing and tearing at the earth with their clawed hands. But the rest kept going, springing into the enemy weapon pits, the brass butts of their rifles slamming into upturned German faces, their razor-sharp shovels cleaving German skulls. And all the while Colonel Dmitrov laughed and laughed and laughed like a man possessed.

Savage knew he was taking a great risk; not the usual one of battle. It was something else. He was risking his men being lined up along the nearest wall and shot as spies if they were captured. For he had ordered something which was not condoned by the Geneva rules of land warfare. He had commanded his men to wear odd bits and pieces of German uniform they had picked up on their way to the River Elbe. He had even taught them a few phases of German that he knew: '*allesklar . . . weitermachen*' and others.

His aim was to trick his way through any German barrier they might encounter on their route to the water. Sergeant Meek had pulled a face when he had given the order, but Savage had explained, 'It's necessary, Sarge, we don't want to fight for every damn German barricade. With luck we'll bluff our way through in the darkness.'

Savage had been proved right. They had passed safely through the few barricades on the road to the Elbe which they had encountered. Most of these barricades were manned by old men of the German Home Guard. From what Savage could see they were ready to drop their weapons and run for it at any moment. Now as they came ever closer to the river, he could hear the final sounds of an intense fire fight. Savage told himself that it had to be the Russians who had successfully attacked beyond the bridge at Lauenburg.

That spurred him on. Now as the April sun began to rise, edging its way over the horizon hesitantly as if some God on high did not want to illuminate the war torn world below, they caught their first glimpses of the river they had suffered so much to reach.

Here the Elbe was at its broadest. To their right was the bridge still intact. To their immediate front there was a cliff-like bank surmounted by the township of Lauenburg. It disappeared into the heavily wooded area running to the next village on the left.

But apart from a few bursts of machine gun fire sweeping the river, these excellent defensive positions seemed definitely undermanned.

Savage was puzzled. Why weren't the Jerries doing more to defend this last major natural barrier to the coast? After all, once the British reached that coast, they had cut off half a million German troops stationed in Denmark and Norway. Anyway, he knew and the Germans knew that the Russians were already on the Elbe ready to attack, so what was going on in the German camp?

It was the same question that was going through the head of the one-eyed colonel of von Rammsau's so called 'Fire Brigade'. He had just been informed at the general's head-quarters outside the city of Bergedorf of the old lecher's plan.

'But, sir,' he protested, 'what have we soldiers got to do with banks and money, especially as the enemy is on the doorstep of our command?'

Von Ramssau had been brought up in the Prussian tradi-tion of *Kadavergehorsamkeit* – the obedience of a corpse. 'Are you questioning my orders, colonel?'

The one-eyed colonel flushed. 'Of course not, sir. But it seems foolish, if I may say so, to take the fire brigade away when it is urgently needed at the front – I think.'

'This is your answer,' the general interrupted harshly. 'You know as I do, we are virtually defeated in the field.

'That doesn't mean our beloved Fatherland is broken and beaten. One day we will regain our rightful position as the leader of Europe. Like the Phoenix, we shall rise again.'

'Of course, general, but the money sir? What has that got to do with it?'

'This, once the allies have taken over they will confis-cate all our assets. At the same time those foreign profi-teers who have made a fortune out of this war at our expense, will sling their hook, with them they will take their foreign currency and return to their homelands and the allies will not be able to stop them. We must ensure that the money remains in German hands and is taken to a safe place before the allies confiscate it.' He raised his voice, '*Leutnant*', he cried.

Almost as if she had been listening behind the door, Jutta appeared. Now she was dressed in the uniform of a staff officer with a purple stripe of the greater general's staff down the side of her tight breeches. She slapped her little riding whip against her highly polished boot and the general gave a shudder of pleasure and apprehension at the sound. He had just spent the last hour polishing those same boots with all his strength while she had belaboured his skinny buttocks with the same whip. She clicked to attention, her spurs jingling. 'Gentlemen, at your service,' she barked as if she was on the parade ground.

'Lieutenant, please explain your plan to the colonel.'

Jutta wasted no time. 'Once we have got the money from the Reinbach Bank we shall transport it to the airport at Hamburg. There a Condor is waiting fully fuelled and ready to take off with a trustworthy patriot at the controls. He will fly the money to a neutral country where it will be hidden in a German colony till the time comes to use it for the Fatherland.'

'Splendid,' the colonel said. Behind his back Jutta winked at Rammsau. He winked back with surprising enthusiasm. They had pulled it off. They were virtually on their way to Spain and sunshine and a new life.

The German Artillery caught Savage's little band completely by surprise. They had grouped at the fishing village of Artlenburg just to the left of the railway bridge. Across from them was a wide stretch of water. Savage had ordered the Wasp to be parked behind the dyke while he considered how to cross the Elbe. 'There is a ferry here somewhere, I guess the locals use it to cut off the miles between here and the bridge. That ferry should have room for at least one Wasp,' he said.

It was then they heard the first terrible shriek of an

eighty-eight millimetre shell like a huge piece of canvas being torn apart. Sergeant Meek, the veteran, ducked instinctively; he knew the sound all too well. Moments later, the rest did the same for the German fire was all too deadly accurate. The first Wasp was hit; whoosh, it exploded immediately. A huge sheet of flame tinged with oil illuminated the scene electrically.

Instantly, Savage reacted and said, 'Look, there's the ferry. Get on it chaps, at the double.'

Charlie, their driver, searched frantically for the starter button of the ferry. As more and more men flung themselves on board choking and sobbing for breath he hit the button. Nothing happened. Frantically he tried again. Again nothing.

'It's too bloody cold,' Meek shouted and pushed Charlie aside. 'There must be a choke.' He pressed hard. Another Wasp was hit. The hiss of that horrific all consuming flame grew louder and louder as it seared the steaming water like a gigantic blow torch. Finally, Meek was lucky, there was a long low groan like some eerie dirge played on the Highland bagpipes. 'Come on you bastard, come on,' Meek cried. His face turning bright red in the scarlet wall of flame.

Behind him Savage hacked away at the tow rope with an axe. Here and there some of the men broke down, they lay on the deck, sobbing nervously with fear. Others prepared to throw themselves into the river. Already the old ferry's paint was beginning to bubble and melt under that awesome heat. It was like the symptoms of some terrible skin disease. Again the Germans on the other side of the river fired but now the ferry was beginning to move. It shook violently as free from the bank it headed into midstream. 'We're moving,' Meek shrieked, 'we are fucking well moving, sir . . .' The rest of his words were drowned by another explosion. All of them on the rusty deck were drenched by a huge wave of water. Then they were moving away putting the German artillery men off their aim.

But even as Savage slumped on the deck, not seeing, not hearing a thing, drained of all energy as if some hidden tap had been opened, he knew with a sinking feeling that they had lost most of their vehicles. Now they were completely at the mercy of the fast flowing river sailing into the unknown.

Four

It was the appalling stench which caught Hetman Dmitrov's attention first.

It was like nothing he had ever smelt before; a thick cloying stink composed of human sweat, infinite misery and the fear of death. The only comparison he could make was it seemed like the rancid penetrating stench he had once experienced in the monkey house of a provincial zoo as a boy; something he had not been able to ban from his nostrils for many a day. Then the Cossack cavalry swung round the bend in the trail alongside the Elbe and they discovered the source of that awful stink. Coming towards them were hundreds of pitiful walking skeletons, men, women and children clad in the striped pyjamas of a concentration camp. They streamed towards the Cossacks crying out in half a dozen languages, '*Voda . . . kleba . . . essen . . . vasser . . . mangare . . .*' stretching out their hands that looked like claws. The hetman reined in his steed. Once he too had been in such a pitiful state just as most of his Black Cossacks had been. Back in the late thirties he and they had been prisoners of one of the Stalag's goulags working themselves to death for being so called defeatists and saboteurs. The war had freed them so that they could go to the front and die for the tyrant in the Kremlin who had sentenced them there. He had pity for these awful wretches, but yet again he had become hardened. Now he searched the ranks of the ex-prisoners for a woman, as in true Cossack fashion he wished to celebrate his recent victory against the German defenders of the Elbe with a woman. Then he spotted her; plump, despite the concentration camp's starvation rations. It would be her. For he knew the type. They had survived the camps by selling their bodies for a crust of bread, a drink of rotgut made from potato peelings or even a couple of spoonfuls of flour to use on their faces as makeup. Perhaps she was Polish. She looked it with her flaxen hair cropped like a man's, light blue eyes and high Slavic cheekbones. Polish women were good in bed or even pressed down on the wet sandy bank of the Elbe. He nodded to Captain Vassily, his second in command. He pointed at the woman in her ragged shapeless pyjamas which still couldn't hide her nubile figure. 'Her,' he commanded, 'I shall have her, captain.'

'Immediately, little brother,' the captain added, an evil grin on his pockmarked face. But that wasn't to be for already both of them heard the boom of German artillery. Immediately they guessed the English were trying to cross and there would be no time for making love (if that was the correct word to nubile Polish women this terrible April day).

'By the holy virgin of Kazan, the English!' The Cossack colonel looked worried.

Around him the pathetic wretches from the concentration camp murmured, 'English . . . English,' as they watched the drifting ferry. 'The English are good, they will help us.'

The hetman frowned. No one would help them really. The prisoners were fated to wander the face of Europe until they disappeared into obscurity. He forgot the concentration camp victims, he had to do something about the English – but what? Next to him Vassily seemed to be able to read his thoughts.

'Colonel, what do a few more dead count, even if they are English. We have killed enough this day, we can kill some more.' He pointed to the victims of the recent battle. They were sprawled out in the violent postures of those recently done to death. One clutched a bottle of looted vodka in his hand but he was minus a head with which to drink it. Another lay on his back, a great yellow obscene snake of his guts clutched in his arms as if he had been trying to thrust back his entrails. Next to him lay a Cossack sergeant, his upper body stripped to the rib cage which glittered through the red gore, like polished ivory. 'Yes,' Vassily said, 'we have killed enough, that's for sure, hetman.'

The hetman wasn't listening or didn't seem to be listening. He snapped his fingers. 'Vodka, Vassily. Vodka, I need to drink in order to think.'

As always the efficient second in command, Vassily brought out a little bottle of pepper vodka and a salt cellar. The hetman spread his thumb and forefinger so that the skin between was ready for the salt. Vassily poured it on. The hetman gave a quick lick and then downed the fiery pepper vodka in one go.

'Now I shall take the Polack woman,' he said thickly. 'I must soothe my nerves. Come, let us find her.'

The Poles among the concentration camp victims muttered in protest as the Cossack colonel led the woman away. Already he had ripped open her striped jacket and was feeling her melon-like breasts. He placed her with her back to him against the nearest tree and grunted, 'Hold tight, I am going to give you a treat.' The woman didn't understand. Soon she did however. Swiftly, he ripped down her pants to reveal she wore no knickers underneath. He pressed his hand cruelly into her plump backside and then without a moment's hesitation he took her in front of the protesting Poles. It was over in a matter of seconds.

Now he turned his attention back to the ferry but already the Poles, angered by this cruel treatment of one of their women folk, decided that they too would do something about the English trapped in the rusty old tub. Forming a human chain they started to wade into the Elbe in order to stop the ferry before it drifted in to even deeper water. The

165

hetman bellowed with rage. He swung himself on to his horse, pulled out his silver sabre, waved it above his head in true Cossack fashion and shouted, '*Urrah, urrah,* Cossacks, charge the bastards.' The men needed no urging. Most of them were pretty drunk by now on the looted vodka they had found. In a rough and ready formation they headed for the bank intent on scattering the Poles. The hetman now knew they would have to kill every last one of the English. There should be no trace of them. If there was an international incident it could not be attributed to his Cossacks. He did not want to disappear back into the gulag where it was likely Stalin would send him, to silence him as a witness just in case.

On board the drifting ferry, Charlie reacted first. He swung himself aboard the Wasp, and swiftly adjusted the controls and nozzle of the flame thrower. He guessed even before Savage that although the poor wretches in their striped pyjamas were trying to rescue them that the Cossack cavalry coming thundering down from the heights wanted the exact opposite. They had murder in their hearts. Hastily Savage cried above the racket, 'Let 'em have it, Charlie!' The Wasp driver didn't hesitate. He pressed the trigger of that fearsome weapon, a fiery rod of flame shot forward. It was the long tongue of some predatory primeval creature reaching out for its prey. But it didn't reach it, instead the flame ended purposelessly in the water sending up a cloud of steam. Savage broke out in a fierce sweat. 'Come on Charlie,' he cried, 'get the bastards before they get us.' For now the Cossacks were scattering the Poles slashing to left and right wildly with their swords, everywhere the would-be rescuers went down. Here and there Cossacks had raised themselves in their saddles with all the Cossack skill of horsemen and were snapping off shots at the men on the ferry.

But neither the Cossacks nor the paras knew that help was at hand. Coming in from the south there were planes flying low; as yet they were mere dots on the morning sky so that they could not be identified. But they were approaching at nearly 400 miles an hour and Savage, with blood now streaming down the side of his face where he had been wounded on his temple, felt a surge of hope. He told himself they weren't German but if he was right they were Allied fighter bombers. Now the planes were directly above the scene of the battle. For what seemed a long while they appeared suspended in mid-air like a hawk which had spotted a mouse in a cornfield far below and was preparing to swoop down upon the unsuspecting rodent. Suddenly the wing leader in front of the V of planes jiggled his wings, once, twice, three times.

It was a signal.

The next instance the leader's plane dropped out of the sky. It hurtled towards the ground at a frightening rate. To the observers on the ferry, it seemed the Allied fighter bomber would never be able to pull out of that death defying dive. Then, when it appeared that the plane must inevitably crash into the ground below, the pilot hit the air brakes and jerked back the stick. The plane shuddered violently. Savage could have sworn he could hear the screaming protest of sorely tried metal. But the plane survived and an instant later, evil black eggs started to tumble in profusion from its blue painted belly. Down below the bombs exploded among the Cossacks bringing their wild charge to an abrupt end.

'Good old Monty,' Meek chortled, as the Allied Fighter bombers came in for their last sortie. Twenty millimetre cannon chattered frantically. 'The seventh cavalry to the rescue sir, eh.'

Savage nodded grimly. 'But we are not out of the shit yet, Meek.' The sweating Poles had nearly towed them out of the river and closer to the bank. He forgot momentarily what was going to happen next if he had guessed right. Above the boom of German artillery he shouted, 'Alright lads, all of you empty your pockets, give these chaps all the chocolates and fags you've got left over, they've saved our bacon, they deserve it.'

Normally the paras were very canny with their chocolate and sweet ration but now they realized how these strange wretches in their striped pyjamas had risked their lives to save them. Hastily they started handing out what they had.

The Poles were pathetically grateful. They grabbed the chocolate and looked at it as if it was manna from heaven. An elderly Pole with a long wispy beard kissed a surprised Savage's hand and said, in broken English, 'You good, sir, this first chocolate I have seen in five years.' He peeled off the blue ration wrapper and was about to take a bite of the precious substance but he never did. A shot rang out and the elderly Pole pitched into the water dead before he reached it. The Cossacks were attacking again. They came charging from their boltholes dodging the steaming pits made by the allied bombs waving their sabres furiously, using all their Cossack skill to avoid being shot by a handful of paras. Some rode with their bodies against the sides of their mounts so that the horse provided their protection. Here and there a few of the more daring swung themselves beneath their mounts and did the same. But the paras knew that once the Cossacks were among them – and they greatly outnumbered the handful of Englishmen – they would be massacred. So they set up a furious scale of fire. Everywhere the riders went down but with the reckless bravery of their kind the surviving Cossacks came on. Now the riders built up their old attack formation with each flank curving outwards while the centre of their ranks took the brunt of the paras fire. Crouched next to Savage, firing wildly, snapping off shots to left and right, Meek shouted, 'They are going to overrun us in a minute if we don't do something.'

Savage, the sweat pouring from his face like opaque

pearls, nodded his head grimly; he knew that without Meek having to tell him. He shouted back, 'Try to spot the leader, Sarge, knock the bastard out and it might just do the trick.'

Meek who was equipped with a sniper's rifle as the paras best shot, swung his weapon from left to right peering through the telescopic sight. Then he had him. A bare-headed dashing figure dressed in the old-fashioned coat, adorned with cartridge cases of the traditional Cossack leader. Meek knew this for as a boy he had seen exiled Cossacks performing in his local circus. He aimed his rifle. Through the gleaming calibrated glass the Cossack leader seemed even larger as he swung his silver sabre back and forth urging his survivors on. Swiftly he adjusted the sights. Now Hetman Dvitrov was neatly dissected by the lines of calibrated glass. The time to fire had come. But Meek, the old hand, knew he daren't hurry. He'd get one bite of the cherry and that would be it. He daren't miss now. He sucked the butt of the rifle into his shoulder, calmed his breathing, counted to three and took first pressure of his trigger. The man he was going to kill had five seconds of life left to him. He took final pressure. The rifle butt slammed against his shoulder, but the weapon itself remained as steady as a rock. The hetman was lifted cleanly out of his saddle by the bullet at such short range. He dropped to the ground, still clutching his sword and squatted there, still not dead. He waved the sabre feebly. '*Davoi, davoi*,' he said in a faint voice, still urging his men onward. Next instance, he keeled over and was dead. His Cossacks came to an abrupt stop. Their leader was dead, what should they do? Captain Vassily, his second in command, did what he expected the hetman wanted. He grabbed the little leather bag of the Cossack's native soil from round his neck, spread it hastily over his face so that he would die and be buried in the land of his birth and then he too fell dead, riddled with bullets. The Cossack attack was over and the paras were free to continue their dash – if that was the word – for the sea.

Half an hour later, the handful of battered paras had left the Elbe behind them. They paused at the crossroads of the country road on which they found themselves. Ruefully Savage realized they had no transport, not much in the way of ammunitions left and no rations. What should he do? Then his eyes fell on the road sign. Printed against a yellow background, he read the words: Wismar 57 kilometres. 'Well lads, can we make 57 kms on our flat feet?'

His answer came back in a deep bass, 'Of course we can, sir, we are the frigging Parachute Regiment aren't we? We can do anything.' They started to move off again. A handful of ordinary British men who had become greater than themselves in this war. Soon they would return to civvy street and become ordinary men once again. But now, for the last time, although they didn't know it, they were going to make history. Five minutes later, they had disappeared from view on their way to the Baltic to fulfil Montgomery's great dream.

AFTERWORD

It has been a damned nice thing . . . the nearest run thing you ever saw in your life . . . By God! I don't think it would have done if I had not been there.

The Duke of Wellington

B rigadier Poett smiled down at Sergeant Meek, noticing that for some strange reason, the grizzled para sergeant, who had been with the regiment since its formation at Churchill's command, had put black boot polish on his thinning hair. He told himself he must ask Savage, standing next to him with the brand new DSO hanging from his dirty camouflaged smock, why he allowed his NCOs to put boot polish on their hair. Then as his adjutant finished reading the citation, he said, 'Congratulations, Sergeant, you put up a very good show.' He then pinned the shining new military medal on the NCO's chest.

'Thank you, sir,' Meek said. 'The lads did it all, sir. Poor sods.' He flashed a look at the handful of survivors, a few of them mouthing 'wets' which meant they expected him to 'push the boat' out for a few beers in due course. But where in God's name could he find even weak German beer in this arsehole of a place, he hadn't a clue.

Poett shook his hand and the award ceremony, carried out here at Montgomery's TAC Headquarters at the Master's express command, was over. The tall brigadier stalked away

171

across the heath with that great lope of his and started chatting to the other senior officers assembled there, all of them throwing glances up the country road, as if they expected something to appear on it soon. But as yet it was empty, save for a lone Daimler armoured car, its gun pointing straight down the road.

Savage joined his handful of survivors. Glad as they were that they had completed their mission and that the shooting was over, they were uneasy. Perhaps it was the place, Savage told himself, and the fact that everyone else seemed 'bulled up' in their best battle dress with burnished brasses and gleaming boots. They, on the other hand, were in obvious shit-order in their dirty tunics and smocks, their boots mud-encrusted, their brasses dull and unpolished these many weeks. Before the award ceremony Brigadier Poett had mentioned in a half-hearted way that he better get 'a grip on the men' seeing they were at HQ. But the brigadier hadn't seemed very serious – in fact, Savage guessed the brigadier might want to show the staff wallahs what the chaps who had done the fighting really looked like. Anyway he, Savage, had done nothing, and even Sergeant Meek had not taken his turnout, save for the boot-polish 'hair cream', too seriously.

Savage listened to the chat all around him. For men who had been through hell and seemed to have aged years in these last few weeks since the crossing of the Rhine, their subdued conversations seemed very mundane: women, grub, the possibility of free beer now the Old Country had won, and that was about it. Idly he wondered if that was it; how they could ever forget what they had seen and done, what they had been through; how, in reality they could ever fit into their pre-war life of pubs, pictures and palais-de-danse. Once again when they returned to civvy street, how they, the young men who had killed without too much compunction, would take to some bloke insulting them in a pub, or any petty little counter-jumper of a council official 'coming the acid' with them. Would they be able to turn the other cheek or be capable of walking away, clenched fists deep in their pockets with suppressed rage? He wondered, knowing that *he* never would be able to do so. He, and all the rest of the handful who had done the real fighting[*] were different from ordinary men. He doubted if they would be capable of ever explaining (he knew he couldn't) of how exactly. But they were different, isolated in a world of memories and emotions that would appear shocking, too violent, even abnormal to the great majority of their fellow citizens. He bit his bottom lip and wondered how the young men all around, weary, but red-faced, hearty with the weeks of outdoor living, full of the strength and confidence of their young years, would cope in the weeks, the months, even years to come.

'Sir, something's going on.' It was Sergeant Meek. With a nod of his blackened head he indicated the road as the senior officers, who obviously knew more than the paras did, shuffled to attention. Another armoured car was driving slowly down the road from the direction of the German lines. Savage recognized it as an old-fashioned Humber, but 'bulled' up as if it was on some kind of 'War Week' parade back in Britain; all gleaming metal and polished wheels. Savage frowned at the sight. Behind it came a camouflaged Mercedes, some sort of metal flag at its bonnet, also proceeding at a snail's pace.

The Humber armoured car rolled past the senior officers. Then came the Mercedes. Here and there the officers saluted. Others clearly declined. They looked down at their feet or away in the distance, as if it was distasteful for them to give the enemy even a military greeting.

The Mercedes stopped. Three German officers, one seemingly uglier than the other. To Savage they seemed perfect

---

[*] In the campaign in Germany, the infantry made up 15% of the fighting force but suffered 70% of the casualties.

173

caricatures of the Nazi officer as presented in the cheap tabloids back home, complete with jackboots, long belted coats that reached to their ankles and, though they might have lost the cartoonist's swagger, they had about them an air of angry pent-up defiance whenever they looked at the senior British officers.

For what seemed a long while they simply stood there in a little group in the wet heather, not speaking to one another, staring at their boots for the most part as if they could see something of significance there. Then the interpreter said something. He didn't look particularly Jewish, as most of the army's top class interpreters were, but he might well be. At all events the Germans definitely didn't like him or taking orders from a lowly captain in a scruffy battledress. Still they moved at his command. For some reason Savage glanced at his watch. It was eleven thirty precisely. He would remember the time always, though he'd never remember why.

For a few moments the four German senior officers stood there awkwardly, self-consciously until one of Montgomery's staff officers gave an order and like green recruits in training they shuffled into position along white lines already painted there. Again they waited, four doomed men in one way or another who wouldn't survive this moment of surrender very long. Savage wondered what must be going on in their minds. He knew he personally would be unable to do what they would soon be expected to do. But then, he told himself, *he* would never surrender.

Suddenly Meek nudged him in the ribs gently. 'His nibs, sir,' he whispered. At the door of the caravan which the four hapless Germans faced, the Master himself had appeared.

Dressed in half uniform, half civilian clothes, perhaps to demonstrate his superiority, he surveyed them silently.

Finally, Montgomery turned to where the interpreter

174

stood. Although he was perfectly aware of who these Germans were, he barked, 'Who are these men?'

Savage grinned suddenly. Monty was running true to form.

Duly, the interpreter told a really uninterested Montgomery the Germans' names, ranks and military positions.

Montgomery listened and then snapped to the interpreter, 'What do they want?' The senior German officer, Admiral von Friedeburg, baggy-eyed and sallow-faced, who would commit suicide before this month was out, explained, 'We have come,' he quavered, 'to ask you to accept the surrender of three German armies now withdrawing in front of the Russians in Mecklenburg.'

Once the captain had translated into English, there was an excited burst of chatter from the war correspondents in their khaki greatcoats who started scribbling in their notebooks immediately. Perhaps this might be the great surrender they had been waiting for?

Montgomery, however, shook his head firmly at the admiral's reply. 'No, certainly not,' he said. 'The armies concerned are fighting against the Russians. If they are to surrender to anybody, it must be to the Russians. Nothing to do with me,' he added casually, as if he were washing his hands of the whole business. He turned as if to go back to his caravan.

Von Friedeburg's face fell. Savage felt pity for the middle-aged admiral. The German looked as if he might break down and begin to sob at any moment. Abruptly, however, Monty seemed to change his mind. Speaking in his hard, clipped fashion, he said rapidly, 'Will you surrender to me all German forces on my western and northern flanks, including all forces in Holland, Friesland with the Frisian Islands and Heligoland, Schleswig-Holstein and Denmark? If you will do this, I will accept it as a tactical surrender on the battlefield of the enemy forces immediately opposing me.'

Just to Savage's right, one of the correspondents, perhaps an American to judge by his accent, whistled softly and said, 'Why the cunning old bugger! He's gonna collar the whole damned shebang and give the Yank army a real nice juicy one in the eye. Ike'll hit the roof when he hears about this.'

But at this moment of triumph Montgomery was no longer interested, Ike was forgotten. All he wanted now was the German's agreement.

Monty pressed home his advantage almost cruelly, knowing the Germans were weakening. 'I wonder if any one of you,' he said, 'if you know the battle situation on the Western Front?'

The German delegation shook their heads.

Montgomery clapped his hands like some latter-day Turkish sultan. As if by magic John Henderson, one of his 'eyes and ears' appeared, unrolling a large map of the British front in Northern Germany, which he and Monty had carefully worked upon once they'd known the German delegation was going to make an appearance. Swiftly and expertly, Montgomery took them the length of his front, covered with a rash of red crayon marks which indicated the progress of his infantry and tank units. The Tommies, or so it seemed to the dumbfounded Germans, were everywhere.

It was too much for Admiral von Friedeburg, the senior delegate. He broke down completely and started to sob.

Savage frowned. It was too much. He had little sympathy for the Germans; he had fought them too long for that. Still why did Monty prolong the Germans' misery like this? There had to be a streak of nasty cruelty in the Master. But the correspondents thought it great fun. They smiled. They held up their thumbs to each other, as if they personally had beaten the Jerries.

Yet as they waited impatiently for the whole damned stage piece to be over (for Savage knew that was what it

176

was in reality) he knew that Monty was gambling for high odds. Without apparently the supreme commander's authority, he was attempting to get the *whole* of the German army to surrender to him. Back at the beginning of April, Montgomery's army had been relegated to what amounted to a side show, now he was after the kudos of final victory over the German armed forces. He might not get Berlin, but he'd get a damned sight more than Ike would with the tame surrender of the German Army Group B in the Ruhr Pocket. Monty was playing for the highest stakes. If he won them, it might well be the British army's last great victory of its whole existence . . .

His men were a little drunk now and Savage didn't particularly mind it. They deserved the cheap German schnapps (the victory beer they had been promised had not arrived and he guessed it never would). They sat around their camp fires away from the main camp, drinking *schlichte* out of great looted fifty-litre German carboys, singing in between toasting Spam and bread, the first white bread they had seen for weeks. They had been through 'Why Are We Waiting?' for everyone from field marshal to simple private soldier was waiting for the Germans to make their decision. Now drunken and a bit bolshy, they were launching into their own version of the old wartime soldier's favourite 'You'll get no promotion this side of the ocean, so cheer up my lads, fuck 'em all . . .'

Savage sitting on a compo ration box next to Sergeant Meek sipped scotch. One of Monty's staff had sent over his NAAFI ration complete with an extra bottle of looted German champagne 'with the field marshal's compliments'. He had suggested sharing the ration and the champagne with the handful of survivors. Meek had said no. 'We don't want 'em getting expensive habits at this stage of the game, sir,' he had objected. 'They'll soon be slung out on their ear into civvy street, then it's back to half a pint of mild-

and-bitter if they're lucky on payday, that is if they've got a job to go to still.' He sniffed. 'My word, sir, bubbly, much too good for 'em.'

Savage laughed, his face a hollowed-out red in the reflection of the flames from the camp fire. 'You are a right little ray of sunshine, Meek.'

'Times like these make you think, sir. You know what the old sweats say, sir. War is hell, but peacetime 'll kill yer.' Again Savage laughed, but without too much conviction.

Suddenly, completely out of the blue, Meek posed a personal question, the first time he had ever done so in all the years the officer and the NCO had known each other. 'What are *you* going to do, sir?'

Savage didn't try to prevaricate. He knew exactly what Meek meant. 'You mean when this little lot is over?' he answered his own question. 'There's not a lot of choice for people like me, Meek. I'll stay in the old Kate Karney in the hope I can serve in a fighting unit. I don't think there'll be much demand for my sort of skills in civvy street – the crafty use of a three-inch mortar, how to get the most out of a ruddy bren gun and the like.' He paused. 'As long as I don't get sent to some bloody depot and have to fight that kind of useless bull. And you, Meek?'

Meek touched his blackened hair. 'Bout the same, sir. Too long in the tooth for anyone else to want me.'

'I thought you were married?'

'Was once.' Meek didn't even seem resentful. 'Went off with a Yank back in '43. Don't blame her, silly cow. No sir.' His voice rose. 'I hope you'll help me to stay in the regiment. It's the only home I know, now, sir.' He tugged the end of his long nose thoughtfully. 'As long as they don't try to push me into the shovel and shit brigade on account of my age. You know, sir, the Pioneer Corps.' He stopped short. 'Something's moving, sir.' It was.

Now as it started to drizzle and grew dark, things were

beginning to move again in the Montgomery camp. Fighter planes had appeared above the tents in that remote wet heath. They circled and circled the area below at just above stalled speed – in case. But there'd be no last minute German suicide attempt on the field marshal. German resistance was broken. This time the Germans were coming back to surrender – *definitely*.

Instead of lording it so cruelly over the German delegation, Montgomery would be all business. He'd dress in dull uniform, unlike his sloppy half-civilian, half-uniform appearance, and this time he'd make sure that the Germans would sign away every resource still under command, including the remote islands such as those along the French coast and the Channel ones they were threatening to defend even if the rest of the German armed forces surrendered. Indeed only moments before the Master prepared to emerge from his caravan to meet the German admirals and generals once more, he had gasped to Major Henderson, 'Christ, Johnny, I've forgotten the bloody Jerry navy.' He thought rapidly for a moment and then added in ink to the surrender document he had clutched in his skinny hand: 'This is to include all naval ships in these areas.' In an instance he had claimed what was left of the *Kriegsmarine*[*] including those U-boats which had almost brought Britain down to its knees in the middle years of the war, as part of the huge booty. Then he opened the door.

Slowly he came down the steps. In his hand he carried the single sheet of paper upon which depended the fate of millions of people this cold wet evening in May 1945. He nodded to the now serious and silent correspondents and senior officers. Over at Savage's little camp the drunken singing died away. Even the young working class paras seemed to realize the world-shaking importance of this moment. Montgomery walked into the large open tent in which the surrender would be signed.

[*]German Navy

179

Stumbling a little on the wet turf, the Germans were led to the tent to meet Montgomery who sat at a simple wooden table covered with a grey army blanket. One of the Germans tried to cover his nervousness by fumbling for a cigarette. Montgomery gave him that same sharp glance that had once stopped Eisenhower from doing the same. The German desisted.

Montgomery cleared his throat. He read out the surrender document. It ended with: 'All hostilities to cease eight hundred hours, British Double Time, Fifth May 1945. The German delegation will now sign. General Admiral von Friedeburg first.' His voice was hard and inflexible. Perhaps he was remembering Dunkirk and the British Expeditionary Force's surrender there – and all the other surrenders which had followed in the black years before El Alamein.

Von Friedeburg's face suffused with grief, perhaps even pain. He rose and signed the document, which was for him one of disgrace. It was as if he wanted to have it over and done with. One by one the others followed. Montgomery watched them like some severe schoolmaster supervising the work of work-shy reluctant school boys. Finally it was over. He raised his voice now so that the army cameramen at the other end of the tent heard, 'Now I will sign –' he paused and gave a kind of curious half-smile as if something had just occurred to him which he thought mildly amusing – 'on behalf of the Supreme Allied Commander General Eisenhower.' He dipped his penny wooden pen in the inkpot and without further ceremony did so. He dropped the pen with a faint sigh. It was all done. The war in North-Western Europe was over and he had brought it to a close, not Eisenhower.

A few moments later he emerged from the tent and posed under the flag. He beckoned to the army cameraman, 'Did you get that picture under the Union Jack?' he asked.

'Yes sir.'

'Good, good.' Montgomery beamed at him and then

around at the gang of correspondents, now huddled in their duffle coats against the drizzle. 'A historic picture,' he said to them. At that moment his gaze caught that of Savage standing a few yards away, a scruffy looking junior officer in a scorched dirty smock, his medal vanished now. The look seemed to say something. It was a kind of bond between those who knew who had really achieved this great victory at last after year after year of bitter defeat, who knew who had done the real fighting. Then Montgomery turned his gaze back to the correspondents. 'Now gentlemen,' he announced, 'it looks as if the British Empire's part in the German War in Western Europe is over . . . I shall now eat my dinner and undoubtedly be persuaded by my staff to drink half a glass of champagne to celebrate.' He chuckled and his listeners did with him. With that Montgomery turned and went back into his caravan slowly, shoulders bowed slightly, head bent as if he might well be thinking deeply.

There was a moment's silence, as if the others realized for the first time what Monty had just said: the war in Europe was over. Standing there with the others Savage stared into the far distance where cherry-red flames flickered on the horizon. They were the camp fires of the Russians. He frowned. *Over*? he asked himself. Next to him Meek broke into his thoughts. He said, 'What was that last bit his nibs said, sir? I didn't quite get it.'

'His nibs . . . Sergeant Meek, you can't talk about your commander-in-chief like that. Don't tell me you're going bolshy like the men as well. Why, you'll be voting Labour at the general election. What did he say?' Savage's bantering tone vanished. 'He said, we've won the war against the Jerries, that's what he said.'

'Oh that's all.' It was Meek's turn to joke in a way. 'I'll miss the war, sort of, sir.'

'Hm, well come on, let's get back to the chaps and then to the regiment before they get up to any more mischief at HQ.'

'Yes sir.' Meek actually saluted, quite smartly in view of the lateness of the hour and the amount of drink he had consumed over this long fateful day. Savage told himself the war was already being forgotten. The peace, for what it was worth, had commenced.

Five minutes later, they were on their way north again, the men snoring loudly in the back of the big three-ton truck, Savage preoccupied with his thoughts and the navigation up front with the driver, disappearing into the darkness – and into the history of World War Two . . .

Man in urban environments

Man in urban environments

Edited by

G. A. HARRISON

AND

J. B. GIBSON

OXFORD UNIVERSITY PRESS · 1976

Oxford University Press, Walton Street, Oxford OX2 6DP

OXFORD LONDON GLASGOW NEW YORK
TORONTO MELBOURNE WELLINGTON CAPE TOWN
IBADAN NAIROBI DAR ES SALAAM LUSAKA ADDIS ABABA
KUALA LUMPUR SINGAPORE JAKARTA HONG KONG TOKYO
DELHI BOMBAY CALCUTTA MADRAS KARACHI

ISBN 0 19 857140 2

© Oxford University Press 1976

Printed in Great Britain
by Thomson Litho Ltd., East Kilbride, Scotland

Contents

Acknowledgements

The chapters of this book are based upon contributions made to a Study Group which the Royal Society established to review the field of human urban biology and to assess the needs for further research. Grateful acknowledgement is made to the Royal Society for its support, for all the facilities provided for the Group and for permitting publication.

G.A.H.
J.B.G.

List of contributors

Dr.D.E.Broadbent, F.R.S.
Department of Experimental
    Psychology,
University of Oxford,
South Parks Road,
Oxford.

Professor Tony J.Chandler,
University of Manchester,
School of Geography,
Manchester, M13 9PL.

Dr.Mary A.M.Eden,
Department of Investigative
    Medicine,
University of Cambridge,
Cambridge.

Dr.Phyllis B.Eveleth,
Institute of Child Health,
Department of Growth and
    Development,
30 Guilford Street,
London WC1N 1EH.

Dr.Ruth Glass,
Centre for Urban Studies,
University College London,
87 Gower Street,
London, WC1E 6AA.

Professor G.A.Harrison,
Department of Biological
    Anthropology,
University of Oxford,
58 Banbury Road,
Oxford.

Professor C.I.Howarth,
Department of Psychology,
The University of Nottingham,
University Park,
Nottingham, NG7 2RD

Dr. Malcolm Carruthers,
St.Mary's Hospital,
Department of Chemical
    Pathology (Research)
Paddington,
London, W.2.

Dr.J.V.G.A.Durnin,
Institute of Physiology,
The University,
Glasgow, W.2

Dr.O.G.Edholm,
School of Environmental Studies,
University College London,
Gower Street,
London, WC1E 6BT.

Dr.John B.Gibson,
Research School of Biological
    Sciences,
Department of Population Biology,
The Australian National
    University,
Box 475, P.O.,
Canberra City, A.C.T. 2601

Professor Jean Gottmann,
School of Geography,
University of Oxford,
Mansfield Road,
Oxford.

Professor R.G.Hopkinson,
School of Environmental
    Studies,
University College, London,
Gower Street,
London WC1E 6BT

Professor G.Howe,
Department of Geography,
University of Strathclyde,
Richmond Tower,
Richmond Street,
Glasgow, G1 1XH

Professor Ivor H.Mills,
Department of Medicine,
University of Cambridge,
Cambridge.

Professor G.A.Rose,
St.Mary's Hospital Mecical
   School,
Epidemiology Department,
Paddington,
London W.2.

Professor R.J.Smeed,
University College London,
Gower Street,
London, WC1E 6BT.

Professor J.M.Tanner,
Institute of Child Health,
Department of Growth and
   Development,
30 Guilford Street,
London WC1N 1EH

Dr.Eric J.Thompson,
Greater London Council,
Director-General's Department,
The County Hall,
London SE1 7PB.

Professor J.K.Wing,
MRC Social Psychiatry Unit,
Institute of Psychiatry,
De Crespigny Park,
London, SE5 8AF.

Members of the Royal Society study group

Professor G.Ainsworth Harrison (Chairman)
Dr.J.B.Gibson (Secretary)
Professor J.S.Weiner (Secretary)
Professor T.J.Chandler
Dr.J.V.G.A.Durnin
Dr.R.H.Fox
Professor D.V.Glass, F.R.S.
Dr.H.W.Hiorns
Professor G.A.Rose
Sir Bernard Katz, F.R.S.
Professor R.Glass
Professor K.M.Gwilliam
Professor N.A.Barnicot
Dr.P.J.Chapman
Professor C.I.Howarth
Dr.O.G.Edholm
Professor J.Gottmann
Professor G.Melvyn Howe
Professor C.H.Waddington, F.R.S.
Professor J.M.Tanner
Professor R.G.Hopkinson
Professor I.Mills
Professor J.K.Wing

1 Introduction

G. A. Harrison and John B. Gibson

URBANIZATION

In 1960 18.8 per cent of the world's population were to be
found in urban centres of over 100 000 people.   The proportion
is likely to increase in the future.   In some countries like
the United Kingdom, where in England and Wales 46.8 per cent
of people live in towns of over 100 000, there is evidence of
outmigration from the centres of large cities to neighbouring
mid-size towns, but this migration,along with the attraction
of these towns for surrounding rural populations,leads to their
own growth and they tend not only to coalesce with each other
but also to become continuous with the cities themselves.   All
the indications are then that most people will continue to live
for most of their lives in urban type situations and any future
population growth is likely to increase the proportion.   The
urban ecosystem is a complex of distinctive physical, biological, and, perhaps most importantly, social factors.   Physical
characteristics include distinctive climatic regimes indoors
and out, high levels of noise, and innumerable new chemical
substances including those responsible for air and water pollution.   Biologically one may note the phenomena of crowding,
dietary changes, physical inactivity, the possibilities for
the adaptive radiation of pathogens,especially viruses, and
the lack of contact with other animals and plants.   Socially,
cities are characterized by an occupational structure of people
employed in manufacturing and increasingly in service industries.   This change in the occupational structure modifies the
way of life of people and in the long-run will have biological
consequences.

There is of course a great variety both within and between
individual urban systems and in this respect the developed
world offers a number of marked contrasts to the developing one.   The Royal Society Study Group concentrated its
attention on the situation in the former, and particularly
that prevailing in the United Kingdom, which would seem to
offer some general characteristics typical of urban situations,
at least in Europe and North America.

URBAN RURAL CONTRASTS

Many of the features of the strictly urban environment in
developed societies are now to be found in some degree in the
surrounding rural areas as a consequence of the general spread
of living conditions brought about by industrial development,

economic growth, and modern medicine. But in the continuum
which connects the metropolis with the countryside there is
a broad range of environmental variation.

In comparison of urban with neighbouring rural groups, mortality from diseases which appear to have a high environmental
component in their etiologies is usually higher in the urban
groups.   These differences, however, are often small by comparison with regional differences. Historically there has, on
the whole,been a correlation between lower mortality and higher
urbanization.

BIOLOGICAL EFFECTS OF URBANIZATION

The urban environments of today differ from those to which
man has been exposed throughout most of his evolutionary experience.   When organisms are exposed to large and rapid environmental changes one expects, and with natural populations
of plants and animals one finds, signs of maladjustment.
Evolutionary time is required for the processes of selection
to build up the new adaptive mechanisms which act to obviate
the stresses in any environment. Man is characterized by remarkable behavioural and physiological adaptability, some of
it acquired in the course of growth and development, but the
range of an organism's adaptability is presumably determined by
the nature of past environments to which ancestral populations
have been exposed. It is highly unlikely that man's adaptability embraces all the processes required for dealing most
efficiently with the many facets of urban environments which
historically are totally new.

Biological changes induced by environmental change may represent alterations in the state of the adaptable mechanisms
whereby organisms attempt to maintain homeostasis, but they
may also represent failures to maintain perfect homeostasis,
and therefore be indicative of changing somatic fitness (which
for present purposes can be equated with health). There are
often difficult problems in deciding whether a biological response is an adaptation or a change in fitness, and this has
contributed uncertainty to the interpretation of the effects
of modern living.

Despite the predictions that urban living involves biological
hazards there is as yet very little substantive evidence for
this.   There is some evidence that coronary heart disease,
particularly in males, is affecting progressively younger age
groups, but it cannot be denied that, at least until very recently, life expectancy in this country has been increasing.
It should not be concluded from this, however, that the biology of urban man is of no practical importance, for there are
many practical reasons why pathologies may be going undetected

and why research should be focused on this area. One important factor which precludes comparison of present-day situations with former ones is the problem of comparable diagnosis. This is of special concern in considering mental illness where, even with an extreme pathology such as schizophrenia, different psychiatrists, even when working on the same population, may reach different estimates of its prevalence.

When it comes to ill-defined neuroses it is quite meaningless to try and compare the past with the present. Nevertheless, evidence is accruing that adolescents, who are both particularly exposed and particularly vulnerable to the conditions of modern life, are displaying more signs of failure of psychological homeostasis than formerly. An underlying pathology can assume the appearance of the norm, thus, for instance, the increase in blood pressure with age found in Europe and North America was for long regarded as part of the natural process of ageing, until it was shown that in other forms of society with other life styles this increase did not occur.

It is evident that even if, as one suspects, there are many components of the urban environment which are harmful, these may well be masked by other technological developments, particularly in the field of palliative medicine. One might well ask how neuroses would manifest themselves without the availability of tranquillizers and sedatives. Of course, as long as medicine manages to keep up with the consequences of new environments one might argue that there is no cause for con-concern, but at least there would still seem to be a need to understand fully what is actually happening.

It is not easy to define precisely what is meant by 'stress', but factors can generally be recognized which act to disturb homeostasis, impose a load on adaptable mechanisms, and are likely to be manifest, chronically if not acutely, in a reduction in fitness. It can be argued that there are stresses in any environment, but the normal consequence of evolutionary adaptation is that they are reduced to a minimum. Because the urban environment is so new and so different from that which has prevailed throughout most of human evolution, it is likely to impose high levels of stress. The consequences of this stress may be expected to be found at every level of biological organization, and to involve physiological, biochemical, and psychological changes. Having said this, it must also be recognized that many of the developments associated with urbanization, particularly in medicine and medical services, have aimed at removing stresses from the environment, and thus in a very general way at making conditions more optimal for human existence.

Much work has been undertaken with experimental animals on the physiological effects of environmental stress. Recently,

this work has been actively developed and applied to human situations, especially by Levi and his colleagues in Sweden, and to some extent also in the United States. There is evidence, particularly in relation to adreno-cortico steroids and catecholamine secretions, that many environments and activities produce biochemically recognizable stress responses. Such responses may vary according to the nature of the stress. So far attention has been primarily directed, at the biochemical level, to rather extreme situations such as in racing drivers and free-fall parachutists, and to the immediate and acute responses to these experiences (see Chapter 13). It seems very likely that more everyday situations are having qualitatively similar effects and that persistent exposure to them will accumulate to produce chronic changes. So far very little attention appears to have been devoted to this, and even in the case of situations giving rise to acute stress there has been little study as yet in the United Kingdom. The dearth of information is even more evident in terms of the long-term psychological effects of chronic mental stress, including competitiveness, which is so widespread and encouraged in modern societies.

Many of the biological effects of urban living have not been recognized so far because sufficient detailed examination has not been undertaken. Many are likely to be subtle, only manifesting themselves slowly over a lifetime. This makes them no less important, but they will require sophisticated techniques and large numbers of subjects to be detected.

MAIN CONCLUSIONS OF THE STUDY GROUP'S REVIEW OF RESEARCH IN URBAN BIOLOGY

1. Urban environments embrace distinctive physical and social characteristics. Interactions between these factors impose constellations of events which are, in evolutionary time, quite new. Only a small proportion of these events have been identified. In the 'work situation', industrial medicine is developing rapidly, but practically nothing is known of the biological effects of the way people spend the rest of their time. And many sections of the community are not involved and never will be involved in organized industry.

2. Established research in urban geography, urban sociology, and epidemiology, environmental design, and transport studies will continue to provide important information on the various aspects of urbanization on man. However, the interpretation of much of this material will be hampered by the lack of information on biological characteristics. The interpretation of urban migration, for instance, may be influenced by whether

migrants are biologically selected, or random samples of the populations from which they come. It would often be helpful to know
whether social groups are genetically different from one another,
and varying resistance, for instance, is of critical concern in
epidemiology. Environmental design and transport systems can
hardly be considered separately from their effects on human physiology and health.

3. Little is known of the nature and extent of biological
variation within and between populations in industrial societies,
although whenever it has been looked for it has been found to be
considerable.

Such variation, whether it be biochemical, physiological, or
psychological, may have genetic and environmental components differing between social and geographical levels.

4. Branches of medical science, for example, epidemiology and
occupational medicine, are concerned with the part of the variation that is pathological, and particular situations have been
identified which account for some of this pathological variation.

5. The majority of the variation is not overtly pathological,
and is usually regarded by biologists as being 'normal'. However,
this variation has itself many components, and whilst some of
that which is environmentally induced represents physiological
adaptability, other parts almost certainly represent failures of
homeostasis and are at least incipiently pathological. There
are also likely to be genetic factors determining the capacity for
adaptability and homeostasis.

The chapters in this book fall into a number of groups. The
first five are concerned with the urban environment itself in
terms of urban geography, demography (particularly migration),
climatology, buildings and architecture, and traffic. There
follow three on normal human biology: nutrition, growth, and
energy expenditure; the last of these is primarily methodological, since a number of methodological problems will have to be
overcome before we have worthwhile descriptive information of
the varying patterns of energy expenditure. Four chapters on
medical and physical health problems with special attention on
the effects of stress, lead on to three papers dealing with behaviour and mental health. The question of genetic variety is
then considered, and the book concludes with a cautionary statement about what constitutes urbanization. Since the book has a
primarily biological-medical focus this last chapter seems to
be particularly important. Human biologists may be prone to enter the field of urban biology with a too naive enthusiasm, ignoring the extensive and sophisticated work which has already
been done in urban sociology.

2 Urban geography and the human condition

Jean Gottman

Urbanization has become a massive phenomenon. Around the world, it is reshaping mankind's habitat. It is both a cause and a product of momentous change in the geographical distribution of people and their activities. The urban phenomenon has been traditionally described first, in terms of density and mass of compact settlement; secondly, in terms of the concentration of non-agricultural economic activities; thirdly, in terms of conglomerates of diverse buildings housing and servicing the agglomerated population; and, finally, as the way of life of a society distinguished by its urbanity and civilization.

Indeed, the growth of cities appeared to coincide in time and space with the birth and progress of civilization. But the urban society, which used to form a minority and an elite living in selected locations, has been rapidly modifying its part in the geography of mankind. In the better-developed countries, it has gradually absorbed most of the modern mass society. A majority of the population in these countries now lives in towns and cities, and the urban condition increasingly describes the mode of living of the developed world, while the developing parts of the world steadily evolve towards urban predominance.

For a long time, the process of urban growth was, however, bemoaned and distrusted. In the past, large cities were accused of concentrating power, wealth, and sin; nevertheless, the urban condition seemed enviable. Today, it is the urban environment rather than the urban dweller that is regarded as evil and in need of reformation. The density, the mass, the congestion, the pollution, the noise, and the turmoil are among the characteristics deplored in the modern city. Urban has come to be contrasted with urbanity. It is often difficult to recognize whether these features are due to urbanization *per se* or to other forces unleashed by the dynamics of modern society.

Perhaps no other discipline has gathered more data on towns and cities than has geography. Geographers are concerned not only with the facts of spatial distribution but also with the organization of inhabited space. Environment, habitat, density, land-use, landscape, and the relationships between human behaviour and physical circumstances have been among the major topics of geographical studies; the urban phenomenon and its consequences for the human condition play a greater role than ever in geographical thought.

PAST ENDEAVOURS

Since ancient times urban phenomena have played a part in the
task of those who attempted to describe, comprehend, and predict
the trends of the spatial organization in which mankind lives.
For at least a century and a half, geographers have been surveying and analysing the urban phenomenon, comparing features of
various cities and categories of towns, and assessing trends in
the form of such settlements. Before the nineteenth century
the description of the variety of the world which was gradually
being discovered by the Europeans fully occupied the endeavours
of most of those who contributed to that sector of knowledge.
Mapping was the principal method used to achieve some precision
and system in organizing the data concerning the geographical
distribution of physical features, people, and cities; and
cartography became the first scholarly expression of geographical
method.

The first treatises that gathered the available geographical
knowledge in a rationalized and systematic form, especially the
early atlases of Varenius' *Geographia generalis* (1650), restricted
their scope to the physical features of the world. These could
be surveyed and correlated in a somewhat safer and more scientific
fashion than the more difficult, disputable, and, indeed, extraordinarily diversified characteristics of human settlements. The
aim of the incipient geographical scholarship was to formulate
some generally recognized relationships and broad features. From
what was known of cities such endeavours seemed too hazardous, so
irregular and diversified were their distribution and characteristics.

However, some maps of cities were included in sixteenth century
atlases and, in the second half of the seventeenth century, a few
scholars concerned themselves with the facts and trends of urbanization. Outstanding among these was Sir William Petty, a true
pioneer of modern geography not only for his surveys of Ireland
but also for his essays on *Political arithmetick* (1683-90). Petty
attempted a comparative evaluation of the size and function of
the major capitals of Europe. He believed London to be the
largest city in Europe; to demonstrate its primacy and rapid
growth, Petty estimated the population on the basis of mortality
rates and went on to describe many of London's spatial and social
characteristics. Observing that the population agglomerating in
and around London increased at a much faster rate than the total
population of England, he predicted, by projecting this trend,
that London would absorb the whole of the English nation by the
1840s unless its growth was controlled. Indeed, William Petty
F.R.S., deserves to be recognized as one of the distant ancestors
of modern human geography. Even though in the 1650s he held the
Professorship of Anatomy at Oxford, posterity ranks his geographical achievements higher than his medical and biostatistical

works. It was meritorious to have forecast the gradual urbanization of English society and the concentration of population
arising around London, despite the flaws in the accuracy of the
statistical lore.

The eighteenth century continued to add many observations to
the available systematic knowledge on the distribution of the
population, its characteristics, and its activities. The improved
and generalized mapping of cities drew attention to their design
and to relations that could be noted between urban layout and the
natural site. The improved mapping of various parts of the world
stressed the inequalities and diverse patterns existing in the
distribution of cities and a few relationships between their
distribution and geographical location. The systematic study
of urban location and site was incorporated in the early principles of human geography as it developed in the nineteenth
century.

The use of cartography not only as a tool for description but
also as a method of analysis greatly benefited after the 1790s
from the statistical data provided by the first population censuses in major Western countries and from the progress of mathematics. The era of enlightenment led scholars to relate human
conditions to the predominating natural and political circumstances. The need arose for a search for logical and rigorous
relationships between human phenomena and the natural environment. It may be noteworthy that two eminent mathematicians
sat on the committee that established the first modern geographical society in Paris in 1821: Laplace was the first president
of the Society, and Fourier was a council member. Mathematics
is the foundation of scientific logic and reason; geographical
knowledge was expected to lead the way to an understanding of the
laws governing the relations of people and nature, and to the
establishment of an orderly management of these relationships.
Much of the data in physical geography lent itself to this
endeavour, but the urban phenomenon was to remain for some time
a sector of chaos.

It was in Great Britain that the Industrial Revolution and
urbanization progressed in parallel in the most spectacular
fashion during the nineteenth century; and it was here that the
movement for urban reform and town planning made its first major
strides. The most important works on the ills of the cities were
written not by geographers but by thinkers deeply disturbed by
the moral and political issues involved in the rapid expansion of
British cities. Best remembered among them are Friedrich Engels'
report on *The condition of the working classes in England* (1842)
and Charles Booth's *Life and labour of the people of London*
(1891-1903), besides many reports by Royal Commissions. All stressed
the conditions of deprivation of the poor concentrated in the
heart of large cities like London and Manchester. The living

conditions of the industrial working class became increasingly
associated with large-scale urbanization, and both were deplored.
Most of the utopian reformers called for breaking up the large
cities into small autonomous units surrounded by rural countryside, and the socialist literature advocated community control
of the ownership of the land and of the management of industry
in each of those new town communities. The lineage of thought
can be easily traced from Thomas More's *Utopia* to Raymond Unwin's
ideas on town planning, as offered around 1900.

Geographers, properly speaking, were not concerned with this
kind of theoretical planning in the nineteenth century; they
seemed to have been too busy gathering and ordering the enormous
flow of new data about their own country and the rest of the
world. They were still surveying, exploring, mapping, and
classifying. Their data and methods were increasingly used for
the management of urban areas by a variety of experts. E.W.
Gilbert has shown how the cartographic method was successfully
used for medical purposes at the time of the cholera epidemics
in London and Oxford in mid-nineteenth century to understand
the source of contagion and to lay the foundations of modern
epidemiological principles (Gilbert 1972).

More general principles gradually emerged from geographical
surveys of the urban phenomena: the facts of density of
population and of the division of labour between city and
country led to the distinction between urban and rural areas and
ways of life; the concentration of the large cities along the
fringe of the land masses, in coastal positions, showed their
frequent location at crossroads of sea lanes and waterways such
as the mouths of estuaries of rivers or straits between the seas;
and, in the case of the British Isles, by far the most urbanized
country in the world by 1900, the obvious correlation was
observed between the map of urbanization and the map of coal-
fields (though with the major exception of London). The last
type of observation led to a variety of generalizations; among
them was the apparently necessary coincidence of the distribution
of large cities and an easy access to coal, a massive use of coal,
and the ensuing 'black country' type of landscape and environment. In his book on the *Evolution of cities* (1915), Sir Patrick
Geddes, one of the scholars most responsible for the development
of both urban geography and town planning in Great Britain,
could still forecast that the growth of urbanization in North
America would conform to the map of the coal basins.

Causal relationships in the interplay between human actions and
natural conditions in the cities remained a traditional concern
of the scholarly geographer. The pattern was set forth in England
in the famous paper read to the Royal Geographical Society in
1887 by Halford Mackinder "On the scope and method of geography".

This paper was the manifesto of the 'new geography' Mackinder had
been preaching in the 1880s; it earned him first a Readership,
then led to the establishment of the School of Geography, in the
University of Oxford.   Mackinder sets the analysis of the relationships between environment and community as a major task for
geographers.   The greatness of London is taken as a case in point;
it is related to the position of London at the centre of the
south-eastern region between its very different sections, and to
the role of the city as a place of trans-shipment between land,
river, and sea traffic.

'Even more pregnant with meaning is the position of the Thames
mouth relatively to that of the Scheldt. It determines the linked
greatness of London and Antwerp, and also much of the continental
policy of England.' But Mackinder emphasizes also that

... the course of history at a given moment ... is the product
not only of environment but also of the momentum acquired in the
past. The fact that man is mainly a creature of habit must be
recognized. The Englishman, for instance, will put up with
many anomalies until they become nuisances of a certain degree
of virulence. The influence of this tendency must always be
kept in mind in geography. Milford Haven, in the present state
of things, offers far greater physical advantages than Liverpool for the American trade; yet it is improbable that Liverpool will have to give way to Milford Haven, at any rate in the
immediate future. It is a case of *vis inertiae* [Mackinder 1887].

Thus, in the new geography, a series of socio-economic considerations were early introduced in the discussion of the size,
function, and evolution of cities. By 1915, when Geddes published
his *Evolution of cities,* urban studies had made considerable
progress, and the philosophy of town planning had diversified
and expanded with the work of many planners such as Ebenezer
Howard and William Morris. By his work and teaching in Edinburgh,
Geddes established a living and fruitful linkage between geography
and urban planning. He was basically interested in the process
of urban growth and the consequences it spelled for the living
conditions of the people. Much in his book reflects the pessimism
of his generation and the undiluted influence of simplified
Darwinism, common at that time. He accepts, though with some
distrust, the rapid and apparently uncontrollable growth and
sprawl of the average city and the rise of the metropolitan
phenomenon (for which he coined the useful term of 'conurbation');
but he foresees the city evolving like the dinosaur towards its
extinction by evolutionary stages of growth from metropolis to
necropolis. Meanwhile, however, Geddes calls for more foresight,
control, and planning. His book points out in useful and elo-
quent fashion many important trends of modern urbanization,
though some of the forecasts were made on the basis of over-
simplified projections, such as the relationship between urban

growth and coal-mining on the one hand, and between urban growth and heavy industry on the other; neither of these has been shown to be essential beyond a short period in history.

The connection outlined between geography and town and country planning has lasted and continues to develop. This association led the geographers to visualize the nature of their discipline as being not only descriptive and analytical, somewhat like an anatomy and a physiology of mankind within its habitat, but also as encompassing an approach with prophylactic purposes (Gottmann 1969).

RECENT CONCERNS AND THEIR EVOLUTION

Urban places have a great many characteristics. A geographical survey of each urban place yields a considerable amount of diversified data. Urban studies in geography deal with natural features of the site and the surroundings, as well as with characteristics of the population, its economic activities, movements, social and political organization, and with the 'built environment' formed by man's physical artifacts. The variety of the urban concerns of the geographer have rapidly increased as he has tried to comprehend a city of some size; the accumulation of the quantity of data concerning the human and socio-economic aspects of towns and cities has proceeded much faster than a single profession can manage. The self-refining division of labour, now common to most scholarly disciplines, has worked within and without geography in the urban field; new sub-specializations have been spawned such as social geography and urban transport economics. To co-ordinate the increase in the number and variety of these sub-dividing specializations, all on urban matters, it has become necessary to establish new schools or scientific organizations for teaching, research, and general policy-making. Interdisciplinary co-ordination has been provided, for instance, by Ekistics, an approach to the study of urban settlements and an international organization, both initiated by the Greek planner, C.A.Doxiadis (Bell and Tyrwhitt 1972), and by special inter-faculty programmes on urban affairs in various universities or by new schools such as that of 'The built environment' at the University of Edinburgh.

The rapid and spectacular development of urban studies has caused urban geographers to concentrate their attention on specific questions more directly concerned with spatial distribution. Traditional geographic work studied the location, size, form, functions, and internal organizations of urban places. As the pace of urbanization has rapidly increased the number of urban places, their average size, and their complexity, urban studies have increasingly become concerned with process, evolution, and interconnections between towns, cities, and suburbs. The ensuing

changes have also intensified the interweaving of size, form,
function, location, and internal structures, creating the
comprehensive concept of an urban environment to be analysed as
well as assessed in terms of its value as a milieu for living,
for the development of individuals, and for the functioning of
society. The human condition in the urban environment had always
been accounted for by geography but in a detached way, as a
phenomenon to be examined or a mechanism to be described; now
it has gradually appeared that geography could not carry on with
such an 'objective', impartial attitude. Description and attempts
at explanation of conditions of living and working imply some
scales of values, value judgments, and frequent concern with
the desirability or dangers of various facts and trends. Geographers have begun assessing the pros and cons of certain urban
features, taking sides in a rising debate to which they bring a
considerable arsenal of ammunition.

Each of the classical concerns of urban geographers has gathered
materials relevant to that debate. Location, for instance, deals
with site and accessibility. It involves the topography, the
climate, the drainage, the water supply, and the natural means of
access; and it can hardly be discussed without putting the town
in its precise place on the networks of traffic and of other cities
and diverse areas with which the place studied maintains relations.
For the environment of an urban settlement cannot be limited to
the locality it occupies. The urban nature connotes density and
mass of settlement; whatever the statistical definition of urban
(which varies from country to country and has in modern times
pursued an upward trend), to be considered urbanized an area must
hold a substantial population distributed in rather dense formation.
Urban also connotes a predominantly non-agricultural economic set
of functions and, therefore, a certain dependence on supplies from
the outside. The description of location must include the systems
of external relations. The larger the concentration of population,
the greater dependence of the urban place on outside connections;
location thus has links with size.

The size of a town, city, or urban district is measured essentially by the population it agglomerates. The extent of area
comprised within municipal boundaries plays a much lesser part.
The statement based on the size of the municipal land area, that
Kiruna, in Northern Sweden, was the largest city in the world was
always received as a sort of joke. The largest cities were the
most populated; in the nineteenth century, if not earlier, London
became the largest city in the world and, indeed, the largest
city that had ever been. The size of urban settlements has been
steadily growing in average as well as in record terms. This
growth accelerated fast in the twentieth century. The famous
cities of ancient times had seldom exceeded the figure of
250 000 inhabitants; this seems to have been the size of Babylon

at its apogee. Rome, Constantinople, and the capitals of China
in the distant past hardly neared a million. By 1800 there were
seven or eight cities of half a million size in the world. By
1900 the great capitals approached or even surpassed the million.
The Japanese architect, Kenzo Tange, has rightly said that a big
city was one that had a population of one million at the beginning of the century but of ten million by 1960; he forecast that
the category would reach the size of a hundred million by the
year 2000.

Indeed, new towns now being built on the periphery of major
conurbations are planned to reach 250 000 inhabitants, as for the
case of Milton Keynes in England, or 400 000, as for several of
the new towns started around Paris. The size of Babylon, so
frightening to people of antiquity, corresponds to a suburban
or satellite role in the contemporary urban system. The old concept of 'urban place', which was opposed to 'rural area' and
seemed to be so compact as to consume hardly any space, has had
to be supplemented with a new terminology for urban systems,
encompassing wider areas, larger masses of people, increased
internal complexity, and greater dependence on a far-flung web
of outside relations. 'Metropolitan' areas, urbanized districts,
'conurbations', and even vaster formations designated as
'Megalopolitan' have thus been defined to describe the larger
modern structures arising as urban man remoulds his habitat.

The rapid increase in size of population has also entailed
expansion in area and new forms. Form and size are closely related. The difficulty of managing very large and crowded cities
has led to suburban sprawl, new patterns of land use, and efforts
to decentralize that have created more-or-less planned new towns
and cities. Size is not, however, the only factor modifying
urban morphology. Technological innovations in transport and
the production of energy have a considerable impact on the spatial
grouping of industries and housing. Manufacturing production,
long dependent on coal, steam, and a large market of nearly
unskilled labour, was responsible for developing a pattern of
industrial 'black country' concentration and for crowding blighted
housing on a large scale next to the factories. Thus grew the
disgraceful picture of the dense industrial urban centre exploit-
ing the poor masses.

The advancement of mechanization and automation liberated the
workers from the hard servicing of machines and shortened working
hours. The railways and, even more, the motor car eliminated
the necessity of clustering workers' housing and industrial
plants close to one another. Freed from many traditional con-
straints, urban settlement scattered and sprawled around the old
centres, and the urban forms and patterns of the growing cities
were also affected by the discussion of social ethics and the
changes in the quality of life. Urban conditions generally im-

proved owing to the rise of the standard of living and better
public health as well as the advance of technology and planning.
The suburban sprawl explosion after 1945 included carefully
planned new towns that were situated on the periphery of,
metropolitan systems. Size also affected land use in many ways.
Almost every town has its slums, but a large mass of these
creates needs for housing and urban renewal which become major
problems. Outdoor recreation may be taken by residents of a
small town in a few gardens or the adjacent countryside. In
a large city the residents need public parks, water spaces, and
sports grounds amounting to a substantial acreage, some of which
may come to be located at a distance outside city boundaries
(Patmore 1970).

Urban geography has been greatly concerned with form, and
still is. Yet the classical relationship of urban land use and
morphology, with emphasis on site, location, and physical conditions, is gradually receding into the background. New geographical concerns focus on the internal features of the structure
of an urban system, and these features, which are powerful among
the environmental forces conditioning urban life, belong to the
'built environment' of the place and the socio-economic characteristics of the population. As Professor Emrys Jones stated, in the
conclusion of his classical study *The social geography of Belfast*:

'at a given cultural stage there was a fairly direct relationship
between the 'natural' environment and land use; this relationship does not hold at the urban stage. At the stage of urban
expansion, residential sectors were moving into human, rather
than physical landscapes; into sectors where social values had
replaced those of soil and site.' *[Jones 1960]*

In the great fluidity of the modern city the social values
attain special importance as anchors and as forces either of
resistance to change or of incentive to movement. Different
cultures react in different ways to the circumstances in which
social values come to determine land use and planning policies.
On the European continent large central cities have often resisted change by pushing manufacturing plants and newly incoming
migrants out to their peripheries. Paris is a classical example
of this trend; the highest social values are still attached to
certain parts of the central core. . In the United States the
trend has been opposite; the vicinity of the 'downtown' at first,
and most of the central city in a metropolitan framework were later
abandoned to the poor newcomers, while the middle class moved
uptown and to elegant suburbs. Social values reflecting cultural
differences deeply affect the morphology and the quality of life
in large cities. The British land-use planning endeavours to
protect rural landscape, green spaces, and to avoid a sprawl of
American style; Professor Peter Hall has directed an interesting
enquiry in the *Containment of urban England* and compared

these efforts to the American megalopolitan growth (Hall 1974;
Hall and Clawson 1973).

Form also evolves with function, and the relationship between
form and function is a basic concern of urban geography (Carter
1972). Urban functions have usually covered the whole span of
non-agricultural economic activities; today, however, functions
such as mining, fishing, and warehousing are carried on outside
urban places, and people employed in these pursuits may reside in
rural territory. With suburban and inter-urban sprawl, 'villages'
that are inhabited by people who work in town and who derive all
their income from urban pursuits are found amid rural countryside.
The nebulous patterns of modern urban morphology (Gottmann 1961)
displace and scatter not only housing but also retail trade and
the other services, which tend to move close to the customer's
doorstep. Manufacturers increasingly move out of the old cores
to peripheral locations, owing partly to the ease of transport by
highway and partly to the pressures of cost, congestion, and
planning regulations. The old central areas continue to play an
important role in the cities where 'quaternary functions', using
white-collar personnel and processing information, are well
developed. The quaternary activities are tightly interwoven;
they include the management of private and public affairs, higher
education and advanced research, mass media, and publishing, etc.,
and need close contact with another. In recent years these have
been the fastest-expanding sectors of employment. These activities
take more space in cities, largely in the form of offices,
libraries, laboratories, and meeting halls. The skyscraper and
the convention hall are architectural expressions of the rising
role of these quaternary, transactional activities. The personnel
so occupied now represents a substantial percentage of total
employment (usually one-fourth to one-third in developed countries),
and its modes of living, quite different from those of the
traditional industrial worker, mark the modern city in many ways
(Gottmann 1974)

The changing characteristics of size, form, and function combine
to modify the internal structure of towns and cities. Usually,
the socio-economic changes develop faster than the physical, and
built-up environment can be recast to fit the new society. The
renewal of the environment attempts to catch up, but generally
lags behind the needs; change has occurred with great celerity
in the twentieth century. Size, form, and function concur to
extend rapidly the space occupied by urban agglomeration. On
average, a lowering of the residential densities has relieved
the crowding caused by the early stages of industrialization.
The daytime densities of those at work in the central or industrial districts of large cities have not necessarily decreased:

present employment in the famous square mile area of the City of London, approximately 250 000 persons, is not very different from what its residential population was a century ago.

The much-improved technology of transport has helped to bind together the various rapidly mushrooming parts of the large modern city. Movement of people and goods within and around the cities has increased faster than any of the other measurable characteristics. Geographers and urban economists have studied carefully the transport and communication networks and the currents of commuting that seem to cause the worst of the congestion. However, the diversity of functions congregating in a lively city, especially one endowed with both manufacturing production and quaternary activities, creates a complex and constantly evolving system of traffic flows that baffles the experts. It has been said that the only real solution to London's traffic problems would be to raze the conurbation and re-build it for its present needs (Buchanan 1963); if such Utopia could be contemplated, it would be safe to expect the needs of a re-built London to be quite different from what they now are and they would be most difficult to foresee.

The fluidity of modern urban space and society has often been described and emphasized. Some experts forecast the almost complete dissolution of cities into such a wide and thin scattering that the concentration of people, activities, equipment, and problems which has always been the essential characteristic of urban centres would cease to be true (Berry and Horton 1970). However, it seems doubtful that the immense amounts of materials and energy required by modern society living at very low densities could be achieved either for economic reasons or for reasons of efficiency. It is even more doubtful that simply to avoid some of the unpleasantness of urban crowding, people would generally prefer an isolated, scattered life and accept rationed social contacts and gregariousness.

The study of the urban environment is, therefore, evolving in stubborn fashion along a road that increasingly subordinates the physical features of that milieu, either natural or manmade,, to economic and technological means first, and to the social and cultural ends second. And the latter are gaining pre-eminence.

There was some surprise, I believe, when, invited as an urban geographer to deliver the Special University Lectures in Architecture and Town Planning for 1967 at University College, London, I chose as my subject 'The growing city as a social and political process' (Gottmann 1967). Scholarly geography had, in fact, for some time analysed cities and urban regions mainly from this viewpoint. The pioneering work by Emrys Jones in his *Social geography of Belfast* (1960) set the tone in the British scene. Other studies such as my *Megalopolis* (1961) or Peter Hall's *London 2000* (1969)

have had a similar slant. In recent years the vogue of stressing
social values and forces, often on the foundation of political
patterns, has broadly invaded urban studies by geographers and
others. David Harvey, a British geographer working in America,
has strongly voiced such views, especially in his *Social justice
and the city* (1973). Two good summaries of these trends in urban
studies have been provided in B.T.Robson's *Urban social areas* (1975)
and P.L.Knox's *Social well-being: a spatial perspective* (1975).

The social problems of modern towns and cities have been compounded
by the diversity and volume of migration currents throughout the
contemporary world. The old concept of a tightly woven, politically
and racially monolithic city seldom applies nowadays. It is regretted, and its re-birth is being sought by many attempts at planning
or re-moulding new or enlarged cities or suburbs in such a monolithic cast. The search, more actively conducted in some countries
than in others, has only led to greater fluidity and to the frac-
tioning of urban systems that depend on the complementarity of the
various components. Hence the acceptance of a picture of the city
as a mosaic of ghettos. Large-scale migrations result from many
factors in modern society and in the international arena. Urbanization is only one of these factors, but the urban places are the
essential receiving environment of the migrations; the ethnic
aspect is thus added to the socio-economic stratification which
always existed to some extent as a source of tensions in the urban
environment.

Studies pointing out recent trends towards the lowering of densities and the gradual scattering of the urban phenomenon may be
misleading for readers who do not realize that, on the world
scale and even in a country such as England, urbanization continues to concentrate people and activities in selected places on
the national territory. These places are more numerous and
spatially more spread out than they used to be, but the urban
phenomenon remains chiefly one of spatial concentration, thinning
out the population in other areas wider than the urban spaces
into which people and buildings are gathered.

The process of concentration causes an unavoidable expansion
on land as well as in height, in and around the older nuclei.
These trends have been considered from various angles (Champion
1972; Gottmann 1966; Hall and Clawson 1973). The crowding
has been accused of affecting the health of the urban dwellers,
causing abnormal psychic pressures, and many other kinds of
unpleasantness. These diverse aspects of the interplay between
urban environment and urban populations are examined further in
this book by competent specialists in the fields concerned.
The urban and political geographers must deal with the urban
phenomenon as a whole. To individuals taken into the dynamics
of the process, the consequences of urbanization may and will
cause tension, trouble and occasionally distress. The process

as a whole cannot be wished away. The fundamental question
that can and should be raised at this stage is whether the
process could be managed in a way that would improve the
human condition as far as it can be surveyed at present;   and,
if so, how could such a result be achieved?

We do not presume to answer these questions in this paper but
it seems possible to point a few fundamental dilemmas, the
realization of which may help to clarify the options before us.

FUNDAMENTAL DILEMMAS

The modern city is a complex, massive, collective, and pluralistic phenomenon;   but as scholars look at the urban environment,
they find the human condition essentially expressed by the
behaviour of individual human beings. The collective behaviour
of populations is extremely difficult to appreciate. Scientific
study has addressed itself to individuals, then tried to assess
the characteristics of the collective with the help of
statistical methods in which the units are again individual
cases. However, observations have often pointed out the diversity
of human reactions to a given situation. Many people like to be
part of a crowd and of collective action - otherwise crowds would
not be forming so frequently - but many others dislike the
situation of being in a crowd on the street. Many people enjoy
standing on a summit with a dominating view, others are afraid
of height or are made uncomfortably by it;   as modern architecture
builds skyscrapers, space on the upper storeys of the high towers
is usually at a premium and a mark of 'status' in office buildings
and hotels, though a substantial minority of the population do not
want such facilities and resent occasions when they have to use
them.

Street crowds and high towers are only two examples of the host
of urban characteristics dividing public opinion about urban life
and design. The modern urban environment is full of such problems.
In some instances the conflict of opinion is more subtle and
engenders worse difficulties, especially when it divides the
individual within himself;   thus, it is obvious to the vast
majority of motor car owners that the motor car, as it works at
present, is a major factor of noise, pollution, and congestion
in the city, but few would be prepared to give up such a convenience even if an alternative mode of transport were provided.
The interests and tastes of one individual do not necessarily
coincide with those of society as a whole or with those of a
group in that society. Hence the difficulty of arriving at
objective standards.

The statistical method may lead us to compute the interests
of an 'average' individual;   but such a mean would not represent
the interests of a large community as a whole accurately, be-

cause the whole has needs and means that are different from
those of its many parts and also because the whole encompasses
a variety of individuals and diverse categories of people that
must be kept living and working together harmoniously. A first
series of difficult dilemmas, therefore, is bound to arise as a
result of the diversity of the individuals and human groups
gathered in an urban place. For, by definition, the urban
community is not homogenized. That could not be expected at
a crossroads constantly receiving newcomers; and it could not
be so even with a stabilized population because the urban
community functions owing to a refined division of labour which
diversifies the society.

Now the geographer uses a spatial approach to dissect the
urban phenomenon. He sees the urban community defined as contained in a certain area, or region, or in an 'urban place'.
His reasons for studying the spatial aspects do not limit his
purposes to space *per se,* for he wants to understand the organization of the place in order to serve ultimately the general
well-being of society. However, the spatial approach emphasizes
the sum total of the population, resources, organizational
features, and problems contained in the units of space considered, even if that space is a 'place' small in extent.
Geography is less concerned with the individual and more
focused on a collective and indeed comprehensive concept of
the urban phenomenon.

To arrive at a comprehensive assessment, urban geography must
reckon with a very large number and variety of characteristics.
A physicist would marvel at the immense diversity of data that
can be gathered on, and may be relevant to, any regional or
urban geographical study. It would seem to him almost unlimited
in comparison with the rather small number of features
recognizable in a defined physical phenomenon. It is indeed
the nature of the urban place, especially in modern times, with
its larger size, faster growth, and greater inner complexity,
to be multi-faceted and pluralistic by essence. The forces at
work within the city stem from a variety of origins and categories; some are natural, others technological, still others
demographic, ethnic, socio-economic, governmental, and so forth.
The choice of the forces and factors to be taken into consideration in each study largely depends on the purpose of the study.
The choice is always difficult. It requires skill and some
knowledge of the wider field of observations related to the
purpose.

The complexity of the task explains why urban geography was
long concerned mainly with location, form, and function and with
physical rather than socio-economic content. As the prophylactic
vocation infiltrated human geography, the geographers rapidly
became aware of the inadequacy of a theory which tried to explain

and determine the human condition in the city by the material
or physical environment alone. The existing physical structures
were recognized as the products of a stage past; they seldom
had perfectly fitted the needs of that stage and they could be
expected to fit the present needs even less. Moreover, although
a city is best described and analysed in terms of its concrete,
physical structures, these, even when modified to fit, determine
only some and not all of the conditions of the population's
well-being. The socio-economic conditions are usually more
decisive, and they change independently of the physical frame.

There are a number of dilemmas inherent in the interweaving
of the urban system. Some are methodological; others affect
the very purpose of any discussion of the urban condition. In
terms of method the geographer is constantly deciding which among
the many components are more relevant, more valuable, in his
analysis. Often he will have to specialize narrowly within urban
geography and to call on the opinion of experts or disciplines
outside geography. Team work in urban affairs becomes increasingly necessary. Many of the important factors at work in urban
problems are not specifically urban. The climate is not urban in
nature, although it is somewhat modified locally by urban
activities; regulation may remove the unpleasant effects of the
urban influences, as the enforcement of the Clean Air Acts has
shown with relation to the fog in London. Motor-car traffic
is certainly a dominant feature and problem of modern cities,
but the motor car is not exactly an urban device, even if manufactured in cities - it can be made in plants located in rural
territory, and it is even more essential for transport in farming
areas than in dense cities.

The urban environment consists of many characteristics, facts,
and forces generated by modern society as a whole, operating in
rural as well as urbanized districts. Are we then justified in
stressing constantly the *urban* character of the environment in
which nations as developed and industrialized as the British live?
Would this environment be better described by another term, related to some other characteristic of modern society?

The adjective 'urban' probably deserves the part it is usually
assigned, because urbanization in its complexity has modified
more deeply and broadly the environment of countries such as Great
Britain than any other single trend. It has modified both the
physical conditions of the habitat and the way of life of the
inhabitants. The term may be used as a synthesis of many forces
and factors, including the technological and the socio-economic.
In the comprehensive concept of urban, the geographer recognizes
two basic features: first the density of population and of land
use, with the ensuing pressures on resources and the facts of
crowding; and, secondly the occupational structure of the
population.

The decisive role of *density* as a feature of the urban environment should not be clouded by the recent trend lowering the residential densities to a slight degree. This is an internal tendency in the remoulding of cities that the richer nations can afford. But the urban character of the environment is rooted in the fact that an overwhelming majority of a nation's population (and in increasing proportion) now lives and works at densities of an urban level, that is, several thousand per square kilometre. This type of spatial distribution is pregnant with certain unavoidable consequences, such as the use of the tools of highly developed technology to insure the supply, movement, and general well-being of the inhabitants; the constant pressure on local resources; the dependence on networks of outside connections; and the development of an involved division of labour. The nuisances that the solutions presently applied entail are not inevitable, as may be demonstrated in many instances. The obstacles to possible improvement usually lie in the economic field, because of cost, and in the political field, because of the need of consensus to organize action.

The rapid spread of nuisances of various kinds in the urban environment has often been blamed on mass and density. Planners and political theorists seem to have accepted human incapacity to deal with the large size of dense agglomeration, particularly in Greater London, and have recommended, on the one hand, deflecting the growth of large agglomerations to smaller units such as new towns and, on the other hand, lowering densities by endeavours to deflect migratory currents towards areas suffering from outmigration. Finally, given modern metropolitan growth and sprawl, various experts expect a controlled generalization of it to dissolve gradually the larger and denser urban nuclei. Could this urban age mean the elimination of the city?

The contradictions in this generally accepted frame of mind are many, and they stem from the dilemmas offered by reality. In fact, the recent worsening of urban conditions coincided in time with the lowering of residential densities and with the expansion of sprawl; this coincidence raises questions concerning the alleged ability of our society to manage better the somewhat lowered densities. Secondly, too much attention has been given to residential distribution, without due accounting of the concomitant trends in the distribution of places of work and of the resulting currents of traffic. A fuller understanding of the consequences of urban densities could be achieved by relating them carefully to the changes occurring in the modes of life as determined by *the evolution of the labour force*.

The main thrust of urban growth and densification is no longer powered by the location of manufacturing production proper. The latter is not an expanding sector of employment. With increasing rationalization and automation, employment of production workers is moving toward numerical decline. The growth of employment is

now taking place in quaternary and transactional work. This
category of workers is more difficult to disperse. Team work,
consultation, interpretation of information, and highly skilled
and responsible personnel are required by this sort of work.
It is better done where all the facilities and services that may
be needed congregate. The dispersal of the places of official
employment can be achieved by policy and regulation, but with
the consequence of constant movement of personnel doing their
work in many places, with frequent visits to the large existing
centres of quaternary activities, in the British case, particularly to London. The dilemma is between greater concentration and
less movement around the country or greater decentralization and
more nomadism.

The nomadism will keep the major centres of information and
quaternary activities busy even if the residential population
and official employment there decline. It may then become
increasingly difficult and costly to maintain in these centres
the facilities for the transient visitors coming to transact
business. In the future, such centres may have to be managed
as cities for national and international transactions and not
any longer in the sole interest and by decisions of their
regular inhabitants. A number of symptoms have pointed that way
for London and for great transactional cities in other countries,
such as New York. New governmental models will have to be
hammered out for such phenomena (Gottmann 1974 and 1974a). The
question may be raised, 'Whom does decentratalization help in the
long run?' The answer may be provided by the desire of the
political personnel to spread as evenly as possible available
resources over the whole territory of the nation, a sort of
geographical egalitarianism.

The logical purpose of urban geography is to lay the foundations
for planning theories and policies that could improve the functioning and the living conditions of urban areas. Planning theory
has been as yet rather monolithic, aiming at one ideal pattern,
expressed in the design of the built environment. The experience
of urban geography and of the history of planning has shown the
utopian weaknesses of such theories: the built environment alone
cannot answer all the problems of the urban community; the
number and variety of factors operating in the equation are so great
as to prevent a rigorous positioning of the problem. The objectivity of physical planning will be distorted by the diversity
of æsthetic options and tastes. The objectivity of economic
planning encounters the pitfalls of a variety of ethical options
and opinions. Finally, a planning design is seldom aimed at
achieving pluralism and fluidity; but then an authoritarian
and single-minded attitude confronts the popular aspirations for
freedom, choice and change. Indeed, physical planning at its best
may be used to correct minor nuisances in a stabilized society
undergoing little growth and change and generally satisfied with

the existing structure. Such communities are seldom found in the restless society of our changing and urbanizing world.

More often than not the geographer will have to rely on historical precedents to assess the quality and evolution of urban phenomena of a rather novel and unprecedented nature. The scholarly distrust of imaginative innovation and the usual attitudes of men, those 'creatures of habit', compound the constant recurrence of dilemmas dictated by modern trends. Amidst the carefully planned redevelopment of Paris by Haussman in the 1850s, the poet Baudelaire wrote of 'the chaos of the living cities'. Despite the traditional human yearning for order, modern trends compel urban population and urban geographers to recognize a strong quantum of chaos in the environment. Future historians may some day be able to describe this process as orderly creation.

REFERENCES

Urban geography has produced an abundant literature including general theoretical works and many case studies. Only modern works specifically referred to in this paper are listed here; several of them contain detailed bibliographies.

BELL, G. and TYRWHITT, J. (eds.) (1972) *Human identity in the urban environment*. Penguin Books, Harmondsworth.

BERRY, B.J.L. and HORTON, F.E. (1970) *Geographic perspectives on urban systems*. Prentice-Hall, Englewood Cliffs.

BUCHANAN, C. (1963) *Traffic in cities*. H.M.S.O.

CARTER, H. (1972) *The study of urban geography*. Edward Arnold, London.

CARTER, H. and DAVIES, W.K.D., (eds.) (1970) *Urban essays: studies in the geography of Wales*. Longmans, London.

CHAMPION, A.G. (1972) *Variation in urban densities between towns of England and Wales*. Research Paper No.1, Oxford School of Geography.

DOXIADIS, C.A. (1968) *Ekistics: an introduction to the science of human settlements*. Hutchinson, London.

GEDDES, P. (1915) *The evolution of cities*. Williams and Norgate, London.

GILBERT, E.W. (1972) *British pioneers in geography.* David and Charles, Newton Abbot.

GOTTMANN, J. (1961) *Megalopolis.* Twentieth Century Fund. New York.

GOTTMAN, J. (1966) Why the skyscraper? *Geog. Rev. 51* 190-212.

GOTTMANN, J. (1967) The growing city as a social and political process, *Trans. Bartlett Soc. 1966-67. 5,* 11-46.

GOTTMANN, J. (1969) *The renewal of the geographic environment* (inaugural lecture). Clarendon Press, Oxford.

GOTTMANN, J. (1974) The dynamics of large cities, *Geog. Jour. 140* 254-61.

GOTTMANN, J. (1974a) *The evolution of urban centrality: orientations for research,* Research Paper No.8, Oxford School of Geography.

HALL, P. (1969) *London 2000* (Rev. edn.), Faber and Faber, London.

HALL, P. (1974) The containment of urban England, *Geog. J. 140* 386-417.

HALL, P. and CLAWSON, M. (1973) *Planning and urban growth: an Anglo-American comparison.* The Johns Hopkins University Press, Baltimore and London.

HARVEY, D. (1973) *Social justice and the city.* Edward Arnold, London.

JONES, E. (1960) *The social geography of Belfast.* Oxford University Press, London.

KNOX, P.L. (1975) *Social well-being: a spatial perspective.* Oxford University Press, Oxford.

PATMORE, J.A. (1970) *Land and leisure in England and Wales.* David and Charles, Newton Abbot.

ROBSON, B.T. (1975) *Urban social areas.* Oxford University Press, Oxford.

3 Patterns of migration

Eric J. Thompson

INTRODUCTION

Contrary to popular belief, migration has a relatively small
effect on the overall population growth of this country, and such
effect as it has had has reduced the rate at which our population
has been growing. Throughout the last hundred years, Great
Britain has been a net exporter of people except for two relatively short periods: first the 1930s - the years of the depression - and secondly the more recent period of rapid inflow
from the New Commonwealth[†] starting about 1954 and ending abruptly
with the imposition of immigration controls in mid-1962. In very
rough terms, there was a net outflow of around 1.0 million
people from England & Wales[‡] between 1871 and 1971. There was
an even greater net outflow - about 2.1 million people - from
Scotland; giving a total net outflow of about 3.1 million people
from Great Britain. During this hundred-year period the population
rose from 26.1 million to 54.1 million, migration having reduced
the potential growth from 31.1 million (the excess of births over
deaths) to 28.0 million. In spite of net outmigration the
population more than doubled in a hundred years.

Once one looks below the national level, a much more varied
picture emerges. This has already been hinted at in the contrasting data for England & Wales and Scotland mentioned in
the last paragraph. Although the former has 9 times as many

---

†The Commonwealth excluding the three 'Old Commonwealth'
dominions of Australia, Canada, and New Zealand. In this context
the major exporting areas to Great Britain are the Indian
sub-continent, East Africa, the West Indies, and the Mediteranean
Commonwealth (Cyprus, Malta, etc.).

‡The ampersand is used to indicate that the whole area is meant
here and is not being treated as two separate countries. (Wales
was 'annexed and united' to England in 1284; and the term
'England' included Wales in statutes from 1746 to 1967. On 1
April 1974 the former county of Monmouth was formally separated
from England and included in Wales. In this chapter, Monmouth-
shire is treated as if it had been in Wales throughout.)

people, net migration from England & Wales has amounted to half
that from Scotland. Figures for England & Wales and for Scotland
are generally presented separately – they have had separate Registrar Generals ever since 1854 and separate volumes of census
statistics and vital statistics are still produced. It is, however, also possible to analyse the data below the national level
and show similar differences between regions within England &
Wales. For this purpose, the standard regions used by government
statisticians in 1971 are used (see General Register Offices
1967, pp.xxvii–xxviii). (These regions were replaced by the new
metropolitan counties on 1 April 1974, but historical series of
data on the new boundaries are not yet available.) Even at this
level of analysis, of course, many substantial changes will be
missed, for regions are little more homogeneous than countries,
and the latter part of this chapter will discuss changes within
Greater London – the largest conurbation – in more detail.

Although at the level of Great Britain as a whole, net migration
is a relatively small component of population change, this is no
longer the case when one looks at some individual regions.
Between 1961 and 1971 net outmigration from Great Britain, at
375 000, was only 12 per cent of natural increase (the excess
of births over deaths) which amounted to 3 070 000. For Scotland
on its own, however, net outmigration (310 000) was 90 per cent
of natural increase (345 000); and for East Anglia, the smallest
of the English regions, with a population of about 1.7 million,
net inmigration (120 000) was substantially greater than natural
increase (85 000).

One reason for the greater importance of migration for smaller
areas is the fact that most moves are relatively short-distance
ones. This can be illustrated by some data collected in the
1966 census.† This asked people for their addresses, not only
in April 1966, but also in April 1965. In England & Wales nearly
1 person in 9 – 10.7 per cent – had changed their address during
those 12 months. Almost half of these, however, had moved within
the same local authority area; and another quarter, though crossing local authority boundaries, had stayed within the same county.
Only 3.3 per cent of people had moved across county boundaries,
and only 2.2 per cent had not lived in the same region in 1965 as
in 1966. (Of these, 1.4 per cent had moved from other parts of
England & Wales, the other 0.8 per cent coming from outside
England & Wales.)

Before discussing migration in more detail, it may be worth
mentioning that there are also differences in natural change at

---

†Scarcely any migration data from the census held in April
1971 were available in June 1974 when this chapter was
written.

regional level. The West Midlands' increase in its share of
Great Britain's population from 9.3 per cent in 1961 to 9.5
per cent in 1971 was due not to net inmigration but to its
relatively high proportion (13.0 per cent) of national natural
increase. (This may in part be itself due to the characteristics
of the migrants moving into and out of the region; for, as we
shall see, migrants are far from being a cross-section of the
population as a whole.) Generally, however, the major shifts
in population result from migration.

REGIONAL PATTERNS

Fig.3.1 shows the way in which the populations of the regions
of Great Britain have grown since the first census was taken in
1801. Because of their varying size, a logarithmic scale has
been used for the populations. This means that similar slopes
correspond to similar rates of increase.

In the early nineteenth century, growth was concentrated in
North and North-West England and South Wales. These areas
contained the early industrial centres, with factories located
near sources of raw materials; and the conurbations grew up
near pits, coal-fields, and iron deposits. By 1851, the Census
Commissioners said that half the population of Great Britain
lived in 'towns'. Later in the nineteenth century, there was
marked growth in South-East England as well as the North. This
was also the period of rapid growth for London, as the 'railway
revolution' made possible the creation of a city based on
commuting. The early twentieth century saw a more even spread
of growth, though it was still rapid in the South East and in
the West Midlands. In the 1920s and 1930s, however, there was
much less growth; and such as there was tended to be concentrated in London and the Home Counties. Concern about the
uneven growth then led, though the 'Barlow Report' (the
Report of the Royal Commission on the Distribution of the Industrial Population, 1940), to increased post-war concern about
regional development.

The Barlow Commission's members included Professor L.P.
(later Sir Patrick) Abercrombie, whose subsequent reports provided
the foundation for much post-war thinking about regional policy.
In the 1950s and 1960s this tended to be summed up in the phrase
'stopping the drift to the South East'. The South East had,
indeed, increased its share of the national population from
28.4 per cent in 1901 to 31.0 per cent in 1951 (though this was
not as rapid a relative increase as that of the North West a
century earlier - from 8.4 per cent in 1801 to 12.1 per cent
in 1851), but this trend was halted during the 1960s. Between
1961 and 1971 there was a net outflow of people from South-East
England, and this appears to have increased in the early 1970s.

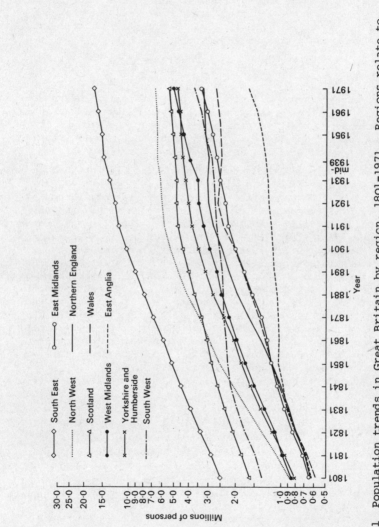

Fig. 3.1 Population trends in Great Britain by region, 1801–1971. Regions relate to areas as constituted in population enumerated at census except for 1939, where mid-year estimates were used. (Sources: Office of Population Censuses and Surveys and Central Statistical Office.)

(Office of Population Censuses and Surveys 1974).

Between 1961 and 1971 the real growth areas were in fact East Anglia and South-West England, followed by the East Midlands. Conversely, Scotland had an exceptionally large net outmigration, with northern England next, followed by North-West England and Yorkshire & Humberside. The distinction was thus not between South-East England and the rest; but between Scotland and the northern regions of England losing population on the one hand, and the diagonal belt from south-west England to East Anglia gaining on the other. South-East England, Wales, and the West Midlands were areas with practically balanced migration.†

One characteristic of the three most rapidly growing regions in the 1960s is their absence of conurbations. There is only one other region without a formally designated conurbation - Wales - and that includes the area round the South Wales coalfields which has many of the characteristics of a conurbation. Of the seven conurbations, only one - West Yorkshire - had an increase in its population between 1961 and 1971, and the increase there (1.4 per cent) was well below the national level (5.3 per cent) and only arose because births exceeded deaths by a margin greater than the excess of outmigrants over inmigrants.

IMMIGRATION FROM ABROAD

Immigrants from outside Great Britain tend to be concentrated in the conurbations, particularly Greater London and the West Midlands. Outside the conurbations, 4 per cent of the population enumerated in the 1966 census had been born outside Great Britain. For Greater London the percentage was 13 per cent, and for the West Midlands it was 7½ per cent. The West Yorkshire and South-east Lancashire conurbations each had about 5½ per cent, just about the national average; but Clydeside and Merseyside (each with 3½ per cent) and Tyneside (with 2 per cent) had far fewer. Table 3.1 shows an analysis of people enumerated in Great Britain by birthplace, and the data for Greater London and the West Midlands are summarized in Table 3.2.

---

† Overall, Wales had a rather lower share of the national population in 1971 than in 1961, and the West Midlands a rather higher one, because of relatively low and high natural increase respectively. This may partially reflect different migration structures.

TABLE 3.1

Persons enumerated in seven conurbations and remainder of Great Britain by birthplace

Area of enumeration	Birthplace						Total persons enumerated (1000s)†
	New Commonwealth	Old Commonwealth	Ireland‡	Foreign	Outside Great Britain§	Great Britain¶	
Conurbations							
Clydeside	8	4	39	14	65	1701	1766
Tyneside	5	1	4	6	18	815	832
West Yorkshire	35	2	25	28	91	1617	1708
South-east Lancashire	30	3	64	35	132	2272	2404
Merseyside	8	2	27	10	48	1289	1338
West Midlands	85	3	71	22	181	2193	2374
Sub-total	171	14	230	114	536	9886	10422
Greater London	368	36	288	281	998	6673	7671
Seven conurbations	539	50	517	395	1534	16559	18093
Remainder of Great Britain	306	72	392	478	1284	31161	32445
Great Britain	845	121	909	873	2818	47720	50538

Source: General Register Offices (1967).

† Due to independent rounding figures in the tables in this chapter may not always add to totals.

‡ Irish Republic and Northern Ireland.

§ Includes visitors born outside Great Britain (69 000 in total).

¶ Includes persons who did not state birthplace (205 000 in total).

TABLE 3.2

Greater London and West Midlands Conurbations, share of persons born in and outside Great Britain

Birthplace	Area of enumeration			Total (%)	Base (1000s)
	Greater London (%)	West Midlands (%)	Elsewhere in Great Britain (%)		
New Commonwealth	44	10	46	100	845
Old Commonwealth	29	2	68	100	121
Ireland	32	8	61	100	909
Foreign countries	32	3	65	100	873
Outside Great Britain	35	6	58	100	2818
Great Britain	14	5	81	100	47 720
Total enumerated in Great Britain	15	5	80	100	50 538

Source: As Table 3.1

See Table 3.1 footnotes.

MIGRANTS' CHARACTERISTICS

Mention has already been made of the fact that migrants are
not a cross-section of the population as a whole. The most
significant aspect of this is probably the fact that, compared
with the whole population, they generally have a distinct age
structure, with a heavy concentration in the late teens and early
twenties. There are nevertheless differences between various
migrant streams - that is, groups of migrants cross-classified
by their origins and destinations. To illustrate this we may
consider movements into and out of Greater London in 1965-6
(that is, the year preceding the last census for which the data
are available).

Fig.3.2 shows the age-sex-marital status structure of four
groups of people: those living in Great Britain outside Greater
London in April 1966, those who had moved from that area to
Greater London in the preceding 12 months, those who had left
Greater London for the rest of Great Britain in that period, and
those living in Greater London in 1966. It is immediately
clear that both in- and out-migrants to and from Greater London
had a higher proportion of people between 15 and 30 than the
population which they left. The concentration is, however,
more marked in the case of inmigrants than that of outmigrants;
and the former tend to be rather younger and to include relatively more people who were not married. There seems a tendency for
London to attract young, single adults particularly, and for
those who leave the metropolis to be somewhat older, married
people. The higher proportion of children under 5 in the outflow further suggest that it includes a high proportion of
married couples with children.

A closer examination of Fig.3.2 shows that the outmigrants
include more people over retirement age than the inmigrants.
This presumably corresponds to a tendency for people to move
home at retirement, and this can be seen more clearly in Fig.3.3
which shows a more detailed sex-age analysis of two particular
migrant streams: migrants from Great Britain outside the South-
East region to Greater London, and migrants from Greater London
to the outer South-East subregion. This last includes movements
to the south coast retirement areas, and there is a distinct
second peak of people in their sixties.

Migrants tend to differ from the population averages in
characteristics other than age, sex, and marital status. They
tend to be better educated, and to be in the higher socio-
economic groups. Non-manual workers move much more than manual
workers. The data from the 1966 census given in Table 3.3 show
that, though more men in most socio-economic groups left
London in 1965-6 than entered it, the numbers were almost equal
in some groups but not in others. Significantly more employers
and managers, foremen and skilled manual workers, intermediate

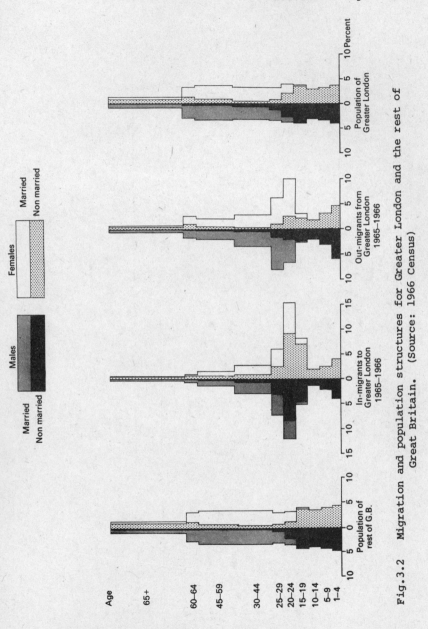

Fig.3.2   Migration and population structures for Greater London and the rest of
Great Britain.   (Source: 1966 Census)

TABLE 3.3

Socio-economic groups of economically active male migrants to and from London 1965-6

Socio-economic groups	Inflow to Greater London from rest of Great Britain		Outflow from Greater London to rest of Great Britain	
	Number (1000s)	Percentage of in-migrants	Number (1000s)	Percentage of out-migrants
Professional	6.8	14.9	9.2	11.8
Employers and managers	6.7	14.6	13.0	16.7
Foremen and skilled manual workers ‡	8.6	18.7	21.3	27.4
Intermediate and junior non-manual workers	14.6	31.9	20.6	26.5
Semi-skilled manual and service workers	5.2	11.4	9.1	11.6
Unskilled manual workers	2.5	5.4	3.0	3.9
Armed forces and unclassified	1.5	3.2	1.6	2.1
Total	45.8	100.0	77.8	100.0

Source: General Register Office (1968)

† Migrants within Great Britain only.

‡ Including non-professional self-employed males.

and junior non-manual workers, and semi-skilled workers left
London than entered it. However, this does not necessarily,
imply that migration was causing London to lose such people.

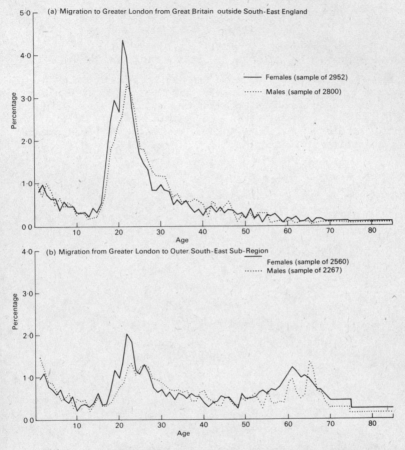

Fig. 3.3   Age comparison of two migrant structures
(Source: 1966 Census)

For one thing, the classification is of people after they moved,
and in some cases people will have changed their socio-economic
group on a promotion which also resulted in their move. Furthermore, London gains people in higher socio-economic groups by
internal promotion within the city and from new entries to the
labour force from higher education.

There is an analogy here with marital status. London gains
single people through migration and married ones move out. If

that were the only source of change, all Londoners would be single by now! In fact of course, people living in London – some of whom have previously entered as single inmigrants – are being married all the time and replenishing the married population of the capital.

EFFECTS OF MIGRATION ON GREATER LONDON'S POPULATION

Fig.3.4 shows the main trends in Greater London's population as revealed by the national censuses from 1901 to 1971. In very rough terms, Inner London's population grew until about 1901, then it was stable for 30 years, but it has been falling since 1931. The population of Outer London, on the other hand, started growing significantly after about 1861, grew rapidly until 1939,

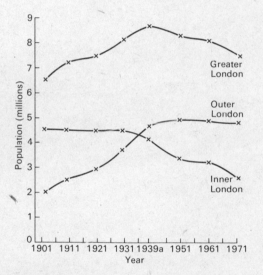

Fig.3.4   Population trends in Greater London, 1901-71
(Source: Registrar General)

but has fallen slightly since 1951. Such rapid changes result primarily from migration. It is the fact that more people have moved out of London than into it since the Second World War that has reduced the number of residents by over 1.3 million from the 1939 peak of 8.6 million. As the data in Table 3.4 show, the population fell by 770 000 between 1951 and 1971 because the 780 000 excess of births over deaths was more than offset by a 1 550 000 excess of outmigrants over inmigrants. The table also shows how migration leads to a redistribution of population

TABLE 3.4

Components of population changes in Greater London, Inner and Outer boroughs

Area	1951-61 (1000s of persons)	1961-71 (1000s of persons)
Inner London Education Area†		
Excess of births over deaths	+150	+200
Excess of outmigration over inmigration	-320	-630
Overall change	-170	-430
Outer London boroughs		
Excess of births over deaths	+180	+250
Excess of outmigration over inmigration	-240	-360
Overall change	-60	-110
Greater London		
Excess of births over deaths	+330	+450
Excess of outmigration over inmigration	-560	-990
Overall change	-230	-540

Source: Registrar Genral Publications (1951-71)

† The Cities of London and Westminster and the London Boroughs of Camden, Greenwich, Hackney, Hammersmith, Islington, Kensington & Chelsea, Lambeth, Lewisham, Southwark, Tower Hamlets, and Wandsworth. (The area of the former London County Council, less that part of the metropolitan borough of Woolwich north of the Thames.)

within the urban area. The excess of births over deaths was
only 80 000 less in Inner than in Outer London, but the excess
of outmigration over inmigration was 350 000 greater in Inner
London.

The differential effect of migration has meant that, though
London's total population in 1971 was much the same as that in
1921, there has been a significant change in the distribution of
that total. Inner London contained 61 per cent of the population
in 1921, but only 37 per cent half a century later. Most of this
change took place in the 30 years between 1921 and 1951, when
Inner London's share fell from 61 per cent to 41 per cent, but
substantial changes are still occurring at the local level. Of
the 655 wards† in Greater London, 77 (12 per cent) had 1971
populations below 80 per cent of their 1961 figures - and all but
14 of these were in Inner London. This makes it clear that, even
within an urban area, migration can have substantially different
effects from place to place.

Fig.3.5 relates the net outmigration experienced by the 32
London boroughs in 1961-71 to their population density in persons
per hectare. For a density over 100 persons per hectare there
does seem to be a positive relationship between net outmigration
and density. Three exceptional cases appear: Islington, where
net outmigration was greater than might have been expected on the
basis of population density alone, and Kensington & Chelsea and
Westminster, where it was less. The last two boroughs contain
the main part of London's bed-sitter area, as well as many hotels
and institutions, and these atypical population characteristics
may account for their position.

It should perhaps be emphasized that the fall in London's
population has occurred despite an increase in the number of
dwellings. Between 1961 and 1971, for example, the numbers of
dwellings in Greater London increased by nearly 200 000, nearly
8 per cent, yet the population living in them‡ fell by over 500
thousand, about 6½ per cent (Garton et al. 1974). However,
though the total population fell, the number of separate private
households was almost the same in 1971 as 1961 (Armstrong et al.
1973). This was associated with a fall in average household size,
reflecting both a substantial increase in the number of one-
person households and a reduction in the number of larger households (particularly those with three or four people in them).

---

† For this purpose, the City of London is treated as if it were
one ward.

‡That is, excluding people in hotels, hospitals, old people's
homes, etc. There were 280 000 people enumerated in non-private
establishments in Greater London in 1961, and 240 000
in 1971.

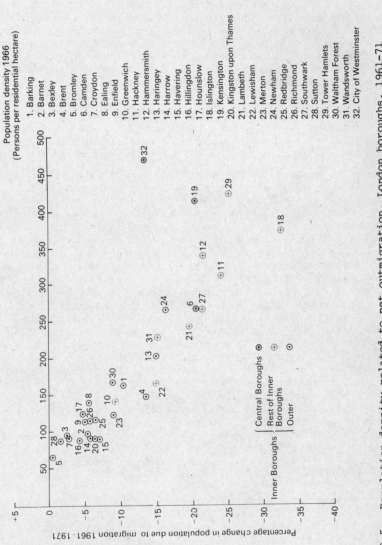

Fig.3.5   Population density related to net outmigration, London boroughs, 1961-71
(Source: Registrar General's annual estimates and GLC Research Report No.8).

With the same number of housholds, and a larger dwelling stock, there were both a reduction in the number of households sharing accommodation and an increase in the number of vacant dwellings. The reduction in sharing may be said to have taken up about 70 per cent of the increased dwelling stock, and the increased number of vacant dwellings the other 30 per cent - but this is an oversimplification of a complicated process as people move from place to place, forming and reforming households. The important consideration in this context is that it is through migration that people are able to improve their housing standards, and the desire for such improvement must be seen as one major factor in causing the reduced level of Greater London's population.

Migration has important effects on the type of people living in Greater London as well as on their numbers and distribution. Three population characteristics will be considered to illustrate this: age, birthplace, and socio-economic group distributions.

The most dramatic effects are probably on age distributions. The atypical age of migrants was illustrated above in Fig. 3.2 To highlight some of their effects on London's population one may take a borough which has a particularly large number of migrants: the Royal Borough of Kensington & Chelsea. This had a population of about 188 000 at the time of the 1971 Census: 30 000 fewer than in 1961. As births in the borough had exceeded deaths by 12 000 outmigration must have exceeded inmigration by about 42 000 in the 10 years from 1961 to 1971, an average of over 4 000 a year. This is a *net* difference. Of the 188 000 people enumerated in the borough in April 1971, about 30 000 had lived outside it in April 1970. Therefore, we can very roughly estimate that about 34 000 people left the borough in the year before the census. (These numbers compare with 2 500 births and 2 000 deaths in the same period.) The migrants would not have typical age patterns. Data on outmigrants as such are not available, but we do know that 52 per cent of the inmigrants were aged 15-24, compared with 24 per cent of the borough's population overall. [†] This latter percentage, however, itself reflects the effects of the inmigration of young adults in earlier years. (The corresponding Greater London percentage was 15 per cent.) We can get nearer to seeing the effects of migration by comparing the age distribution of the borough's population with what might be expected on the basis of births in earlier years.[‡] Thus the 7 310 people aged 23 in Kensington &

[†]Putting this another way, 34 per cent of the people aged 15-24 in the borough in April 1971 had lived outside it in April 1970. (Another 10 per cent had moved house within the borough, so over-all 44 per cent had different addresses in 1970 and 1971.)

[‡]This is not an exact comparison, as the births include those to inmigrants in earlier years, and exclude those to parents who had left the borough.

Chelsea in 1971 can be compared with the 3 815 children born
in the area in 1948. The results of such a comparison are
shown in Fig.3.6 for people aged up to 50, after which significant differences arise from deaths as well as migration. Clearly,
the age pattern of Kensington & Chelsea's population is affected
far more by migration than by past variations in births, substantial though these are.

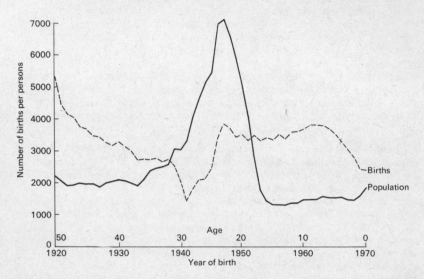

Fig. 3.6 Population of Kensington & Chelsea aged 0-50 in 1971,
by single years of age, and numbers of live births in Kensington
& Chelsea, 1970-1. (Source: 1971 Census).

Kensington & Chelsea is an extreme case, and it needs to be
emphasized that, just as that borough has relatively many more
migrants than the country as a whole, there are other parts of
Greater London - particularly the boroughs to the east of the
City of London - with populations who moved less than the national
average. Thus the London Borough of Barking, with April 1971
population of 161 000, had only 6 000 inmigrants in the preceding
year (and perhaps 8 000 or so outmigrants), so 96 per cent of
its population had lived within the same borough for at least
a year, compared with 84 per cent of Kensington & Chelsea's
population. Overall, indeed, the 1966 Census showed that the
number of Londoners who had moved house in the previous twelve
months was little more than the national average.

Another way of classifying London's population is according
to where they were born. The 1966 Census showed that 68 per

cent of people enumerated in Greater London were born there, and
another 19 per cent were born in the rest of Great Britain.
The remainder were born in Ireland (4 per cent), the Commonwealth
(5 per cent), and other countries (4 per cent).

The 1971 census only asked about people's country of birth, but
this does enable one to see how one aspect of London's population
changed over the preceding decade. This is summarized in Table
3.5, which shows that not all the birthplace subgroups changed
in the same way. Greater London had a net reduction in the number
of its inhabitants born in the United Kingdom of about 850 000
(12 per cent), but an increase in the number born outside the
United Kingdom of some 265 000 (31 per cent). This latter was
mainly due to the increase in the number of people born in the
'New Commonwealth'. These changes include the effects of births
and deaths, but resulted primarily from migration. Most of the
increase in the number of Londoners born in the New Commonwealth
would, because of legislative changes, have occurred in the first
part of the intercensal decade.

Immigrants from abroad do not settle uniformly over Greater
London. There are, for example, relatively high proportions of
people born in the Irish Republic in Brent and Hammersmith;
people born in the Old Commonwealth are found particularly in
Kensington & Chelsea; and those born in continental European
countries in Kensington & Chelsea, Westminster, and Camden. As
far as the 'New Commonwealth' is concerned, those born in Africa
are found particularly in Brent, Islington, and Lambeth; those
born in India in Ealing, Hounslow, and Brent; those born in
Pakistan in Tower Hamlets and Waltham Forest; and those from
Cyprus and Malta in Haringey and Islington (Field *et al.* 1974).

The effects of migration on London's age and birthplace
characteristics are not independent, of course, and migrants
from abroad generally tend to be concentrated in their early
twenties like other inmigrants. This meant that, though only
5.8 per cent of female Londoners in 1971 had been born in the
New Commonwealth, 17.1 per cent of children born in London in
that year had mothers born in the New Commonwealth. (This
percentage was the same in 1971 as 1970, and increased mar-
ginally to 17.6 per cent in 1972 (Office of Population Censuses
and Surveys 1973).) Over London, the percentage ranged from
2 per cent in Havering to 36 per cent in Haringey in 1972,
reflecting the varying composition of London's population.

A third facet of the characteristics of migrants, socio-
economic group, has had rather less effect upon the nature of
Greater London's population during recent years than either
age or birthplace. Although the 1971 count is of enumerated,
rather than resident, population, columns (A), (C), and (E) in
Table 3.6 indicate reasonably consistent trends in the changing

TABLE 3.5

Persons enumerated in Greater London by birthplace, 1961 and 1971 (units are 1000s of persons)

	1961	1971	Change	Percentage change
Enumerated population	7997	7452	-545	(-7)
People not stating their birthplace	31	69	+ 38	(+123)
People stating their birthplace	7966	7383	-583	(- 7)
People born in United Kingdom	7119	6270	-849	(-12)
People born outside United Kingdom	847	1113	+266	(-31)
Visitors born outside United Kingdom	37	44	+ 7	(+19)
Residents born outside United Kingdom	810	1069	+259	(+32)
Irish Republic	254	241	- 13	(- 5)
Canada, Australia, New Zealand	33	41	+ 8	(+24)
'New Commonwealth'	242	476	+234	(+97)
Other countries and at sea	281	311	+ 30	(+11)

Source: Census data: see Field *et al.* (1974, p.8).

TABLE 3.6

Social-economic groups of economically active males, 1961, 1966, and 1971, and net migrants 1965-6 (10 per cent samples)

Socio-economic groups	1961 Economically active resident males in Greater London Number Percentage	Migration: net flow between Greater London and rest of Great Britain 1965-6	1966 Economically active resident males in Greater London Number Percentage	Migration: net changes as percentage of 1966 resident population (B as percentage of C)	1971 Economically active survive males enumerated in Greater London Number Percentage
	(A)	(B)	(C)	(D)	(E)
1. Employers and managers in central and local government, industry, commerce, etc. (small establishments	11 666 (4.4)	-224	11 224 (4.5)	-2.0	9380 (4.1)
2. Employers and managers in industry commerce, etc.(small establishments)	18 931 (7.2)	-402	18 467 (7.5)	-2.2	22 509 (9.8)
3. Professional workers - self-employed	2287 (0.9)	- 17[1]	1970 (0.8)	-	2492 (1.1)
4. Professional workers - employees	10 056 (3.8)	-216	11 968 (4.8)	-1.8	11 454 (5.0)

5. Intermediate non-manual workers	12 547 (4.8)	-198	13 263 (5.4)	-1.5	14 943 (6.5)
6. Junior non-manual workers	48 015 (18.2)	-401	44 724 (18.1)	-0.9	39 034 (16.9)
7. Personal service workers	3990 (1.5)	+ 29[1]	4207 (1.7)	-	4097 (1.8)
8. Foreman and supervisors - manual	8295 (3.1)	-133	8215 (3.3)	-1.6	6858 (3.0)
9. Skilled manual workers	74 348 (28.2)	-952	67 878 (27.5)	-1.4	56 173 (24.4)
10. Semi-skilled manual workers	34 341 (13.0)	-382	31 299 (12.7)	-1.2	26 431 (11.5)
11. Unskilled manual workers	22 128 (8.4)	- 56	19 664 (8.0)	-0.3	16 527 (7.2)
12. Own account workers (other than professional)	9778 (3.7)	-179	10 306 (4.2)	-1.7	12 365 (5.4)
13. Farmers - employers and managers	126)	- 9)	92)	)	92)
14. Farmers - own account	85) 336 (0.2)	- 10) -51	70) 482 (0.2)	) -10.6	60) 430 (0.2)
15. Agricultural workers	425)	- 32)	320)	)	278)
16. Members of armed forces	2004 (0.8)	- 23[1]	1297 (0.5)	-	1358 (0.6)
17. Inadequately described	4954 (1.9)	+ 9[1]	1866 (0.8)	-	6448 (2.8)
Total	263 979 (100.0)	-3196	246 830 (100.0)	-1.3	230 499 (100.0)

(1) Smaller than the simple standard error.   (2) There have been no adjustments for under-enumeration

Sources: General Register Office (1968), 1961 Census Occupation Tables, 1966 Census, Economic Activity Tables, and 1971 Census Small Area Statistics.

social composition of male workers living in London between
1961 and 1971. Managers of small establishments, professional
employees, intermediate non-manual workers, and own-account
workers all increased proportionately during both halves of
the decade. On the other hand, junior white-collar workers
and manual workers of varying degrees of skill decreased as a
proportion of Greater London's economically active† male population. The remaining groups, such as managers of large
establishments and foremen, showed no clear trends. The general
change through the decade was one of increases in the number of
white-collar workers, but decreases in the number of manual
workers, within an overall reduction in the economically active
male population from 2.6 to 2.3 millions. This pattern held
for both Inner and Outer London.

Can these changes be seen as the net result of selective
migration?   Unfortunately, no data are yet available on the
socio-economic group of in- and outmigrants in the one and five
years preceding the 1971 Census. Turning to the 1966 Sample
Census, both the 1965-6 and 1961-6 flows are available, but
the data for the five-year period have to be treated with
caution (Gray and Gee 1972).

Falling as they do in the middle of the decade, flows for
the year up to April 1966 may be taken to provide a pointer to
the impact of migration upon Greater London's social composition
between 1961 and 1971. The flows between Greater London and
the rest of Great Britain were outlined in Table 3.3, and the
propensity of white-collar workers to move more frequently
and further than those in manual occupations is well established.
Looking at the net result of these flows, it can be seen from
Table 3.6 that, in the case of the major groups resident in
1966 - those numbering more than 100 000 -, the largest proportionate decreases (column D) resulting from migration as such
were of white-collar or own-account workers. The net decreases
of manual workers other than foremen were 1.5 per cent or less
with the unskilled showing the smallest proportionate outflows.
An unpublished analysis of migration within Greater London
during the same period (1965-6) confirms that not only did white-
collar workers move more than manual workers, but they moved
outwards, both within and beyond Greater London, to a greater
extent. Similarly, skilled manual workers showed a greater
propensity to migrate than did the unskilled. It is worth noting
at this point that Gould and Lacy (1973) have shown that the
majority of movers out of the rest of the South-East region in
the previous year already no longer worked in London by April
1966.

---

†That is, in work or looking for a job on census day.

These findings of a larger net outmigration of white-collar groups in the year before the 1966 census contrast with the observed increase during the whole decade. It is true that a single year's data can only be taken as a pointer; but migration data for the period 1961-6, although less reliable, again suggest larger net outflows of white-collar workers from both Inner and Outer London. The explanation must lie in the joint effects of moves to and from Great Britain and economic mobility within Greater London - people leaving school, getting promoted, and retiring. As Waugh (1969) points out, 'it is wrong to regard selective internal migration as the greatest factor in socio-economic change. A healthy regional economy provides opportunities for occupational mobility among the resident population irrespective of inter-regional migration.' Social mobility in Greater London apparently offsets the effects of physical moves suggested by 1965-6 migration data.

Migration has clearly been of importance in determining the numbers, spatial distribution, age, birthplace, and social group of Londoners, throughout the city's history, but it is essential to examine the data closely. In some cases, such as the outflows of people from the Inner London boroughs during the last three decades, or the unusual age structure of the population in Kensington & Chelsea, the impact of migration has been considerable. It would, however, be quite erroneous to point to migration data alone and assume that Greater London is gradually losing all its white-collar workers or married couples: migration represents one, albeit an important one, of the dynamics of the city.

REFERENCES

ARMSTRONG, W. *et al.*(1973). *1971 Census county report for Greater London: selected topics and historical comparison - I* Intelligence Unit Research Memorandum 415. GLC. London.

FIELD, A.M. *et al.* (1974). *1971 census data on London's overseas-born population and their children,* Intelligence Unit Research Memorandum 425. GLC. London.

GARTON, B. *et al.*(1974) *1971 census county report for Greater London: selected topics and historical comparison - II,* Intelligence Unit Research Memorandum 421. GLC. London.

General Register Offices, London and Edinburgh (1967). *Sample census 1966, Great Britain, summary tables.* HMSO. London.

General Register Office (1968). *Sample census 1966, England & Wales, migration. Regional report south eastern region* HMSO. London.

GOULD, T. and LACY, S.   (1973). *A note on migration and commuting in the south east region, 1965-66,* Greater London Intelligence Quarterly No.25 GLC. London.

GRAY, P. and GEE, F.A. (1972). *A quality check on the 1966 ten per cent sample census of England and Wales,* HMSO for OPCS Social Survey Division. London.

Office of Population Census and Surveys (1973), *The Registrar General's quarterly return for England and Wales,* No.498, Appendix D. HMSO. London.

Office of Population Censuses and Surveys (1974). *The Registrar General's quarterly return for England and Wales,* No.500, Appendix J. HMSO. London.

Royal Commission of the Distribution of the Industrial Population (1940). Chairman: Sir Montague Barlow): *Report* (Cmd. 6153) HMSO. London.

Waugh, M. (1969). *The changing distribution of professional and managerial manpower in England and Wales between 1961 and 1966.*   Reg.Stud. 3, 157-69.

4 Human settlements and the atmospheric environment

Tony J. Chandler

Urbanization is a global phenomenon: already 30 per cent of the world's population live in towns of 5 000 or more persons and 18 per cent in cities of more than 100 000. What is more, the proportions are increasing fast. Almost everywhere in the developed and developing world, brick, stone, concrete, and tar macadam are replacing field, forest, and farm, as new towns are established, existing towns grow into sprawling cities, and cities merge into vast conurbations. In almost every country, towns are expanding to consume more and more land, so that in many countries, considerable proportions of their total land area are built upon; in England and Wales, for instance, about 12 per cent of the surface is covered by buildings, and it is estimated that by the year 2 000, this proportion will have increased to nearly 16 per cent (Best 1968).

It is clear that the urban environment provides the life framework for a large and growing proportion of the world's population, and it is therefore important to remember that, when buildings are congregated in villages, towns, and conurbations, the physical and chemical properties of the air between and above, as well as within, the buildings are radically changed. Urban dwellers therefore spend much of their lives in a quite distinctive type of man-modified climate, some of the more undesirable attributes of which are best avoided by purposeful planning, whilst others can be used to advantage. The study of these modifications of climates by towns is clearly of more than academic interest, being of practical importance in human bioclimatology and the proper design of buildings and cities.

In built-up areas, the effects of the surface's complex geometry, the particular thermal and hydrological properties of the urban fabric, the heat from metabolism, the various combustion processes taking place in the city, and the chemical composition of the air combine to create a climate which is quite distinct from that of extra-urban areas. All the meteorological elements are changed. Strong winds are decelerated and light winds are often accelerated as they move into towns; air turbulence is increased; relative humidities are reduced though absolute humidities are little changed and may well be higher inside towns during the night; the chemical composition of the air is changed; receipts and losses of radiation are both reduced; temperatures are substantially raised; fogs are made thicker, more frequent and more persistent; and rainfall is sometimes increased. The most important of these changes will now be considered in more detail.

AIR FLOW IN URBAN AREAS

The flow of air over an urban area is affected by a rougher surface than in rural areas and by the frequently higher temperatures of the city fabric. The buildings exert a powerful frictional drag on air flowing over and around them, and winds in cities are more turbulent than outside. Because of this, the characteristic mean horizontal wind profile in urban areas is changed, with a more gentle gradient through a deeper boundary layer than above rural and sea areas (Fig.4.1). Height for height, mean horizontal wind speeds in cities are less than above rural areas but the precise reduction in speed is very dependent upon the prevailing meteorological and topographical conditions.

It is, in fact, very difficult to obtain representative measurements of wind in urban areas because of the spatial and temporal complexity of the airflow above a very diverse surface. In cities, wind speed and direction change rapidly over very short distances and intervals of time. Most observations of wind are made above the roofs of tall buildings or in parks and other open spaces, these sites avoid some of the very small-scale fluctuations of speed and direction which always occur in streets and courtyards, but they are still strongly influenced by almost unique local circumstances of the urban environment.

Wind speed

Studies in many cities have shown that average wind speeds are lower in the built-up areas than over rural areas (Chandler 1965; Graham 1968; Landsberg 1956; Munn 1970) but Chandler (1965) and Bornstein (1969, 1973) have analysed data for London and New York respectively to show that the difference in strength between town and country is a function of the regional near-surface wind speed and the wind profile. When winds are light, speeds are greater in the built-up area than outside, whereas the reverse relationship exists when winds are strong. In a comparison between winds speeds in central London and contemporaneous measurements at London Airport, on the western fringe of the city, Chandler showed that when the wind speed at London Airport was less than 3-5 ms^{-1}, winds accelerate towards the centre of the city. He also demonstrated that, on average, nighttime wind speeds in central London were 14 per cent stronger than at London Airport whilst daytime winds were 24 per cent weaker.

Chandler attributes these contrasts in the urban influence to differences in the effect of increased surface roughness upon airflows having dissimilar velocity profiles. When surface winds are relatively calm, as commonly happens by night, there are frequent inversions above country areas associated with weak turbulence and a sharp wind gradient in the boundary layer. In

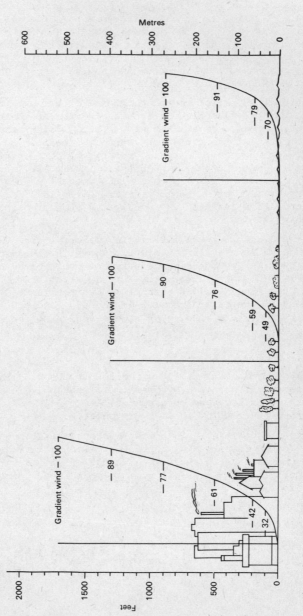

Fig. 4.1   Profiles of mean wind velocity over level terrains of differing roughness.
(After Davenport 1965)

the city, the increased roughness and higher near-surface temperatures cause stronger turbulence and a more even velocity profile
through a deeper boundary layer. Surface winds are therefore
reduced in rural areas, but in urban areas there is a downward
transport of momentum to increase near-surface speeds. With
stronger regional winds there is active turbulence even in rural
areas and the increased overturning in the city with a net
downward transport of momentum is insufficient to compensate for
the enhanced frictional drag.

Such meteorological considerations are obviously relevant to the
day-to-day and seasonal differences in wind speed between cities
and rural areas. In autumn, winter, and spring, for instance,
when regional winds tend to be strong, speeds in central London
are reduced by about 8, 6, and 8 per cent respectively, whilst
in summer, with lighter winds, there is little or no difference
in mean urban and rural speeds. The overall annual reduction in
wind speed in central London for all winds is 6 per cent, but
for winds of more than 1.5 ms $^{-1}$, the reduction is 13 per cent
(Chandler 1965).

In the light of the above, it is not surprising that there are
fewer calms in the air immediately above the buildings of a city
than above the surrounding country, although between the buildings
calms might be more frequent. Equally, however, there will be
times when winds will be channelled and accelerated along streets
oriented in the same direction as the wind and eddies will form
across the streets running at rights-angles to the wind.

Wind direction

As already indicated, the direction of the wind in cities is
very closely controlled by the form of the buildings and the
pattern of streets and open spaces, as well as, of course, by the
topography upon which the city is built.

Above the buildings of a city, winds blow at an appreciable
angle to the isobars because of the powerful surface friction.
Measurements of this angle in a number of cities vary from 15°
at times of strong instability to more than 40° during temperature
inversions.

Turbulence over cities

In urban areas, wind speeds and directions vary more rapidly
in space and time than in the country, but the details are very
particular to the geometrical form of individual cities (Graham
1968).

Local airflows

Studies in a number of cities (Fosberg *et al.* 1973; Pooler 1963; Georgii 1968; Chandler 1961) have shown that on calm, clear nights, when a strong 'heat-island' develops over a city, there is a surface inflow towards the centre(s) of warm air. These inblowing, cool winds are linked to rising air over the city and a return flow from city to country at a higher level, though there have been few observations of this. The centripetal winds near the surface are very light, normally less than 4 ms^{-1} and for this reason they are quickly decelerated by surface friction in the suburban areas of many large cities. Here they occur as pulsating flows across the margins of the warm air or 'heat-island' above the city.

Airflow around buildings

Air motions above and between buildings, but more particularly those around modern high-rise buildings, constitute a very important and distinctive element of the urban climate, frequently giving rise to quite serious environmental problems. But more than this, they are a vital factor controlling the distribution of other elements, particularly air pollution.

The patterns of airflow induced by tall slab and tower blocks (Fig.4.2) have sometimes created almost intolerable environmental conditions for pedestrians in nearby streets and shopping precincts. More applied research and awareness by architects and planners are needed to avoid these circumstances. Similarly, airflow patterns immediately above the city are very relevant to the structural and service design of modern high-rise buildings. On a broader scale, they are important in the planning of the whole towns - including, for instance, the achievement of adequate but not excessive ventilation of city streets - and in deciding the most suitable locations for certain industries, power stations, and other major sources of air pollution.

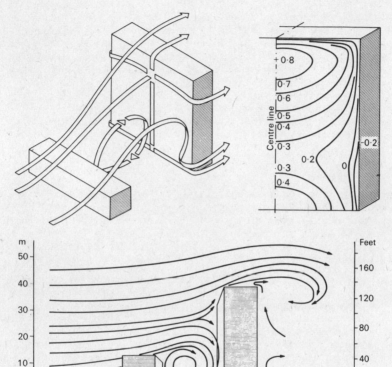

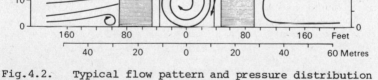

Fig.4.2.   Typical flow pattern and pressure distribution
on the windward face of a slab block with a low building to
windward.   Pressures are given in terms of a pressure
coefficient $c = p/p_0$ where p is the local pressure and p_0
is the velocity pressure of the wind (After Wise 1971).

ATMOSPHERIC POLLUTION

   Man has always treated the atmosphere as an open sewer,
into which he wantonly discharged the hundreds of varieties
of waste products, gaseous liquid, and solids which are released from house and factory chimneys and from cars, lorries,

trains and ships. Nevertheless, man, much less urbanized
man, is not solely responsible for the contamination of his
atmospheric environment. In the sparsely settled parts of the
globe, most of the air pollutants are the products of natural
processes, being comprised mainly of pollen, mineral dust, and
the smoke from forest and bush fires. Even so the concentration
of Aitken nuclei (particles having a radius of less than 0.2 µm)
in cities is, on average, 16 times greater than over inland rural
areas and 160 times greater than over the oceans (Landsberg 1962).

The problem of polluted urban atmospheres has been recognized
for a long time. Romans complained about the soot that soiled
their togas and a fourteenth-century English artificer was hanged
for violating a Royal Proclamation against the burning of coal in
London. But in spite of the long-suspected danger to health
(Lawther 1973), and the obvious destruction of urban fabric and
amenity, the skies above many of the world's cities have been
darkened by a shroud of smoke mixed with a variety of other
chemicals, more particularly carbon dioxide and sulphur dioxide.

More recently, the widespread conversion from coal to oil,
electricity, and gas as sources of industrial and domestic power
has greatly reduced the emissions of smoke. In England and
elsewhere this economic process has been acclerated by clean-air
legislation and because serried ranks of terrace houses with
their forest of chimneys have often been replaced by centralized
space-heating systems burning smokeless fuels. In many cities,
emissions of smoke have fallen dramatically in recent years
(Reay 1973), often helped by more turbulent atmospheric conditions.
In London, for instance, they are already only a fifth of what
they were 10 years ago, and average ground-level concentrations
of smoke have fallen by a similar amount. Because local concentrations of smoke are derived mainly from nearby sources (Marsh
and Forster 1967; Williams 1960) the pattern of smoke in cities
is often extremely complicated. Low level sources such as house
chimneys are the most serious pollutants of the urban environment,
the fumes from tall industrial and power-station chimneys
generally not reaching the ground until the concentration of
pollutants has been substantially diluted. Because domestic
sources are so dominant in the make-up of ground-level concentrations of smoke in mid and high-latitude towns, amounts are
generally much higher in winter than summer, and during the day
there are often two peaks in the early morning and evening when
fires are lit or recharged. Much will, of course, depend upon
the prevailing meteorological conditions; high ground-level
concentrations being associated with light winds and a stable
atmosphere up to the effective height of emission (Stern 1968;
Singer and Smith 1970). Because of the close relationship
between concentrations and local emissions, the amount of lateral
drift across cities and from city to country is, near the
ground, surprisingly small (Chandler 1965), although smoke and

sulphur dioxide can often be traced for hundreds of kilometres and that at a higher level, perhaps trapped and concentrated under a temperature inversion, may be brought down to the ground again by the increased turbulence above a city lying downwind of the source (Marsh and Forster 1967; Parry 1970). Sulphur dioxide, an invisible pollutant from the burning of fossil fuels, is emitted into the atmosphere in enormous quantities, much of it from industry and power stations. In England and Wales, for instance, about 85 per cent of the emission of sulphur dioxide is from these sources; but three-quarters of the average ground-level concentration, on the other hand, is of domestic origin. Ground-level concentrations of pollution are inversely proportional to the square of the effective height of emission so that tall chimneys, and a hot plume with a high efflux velocity all help to reduce ground-level concentrations of smoke. The pollution may not reach the ground locally at all, although in cities there is always the danger of downwash by the eddies which commonly form around buildings (Singer and Smith 1970).

In recent years what might be called the traditional pollutants of smoke and sulphur dioxide from the burning of coal and heavy oil have been joined in almost all cities by a great variety of pollutants from the carburettors and exhausts of the vehicles which increasingly congest the streets of most modern cities. These include various oxides of nitrogen, polycyclic hydro-carbons (including 3:4 benzpyrene), carbon monoxide, and inorganic lead bromides and chlorides. In cities such as Los Angeles and Mexico City, having strong radiation receipts, there are complex photochemical reactions upon the enormous quantities of these gases released into the air and one of the products is ozone which, contrary to popular opinion, is toxic not tonic. In cities such as London, having stronger winds and street ventil-ation and weaker sunshine, such photochemical reactions are less important, but even here, in the bottom of deep street chasms congested by slow-moving traffic, concentrations of carbon mon-oxide can reach 200 p.p.m. for short periods (Reed 1966). The diesel engine produces virtually no carbon monoxide, although when overloaded or badly maintained it does generate clouds of malodorous black smoke.

Even in cities, atmospheric pollutants are not confined to the unburnt products of various fossil fuels: oil refineries, cement and asbestos manufacturers, and brickworks are among those where the most serious pollutants come from the materials of manufacture rather than the fuels of combustion. The chemistry of their emissions is frequently complex, and although many gases are present in concentrations of only a few parts per million, they sometimes give rise to pungent smells and medically suspect air. The fluorine in some brickwork plumes can lead to the contamination of grass and fluorosis in cattle.

Lord Richie Calder has described pollution as a crime compounded of ignorance and avarice, and if we are to reduce air pollution so that healthy and attractive atmospheric environments can exist in towns, action will be needed on a number of fronts: technical, planning, legislative, and social.

Substantial technical progress towards cleaner air has already been made by reducing the pollution content of fuels, by more efficient combustion processes and by the removal of certain pollutants from plumes and exhausts.   Steady legislative progress towards cleaner air is also being made in many countries.   The wise location of industry with respect to the drift of pollutants, more particularly at times of light winds and inversions of temperative in the boundary layer, can also bring improvements in the residential areas of towns.

VISIBILITY

Because of the high aerosol concentrations in urban area, visibilities are lower (Pritchard and Chopra 1973), and because of the motes, fog droplets form more readily and evaporate more slowly than in rural areas.   The densest fogs are often found in the suburbs rather than in city centres, which are warmer and have lower absolute humidities.   Central London, for instance, had, before the Clean Air Act of 1956, almost twice as many hours of fogs (visibilities of less than 1000 m) per year as rural areas around the city but only about the same numer of hours of dense fog (visibilities of less than 40 m).   The London suburbs, on the other hand, had only between 1.14 and 1.28 times as many hours of fog as the rural areas beyond the city but up to 4 times as many dense fogs (Chandler 1965).

The warmer air and gentler winds of city centres also delay the formation of evening fogs and their dispersal the following morning, so that in the evening the fog lies like an annulus around a gradually disappearing clear centre, and in the morning the fog clears in the stronger winds and more rapidly rising temperatures of rural and suburban areas to leave fog only in the centre of the city.

Since the Clean Air Acts (1956 and 1968) in England, there has been a dramatic improvement in visibilities in London and other cities, where the emission of smoke has been reduced (Brazell 1964;   Freeman 1968;   Atkins 1968) though some of the improvement might be because of stronger winds (Schmidt and Velds 1969).

RADIATION AND SUNSHINE

Because of the blanket of pollution which shrouds many areas, radiation receipts at the ground are often severely reduced,

more espeically at times of low solar elevation so that the
effect is particularly noticeable in high-latitude cities
during the early morning and late evening in winter. From
November to March, and before the reductions in air turbidity
following the Clean Air Acts, many polluted British cities
received between 25 and 55 per cent less radiation than nearby
rural areas. In central London the loss of sunshine amounted
to about 270 hours per year, there being a reduction of more
than 50 per cent in December (Chandler 1965). With the more
recent improvements in air clarity, winter sunshine receipts
have increased by 50 per cent, being as much as 70 per cent in
January (Jenkins 1969).

Investigations in many cities have shown an increase in
radiation receipts at weekends when industrial emissions of
pollution are generally reduced (Chandler 1965; Mateer 1961;
McCormick and Kurtis 1966).

The most serious reduction of radiation is in the short wavelength, ultraviolet part of the spectrum (Nader 1967), and on
extremely smoggy days in Los Angeles this could amount to more
than 90 per cent; but because much of the radiation scattered
by the pollution particles is directed downwards, the reduction
in surface receipts may often be mainly by absorption (Sheppard
1958), thus making the air more stable above urban areas and
indirectly helping to increase the amount of pollution.

TEMPERATURE

The warm air, which more often than not (and particularly by
night) covers built-up areas, is known as a 'heat-island'.
On calm, clear nights the air in cities has frequently been
measured as 5° C warmer than above nearby rural areas, and
occasionally 10° C differences have been recorded. The aerial
extent of the city seems to matter much less than the building
densities in controlling the maximum intensity of the heat-
island (Chandler 1965), large temperatures differences being
recorded on calm, clear nights in quite small, though densely
settled, towns. On nights when there is a moderate wind the
size of the city is clearly more important through its control upon wind speeds and turbulence, but even the, the strong
relationship with local buidling densities is shown in the
close correspondence between the pattern of a heat-island and
the morphology of the city. Frequently there is a sharp edge
to a heat island parallel to the margin of the built-up area
(Fig. 4.3); this reflects the close relationship between air
temperature and local building densities, and within the heat-
island there are often further sharp temperature gradients defining the boundaries of city regions with particular types of
building development. Any correlation between population size

and heat-island intensities (Oke 1973) is likely to be an indirect relationship through a correlation of urban densities and urban population.

Temporal variations in the intensity of heat-islands

Because of the many meteorological and topographical controls upon heat-island intensities these vary a good deal spatially and temporally. A diurnal variation, with a maximum warmth by night and minimum intensities or even a 'cold-island' (lower temperatures in the city than the surrounding country) by day, is almost universal. Table 4.1 gives the mean temperature in and around London for the period 1931-60.

Table 4.1

Average annual temperature in and around London, 1931-60

	Average height (m)	Maximum (^{o}C)	Minimum (^{o}C)	Mean (^{o}C)
Surrounding country	87.5	13.7	5.5	9.6
Suburbs	61.9	14.2	6.4	10.3
Central districts	26.5	14.6	7.4	11.0

The air in central London is colder than around the city on about one day in three on average and one day in two from February to April, whilst cold-islands occur on only about one night in five, with a clear winter peak.

Many cold-islands are related to the passage of fronts or to local differences in cloud amounts, pollution, and fog densities between central city, suburban, and country areas, but perhaps their most important cause is the more rapid increase of daytime temperatures in the open country compared with the city, owing to differences in the thermal conductivity, thermal capacity, and active mass of their surfaces. The nature of the city fabric produces a thermal lag which tends to produce weak heat-islands or cold-islands by day and stronger heat-islands by night (Mitchell 1962). Cold-islands commonly form above built-up areas when regional temperatures are rising, often occurring in groups of several days.

Daytime street temperatures in the central core of cities are sometimes less than in the surrounding downtown area because of shading by very tall buildings (Ludwig 1970), and suburban areas are cooler still so that temperatures rise then fall in a traverse

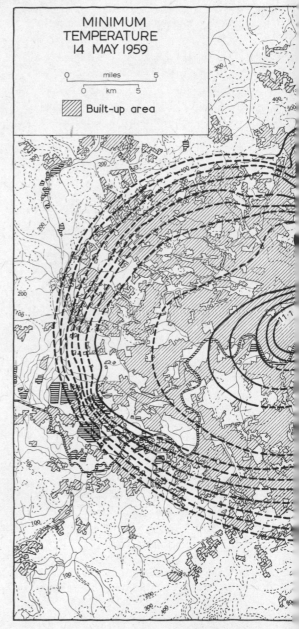

Fig. 4.3   Typical heat-isl

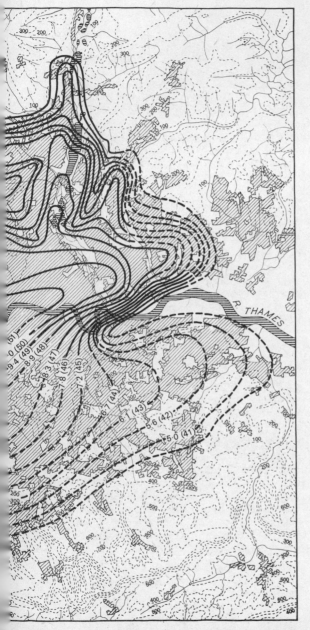

er London associated with clear skies and calm

from the margins to the centre of the city.

Seasonal variations in the intensity of heat-islands are more marked in some cities than others and, indeed, annual patterns are sometimes reversed. There is, for instance, a clear summer peak of intensities in London, but in Japanese cities the strongest heat-islands occur in winter, and many investigations in North American and European cities show only small seasonal differences (Mitchell 1961; Sundborg 1950; Landsberg 1956; Steinhauser *et al.* 1955). These differences between cities are probably due not only to contrasts in their urban morphology and the relative importance of the liberated heat of combustion but also to differences in the general climates of their regions, more particularly in relation to seasonal changes in wind speed, cloud amounts, and the incidence of inversions.

In addition to diurnal variations in the mean intensities of heat-islands, there are also hour-by-hour changes resulting from differences in the general synoptic situation.

Studies in a number of cities have highlighted the importance of wind speed, cloud amount, evaporation rates, and some index of the stability of the lower atmosphere amongst the several meteorological controls upon heat-island intensities (Nappo 1973; Miller *et al.* 1973). The strongest heat-islands are nearly always associated with calm air, clear skies, and an inversion of temperature in the lower 100 - 300 m of the atmosphere. Ludwig (1970), using nocturnal transverse data from a dozen cities in North America and England, showed the paramount importance of the near-surface temperature lapse rate as a control of heat-island intensity. This is readily understandable since only with a stable lower atmosphere, light winds, weak turbulence and a shallow mixing layer can the warm air of the heat-island be prevented from being eroded and its warmth diffused.

As wind speed and turbulence increase, so the urban-rural temperature differences are diminished, and because the size of the city is critical to changes in airflow, this might be an important factor in explaining why, on average, larger cities tend to have stronger heat-islands. The generally greater development densities found in the larger cities are also relevant here. At times of calm, city size is much less critical, and even small settlements with high building densities can develop strong heat-islands.

Oke and Hannell (1970) analysed the critical wind speeds for the elimination of the heat-island effect in several cities and derived the following relationship :

$$U = 11.6 + 3.4 \ln P,$$

where U is the critical wind speed and P is the city population

(used as an index of the spatial extent of the city). ln P
and U were highly correlated (+0.97). For London (population
5.5 million) the critical speed for the elimination of the heat
island was 12 ms $^{-1}$; for Montreal (population 2 million)
11 ms $^{-1}$; for Reading, England (population 120 000) 4.7 ms $^{-1}$
and for Palo Alto, California (population 33 000) 3.5 ms $^{-1}$.
Using the formula, the authors estimated the smallest settlement
to form a heat-island would have a population of 2 500, but
the original analysis was based upon a very limited sample and,
in fact, very small settlements and even groups of just a few
buildings have produced measurable heat-islands (Chandler 1965;
Landsberg 1970).

Spatial variations in intensity

The pattern of temperature in a city and the absolute values
are profoundly influenced by site conditions (Norwine 1973;
Chopra and Pritchard 1973) and by the prevailing weather conditions (Chandler 1961a; Clarke and Peterson 1973; Oke and
Hannell 1970). In general, because of the advection of cold
air into the windward areas of cities, the highest temperatures,
though still related to the areas of high building densities, are
displaced somewhat downwind. On calm nights, the correlation
between heat-island intensities and building densities is very
high as noted by Clarke and Peterson (1973) in St.Louis and by
Chandler in a comparative study of Leicester and London (1967).

Much less is known about the vertical than about the horizontal
pattern of temperatures in heat-islands. Meteorological towers
and tall buildings carrying temperature recorders have been used
in several cities (De Marrais 1961; Munn and Stewart 1967), but
perhaps the most detailed results have come from a study by
Clarke (1969) of temperatures over Cincinnati using a helicopter.
All of the studies show that nighttime inversions of temperature
are more frequent, stronger, and shallower over the country
than over the city, although there is often little difference
between the two environments by day.

In his study in New York City, Bornstein (1968) recorded multiple
elevated inversions over the surrounding country. Between the
ground and heights of up to 300 m over the city, temperatures
were generally higher than over the country and the lapse rate was
pseudo-adiabatic. Above about 400 m, temperatures over the city
were generally lower than those above the surrounding country.
This 'crossover' of urban and rural temperature profiles with colder
air above the city than the country at a level of about 300 – 400 m
above ground has not been fully explained, but it is suggested
that it may be related to long-wave radiation from a high-level
pollution haze over the city. A similar 'cross-over' was found
above San Francisco by Duckworth and Sandberg (1954) and above
Montreal by Oke and East (1971).

Clarke (1969), measuring temperatures above Cincinnati, at times of clear skies and light winds found evidence of an 'urban heat plume' rising above the city and then spreading several miles downwind at intermediate heights. Upwind of the urban area, there was a strong deep radiation inversion, whilst over the built-up area, temperature lapse conditions prevailed up to about 60 m above the ground. Downwind of the urban area there was a strong but shallow inversion at the surface, above which there was a weak lapse condition in the urban heat plume, followed at higher levels again by the upper part of the regional nocturnal radiation inversion.

Causes of the heat-island

There is little doubt that a variety of topographical and meteorological parameters are responsible for the existence and varying intensity of urban heat-islands. Some of these are connected with contrasts in the thermal and hydrological properties of urban and rural surfaces, others are related to differences in airflow, a third group includes processes affected by atmospheric turbidity, and a fourth group is concerned with the addition of heat from a variety of sources (Terjung 1970; Terjung and S.F. Louie 1973).

Shortly before dawn, temperatures over cities are normally higher than above the surrounding country, but after sunrise, the higher heat capacity, surface area, and heat conductivity of the city fabric means that the city will not warm as quickly as the vegetation-covered soils of the country. The rise of air temperature over the city will also be reduced by a haze-hood or morning fog and by the rougher surface and stronger turbulence of the built-up area. Thus, in spite of a higher albedo and more evaporation cooling in rural areas, these areas soon warm to temperatures almost equalling and sometimes above those of the city, and in the generally unstable conditions and gentle breezes of daytime the heat stored by the buildings and roads of the city plus that released by combustion is relatively easily and efficiently dispersed. By night, several factors will cause urban temperatures to fall less rapidly than those of the country. One of these is tye heat contribution of industrial boilers, vehicles, and human metabolism plus, in middle and high latitudes, the energy from domestic space-heaters. Manmade energy in many mid-latitude cities represents from a sixth to a third of the net all-wave radiation available at the ground (Kratzer 1956; Garnet and Bach 1965; Bornstein 1968). In winter, in New York City, the amount of heat from combustion is more than twice that reaching the ground from the sun but in summer, the factor drops to a sixth. But in spite of the tremendous amount of heat released from the various combustion processes in a city, and more parti-

cularly from low domestic chimneys in winter, most authors agree
that it is rapidly diffused and, overall, not first in importance
in explaining urban heat-islands (Sundborg 1950; Chandler 1965;
Craddock 1965; Myrop 1969). Far more telling is the release of
stored heat by the fabric of the city, back radiation into streets
from the walls of tall buildings, fogs and a pollution haze, and
the reduced mixing by turbulence of warm air in the bottom of
streets and courtyards (Chandler 1967; Miller *et al.* 1973).
Although mixing between the buildings is reduced, that above the
rooftops is increased by the serrated surface of the city, and
this increased turbulence in the boundary layer may also caused
a downward transport of heat from the level of the inversion.

Empirical and theoretical studies of heat-islands have recently
yielded a number of physical models which offer the hope that one
day it might be possible to predict local intensities. Such
predictions would be of interest, amongst others, to those studying air pollution in cities for, as has already been shown, heat-
islands generate local wind circulations, centripetal to the
centre of the city at the surface, which affect pollution patterns
and help to maintain the characteristically sharp pollution gradients
found near the margins of built-up areas. The higher temperatures
themselves can be regarded as either an advantage or disadvantage
depending upon the regional climatic setting. In cold climates,
towns could be purposefully designed to accentuate the heat-island,
whilst in other circumstances a more vigorous and turbulent airflow might be sought in order to prevent stagnation of uncomfortably warm air in the bottom of street chasms and sheltered pedes-
train precincts.

HUMIDITY

There have been relatively few comparative studies of the
moisture content of urban and rural atmospheres and the observational evidence is not conclusive. Much of the urban surface
is, of course, sealed by concrete, asphalt, and other impervious
and semi-impervious materials, although the still fairly large
amount of open ground has often been overlooked. Certainly a
lot of rainwater is led quickly underground, but the amount of
moisture absorbed by bricks and tiles is frequently underestimated.
Nevertheless, there is no doubt that evaporation rates in cities
are substantially less than from vegetation-covered soils. On
the other hand, amounts of dew are almost certainly greater in
rural areas and the added moisture from combustion is greater in
the city.

Evaporation rates are likely to manifest themselves in differences
in absolute humidity only when the atmosphere is calm. Average
annual or monthly vapour-pressure contrasts between urban and rural
areas for this reason are likely to be very small. Chandler (1965)

for instance, found that the mean annual vapour pressure in
London was only 0.2 millibars lower than at a nearby rural
climatological station. On calm nights, however, the moisture
content of the air above London and above another English town,
Leicester (population 270 000), was highest in the centre of
the city, being 1.5 - 2.0 millibars higher here than above the
surrounding country. The reason for this was explained in terms
of the low rates of diffusion of air 'trapped' between tall
buildings, so that it retained its characteristically high
daytime humidities.

Relative humidities, being in part a function of prevailing
temperatures, are inversely proportional in towns to the
intensity of the urban heat-island, and average annual urban-
rural differences of about 5 per cent have been widely reported.
On individual nights, the pattern of relative humidity in
cities is closely related to the detailed form of their heat-
island, which in turn depends upon the distribution of urban
building densities (Chandler 1967). Relative-humidity
differences between town and country can then amount to between
20 per cent and 30 per cent.

RAINFALL

It has been said that 'in contrast to analyses of [other]
near-surface phenomena, much of the literature on urban precipitation is primarily concerned with establishing whether or
not the urban area has any effect at all on the precipitation
distribution' (Atkinson 1970). It seems, at first sight,
plausible to postulate that, because of increased pollution with
active condensation and freezing nuclei (Schaefer 1969) as well
as the more active thermal and mechanical turbulence, there will
not only be increased cloud but also more precipitation above
cities. Lansberg (1956, 1962) and Changnon (1968, 1969, 1973)
have summarized the theories and field evidence for a number
of cities in Europe and the United States, whilst Atkinson
(1968, 1969, 1970) has produced a number of synoptic analyses for
London.

Simple comparisons of precipitation inside and outside urban
areas prove very little, because of the well-known fickleness of
the element, the relatively poor sampling inherent in normal
rain-gauge measurements, the drift of city pollutants into rural
areas, and the important orographic controls of the ground sites
of most cities. Also, more recent studies have emphasized the
time involved in precipitation processes and have pointed to the
displacement of positive anomalies downwind of their initiation.
Changnon (1968), for instance, has drawn attention to the
increase precipitation and days with heavy rain and hail at La
Porte, Indiana, 30 miles downwind of a large, heavy industrial

complex between Chicago and Gary. The annual precipitation at
La Porte was 31 per cent higher than in rural areas and the
number of summer thunderstorm days 63 per cent higher, although
not all of these differences could be accredited to the urban
effect alone. Increases of the order of 5 - 8 per cent in
annual precipitation (being greater in the cold season) and of
17 - 21 per cent in the number of summer thunderstorms were found
more typical of other cities in the United States less affected
by local topographies such as Lake Michigan (Holzman and Thom
1970; Ogden 1969).

Cities are unlikely to make very substantial differences in the
frequency of snowfall, for snow falls at times of the year and in
meteorological conditions generally inhibitive to strong heat-
islands which could otherwise act both as a trigger to instability
and a means of melting the flakes. But in the absence of orographic
controls, fallen snow will melt more quickly in central urban
parks than in suburban gardens, where it will often disappear
several days before that covering the farmlands around a city.

CONCLUSION

There are still large gaps in our understanding of the manner,
degree, and mechanisms by which urban climates are differentiated
from those of the surrounding country, but because rural atmospheres are being increasingly modified by human activity, this
comparison can be regarded less and less as between 'artificial'
and 'natural' climates. There are very few 'natural' climates
remaining, even in remote rural areas of the globe, because of
the spread of pollutants from other areas.

As in so many branches of applied climatology, theory and
application need to be more positively related and co-ordinated
than they have in the past. Meteorologists, urban climatologists,
architects, engineers, planners, and health experts must seek
every opportunity to exchange information and ideas so as to
maximize the advantages and minimize the disadvantages of the
known and still to be discovered aspects of urban climates.
These features are and will continue to be an important aspect
of the human environment for a large and growing proportion of
the world's population.

REFERENCES

ATKINS, J.E. (1968) Changes in the visibility characteristics
at Manchester/Ringway Airport, *Meteorol.Mag.* 97, 172-174.

ATKINSON, B.W.   (1968)   A preliminary examination of the possible effect of London's urban area on the distribution of thunder rainfall, *Trans. Inst. Br. Geogr.* 441, 97-118.

ATKINSON, B.W. (1969)   A further examination of the urban maximum of thunder rainfall in London, 1951-60, *Trans. Inst. Br.Geogr.*   48, 97-119.

ATKINSON, B.W. (1970)   The reality of the urban effect on precipitation: a case study approach, *Urban Climates,* Technical Note 108, 342-60. WMO, Geneva.

BEST, R.H. (1968)   Extent of urban growth and agriculture displacement in post-war Britain,   *Urban Stud.* 5, 1-23.

BORNSTEIN, R.D. (1968)   Observations of the urban heat island effect in New York City. *J. appl. Meteorol.* 7, 575-82.

BORNSTEIN, R.D.   (1969)   *Observed urban-rural wind speed differences in New York City.*   Paper presented at the American Geographical Union meeting, San Francisco, 1969.

BORNSTEIN, R.D., JOHNSON, D.S., and LORENZEN, A.   (1973) Recent observations of urban effects on winds and temperatures in and around New York City. *Conference on urban environment and second conference on biometeorology,* pp.28-33. American Meteorological Society, Philadelphia.

BRAZELL, J.H. (1964)   Frequency of dense and thick fog in central London as compared with frequency in outer London. *Meteorol. Mag.*   93, 129-35.

BRYSON, R.A. (1968).   All other factors being constant. *Weather,* 21, 56-61.

CHANDLER, T.J. (1961)   Surface breeze effects of Leicester's heat island. *E.Midland Geogr.*   15, 32-8.

CHANDLER, T.J. (1961a)   The changing form of London's heat island. *Geography* 46, 295-307.

CHANDLER, T.J. (1965)   *The climate of London.*   Hutchinson, London.

CHANDLER, T.J. (1967)   Night-time temperatures in relation to Leicester's urban form. *Meteorol. Mag.*   96, 244-50.

CHANGNON, S.A. (1968)   The La Porte weather anomaly - fact or fiction?   *Bull. Am. Meteorol. Soc. 50,* 411-21.

CHANGNON, S.A., SEMONIN, R.G. and LOWRY, W.P. (1973). Results from Metromex, *Conference on urban environment and second conference on biometeorology*, pp.191-7, American Meteorological Society, Philadelphia.

CHOPRA, K.P. and PRITCHARD, W.M. (1973)   Urban shopping centres as heating islands, *Conference on urban environments and second conference on biometeorology*, pp. 310-17. American Meteorological Society, Philadelphia.

CLARKE, J.F. (1969) The nocturnal urban boundary layer over Cincinnati, Ohio. *Mly Weather Rev.* 97, 582-89.

CLARKE, J.F. and PETERSON, J.T. (1973) The effect of regional climate and land use on the nocturnal heat island. *Conference on urban environments and second conference on biometeorology*, pp. 147-52. American Meteorological Society, Philadelphia.

CRADDOCK, J.M. (1965) Domestic fuel consumption and winter temperature in London, *Weather 20*, 257-8.

DAVENPORT, A.G. (1965) The relationship of wind structure to wind loading. In *Wind effects on buildings and structures*, Vol. 1, pp.54-102. National Physical Laboratory, HMSO, London.

DE MARRAIS, G.A. (1961) Verticial temperature difference observed over an urban area. *Bull. Am. Meteorol. Soc.* 42, 548-60.

DUCKWORTH, F.S. and SANDBERG, J.S. (1954), The effect of cities upon horizontal and vertical temperature gradients. *Bull. Am. Meteorol. Soc.* 35, 198-207.

ECKEL, O. and SAUBERER, F. (1957) *Klime und Bioklima von Wien*, Teil 11. Vienna.

FOSBERG, M.A., RANGO, A. and MARLATT, W.E. (1973) *Wind computations from the temperature field on an urban area. Conference on urban environments and second conference on biometeorology*, pp.5-7. American Meteorological Society, Philadelphia.

FREEMAN, M.H. (1968) Visibility statistics for London/Heathrow Airport, *Meteorol. Mag.* 97, 214-218.

GARNETT, A. and BACH, W. (1965) An estimation of the ratio of artificial heat generation to natural radiation heat in Sheffield, *Mly Weather Rev.* 93, 383-5.

GEORGII, H.W. (1968) The effects of air pollution on urban climates. *Urban climates*, Technical Note 108, pp.214-37, WMO, Geneva.

GRAHAM, I.R. (1968) An analysis of turbulence statistics at Fort Wayne, Indiana. *J.Appl.Meteorol.* 7, 90-3.

HOLZMAN, B.G. and THOM, H.C.S. (1970) The La Porte precipitation anomaly, *Bull. Am. Meteorol. Soc.* 51, 335-7.

JENKINS, I. (1969) Increases in averages in sunshine in central London. *Weather, 24,* 52-4.

KRATZER, P.A. (1956) *Das Stadklima,* Braunschweig.

LANDSBERG, H.E. (1956) The climate of towns, *Man's role in changing the face of the earth,* W.L.Thomas, (ed.) University of Chicago, Chicago.

LANDSBERG, H.E. (1962) *City air - better or worse. Symposium: air over cities,* pp.1-22, U.S. Public Health Service, Cincinnati, Ohio.

LANDSBERG, H.E. (1970) Micrometeorological temperature differentiation through urbanization, *Urban Climates*, Technical Note 108, pp.129-36, WMO. Geneva.

LAWTHER, P.J. (1973) Medical effects of air pollution. *Fuel and the environment,* pp.123-7. The Institute of Fuel, London.

LUDWIG, F.L. (1970) Urban temperature fields. *Urban Climates,* Technical Note 108, pp.80-107, WMO, Geneva.

McCORMICK, R.A. and KURTIS, K.R. (1966). The variation with height of the dust loading over a city as determined from the atmospheric turbidity, *Q.Jl.R.meteorol.Soc.* 92, 392-6.

MARSH, K.J. and FORSTER, M.D. (1967). An experimental study of the dispersion of emissions from chimneys in Reading - 1: The study of long-term average concentrations of sulphur dioxide. *Atmos.Environ. 1,* 527-50.

MATEER, C.L. (1961) Note on the effect of the weekly cycle of air pollution on solar radiation at Toronto. *Int.J.Air Water Pol. 4,* 52-4.

MILLER, E.L., JOHNSON, R.E., and LOWRY, W.P. (1973) The case of the muddled metromodel. *Conference on urban environment and second conference on biometeorology,* pp.77-82. American Meteorological Society, Philadelphia.

MITCHELL, J.M. (1961) The temperature of cities, *Weatherwise* 14, 224-9.

MITCHELL, J.M. (1962), The thermal climate of cities, *Symposium: air over cities,* pp.131-45. U.S. Public Health Service, Cincinnati, Ohio.

MUNN, R.E. (1970) Airflow in urban areas. *Urban climates,* Technical Note 108, pp.15-39, WMO, Geneva.

MUNN, R.E. and STEWART, I.M. (1967) The use of meteorological towers in urban air pollution programs. *J. Air Poll.Cent. Ass.* 17, 98-101.

MYROP, L.O. (1969) A numerical model of the urban heat-island. *Appl.Meteorol.* 8, 908-18.

NADER, J. S. (1967) *Pilot study of ultraviolet radiation in Los Angeles October 1965.* Public Health Service Publication. U.S. Department of Health, Education and Welfare, National Centre for Air Pollution Control, Cincinnati, Ohio.

NAPPO, C.J. (1973) A numerical study of the urban heat-island. *Conference on urban environments and second conference on biometeorology,* pp.1-4. American Meteorological Society, Philadelphia.

NORWINE, J.R. (1973) Heat island properties of an enclosed multi-level suburban shopping center. *Conference on urban environments and second Conference on biometeorology,* pp.139-43. American Meterological Society, Philadelphia.

OGDEN, T.L. (1969) The effect on rainfall of a large steelworks. *Appl. Meteorol. 8,* 585-91.

OKE, T.R. (1973) City size and the urban heat island. *Conference on urban environment and second Conference on biometeorology,* pp.144-47. American Meteorological Society, Philadelphia.

OKE, T.R. and HANNELL, F.G. (1970) The form of the urban heat island in Hamilton, Canada. *Urban climates,* Technical Note 108, pp.113-26, WMO, Geneva.

OKE, T.R. and EAST, C. (1971) The urban boundary-layer in Montreal *Boundary-layer meteorology.* 1(4), 411-437.

PARRY, M. (1970) Sources of Reading's air pollution *Urban climates,* Technical Note 108, pp. 295-305, WMO, Geneva.

POOLER, F., Jr. (1963) Air flow over a city in terrain of moderate relief. *J.appl. Meteorol.* 2, 446-56.

PRITCHARD, W.M. and CHOPRA, K.P. (1973) Effect of air pollution on urban visibility statistics. *Conference on urban environment and second Conference on biometeorolgy*, pp.241-8. American Meteorological Society, Philadelphia.

REAY, J.S.S. (1973) Monitoring of the environment. *Fuel and the environment*, pp.105-10. The Institute of Fuel, London.

REED, L.E. (1966) Vehicle exhausts in relation to public health. *R.Soc.Hlth Jl.* 86, 231.

SCHAEFER, V.J. (1969) The inadvertent modification of the atmosphere by air pollution. *Bull.meteorol.Soc.* 50, 199-206.

SCHMIDT, F.H. and VELDS, C.A. (1969)   On the relation between changing meteorological circumstances and the decrease of the sulphur dioxide concentration around Rotterdam. *Atmos.Environ.* 3, 455-60.

SHEPPARD, P.A. (1958) The effect of pollution on radiation in the atmosphere. *Int.J. Air Water Poll.* 1, 31-43.

SINGER, T.A. and SMITH, M.E. (1970) A summary of the recommended guide for the prediction of dissersion of air-borne effluents *Urban climates*, Technical Note 108, 306-24, WMO, Geneva.

STEINHAUSER, F., ECKEL, O., and SAUBERER, F. (1955, 1957, 1959) *Klima und Bioklima von Wien*, Pts. I, II and III, pp.120, 134, and 136.

STERN, A.C. (ed.) (1968) *Air pollution* (2nd ed.) Academic Press, New York.

SUNDBORG, A. (1950) Local climatological studies of temperature conditions in an urban area, *Tellus*   2, 222-32.

TERJUNG, W.H. (1970) Urban energy balance climatology: a preliminary investigation of the city-man system in downtown Los Angeles. *Geog. Rev.* 60, 31-50.

TERJUNG, W.H. and S.F. LOUIE, S. (1973) Solar radiation and urban heat islands. *Ann. Ass. Am. Geogr.* 63(2), 181-207.

WILLIAMS, F.P. (1960) Pollution levels in cities, *Proceedings of the Harrogate Conference*, pp.83-8, National Society for Clean Air, London

WISE, A.F.E. (1971) Effects due to groups of buildings. *Phil. Trans.Soc. A.* 269, 469–85.

5 Urban man in buildings

R. G. Hopkinson

ARCHITECTURE AND ENVIRONMENTAL DESIGN

New and more sophisticated methods of building and environmental engineering having been tried and found wanting, the interaction of man with his built environment has become the subject
of intensive study.   Some of the stresses suffered by urban
man arise from the inadequacy of the architectural and engineering design of modern buildings, buildings both for living in
and working in.   Tall buildings, excessively glazed, with no
protection against unwanted solar radiation, and with inadequate
insulation against the excessive noise of traffic and aircraft;
rooms in which the occupant has a choice of acute thermal
discomfort from solar heat if he closes the windows to keep out
the noise, or the impossibility of speech communication if he opens
the window to relieve his thermal stress - these have become
all too common, with the result that there is a revolt and a
move back to the traditional building with massive walls of
great heat capacity and windows on a more human scale.   The
cult of Le Corbusier (Le Corbusier 1933) and of Mies Van de
Rohe is at last passing, but the environmental atrocities which
their inadequately briefed disciples have created over the past
30 years are still with us, and are liable to go on creating
environmental stresses for the years to come.

A building should act as a filter to the natural environment,
modifying features such as excessive cold, excessive air movement,
excessive light and solar radiation, and excessive moisture, in
order to create an internal environment more in keeping with
the range of environment parameters to which man has adapted
and evolved over the centuries.   A building must also create
an environment over and above that available from outdoors,
by supplying light, heat, air movement, etc. by artificial means
(nowadays more than ever before) and by integrating the
natural and artificial components of the environment to produce
the ideal conditions suitable for work or leisure.   This is the
purpose of environmental design;   where it fails it may be
partly due to ignorance of the fundamental requirements, but
failure is more often due to the ignoring of these fundamentals
in the interests of architectural fashion or economic restrictions.

Standards of environmental design were, until recently, based
upon evolution and tradition, trial and error over the centuries,
and the adoption of the best solution for particular circumstances.
The need for more concentrated study and the development of
experimental techniques for expanding knowledge of the internal

environment came with the increasing sophistication of industrial
urban activities and the availability of new forms of fossil
fuels and of building materials and methods of construction.
The changeover from traditional to experimental standards has been
gradual. The first industrial buildings relied upon natural light,
but in those which required good light for continuous working
around the clock, methods of artificial lighting were introduced
and steadily improved until now almost every industrial building
is provided with permanent artificial lighting, and many are
provided with artificial light of the same quantity as that of
good natural daylight.

The replacement of traditional standards with those based upon
controlled experiments has been a slow process. This was due
largely to the reluctance of builders, architects, and occupants
to accept changes which cost more money or require a higher level
of design thinking or which call for changes in occupational
habits. Laboratory experiments under idealized conditions,
apparently remote from the real conditions in which the results
are to be used, give rise to criticisms that can only be overcome
by the subsequent validation of the standards which are derived
from them. The proof of the pudding has to be in the eating thereof.
The criticism of standards derived from controlled experiments
takes many forms, and at present it is manifesting itself in
planners basing undue reliance on social surveys. It cannot be
pointed out too often that social surveys can only assess what
people have and their reaction to what they have; a survey
cannot, except in unusual circumstances, predict what will be a
person's response to conditions which they have never experienced.

Adaptation and the effect on standards

One of the criticisms that is often made of environmental
standards is that they are constantly changing. Our grandfathers
recall that in their youth a room temperature of 60° F (15° C) was
considered ideal. Nowadays 68° F or 70° F (20 or 21° C) is
considered the norm in this country, while higher standards, 75° F
or even 78° F (24 or 25° C), are considered desirable in North
America. In the same way one can find papers in the technical
journals of around 1900 which state that one foot-candle (that
is, the amount of light cast by an ordinary wax candle on a
book one foot away) is 'a very comfortable illumination by which
to work' and this was the standard of lighting recommended for
work at the time. The standard crept up to 10 foot-candles by
the 1930s, and the recommended working lighting at the time of
writing is about 500 - 1000 lux, which corresponds to 50 - 100
foot-candles - that is, between 50 and 100 times the lighting
level considered adequate only 70 years ago. (IES Code 1936,
1941, 1946, 1955, 1961, 1968, 1973).

These upgradings in environmental standards have been brought about essentially by economic changes, chiefly the more ready availability of energy from fossil fuels and the provisions of more efficient methods of creating heat and light artificially. They are not due to any changes in human beings themselves. People can see no worse in an illumination of 1 foot-candle than they could in 1900, but they are much less willing to put up with the difficulties of seeing in inadequate lighting than they were previously. In 1900 it was assumed without question that it is more difficult to see by artificial light than it is by daylight and one put up with the difficulties - one adapted.

This is the difficulty of setting standards generally. The human sensory mechanism is capable of a wide range of adaptations, and people will adapt either consciously or unconsciously, if the environmental conditions are not optimum. The average noise level inside buildings (due either to traffic noise coming in from outside or internally generated noise) has been steadily rising, and in many urban situations has reached a level which 30 years ago would have given rise to acute complaint. However, the change has been gradual and people have adapted to and accepted these high noise levels. But the human adaptation process is not limitless, and in many environmental situations the limits have now been reached. About 20 years ago the excessive glare caused by very large windows in some urban buildings on the one hand, and excessively bright unscreened fluorescent lighting, on the other, exceeded the tolerable limits, and entirely new lighting standards called 'limiting glare indices' were introduced (IES Code 1961) in codes of practice all over the world to combat this menace. Ten years later the limit was reached for excessive noise due to aircraft and heavy traffic, and the Wilson Committee (Wilson 1963) was set up to investigate the nuisance. Standards were laid down for the upper limits of tolerance of these and other forms of noise in the working environment.

Human adaptation is characterized by a 'hysteresis' effect - a slowness to respond to change. There are both short-term and long-term hysteresis effects. If the temperature in a room gradually falls, people will not feel cold immediately, but there will be a delay of perhaps several minutes before the fall in temperature gives rise to some comment or complaint. If the cloud density on an overcast day gradually changes, people will not notice for some time that the lighting level has fallen and the cloud cover may change back and the lighting level be restored without anyone noticing. In the long term the gradual changing of the noise pattern in a city with increasing traffic or the increasing proportion of heavy goods vehicles may pass unnoticed for several weeks or months, until at last a point is reached where complaints become frequent and vociferous. This 'threshold of complaint' is a critical parameter in environmental design.

Environment and well-being

The effect of the environment on man in urban buildings can be considered under several headings. Each is of equal importance but one may have to be given priority over the others, depending upon the circumstances.

First, there is the effect of the environment on working efficiency and performance. If the lighting is inadequate, visual performance will be affected, mistakes will be made, and work will be done more slowly, but it does not necessarily follow that anybody will complain about inadequate lighting or that anybody will suffer from visual fatigue. Next, there is the effect of the environment on comfort. Ideal conditions for most efficient work may not necessarily be those which provide the greatest comfort. On the other hand, it is unlikely that work will be performed efficiently if people are acutely uncomfortable. There are some environments, for example, that for patients in a hospital, where environmental comfort is of high priority, and this also applies to people in their homes. But in a working environment, the conditions most conducive to efficient and productive work, consistent with the absence of discomfort, are the criterion.

Finally, there are the effects of the environment on health, both in the short term and the long term, and upon the physiological and psychological cost to the human being. It is possible to envisage an environment in which a person works efficiently and is unaware of any discomfort, but in which he is 'nothing himself up' to perform, at some subsequent physiological or psychological cost to himself. These are situations which need to be recognized, but they cannot readily be detected by social surveys.

The immediate effects of the environment upon efficiency and comfort can be investigated using well-attested techniques. The short-term effects on health, such as temporary deafness, eye-strain or blurred vision, and feelings of excessive warmth or cold or of draughts are also relatively easy to detect. It is the long-term effects which are insidious in their onset, and which give rise to fears, rational or irrational, that are at last becoming the subject of serious study. For decades the noises characteristic of engineering factories were tolerated by workers, and the resultant deafness in old age was accepted as something which was part of the normal ageing process. In the same way, rises in blood pressure and greater incidence of heart conditions with age were accepted as the disadvantages of growing old, until it was demonstrated that people living in rural environments in undeveloped countries did not suffer these ageing effects and that the complaints were characteristic of the urban civilization of 'western man'. Serious consideration is now being given to

the onset of deafness and other long-term effects caused by
continuous levels of noise below the threshold of acute
discomfort.

Research is urgently needed into the effect of concurrent
environmental stresses. Nobody knows yet what happens when
people are subjected to a number of stresses at the same time
(but see Chapter 14). In the short term, many of the effects
of environmental stress are known; however, it is not easy to
see how they act in an additive way, for example the thermal
stresses down a coal-mine result in a miner having reduced
sensitivity to glare from the mine lighting, but it is not
known whether the submersion of one form of discomfort under
a greater form of discomfort causes a summation of the
physiological costs of the two. There is every reason to
believe, from a common-sense point of view, that it does, but
it must be proved by experiment or experience before action
which costs money can be expected to be taken.

The order in which environmental effects occur is not always
predictable, although there is a general pattern which can be
recognized. As long ago as 1935 Bartlett and Pollock pointed
out that in the case of discomfort from noise and from glare,
subjective effects causing complaint (and sometimes acute
complaint) were present long before there was any measurable
effect upon performance. These studies were done in factories
for the then Industrial Health Research Board. Whether this
is still true in industry - with full employment and more
powerful trade unions compared with 1935 when fear of unemployment lead to strong motivation to work - is not known, but the
findings of Bartlett and Pollock (1935) seemed to indicate
that unfavourable environments that give rise to discomfort
and complaint of discomfort are not usually sufficiently bad
to affect performance. If performance *is* affected by environmental factors then the situation is already one which would
cause acute complaint.

In the same way, the conditions which cause permanent impairment of the sensory processes may or may not be the conditions
which impair efficiency or give rise to discomfort. In general,
however, as an environment progressively moves from the optimum
there is first a feeling of discomfort, then an impairment of
efficiency and performance, and finally a short-term and then
a long-term change in the sensory process. In other words, the
complaint of a human being about his environment should be taken
as a first warning that all is not well. Unfortunately, in many
environmental situations impairment in the short or long term
can result without the subject being aware that anything serious
is wrong.

A word of warning about the use of statistical methods to
evaluate the long-term effects of environmental inadequacies:

a classic example is that of the suspected relationship between
bad lighting and poor eye-sight. Not long ago it was considered
that bad light caused bad sight, (Luckiesh and Moss 1937) and
that in particular the onset of adolescent myopia was due to bad
lighting in schools. The apparently close statistical correlation
between short-sight in children, the amount of book-
work which they did, and the poor artificial lighting in schools
where they worked, was considered as valid beyond question. However, Sorsby and his collaborators (Sorsby *et al.* 1961) showed
that the onset of adolescent myopia was conditioned chiefly by
inherited physiological genetic characteristics. Children who
were intelligent enought to become 'bookworms' were shown to
come from families whose inheritance includes not only cleverness
but also the tendency to rapid physical growth in adolescence,
which is often accompanied by increasing myopia. In the years
which have since elapsed, Sorsby's findings have been vindicated.
There has been, for example, no reduction in the frequency or
period of development of adolescent myopia, in spite of the
fact that all schools in this country are well lit both by day and
in the evening, and that schools built during the last 30 years
which received special attention to their lighting because of
the 'school myopia' situation, have no apparent advantages in
this respect over the older schools. Those who deduce causal
relationships from statistical correlations might take warning.

The determination of environmental standards

The standards of lighting, heating, ventilation, acoustics, and
other environmental factors are no longer determined from
tradition and experience but almost entirely rest upon the
results of carefully controlled experiments in the laboratory
and in the field.   There are three processes involved (Hopkinson
1965).

First, there must be experiments to observe the behaviour of
people under different environmental conditions, which measure
their performance, or which ask for their responses and their
preferences. Such experiments necessarily have to be conducted
with only a limited number of subjects. There must follow
validation of the standards so derived, by testing them in the
field (that is, under conditions representative of the conditions
in which they will be operative) and demonstrating on a sufficient sample that the standards are reasonably representative
and adequate for their purpose.

The next stage is to devise methods of design which architects
and building services engineers can use and put into practice,
and to put pressure upon them to use these methods so that they
can be built into buildings which can be subsequently tested.
This is the final stage, the validation in buildings, with real

people in real situations, if necessary over a period of years.
This is the only final test of the experimental approach.   It
is an approach which has been strongly criticized by academic
psychologists but the standards of thermal comfort, and of
lighting, which were laid down on the basis of psychophysical
experiments of this kind during a period between 20 and 40 years
ago, have not required any changes as a result of any inadequacy
of the experimental approach.   In the instances where standards
have changed, these have been in the direction of upgrading the
standard to one more in accordance with the experimental results,
because an improved economic situation or better technology
permitted it.

The main gap in our knowledge is still, however, that we do
not understand sufficiently what happens when the human being
is subjected to stresses which are well below the breakdown
point and may even be below the threshold of complaint. Conditions
of stress, particularly thermal stress, at or near the breakdown
level have been investigated for limiting climatic conditions
of both heat and cold, and noise conditions which result in
the permanent impairment of hearing are being closely studied.
But more attention needs to be given to those environmental
conditions which are outside the comfort zone, while still
within the zone of tolerability - particularly when work motivation influences acceptances of inferior conditions.

LIGHTING AND VISION IN BUILDINGS

When it was accepted without question, as it no longer is,
that buildings had windows to provide light and a view, it
was the play of natural light which, more than any other environmental factor, determined the character of the building.   The
architect consequently made a detailed study of light and window
design.   Principles that were laid down by the architects of
the classical period, and which are embodied in the writings of
Vitruvius were respected and followed. In the
'environmental period', that is, from say 1900 onwards, advances
in window design were made, in the sense that research revealed
the fundamental principles of vision that led to the success
of the traditional designs.   Refinements were made and design
principles laid down, particularly with regard to the creative
use of internally reflected light.

It is in the field of artificial lighting that the major
modern advances have been made.   With the development first
of the incandescent tungsten filament lamp and subsequently of
the tubular fluorescent lamp, the designer had been provided
with reasonably cheap light sources that can give adequate
levels of working and environmental light.   At first the
technology of artificial lighting was in the hands of 'illuminating engineers' who providing the maximum working light for the mini-

mum expenditure of energy. Subsequently, however, the role of the illuminating engineer has diminished, while that of the lighting designer has increased. The lighting designer is the creator of a visual environment which provides not only light on the work but also an environment that is comfortable and pleasant and which may evoke positive pleasure.

For 50 years the art of the artificial lighting technologist and of the architect were entirely independent. The contrast between the imaginative use of natural light in buildings and the prosaic efforts of the 'illuminating engineer' after dark were all too apparent, not only in churches and cathedrals, where the contrast was most marked, but also in schools and hospitals. It is only in the last 15 years that the marriage of natural and artificial lighting has taken place. But even now few architects really understand the potential for creative visual design with artificial light. Bland lighting by uniformly spaced fluorescent fixtures is an integral part of the urban scene; the best that can be said for it is that, so far as we know, it does nobody any positive harm.

Integration of the natural and the artificial lighting environments has been achieved as the result of an approach from entirely opposite beginnings. Natural lighting proceeds from the sky, through the window, and so the light source, as seen from the interior of the building, is a large area of light, often of interest in itself, with the play and movement of clouds. Windows are usually in the side walls rather than the roof of the building and so the lighting has strong directional characteristics, which model the objects seen in the building as well as providing the working light. Artificial lighting, on the other hand, comes either from a point source (the filament lamp) or from a linear tubular source, (the fluorescent lamp) and is usually placed in the ceiling, creating a downward modelling effect, which at best is unnoticed and at worst is baleful and unflattering. The technology of natural lighting therefore developed from a consideration of the effects of massive amounts of light coming from large sources, while the technology of artificial light started from small point sources producing inadequate amounts of light, which had to be harnessed by mirrors and lenses and directed for economic reasons on to the work and nowhere else. As artificial lighting became more and more within the means of everyday people, more and more light could be spared for the lighting of the environment as well as the working area, and so gradually the techniques of natural lighting, with their regard for appearance and modelling and their disregard for quantity (since daylight was free), became part of artificial lighting technology. The final marriage took place in the mid-1950s, with the development of the technique of Permanent Supplementary Artificial Lighting in Interiors (known

as PSALI).   In this system an artificial lighting supplement
is designed as an integral part, along with the windows, of the
total lighting of the building during daytime, and the same
lighting scheme, with modifications, operates at night (Hopkinson, 1963, Hopkinson and Longmore 1959, Hopkinson and Kay 1969).

The lighting-vision relationship

As with all sensory processes, there is a comfort range for
lighting.   If there is insufficient light, it is not possible
to see well.   If there is too much light there is a feeling
of discomfort, even though vision may not be impaired.   If
there is very much too much light, vision is impaired and there
is an acute feeling of discomfort or even pain.

The comfort range depends upon the nature of the visual task.
It is often said that the ideal levels of light are those out
of doors on a sunny day, levels which are very much
greater than those at present current in building interiors.
The argument is that the eye evolved to be at its most comfortable in daylight conditions.   While this is certainly true
for the kind of circumstances in which people find themselves
out of doors, these are not the circumstances in which people
find themselves indoors.   Human vision did not evolve around
the reading of black print on white paper, but it evolved
around the need to hunt for food in the natural environment.
The landscape reflects, on average, only about one-tenth
of the light that it receives.   White paper, on the other hand,
reflects about 80 per cent of the light - and this is only one
of a number of important differences.

The basic relationship between sharpness of vision (visual acuity)
and the level of light (that is, the illuminance) is shown in
Fig.5.1 (Hopkinson 1963).   At low and moderate levels of
illuminance the relationship is logarithmic, that is, equal ratios
of increase in illuminance produce equal changes in visual
acuity.   However, at the levels of illuminance common in everyday life, this logarithmic relationship gives place to a situation
of diminishing returns.   Eventually, at the levels of illuminance
characteristic of natural lighting out of doors, changes in
illuminance make little or no difference to sharpness of vision.
Beyond the level corresponding to direct sunlight, sharpness of vision
falls off markedly. The relationship in Fig.5.1 shows that if
the lighting is already adequate there is only very little to
be gained, so far as visual performance is concerned, by increasing the level of lighting.   The precise relationship
between lighting and visual performance depends upon the individual.   There is a wide variance even among individuals with
'normal' vision.   If the effects of age are taken into account
as well, this variance is even wider, as Fig.5.1 shows.

Environmental codes of practice for lighting lay down certain optimum levels of illuminance for different types of work. Of these various codes, that produced by Illuminating Engineering Society (IES Code 1936, 1941, 1946, 1955, 1961, 1968, 1973) is the most comprehensive and also the most authoritative, and it serves as the basis for codes for special circumstances, including the recommendations and regulations put forward by

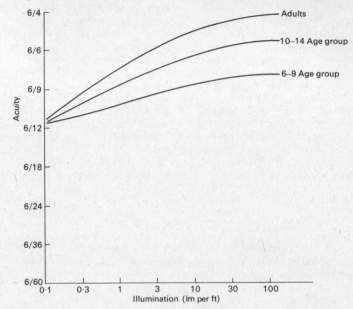

Fig. 5.1 Typical relationship between the amount of light on the visual task, and the resultant visual acuity, measured by recognising letters on a Snellow chart. The acuity is a function of experience in recognition as well as of inherent response of photo-receptors. The relationship is characterized by its asymptotic approach to a maximum acuity, at about 30/100 lumens/ft^2 (average dull daylight out of doors) beyond which further increases in light result only in marginal further improvement in acuity. (After Hopkinson 1963).

Government Departments. The levels of illuminance recommended by the IES for interior lighting are generally comparable with those which result from natural lighting through sensibly designed windows. These levels are of the order of 300-600 lux, that is, about one-tenth of that provided by the unobstructed natural sky. Certain visual tasks of great difficulty, such as the work of the surgeon on the operating table, require very much higher levels of lighting than this, though only for the short period of the duration of the visual activity.

Lighting codes now also specify a 'limiting glare index', because it is recognized that, whether the light comes from a window or from an artificial lighting fixture or array of fixtures, excessive brightness of the source of light can give rise to discomfort. However, absence of visual discomfort is not considered to be a pre-requisite, and in some circumstances it may be stimulating to an otherwise bland environment if a glimpse of the bright light sources is afforded. For this reason the comfort index, in the form of a 'limiting glare index', recommends different values of this index for different environments. Environments which must be completely free from visual discomfort, such as a sick ward in a hospital, are given the lowest value of limiting glare index. Environments where glare does not matter, provided that it is not beyond the limit of tolerability, are given a high value of limiting glare index. This latter would apply to places like factory stores, for example, which are only visited occasionally. Towards the middle and lower end of the range are environments like offices and schools, where glare discomfort should be kept to a minimum but not to the extent of limiting the designer's freedom to provide some visual stimulation from the windows or the lighting fixtures.

Lighting the building and the work

In the early days of lighting technology, the architect, in arranging the natural lighting, gave more attention to lighting the building itself, often neglecting the need for working light by the people who inhabited the building, while the illuminating engineer, who designed the artificial lighting, gave almost total attention to lighting the work and little attention to the lighting of the environment. For example, in a church, by day the beauty of the architecture of the building would be revealed by the play of light from the windows, but the glare from the altar window would prevent the congregation from seeing the performance of the Mass. By night, people would be able to read their hymn books, but the form of the church would be lost in the gloom and shadow.

This is no longer the case. Artificial lighting is now sufficiently plentiful (apart from problems arising as a result of the recent energy crisis) to enable the same pattern of thinking to be applied to both the natural and the artificial lighting of a building. This patter of thinking draws a distinction between, though does not segregate, the lighting of the building and the environment generally and the lighting of the visual tasks which go on in the building. More often than not the same lighting system functions both as building

lighting and as work lighting, and, if this is possible, then
it is all to the good. For some types of visual task, however,
it is far better to consider the lighting of the building environment and the lighting of the work as coming from two different
systems. This is particularly the case where the work demands
the maximum of attention and where the environment should form
nothing more than a non-distracting background. In general,
the eye is attracted naturally to those objects which are the
brightest, the most contrasting, or the most colourful in the
visual field, and is correspondingly distracted by bright, colourful, or contrasting objects. In an industrial environment the
work lighting should therefore be *focal* lighting, that is, light
which attracts the· eye to the work as a focus of attention. The
building lighting should be non-distracting and therefore should
be free of wide changes in colour, levels, and contrast.

These ideals, which are fully quantified in the present-day
technology of the lighting designer, are easier to achieve by
artificial light than they are by natural lighting. Natural
lighting by side windows necessarily produces a dual focus of
attention - the work itself and the view through the window.
In practice, however, this seems to be of far less concern than
might be expected. In fact, there is plenty of evidence that
the eyes require 'visual rest centres' to which they can turn
away from the work, to relax the accommodation and convergence
for a few moments before returning to close activity. The view
through the window provides just this kind of visual rest centre,
and seems to constitute far less of an unwanted distraction than
would an artificial lighting situation of comparable brightness
and size.   Nevertheless, the problem is one which is not fully
understood, and arguments one way or another are used to support
the retention or the elimination of windows.

The windowless environment

The arguments in favour of windowless buildings are based partly
on economic grounds and partly on environmental considerations.
A building without windows can be thermally isolated from the
environment so that the losses of internally generated heat in
winter can be kept to a minimum and the unwanted gains from solar
radiation in summer can also be minimized without the cost of
expensive air-cooling systems and sun controls over windows. The
economic balance will be different for different climates and will
depend upon the cost of power for heating and lighting and on costs
of maintenance.

On environmental grounds the arguments are that the environment
can be controlled within close limits of temperature and humidity
and that a uniform and non-fluctuating level of lighting can be
provided throughout the working period. These arguments carry

weight where the manufacturing process requires close temperature and humidity control and where work has to go on round the clock. The arguments also carry weight in areas where the external climate is highly unfavourable to human activity, areas such as those where it is very cold or very hot and dry.

A third and new argument in favour of windowless buildings is that they reduce the risk of damage through vandalism in towns. In some cities of North America vandalism in schools, where the vandals have broken in through windows, has become so serious that this argument cannot be ignored.

The arguments against windowless buildings are almost entirely psychological. While it is true that no concerted research effort has been made to assess the physiological cost of working in a windowless environment, nevertheless if there were serious health hazards involved these would have made themselves apparent by now. In many countries of the Western world and in Russia windowless buildings have been in use for several years, and evidence of serious physiological harm has not been forthcoming.

The psychological factors which operate in windowless buildings are more evident but by no means fully understood, and the evidence is full of contradictions. People occasionally express a dislike of working in buildings without windows, but it is said that the complainants are often the kind of people who would find something to complain about in any environment. A great many people, on the other hand, continue to work in windowless buildings without any unsolicited comment or complaint Although many of these, when specifically asked, will say that they would prefer to work in a building with windows, they are not particularly bothered by the environment in which they find themselves. Distress caused by a windowless environment is considerably relieved if there is some other access to a view of the world outside. People do not then feel claustrophobic. The greatest complaint arises if there appears to the worker no good reason for cutting out the daylight except profit to the management. In offices people doing routine work, such as audio-typing, which nevertheless demands attention, seem less worried by a windowless environment than are people whose work allows the attention to wander. An executive alone in a windowless office suffers more than the secretaries in the typing pool next door..

It is perhaps significant to the discussion that 'good natural light' in a building is an amenity which is considered to justify an increase in rental, while the absence of windows is also an accepted argument for additional remuneration of work people.

Lighting design is able to alleviate the psychological feelings of deprivation in a windowless building to some extent, but

much can be done by intelligent attention to the design of the building. In particular the use of large glass-partitioned spaces within a large windowless building, giving the greatest possible viewing distance, can do more than almost any other design feature. The provision of false or symbolic windows, the use of 'warm' coloured light behind a partition to give the illusion of a shaft of sunlight coming into the room, and the distribution of light in such a way as to create an illusion that the ceiling is higher or the room larger are all useful design techniques.

There is no evidence so far that working in a windowless building has any short-term or long-term effects on vision. Absence of evidence does not, of course, mean absence of effect, but in this case there is no cause to expect that good artificial lighting to an adequate level of illuminance will have any long-term effects on human vision different from those produced by the same level of natural daylight. However, medical staff responsible for the health of staff working in windowless buildings should be aware of the possible problem.

The control of daylight and sunlight - the daylight code

The existing regulations and by-laws of Government and local authorities for the admission of daylight to buildings are based on the assumption that during daylight hours much of the work and activity which goes on in buildings makes use of natural light. These codes of practice make recommendations for the controlling (a) of the spacing of buildings so that adequate amounts of natural light reach the facades of buildings and (b) the provision and positioning of windows to ensure that adequate light at the facade penetrates all the working areas of the building. These two sets of codes are, of course, interlinked, but the relationship is of particular importance in urban situations. (British Standard Code of Practice 1964, Planning Criteria and Design of Buildings 1971).

The general basis of daylight regulation is that a minimum percentage, usually 2 per cent, of the available light from the sky (exclusive of direct sunlight), should be allowed to penetrate to the remotest part of the working environment. The ratio of the interior lighting to that available to the whole sky outside is called the 'daylight factor', and this 2 per cent daylight factor has become a general guide to building designers over the past 30 years. In order to achieve it in buildings of conventional (as opposed to 'open plan') design it is necessary to provide windows in the side walls of not less than an eighth and usually nearer a quarter of the floor area.

This is a considerable amount of glazing, and, as a result, the 2 per cent daylight factor has caused the building of a rash of 'greenhouse buildings', excessively glazed because the designers wished to meet the codes of practice requirements without going to the trouble of careful design and placing of windows.

The major discomforts from excessive glazing arise from (a) too much sunlight and solar heat gain; (b) a high degree of discomfort and disability due to glare from the bright sky even if not from a direct view of the sun; and (c) thermal discomfort in winter due to heat loss through the window and radiation loss from the human body.

The Town Planning Daylight Code, operated by many local authorities (Planning Criteria and Design of Buildings 1971) and especially the Greater London Council, was devised to permit the building of high blocks in towns without contravening the daylight requirements. It was shown that if high tower blocks are placed judiciously in relation to one another, daylight can penetrate between them even to the lowest floors. The 'canyon' effects of the closely-packed American skyscrapers are thereby avoided. The Daylight Code has been a major factor in determining the skyline of London and other big cities during the last 30 years. Setting on one side for the moment the social and psychological disadvantages of high-rise building, the Daylight Code has at least had the effect of providing a framework for good environmental design. As a result the grouping of tall buildings nowadays is a vast improvement upon the American practice typified in downtown New York.

More recently a new form of recommendation has been put forward. This is in the form of 'guidelines'rather than 'regulations', with the intention of encouraging the architect to use his design skill rather than conforming to a regulation pattern. These new guidelines on the provision of daylight in buildings (at the moment this form of code applies only to educational buildings) distinguishes between the two main functions of a window in the way that the daylight factor code did not. These two functions are (a) providing working light, and (b) providing a view outside. The new guidelines recommend that there should be a certain level of working light, provided either by windows or by artificial lighting or a combination of both, and that in addition windows should occupy a certain proportion of the external walls of the space, in order to ensure that there is an adequate view of the world outside. The present guidelines are based upon a systematic investigation which showed that there is a critical minimum size of window below which some of the troubles of windowless buildings can arise and also that the shape and position of windows needs to be related to the nature of the view outside - research has

shown that both the American-type horizontal-view window and
the vertical slit window are unsatisfactory.

Visual stress - discomfort and annoyance (Hopkinson and Collins
1970)

A number of stress effects from both natural and artificial
lighting have been investigated over the years (particularly
during the previously mentioned period when it was believed that
there was a causal relationship between bad lighting and the
onset of visual defects such as myopia in children.) Some of this
work is now seen to be irrelevant but there are still outstanding
problems, particularly glare, flicker, and poor colour rendering
by fluorescent light sources, which cause complaint and have not
been satisfactorily resolved.

It can be said with confidence that neither the onset of
adolescent visual defects nor the onset of presbyopia in mature
adults is significantly influenced by inadequate lighting. This does
not mean to say that people suffering from the defects are not
considerably helped by the provision of good lighting. Most people
with visual defects are aware that they can see better in good
light and that the assistance which good light gives them is greater
than that which it gives people with normal vision.

It is also necessary to distinguish between subjective feelings of
'eye-strain' and any form of true 'visual fatigue'. People often
complain of eye-strain, which they blame on the lighting, even though
there are no measurable objective symptoms which can be detected.
Such complaints need to be investigated, even though it is often
proved that non-visual causes are at the root of the trouble.
Middle-aged people avoiding, or unaware of, the need for their
first pair of reading spectacles may complain of the lighting. The
fault, however, lies in their eyes and not in the lighting.

The elimination of glare is still a problem for the lighting
designers. There are two forms of glare, one form, called 'disability
glare', results from the scattering of light in the optic media.
The other form of glare, called 'discomfort glare', can exist
independent of whether or not any disability is present. The remedy
is to reduce the brightness by screening or diffusing the light
sources, and the methods for doing this are part of current
techniques of lighting design. This form of glare is controlled
by the limiting glare index of the Illuminating Engineering
Society's code of practice (see p.84)

Flicker is a problem associated with flurorescent and other forms
of non-incandescent lighting. People vary widely in their
sensitivity to flicker, and lighting which causes acute annoyance
to one person may be perfectly satisfactory for another. Very

few people are so sensitive to flicker that they cannot work in
fluorescent lighting - those who do suffer in this way often
cannot watch television either (and so this is a good test for
malingerers). The remedies are primarily electrical, that is,
the lamps are wired into circuits in which the alternations of
the light from adjacent lamps are out of phase to give a more-
or-less uniform output of light.

Poor colour rendering, particularly of natural colours such
as the complexion or the colour of foodstuffs, was characteristic
of the early forms of fluorescent lighting, but there have been
major improvements over the years. It is still true that the
forms of fluorescent lighting which give the greatest advantage
so far as light output per unit of electrical power is concerned
are those which give the poorest rendering of colours. On the
other hand, if a lower light 'efficiency' can be accepted, as it
usually can, fluorescent lighting can give colour rendering which
is acceptable even in critical colour-judgement situations.

There is no evidence that any of the 'stress' effects of lighting have any effect on vision, either in the short term or the
long term. When fluorescent lighting was first introduced
there was a considerable amount of misgiving, particularly among
some medical people, that fluorescent lighting would cause real
harm to eyesight. At one period, for example, fluorescent
lighting was banned in the schools of France, and for many years
some hospital authorities would not permit fluorescent lighting
in hospitals. But if there had been any deleterious effect
on vision due to fluorescent lighting, this would have made itself apparent by now; many people have been working in fluorescent lighting for more than 20 years and there is no evidence
that the vision of any of them has deteriorated specifically
for this reason.

Direct sunlight probably causes the greatest visual distress
of any form of lighting, and it can even cause impairment of
vision. In the urban environment, man has a love-hate relationship with the sun, which creates many problems for the designer.
In the late 1940s the Post-War Building Study group in this
country made recommendations for the admission of sunlight into
buildings. The interpretation of these recommendations gave
rise to levels of insolation which were subsequently shown to be
excessive both on visual and thermal grounds. More recently
work has been completed which puts into better perspective
the compromise between admitting sunlight for its amenity value
and controlling or eliminating sunlight from rooms when there
is too much of it. The technology of design for the control
of sunlight and solar radiation is well developed, and the only
obstacle to its proper use is an economic one. In the climate
of Great Britain sunlight is not sufficiently frequent to demand
the relatively costly forms of solar control which are essential

for building in the tropics and in semitropical areas, for
example, the southern United States. Nevertheless, these
sophisticated techniques do exist and are available for use
even if, in practice, most people are content with simple
curtains or venetian blinds.

ACOUSTICS AND NOISE (Parkin and Humphreys 1958; Building
Bulletin 1975)
   Three factors have caused a radical change in the thinking
behind acoustic technology during the past few years, in
relation to buildings in cities and towns. These are, first,
the considerable increase in the volume of traffic and aircraft noise, second, the development of deep and open-plan
buildings and a consequent increase of internally generated
noise, and, finally, the changing pattern of response by people
to noise, of greater awareness and concern on the part of the
middle-aged and elderly, and the cult of noise by the adolescent.
As a result many of the basic psychophysical assumptions of
the earlier science of acoustics in buildings no longer apply.

   Until recently acoustic design in buildings was concerned
with two primary matters. First, there was the need to provide
the maximum acoustic insulation between one space and another,
both between adjacent internal spaces and between the building
and the world outside. Second, there was the need to create
reverberation characteristics in the space appropriate to the
activity. Of these the second was creative, but the first was
entirely prohibitive. The situation today demands that very
often it is necessary to create a 'masking background' against
which the sounds that one needs to hear are silhouetted, whereas
previously acoustic design attempted to create an environment in
which the wanted sounds were to be heard against a background of as
near silence as could be achieved.

   Spaces in buildings can be divided into different categories
according to the acoustic requirements. First, there are
acoustically isolated spaces, conforming to the old pattern,
for which there is still a considerable need. These are either
spaces which require complete quiet because of the activity
which goes on in them (for example, a doctor's consulting room)
or because the activity which goes on in them, if allowed to
penetrate outside, would cause annoyance to others (for example,
a noisy workshop in a school or a kitchen in a hospital).
Second, there are places which do not need to be completely
acoustically isolated, because people in them want to be aware
of the world outside, but where the amount of external noise
which penetrates should not be sufficient to cause interference
and annoyance. Hospital wards and domestic interiors are
examples - all the evidence is that people who are ill or people

living in their homes do not want to be totally isolated from
what is going on in the world outside, but do not want it to
intrude too much. Again, there are spaces where speech communication is important, but in which there are a number of different
conversations going on at the same time. This is the case in
open-plan buildings, and the requirement here is that speech in
the immediate communication group can be heard clearly but speech
from other groups should not obtrude and distract the attention.
In such spaces, above all, the need for masking noise of just the
right level is critical.

Acoustical design in buildings therefore has to do two essential
jobs. First, any communication between people, whether of speech,
music, or whatever, must be heard clearly and with no unnecessary
interference. Second, the acoustic character of the space must be
defined - whether it is to be dull, or lively and resonant, etc.
The analogy with lighting is clear. Just as good lighting enables
people to see well and also defines the visual character of the
space, so good acoustics enable people to hear well and also define
the aural character of the building.

Analogies between lighting and acoustics in buildings are helpful,
but should not be pressed too far. One significant difference is
that people are, as yet, not aware that the acoustic environment
is an artifact. While it is obvious to them that the lighting
environment is created by virtue of the provision of windows or
electric lighting, few people are aware that the materials of the
walls of the building, the carpets on the floor, the curtains,
the furniture, and even the people themselves all constitute part
of the created acoustic environment. To them the acoustic
environment 'just happens' - it is not part of the 'environmental
design'. However through the more common use of remedial measures
like double-glazing, people are slowly becoming conscious that
the sound pattern in a building can be controlled.

There are significant differences between the levels of energy
involved in lighting and accoustical design. The relationship between acoustic acuity and energy incident on the ear is very much
the same as in Fig.5.1 for lighting but the essential difference
is that far less can be done to control the amount of acoustical
energy than can be done to control the amount of light. The
only analogy here with the lighting situation is in the public-
address system, where the amount of energy produced by the human
voice is magnified and controlled to a level which permits every
individual in a large audience to hear clearly. In other
circumstances the hearer has to make do as best he can with the
amount of acoustical energy which reaches his ear. Nevertheless
it is useful to know that the response of the ear to sound
energy is very similar to that of the eye to light energy. In
the first place, there is the basic logarithmic response, that

is, equal ratios of incident sound energy produce equal differences in the sensory response. Again, there is also the
saturation effect as the limits of hearing are approached. Excessive sound causes acute discomfort and pain and finally the
destruction of the sensory process, as in the case of excessive
light falling on the eye. Adaptation to sound levels, however,
does not take place in the same way as adaptation in the visual
field. A good colour photograph of a scene projected on to a
screen at a level of lighting intensity perhaps 100th of the
original can still give a very accurate representation of the
original. An accurate sound recording of an event, played at
a much lower level of sound than the original, will not give
an accurate rendering, because the ear does not adapt in the
same way as the eye does. In compensation, though, the ear has
ways of selecting wanted sounds from a whole range of unwanted
sounds in a way which has some resemblances to, but many
differences from, the selection of wanted information by the
eye. It has become customary to refer to the wanted sound as
the 'signal' and to the unwanted sound in the background as the
'noise'. This custom arose from the development of telephone communication systems, where the requirement was to enhance
the wanted speech and reduce the unwanted background noise
that derives from the inherent limitations of the communication
system.   However, the analogy has been taken much farther and
has proved a useful one. At a cocktail party, for example, the
conversation with one's immediate interlocutor is the 'signal',
and all other conversations are the 'noise'. On the other hand,
if the conversation which is going on immediately to one's
right proves to be much more interesting then the attention can
be directed towards this other conversation, which then becomes
the 'signal' and all else including the uninteresting interlocutor then becomes the 'noise'. (This signal-and-noise concept
could also be applied in the visual field. To most people, the
picture hanging on the wall is the 'signal' and the pattern on
the wallpaper is the 'noise' - but to a wallpaper designer who
recognizes an original William Morris design, the reverse will
be true.)

Acoustic standards in buildings (British Standard Code of
Practice 1960)

   There are at the moment two forms of acoustic standard and
codes of recommended practices. First, there are the building
regulations, which lay down certain requirements, particularly
for sound insulation in buildings where external and internal
noise can be a serious problem. Second, there is the new
form of official 'guidelines', which offer quantitative advice
to the designer of an advisory rather than a mandatory form.
Both forms of code of practice have their particular value.

Most of the mandatory regulations are concerned with sound insulation. In dwellings, the chief problem is to isolate attached dwellings, whether flats or houses, from the noises of their neighbours. Other people's noises are much more trouble-some in dwellings than are the noises of the world outside, in general. Acoustic insulation in dwellings is, however, expen-sive because the nature of sound is such that the only satisfactory means of isolating one space from another is by the interposing of a massive, and therefore expensive, partition. Acoustic in-sulation regulations are a compromise between what is desired and what can be afforded. For example, the Building Research Station puts forward two standards of insulation recommendation for flats. The lower (BRS grade 2) corresponds to the lowest acceptable for the insulation between flats occupied by people in a relatively undemanding community where minimum cost is the overriding criterion. The higher grade of sound insulation (BRS grade 1) is acceptable in all normal situations and to most people, provided that there is no excessive source noises (such as that from audio amplifiers).

All the value of an expensive sound-insulating partitiion can be lost, however, if there is an air path between the source of sound and the receiver. Some air gaps are controllable, for example, open windows may be closed. But other air gaps occur around doors or through voids in the ceiling or along the ducts of the ventrilation of heating system. (A classical case of air-gap sound transmission occurred in a hospital in which no ex-pense had been spared in providing massive sound insulation to keep out the noise of the traffic from outside but the ducting for the heating and ventilating system permitted conversation in adjacent consulting rooms to be heard clearly.)

Sound insulation is assisted by attention to sophisticated details of design - for example, the 'double leaf' or 'cavity' construction, in which the partition, instead of consisting of one massive wall, consists of two separate walls (or in the case of a window, sheets of glass) with an air space in between. The principle is to absorb the incident energy at the first leaf and so break up the continuity of the sound path, absorbing as much of the transmitted sound in the cavity as possible and so limiting the amount of sound which has to pass through the second leaf. The design, spacing, sealing, and sound-absorbing characteristics of the leaves and intervening spaces are critical for optimum performance.

The acoustic character of a space is partly governed by the amount of external sound which the sound insulation permits to penetrate into the space, but is affected to a greater extent by the reflecting and absorbing characteristics of the internal surfaces of the space. The hard tiling of a bathroom

produces a totally different acoustic character to that of a
living room with thick-piled carpet and heavy curtains. The
sound-reflecting and -absorbing characteristics of the surfaces
of a room determine the reverberation time, that is, the time
which sound takes to die away to an imperceptible level. (This
is not the same as an 'echo', which is the unimpaired reflection
of an incident sound - the reverberant sound in a room is diffused by multiple reflections, so that its coherence is largely
lost.) The ideal reverberation time in a room depends on the
nature of the activity. Ordinary conversation and domestic
activities require a relatively short reverberation time, say
half a second or less, leading to the general use of carpets,
soft furniture, and heavy curtains to create the desirable
'warmth' of a domestic interior. At the other end of the scale,
concert halls and cathedrals need much longer reverberation times,
of the order of 1.5 - 5 seconds. In the case of a concert hall
there needs to be a compromise between 'clarity' and 'richness',
the former requiring a short reverberation time and the latter
a longer reverberation time. Requirements for lecture halls
and teaching spaces are between these extremes.

Architects are therefore faced with the problem of reaching a
compromise between the cost and effectiveness of acoustic
design. The compromise is quite different in different situations. It is the achieving of the correct compromise which
constitutes the technology of acoustics. The urban building
problem is entirely different from that of buildings isolated
in the country. While in theory it is possible (although
at great cost) to achieve the acoustic isolation of a building
even in a noisy urban environment, in practice this is difficult
or impossible. A building can be isolated from the higher
frequencies of external noise but the lower frequencies, at the
lower threshold of hearing, cannot be so easily removed. To
a great many people the 'thump, thump' and rumble of the lower
frequencies generated by heavy traffic are actually more
distressing in the absence of the higher frequencies. Again,
if a great deal of money is spent on achieving acoustic isolation
from the world outside, it is totally false economy to save
money on the acoustic insulation in the building itself. More
distress may be caused by the internally generated noises
penetrating into quiet rooms, such as consulting rooms in a
hospital, or libraries in a school, than would be caused by
traffic noise.

A typical example of new thinking in acoustic design is
illustrated by *'Guidelines for environmental design of educational
buildings'*, (1972). These guidelines lay down criteria for
different types of teaching area. In open plan teaching
areas teaching takes place in the form of small groups of
perhaps four to ten children with a teacher or group leader,
and there may be five or six such groups in the same large

room. For such spaces, the *Guidelines* recommend that there
should be a background 'masking' noise, which should be kept
strictly within an upper and a lower limit. If the masking
noise is too loud, then it obtrudes on the teacher and causes
irritation and annoyance. On the other hand, if the background
is too quiet, the activities of groups overlap and teaching is
difficult. The background noise should be just high enough not to
cause annoyance and yet to mask the sounds from other groups.
This masking noise can be generated partly by admitting a limited
amount of noise from outside and partly by allowing internally
generated noise to build up through the medium of internally
reflected sound. In an urban area traffic noise itself will almost certainly provide an ample source of background noise, and
the skill of the acoustic designer lies in filtering this noise
through the outer leaf of the building in such a way that the
level and frequency distribution of the admitted sound is of the
right order to act as a mask to speech. It so happens,
fortuitously, that the frequency distribution of traffic noise,
and the insulating characteristics of many forms of building
construction do permit just such a required masking characteristic to be achieved. The theoretical principles are complex,
but fortunately the application in practice is well within
the competence of the acoustics consultant or environmental
designer. A similar, though not identical, form of acoustic
design is required in hospital wards. Many patients who have
been transferred from a hospital in a town to a hospital in the
country find that the transition is not as idyllic as they had
hoped. In the absence of traffic noise, internal noises in the
ward, no longer masked by the traffic noises, become intrusive
and distressing. In hospitals with heavy traffic during the
week but light traffic at the weekends, patients have been known
to express a longing for the weekend to end quickly so that the
traffic noise would start again. Consequently, while the same
principles apply in hospital wards as in open-plan teaching
spaces, the precise requirements are different, because the
internally generated noises are not the same, and the requirements for communication are not the same, (the doctor or
nurse speaking to the patient is much closer than the teacher
speaking to a group of children and there is need for privacy
which there is not in the open-plan classroom) and so the
frequency characteristics and loudness level are quite different
in the two cases.

Acoustic stress conditions

As in the case of lighting, the 'complaint' level for noise
is lower than the level which is likely to cause impairment of
work performance. It is generally recognized that unfavourable
acoustical conditions produce a feeling of distress, discomfort,

or annoyance simply due to the presence of noise. Although
noise by itself can cause general fatigue, if, (as in the classroom situation) information has to be communicated by speech,
there is an additional problem of straining to hear above the
background noise, and this will add to the general feeling of
fatigue, annoyance, or tiredness caused by the noise itself.
Such difficulties can occur at quite moderate levels of sound,
well below those likely to give rise to temporary or permanent
hearing loss. The next stage in the stress effects of noise
occurs when the levels of sound are sufficiently high to give
rise to a temporary hearing loss. Although the adaptation process of the ear is different from that of the eye, nevertheless
there is some slight analogy in the sense that, just as when
one goes out into a poorly lit street at night from a brightly
lit interior some minutes elapse before one can see clearly,
so also if one has been subjected to a high level of noise
(say from a pneumatic drill) then on returning to a normal
speech-communication situation it may be a little time before
one's hearing has recovered sufficiently to hear clearly what
is being said. This is temporary hearing loss. In normal
circumstances no permanent damage results, but it has now
been shown that continuous exposure to noise which occasions
temporary hearing loss may result, in the long term, in some
permanent hearing loss. This, therefore, is the final stage
of stress effects, the development of permanent hearing loss
due to exposure to noise. If the noise levels are very considerable, then the permanent hearing loss may occur either
instantaneously or after only a short period of exposure. At
lower levels the time of exposure which gives rise to permanent
hearing loss may be much longer. The relationship between time
of exposure, level of incident sound and loss of hearing is
now much better understood (Kryter 1970).

The problems from discontinuous sound produced by traffic,
on the one hand, and aircraft, on the other, are different.
In the case of traffic noise in towns, a busy traffic route will
produce an almost continuous rumble, on which the noises of
individual cars or lorries will be superimposed. In the case of
aircraft noise, there are periods of relative quiet, even near
a busy airport in between the noise of each passing aircraft.
In either case the problem is to evaluate the sound in terms of
one single 'noise index' which will correlate satisfactorily
with the opinions of people who experience the sound. In the
case of traffic noise the solution has been to measure the
sound level over a long period and to express the intensity
of the sound in terms of that level which is exceeded for only
10 per cent of the measuring time. It will be appreciated that
this is a compromise between the peak levels that occur when
a single heavy lorry goes by and the average levels, which do

not take adequately into account the annoyance caused by the peak levels. Since it is usual to make the measurements for the period of 18 hours from 6 a.m., when the volume of traffic usually begins to be noticeable, to 12 midnight, when it usually diminishes considerably, this traffic-noise measurement is known as the 'L_{10} 18-hour level'. This parameter is often referred to in statements about traffic-noise levels.

The Government Committee on the Problem of Noise (the Wilson Committee) (Wilson 1963) has made recommendations for the tolerable values of this L_{10} traffic-noise parameter for various situations. More recently, the Urban Motorways Committee of the Department of the Environment recommended that, where motorways and other major traffic routes were built through towns, those dwellings which received an L_{10} 18-hour noise level in excess of a certain value (originally 70 dBA since revised to 68 dBA) should be assisted by compensation payments to insulate their dwellings against such traffic noise (by double-glazing or roof-glazing.

In the case of aircraft noise, the L_{10} value does not apply. Instead, a different form of evaluation, termed the 'noise and number index' (NNI), is used. This is an index based on a formula which takes into account the noise level produced by the aircraft and also the number of aircraft which fly over during the relevant period.

The existence of these two different criteria for the evaluation of noise disturbance illustrates the problems that the environmental designer and legislator have to face. There are no simple methods of evaluating disturbance, distress, and harm from noise, and each type of situation has to be considered independently on its merits. It is highly probable that when the mechanism of noise assessment by the brain is more fully understood, a single uniform method of evaluating noise in urban situations will be forthcoming, but at the moment there is no sign of a breakthrough, and the present rather unsatisfactory empirical approach has to be accepted as the best which is available.

THE THERMAL ENVIRONMENT IN URBAN BUILDINGS (Bedford 1948; IHVE Guide)

The problems of thermal comfort in urban buildings differ little, if at all, from those in rural areas - a situation which is not the same as that encountered with lighting and acoustics. The thermal environment also differs in that no primary sensory process is involved and it transmits no 'information'. The human body is in a situation of passive rather than active response. In addition, while the problems of lighting and acoustics demand a detailed knowledge of the special sense, those of thermal comfort can be readily appreciated by the non-

specialist physiologist or biologist. There is therefore no need to treat the thermal-comfort problem here in the same detail as that of lighting and vision, hearing and acoustics.

Such special problems as there are regarding the thermal environment in buildings in urban situations are associated more with the methods available for heating and ventilating buildings than with the responses of the people in the buildings. The close proximity of buildings in towns means that methods of heating such as district heating and the use of 'waste' heat from power stations can be considered; thus good standards of thermal comfort can be achieved economically. To a lesser extent also, the large amount of waste heat from buildings raises the temperature of the central parts of large cities (1 or 2°C) so that the difference between inside and outside temperatures is less; and in theory, it should be cheaper to heat a town building by whatever means is used. This urban climatic effect (see Chapter 4), which is well attested by measurement, nevertheless plays little or no part in the design of heating systems for town buildings.

As in the cases of lighting and acoustics, the environmental design problems associated with producing an acceptable thermal environment involve first, the nature of the activity which is going on in the building, and, equally important, the comfort and health of people in the building. The relationship between thermal environment, the activities of people, and the kind of clothing which they wear has been thoroughly studied over the years, and there is no lack of data upon which designs can be based. For example, in *Guidelines for environmental design of educational buildings* (1972) there are different standards for the thermal environments of areas where there is intense activity (such as gymnasia), for areas where there is normal activity (such as conventional teaching rooms), and for areas where there is little or no activity (such as libraries, quiet rooms, or teaching spaces for disabled children). These different types of space need different kinds of thermal treatment (Humphreys 1973; Humphreys and Nicol 1970).

For a given level of activity and clothing characteristics, the problem is to design a thermal environment which will be comfortable and which will permit efficient work or activity appropriate to the purpose. The thermal response of the body to the environment is governed by a number of factors which are linked physically in the environment itself and linked physiologically in the metabolic system of the human being. Four main factors are the air temperature, the humidity of the air, the rate of air movement, and the mean radiant temperature of the surfaces of the space (the walls, floor, ceiling, and, above all, the windows, especially if these are large, as in many modern buildings). Both the physical and the physiological links are complicated, and as a result all attempts

to produce one single figure as a measure of the comfort of the thermal environment have proved abortive. Of the various thermal comfort indices that of 'equivalent temperature', which has been widely used in Great Britain, is probably the best in that it takes into account air temperature, air movement and the effects of radiation from surrounding surfaces. The index is criticized because it does not take into account humidity, and so improved scales have been developed, although, so far, they have not received much currency. The latest standards of thermal comfort recommend standards of air temperatures and mean radiant temperature only (the mean radiant temperature is the average temperature of the surrounding surfaces in the room).

As with many comfort indices, a relatively simple index can be used if like is being compared with like. For example, in comparing two buildings, both provided with conventional hot-water-radiator heating systems, comparison of the air temperature will probably give all the necessary information about the relative degree of comfort to be experienced in each. On the other hand, if one building is heated by hot-water radiators and the other by a warm-air-circulating system, which warms the air but does very little to heat the walls of the space, comparison of air temperature will give a misleading impression: for the same air temperature the hot-water-radiator building in winter will be more comfortable than the warm-air system, especially to somebody sitting near to a window. It is where like is compared with unlike that there is a need for more sophisticated thermal comfort indices.

The building-engineering problem of design for thermal comfort is threefold. First, there is the design of the heating system itself, to generate enough heat inside the building to raise the interior temperature conditions to a level sufficiently far above those prevailing outside, ensuring the continuing thermal comfort of people inside the building. Second, there is the problem of providing an outer skin to the building with insulating properties which will prevent as much as possible of this internally generated heat from escaping to the outside. Finally, there is the problem of designing the building in such a way that in the hot days of summer solar radiation is allowed to penetrate into the building only to an extent sufficient to warm it to the comfort level and not beyond.

The first problem is to define the required internal temperature conditions and to relate these to the expected external conditions, which, of course, can only be predicted on a statistical basis. The heating engineer therefore has to design a heating plant which is sufficient to cope with the heating of the building on the coldest days yet will be flexible enough to adjust to short-term and long-term

fluctuations. While a great deal of adjustment is possible through ventilation (that is, by allowing heat to be removed from the building by air current), this is obviously expensive because ventilated heat is waste heat. More sophisticated environmental control systems are desirable if heat can be conserved when it is not required and made available when it is. One solution to the problem of predicting the external temperature conditions is to provide a main heating system which has just sufficient capacity to raise the building temperature to the comfort zone on days when the outside temperature is no lower than some value well above the expected minimum. A secondary heating system is provided for 'topping up' on really cold days. Such a dual system may be cheaper in operating costs but it will be more expensive in capital costs and may involve the problem of creating space for two kinds of heating unit at the expense of other priorities such as storage space in a school classroom or a hospital ward. The problems of heat loss and insulation in winter and heat gain and solar protection in summer are similar though not identical. Internally generated heat is a different (long-wavelength) form of radiation to solar radiation (short-wavelengths), and some building materials, particularly glass, have completely different transmitting characteristics to the two forms of radiation. Glass is highly transmitting to direct solar radiation but has a much lower transmission to radiation from warm surfaces in the room (this, of course, is the origin of the well-known 'greenhouse' effect). Heat is lost from a building by conduction through the external walls, the floor, the ceiling and roof, and the windows, by convection (for example, by the ventilation system) and by radiation to the outside air. Loss by radiation will not occur if the insulation of the external walls is so good that no heat is allowed to reach the external radiating skin of the building. This is in practice impossible, and so buildings act just like any other radiators and lose heat more when the external conditions are conducive to the loss of heat from the earth generally (for example, on cold, cloudless nights in winter). Heat loss by convection can be minimized by limiting the number of openable windows and doors through which warm air can escape.

The major loss of internally generated heat is by conduction through the walls. The laws of thermal insulation are different from those of acoustic insulation, and part of the environmental designer's problem is to produce external walls which are both thermally and acoustically insulating to the required degrees. Whereas the air space between leaves of the building is critical to acoustic insulation in the case of thermal insulation it is less so. The design of the insulating system, so far as the air spaces are concerned, may be governed by acoustic consider-

ations, but where the mass, density, porosity, and reflectivity to radiation are concerned, thermal considerations will be given greater importance. An external wall system may therefore consist of two or more main leaves, for example, an external layer of brick and an internal layer of brick or breeze block, with one or more intervening cavities which may be filled with light, air-retaining porous material.

Even a complicated design of external wall system would not be entirely satisfactory for its purpose unless the skin on the internal wall is of a material of very low thermal conductivity, such as a layer of expanded polystyrene. Such a wall will then have a sufficiently high surface temperature to avoid 'cold-radiation' effects for people sitting close to it.

The thermal insulation properties of external walls are not the only properties to be taken into account. The thermal capacity of the building as a whole, including the external walls (that is, the capacity of the building to absorb and retain heat) has a profound effect on thermal comfort. In a school, in which the heating system is shut down in the early evening, a construction of high thermal capacity will take much longer to warm up in the morning, and so for the first two or three hours of the school day the surface temperatures will be too low, even though the air temperature is up to the required standard. A building with high thermal capacity is slow to respond to changes in the internally generated heat and also to changes in the air temperature outside. On the other hand, a building with high thermal capacity is preferable where the use is fairly continuous, because the high thermal capacity creates a 'fly-wheel effect' which evens out fluctuations and preserves a more regular thermal environment.

The problem of solar-heat control (Hopkinson 1967) in summer is more difficult, because it is related to people's often irrational response to sunlight and solar heat. In the climate of Great Britain, people will often willingly accept degrees of thermal discomfort from the sun which they would never accept from a manmade heating system. This is not true, however, in tropical countries, where the sun is all too constant and prominent a feature of the natural environment. As a result, solar-heat control systems which have been designed for sunny countries are not acceptable in Great Britain.

Solar radiation can enter a building (a) through the windows and (b) through the roof and walls. Solar radiation through the windows poses the greater psychological problems. In a particular environment or even on a particular occasion, the visual and thermal effects of sunlight may produce entirely opposite reactions. People may want sunlight to come into the room to cheer it up or to enhance the visual character, but the resultant temperature rise may be unacceptable. The ideal answer would be a type of glazing that admitted light radiation but excluded the longer-

wavelength radiation which causes the greater part of the
heating effect.   This, of course, is the purpose of the
various forms of heat-absorbing or heat-reflecting glass
which architects who design fully glazed buildings have been
forced to use.

The use of blinds to exclude solar radiation also poses
certain problems.   In order to avoid internal temperature
rises, it is necessary to exclude solar radiation of all wave-
lengths before it passes through the glass.   Once in the
building the radiation will warm up internal surfaces, including any blind which is hung internally behind the glass,
and these surfaces will then act as secondary radiators.
Such secondary radiation will be of too long a wavelength
to escape back through the glass, and so the temperature of
the interior will rise.   Ideally, therefore, blinds should be
outside the window, as is customary in tropical countries, but
there are then problems of deterioration and maintenance.

Solar radiation passing in through the fabric of the
building can be controlled, but not necessarily by the same
methods which are used to prevent the escape of internally
generated winter heat to the outside.   Highly reflecting
surfaces, whether with white diffusing characteristics (like
paint or white chippings) or with metallic reflecting properties such as an aluminium reflecting skin, are efficient
means of reducing fabric-gained radiation.

The thermal-capacity characteristics of the building are
also important in the solar-radiation problem.   A building of
high thermal capacity will take time to heat up, and so,
during the early part of the day, after a cold night, while
the building is at a lower temperature than the air, and
provided that solar radiation through the windows is excluded,
thermal conditions inside the building may be fully acceptable.   But when the building has heated to the air temperature
the high thermal capacity will no longer be useful.   However,
this 'heat-sink' effect in buildings of high thermal capacity
is of value in tropical and semi-tropical countries where the
work pattern is different and allows for an afternoon siesta.

Natural and mechanical ventilation and air-cooling and conditioning

As the design of buildings becomes more sophisticated the
traditional use of windows for providing natural ventilation
becomes less acceptable to the environmental designer, because
it is not under his control.   Recourse to mechanical ventilation,
then to ventilation with air-cooling, and finally to full air-
conditioning, which controls temperature, humidity, cleanliness,
and amount of air moving through a building becomes an integral
part of the environmental design.   A total artificial environment

is the logical conclusion of this increasing sophistication in building services engineering. Other thermal parameters, hitherto negligible, become important. In a highly insulated building, with restricted windows, the amounts of energy necessary to provide adequate lighting in the absence of daylight provide such a high proportion of the total thermal load that in some buildings the lighting heat, combined with the heat radiated by the human inhabitants (ten inactive people or five active people are the equivalent of 1 kW of electrical heating), may be sufficient to heat the building adequately on all but the coldest winter days. In summer this heating load, together with the solar radiation intake, may make air-cooling and air-conditioning absolutely essential. The logic of the situation has then led inevitably to what is now called 'integrated environmental design'. This is a term which can now no longer be used in a general sense because it has been appropriated by the Electricity Council in Great Britain for the special form of building design which the Council has developed for its own office and other buildings. These buildings are characterized by walls of high thermal insulation, with narrow vertical slit windows, double-glazing, and a totally controlled artificial environment which makes the fullest use of heat from the lighting by fluorescent lamps, the body heat of the inhabitants, and the heat generated by internal machinery such as business machines. Some architects, especially those concerned with school buildings, feel that there is an element of inhumanity in such exclusion of the outside world from the working environment. But it is not possible to put an 'amenity factor' into the heat-balance equations. In physical and economic terms, 'integrated environmental design' may have a case. In psychological terms, it may fail completely. So runs the argument.

CONCLUSION

The interaction between people and buildings in cities and towns, in terms of environmental design, is highly complex and only a few of the salient points have been mentioned here. Many other factors, of paramount importance in certain special types of building, have either been glossed over or not mentioned at all. But enough has, perhaps, been indicated of the stress conditions which can arise from faulty environmental design - faulty either through ignorance or through lack of resources.

Many valuable contributions were made to the study of environmental design in the 1950s by the setting up of joint committees of the Medical Research Council and the Building Research Board, in which physicists and engineers, architects, and medical authorities sat round the table and discussed a great many general and special problems of environmental design, from ventilation

rates in schools and hospitals to problems of stress through
noise, and the lighting of schools for the partially sighted.
These formal opportunities for joint discussion of mutual
problems are of value, because although informal co-operation
between medical and non-medical specialists is greater than
it once was, nevertheless the two groups do tend to operate
more independently than is desirable.

There are many problems where co-operation between planners,
sociologists, and building engineers is still essential -
problems which remain unsolved for lack of such co-operation.
For example, the building of high-rise dwellings was a development for which architects and town planners were essentially
responsible. Warnings from environmental engineers of the
thermal, visual, and acoustic problems generally went unheeded,
even though these warnings were well documented with physical
facts and predictions. Warnings from sociologists also received less than full consideration. It is too late now to
rectify these particular mistakes, but it may not be too late
to prevent the next round of mistakes being made. It has been
suggested that a form of city building which ought to be studied
as a possible alternative (Hopkinson 1965) to the high-rise
dwelling block is a form of development of the old mediaeval
idea of 'living over the shop', that is, work places and
living places in the same building, with consequent reduction
in commuter travel. There are, of course, objections to the
system, particularly now that people have grown used to the
idea of living away from their work; but things were not always
so, and a change back could occur. Certainly if urban travel
becomes only slightly more difficult than it is at the moment,
the idea of 'living over the shop' could prove to be as attractive as it once was. It is in directions such as these that
urgent work is needed.

Another area in which adequate study is lacking is that of the
physiological cost of working in an environment which is outside the limits of comfort but within the limits of tolerability.
There is a great deal known about the behaviour of the human
body in environmental conditions approaching tolerability
limits, but not about our reactions in just-bearable conditions.
For example, there is very little known of the effect on teachers
and children of working in school in a hot summer's day in a room
with big windows and no blinds, with the temperatures up beyond
30 °C, far too hot to be comfortable but not too hot to give up
and send everybody home. People in offices and factories suffer
similarly, but because next morning they appear to have fully
recovered from overheating the day before then no one expresses
concern. The powers of recuperation of the human body are
certainly remarkable, but, as in the case of prolonged exposure to
noise, it may be proved that exposure to visual or thermal discomfort also has long-term effects.

REFERENCES

BARTLETT, F.C. and POLLOCK, M.G. (1935) *Industrial Health Research Board Report,* No.65 HMSO, London.

BEDFORD, T. (1948) *Basic Principles of Ventilation and Heating.* H.K.Lewis, London (2nd ed. 1964).

BRITISH STANDARD CODE OF PRACTICE CP3, (1960) Chapter 3. *Sound Insulation and Noise Reduction.* British Standards Institution, London.

BRITISH STANDARD CODE OF PRACTICE CP3, (1964) Chapter 1, Part 1. *Daylighting.* British Standards Institution, London.

Guidelines for Environmental Design of Educational Buildings (1972) Department of Education and Science, London.

HOPKINSON, R.G. (1963) *Architectural Physics: Lighting.* HMSO, London.

HOPKINSON, R.G. (1965) *The Evaluation of the Built Environment.* H.K.Lewis for University College, London.

HOPKINSON, R.G. (ed.) (1967) *Sunlight in Buildings.* Bouwcentrum International, Rotterdam for the Commission Internationale de l'Eclairage.

HOPKINSON, R.G. and COLLINS, J.B. (1970). *The Ergonomics of Lighting.* Macdonald, London.

HOPKINSON, R.G. and KAY, J.D. (1969) *The Lighting of Buildings.* Faber, London (2nd edn 1972).

HOPKINSON, R.G. and LONGMORE, J. (1959) The permanent supplementary artificial lighting of interiors. *Trans. Illum. Engng. Sc.* (London) 24, 121-46.

HUMPHREYS, M.A. (1973) Classroom temperature, clothing and thermal comfort - a study of secondary school children in summertime. *JIHVE,* 41, 191-202.

HUMPHREYS, M.A. and NICOL, J.F. (1970) An investigation into thermal comfort of office workers. *JIHVE,* 38, 181-9.

IES Code. (Editions 1936, 1941, 1946, 1955, 1961, 1968, 1973). *Recommended Practice for Good Lighting.* Illuminating Engineering Society, London.

THE IHVE GUIDE (annually)   Institution of Heating and
Ventilating Engineers (London).

KRYTER, K. (1970)   *The effects of noise on man (pp.140-44)*
Academic Press, New York.

LE CORBUSIER (JANNERET, C.) (1933) *La Ville Radieuse.* Edns.
d'Arch. d'aujourd'hui, Boulogne.

LUCKIESH, M. and MOSS, F.K.   (1937)   *The Science of Seeting.*
D. van Nostrand, New York.

PARKIN PARKIN, P.H. and HUMPHREYS, H. (1958 and subsequent reprinting)
Acoustics, Noise,and Buildings. Faber, London.

PLANNING CRITERIA AND DESIGN OF BUILDINGS (1971)   *Sunlight and
Daylight.*   HMSO, London.

SORSBY, A., BENJAMIN, B. and SHERIDAN, M. (1961)   Refraction
... during the growth of the eye ...   *Med.Res.Counc.Sp.Rep.
Ser. No. 301.*

VITRUVIUS MARCUS POLLIO   (c.55 B.C.)   *De Architectura.*
Translated as   *The Ten books on architecture* by M.H. Morgan
(1914) re-issued by Dover, New York.

WILSON, A. (Chairman) (1963)   *Noise - Final Report of the
Committee on the Problem of Noise.*   HMSO, London.

6 Traffic problems in towns considered quantitatively

R. J. Smeed

The congestion difficulties now occurring in our towns are, of course, due to the large amounts of traffic relative to the facilities available for dealing with them. It is desirable, therefore, to consider the matter quantitatively, and a summary of the results of an attempt to tackle the subject in an approximate quantitative manner is given in this chapter. Inevitably, however, in an article of limited length a number of major points have had to be glossed over or omitted altogether, but further details are given in the original papers to which reference is made.

A natural starting point is to examine the relationship, if any, between the speed of traffic and its amount on a single road. An extensive survey of the speeds and amounts of traffic between controlled intersections on major roads of various widths was carried out by the then newly-formed Traffic and Safety Division of the Road Research Laboratory in the late 1940s. The observations were analysed by Wardrop (1952) and his main results are shown in Fig.6.1.

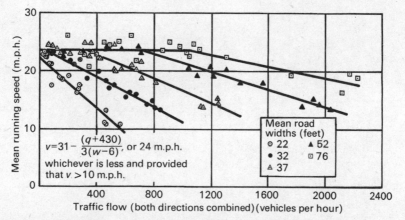

In the figure:

$$v = 31 - \frac{(q+430)}{3(w-6)}, \text{ or } 24 \text{ m.p.h.}$$

whichever is less and provided that $v > 10$ m.p.h.

Mean road widths (feet)
⊙ 22   ▲ 52
● 32   ☐ 76
△ 37

Fig. 6.1 Relations between mean journey speed and flow in Central London (after Wardrop 1952).

It will be seen that for speeds above 10 m.p.h. the mean speed
of traffic could be deduced, to a considerable extent, from the
width of the road and the number of vehicles travelling on it per
unit time. The quantitative relationship is of the kind that
would qualitatively have been expected. For a given amount of
traffic, the wider the road the higher the average speed. For a
road of given width, the greater the volume of traffic the slower
the speed.

Fig.6.1 applies to stretches of road between controlled intersections. The phenomena at intersections must be considered in a
different manner. The saturation flow — that is, the number of
vehicles that can pass through a signal controlled intersection
per hour of green phase time — had been investigated before the
Second World War in Great Britain and elsewhere. Some results of
a comprehensive investigation by the Road Research Laboratory,
published by Webster (1958), are shown in Fig.6.2. In that figure

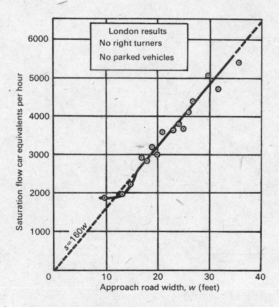

Fig. 6.2 Effect of approach road width on saturation flow in
London (after Webster 1958).

the amounts of traffic are expressed as car equivalents, a motor-
cycle being equivalent to 0.5 car, a medium commercial vehicle to
2 cars, and a heavy commercial vehicle or bus to 3 cars. The

graph suggests, again as might be expected, that the number of
vehicles that can pass through a given intersection in a given
direction in a given time is roughly proportional to the duration
of that time and to the width of the road.   It is also dependent
on the number of right turners and is affected by parked vehicles.
With a knowledge of (a) the effects of such factors on saturation
flow, (b) the green and red times on a given approach road, (c) the
numbers of vehicles of various kinds on the road concerned, and
(d) the numbers of right turners and the amounts of parking, it is
possible to deduce the average delay experienced by the vehicles
on the approach roads concerned.   Agreement between observed and
calculated delay is reasonably good as is shown in Fig.6.3.

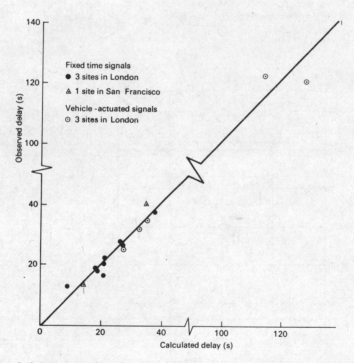

Fig.6.3 Observed and calculated average delays at traffic signals.

The results shown in Figs.6.1 and 6.2 give us knowledge of the
effects of the amount of traffic on speed between intersections
and on delay at intersections.   Clearly it should be possible to
combine the two results and obtain a relation between amounts and
journey speed of traffic.   A comprehensive analysis was carried

out by Wardrop (1968) and his main results are given in Fig.6.4.

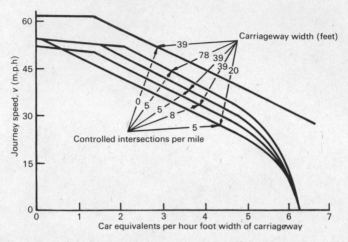

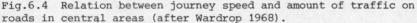

Fig.6.4 Relation between journey speed and amount of traffic on roads in central areas (after Wardrop 1968).

It will be seen that the journey speed is related to the number of controlled intersections per unit length of road and to the flow of traffic per unit width of carriageway. However, detailed analysis shows that, for widths greater than about 30 feet, the width effect is not important and the mean speed of traffic is largely controlled by the flow per unit width and by the number of controlled intersections per mile of road.

Since the number of controlled intersections per mile of road averages about five in Central London and since, at simple inter-sections, about half the signal cycle time is green for any approach flow, it is possible to deduce an average relation for an average road in Central London greater than 30 feet in width. This was done by Wardrop in 1968, and his formula and curve, with the results of some measurements by Thomson (1967) are shown in Fig.6.5.

This formula may — for analytical purposes — be interpreted as meaning that, on average, each car using a road during a one-hour period requires a width $1/(68-0.13\ v^2)$ feet. A bus or heavy commercial vehicle would require three times this width. The formula should not, of course, be interpreted as meaning that on a road w feet wide one car per hour can travel at $v = 10$ m.p.h. on a piece of road 1/55 foot wide, but that 55w cars per hour can travel at 10 m.p.h. on a road w feet wide providing that w is

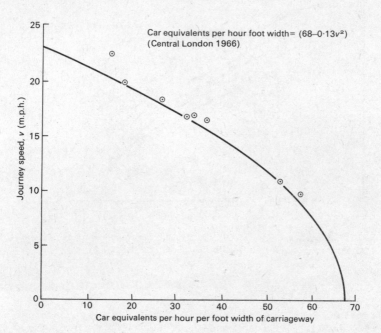

Car equivalents per hour foot width= $(68-0.13v^2)$
(Central London 1966)

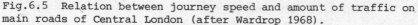

Fig.6.5 Relation between journey speed and amount of traffic on main roads of Central London (after Wardrop 1968).

greater than 30 feet (Smeed 1968).

Some results (Smeed 1968) of assuming that this formula applies to town centres in general, not merely the individual roads of Central London, will now be examined. Let the ground surface of the central area of a town have an area A square feet, where the central area is defined as that area in which the number of controlled intersections per mile is high, usually three or more. This area will usually be small, and the great majority of vehicular journeys will be between points within the central area and points outside it. Let the average distance travelled within the central area be d. Then, for areas of the same shape and similar road networks, it is to be expected that d would be proportional to $A^{\frac{1}{2}}$. Calculations of the average distance between points on the boundary of A and random points on the road network within it have been carried out in a large number of idealized and actual road networks, and some examples are shown in Fig.6.6, in which equal

numbers of vehicles have been assumed to enter or leave the area
at each point at which a road meets the boundary. The figures
suggest that the constants of proportionality do not vary greatly
with the shape of the area and the design of the network. It is
not, however, necessary to postulate this, and it will be assumed
that in any town the average distance travelled is KA^2, K possibly
being different in different towns. Since each vehicle per hour

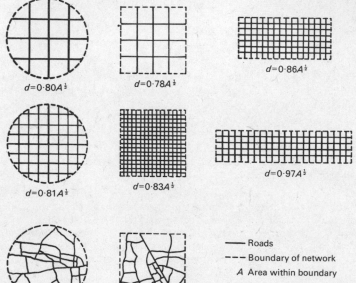

$d = 0.80A^{\frac{1}{2}}$ $d = 0.78A^{\frac{1}{2}}$ $d = 0.86A^{\frac{1}{2}}$

$d = 0.81A^{\frac{1}{2}}$ $d = 0.83A^{\frac{1}{2}}$ $d = 0.97A^{\frac{1}{2}}$

$d = 0.89A^{\frac{1}{2}}$ $d = 0.86A^{\frac{1}{2}}$

—— Roads
--- Boundary of network
A Area within boundary
d Average distance travelled

Fig.6.6 Average distance travelled on some imaginary and real
road networks.

requires a width of road $1/(68-0.13\ v^2)$ feet and a length of road
$KA^{\frac{1}{2}}$ feet, it requires an area of carriageway $KA^{\frac{1}{2}}/(68-0.13\ v^2)$ square
feet. If Q car equivalents cross the boundary of the town centre
per hour, the total area of carriageway required to accommodate
the vehicles is $KQA^2/(68-0.13\ v^2)$ square feet. If the fraction of
the town centre used for carriageway is f, the total area of
carriageway available is fA square feet. Since these two expressions for the area of carriageway must be equal to one another,†

---

† Strictly it should be assumed that the area needed is equal to
the area available in every small ·division of the town centre, but

it follows that

$$\frac{KQA^{\frac{1}{2}}}{68-0.13 \ v^2} = fA,$$

and that

$$Q = \frac{1}{K} \ (68-0.13 \ v^2) \ fA^{\frac{1}{2}}.$$

Smeed (1968) gives some values for Q, v, f, and A for eleven British towns, and it is possible to deduce the values of K for each town from these data. All the values lie between 1.89 and 3.78 and it follows that Q varies between $(18-0.0345 \ v^2) \ fA^{\frac{1}{2}}$ and $(36-0.069 \ v^2) \ fA^{\frac{1}{2}}$.

In either case, the speed under light traffic conditions can be found by putting $Q = 0$, and is the same in both cases,

$$\sqrt{(\frac{18}{0.0345})} = \sqrt{(\frac{36}{0.069})} = 23 \ \text{m.p.h.}$$

The quantity $Q/fA^{\frac{1}{2}}$ is, according to these results, a function of speed, and its values, deduced from the above formulae, are given in Table 6.1.

Now it is found by experience that, at peak periods, the speed of traffic in the central areas of most towns is between about 8 m.p.h. and 12 m.p.h. Table 6.1 suggests that, at these speeds, $Q/fA^{\frac{1}{2}}$ would lie between, say, 13 and 31, and it seems worthwhile investigating the accuracy of this prediction. Some values of $Q/fA^{\frac{1}{2}}$ at peak periods for the central areas of various towns are therefore given in Table 6.2.

It will be seen that agreement between measured and predicted values is fairly good at peak periods. It is also fairly good at lightly trafficked periods, since average journey speed cannot reach the permitted running speed values of 30 m.p.h. because of the presence of controlled intersections and because some drivers do not desire to travel as fast as this. These results suggest that the formulae can be fairly reliably used in problems requiring some knowledge of the relation between the speed of traffic in towns and its amount.

---

since road-layout designers have tended to build roads at the places at which they are required, and since vehicle drivers tend to choose routes which have road space available, it is sufficient to use one overall equation.

TABLE 6.1

Calculated limits of value of $Q/fA^{\frac{1}{2}}$ at various speeds

Speed (m.p.h.)	$Q/fA^{\frac{1}{2}}$	
	Lower limit	Upper limit
0+	18	36
5	17	34
7.5	16	32
10	15	29
12.5	13	25
15	10	20
17.5	7	15
20	4	8
22.8	0	0

TABLE 6.2

Values of $Q/fA^{\frac{1}{2}}$

Great Britain		Elsewhere	
Edinburgh	12	St. Helier, Channel Islands	9
Bradford	14	Salisbury, Rhodesia	11
Maidenhead	15	Leiden, Netherlands	12
Darlington	15	Dublin, Ireland	12
Liverpool	17	Hamburg, Germany	14
Hull	19	Lisbon, Portugal	14
Nottingham	19	Tel-Aviv, Israel	14
Leeds	21	Denver, Colorado, USA	17
Sheffield	21	Stockholm, Sweden	18
Exeter	23	Göteborg, Sweden	24
Cardiff	24	Madrid, Spain	26
Birmingham	24	Washington, D.C., USA	26
Coventry	25	The Hague, Netherlands	26
Watford	25	Copenhagen, Denmark	29
Bristol	25	Los Angeles, California, USA	30
Reading	25		
Leicester	25		
Maidstone	27		
London	30.5		
Glasgow	32		

Q = car equivalents in peak hour in peak directions.
A = area of a town centre in square feet.
f = fraction of ground area that is carriageway.

THE MAXIMUM NUMBER OF WORKPLACES IN A TOWN CENTRE
TO WHICH ALL COMMUTERS CAN TRAVEL BY CAR

It has been shown above that the maximum number of car equivalents that can enter a town centre per hour is about 30 $fA^{\frac{1}{2}}$. If
the proportion of non-car traffic is p, then the number of cars
that can enter per hour is $30(1-p)fA^{\frac{1}{2}}$, and the number that can
enter in time t is $30(1-p)ftA^{\frac{1}{2}}$. If the average number of car
occupants per car is c, then the number of commuters who can enter
by car in time t is $30(1-p)fctA^{\frac{1}{2}}$.

If the total number of workplaces in a town centre is N, and if
the mean ground surface area occupied by a commuter is G, then
$A = NG$, and all the commuters will be able to travel by car if
$N < 30(1-p)fctN^{\frac{1}{2}}G^{\frac{1}{2}}$, that is, if $N < 900(1-p)^2f^2c^2t^2G$.

During the morning and evening peak travel periods, p is usually
about 1/3 and c about 1.4. The median value of G for a town centre
is usually about 250 square feet, whilst for British town centres
f is characteristically about 0.14, but is about 0.25 for many
North American and Continental towns. Taking the value of 0.14,
we find that for everyone in a town centre to travel to work by
car the working population must be less than 3840 t^2. Thus,
making the above assumptions, the maximum working population in
a town centre to which everyone can travel to work by car is about
1000 if their work starting times are spread over 30 minutes,
about 4000 if they are spread over an hour, and about 15 000 if
they are spread over two hours. If, however, the proportion of
the ground surface area used for roads were double that assumed
above, the size of town to which everyone could travel by car would
be four times the figures given above. Again, if car occupancy
were to be 2.8 instead of 1.4 the above figures for the size of
town centre to which everyone could travel to work by car would
again be multiplied by a factor of 4, whilst if other traffic could
be forbidden to use the road system during the peak travel period
the above figures would be multiplied by a factor of 2.25. Thus,
if there were no other traffic, if 28 per cent of the town centre
were used for roads, if average car occupancy were to be 2.8, and
if the peak period lasted two hours, then the working population
of the town centre of appropriate area to which everyone could
commute by car would be about half a million.

Other ways of increasing the numbers of people who could travel
by car into a town centre would be to increase the capacity of
those crossroads at which traffic reaches capacity by building
underpasses, by widening roads or by building a high-capacity ring
road around the town centre. These will be discussed later in
this chapter. It is, however, clear that the number of persons
who can travel to a town centre by car varies enormously with the
conditions.

PARKING REQUIREMENTS

When considering the possibilities of urban car travel, it is, of course, also important to consider parking requirements. Measurement shows that car parks usually require about 250 square feet per car. At an average car occupancy of 1.45 persons, this is equivalent to about 172 square feet per commuter. In a six-storey car park, this amounts to about 29 square feet of ground space per commuter, or about 9 per cent of the ground space in a town centre with the average workplace density of Central London ($G = 333$ square feet). The proportion would, of course, be much higher in some parts of London, but much less in others.

THE EFFECTS OF THE DESIGN OF THE ROAD SYSTEM AND THE TRAVEL PATTERN ON THE DISTRIBUTION OF TRAFFIC OVER A TOWN

An attempt has also been made (Smeed 1970 and 1971) to obtain some appreciation of the effects of the design of the road system and of the travel pattern on congestion by calculating the effects of highly *idealized* origin-destination patterns and road systems. There is evidence that these idealized patterns give results which bear some relationship to that of real road systems.

Types of journey

Three types of journey have been considered:

(a) *Internal journeys*. Both origin and destination are within the town's boundaries.

(b) *Cross-cordon journeys*. One trip end is within the town, the other outside. As far as travel within the town is concerned, the latter trip end may be taken to be on the town boundary.

(c) *Through journeys*. Both origin and destination are outside the town but the journey route lies partly within the town. As far as the calculation is concerned, both origin and destination are taken to be on the town's boundaries.

Numbers of journeys and density of trip ends

In the cases considered here it is supposed that the town is circular and of radius R and that the total number of journeys is N. The density σ of trip ends is taken either to be uniform or to vary inversely with ρ the distance from the centre of the town, as is the case in London and many other towns approximately. It is supposed that journeys are made from every trip end to every other trip end.

The road networks and routeing systems considered

The road networks and routeing systems considered are described in further detail below.

Direct. Straight roads run from each origin to each destination. It is not, of course, normally possible to provide such a road network, but the case is of interest because it gives lower limits to journey lengths and because it provides — after suitable adjustments — a basis for other more relevant calculations. *Route*: Journeys are made by travelling along the straight line joining the origin and destination.

Radial-arc. Radial roads run from the centre in all directions, and there are circular roads concentric with the boundary of the town at all distances from the centre. *Route*: If the origin is nearer than the destination to the centre, travellers take the circumferential road from their origin to the radial along which their destination lies by the shortest of the two available routes, and then travel along the radial to their destination. If the origin is further than the destination from the centre, travellers take the radial road from the origin until they reach the circumferential road on which their destination lies, and then travel along that road to their destination by the shortest of the two available routes.

Ring. Radial roads run from the centre to the boundary in all directions and there is a single ring road concentric with the boundary of the town. The radial roads are not connected at the centre, except where the radius of the ring road is zero. *Route*: Journeys are made along a radial to the ring road, then along the ring road by the shortest of the two alternative routes until the radial on which the destination lies is reached, and then along that radial to the destination.

Radial. Ring routeing when the radius of the ring road is zero.

Radial-arc/Radial. Radial roads, connected at the centre, run in all directions from the centre and there are closely spaced circular roads concentric with the boundary of the town. *Route*: Travellers can use either radial-arc or radial routeing and choose the quickest, shortest, or cheapest route.

Ring-radial. Radial roads, connected at the centre, run in all directions from the centre, and there is a single ring road concentric with the boundary of the town. *Route*: Travellers have the choice of ring or radial routeing and choose the quickest, shortest, or cheapest route.

Route choice. In the above definitions of radial-arc/radial and ring-radial routeing, drivers choose the quickest, shortest, or cheapest routes. It is convenient, however, to assume that they choose the one giving the shortest journey time when the speeds are v on the radial roads and V on the circular ones. Since, however, the assumption of shortest time is identical with that of shortest distance when $V/v = 1$, the results for shortest distance may be deduced from those for shortest time by putting $v = V$.

The method of calculation

It is neither possible nor desirable in this short chapter to give the calculations in full, but three cases which can be dealt with very simply are analysed below to illustrate the method. All these cases apply to cross-cordon journeys and it will be supposed that the journeys are all from the outskirts to random points within the town.

Ring routeing, the ring lying on the boundary of the circular town

Journeys are made from the origin along the ring road until the radial on which the destination lies is reached. The traveller then turns on to this radial and travels along it until he reaches his destination.

The number of journeys to points within a circle of radius ρ ($\rho < R$, the radius of the town) concentric with the boundary of the town is $N\rho^2/R^2$. Each of these journeys involves travelling a distance $d\rho$ in the annulus between the circles of radii ρ and $\rho + d\rho$, and the total distance travelled within this annulus is therefore $(N\rho^2/R^2)d\rho$. Since the area of this annulus is $2\pi\rho d\rho$, the distance travelled per unit area at a distance ρ ($\rho < R$) from the town centre is $N\rho/2\pi R^2$.

The flow on the ring road can also be calculated easily. Since a traveller starting from any point on the ring road is equally likely to wish to travel to any other point, the maximum distance he will travel is πR and the average distance travelled is $\pi R/2$. Hence, the total distance travelled is $N\pi R/2$. Since the total length of the ring road is $2\pi R$, the flow past any point is $N/4$.

Radial routeing

A person travels from his origin directly to the centre of the town and then turns on to the radial on which his destination lies and travels directly towards it. Now all travellers cross the $\rho, \rho + d\rho$ annulus when travelling towards the centre, and all those with destinations outside the ρ annulus, and no others, cross it again in the outward directions. Hence, the number of crossings of the ρ annulus is $N(2 - \rho^2/R^2)$. Making use of the fact that both of these crossings involve travelling a distance $d\rho$ in the annulus and that the area of the annulus is $2\pi\rho d\rho$, the distance travelled per unit area is clearly

$$\frac{N}{\pi R}(\frac{R}{\rho} - \frac{\rho}{2R}) .$$

Radial-arc routeing

It is supposed that a traveller travels along the radial on which his origin lies until he reaches the circle on which his

destination lies, and then travels along this circle to his destination.

The number of destinations in the $\rho, \rho+d\rho$ annulus is $N\, 2\pi\rho d\rho/\pi R^2$ and, since any traveller is equally likely to travel any distance between 0 and $\pi\rho$ in this annulus, the average distance travelled is $\pi\rho/2$. The total distance travelled along this annulus is therefore $N\, \pi\rho^2\, d\rho/R^2$.

All travellers to destinations within the circle of radius ρ travel a radial distance $d\rho$ within the annulus, and the radial distance travelled by these travellers in the annulus is therefore $(N\, \rho^2/R^2)\,d\rho$. Since the area of the annulus is $2\pi\rho d\rho$, the total distance travelled (along plus radially) per unit area in the annulus is

$$\frac{N(1 + \pi)\rho}{2\pi R^2}\ .$$

The distance travelled per unit area is plotted against the distance from the town centre for each of the three cases considered in Fig. 6.7.

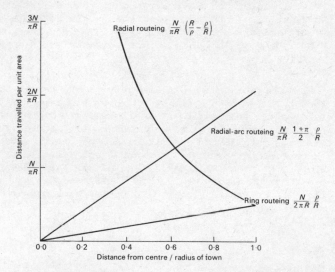

Fig. 6.7 Distance travelled per unit area in cross-cordon journeys when density of trip ends is uniform.

The formulae and the figure show the enormous effect of the routeing and road system on the distribution of traffic over the town.
With radial routeing, which the road systems of many British towns
encourage, the distance travelled per unit area becomes very high
at the centre of the town; with radial-arc or ring routeing it is
low at the centre but a maximum at the outskirts of the town, where
it will often do less harm to the amenities.

The total distance travelled within the town can, of course, be
calculated from the above expressions by multiplying each of them
by $2\pi\rho d\rho$ and integrating. It follows that the average distance
travelled within the town is $0.33 R$ for ring routeing, $1.38 R$ for
radial-arc routeing, and $1.67 R$ for radial routeing. In the case
of ring routeing, however, there is an extra distance $\frac{1}{2}\pi R = 1.57 R$
to be added for distance travelled on the ring road. However, as
speeds are often much faster and more uniform on an external ring
road than on journeys within a town centre, such journeys are often
cheaper and less time consuming than journeys using other routes.
They will, therefore, often be used.

The distance travelled per unit area

The travel intensity — the distance travelled per unit area — for
a number of other cases for which it has been calculated (Smeed
1970) are shown in Fig. 6.8. They suggest a number of conclusions,
some at least of which might have been expected. For example,

(a) Whether or not the speed on the circumferential roads is
greater or less than $\frac{1}{2}\pi$ times the speed on radial roads is crucial
in determining the travel intensity when routeing is radial-arc
radial, or ring-radial. When the circumferential speed is above
this limit, the travel intensity is low near the town centre; when
the circumferential speed is below this limit, the travel intensity
is high at the centre.

(b) Although many of the origin-destination patterns are fundamentally different, consisting as they do of internal, cross-cordon
and through journeys and of densities of trip ends both uniform and
varying inversely with distance from the town centre, the shape of
the (travel intensity)-(distance from city centre) curve is mainly
determined by the road network and routeing method rather than by
the origin-destination pattern.

Some data for real towns

Although the assumptions made above relate to idealized origin-
destination patterns and road networks, the common sense of the
results suggests the likelihood of all the tendencies being appli-
cable to real towns. It therefore seems desirable to examine the
extent to which they do so and, although it is not possible to
find towns in which either the road network or the origin-destination pattern corresponds exactly to those assumed, something can

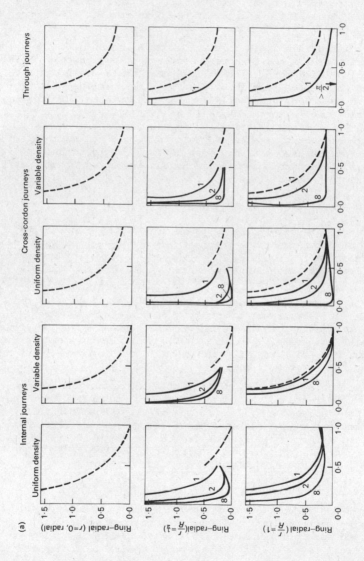

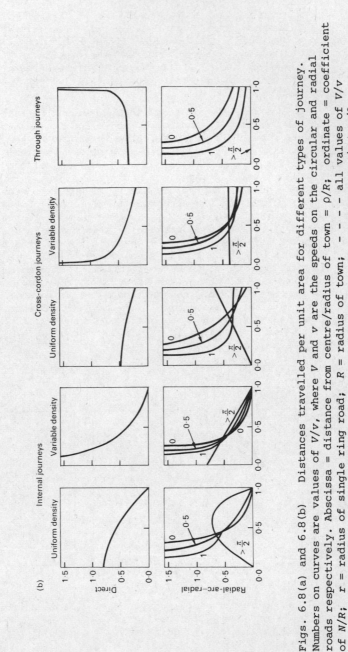

Figs. 6.8(a) and 6.8(b)　Distances travelled per unit area for different types of journey.
Numbers on curves are values of V/v, where V and v are the speeds on the circular and radial
roads respectively. Abscissa = distance from centre/radius of town = ρ/R; ordinate = coefficient
of N/R; r = radius of single ring road;　R = radius of town; - - - - all values of V/v
(including 0 for $\rho > r$);　> $\pi/2$ means that top curve applies for values of V/v > $\pi/2$.

be done. Analysis (Smeed 1970) shows that the fact that roads are always a finite distance apart,and not infinitely close as assumed above,does not make a great deal of difference to the distribution of travel intensity in large towns,and the results in Figs. 6.8(a) and 6.8(b) suggest that quite fundamental differences in the trip-end pattern do not always alter fundamentally the travel intensity pattern.

Now trip ends in real towns are,to some extent,distributed in the variable density pattern considered above,and it is to be expected that drivers attempt,to an appreciable extent,to travel in as direct a manner as possible between their origins and destinations. It is clear that in a town with a rectangular road system the road distance between any two points is $d(\cos\theta+\sin\theta)$ where d is the straight line distance between the points and θ the angle between the line joining the points and the direction of the roads of the system. If the mean of a varying quantity is denoted by a horizontal bar over the quantity,the mean road distance between two points selected at random but at air-line distance d apart in a town with a rectangular network is $d(\overline{\cos\theta}+\overline{\sin\theta})$ and, since $\overline{\cos\theta}=\overline{\sin\theta}=2/\pi$, it is clear that the mean road distance between randomly selected pairs of points at air-line distance d is $4d/\pi=1.27d$. The same mean value would be expected to apply to roads selected at random in a town with a road system with straight roads in random directions. Fig. 6.9 gives the ratio of the road distance to the straight-line distance for a number of randomly selected pairs of points in a number

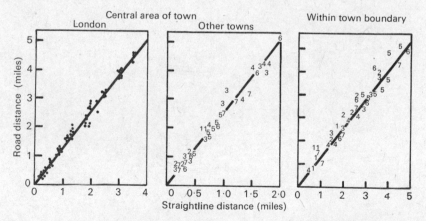

Fig. 6.9 Road distance compared with direct distance for randomly selected pairs of points in urban areas.
1 Cardiff; 2 Darlington; 3 Edinburgh; 4 Leeds; 5 Leicester; 6 Hull; 7 Washington, D.C., USA.

of towns and shows that the points lie very close to the line that
would be expected if the roads were in random directions. If,
therefore, drivers in real towns select routes as close as possible
to the straight lines joining their origins and destinations, it
seems that the calculations referred to above for direct routeing
may well apply to travel in real towns, provided that the estimates
of distance travelled per unit area are multiplied by 1.27. The
ratio of the distance travelled per unit area to the total distance
travelled in the town is plotted in Fig.6.10 against the ratio of the

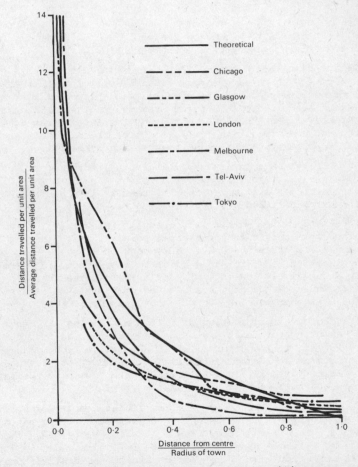

Fig. 6.10 Actual traffic intensity in various cities compared
with that in a theoretical model city.

distance from the town centre to the radius of the town. The corresponding 'theoretical' curve, as deduced from the data in Fig. 6.8, is also given. The 'theoretical' curve is seen to have approximately the same shape as the corresponding curves for real towns, and this gives some confidence in the conclusions drawn from the calculations on the general effects of the design of the road system on travel intensity in towns.

CONCLUSIONS ON THE EFFECT OF ROAD NETWORK DESIGN ON THE DISTRIBUTION OF TRAFFIC IN A TOWN

The main conclusions on the effect of road network design on traffic intensity in towns and on desirable road systems in towns derived from the above analysis are given below.

1. The type of road network and the routeing methods used have much less effect on the average distance travelled than on the distance travelled per unit area, called, in this chapter, the intensity of travel. Some routeing systems result in high intensities of travel near the town centre and low intensities at the outskirts. Others result in low intensities of travel at the town centre and relatively high intensities at the outskirts.

2. (a) Travel in a town via radial routes, that is, routes in which travel takes place from origin to town centre and thence to destination, naturally results in a very high intensity of travel at the town centre.

    (b) Ring routes — that is, routes in which travel takes place from origin to the nearest point on a single ring road, then along the ring road to the point on it nearest to the destination, and from this point to the destination — result in a relatively low intensity of travel in the region surrounded by the ring road, especially when the ring road has a high proportion of trip ends outside it.

    (c) Routes approximating to direct ones — that is, those in which travel takes place on roads as near as possible to the straight line joining origin and destination — can often be used on some road systems. The intensity of travel due to such routes is, in most parts of the town, intermediate between that for ring and radial routes.

    (d) Radial-arc routes — that is, routes based on a number of radial roads together with a number of circumferential roads — result in intensities of traffic higher than those due to a single ring route, except in the neighbourhood of the ring road itself, but lower than those resulting from direct or radial routes near the town centre.

3. Since there is often a social requirement for low intensities of travel near town centres, the conditions under which drivers

will of their own accord use ring roads require consideration.

(a) Provided that drivers select the quickest route, drivers faced with a choice of radial-arc or radial routes will always choose the radial-arc ones, provided that the speed on the circular roads is more than $\frac{1}{2}\pi$ times that on the radial road system.

(b) Faced with a choice of ring or radial routes, drivers using the quickest routes will always use the ring route if both trip ends are external to the ring road, and if the speed on the ring road is more than $\frac{1}{2}\pi$ times that on the radial roads.

(c) There is a large difference in the intensity of travel on the two sides of a single ring road, especially if it is near the centre of a town.

(d) In the cases examined, the single ring road which minimizes travel in other parts of the town has about as many trip ends in the area which it surrounds as in the area surrounding it.

(e) Provided that the destination of a journey from any origin is equally likely to lie on any line diverging from the town centre, then one-quarter of all journeys will pass any point on the single ring road if all journeys use it Since a high proportion of journeys are likely to use a ring road if speeds on it, relative to those on other roads, are high, large flows are likely on single ring roads in large towns. In such cases, a series of ring roads — approximating radial-arc routeing — have advantages if it is desired to minimize traffic at the town centre.

Two of the common desiderata in urban road planning are a minimum total travel distance and a small value for the distance travelled per unit area in the town centre for any likely origin-destination pattern. The analysis suggests that for a large range of origin-destination patterns both these objectives may, to a considerable extent, be achieved by arranging for:

1. An inner ring road around the central area on which speeds are fast relative to speeds within the area;

2. A series of ring roads beyond the first together with a series of radial roads leading outwards from the innermost ring road; the ring roads should be designed so that the average speed on any one of them is appreciably faster than on the radial roads leading to it from the town centre;

3. Radial roads — unconnected with one another — leading from near the town centre to the ring roads.

The first two arrangements may, however, often be enough to achieve the objectives desired, especially if the road system does not encourage traffic to travel to the centre of the city.

REFERENCES

SMEED, R.J. (1968)   Traffic studies and urban congestion.
J. Transport Econ. Policy, 2, 33-70.

SMEED, R.J. (1970, 1971)   The effects of the design of the road network on the intensity of traffic movement in different parts of a town with special reference to the effects of ring roads.
Proceedings of the Tewksbury Symposium, Melbourne, 1970 and *Technical Note 17,* CIRIA, London (1971).

THOMSON, J.M. (1967)   Speeds and flows of traffic in central London.   2. Speed-flow relations.
Traff. Eng. Control, 8, 721-725.

WARDROP, J.G. (1952)   Some theoretical aspects of road safety research.
Proc. Instn. Civ. Engrs, 1, 325-378.

WARDROP, J.G. (1968)   Journey speed and flow in central urban areas.
Traff. Eng. Control, 9, 528-532, 539.

WEBSTER, F.W. (1958)   *Traffic Signal Settings.*
Department of Scientific and Industrial Research, Road Research Paper No. 39, HMSO, London.

7 Nutrition

J. V. G. A. Durnin

A shift from a preponderantly rural-agricultural to an urban-industrial economy, with its attendant population drift to the cities, obviously has potential nutritional importance. The effects on health and nutrition of the rapid urbanization affecting many *developing* countries has been the subject of several WHO and FAO publications in recent years. The eating patterns of these migrants may change drastically and abruptly. Often they have come from some form of subsistence agriculture where most of the food is grown or gathered, or where animals are hunted or perhaps where domestic animals are herded as a source of food; they move to an urban situation where strange and expensive food (perhaps much of it processed, tinned, and packaged) is purchased in shops or markets. With the urban shift the population balance is altered, and changes occur in living conditions, in access to traditional foods, in alcohol consumption, and in general standards of health. Very significant modifications in eating habits take place in such migrant populations, and diseases which have a strong nutritional component may become common (for example, obesity, diabetes, coronary heart disease, and dental caries).

However, in some respects the problem of 'urbanization and nutrition' is more complex in the industrially *developed* countries. The change of life style from that of a rural environment to an urban environment has progressed more gradually and during a very much longer period. Also, because of the present-day availability of transport and ease of communication, nutritional differences between town and country are often somewhat blurred. Nutritionally indeed we have returned to the equivalent of the early stages of urbanization, more than 2000 years ago, when, with few exceptions, cities were relatively small and depended for their food supplies on the adjacent land, with the result that the diets of town dwellers and rural food-producers were very similar.

GENERAL INFLUENCES ON NUTRITION

Many social and economic circumstances can exert an influence on nutrition. For example, between rural and urban communities there may be differences in family income; the nature of occupations and the physical effort required by them; levels of unemployment; the contribution from women's earnings to the family budget (there is some evidence that the amount of money earned by the women in the family may increase the amount spent

on food); opportunities for higher-grade schooling and higher
education; and vocational training facilities. At present,
there is little direct information about the relative importance
of these influences and much of this section must, of necessity,
be speculative.

HISTORICAL

The effects of urbanization and industrialization on food
consumption during the past 200 years have been well documented
in the U.K. in the classic work *The Englishman's food*
(Drummond and Wilbraham 1939) and in other historical surveys
of food habits (Ashley 1928; Burnett 1966, 1969; Crawford and
Broadley 1938; Curtis-Bennet 1949; Fenelon 1952; Oddy 1970).
Hollingsworth (1974) has tabulated the interesting changes in
patterns of food consumption in Britain from 1880 to the
present day. Table 7.1 shows that the most noticeable features
have been (1) gradual increases in the proportions of energy
derived from oils and fats, from dairy products and, except for
wartime and post-war shortages, from sugar and syrups; (2)
a relative stability in the energy derived from meat; and (3)
a marked decline in the use of grain products for human consumption and, to a lesser extent, of potatoes. When these trends
are analysed as a function of income, general patterns, which have
been found in many countries (Perisse, Sizaret, and Francois 1969),
become apparent, With rising income, the proportion of energy
derived from animal fats rises steeply, that from carbohydrate
falls (except that sugar intake rises), and total protein remains
much the same, although animal-protein intake increases. The
consumption of sugar has shown the most consistent and spectacular
rise of any foodstuff intake, and Aykroyd (1973) has written
categorically that this increase is associated with urbanization.
Whether his statement is valid for developed countries is
questionable.

Although historical accounts provide interesting descriptions
of past trends, which superficially might seem the result of a
change from a mainly rural to a predominantly urban life style,
such analyses probably have little direct relevance to present-
day urban-rural differences in nutrition. Working conditions, the
amount of leisure time, the changes brought about by the motor
car, television and the cinema, the relative economic prosperity
of a large proportion of the population, an ubiquitous transport
system that allows rural dwellers access to the same range of
foods as urban inhabitants - all these have an impact today
which is not mirrored by anything comparable in the past.

PATTERNS OF EATING AND MODERN FOODSTUFFS

Paradoxically, in spite of shorter working hours, the time

TABLE 7.1

Estimated percentage distribution of United Kingdom's supplies of food energy for selected years between 1880 and 1972

	1880 (i)	1909-13 (i)	1924-8 (i)	1934-8 (ii)	1942 (ii)	1952 (ii)	1962 (iii)	1972 (iii)
Dairy products (excluding butter)	8	8	9	9	11	11	11	12
Meats	13	18	18	17	14	13	17	17
Oils and fats	7	9	12	17	16	17	18	18
Sugar and syrups	11	14	15	15	11	14	17	18
Potatoes	8	7	6	5	5	6	5	5
Grain products	48	37	33	30	37	32	25	22
Other foods	5	7	7	7	6	7	7	8
Total	100	100	100	100	100	100	100	100

(i)   From Greaves and Hollingsworth (1966)

(ii) From Ministry of Agriculture, Fisheries and Food (1968)

(iii) From Ministry of Agriculture, Fisheries and Food (1973).

available for buying, preparing, and eating food is often
less than previously, and this influences the types of food
that are eaten. Working in large cities often necessitates
much time being spent in commuting. Snacks, sometimes
including beer or spirits, may be the usual lunch for many
office workers. Breakfast is frequently a hurried bite of
food or may be completely omitted, even by school children,
and perhaps the only sizeable meal of the day is eaten in the
evening. A dietary pattern of this nature, consisting of only
one or two meals in the day, may result in an increased
efficiency of utilization of the energy available in the
food (Fabry 1969) and may indirectly predispose to the development of obesity.

'MODERN' FOODSTUFFS

The nature of the foodstuffs eaten in our modern society
has undergone much modification with the result that our
present-day diet causes anxiety to people concerned with the
health of the community. Food is now softer because its
natural fibre is often removed and sweeter because of added
sugar, and it has a much higher fat content. Whereas man's
diet was once based largely on wholemeal cereals, fresh
vegetables, fresh fruit, and a little meat, now it may contain
much refined flour, sugar, fried foods, cakes and pastries,
processed vegetables, and canned fruits. For large numbers
of people, the diet is not well balanced.

The increasing affluence in developed countries, especially
of young adults, has resulted in more food being consumed in
restaurants and snack bars; in addition, many works and offices
have canteens, and so traditional and family influences on
the types and amounts of food eaten are eroded. The popularity
of 'foreign' dishes - Italian, Chinese, Indian and Spanish
has had a further effect on altering customary eating habits.

The time occupied by work and by travel, combined with the
many attractions (mostly sedentary!) available to fill leisure
hours, mean that many people spend little time in cooking or
eating meals. If the wife is also working, the tendency is
more marked. The shorter time available for cooking means
an increased reliance on processed foods.

The variety of packaged and tinned foods now widely obtain-
able constitutes an enormous and continually increasing market.
When processing is carried out efficiently it may improve
palatability and will increase the shelf-life of cooked and
uncooked foods, as well as conserving the nutrient content of
these foods (the process of freeze-drying probably brings about
the smallest changes in both flavour and nutritional quality).

Heat treatment may sometimes actually increase digestibility or remove minor toxicity of certain foods, such as some varieties of beans and maize.

Foods such as flour and many commercial cereal-based packaged foods have minerals and vitamins added. However, many food products have artificial flavouring, sweeteners, emulsifiers, and preservatives added to them to improve colour, flavour, or acceptability.

All of these methods of interference with 'natural' foods will have nutritional implications. Many of the preserving and flavouring techniques appear entirely beneficial but, from time to time, dangers attached to their widespread use become apparent. Nowadays, owing to easy transport and widespread advertising, these dangers probably exist to the same extent in town and country, and urban man is no more at risk than his rural counterpart. Differences between town and country in the family purchases of processed foods are steadily decreasing; village shops tend more and more to stock similar goods to those in city stores.

FOOD CONSUMPTION IN THE U.K.

Nevertheless the annual reports of the National Food Survey Committee (1966, 1969, and 1973) show not only that there are still differences between geographical areas but that these are constantly changing. In 1973 rural areas had consumptions *above* the national average of 44 per cent for margarine, 34 per cent for sugar, 26 per cent for flour, 15 per cent for cooking fat, and 11 per cent for butter, and had consumptions *below* the national average of 21 per cent for fish and 14 per cent for cakes and biscuits. However, the variability in these differences during the space of a few years is very large. Table 7.2 shows how, in rural areas, the consumption of flour, sugar, and green vegetables has fluctuated very considerably in recent years. London has a more consistent set of differences from the national average, with a remarkably constant consumption of fresh fruit, green vegetables, and cheese, all appreciably more than the national average, and cooking fats and bread considerably less than the national average.

There are small but interesting differences in the total energy and nutrient consumption in rural and urban areas, as tabulated in these reports. People in rural areas consistently consumed about 200-300 kcal per day per head more than Londoners. People in provincial conurbations had an intake of energy between these two. However, at least as important as this difference is the small but steady decrease in the average energy intake throughout this period, from just under 2600

kcal per head per day in 1966 to 2400 kcal per head per day
in 1973 - almost certainly symptomatic of a slight but

Table 7.2

*Consumption of certain foodstuffs above (+) or below (-) the
national average for the United Kingdom (percentages)*

	1966	1969	1973
Rural areas			
Flour	+30	+57	+26
Sugar	+10	+ 6	+34
Green vegetables	0	+31	+11
London			
Fresh fruit	+25	+27	+32
Green vegetables	+19	+28	+16
Cheese	+14	+ 9	+ 8
Cooking fat	-18	-21	-34
Bread	-12	-13	-15

steady decrease in the general level of physical activity in
the population as a whole.

INFANT FEEDING : BREAST-FEEDING AND BOTTLE-FEEDING

An important influence which affects infant and child
nutrition is whether or not the child's mother is working
outside the home. The most immediate effect on infant
nutrition relates to breast-feeding. In both developing and
developed countries breast-feeding is becoming less common,
and it is possible that this is more marked in urban dwellers.
The trend seems to vary also with socio-economic status,
although there are geographical variations and fashions which
change from time to time. In a nutritional study conducted
in the Glasgow area in 1968-69, almost 70 per cent of women
of social class I breast-fed their babies during a minimum of
4 weeks, whereas only a small percentage of women from the
poorer social groups (IV-V) breast-fed their babies at all.
These differences between social groups remained the same
no matter whether the women were living in the city, in a
country town, or in a rural area. The numbers involved in the

survey were small (400 infants with a similar number of mothers),
but they were a random sample of the appropriate population.
In a survey of 4365 Scottish infants, Arneil (1967) found that
70 per cent were not breast-fed at all and that only 10 per cent
of mothers were breast-feeding beyond 2 months. These figures
are similar to those obtained by surveys in England and Wales;
Shukla, Forsyth, Anderson, Marwah (1972) found that most mothers
had stopped breast-feeding by the end of the first month.

However, the nutritional significance of breast-feeding is a
matter for dispute, so that even if there were a lower prevalence
of breast-feeding in urban areas this might have little relevance
to general nutrition. On the other hand, certain indirect effects
involving physical health are associated with bottle-feeding.
The dangers of gastro-enteritis are greater in young infants who
are bottle-fed. Also, since solid food (often tinned) may be
introduced to bottle-fed babies at a very early age, sometimes
when the baby is only 3 or 4 weeks old, the result is frequently
a larger food intake by the infant, bringing about accelerated
growth and leading to a greater proportion of fat babies in the
population. There is contradictory evidence about whether or
not fat babies are likely to become fat adults (Mellbin and
Vuille 1973; Asher 1966; Eid 1970), but there seems at least
a chance that this will happen, because of the possible increase
in the number of fat cells in the infant's body as a result of
overfeeding.

The purchase of tinned and packaged baby foods may involve
considerable extra expense to the family, and this may lead
to reduced expenditure on other foodstuffs. This in itself
may have a significant effect on the nutrition of some families.

Whether or not progressive 'improvement' in the nutritional
status of infants and children during recent decades has been
mostly responsible for the increase in stature of children
is unknown. There are differences in heights and weights
between urban and rural children and this may suggest that
factors other than nutrition are also operating, but again
this, at present, is a matter for speculation only. Tanner
and Eveleth, in their chapter on Urbanization and Growth
(Chapter 8) deal with this subject in some depth.

WORKING MOTHERS AND ONE-PARENT FAMILIES

Working wives and mothers now form an appreciable proportion
of the labour force, especially in urban areas. This situation
has conflicting influences on the nutritional status of the
urban family. Perhaps more money is now available for food for the
household, but on the other hand, the children may be left more
to fend for themselves, and will very often have to cook or
otherwise obtain one meal a day by themselves. Many children

prefer to eat sweets, biscuits, and pastries and to drink
Coca-Cola rather than to eat better-balanced meals and this
may have both short- and long-term consequences in an increased
susceptibility to obesity, to dental caries, and even (eventually)
to coronary heart disease.

The growing number of one-parent families, where the single
parent needs to go out to work, may again have undesirable
nutritional implications.

NUTRITION AND THE UNEMPLOYED

A very large group of people, who are not often considered
to have specifically nutritional problems, are the unemployed.
Their number frequently constitutes between 5 and 10 per cent
of the total population, and in some depressed urban areas
the percentage is much higher. Most unemployed people live in
towns or large cities. Very little is known about the effects
on nutritional status of the serious socio-psychological and
economic problems which must be faced by the chronic unemployed,
and this is an area where research is urgently needed.

THE NUTRITIONAL NEEDS OF FOREIGN IMMIGRANTS

Immigrants are another population group which may have
nutritional problems in the urban environment of developed
countries. Such immigrants tend to settle in urban areas and
often in the larger conurbations. They often retain their
traditional feeding habits as part of an attempt to maintain
the old culture. This sometimes leads to malnutrition. As
an example, rickets is a nutritional deficiency which has been
virtually non-existent in the U.K. in white populations for
30 years and more, yet in the past 10 years it has been found
to be common in children of immigrants from the Indian sub-
continent. This is apparently due to the combined effect of a
diet deficient in Vitamin D and the absence of exposure of
the skin to the available sunlight. A traditional diet, the
maintenance of traditional dress and custom, and living in
cities have resulted in the development of rickets by a
considerable percentage of Pakistani immigrant children in
Glasgow and in the Midlands of England (Ford, Colhoun,
McIntosh, and Dunnigan 1972; Holmes, Enoch, Taylor, and
Jones 1973).

Anaemia, of a nutritional origin, is also found among
certain immigrants whose diet is strictly determined by
religious beliefs. This is especially true of orthodox
Hindu women, who may eat a relatively poor and entirely
vegetarian diet.

PHYSICAL ACTIVITY AND ENERGY BALANCE

One indirect but important influence on nutrition is related to physical activity. In the recent past in most developed countries, urbanization and increasing mechanization of industry, coupled with widespread use of public and private transport, has inevitably led to a reduction of physical activity in the whole population. The physical effort involved in most occupations has lessened markedly. Occupational activity usually determines total activity. In an analysis of over 1000 men and women employed in a variety of occupations, it was found that total physical activity, as an average over several consecutive days (including weekends), was highly dependent on the physical activity of the occupation (Durnin 1973). In leisure time, the two great destroyers of physical activity – television and the motor car – increasingly encompass the general population. Both voluntary and compulsory physical effort by the general public is continually diminishing.

Decreased physical activity and nutritional needs form a vicious circle, as follows. If average daily energy expenditure is already low, because of comparatively little necessity for physical effort at work, and is becoming lower, then smaller quantities of food are necessary to maintain energy balance. Often these small quantities are unsatisfying and larger amounts are eaten. Obesity then occurs, and an obese individual frequently indulges in even less physical movement. Measurements, of total daily energy expenditure in a large series of individuals show a clear negative relationship between the time spent in all physical activity throughout the day and the degree of obesity (Durnin 1967).

Corroboration of the possibility that at least some fat adults maintain weight on low energy intakes has been provided by the study of Miller and Parsonage (1975), where nine out of a group of 29 moderately obese women did not lose weight during a 3-week period of eating a 1500 kcal per day diet.

It is well known clinically that obese young adolescents are an extremely difficult group to treat by dieting and eating habits in these children probably more nearly approaches the 'normal' than those of 'obese' adults. Several studies have shown low intakes of food in obese adolescents (Johnson, Burke, and Mayer 1956; Hampton, Huenemann, Shapiro, and Mitchell 1967). In our own cross-sectional study on 14 year-old Glasgow adolescents in 1964 and in 1971 (Durnin, Lonergan, Good, and Ewan 1974) some interesting differences between the boys and the girls were apparent. Whereas there was no difference between the amounts of energy consumed in the food by the fattest and by the thinnest boys, the thinnest girls ate considerably more food than the fattest (2200 kcal per day compared to 1700 kcal per day), presumably illustrating the much greater degree of

inactivity of the fat girls. Also, both the boys and the girls
studied in 1971 showed an appreciable reduction in the energy
intake compared to the groups studied in 1964 (2800 kcal per
day down to 2610 kcal per day for the boys and 2270 kcal per
day down to 2020 kcal per day for the girls). Even in the
relatively brief space of time of 7 years the physical
activity involved in the way of life of these urban children
had diminished. There have been no comparable measurements on
rural children, but it seems unlikely that similar results would
be found.

Apart from its important role in energy balance, physical
inactivity and coronary heart disease may also be connected,
although the relationship is complex and confounded by many
other factors (Keys 1970). Quantitative measures of the
physical activity of individual people are notoriously difficult
(Taylor 1967; Wyndham 1972). However, Morris and his
colleagues have described (using a large group of bank employees)
a technique of classifying physical activity (Morris, Adam,
Chave, Sirey, Epstein and Sheehan 1973). Their investigations
showed a significantly lower incidence of coronary heart disease
among men who were physically active. The technique could
perhaps be widely employed and thus provide a means of assessing
more exactly the effect on physical activity of living in an
urban environment. Alterations in patterns and total quantities
of physical activity could be the most important factors related
to physical health which are altered by urbanization and by
progressive industrialization. Often, even when urban dwellers
appear to be physically active, the form of the activity in which
they indulge is such as is seldom found in peoples living in
'natural' circumstances. For example, it seems relatively
uncommon that individuals in non-industrialized societies ever
partake of very severe exercise. Exercise for them, either when
working or at leisure, involves moderate, or, occasionally,
moderately severe levels of energy expenditure - requiring
perhaps 5-10 kcal per min, and heart rates of around 100-150
per min. Exercise for those of us in urban environments is
often of short duration and violent; in many sports and
recreations, energy expenditures of 10 - 15 kcal per min and
even higher occur, and heart rates of between 150 and 200 per
min are not unusual. Such exercise may be done infrequently
and sporadically and may last, at fluctuating levels, for an
hour or less. For the remainder of the 24 hours of an average
day, physical activity is often minimal. Whether or not this
pattern of 'unnatural' activity is entirely beneficial and
whether or not it usually occurs only in urban populations are
questions which warrant investigation.

In Sweden it has already been decided that insufficient
exercise is dangerous to the health of the population, and

the Swedish National Board of Health and Welfare (1972) have
published a report giving advice on diet and exercise. The
objectives are mostly admirable, although the likelihood of
their being accomplished is perhaps doubtful: 'adjust energy
intake to the energy output; limit consumption of sugar and
saturated fats; increase supply of essential nutrients; increase
physical activity.'

TWO UNRESEARCHED URBAN PROBLEMS

Obesity

Whatever the relative importance of the various aetiological
factors in obesity - whether it arises from lack of exercise,
simple overeating, or for more complex reasons - it is probably
the major disability which is most immediately connected with
modern urban life (see Chapter 10). It is supposed to affect
up to one-third of the total population in the U.K. but no
reliable estimates are available on large unselected populations.
Obesity is thought to have medical dangers, but these have
never been properly assessed, and it is likely that the dangers
are different for women, especially prior to the menopause, than
for men.

The varying distributions of body fat at different sites
of the body and between the subcutaneous and internal tissues,
and alterations that occur with ageing and in different types
of physique, are virtually unknown. The importance of social
factors, psychological influences, patterns of eating, and
economic circumstances in the context of obesity are subject
to speculation, with little reliable evidence to give assistance.
It is surely reprehensible that our knowledge of such a widespread concomitant of modern urban life is so unsatisfactory.

Alcohol consumption

A health and social problem of apparently increasing magnitude
relates to alcoholism and the steady and rapid increase in the
consumption of alcohol in the community. This is not exclusively
an urban phenomenon. The nutritional importance of alcohol
consumption is perhaps less than its importance as a health
hazard, but alcoholic drinks do provide a considerable energy
source for many people and have effects on the food budget
for a household, on the types of foods eaten by the individual,
and on his or her total energy balance (and likelihood of obesity).
Our knowledge is inadequate at present on these widespread problems.

CONCLUSION

The nutritional effects of urbanization on the populations
of developed countries are the subject of much emotional
conjecture but only a little hard scientific appraisal. The
Reports of the National Food Survey Committee in the U.K.
still show differences in the diets of urban and rural communities.
but these are no greater than differences found between certain
regions, and the differences seem to change from year to year.
Therefore it is uncertain whether variations in food-consumption
pattern between rural and urban communities are of much direct
nutritional significance.   However, indirect influences on
nutrition, caused by local customs, by socio-economic differences,
by factors such as unemployment, and by the general life style
may be of considerable importance to the health of urban
communities.

Urbanization in *developing* countries undoubtedly creates
specific nutritional problems.   In *developed* countries the
situation is entirely different.   Undernutrition is virtually
non-existent.   However, malnutrition, including 'overnutrition',
may be widespread and may be more concentrated in certain urban
environments, leading to a high prevalence of obesity, various
metabolic and degenerative diseases, dental caries, and
gastro-intestinal and other nutritional disorders affecting the
whole age spectrum of the population.   The direct relevance
of urbanization to these aspects of malnutrition needs investigation.   Our economic, industrial, and social existence may well
change radically in the near future, and a suitable food policy
will require much more complete nutritional information.

REFERENCES

ARNEIL, G.C.   (1967).   *Dietary study of 4365 Scottish infants.*
Scottish Health Service Studies No.6, Scottish Home and
Health Dept., Edinburgh.

ASHER, P.   (1966).   Fat babies and fat children.   *Archs.Dis.
Child.* *41*, 672-77.

ASHLEY, W. (1928).   *Bread of our forefathers.*   Clarendon Press,
Oxford.

AYKROYD, W.R. (1973).   The consumption of sugar.   *Br.Nutr.Found.
Bull.* *8*, 21-9,

BURNETT, J. (1966)   *Plenty and want.*   Nelson, London.

BURNETT, J. (1969). *A history of the cost of living.* Pelican, London.

CRAWFORD, W. and BROADLEY, H. (1938) *The people's food.* Heinemann, London.

CURTIS-BENNETT, N. (1949). *Food of the people: being the history of industrial feeding.* Faber. London.

DRUMMOND, J. and WILBRAHAM, A. (1939) *The Englishman's food* (2nd ed.) revised by D.Hollingsworth (1958) Jonathan Cape, London.

DURNIN, J.V.G.A. (1967) Activity patterns in the community, *Can. med. Ass. J. 96,* 882-6.

DURNIN, J.V.G.A. (1973) Body weight, body fat and the activity factor in energy balance. In *Energy balance in man,* pp.141-50. Masson et Cie, Paris.

DURNIN, J.V.G.A., LONERGAN, M.E., GOOD, J., and EWAN, A. (1974). A cross-sectional nutritional and anthropometric study, with an interval of 7 years, on 611 young adolescent schoolchildren. *Br.J.Nutr.* 32, 169-79.

EID, E.E. (1970) Follow-up study of physical growth of children who had excessive weight gain in the first 6 months of life. *Br. med. J.* ii, 74-6.

FABRY, P. (1969) *Feeding patterns and nutritional adaptations.* Butterworths, London.

FENELON, K.G. (1952) *Britain's food supplies.* Methuen, London.

FORD.J.A., COLHOUN, E.M., McINTOSH, W.B. and DUNNIGAN, M.G. (1972) Rickets and osteomalacia in the Glasgow Pakistani community 1961-71. *Br.med.J.* ii, 677-80.

GREAVES, J.P. and HOLLINGSWORTH, D.F. (1966). Trends in food consumption in the U.K. *Wld. Rev. Nutr. Diet.* 6, 34-89.

HAMPTON, M.C., HUENEMANN, R.L., SHAPIRO, L.R., and MITCHELL, B.W. (1967). Caloric and nutrient intakes of teenagers. *J.Am. diet. Ass.* 50, 385-96.

HOLLINGSWORTH, D. (1974) Changing patterns of food consumption in Britain. *Br.Nutr.Found.Bull.* 12, 31-41.

HOLMES, A.M., ENOCH, B.A., TAYLOR, J.L. and JONES, M.E. (1973)
Occult rickets and osteomalacia amongst the Asian immigrant.
population, *Quart. J. Med.* 42, 125-49.

JOHNSON, M.L., BURKE, B.S., and MAYER, J. (1956). Relative
importance of inactivity and overeating in the energy balance
of obese high school girls, *Am. J. clin. Nutr. 4*, 37-44.

KEYS, A. (1970) *Coronary heart disease in seven countries.*
Monograph No. 29, *American Heart Association.*

MELLBIN, T. and VUILLE, J.C. (1973) Physical development at
7 years in relation to velocity of weight gain in infancy with
special reference to incidence of overweight. *Br.J.prev.
soc. Med.* 27, 225-35.

MILLER, D.S. and PARSONAGE, S. (1975) Resistance to slimming:
adaptation or illusion. *Lancet i.* 773-5.

MINISTRY OF AGRICULTURE, FISHERIES AND FOOD (1968) Food
consumption levels in the U.K. *Bd. Trade J.* 194, 753-9.

MINISTRY OF AGRICULTURE, FISHERIES AND FOOD (1973). Energy
of food supplies moving into consumption. *Food facts.* No.72.

MORRIS, J.N., ADAM, C., CHAVE, S.P.W., SIREY, C, EPSTEIN, L.
and SHEEHAN, D.J. (1973). Vigorous exercise in leisure-time
and the incidence of coronary heart-disease. *Lancet i.*
333-9.

NATIONAL BOARD OF HEALTH AND WELFARE (1972) *Diet and Exercise.*
Stockholm.

NATIONAL FOOD SURVEY COMMITTEE (1966) *Household food consumption
and expenditure.* Annual Report. HMSO, London.

NATIONAL FOOD SURVEY COMMITTEE (1969) *Household food consumption
and expenditure.* Annual Report HMSO. London.

NATIONAL FOOD SURVEY COMMITTEE (1973) *Household food consumption
and expenditure.* Annual Report. HMSO. London.

ODDY, D.J. (1970) Food in nineteenth century England: nutrition
in the first urban society. *Proc.Nutr.Soc.* 29, 150-57.

PÉRISSÉ, J., SIZARET, F. and FRANÇOIS, P. (1969). The effect
of income on the structure of the diet. *Fd. Agric. Org. Nutr.
Newsletter* 7 No.3, 1-9.

SHUKLA, A., FORSYTH, H.A., ANDERSON, C.M., and MARWAH, S.M. (1972)   Infantile overnutrition in the first year of life: a field study in Dudley, Worcestershire.   *Br.med.J.* iv. 5o7–15.

TAYLOR, H.L. (1967)   Occupational factors in the study of coronary heart disease and physical activity.   *Can. med. Ass. J.* 96, 825–31.

WYNDHAM, C.H. (1972)   *Coronary heart disease in relation to physical activity.*   Morton Press, Johannesburg.

8 Urbanization and growth

J. M. Tanner and Phyllis B. Eveleth

In recent years there has been considerable discussion amongst auxologists and paediatricians about the effects of urbanization on the growth and health of children and adolescents. Particular interest has been focused on the tendency for children to grow up faster than previously, that is to be larger nowadays at each age than they were 50 years or even 20 years ago and to attain full adult physical status earlier (see Tanner 1965; 1973). This tendency has been general throughout Europe during the last 50 - 100 years. 'Urbanization' has been held responsible for this. In the Austrian province of Carinthia, during the years 1953-61, the average age of reaching menarche,(the first menstrual period) decreased in girls in the towns (from 13.8 to 13.1 years) and 'industrial settlements' (from 14.1 to 13.4 years), more than in girls remaining on isolated upland farms (from 14.5 to 14.3 years) (Wurst 1964). Some authors (for example, Bennholdt-Thomsen 1952), seemingly regretful, demonstrate perhaps the ruro-humeral prejudices of Quarinonius (1610), a seventeenth century writer who described exactly the problem we are to discuss:

> The peasant girls in this landschaft in general menstruate much later than the daughters of the townsfolk or the aristocracy, and seldom before their 17th, 18th or even 20th year. For this reason they also live much longer than the townsfolk and aristocratic children and do not become old so early. The townsfolk have usually borne several children before the peasant girls have yet menstruated. The cause seems to be that the inhabitants of the town consume more fat food and drink and so their bodies become soft, weak and fat and come early to menstruation in the same way as a tree which one waters too early produces earlier but less well-formed fruit than another.

We shall be mainly concerned with the obvious, and majority view, that urbanization (in the European sense) brings increased economic benefits which are reflected in improved nutrition and child care. But some writers, believing that urbanization covers a multitude of sins as well as virtues, have stressed the supposed contrast in life style between town and country dwellers, especially adolescents. In particular increased sexualization of the youth

---

† Based on a chapter of *World-wide variation in human growth* by Phyllis B.Eveleth and J.M.Tanner published by Cambridge University Press in International Biological Programme Monographs, 1976.

cultures of Europe and North America has been said to stimulate development, if not growth (for example, Brown 1966). It is necessary to say that modern knowledge of the endocrinology of growth (see Tanner 1975) does not permit us to rule this out as being a physiological impossibility. Nevertheless, it is not a view that is easy to take seriously when one recalls that in every instance where children have matured earlier sexually they have already been more advanced physically by the age of 5 or 6 (as judged by percent of final size attained).

A more bizarre suggestion is that the increased lighting of towns, and presumably the long winter evenings spent crouched over the TV screen, brings on earlier maturation (as does indeed the lengthening daylight of spring, in some seasonally breeding animals). This time, however, such physiological facts as we have seem to run *contra*, for blind children that is those who cannot distinguish light from darkness, grow up if anything faster than the sighted (Zacharias and Wurtman 1969).

The crux of the matter is what we imply by urbanization. Simply a high density of population is not in itself sufficient; the shanty slums of South America and some other parts of the world do not come within our definition (though we shall discuss them later), and a European or North American city is considerably different from an urbanized area in Africa, or even a city in India or Japan. From our point of view, life in a city implies first and foremost a regular supply of goods and services, and the existence of institutions associated with this provision. In rural areas children, and pregnant and lactating mothers also, may well go without food for a period before the new harvest; in the city techniques of storage and distribution prevent this. Urbanization, in its most modern form, abolishes the seasons. Moreover, the city child has the advantages of more developed and immediately available sanitation and health services, large medical institutions, and large educational, recreational, and welfare facilities. As against this, the child in the country has the benefits of more open space, less air pollution, and the possibility, not always realized, of a greater variety of physical exercise and experience. He lives less in a depersonalized world of hurrying strangers and dangerous noise.

Seen thus, it is not necessarily obvious which child is healthier. It is in this context that the study of growth is important, for growth rate (of height though by no means of weight) appears to be the best overall guide to health that we have at present at our disposal.

In investigating the sources of any differences, we cannot escape the normal task of the human biologist: to keep in unwavering stereopsis the views from the twin eyes of environment and heredity. Not only are most urban samples of children

living under better environmental conditions than the corresponding
rural samples, but also they are often drawn from genetically
dissimilar pools.

The genetic, or even ethic, difference may arise in two ways, which
may be called 'migrant sampling', and 'urban heterosis'. Many
city folk are immigrants from the countryside: in Poland in
1956, for example, nearly 50 per cent of urban dwellers were
born and raised in the country (Gorny 1972). One must therefore
ask whether those who migrated from country to town were a random
sample of people living in the country, or whether they were
selected or selected themselves, for qualities that may be in
part genetically controlled. The best evidence that migrants
are sometimes a select group comes from Shapiro's (1939) classical
study showing that Japanese immigrants to Hawaii were significantly
different from the Japanese remaining in Japan (sedentes). In
the United Kingdom Martin (1949) demonstrated that amongst men
measured for induction into the armed forces in 1939 (that is, a
complete national sample) those who were living in counties
different from their county of birth were 0.8 cm taller than those
still living in their county of birth. However, not all studies
agree that migrants are a select group physically. In South
Africa, Venda men migrating to Johannesburg 10 or more years
prior to the study were not different in length measurements from
those remaining in rural Venda areas (though they were greater
in weight and skinfolds, as one might imagine) (De Villiers 1971).
Thus, it remains inconclusive that migrants themselves are always
selected, since frequently studies deal with immature adults
or children of immigrants who have benefited from an improvement
in the environment. In certain countries too, particularly in
Central and Southern America, the distinct ethnic groups making
up a post-colonial population may be differently distributed in
urban and rural areas. In Peru, for example, one might expect
to find more people of predominantly Spanish ancestry in central
Lima than in the surrounding urban slums and rural villages.
There, Amerindian genes, conferring perhaps a different potentiality
for growth, would be more represented.

As for urban heterosis: cities are more genetically heterogeneous
than rural villages. Though there is no evidence that outbreeding
affects rate of maturation, it may affect the ultimate adult
height attained (and hence to a small extent children's heights
for given age). Outbreeding would increase stature only if some
degree of dominance exists in the many genes controlling it; that
is, if on average the offspring of a tall and a short parent lies
not exactly halfway between the two, but a little closer to the tall
parent. Thus the (outbred) person with many heterozygote pairs
amongst his stature-controlling genes would be slightly nearer the
(inbred) person with many 'tall' homozygotes than to the (inbred)
person with many 'short' homozygotes. Whether such dominance does
occur in man is not at present clear, owing to the formidable

number of parent-offspring pairs that have to be measured
before the findings become significant either way (Tanner and
Healy 1954). Hulse (1957) has shown that the breaking up of
rural islates in the Ticino, Switzerland, led to an increase
in body size in products of out-marriages, and others (Saldanha
1962; Wolanski, Jarosz, and Pyzuk 1970) have found the same.
However, such studies are not in themselves conclusive since
this process involves migration to new and usually better
environments.

MIGRANTS TO A NEW TOWN IN POLAND

An unusually clear example of rural-urban migration occurred
in Poland when the new industrial city of Nowa Huta was created
in 1949 on the outskirts of Cracow. The population increased
sevenfold in the 15 years from 1950 to 1965 through immigration
from rural areas, principally a region called 'little Poland'.
By 1965 the population was 1599 inhabitants per square kilometre, comparable with that of Liege, Belgium.

The growth of the school children of Nowa Huta was studied
in 1967 as part of the International Biological Programme
(Panek and Piasecki 1971). These children had lived in Nowa
Huta for at least 10 years or since birth, their parents
having arrived before 1958, mostly from rural villages (rural-
to-Nowa Huta children) though some from other small towns
(urban-to-Nowa Huta children). Thus the great majority were
Nowa Huta born and reared: but some of the adolescents had
spent their early childhood elsewhere. Children remaining in
Little Poland areas were simultaneously measured.

The urban-to-Nowa Huta children were on average about 4.3 cm
taller and 1.5 kg heavier at ages 4-14 than children who had
reamined in the rural area. Fig.8.1 illustrates the curves
for boys; those for girls are similar. The urban-to-
Nowa Huta boys were a little larger than the rural-to-Nowa
Huta boys, by about 1 cm in the early years rising to nearly
3 cm at age 14. Evidently the urban-to-Nova Huta boys
matured earlier, as can be seen from the shapes of the curves.
Since the urban-to-Nowa Huta children and the rural-to-Nowa
Huta had both lived for the same period in Now Huta, the
difference between them probably reflects the migrant
selection - not to Nowa Huta, but in the previous move from the
country to the town. It may also reflect an environmental
amelioration of the conditions of the mothers during their growth
period, resulting in better intra-uterine growth of the urban-to-
Nowa Huta children. Unfortunately, birth weights are not give
but second-generation effects of this sort are well documented
(Thomson 1959). That townspeople have a greater average height
is an observation made in various regions of Poland (Panek and
Piasecki 1971 pp.218-19; Wolanski and Lesotes 1964).

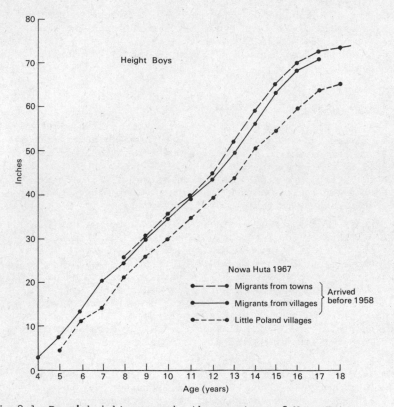

Fig.8.1 Boys' height means in the new town of Nowa Huta,
Poland, 1967 contrasting those who migrated from towns and those
who migrated from villages (Panek and Piasecki 1971.) These are
compared with boys 9-14 years from 'Little Poland', origin of
78 per cent of Nowa Huta migrants, and with rural villages of
Kurpie and Suwalki at other ages (Wolanski, unpublished data.)

Nowa Huta children matured earlier than rural ones, as indicated
by earlier menarche and accelerated tooth eruption. The urban-
to-Nowa Huta girls had significantly earlier menarche than the
rural-to-Nowa Huta girls, though there was no significant
difference in dental eruption.

URBAN-RURAL COMPARISONS IN HEIGHT AND WEIGHT: EUROPE, UNITED STATES, AND AUSTRALIA

Studies in some other European countries also show that children in the cities are larger than those in rural areas. Figs. 8.2 and 8.3 give means for heights and weights from Finland Backström-Jarvinen 1964), Greece (Valaoras and Laros 1969),

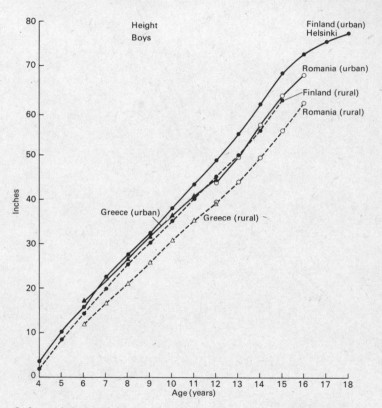

Fig.8.2 Heights of boys in urban and rural areas in Romania, Finland, and Greece. For source of data see text

and Romania (Cristescu 1969). The amount by which urban children are taller or heavier varies. Eight-year-old boys in Helsinki for example, were 2.4 cm taller and 1.6 kg heavier than rural Finnish boys, while in Greece the urban-rural differences were twice as great, amounting to about 5.7 cm

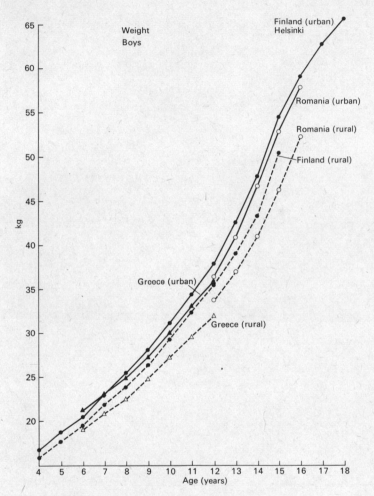

Fig.8.3 Weights of boys in urban and rural areas in Romania, Finland, and Greece. For source of data see text.

and 2.5 kg. During puberty the differences became greater, presumably because of the earlier appearance of the adolescent growth spurt in city children.

While part of the urban-rural difference results from earlier maturation, part at least persists into adulthood (Fig.8.4).

Comparisons of adults are always fraught with difficulties about
the age at which final height is reached in different populations
(see Tanner 1966) but it appears that in the 1960s in Romania,
Poland, Greece and Norway, but not East Germany, urban men were
taller than rural.

Other European countries, however, show smaller urban-rural
differences, or none at all. In Holland, where a large sample
of children fully representative of all parts of the country

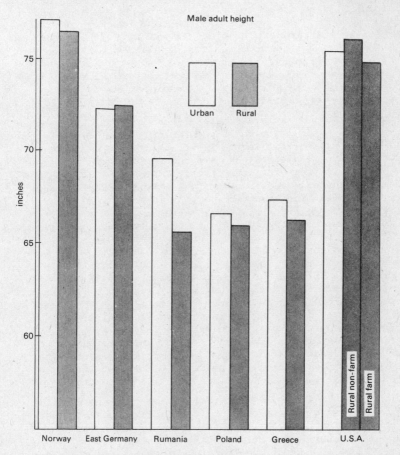

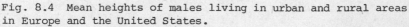

Fig. 8.4 Mean heights of males living in urban and rural areas
in Europe and the United States.

was measured in 1965, no difference was found in mean height
between children in towns and rural areas, though rural
adolescents, particularly girls, were heavier (van Wieringen,
Wafelbakker, Verbrugge, and De Haas 1971). Differences
associated with socio-economic status were present, and
differences in adults linked with a geographical north to south
gradient.

Recent studies from Australia (Jones, Hemphill, and Meyers 1973)
and the USA (Hamill, Johnston, and Lemeshow, 1972) both showed no
significant differences in height and weight between city and
country children. The comparisons, however, are very different
from those in most parts of Europe. In the Australian study the
Sydney metropolitan area was compared with an inland country
town already wholly urbanized in terms of goods and services and
in no way comparable to the rural communities of parts of Europe
stretching back hundreds of years. The comparison is really
between a large and a small urban area.

The American study concerns that extreme rarity, a representative sample drawn from the whole population. Moreover, the
analysis standardizes for income level. At the same income
level there were no discernible differences of height or weight
between 6- to 11-year-old rural farm children and children in
24 central cities ranging from New York City to Columbia, South
Carolina. Differences appeared when the lower-income rural
population was compared with either the high-income-urban or
rural populations. These results are substantiated by the
earlier report on American adults (Hathaway and Foard 1960)
which showed no consistent differences in height or weight in
relation to urbanization (Fig.8.4). It seems likely then that
the urban-rural differences in Central, South, and Eastern
European populations reflect primarily an economic differential
between town and country. They may reflect also the degree to
which life styles really differ in the two localities; in
still-developing rural areas, the children may walk several
kilometres to school each day, and help on the farm with
considerable expenditure of physical labour, in a relatively
marginal nutritional situation, as Wurst (1961) and Wolanski
and Pyzuk (1973) showed in Austria and Poland respectively.

All the same this possibly critical balance between exercise and
nutrition does not prevent the rural children being relatively
heavier than urban ones in those countries in which they are
smaller. In Finland, Greece, and Romania rural boys had a greater
weight for given height than urban boys at most ages studied.
Probably this reflects primarily a greater amount of muscle, for
skinfolds, representing fat, are less in the rural groups studied
(see below). In urban situations a similar difference may occur
in relation to socio-economic class; in Birmingham, England
children of lower economic groups, though smaller than others, had
greater weight for height (Healy 1952). Fat may be involved in

urban groups, for Whitelaw (1971) showed that skinfolds are consistently greater in London lower social classes. Furthermore, in London, New York, and three Eastern American cities, it has been reported that obesity is more prevalent among the less well-off classes. (Stunkard, d'Aquilo, Fox, and Filion 1972).

URBAN-RURAL COMPARISONS IN HEIGHT AND WEIGHT: AFRICA, ASIA, AND CENTRAL AMERICA

In developing countries the cities are often newer, and usually growing more rapidly, than the Old European centres of population, and by the side of often quite rich urban areas grow up the shanty slums of the urban poor. Here our question takes on a more serious urgency; are such 'urban' slums better or worse than the slums of the impoverished countryside that the migrants have left?

In Nigeria (Janes 1970; Morley, Woodland, Martin, and Allen 1968) and Costa Rica (Villarejos, Osborne, Payne and Arguedes 1971) urban slum children had heights and weights that were not significantly different from those of rural children. In one instance only have urban slum children been reported as larger than children in the corresponding rural areas; this was in Bombay, where even the urban poor were said to have received more food in the first two years after birth than the children in the rural areas (Pradke and Kalkurni 1971).

Adult height means in Nigeria (Janes 1970), Puerto Rico (Fernandez, Burgos, Asenjo, and Rosa 1971), and Jamaica (Ashcroft, Ling, Lovell, and Miall 1966) (Fig.8.5) did not differ greatly between urban and rural poor, although the urban populations were slightly taller. In Chad (Crognier 1969) and Malawi (Nurse 1971) differences were greater. Because of the nature of these new urban areas it is difficult to know what proportion of the adults studied were actually urban-born and reared and what proportion migrated to the cities after they were full grown. These problems for Africa are discussed more fully by Nurse (1971) and de Villiers (1971).

Better-off urban children, that is, children who live in parts of towns that we would classify as urban in the European sense, are considerably taller and heavier than rural children, as one would expect from consideration of the European data. Figs.8.6, 8.7, and 8.8 show this for children in Costa Rica (Villerejos *et al.* 1971) and children of Negro or predominantly Negro parentage in Kingston, Jamaica (Ashcroft, Heneage, and Lovell 1966). It is significant that in Jamaica the difference seems almost entirely one of rate of development and not of ultimate height. The 16-, 17- and 18-year-old rural girls come up to the urban girls in height and weight and the 18-year-old

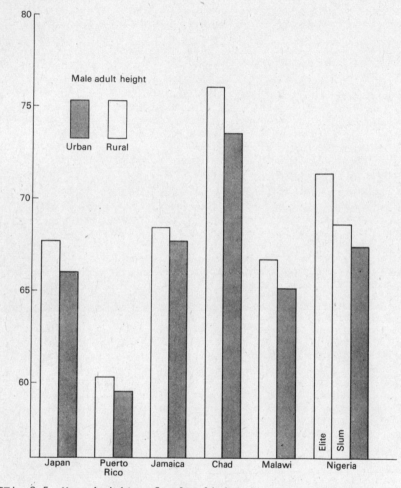

Fig.8.5 Mean heights of males living in urban and rural areas
in Africa, Japan, and the Caribbean.

rural boys, though still below the urban 18-year-olds appear to
be still growing. This very small difference in male adults,
illustrated in Fig.8.5, indicates that the rural boys also
catch up with the urban by the end of their growing period.
Thus we see in this society the intermediate stage of the

economic effect on growth, the further stage being that which involves a smaller final size as well as a longer time needed to reach it.

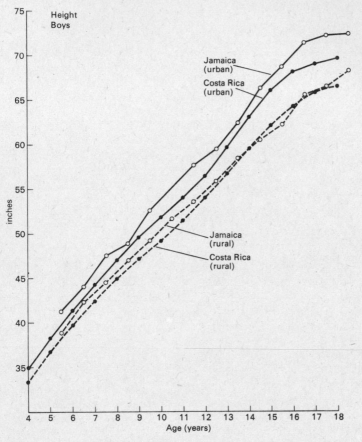

8.6 Heights of boys in urban and rural areas in Jamaica predominantly of Negro ancestry, and in Costa Rica predominantly of European ancestry.

In Costa Rica (Villarejos *et al*. 1971) there is a substantial middle class in both rural and urban areas, and the mostly white sample represented different socio-economic groups. Again the urban children were larger. The Indian National Survey, however, showed that in most parts of India urban children were only

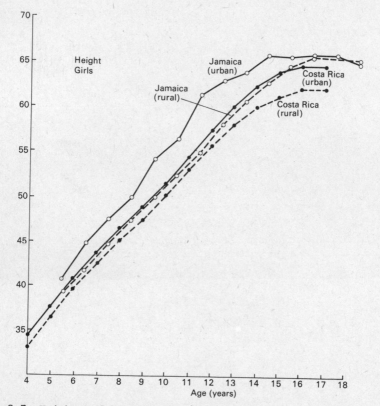

Fig.8.7 Heights of girls in urban and rural areas of Jamaica predominantly of Negro ancestry and in Costa Rica predominantly of European ancestry.

slightly taller and heavier than rural ones; indeed such differences as existed were mainly in weight. (Indian Council of Medical Research 1972). It seems that in most of India urban and rural children experienced not dissimilar conditions unless they came from really well-off families, in which case they did indeed grow to be considerably larger (Ragahavan, Singhard, and Swaminathan 1971).

Reports have come from a number of other nations and urban-rural differences in child growth, and all are in agreement

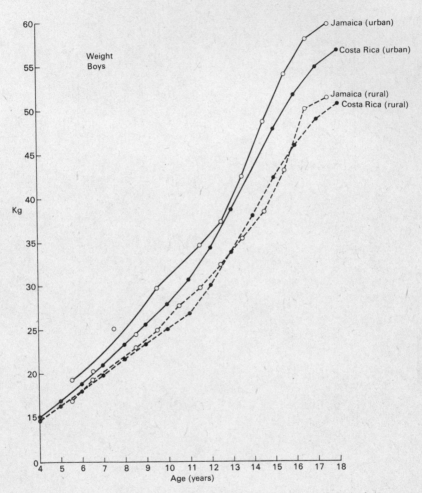

Fig.8.8 Weights of boys in urban and rural area of Jamaica predominantly of Negro ancestry and in Costa Rica predominantly of European ancestry.

that the urban children are generally larger than rural. Further details will be found for the Central African Republic in Gody (1971); for South African Bantu in Richardson (1973); for South Africans of European descent in Grobbelaar (1964); for

TABLE 8.1

Comparison of secular increase in height in Tokyo and rural Japan from 1907 to 1953 calculated from Shigeta 1962

	Age	Actual increase in height means 1907 to 1953, cm. †		Relative increase in height Means from 1907 to 1953‡	
		Boys	Girls	Boys	Girls
Seishi	6+	1.71	3.81	1.54	3.52
Elementary	7+	–	3.66	–	3.21
School, Tokyo	8+	2.78	3.57	2.28	2.98
	9+	3.10	5.40	2.44	4.33
	10+	4.74	5.83	3.61	4.47
	11+	5.78	6.72	4.23	4.91
Iwaizumi	6+	4.56	4.08	4.25	3.85
Elementary	7+	5.15	5.50	3.21	4.97
School, (rural)	8+	6.96	8.72	5.90	7.51
	9+	5.37	7.84	4.37	6.45
	10+	4.09	8.65	3.22	6.80
	11+	5.74	9.50	4.35	7.15

† $\bar{X}_{1953} - \bar{X}_{1907}$

‡ $\dfrac{\bar{X}_{1953} - \bar{X}_{1907}}{\frac{1}{2}(\bar{X}_{1953} + \bar{X}_{1907})} \times 100$

Koreans in the Yonsei University report (1967-8); and for Japan in Shigeta (1962). The last study is particularly interesting because in addition to urban-rural comparisons there is information on the secular increase in height and weight. Children in a Tokyo school were taller and heavier both in 1907 and 1953 than children in a rural school in Iwate prefecture. However, between 1907 and 1953 rural children gained more in height than the urban children, both actually and relatively, so that the 1953 differences were considerably smaller than the 1907 ones (Table 8.1). This result, of course, argues against such things as urban psycho-sexual stimulation being a predominant influence on growth and reinforces the view that nutritional causes are paramount.

URBAN-RURAL COMPARISONS OF SKINFOLDS, AND INCIDENCE OF OBESITY

Skinfolds have been used in a very large number of studies as measures of fatness and hence nutritional status (for example, South Africa, Nigeria, Britain, USA, India, Honduras, Jamaica, and Puerto Rico). Many of these studies show larger skinfolds in urban than in rural populations both of children and adults. In South Africa, Richardson (1973) found greater average triceps skinfolds at nearly every age in comparably selected groups of white and Bantu urban schoolchildren as compared with rural. More of the urban children were judged to be either overweight or obese. Adult Bantu showed a similar picture, tending toward overweight with increasing urbanization (Walker, Richardson, Nurse, and Walker 1965).

In Puerto Rico schoolchildren, adolescents, and adults over 60 years living in urban areas had a higher prevalence of obesity than rural people (Fernandez, Burgos, and Asenjo 1969). At all ages the city dwellers had greater average subscapular skin-folds. In Poland and Greece children in rural areas had on average considerably smaller skinfolds than their urban peers (Charzewska, unpublished data; Wolanski, unpublished data; Valaoras and Laros 1969).

In contrast to this, adults, particularly women, in rural areas in Czechoslovakia have been reported to have a higher prevalence of obesity than those in Prague (Osanova and Hejda 1972).

RATE OF MATURATION IN URBAN AND RURAL AREAS

A good indication of the rate of maturation is given by age of menarche. In every urban-rural comparison so far reported urban girls have a earlier menarche than rural girls (Fig. 8.9). In Romania (Cristescu 1969), Finland (Kantero and Widholm 1972), Poland (Laska and Mierzejewska 1970; Milicer and Szczotka 1966), India (Indian Council for Medical Research 1972),

and South African (Bantu) (Walker *et al*. 1965 (girls appear to
mature earlier in the cities. In the Australian comparison
of Sydney with an inland town, discussed above, however, there
was no significant difference in menarcheal age, just as there
was none in height and weight (Jones *et al*.1973). As with
growth in the body size, age at menarche is closely related to the
health and nutritional level of an individual or a population.

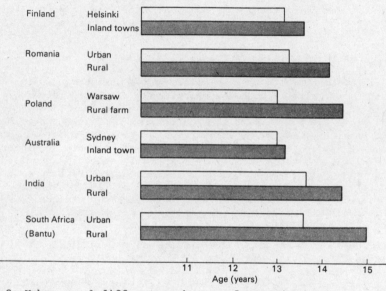

Fig.8.9 Urban-rural differences in age of menarche in
various countries.

Though there seem to be no reports contrasting skeletal
maturation in urban and rural groups, the timing of the
eruption of the deciduous dentition in well-off urban children
in Ibadan, Nigeria has been contrasted with those of village
children north-east of Ibadan; the urban children had earlier
eruptions (Enwonwu 1973). Charzewski (1963) had also noted
that Polish village children erupted their permanent teeth
on average later than urban children.

SUMMARY AND CONCLUSIONS

Children growing up in the towns of most European and some
other countries (Finland, Poland, Greece, Romania, Jamaica,
Spain, Czechoslovakia), are larger at each age, and reach

maturity sooner than children growing up in the villages.
Despite having more subcutaneous fat they are lighter for
given height, and thus presumably more 'linear' and less
'lateral' in build. Even as adults they are taller in many
countries (Poland, Greece, Romania, Norway). However, in some
places (for example, Jamaica) the urban children's greater size
is wholly due to their earlier maturation, and the rural children
eventually catch up to equal them. These differentials are all
evident in early childhood and clearly develop right from birth.

In some European countries (for example, Holland) there is now
no difference in growth between urban and rural children nor
between urban-grown and rural-grown adults (East Germany). In
Australia no difference was shown between the capital city and
a smaller inland town. A representative and nation-wide
survey in the United States showed an urban-rural difference,
but this disappeared when the parents' incomes were equated.
It would seem that in rural areas where the traditional rural
patterns and isolated farms and small villages exist the children
are small and delayed in growth, whereas in rural areas where
the agricultural pattern is 'industrialized' the children grow
the same as in the towns.

In the economically impoverished urban areas of Asia, Africa,
and South America the shanty-town slum dwellers are mostly not
larger than their rural counterparts, though children living in
the middle-class areas of the cities are. In general urban-
rural differences mirror the differences seen between children
in different social classes, whether in the urban or rural
population.

However it does, have to be borne in mind that outbreeding
is greater in towns than in rural villages and that if heterosis
for stature occurs in man, as it may, then this in itself would
cause the adult height (though not the rate of maturation) to be
greater in the towns. In addition those people who migrate from
the villages to settle in towns are usually not a random sample
of the village population, but may be taller and heavier than
average. Thus some part of the greater adult stature of the urban
population, where it occurs, maybe due to these selective
genetical mechanisms.

Thus it seems highly probable that most, if not all, urban-rural
differences are due to the economic differential between town
and country dwellers, resulting in the better feeding of the
well-off. In some rural communities, also, children may still
expend more energy than they do in life in the city. Other
theories advanced as to the cause of earlier maturation in cities,
such as differences in life style, in particular supposedly
greater psychosexual stimulation, have no solid evidence to support
them. The nutritional-economic effect is in any case so predominant as to make investigation of other effects very difficult
except in a few countries.

ASHCROFT, M.T., HENEAGE, P., and LOVELL, H.G. (1966) Heights and weights of Jamaican schoolchildren of various ethnic groups. *Am. J. phys. Anthrop.* 24, 35-44.

ASHCROFT, M.T., LING, J., LOVELL, H.A., and MIALL, W.E. (1966) Heights and weights of adults in rural and urban areas of Jamaica. *Br.J.prev.soc.Med.* 20, 20-26.

BACKSTROM-JARVINEN, L. (1964) Height and weights of Finnish children and young adults. *Ann.Paed.Fenniae*, suppl. 23.

BENNHOLDT-THOMSON, S. (1952) Uber das akzelerationsproblem, *Z.Mensch. Vererb. Konstlehr.* 30, 619-34.

BROWN, P.E. (1966) The age at menarche. *Br.J.prev.soc.Med.* 20, 9-14.

CHARZEWSKI, J. (1963) Some problems of the cutting of permanent teeth in children and youths in urban and rural environments. *Prace Mat. Naukowe IMD (Res Rep.)* 1, 65-80.

COLLEGE OF HOME ECONOMICS AND COLLEGE OF MEDICINE, YONSEI UNIVERSITY, KOREA (1967-8). *A study on the food intake and nutrititional status of elementary school children and the family in urban and rural Korea.*

CRISTESCU, M. (1969) *Aspecte ale cresterii si dezvoltarii Adolescentilor din Republica Socialista Romania.* Ed. Acad. Repub. Soc. Romania, Bucarest (In Rumanian; French summary.)

CROGNIER, E. (1969) Données biometriques sur l'état de nutrition d'une population africain tropicale: les sara dutchad. *Biomet. hum.* 4, 37-55.

DE VILLIERS, H. (1971) A study of morphological variables in urban and rural Venda male populations. In *Human biology of environmental change* (ed. D.J.M. Vorster) I.B.P., London.

ENWONWU, C.O. (1973) Influence of socio-economic conditions on dental development in Nigerian children. *Archs. oral Biol.* 18, 95-107.

FERNANDEZ, N.A., BURGOS, J.C., and ASENJO, C.F. (1969). Obesity in Puerto Rican children and adults. *Bol.Ass.Med. (Puerto Rico)* 61, 153-7.

FERNANDEZ, N.A., BURGOS, J.A., ASENJO, C.F., and ROSA, I. (1971) Nutritional status of the Puerto Rican population. *Bol.Ass.Med. (Puerto Rico)* 63, 1-46.

GODY, J. (1971) L'Enfant en Republique Centrafricain (ed. Bergeret) Bordeaux. (These pour le doctorate en medicine).

GORNY, S. (1972) Anthropometric survey of Poland. Part I. Measurements of adults, 1955-56. *Mat. I. Prace Anthrop.* 223 (In Polish, English summary)

GROBBELAAR, C.S. (1964) *Suggested norms of physical status for white South African males aged 10-26 years, based on anthropometric survey.* Struick, Cape Town.

HAMILL, P.V.V., JOHNSTON, F. and LEMESHOW, S. (1972) *Height and Weight of Children: socioeconomic status.* DHEW Publ. No. (HSM) 73-1601; Vital Health Statistics, series 11, no.119. U.S. Government Printing Office, Washington.

HATHAWAY, M.L. and FOARD, E.D. (1960) *Heights and Weights of Adults in the United States.* Home Econ. Res. Rep. No.10. U.S. Government Printing Office Washington.

HEALY, M.J.R. (1952). Some statistical aspects of anthropometry. *J.R. Stat.Soc.* 14 164-84.

HULSE, F. (1957) Exogamy and heterosis. *Yearb. phys. Anthrop.* 9, 240-57.

INDIAN COUNCIL OF MEDICAL RESEARCH (1972) *Growth and development of Indian Infants and children.* Technical Report Series, No.18, New Delhi.

JANES, M.D. (1970) The effect of social class on the physical growth of Nigerian Yoruba children. *Bull. Int. epidemiol. Ass.* 20, 127-36.

JONES, D.L., HEMPHILL, W. and MEYERS, E.S.A. (1973) *Height weight and other physical characteristics of New South Wales children.* New South Wales Department of Health, N.S.W. Australia.

KANTERO, R. and WIDHOLM, O. (1972) A statistical analysis of the menstrual patterns of 8,000 Finnish girls and their mothers II. The age of menarche in Finnish girls in 1969. *Acta Obstet. Gynecol. Scand. Supp.14.*

LASKA, M. and MIERZIJEWSKA, T. (1970) Effect of ecological and socio-economic factors on the age of menarche, body height and weight of rural girls in Poland. *Hum.Biol.* 42, 284-92.

MARTIN, W.J. (1949) *The physique of young adult males.* Medical Research Council Memorandum No.20, HMSO. London.

NURSE, G.T. (1971) The body size of rural and peri-urban adult males from Lilongwe District. In: *Human biology of environmental change* (ed. D.J.M.Vorster) IBP, London.

OSANOVA, K. and HEJDA, S. (1972) Incidence and prevalance of obesity in Czechoslovakia. *Nutr.Rep.Internat.* 6 191-98.

PANEK, S. and PIASECKI, (1971) Integration of population of Nowa Huta in the light of anthropometric data. *Mat.I. Prace Anthrop.* 80, 249. (In Polish, English summary).

PRADKE, M.V. and KALKARNI, H.D. (1971) Growth and development in the underprivileged sections in the Bombay area. *Proc. Nutr. Soc. India* 10, 167-76.

QUARINONIUS, H. (1610) *Die grewel der verwurslung menschlichen Geschleckhts.* Innsbruck.

RAGAHAVAN, K.V., SINGH, D., and SWAMINATHAN, M.C. (1971). Heights and weights of well-nourished Indian children. *Ind.J.Med.Res.* 59, 648-54.

RICHARDSON, B.D. (1973) Studies on nutritional status and health of Transvaal Bantu and white pre-school children. *S.Afr. Med. J.* 47, 688-98.

SALDANHA, P.H. (1962) The genetic effects of immigration in a rural community of Sao Paulo, Brazil, *Acta Genet. Med. Gemell.* 11, 158-224.

SHAPIRO, H.L. (1939) *Migration and environment.* Oxford University Press, London.

SHIGETA, S. (1962) A study on the change in physique of the Japanese. *Res.J.Phys.Educ.* 6, 23-39.

STUNKARD, A., D'AQUILI, E., FOX, S.S. and FILION, R.D.L. (1972) Influence of social class on obesity and thinness in children. *J.Am.med.Ass.* 221, 579-84.

TANNER, J.M. (1965) The trend towards earlier physical maturation. In *Biological aspects of social problems,* ed. J.E. Meade and A.S.Parkes, pp.524-39. Oliver and Boyd, London.

TANNER, J.M. (1973) Trend towards earlier menarche in London, Oslo, Copenhagen, the Netherlands and Hungary, *Nature,Lond.* 243, 95-6.

TANNER, J.M. (1975) Growth and endocrinology of the adolescent. In: *Endocrine and genetic diseases of childhood* (2nd ed.) (ed. L.Gardner) Saunders, Philadelphia and London.

TANNER, J.M. and HEALY, M.J.R. (1954) Lack of sex-linkage and dominance in genes controlling human stature. *Caryologia* suppl. 933-4.

THOMSON, A.M. (1959) Maternal stature and reproductive efficiency. *Eugen.Rev.* 51, 157-162.

UDJUS, E.G. (1964) *Anthropometrical changes in Norwegian men in the twentieth century*. Universitetsforlaget, Oslo.

VALAORAS, V. (1970) Biometric studies of army conscripts in Greece. *Human Biol.* 42, 184-201.

VALAORAS, V. and LAROS, K. (1969) Biometric characteristics of Greek pupils in elementary schools. *Iatriki* 15, 266-76. (In Greek).

VAN WIERINGEN, WAFELBAKKER, F., VERBRUGGE, H.P., and DE HAAS, J.H. (1971) *Growth diagrams 1965: Netherlands*. Netherlands Institute for Preventive Medicine, TNO, Leiden.

VILLAREJOS, V.M. OSBORNE, J.A., PAYNE, F.J. and ARGUEDES, J.A. (1971) Heights and weights of children in urban and rural Costa Rica. *Env.Child Hlth*. 17, 31-43.

WALKER, A.R.P., RICHARDSON, B.D., NURSE, A. and WALKER, B.F. (1965) The changing pattern of growth and other parameters in South African Bantu children. *S.Afr.med.J.* 39, 103-4.

WHITELAW, A.G.L. (1971) The association of social class and sibling number with skinfold thickness in London schoolboys. *Hum.Biol*. 43, 411-20.

WOLANSKI, N. and LASOTA, A. (1964) Physical development of countryside children and youths aged 2 to 20 years as compared with the development of town youth of the same age. *Z.Morph. Anthrop*. 54, 272-92

WURST, F. (1964) Untersuchungen zur akzeleration auf dem Lande. Off Gesundli-Dinst. 26, 179-86.

WURST, F., WASSERTHEURER, H. and KIMESWENGER, K. (1961) *Entwicklung und Umwelt des landkindes*. Ostrereichicher Bundesverlag. Wien.

WOLANSKI, N., JAROSZ, E. and PYZUK, M. (1970) Heterosis in man's growth in offspring and distance between parents' birthplaces. *Soc.Biol*. 17, 1-16.

WOLANSKI, N., PYZUK, M. (1973) *Studies in human ecology*, Polish Scientific Publishers, Warsaw.

ZACHARIAS, L. and WURTMAN, R.J. (1969) Blindness and menarche. *Obstet. Gynecol*. 33:603.

9 The use of socially acceptable monitoring instruments (SAMI)

O. G. Edholm

When the International Biological Programme (IBP) was in its initial stages, it began to be clear that in the Human Adaptability section there would be considerable problems in devising methods for making physiological measurements on a very large number of subjects. In general, physiologists were familiar with studies in the field of up to 10 individuals, and even this number strained resources. Now they were faced with studying 100 or more individuals, whose ordinary lives should not be disturbed, and who would not tolerate many elaborate measurements. A large number of people had to be studied using as small a team of observers as possible, both because of difficulties due to cost and to interference. Hence there was a need to design equipment which would be light and inconspicuous so that it could be worn by the subject without altering his/her habitual activity. On the other hand, continuous recording in a conventional form would generate a very large amount of information which would be difficult to analyse and interpret, and so it was decided that integrated information would be obtained, which was in many cases the end point of the laborious analyses of continuous records.

Once the basic design for a SAMI was formulated, the signal to be transduced was discussed. There was general agreement that heart-rate should be included, as this could be the basis for estimates of energy expenditure. Other signals have included environmental temperature, skin and body temperature, and posture. Up to the present, by far the greatest interest has been shown in the heart-rate SAMI, and most of the account given in this section will be concerned with experience gained in the use of this instrument.

It will be realized that the problems of measurement on a large number of subjects are similar to the methodological problem involved in studying physiological aspects of urban human biology. Amongst the information required is an estimate of daily energy expenditure, hence the importance of assessing the use of heart-rate SAMI for this purpose.

THE HEART RATE INTEGRATING SAMI RECORDERS

The instrument used in our tests was a one-E-cell SAMI. The information obtained was the total number of heart-beats recorded during the period of time the instruments were connected. Our purpose was to use heart-rate as an index of

energy expenditure.

The procedure used by different investigators operating this instrument has varied. The simplest has been to measure heart-rate during a night's sleep in bed, followed by a second record-ing of heart-rate during the day, from the time of rising to going to bed at night, and a third recording during the subsequent night. The mean rate during the two nights' sleep is taken as the resting level, and the difference between day and night rates as an index of energy expenditure. This procedure provides a guide to energy expenditure making it possible to rank individuals according to their day-night differences. In the absence of other information, such a ranking order is useful, but it is not possible to assign energy expenditure values in joules or calories. To do this it is necessary to calibrate each subject by measuring oxygen consumption and heart-rate at rest and three levels of increasing energy expenditure, using a bicycle ergometer, or a treadmill, or stepping on and off a stool at different rates. Acheson (1974) has also shown that in a long-term study it is important to repeat such calibrations at approximately monthly intervals. There is a linear relation-ship between heart-rate and oxygen consumption; so provided heart-rate is known, energy expenditure can be derived.

The heart-rate/oxygen relationship, although invariably found when a relatively wide range of oxygen consumption is used, is not generally clear in light activities, that is, with oxygen consumption below about 750 ml/per minute. If, for example, resting or sleeping heart-rate is 60 per min, then up to heart-rates of approximately 80 beats per min, the relationship to oxygen consumption can show a considerable scatter. Hence, if the overall daily energy expenditure is low, there may be a large error in estimating expenditure from the nett heart-rate The departures from linearity are due to the following.

1. *Static compared with dynamic work.* Static work results in a greater increase in heart-rate than dynamic work at the same level of oxygen consumption.

2. *Posture.* Heart-rate is higher standing than sitting or lying.

3. *Emotional effects.* For example, excitement, apprehension, anger, and alarm; all these cause an increased heart-rate.

With very few exceptions heart-rate from any of these causes - static work, posture, and emotion - is higher than predicted from the linear relation. So usually, at low to moderate levels of energy expenditure, overestimates are made on the basis of heart-rate recording.

STUDIES WITH HEART-RATE SAMI

An Israeli study (Edholm *et al.* 1973) of Yemenite and Kurdish
Jews living in agricultural villages in Israel has been made.
It included the assessment of daily energy expenditure. Assess-
ments were made using a single-E-cell SAMI and separately by
observing and timing an individual subject's activities and
measuring the oxygen consumption associated with different
activities. The heart-rate was measured for approximately 36
hours (for example the first night, during the day, and the
second night), providing the total beats recorded in each of
three periods. There were 160 subjects, men and women, and they
were tested in the summer and winter. The subjects carried out
their ordinary activities.

The problems arising from the use of the heart-rate SAMI
included faults in the equipment and faults in the use of the
equipment. As regards the first, there were occasional
difficulties, due to dry joints or to the E cell not making
proper contact. If the subject rode on a tractor, and hence
experienced vibration and occasional violent movement, then
false signals were often generated. These were due to shaking
the recorder and were overcome by more careful sealing of the
components. It was necessary to have careful and expert maintenance to ensure that the SAMIs continued to function, and
calibration had to be checked regularly. User-faults were due
first to a high skin resistance. Careful preparation including
abrasion of the skin to reduce resistance below approximately
10 kΩ is essential. It proved desirable to check skin resistance at the end of 24 hours, as frequently it had increased to
an unacceptably high level. Useful measures to combat this
included using a suitable electrode jelly (see de Looy and
James 1972) and the technique of skin abrasion (Lourie 1971).
A common cause of failure was detachment of the electrodes
from the skin, and this was more frequent if the subject was
sweating freely. A good adhesive was the best antidote. The
next commonest fault was a break in the lead from the electrodes
to the recorder, usually associated with hard work involving the
arms and chest. It could be avoided by ensuring an adequate
lead and a suitable place for the subject to wear a recorder.

In the Israel study, 70 of the subjects were calibrated, that
is, oxygen consumption and heart-rate were measured at rest
and on a bicycle ergometer at three or four different levels
of work, usually up to a maximum level. Details are given in
Edholm *et al.* (1973).

The results were assessed by comparisons with the estimates
of energy expenditure calculated from the timed activity by
the measured values of oxygen consumption. The daily energy
expenditure of the individual subjects were compared with the
day heart-rates minus the night heart-rates. When subjects

were ranked in order of heart-rate there was some correspondence
with rank order of estimated energy expenditure, but there were
many discrepancies.   When energy expenditure was calculated
from heart-rate using the oxygen consumption heart-rate calibration
for the individual, the values obtained were substantially higher
in most cases that those calculated from the time activity
studies. The difference ranged from O to 25 per cent and
averaged 16 per cent. A similar difference has been observed
by Acheson (1974) from careful studies on a small group of
subjects examined throughout one year.

It was concluded from the Israel study that the SAMI heart-
rate technique was feasible and acceptable and could be used
on a large scale, although skilled and unremitting maintenance
of the instruments was essential. However, the results obtained
were not considered to be sufficiently reliable for using to
estimate daily energy expenditure. This judgment depends on the
validity of the timed-activity oxygen-consumption technique.
This method has been extensively used in many surveys by a number
of workers, and the mean results in any one survey usually
agree closely with the mean value for food intake. The mean
energy expenditure calculated from the heart-rate was substantially
and significantly higher than the estimate from the timed-
activity survey, hence the conclusion was drawn that the heart-
rate estimate was too high.

Apart from the use of heart-rate measurements to estimate energy
expenditure, other information was obtained from the recordings.
In the Israel study, the night or resting heart-rates showed a
small but highly significant difference between summer and winter.
Rather surprisingly, the night heart-rates were higher in the
summer.

Payne and his colleagues (1971) have used the heart-rate SAMI
to study energy expenditure in elderly people. The subjects were
carefully calibrated, and excellent linear relations between heart-
rate and oxygen consumption were obtained. Heart-rate was
measured both in the day and during the night and the energy
estimates so obtained agreed well with estimates of food intake.

Beeghly (1972) has used the SAMI heart-rate recorder in a
study of villagers in the Philippines; both a one and a three
E-cell SAMI were employed. Beeghly concluded the estimates of
energy expenditure derived from heart-rate were too high as
compared with food consumption 'and there seems little choice
but to conclude that some of the results derived from SAMI data
must be considered suspect.' However, it appears from the text
of the report that it is the derivation which is suspect rather
than the heart-rate recording.

Acheson (1974) has studied energy expenditure and food intake
at a British base in the Antarctic (Halley Bay). His main

object was to compare different methods for measuring food
intake and energy expenditure, and he used the single-E-cell
SAMI.   Although only six subjects were examined, measurements
were made on each of them for a continuous period of seven
days every month for nearly a year. One subject was studied
for a total of 319 days. From measurements of food intake and
changes in body fat over the course of a year (42-44 weeks)
an estimate was derived of the mean daily expenditure for each
subject. This was used as a standard with which to compare
results obtained by other methods. In general, methods based
on heart-rate overestimated energy expenditure, and those
based on diary cards combined with measurements of oxygen
consumption for specific tasks underestimated energy expenditure.

  There are a number of differences between the Acheson and
Beeghly studies, both in methods and results. Beeghly used
the three-cell SAMI during the working day, for an average
period of 10 hours each day. Subjects were calibrated working
on a bicycle ergometer in an air-conditioned room. The energy
expenditure for the 10-hour working period of the day was
calculated using the appropriate heart-rate/oxygen-consumption
calibration. A period of 8 hours sleep was assumed to be at
the average resting metabolic rate. The energy expenditure
during the remaining 6 hours was assumed to be midway between
the sleeping and working rate. Although this is a considerable
assumption, it appears from the figures given by Beeghly that
the energy expenditure for the 10-hour working period computed
from the heart-rate substantially exceeded the total energy
intake of the subject (estimated from food intake). Hence it
may be reasonably concluded that the heart-rate technique
overestimated actual energy expenditure by a very large
factor. Beeghly concludes that one important reason for the
discrepancy is that the villagers were working out of doors
in a hot and humid climate with high levels of solar radiation,
and as a result heart-rate was greatly increased. No figures
are given for body temperatures either during the working period
or at rest nor are any climatic data included. The increased
heart-rate during work in hot compared with cool conditions
is mainly due to the rise of body temperature (Edholm *et al.*
1962), although some rise may be associated with the increased
blood-flow in the skin. Beeghly cannot be said to have
demonstrated unequivocally that the main reason for an overestimate was due to the effect of heat, as the effect would
have had to have been large, which seems improbable in subjects
who were presumably fully acclimatized to heat.

  Poleman (1972) in studies in Sri Lanka also found very big
differences between energy-expenditure estimates derived from
measurements of oxygen consumption and heart-rate, and concluded
that the latter gave unacceptable values.

On the other hand, Acheson's work was conducted with meticulous detail, on a small number of subjects, over a long period of time. He compared energy expenditure in a variety of ways; using the regression of heart-rate on oxygen consumption for standarized exercise on a bicycle ergometer (repeated each month) or for habitual activities or for a combination of habitual exercise and standardized exercise. In addition, he used diary cards combined with many measurements of oxygen consumption during the performance of each activity recorded by the subject. A single-E-cell SAMI was employed and the total heart-beats for 24 hours were recorded. There was no separate recording for sleep and activity. When the results for the different methods were compared with food intake, corrected for change in body fat over the course of 44-46 weeks, all the heart-rate methods over-estimated and the diary-card techniques underestimated energy expenditure. There was also very large individual variation, so that, although the mean for all six subjects using the habitual-activity regression time was only 3 per cent greater than the 'standard', the range for individuals was -21 per cent to +51 per cent. Acheson concluded that there are such large variations in the individual for the heart-rate associated with any particular activity that it is not feasible to obtain consistent results for energy expenditure using a SAMI.

Goldsmith, Miller, Mumford, and Stock (1967) compared oxygen consumption with heart-rate using the single-E-cell SAMI. They obtained good agreement between the two methods; the mean for the group was 2.29 kcal per min from measured oxygen consumption and 2.27 kcal per min predicted from heart-rate. Their subjects were students, 19-22 years old, who spent most of the day indoors in a thermally neutral environment.

DISCUSSION OF THE HEART-RATE SAMI RESULTS

The reports by different investigators using the SAMI heart-rate recorder and briefly reviewed above reveal differences in methodology and interpretation. There is general agreement that the heart-rate SAMI is socially acceptable, even amongst unsophisticated subjects.

Amongst old people, leading inactive lives, Payne *et al.* (1971) found good agreement between energy expenditure derived from heart-rate and food intake. Goldsmith *et al.* (1966) also obtained satisfactory results comparing heart-rate and measured oxygen consumption on young relatively inactive subjects. Three field studies have been carried out in warm to hot climates and one in the Antarctic.

In Israel, studies were carried out on a semi-arid zone amongst people who were primarily farmers, both in the hot, dry summer and in the relatively warm winter. In Sri Lanka and

the Phillipines the subjects were field workers exposed to a hot and humid climate. In all three cases energy expenditure calculated from heart-rate exceeded estimates derived from either direct measurement or from food intake.

In the Antarctic, in a very cold climate, estimates of energy expenditure derived in various ways from heart-rate recordings, were in general higher than those based on food intake and measurement of changes in total body fat. The most striking finding was the great variability between subjects, so the chances of making moderately accurate determinations on any one individual were not considered to be good.

Should one then dismiss the SAMI heart-rate integrator as of minimal use in the determination of daily energy expenditure? This question cannot be answered by a simple 'yes' or 'no'. In the first place, it would appear that in some circumstances satisfactory results can be obtained, specifically in relatively inactive groups. Indeed, as regards group averages not individual results, estimates of energy expenditure based on heart-rate may be too high, but in the Antarctic group the difference between food intake estimates and heart-rate estimates was only 3 per cent. In hot and warmer conditions errors appear to be larger, and this could be due to a raised body as well as skin temperature.

In view of the convenience and acceptability of the SAMI and the laborious alternative techniques for measuring energy expenditure it would be rash to discard the SAMI, especially for use in a temperate climate and for subjects who might be very difficult to study in any other way. Provided, and this is an important technical proviso, that the heart-rate obtained from the SAMI is reliable then useful information can be obtained which may be related to other conditions than energy expenditure, for example, environmental levels of temperature and noise, awkward working postures, and fatigue. In general then, the heart-rate SAMI (especially in some of the more recent forms, which are currently being tested) should not be discarded, but it cannot be expected to give an exact answer to a very difficult question, that is, the accurate measurement of daily energy expenditure.

OTHER USES FOR THE SAMI

At the beginning of this chapter mention was made of the other uses of the SAMI, one of which was the recording of environmental temperatures. Here the temperature-sensitive end organ is worn on the surface of the subject's clothing, and an integrated record of temperature is obtained.

Corkhill, Holland, Fox, and Mee (1972) have written a paper entitled 'A study of exposure to environmental temperatures on a population sample using the temperature SAMI'. Environmental

temperatures were measured day and night for 48 hours on 112
subjects aged 35-74. Of the 448 possible measurements, 108
were not obtained, mainly due to human errors by subjects and
observers. Four of the failures were due to failure of the
instrument, but there were a number of faults in the E cells.
The technique was acceptable, and there were only a small
number of minor complaints. However, careful supervision was
necessary.

Although the temperature SAMI has not been extensively used
so far, various personal reports have been obtained which
support the opinions expressed by Corkhill *et al.* that the
technique is feasible and useful.

Other applications of the SAMI technique are currently being
tested, and it seems probable that with further development
much field work which hitherto has been desirable but
impracticable will be possible, and physiologists may successfully examine the very large number of subjects that are
necessary for genetic and epidemiological studies.

REFERENCES

The American Journal of Clinical Nutrition, Volume 24, contains
a number of papers on the measurement of energy expenditure.
The use of heart-rate and the SAMI heart-rate integrator is
discussed in a number of these papers, some of which are cited
below.

ACHESON, K.J. (1974) *The assessment of techniques for measuring
energy balance in man.* Ph.D. Thesis, University of London.

BEEGHLY, W.M. (1972) Nutrition, employment and working efficiency:
towards measuring human activity in the rural Tropics. *Cornell
Agricultural Economics Staff Paper,* No.72-3.

BRADFIELD, R.B. (1971) A technique for determination of usual
daily energy expenditure in the field. *Am.J.clin. Nut.* 24,
1148-54.

BRADFIELD, R.B., CHAN, H., BRADFIELD, N.E., and PAYNE, P.R.
(1971) Energy expenditure and heart-rates of Cambridge boys
at school. *Am.J.clin.Nutr.* 24, 1461-6.

CORKHILL, R.T., HOLLAND, W.M., FOX, R.H., and MEE, M.S.R.
(1972). A study of exposure to environmental temperature in
a population sample using the temperature SAMI. *Br.J.prev.
soc.Med.* 26, 40-5.

EDHOLM, O.G., ADAM. J.M.. and FOX. R.H. (1962) The effects of work in cool and hot conditions on pulse rate and body temperature. *Ergonomics* 5, 545-56.

EDHOLM, O.G., HUMPRHEY, S., LOURIE, J.A., TREDRE, B.E., and BROTHERHOOD, J. (1973). Energy expenditure and climatic exposure of Yemenite and Kurdish Jews in Israel. *Phil. Trans. R.Soc.* B266, 127-40.

GANDRA, Y.R. and BRADFIELD, R.B. (1971). Energy expenditure and oxygen handlings efficiency of anaemic school children. *Am.J.Clin.Nutr.* 24, 1451-56.

GOLDSMITH, R., MILLER, D.S., MUMFORD, P., and STOCK, M.J. (1966) The use of long-term measurements of heart rate to assess energy expenditure. *J.Physiol.* 189, 35.

HEYWOOD, P.F. and LATHAM, M.C. (1971) Use of the SAMI heart-rate integrator in malnourished children. *Am.J.clin. Nutr.* 24, 1446-50.

deLOOY, A. and JAMES, S. (1972) Electrical resistance and skin reaction to eight electrode jellies. *Proc. Nutr. Soc.* 31, 88A.

LOURIE, J.A. (1971) *Anthropometry of Middle Eastern Jews in Israel. Ph.D. Thesis,* University of London.

PAYNE, P.R., WHEELER, E. and SALVOSA, C. (1971) Prediction of daily energy expenditure from average pulse rate. *Am.J. clin. Nutr.* 24 1164-70.

POLEMAN, T.T. (1972) Estimation of energy expenditure from the measurement of heart-rate. *Cornell Agricultural Economics Staff Paper* No.72-35.

SALVOSA, C., PAYNE, P.R., and WHEELER, E. (1971) Energy expenditure of elderly people living alone or in local authority homes. *Am.J.clin.Nutr.* 24 1467-70.

10 Aspects of medical geography in Great Britain

G. M. Howe

Medical geography, also known as nosogeography (from the Greek *nosos,* disease) deals with the geography of human disease. In so far as disease represents lack of harmony in environments, medical geography may be defined as the study of human maladjustments or maladaptations in the environment or habitat which result, or threaten to result, in some form of human pathological condition. The study is concerned with differences in environments and ways of life in various geographical areas and among various social groups which make for diversity in the prevalence and nature of disease.

As a technical term medical geography is sometimes equated, at least in part, with geographical pathology, medical ecology, geo-medicine, disease ecology, epidemiology, and, by some, with human ecology. The differences are largely of approach and emphasis. More recently, and particularly in the USA, medical geography has come to embrace also the geography of health care.

In Western, industrial countries such as Great Britain, Germany, Sweden, and the USA there has been in recent years a striking change in the relative importance of the various forms of disease. Many of the infectious diseases such as tuberculosis, diphtheria, and poliomyelitis have been brought under control or eliminated by a combination of antibiotics and vaccines, and the worst kinds of poverty such as result in undernourished children and high mortality have been removed. And yet the overall death rate has changed but little over the last quarter of a century. All that has happened is that deaths from heart disease, strokes, cancer, and road accidents have taken the place of previous diseases.

Degenerative diseases of middle and later life are now the principal causes of suffering and death. Their aetiology is still, to a large extent unknown. They are termed 'degenerative'; but there is growing evidence to suggest that environmental factors play an important part in their development. It seems reasonable to assume therefore that a more exact description of environmental factors may prove of value in increasing understanding of the causation of those disorders which now scourge society in the developed world.

In Great Britain, the National Health Service, was set up more than 25 years ago. Medical care is now available to all residents regardless of whether or not they contribute

to National Insurance, and the duration of entitlement to treatment is unlimited. Using data obtained under the National Health Service - and such data is available for the whole population - it is possible, after standardizing for sex and differences in age structure of local populations, to examine geographical distributions of mortality experience. Where significant regional differences occur it is often possible to measure the degree of co-extensiveness between disease and other spatially varying factors and thus to test whether spatial associations are causally related. In practice, most spatial relationships of disease are found to be multivariate and are best analysed by a combination of cartographical representation, multiple regression, and/ or factor analysis methods.

Mortality data for the major causes of death, published annually by the Registrars-General in London, Edinburgh, and Belfast, are available for the individual metropolitan boroughs of London, the county boroughs, and the urban and rural districts within each administrative county of the United Kingdom. Many of these data have been standardized and expressed cartographically on demographic maps (Figs. 10.1, 10.4, 10.5, 10.9, and 10.12. In each map the index number 'SMR (standardized mortality ratio) 100' is the national expectation of mortality for the particular disease. Standardized mortality ratios in excess of 100 denote unfavourable mortality experience from that cause of death while values less than 100 are taken to represent favourable mortality experience. On the maps those areas classified as 'urban' are represented by squares of a size proportionate to the population 'at risk' in those areas: the rural areas are represented by diamonds similarly proportionate to the local population.

ISCHAEMIC HEART DISEASE - (ARTERIOSCLEROTIC HEART DISEASE, INCLUDING CORONARY DISEASE)

Heart disease is the main cause of untimely death in Great Britain, certified in almost a third of the deaths in middle-aged men. The most obvious feature of the distributional pattern of standardized mortality ratios for ischaemic heart disease (see Figs.10.1 and 10.2) is the concentration of high ratios in the north of the country and low ratios in the south. The dividing line runs from the Mersey to the Humber, although South Wales and certain London boroughs are obvious exceptions. Major areas of particularly unfavourable mortality experience occur in Lancashire, Yorkshire, Teeside, Scotland, and Northern Ireland.

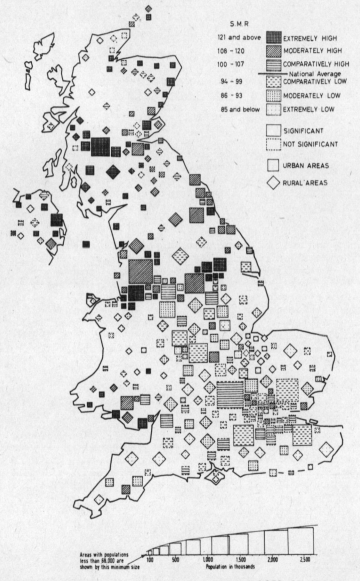

Fig. 10.1 Ischaemic heart disease, males, 1959–63 (after Howe
1970.)

Heart disease, like cancer, is not caused by any specific microbe but by a multitude of factors inextricably woven into the life-style and social habits of men and women in industrial society. Internationally, coronary heart disease strikes more frequently in nations which are economically rich and whose populations are predominantly sedentary and well fed. Within Britain the reverse appears to be the case with the economically more prosperous South East of the country enjoying the more favourable mortality experience.

At least eight factors have been deemed significant in ischaemic heart disease: high blood lipid (fat) levels, hypertension, cigarette smoking, physical inactivity, obesity, nervous stress, diabetes mellitus, and genetic factors. There is considerable speculation on the role played by each of these risk factors and on their relative importance. The obese for example, are prone to diabetes; people under stress take little exercise; racial and genetic differences are often associated with differences in diet. Obesity, exercise, and diet are themselves interrelated. Consequently, when correlations between disease and any single factor are being examined it is almost inevitable that other factors tend to complicate conclusions.

Cardiovascular mortality is thought to be inversely correlated with the hardness of the water supply (Fig.10.3). One study found more arteriosclerosis among the male population of Glasgow, which has a soft water supply, than among the male population of London, with its generally hard water supply. (Morris, *et al*. 1968). On the other hand, a detailed study within Glasgow revealed several wards (administrative areas) within the city enjoying mortality experience 20—30 per cent *below* the national average (Howe 1970).

Diets vary greatly within Britain. In the London area, for example, household consumption for all selected items of food except margarine, cakes, and biscuits is above the national average. The consumption of all selected items is below the national average in Scotland except for cakes, biscuits, margarine, beef, and veal. The high consumption of butter in Wales is noteworthy, as is the high consumption of pork, mutton, and lamb in the Midlands. Such regional variations are worthy of note in the context of dietary fats, blood cholesterol, and the intake of sugar.

In a country in which over 80 per cent of the population is classified as 'urban' (residential location) and in a society in which a high proportion of the population experience different environments during their lifetime, or even in their daily round (at home, at work, for leisure) it seems unlikely that urban-rural differences in mortality would be revealed.

Fig.10.2   Key to Figs.

COUNTIES

AB	Aberdeen	DO	Dorset	L (E)	East Lothian	SR	Stirling
AG	Anglesey	DU	Durham	L (M)	Midlothian	ST	Staffordshire
AH	Armagh	DW	Down	L (W)	West Lothian	SU	Sutherland
AN	Angus	E (I)	Isle of Ely	M	Moray	SY	Surrey
AR	Argyll	EX	Essex	ME	Merionethshire	S (E)	East Suffolk
AT	Antrim	F	Flintshire	MO	Monmouthshire	S (W)	West Suffolk
AY	Ayr	FE	Fermanagh	MT	Montgomeryshire	SX (E)	East Sussex
BA	Banff	FI	Fife	MX	Middlesex	SX (W)	West Sussex
BD	Bedfordshire	GC	Gloucestershire	M (I)	Isle of Man	TY	Tyrone
BE	Berkshire	GH	Glamorgan	N	Nairn	WA	Warwickshire
BK	Berwick	HA	Hampshire	NF	Norfolk	WE	Westmorland
BR	Breconshire	HE	Herefordshire	NO	Northamptonshire	WG	Wigton
BT	Bute	HF	Hertfordshire	NR	Northumberland	WI	Wiltshire
BU	Buckinghamshire	HU	Huntingdonshire	NT	Nottinghamshire	WO	Worcestershire
C	Caithness	IN	Inverness	OR	Orkney	W (I)	Isle of Wight
CA	Caenarvonshire	K	Kent	O	Oxfordshire	Y (E)	Yorkshire
CB	Cambridgeshire	KI	Kincardine	P	Pembrokeshire		(East Riding)
CD	Cardiganshire	KR	Kinross	PB	Peebles	Y (N)	Yorkshire
CH	Cheshire	KU	Kirkcudbrightshire	PE	Soke of		(North Riding)
CL	Clackmannan	LA	Lancashire		Peterborough	Y (W)	Yorkshire
CM	Carmarthenshire	LC	Leicestershire	PR	Perth		(West Riding)
CO	Cornwall & Isles of	LK	Lanark	R	Radnorshire	Z	Zetland
	Scilly	LO	Londonderry	RE	Renfrew		
CU	Cumberland	L (H)	Lincolnshire	RO	Ross and Cromarty		
D	Denbighshire		(Parts of Holland)	RU	Rutland		
DB	Derbyshire	L (K)	Lincolnshire	RX	Roxburgh		
DE	Devon		(Parts of Kesteven)	SE	Selkirk		
DM	Dumfries	L (L)	Lincolnshire	SH	Shropshire		
DN	Dunbarton		(Parts of Lindsey)	SO	Somerset		

COUNTY BOROUGHS
Counties of Cities in Scotland

AB	Aberdeen	CR	Croydon	LI	Liverpool	S.H.	St. Helens
B	Bournemouth	DA	Darlington	LO	Londonderry	SL	Sunderland
BB	Blackburn	DB	Derby	M	Manchester	SM	Smethwick
BD	Bradford	DC	Doncaster	MI	Middlesbrough	SN	Southampton
BF	Belfast	DD	Dudley	M.T.	Merthyr Tydfil	S.o.T.	Stoke on Trent
B.F.	Barrow in Furness	DU	Dundee	NE	Newport	SP	Stockport
BG	Brighton	DW	Dewsbury	NO	Northampton	S.S.	South Shields
BH	Bath	E	Exeter	NT	Nottingham	SW	Swansea
BI	Birmingham	EB	Eastbourne		Newcastle upon	T	Tynemouth
BK	Birkenhead	ED	Edinburgh		Tyne	W.B.	West Bromwich
BN	Barnsley	EH	East Ham	NW	Norwich	WG	Wigan
BO	Bootle	GA	Gateshead	O	Oxford	W.HL.	West Hartlepool
BP	Blackpool	GC	Gloucester	O	Oldham	W.H.	West Ham
BR	Bristol	GL	Glasgow	P	Portsmouth	WK	Wakefield
BT	Bolton	GY	Grimsby	PL	Plymouth	WL	Walsall
B.T.	Burton upon Trent	H	Hastings	P	Preston	WO	Worcester
BU	Burnley	HF	Huddersfield	R	Reading	WR	Warrington
BY	Bury	HX	Halifax	RC	Rochdale	WV	Wolverhampton
C	Canterbury	IP	Ipswich	RO	Rotherham	WY	Wallasey
CA	Carlisle	K.H.	Kingston upon Hull	S	Southport	Y	Great Yarmouth
CD	Cardiff	L	Lincoln	SA	Salford	YO	York
CH	Chester	LC	Leicester	SD	Southend on Sea		
CO	Coventry	LE	Leeds	SF	Sheffield		

METROPOLITAN BOROUGHS

1	City of London	9	Fulham	17	Lambeth	25	Stepney
2	Battersea	10	Greenwich	18	Lewisham	26	Stoke Newington
3	Bermondsey	11	Hackney	19	Paddington	27	Wandsworth
4	Bethnal Green	12	Hammersmith	20	Poplar	28	Westminster
5	Camberwell	13	Hampstead	21	St.Marylebone	29	Woolwich
6	Chelsea	14	Holborn	22	St.Pancras		
7	Deptford	15	Islington	23	Shoreditch		
8	Finsbury	16	Kensington	24	Southwark		

10.1, 10.4, 10.5, 10.9 and 10.12

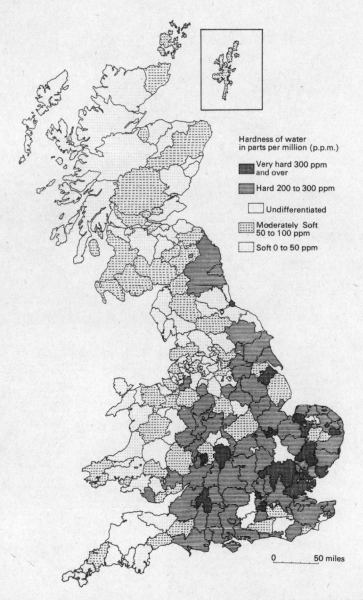

Fig.10.3   Character of public water supplies in the United
Kingdom (Based on data in the *Water Engineer's Handbook* 1970).

In the case of ischaemic heart disease regional and inter-
urban differences rather than urban-rural differences tend
to prevail.

CEREBROVASCULAR DISEASE - (VASCULAR LESIONS AFFECTING THE
CENTRAL NERVOUS SYSTEM)

The areal distribution of standardized mortality ratios
reveals a regional pattern distinguished by values in excess
of the national average north of a line from the Bristol
Channel to the Wash, and values below the national average
south of this line (Fig.10.4). Exceptions to this
generalization include the aggregates of municipal boroughs
and urban districts in Bedfordshire and Oxfordshire (though
not Oxford itself), and also Northampton and Bristol. These
have relatively high ratios in a region of favourable
mortality experience.

The reliability of the reported differences in records of
stroke mortality is unknown. Evidence suggests that there
is room for regional variations in the degree of clinical
overdiagnosis to account for reported mortality differences.
Validating studies are practicable and would be worthwhile.

Effective treatments for high blood pressure would have
become available within the last quarter of a century and may
perhaps have an important effect on the incidence of strokes.
Regional variations in the availability and use of such
treatments may therefore now contribute to regional
inequalities in stroke mortality.

The regional differences are strikingly correlated with
those for ischaemic heart disease. This is not surprising,
since high blood pressure and arteriosclerosis play a part
in both conditions. It is the more remarkable that in a few
areas (notably Northern Ireland) there are high rates for
ischaemic heart disease and low rates for strokes. This paradox
merits further enquiry.

Hardly anything is known of regional variation in blood
pressure levels. Mortality from hypertension shows some geographical correlation with that for strokes: possibly then
the incidence of strokes could be related to local differences
in the incidence of hypertension.

The influence of factors linked with urbanization seems to be
relatively weak, so that the generally favourable rates for
the South and East extend even to the towns and cities in those
regions. If real, and not due to medical-care differences,
this distribution pattern would perhaps favour an explanation
linked with environmental or geographical factors rather than

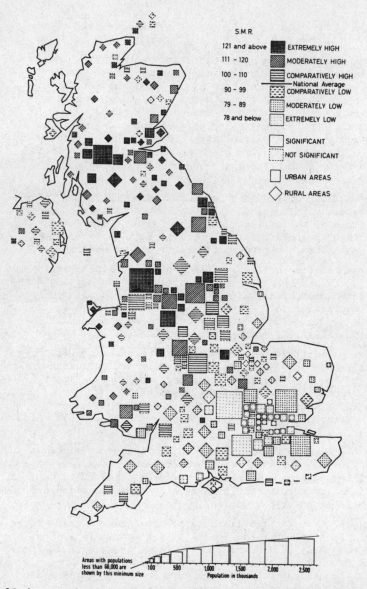

Fig.10.4   Cerebrovascular disease, males, 1959-63. (After Howe 1970.)

with socio-economic differences.

CANCER - (MALIGNANT NEOPLASMS)

Owing to their histological implications cancers have
traditionally been considered a collection of diseases
rather than a single type. Studies of the spatial variability
of cancers are thus complicated by a wide variety of
differential occurrence rates recorded by histological site.
In addition, different ratios by site have been attributed
to differences in séx, age, race, place of residence, individual
behaviour, specific environment, and many other 'non-medical'
factors.

Cancer of the trachea, lung, and bronchus

Greater London, Merseyside, South-east Lancashire, North-east
England and Central Scotland are areas of particularly
unfavourable mortality rates (Fig.10.5). There are two
lesser concentrations of high mortality in West Bromwich and
in Kingston-upon-Hull. In contrast, South-west England, the
West Country, extreme South-east England, Wales, Northern
Ireland, Southern Scotland and the Borders, the Scottish
Highlands, the Scarplands of Eastern England, the Fenlands
and East Anglia have favourable mortality experience.

The evidence of the map (Fig.10.5) suggests an urban-rural
gradient in mortality experience from lung-bronchus cancer.
The most densely populated and industrialized areas have
higher standardized mortality ratios; those for rural areas
are below the national average.

The modern town, the social habitat of industrialized man,
is characterized by high-density living, overcrowding, and an
atmosphere polluted by smoke, dust, and a wide variety of
chemical substances arising from coal and fuel oil and the
exhaust gases of motor vehicles. In addition, there are
pollutants of local importance associated with oil refineries,
enamelling works, some steel works, artificial fertilizer
plants, aluminium-processing plants, bakeries, cotton mills,
carpet mills, jute mills, etc. An areal correspondence,
though not necessarily a causal association is apparent
between the distribution of lung-bronchus cancer and smoke and
sulphur dioxide - two parameters of atmospheric pollution.
The correspondence with the stress effects of atmospheric
pollution revealed in lichens (Fig.10.6) is of particular
interest in this context (Hawksworth and Rose, 1970).

Further statistical work may reveal the extent to which the
distribution of lung-cancer mortality is explainable in terms

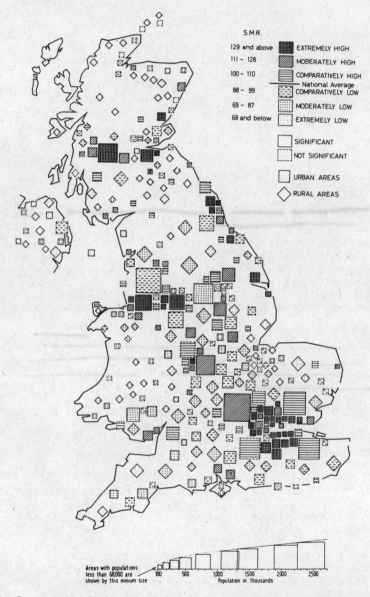

Fig.10.5 Cancer of the trachea, lung, and bronchus, males
1959-63 (After Howe 1970.)

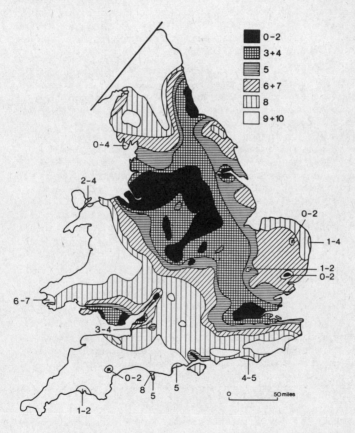

Fig.10.6   Zonation patterns of epiphytic lichens in England
and Wales as indicators of varying concentrations of mean winter
sulphur-dioxide atmospheric pollution.   (Based on Hawksworth
and Rose 1970.   The heaviest concentrations are indicated by
the black shading (scale 0-2).

of the distribution of atmospheric pollution or other factors, and how far it remains unexplained. Lack of explanation is of the utmost value, since it points to the existence of further, but as yet unknown factors. The indications of the existence of further factors can be used as feedback to stimulate exploration by renewed basic research. Why, for instance, is the mortality experience for women only 20 per cent of that for men despite the fact that in towns they are presumably exposed to the same polluted atmosphere?† The inference is that atmospheric pollution *per se* is not necessarily a dominant causal factor in lung-bronchus cancer; it does, however, have an adverse effect on the health and well-being of millions of city dwellers, and its control is now one of the most important tasks of our day.

Areal concentrations of atmospheric pollution vary slightly from one year to the next though there has been a national improvement in the amount of smoke pollution (though less so for sulphur dioxide) since the introduction of the Clean Air Act in 1956 (Figs.10.7 and 10.8). There are, however, occasional days in winter when local pollution levels rise appreciably above the average. These are usually 'smog' (smoke and fog) days, when, under conditions of high atmospheric pressure, relative quietude and temperature inversion, the upward movement and evacuation of chimney and exhaust products is checked and the intensity of the impurities in the air increases (see Chapter 4). The effects of temporarily acute air-pollution incidents have in the past been dramatic - for example, the London smog of 5th-8th December 1952 - but the longer-term chronic effects are probably more important. Urban air is poor in positive stimuli, and at the same time it is loaded with contaminating substances which produce general and local effects and are thus injurious to human health. The injury caused is thus the result not so much of individual air pollutants as of their complex action.

There are medical arguments against cigarette smoking. Indeed it is thought that no greater benefit could be conferred on the health of the British people particularly

---

† The pattern of sex distribution of lung cancer, with predominance of males, has not changed since the nineteenth century. Several authorities in the 1890s reported that lung cancer was predominantly a male disease with sex ratios ranging from 3:1 to 13:1. The ratio did not change in the early decades of the twentieth century when cigarette smoking was still not very popular.

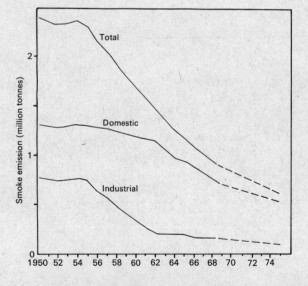

Fig. 10.7 Smoke emission in the United Kingdom (After
Craxford and Weatherley 1971.)

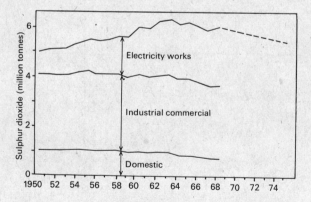

Fig.10.8 Emissions of sulphur dioxide in the United Kingdom (After Craxford and Weatherley 1971.)

in the context of lung cancer than the abolition of cigarette
smoking. On a yearly basis the Scottish male cigarette smoker
consumes an average of about 7400 cigarettes and the English
and Welsh about 6700 - a difference of about 11 per cent.
Furthermore, the Scots smoke a higher proportion of non-
tipped cigarettes (Todd 1966). Yet, despite the non-
availability of detailed information about the distribution
of cigarette smoking in Great Britain, it seems unlikely
that it would help to explain the regional incidence of lung
cancer shown in Fig.10.5.† Either way, anti-smoking propaganda
has had virtually no permanent effect, except on doctors.

Stomach cancer

The spatial variations of standardized mortality ratios for
stomach cancer are markedly different from those for lung-
bronchus cancer. Areas with markedly unfavourable mortality
experience occur in Lancashire-Cheshire, North-East England,
Wales, and the Potteries (Fig.10.9). Extremely high mortality
ratios occur sporadically in parts of the Midlands, the London
area, Central and North Wales, Scotland, Northern Ireland, and
the Fenlands, but in such areas there are only relatively small
populations at risk.

No particular urban or rural distributional pattern is
revealed for stomach cancer. This would suggest that the
relationship, if any, whether direct or indirect, is with a
factor or factors common to both urban and rural environments.
Stomach cancer is almost certainly a disease of many causes.
A range of risk factors has been postulated as being
associated with the disease in different parts of the world.
These are thought to include trace elements in soil and water,
dietary factors, and hereditary predisposition.

Soils derive their trace elements from the parent rock and
from applied fertilizers, agricultural dusts, and sprays.

---

† Some workers consider the aetiological indictment of cigarette smoking to be an oversimplification. They draw attention
to the fact that lung cancer is still predominantly a disease
of men and that the sex ratio is relatively constant despite the
prodigious increase in cigarette smoking among females during
the past four decades. (Rosenblatt 1974).

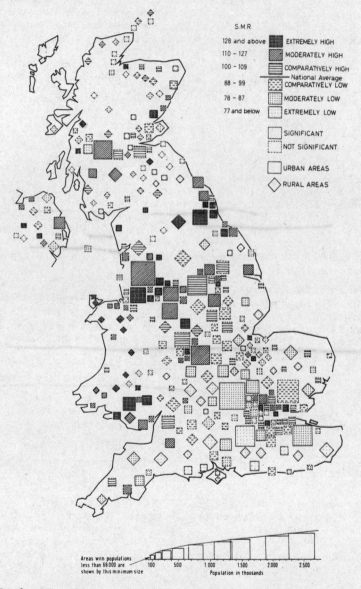

Fig.10.9 Stomach cancer, males, 1959-63. (After Howe 1970.)

Trace element characteristics are passed on from soils to grass and vegetable matter growing on them. Vegetable matter used as food may thus reflect the trace element peculiarities of local soils and of the parent geological material. Soils with a high zinc and low copper content are suspect. The addition of nitrogenous fertilizers is known to cause copper deficiences which in turn may be carcinogenic. The role of trace elements in gastric cancer requires careful investigation because the artificial addition of these elements to soils to increase their productivity may have serious deleterious effects on man.

The spoil heaps and workings of defunct lead, zinc, and copper mines in Britain contain residual amounts of these metals, generally as sulphides. These are changed to more soluble form by aerial oxidation and the action of acidic water. The streams and rivers in the vicinity of mine dumps in Wales and elsewhere are polluted by mine effluent containing these metals. Even very slight amounts of zinc and lead have been shown to be fatal to fish life. Selenium, silver, bismuth, arsenic, and antimony also occur in galena, the main source of lead. The evidence, such as it is, suggests that zinc-copper ratios in soils and/ or lead in water, act more as co-factors rather than as a complete determinants in the genesis of stomach cancer. In this same context the action of plumbo-solvent waters on the lead piping in some older properties may not be without significance. It may well be that the factor or factors responsible for a high incidence of deaths from gastric cancer merely tend to move parallel to lead pollution of water or the zinc-copper ratio of soils, these being themselves irrelevant.

Finally in this context it may be noted that a recent study suggests that with high nitrate intake, carcinogenic nitrosamines are formed in the urinary bladder and that these give rise to gastric cancer (Hill *et al.* 1973). Gastric carcinoma is said to be significantly higher in people with blood group A. The distribution pattern (Fig.10.10) does not appear to support this statistical correlation. On the contrary, Lincolnshire-Norfolk with high frequencies of blood group A in the population have low standardized mortality ratios for gastric cancer. Alternatively, it may well be that in the areas of unfavourable mortality experience it is only those memebers of the community with blood-group A who are predisposed to gastric cancer - that is, gastric cancer reflects both 'nature' and 'nurture'.

Cancer of the stomach is a well-recognized complication of pernicious anaemia. Fig.10.11 is based on the results of a collective investigation conducted by the College of General Practitioners (Scott 1960) and reveals a distributional pattern broadly similar to that for stomach cancer.

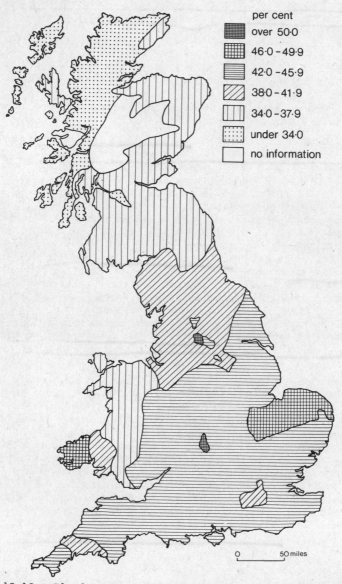

Fig.10.10.　Blood group A (based on Kopec 1970; Brown 1965 and unpublished data from the Glasgow and West of Scotland Blood Transfusion Service.)

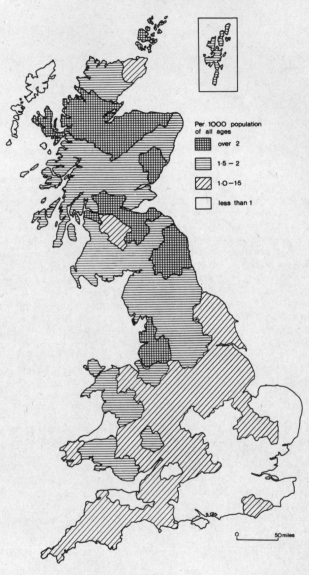

Per 1000 population
of all ages

over 2

1·5 – 2

1·0 – 1·5

less than 1

0   50 miles

Fig.10.11   Pernicious anaemia.   (Based on Scott 1960.)

BRONCHITIS

The areal pattern of standardized mortality ratios is dominated
by extremely high ratios in parts of London, South-east Lancashire, Merseyside, the Midlands, the West Riding of Yorkshire,
South-east Wales, and west Central Scotland. Ratios on Tyneside-
Teeside are moderately high. Experience in other parts of the
country is general favourable (Fig.10.12). The origins of the
disease are not fully known, but the evidence of the distributional
pattern suggests that it is a town disease. It appears to
correlate with heavily industrialized and polluted areas; rural
areas with slight atmospheric pollution seem to escape. As
already noted the atmosphere in industrialized areas is polluted
by smoke from domestic and factory chimneys, and gases from a
wide variety of factories, motor vehicles, railway locomotives,
power plants, and refuse disposal. The subject of atmospheric
pollution is well documented, but the lasting effects of chronic
pollution on man's health are not fully known. Chronic
bronchitis, lung cancer, emphysemia mesothelioma, and asbestos
are among the diseases or disorders commonly associated with
atmospheric pollutants and thought to be aggravated by them.
On the other hand, in the case of chronic bronchitis it has also
been observed that unskilled workers and their wives suffer the
highest mortality, the rate falling progressively to the lowest
among professional men and their wives. Does the higher
bronchitis mortality of certain towns reflect urban atmospheric
pollution or does it reflect urban class structure and associated
social conditions?   Cigarette smoking, a habit indulged in
universally by both males and females throughout Great Britain,
has long been considered to be a contributory causal factor in
chronic bronchitis. A constitutional or genetic element
in susceptibility may also be implicated.

The worst episode of bronchitis mortality so far recorded in
Britain was during the London smog of December 1952 when, in 4 days,
there were nearly 4000 deaths largely attributable to bronchitis.
Such mortality was as dramatic as the worst days of cholera in
the nineteenth century or the plague in the fourteenth and
seventeenth centuries. Since then the combination of clean-air
legislation and the use of antibiotics has slowed down the
mortality rate from this, the so-called 'English disease'.

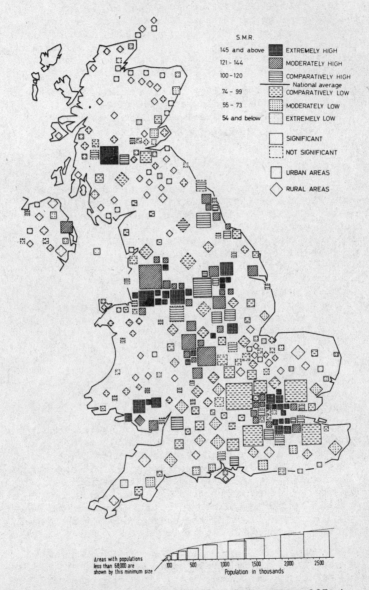

Fig.10.12 Bronchitis, males, 1959-63. (After Howe 1970.)

INFANT MORTALITY

The overall pattern of infant mortality in England and Wales in 1971 (see Figs.10.13 and 10.15) shows high rates in the Merseyside conurbation (Liverpool, Birkenhead, St.Helens, etc.), South-East Lancashire conurbation (Manchester, Oldham, Bolton, etc.), and West Yorkshire conurbation (Leeds, Bradford, Halifax, etc.) in the North, and in the Greater London boroughs of Camdem, Haringey, Hackney, Tower Hamlets and Lewisham in the South-east.

Areas with high infant mortality rates are usually those with relatively high levels of unemployment, low wages, large families, and low educational standards. With poverty are normally associated poor hygiene, overcrowding and faulty diets.

ALL CAUSES OF DEATH

The summation of community responses to the total complex of environmental factors and ways of life in the several parts of England and Wales in the twentieth century and to the effective-ness of medical and public health services, antibiotics, and vaccines is shown in Fig.10.14.   Compared with the England-Wales death rate (11.6 per 1000 of the home population in 1971), the mortality experience of the South and East of the country is generally favourable. The exceptions are Barking, Tower Hamlets, Hackney, Hammersmith, and Southwark. Lifespan in the favoured areas is on the whole longer than the national average (69 years for males and 75 years for females in England and Wales in 1972). Elsewhere, expectation of life is less than average. It is obvious, therefore, that from the point of view of health and life expectancy, marked regional inequalities exist.

COMMENT

If Great Britain was an environmentally homogeneous country, regional variations in mortality experience would be a grave indictment of the National Health Service 25 years after its inauguration. But the differences noted may well be associated with, and accounted for, by differences in the various physical and socio-economic environments. That those in authority appreciate that noticeable environmental and occupational hazards to health occur in some parts of the country and not in others, is, however, open to doubt.

In the short term it may appear expedient in Government planning to give priority to purely economic considerations, whether they relate to industrial production, road and rail construction, or improved air communications. There is un-doubtedly a case for multiplying wealth, to increase the gross

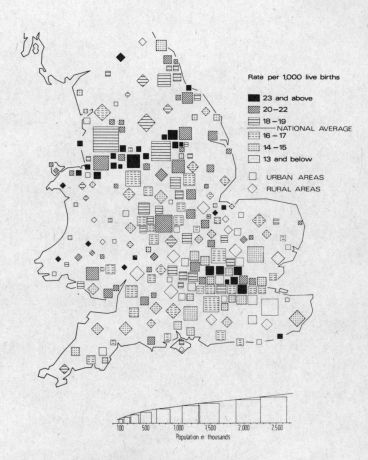

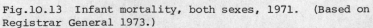

Fig.10.13 Infant mortality, both sexes, 1971. (Based on
Registrar General 1973.)

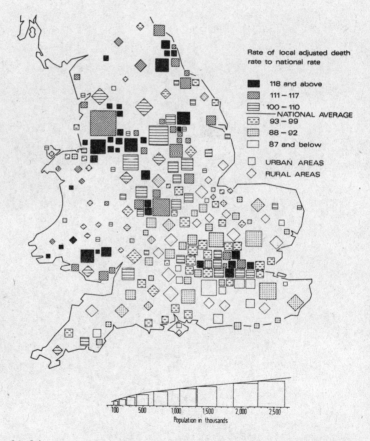

Rate of local adjusted death
rate to national rate

■ 118 and above

▨ 111 – 117

▤ 100 – 110
—————NATIONAL AVERAGE
⊡ 93 – 99

▦ 88 – 92

□ 87 and below

□ URBAN AREAS

◇ RURAL AREAS

Population in thousands

Fig.10.14 Mortality from All Causes, males 1971. (Based on
Registrar General 1973.)

national product in order to obtain the finance necessary
for social improvements. A reduction in mortality and
morbidity rates brought about by social improvements in the
less favoured areas would be of immense economic value. In
preventing morbidity and premature death among the working
population such benefits as fewer days' absence from work, and
increased amounts of tax the people concerned will pay as a
result of having a longer and healthier working life, would
accrue. This is based on the assumption that the value of the
individual to society depends solely on his productive work
and that his earnings are a measure of the value of his work.
To many such a conclusion would be ethically unacceptable.
Crude economic reasoning, the constant bowing to the House
of Mammon, overlooks a whole range of social considerations,
not least the nebulous but important concept 'quality of
life'. This depends on health, population pressure, social
security, fulfilment of individual needs, job satisfaction,
and other social indicators.

There is need for medical men and planners, in their
several ways, though preferably in a concerted and co-ordinated
effort, to examine critically areas of social deprivation,
i.e. the areas where death rates are relatively high and life
expectancy relatively low. They should advise on measures,
remedial or preventive, thought most likely to bring about
an amelioration in such areas, and supervise their
implementation.

Human progress should be judged by social as well as economic
criteria. The provision of an improved environment is a
prerequisite for a healthier nation. Society cannot be
satisfied until the prospects of existence, of life expectancy
and quality of life, are comparable in all parts of the country
and for people in every walk of life. A state of complete
physical, mental and social well-being is surely the birth-
right of everyone.

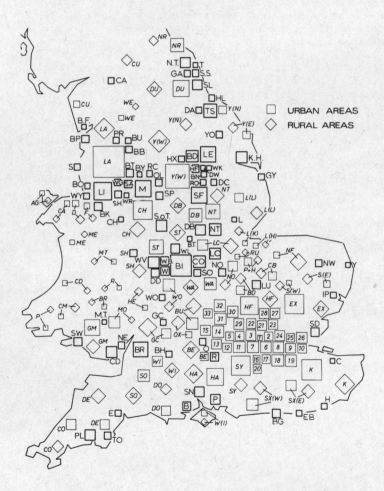

Fig.10.15   Key to Figs.10.13

COUNTIES

AG	Anglesey	GC	Gloucestershire	P	Pembrokeshire
BD	Bedfordshire	GM	Glamorgan	P&H	Peterborough and Huntingdonshire
BE	Berkshire	HA	Hampshire	R	Radnorshire
BR	Breconshire	HE	Herefordshire	RU	Rutland
BU	Buckinghamshire	HF	Hertfordshire	SH	Shropshire
CA	Caernarvonshire	K	Kent	ST	Staffordshire
CB	Cambridgeshire	LA	Lancashire	SY	Surrey
CD	Cardiganshire	LC	Leicestershire	S(E)	East Suffolk
CH	Cheshire	L(H)	Lincolnshire (Parts of Holland)	S(W)	West Suffolk
CM	Carmarthenshire	L(K)	Lincolnshire (Parts of Kesteven)	SX(E)	East Sussex
CO	Cornwall & Isles of Scilly	L(L)	Lincolnshire (Parts of Lindsey)	SX(W)	West Sussex
CU	Cumberland	ME	Merionethshire	WA	Warwickshire
D	Denbighshire	MO	Monmouthshire	WE	Westmorland
DB	Derbyshire	MT	Montgomeryshire	WI	Wiltshire
DE	Devon	NF	Norfolk	WO	Worcestershire
DO	Dorset	NO	Northamptonshire	W(I)	Isle of Wight
DU	Durham	NR	Northumberland	Y(E)	Yorkshire (East Riding)
EX	Essex	NT	Nottinghamshire	Y(N)	Yorkshire (North Riding)
F	Flintshire	OX	Oxfordshire	Y(W)	Yorkshire (West Riding)

COUNTY BOROUGHS

B	Bournemouth	CR	Croydon	M	Manchester	SN	Southampton
BB	Blackburn	DA	Darlington	M.T.	Merthyr Tydfil	S.O.T.	Stoke on Trent
BD	Bradford	DB	Derby	NE	Newport	SP	Stockport
BF	Barrow in Furness	DC	Doncaster	NO	Northampton	S.S.	South Shields
BG	Brighton	D	Dudley	NT	Nottingham	SW	Swansea
BH	Bath	DW	Dewsbury	N.T.	Newcastle upon Tyne	T	Tynemouth
BI	Birmingham	E	Exeter	NW	Norwich	TO	Torbay
BK	Birkenhead	EB	Eastbourne	O	Oxford	TS	Teesside
BN	Barnsley	GA	Gateshead	OL	Oldham	W	Warley
BO	Bootle	GC	Gloucester	P	Portsmouth	W.B.	West Bromwich
BP	Blackpool	GY	Grimsby	PL	Plymouth	WG	Wigan
BR	Bristol	H	Hastings	PR	Preston	WK	Wakefield
BT	Bolton	HA	Hartlepool	R	Reading	WL	Walsall
B.T.	Burton upon Trent	HF	Huddersfield	RC	Rochdale	WO	Worcester
BU	Burnley	HX	Halifax	RO	Rotherham	WR	Warrington
BY	Bury	IP	Ipswich	S	Southport	WV	Wolverhampton
C	Canterbury	K.H.	Kingston upon Hull	SA	Salford	WY	Wallasey
CA	Carlise	L	Lincoln	SD	Southend on Sea	Y	Great Yarmouth
CD	Cardiff	LC	Leicester	SF	Sheffield	YO	York
CH	Chester	LE	Leeds	S.H.	St. Helens		
CO	Coventry	LI	Liverpool	SL	Sunderland		

GREATER LONDON BOROUGHS

1.	City of London		12.	Richmond		23.	Hackney
2.	Tower Hamlets		13.	Hounslow		24.	Newham
3.	Westminster		14.	Ealing		25.	Barking
4.	Kensington and Chelsea		15.	Hillingdon		26.	Havering
5.	Hammersmith		16.	Kingston		27.	Redbridge
6.	Southwark		17.	Merton		28.	Waltham
7.	Lambeth		18.	Croydon		29.	Haringey
8.	Lewisham		19.	Bromley		30.	Enfield
9.	Greenwich		20.	Sutton		31.	Brent
10.	Bexley		21.	Islington		32.	Barnet
11.	Wandsworth		22.	Camden		33.	Harrow

and 10.14

REFERENCES

BROWN, E.S. (1965). Distribution of the ABO and rhesus (D)
blood groups in the North of Scotland. *Heredity* 20, 289.

CRAWFORD, M.D., GARDNER, M.J., and MORRIS, J.N. (1968).
Mortality and hardness of local water supplies. *Lancet* 1,
827.

CRAXFORD, S.R. and WEATHERLEY, M.-L.P.M. (1971). Air pollution
in towns in the United Kingdom. *Phil.Trans.R.Soc.* A, 269, 503.

HAWKSWORTH, D.L. and ROSE, F. (1970). Qualitative scale for
estimating sulphur dioxide and pollution in England and Wales
using epiphytic lichens. *Nature. Lond.* 227, 145.

HILL, M.J., HAWKSWORTH, G., and TATTERSALL, G. (1973). Bacteria,
nitrosamines and cancer of the stomach. *Br.J.Cancer* 28, 562.

HOWE, G.M. (1970a)   Some aspects of social malaise in Scotland.
Health Bull. 28(1), 1.

HOWE, G.M. (1970b)   *National atlas of disease mortality in the
United Kingdom* (2nd edn.) Nelson, London.

HOWE, G.M. (1972)   *Man, environment and disease in Britain*.
David and Charles, Newton Abbot. (Pelican Books, Harmondsworth, 1976)

KOPEC, A.C. (1970)   *The distribution of the blood groups in the
United Kingdom*. Oxford University Press.

MINISTRY OF AGRICULTURE, FISHERIES AND FOOD (1969). Domestic
food consumption. *Annual Report of the National Food Committee*
HMSO, London.

MORRIS, J.N., CRAWFORD, M.D., and HENDRY, J.A. (1968). Hardness
of local water supplies. *Lancet* 1, 827.

REGISTRAR GENERAL (1973)   *Statistical Review of England and
Wales for the year 1971.*   Part I. Tables, Medical. HMSO.
London.

ROSENBLATT, M. (1974). Lung cancer and smoking - the evidence
re-assessed. *New Scient.* 62, 897.

SCOTT, E. (1960). Prevalence of pernicious anaemia in Great
Britain. *J.Coll.gen.Pract.* 3, 80.

TODD, G.F. (ed.) (1966). *Statistics of smoking in the United
Kingdom* (4th edn.) Tobacco Research Council. Research Paper
No.1.

11 Epidemiological evidence for the effects of urban environment

G. A. Rose

THE EPIDEMIOLOGICAL APPROACH TO HEALTH

Epidemiology is the quantitative study of health in populations. Standardized measures of morbidity or mortality are used to enumerate cases, which are then related to the populations from which they were derived so as to yield rates. The distribution pattern for these rates in regard to place, time, and personal characteristics often yields clues to the causes of illness, and it also enables the community to define its health problems.

For its success the epidemiological approach depends substantially on the identification of contrasts. For example, in a population where all persons were equally exposed to physical inactivity or to a rushed and competitive existence, any health consequences from these factors would also be homogeneously distributed, and epidemiology would fail to identify them; and if the environment were uniformly polluted, the effects of pollution would be likely to pass unrecognized. In an affluent and mechanized society many features of the environment and way of life which were formerly concentrated in cities are now more evenly distributed. This makes it less likely that there will be any large urban-rural differences in disease rates, even if health were substantially influenced by urbanization. This situation is illustrated by an American study of urbanization and coronary heart disease. The mortality rates in various counties of a state were found to correlate with their degree of urbanization; but in the more urbanized counties the excess risk was shared by the rural as well as the urban residents (Tyroler and Cassel 1964).

Epidemiology depends on averages and generalizations, rates in one whole class of individuals being compared with those in another. This is both a limitation and a strength. It is a limitation because broad averages may conceal local differences; to consider mortality, for example, in conurbations taken as a whole may hide big differences which occur within one city between adjacent areas. Generalization, however, is also a major source of strength; for in contrasting the health experience of conurbations and rural districts it may be expected that local irregularities will tend to cancel one another out, so that a general tendency is shown up more clearly.

DEFINING THE ENVIRONMENTAL QUESTIONS

The simplest test of an urban factor in health might be to ask "How do disease rates for residents of large cities compare

with those living in small towns or in the country?' Much of
the information which follows in this chapter will be in this
form; but in interpreting such data it must be remembered
that the persons whose health is being contrasted differ
systematically from one another in many respects besides their
urban residence. The cities of Great Britain are not randomly
distributed geographically, nor are their inhabitants randomly
assigned to their place of residence. The true health effects
of urban living may be confounded with regional and social
class differences or with the complex factors governing the self-
selection of migrants.

This problem of interpreting a simple factual observation can
be illustrated by the example of gonorrhoea. In recent years
there has been a very steep increase in the number of new cases,
concentrated in the large cities and especially in London.
The explanations of this phenomenon probably include not only
the effects of city life on sexual promiscuity but also
selective migration into the cities of socially rootless young
people, as well as the tendency for cultural change to appear
first in the large cities, especially London.

The same trend was seen in the case of lung cancer, where the
rise and subsequent plateauing in incidence occurred first
in London, later spreading to other towns and on into rural
areas; the situation now approaches an even distribution of
rates. It seems that this pattern simply mirrored the spread
of cultural change - in this case, the habit of cigarette smoking.
In instances such as this an urban excess in disease is only
temporary; and in the future such phases may become even
briefer and less marked, as urban-rural cultural differences
tend to diminish.

In order to reduce the problem introduced by these confounding
variables, we could seek to eliminate their effect by some form
of standardization, asking 'How do urban and rural disease rates
compare, after adjusting for other relevant factors?' For some
simple factors, such as age or cigarette-smoking habit, this
is possible and reasonable; but for more subtle factors it
becomes impracticable, since those who choose to move into the
big city differ in many undefinable ways from those who remain
outside. More fundamentally, however, it may be objected that
this is not a realistic approach. For example, in seeking to
control the urban epidemic of gonorrhoea, the problem is to find
causes and remedial action appropriate specifically to the mobile
and sexually promiscuous young people who preferentially
congregate in cities. The operational question therefore to
which we should most of all wish the epidemiological evidence
to point an answer is, 'What are the modifiable features of the
urban environment and way of life which adversely affect the
health of those who are living there?'

ALL-CAUSES MORTALITY: THE CHANCES OF LONGER LIFE IN RURAL
AREAS

Before considering particular diseases we may enquire how
urban-rural status is reflected in overall survival prospects,
taking into account differences in age and sex distribution.
Table 11.1 shows the strong relationship between urban residence

TABLE 11.1

*Urban-rural differences in mortality at birth and in the first
year of life (England & Wales 1971, HMSO 1973)*

Parental residence	Still-birth and infant deaths per 1000 births per year
Conurbations	31.7
Other towns >100 000 population	31.4
Other towns 50-100 000 population	29.4
Other towns <50 000 population	28.8
Rural districts	27.0

and the probability that a child will either be born dead or will
die before the first birthday. As compared with rural districts
the risk in large cities is almost 15 per cent greater. This
is extremely disturbing, since it is thought that a substantial
proportion of these deaths are preventable. The problem,
however, has many causes, arising probably both from socio-
economic predisposing factors and the quality and utilization
of medical-care services.

Table 11.2 shows the picture for subsequent ages of life. For
simplicity's sake rates are given only for conurbations and rural
areas (the extremes of the Registrar General's residence
classification). Rates for other sizes of town fall more or less
intermediately. In every age group there is some disadvantage
to the urban residents, but it is small except in the case of
middle-aged and older men. Thus, overall, the life expectancy
for city dwellers is distinctly diminished, especially for males.

For adults some part of the disadvantage can be attributed to
their earlier acquisition of the smoking habit. In the early

TABLE 11.2

*Rates for all-causes mortality in conurbations and rural districts
(England and Wales 1971, HMSO 1973*

| Age group (years) | Death per 1 000 per year | | | |
| | Males | | Females | |
	Conurbations	Rural districts	Conurbations	Rural districts
1–15	0.53	0.51	0.38	0.36
15–44	1.39	1.37	0.85	0.80
45–64	14.40	11.76	7.60	6.70
65+	79.76	70.76	56.56	53.38
Standardized mortality ratio (per cent)	106	91	103	97

1950s it was estimated that the proportion of cigarette smokers
among men was 61 per cent in conurbations but only 54 per cent
in rural districts, although by 1968 this difference had almost
disappeared (Todd 1969). Changes in smoking habit have a large
but delayed effect on mortality, and it may be that the present
rural advantage in all-causes adult mortality will diminish.

THE EFFECTS OF CROWDING

Historically the great killing diseases were infectious, and their
spread was facilitated by crowded living conditions. For various
reasons (more social than medical) their importance has declined,
their place being now largely taken by chronic non-infectious
conditions. However, infectious diseases have not disappeared,
and neither has their association with the more crowded living
conditions of urban life, with its facilitation of the spread of
droplet-borne infections (Table 11.3). The gradients, however,
are not uniform. Rural districts fare consistently and substantially
best; yet it is the larger towns, not the conurbations, which
come off worst. The differences are large, and doubtless represent the effect of other urban-related factors besides
domestic overcrowding (for example, the concentration in certain
areas of Asian immigrants with a high prevalence of respiratory
tuberculosis.

TABLE 11.3

Examples of urban-rural differences in rates for various conditions related to droplet-borne infections (England and Wales, 1971, HMSO 1973

	Conurbations	>100 000	Other towns (populations) 50 000 100 000	<50 000	Rural Districts
Respiratory tuberculosis men (Standardized mortality ratio)	124	145	79	86	64
Rheumatic heart disease, men (Standardized mortality ratio)	114	119	90	88	86
Measles under age 1 year (notifications per 1000 per year)	8.52	9.05	10.47	8.73	7.74
Common cold (GP consultations per 1000 per year)	77	87	88	78	62

TABLE 11.4

Mortality from road-traffic accidents in conurbations and rural districts, analysed by age and sex (England and Wales 1971 HMSO 1973)

Age (Years)	Deaths per 100 000 per year			
	Males		Females	
	Conurbations	Rural districts	Conurbations	Rural districts
0-4	8.1	8.0	3.7	5.5
5-14	8.5	11.3	4.9	6.3
15-44	19.2	33.6	4.6	8.9
45-64	15.0	22.1	7.5	9.8
65+	40.5	34.1	29.0	17.8
All ages standardized mortality ratio (per cent)	88	126	101	111

Fatal influenza - not currently a condition of great importance numerically - is a curious exception to the otherwise
advantageous position of the countryman. The explanation is not
clear, unless it is that by virtue of less frequent attacks he
loses his immunity; and if he then by misfortune at last meets
the virus, he is liable to a more severe illness. Certainly
there are instances where influenza on first reaching an
isolated community has proved to be exceptionally virulent.

AIR POLLUTION AND ITS EFFECT ON HEALTH

This is one of the socially unpleasant features of the urban
environment. It is also a major hazard to health. Bronchitis
is the leading cause both of absence from work through
sickness and of chronic disability, and in men it is the
third commonest cause of death. A major factor in its aetiology
is air pollution, chiefly that arising from low-level emission
from domestic coal-burning rather than from tall factory
chimneys (more obvious but less dangerous) or from motor-car
exhausts (which arouse emotion because we only suffer from
emissions for which others are responsible).

Standardized mortality ratios for chronic bronchitis in men
in England and Wales range steadily upwards from 77 per cent
in rural districts to 118 per cent in conurbations, and this
is the main reason for the excess mortality of older urban
men. The adverse effect, however, begins early in life.
Figure 11.1 is taken from a study of the prevalence of persistent
cough among more than 10 000 schoolchildren from three selected
areas, representing respectively low, intermediate, and high
levels of air pollution (Colley and Reid 1970). Within each
social class group - and especially in classes IV and V - there
is a clear effect of area of residence: the proportion of social
class IV/V children with persistent cough is 55 per cent
higher in the areas with higher pollution.

There is evidence that children who are re-housed from an area
of higher to an area of lower pollution can subsequently lose
much of their bronchitic tendency. By later in life, however,
a great deal of irreversible damage has occurred. Studies comparing urban and rural postal workers (Holland and Reid 1965)
have shown that the urban group tend to suffer more, not only
from bronchitic symptoms but also from serious and disabling
impairment of ventilatory function. Studies of lung cancer
suggest that here too there is a contribution from domestic
air pollution, but that its effect is small relative to the
dominating influence of cigarette smoking.

Legislation in recent years for the control of air pollution
has resulted in considerable progress: the urban-rural gradient

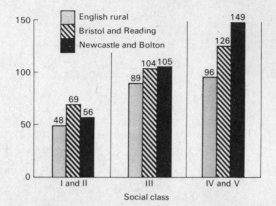

Fig.11.1 Age-adjusted morbidity ratios for chronic cough among 10 887 children aged 6-10 years living in contrasting urban and rural areas. (From Colley and Reid 1970)

in bronchitis mortality is substantially less than 20 years ago. Tragedies like the great London smog of 1952, which killed 4000 within one week are now, one hopes, a thing of the past; but even in 'clean-air' zones the concentrations of sulphur dioxide are still high, urban-rural gradients in chronic bronchitis are still large, and recent changes in the national fuel situation could well lead to increased burning of smoky coal in domestic grates. The danger has by no means passed.

DEATH FROM ROAD-TRAFFIC ACCIDENTS

Accidents (all forms) rank fourth as a cause of death in Great Britain today, and among young men road-traffic accidents rank easily first. Any factor influencing their occurrence is therefore of great social importance. Table 11.4 shows that place of residence is one such factor. In general, the city resident is at lower risk, especially if male. The little boy living in the conurbation seems largely to avoid the hazards of travel to school, which in the country take a considerable toll. The advantage persists throughout adult life, except that among old men pedestrian fatalities occur more frequently in the cities. However, in both urban and rural areas, and at every age, it is the aggressive male who is more at risk than the cautious female.

TABLE 11.4

Mortality from road-traffic accidents in conurbations and rural districts, analysed by age and sex (England and Wales 1971, HMSO 1973)

Age (years)	Deaths per 100 000 per year			
	Males		Females	
	Conurbations	Rural Districts	Conurbations	Rural districts
0–4	8.1	8.0	3.7	5.5
5–14	8.5	11.3	4.9	6.3
15–44	19.2	33.6	4.6	8.9
45–64	15.0	22.1	7.5	9.8
65+	40.5	34.1	29.0	17.8
All ages, standardized mortality ratio (per cent)	88	126	101	111

EMOTIONAL STRESS IN THE URBAN ENVIRONMENT

Certain types of stress are supposedly more prevalent among city dwellers, particularly stress due to time pressure, competitiveness, and a less individualized micro-environment. Some of the signs of emotional trauma will be considered elsewhere (see Chapters 12 and 16). The relevance of place of residence can, however, be clearly seen even in the crude statistics for successful suicide: in young adults of both sexes, and in old women, there is a substantial excess among residents of conurbations.

A similar gradient is shown by general practitioner consultations for 'psychoneurotic disorders', and also for peptic ulcers (Table 11.5). (Peptic ulcer comprises both gastric and duodenal ulcer, and in the latter there is evidence for the aetiological importance of emotional stress.) As with some of the previous examples, there are only rather irregular differences between the various large urban classes; but the rural districts, and to a lesser extent the small towns, show a definite advantage.

TABLE 11.5

*Urban-rural differences in general-practitioner consultation
rates for conditions related to emotional stress*

Diagnosis	Consultations per 1000 per year				
	Conurbations	Other towns populations			Rural districts
		>100 000	50 000–100 000	<50 000	
Psychoneurotic disorders	32	32	25	27	23
Peptic ulcer	15	18	15	14	10
All causes	610	593	607	582	567

From Logan and Cushion 1958

Mortality statistics (suicide rates, for example) have the
advantage of objectivity, but they represent only the extreme
of the whole spectrum of disability. Data from general practice
relate to a wider part of the range, but it must be remembered
that they reflect not only the incidence of disorders but also
the tendency of sufferers to seek medical help and the
diagnostic proclivities of the doctors. It may be that urban
residents are more ready to go to their doctors, either
because of greater physical proximity or from cultural
differences in attitude to illness and to seeking help. Thus
the pattern for 'psychoneurotic disorders' seen in Table 11.5
is only an exaggeration of the pattern for the total of 'all-
causes' consultations.

CORONARY HEART DISEASE IN THE URBAN ENVIRONMENT

The vast pandemic of this disease is responsible each year
for about 150 000 deaths in England and Wales alone. The
pattern of its growth, and of its distribution around the world,
links it closely with affluence, industrialization, and
urbanization. The problem is to dissociate, among a whole
complex of social changes, the causally important factors
from those which are only coincidentally associated. A diet

over-rich in fats, cigarette smoking, and physical inactivity
seem to be the major culprits. Each of these social habits,
with the possible exception of a fat-rich diet, first became
prevalent in the large cities. However, as explained earlier,
there is a strong tendency towards rapid obliteration of urban-
rural differences in habits and way of life. Both dietary and
smoking habits are now relatively homogeneous. Subjective
impression suggests that the townsman tends to get less exercise,
although this has not been properly quantified.

In an important American study (Rosenman, Friedman, Strauss,
Jenkins, Zyzanski and Wurm 1970) members of a population
sample were classified by psychologists according to whether
they were thought to show a particular behaviour pattern
('type A'), characterized essentially by a sense of time-urgency
and competitiveness - a pattern which might be thought to be
encouraged by the conditions of modern urban life. During the
follow-up phase of this study it was found that the incidence
of coronary heart disease in 'type A' individuals was about
twice as high as in 'type B' (the remainder). The difference
could not be explained in terms of the other familiar risk
factors, and it has been proposed that the stress associated
with 'type A' behaviour is a major aggravating factor in this
disease, perhaps through the intermediary of excessive release
of catecholamines. This is clearly an important hypothesis,
although at the moment the only direct evidence in its support
comes from this one study.

The earlier arrival and perhaps heightened concentration
in cities of each of these suspect causes would lead one to
expect some major urban-rural differences in heart disease
incidence and mortality. It comes therefore as a surprise to
find (Table 11.6) that the rural advantage, though present,

TABLE 11.6

Urban-rural differences in mortality from coronary heart disease
(England and Wales 1971, HMSO 1973)

Place of residence	Standardized mortality ratio (per cent)	
	Men	Women
Conurbations	102	99
Other towns, >100 000 population	105	105
Other towns 50 000-100 000 population	100	97
Other towns <5 000 population	103	102
Rural districts	90	96
England and Wales	100	100

is not great; and within the range of urban aggregates, from small towns up to conurbations, there are no consistent differences at all. Furthermore, if one goes back to the statistics of 20 years ago the pattern was essentially the same.

CONCLUSIONS

As compared with many countries of the world, the epidemiological picture in Great Britain is one of a comparatively even distribution of disease, doubtless because in the compact British society there is less socio-economic and cultural variety than elsewhere. Factors such as higher living standards, and the use of mechanized transport and manufactured processed food, are in Great Britain almost as evident in rural areas as in cities. Compared with most other countries there is more homogeneity in medical services and their utilization. In these senses it could be said that nearly all the British are effectively urban residents, and this makes it correspondingly difficult to research into the health consequences of our modern urban-type way of life.

Having pointed out a relative homogeneity it is important to emphasize that this is by no means complete. For the statistics considered here it is only in regard to fatal road traffic accidents that the urban residents show an advantage, and even this does not extend to all pedestrian accidents. Overall, it is the countryman who lives a little longer, although there is no indication that residents in conurbations are any worse off than those in other large towns. There is some evidence too of higher rates for psychological disorders in the large towns, but it is not possible to apportion responsibility for this between, on the one hand, the consequences of urban life style, and, on the other, the effects of selective internal migration and of cultural differences in seeking medical help.

The adverse health position of urban residents has complex socio-economic explanations, but we may identify a number of potentially remediable factors. The excess in perinatal mortality is related to a number of preventable obstetric factors. Subsequently domestic overcrowding facilitates the spread of respiratory and other infections, both minor and major. Air pollution, especially that emanating from domestic coal fires, is still a major factor in chronic bronchitis and its attendant disability, and it makes some contribution also to the incidence of lung cancer. Overdependence on mechanized transport may well be a factor in the massive mortality from coronary heart disease. The possible harm to health and happiness from the time-pressures and

competitiveness characteristic of the urbanized life style
is hard to evaluate: it may be large.

REFERENCES

COLLEY, J.R.T. and REID, D.D. (1970)   Urban and social origins
of childhood bronchitis in England and Wales.   *Brit.med.J. 2*,
213-17.

HOLLAND, W.W. and REID, D.D. (1965)   The urban factor in
chronic bronchitis.   *Lancet* i, 445-8.

LOGAN, W.P.D. and CUSHION, A.A. (1958)   *Morbidity statistics
from general practice,* Volume 1 (general).   General Register
Office: Studies on Medical and Population Subjects No.14.
HMSO, London.

*Registrar General's Statistical Review of England and Wales for
1971.*   (published 1973), Part I, Tables, Medical, HMSO, London.

ROSENMAN, R.H., FRIEDMAN, M., STRAUS, R., JENKINS, C.D.,
ZYZANSKI, S.J. and WURM, M. (1970)   Coronary heart disease in
the Western Collaborative Group Study.   A follow-up experience
of 4½ years.   *J.chron.Dis.* 23, 173-90.

TODD, G.F. (ed.) (1969)   Statistics of smoking in the United
Kingdom.   Research Paper No.1, 5th ed.   Tobacco Research
Council, London.

TYROLER, H.A. and CASSEL, J. (1964)   Health consequences of
culture change II.   The effect of urbanization on coronary
heart mortality in rural residents.   *J.chron.Dis.* 17, 167-77.

12 Social disturbances affecting young people in modern society

Ivor H. Mills and Mary A. M. Eden

The social health of a society may be judged by the behaviour of its members. Changes which occur with time will indicate whether the society is improving or regressing. Some activities of the member groups may be defined as contrary to the well-being of the population as a whole, but there might be disagreement as to what should be included in such a definition. Whereas there would be general agreement that an increase in crimes of violence would represent a regressive feature, the offsetting effect of a parallel increase in visitors to museums would be hard to assess.

There is little doubt that changes have been taking place relatively rapidly in our society in the last 20 years, but while some features may be quantified and studied others are not sufficiently concrete for scientific assessment. The interpretation of the changes will undoubtedly depend upon the viewpoint of the observer. The increased freedom which has been generally referred to as the development of the permissive society is likely to be seen by the young as progress but by their parents and grandparents as retrogression. In so far as it leads to an increase in ill-health of individuals (for example, gonorrhoea) it would be placed by most people of middle age or older on the debit side of the social-health account.

Initially it is of importance to establish a number of facts before attempting any interpretation of them. The conditions on which data are available tend to be predominantly on the negative side of the balance sheet because they are most easily collected via the health services or via police statistics. It is important, therefore, to attempt to see them in the wider perspective of society as a whole.

ATTEMPTED SUICIDE

The term 'attempted suicide' is an emotive one, and some people would prefer a euphemistic one such as self-injury or self-poisoning. If the action taken by an individual carries with it an unknown risk of death it seems appropriate to use the term 'attempted suicide'. Perhaps the most impressive evidence of the change in the incidence of this activity is that provided by the numbers of admissions to the Poisons Unit in the Royal Infirmary at Edinburgh (Fig.12.1) (Matthew and Lawson 1967). These data are particularly useful because they

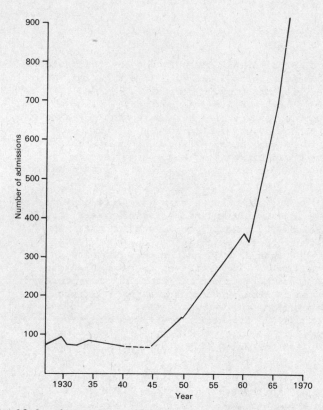

Fig.12.1   The numbers of patients admitted each year to the
Poisons Unit at the Royal Infirmary, Edinburgh from 1928 onwards
(From Matthew and Lawson 1967)

go back to 1928 and therefore precede most other available data.
Up to the outbreak of the Second World War the numbers of
admissions did not change very greatly, but a steep rise is
apparent from the end of the war until about the year 1960.
From then on the rise becomes very steep indeed for the next
10 years.   Although knowledge of the existence and value of the
Unit may have increased with time, so that a higher percentage
of the cases of self-poisoning was sent there, this could not
explain the very large increase that has taken place.

The biphasic nature of the change in attempted suicide since
1950 is also shown in data from other cities (Fig.12.2).   The
data from the Cambridge area and that from the Cardiff area
(Graham and Hitchens 1967) show that the increase in incidence

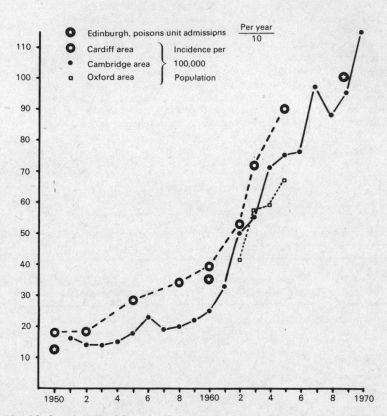

Fig.12.2 The incidence of attempted suicide per 100 000 population for the Cardiff area, the Cambridge area, and the Oxford area for the years from 1950 to 1970. The numbers of admissions to the Poisons Unit, Edinburgh divided by 10 are shown by stars for the years 1950, 1960, and 1969.

rate took a much steeper rise after 1960 than was occurring during the 10 years prior to this date. The more limited data from the Oxford area (Evans 1967) show a similar rising incidence rate during the 1960s.

Even so, all these sets of data represent university towns, and it is possible that the figures so obtained do not reflect what was occurring throughout the rest of the country. In

1969 a report was published on the treatment of self-poisoning in hospitals. Included in that are data obtained from a
10 per cent survey of deaths in, or discharges from, all
National Health Service hospitals in England and Wales. The
figures are given in Table 12.1. The total cases rose from
20 000 in 1959 to 50 400 in 1964, while the percentage that
these cases were of all medical admissions rose from 3.2 per cent
to 6.8 per cent. Attempted suicide admissions expressed as a
percentage of all medical admissions to Addenbrooke's Hospital,
Cambridge each year are also shown in Table 12.1. The
percentages are slightly higher than the national 10 per cent
survey because the figures include patients who were kept in
the Admission Unit until they were fit to go home and so were

TABLE 12.1

Cases of self-poisoning

10 per cent survey in England and Wales			Addenbrooke's Hospital
	Cases	As percentage of all medical admissions	As percentage of all medical admissions
1959	20 000	3.2	
1960	23 000	3.6	
1961	27 900	4.1	5.9
1962	33 600	4.8	7.0
1963	45 900	6.2	7.4
1964	50 400	6.8	10.0
1965			10.7
1966			11.9
1967			13.0
1968			11.1
1969			13.5
1970			13.0

not technically admitted to the wards. It seems probable that
the national figures will have increased in a comparable fashion
to those of the Cambridge area, and from this it can be
calculated that there are now approximately 100 000 cases of
attempted suicide each year in England and Wales.

The age distribution of the patients attempting suicide is
shown in Fig.12.3 for the Cambridge area for the years 1961-70

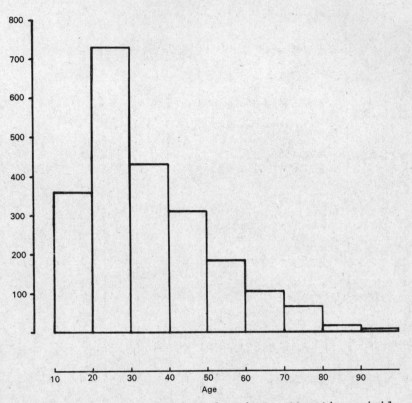

Fig.12.3 The age distribution of patients attempting suicide in the Cambridge area, 1961-70.

inclusive. There is a striking peak in the age group 20-29 years. The actual numbers in the age group 10-19 are approximately half those in the next decade, but since almost all of these are in the age group 15-19, the incidence rate for late teenagers is similar to that for those in their twenties. The peak, in the latter half of the 1960s, was formed by individuals of 19, 20, and 21 years of age, but these figures must be influenced by the presence of some 10 000 University students, which approximately doubles the town's population in the age group 15-24 years. In the years 1966-9 inclusive, in the Cambridge area, the age group 15-24 years, which we shall

TABLE 12.2

Total drug overdosage admissions in the Cambridge area

Age groups	1961		1962		1963		1964		1965		1966		1967		1968		1969		1970		Total		Total
0-9	6	3	9	5	12	5	11	5	15	4	15	25	31	15	35	36	46	36	31	11	211	145	356
10-19	8	11	5	15	6	11	4	22	10	20	18	24	35	17	14	27	23	38	22	30	145	215	360
20-29	8	14	15	24	17	28	23	43	26	44	17	37	37	49	39	52	52	69	53	83	287	443	730
30-39	7	14	9	10	12	28	18	22	11	27	13	45	19	45	18	32	23	34	19	46	149	282	431
40-49	1	7	7	12	5	13	10	24	8	25	12	27	13	22	9	30	13	34	19	33	97	227	324
50-59	4	5	5	11	8	11	6	13	7	12	10	12	10	9	8	12	8	12	6	12	74	109	183
60-69	3	3	2	6	2	5	3	6	5	8	11	6	2	12	2	7	4	10	3	10	37	66	103
70-79	2	2	0	8	4	0	1	4	3	8	2	3	2	7	0	5	2	3	2	7	18	47	65
80-89	0	1	1	3	0	1	0	0	1	2	1	1	0	2	1	3	0	0	0	2	4	15	19
90+	0	0	0	1	0	0	0	0	0	3	0	0	0	1	0	0	0	0	0	0	0	5	5
Total	90		150		168		215		232		258		328		330		407		389		1022	1551	2576

Totals all ages

Total excluding children under 10 years   2220

Columns on the left are males and on the right females in each year.

look at repeatedly in examining social disturbance, contained
almost 40 per cent of all the attempts at suicide, and in the
years 1961-70, 50 per cent were in the age group 10-29 years.

For the sample as a whole the females comprised approximately
63 per cent of all the admissions for self-poisoning; however,
when the individual age groups are looked at separately there is
a striking change after the middle of the 1960s, especially in
the teenagers. The numbers of teenage male self-poisoning
rose sharply after 1964 and in the year 1967 the numbers of
teenage male self-poisonings considerably exceeded the numbers
of females and almost equalled the males in their twenties.
The higher number of teenage males persisted for the rest of
the decade, though in all the years other than 1967 the female
teenagers exceeded the male ones (Table 12.2). Since these
teenagers were mainly unmarried this change altered the ratio
of married to single men for the sample in the latter half of
the decade from 1.2 in the early 1960s to 0.5 in the late
1960s. Amongst the women the ratio of married/single remained
fairly close to 2.1.

THE INFLUENCE OF BROKEN HOMES

Greer and Gunn (1966) pointed out that a higher percentage of
his self-poisoned patients, compared to his control group,
had either a broken marriage or came from a broken parental
home: 47 per cent of self-poisoned patients against 25 per
cent of the control group. In Table 12.3 are shown the figures
from the analysis of 167 patients living in the city of
Cambridge who attempted suicide in 1969. Amongst the women
approximately two thirds were married and 53 per cent of the
married women had children aged 15 years or younger; 21 per
cent of the women were either from a broken home or their own
marriage had been disrupted. Amongst the men 48 per cent of
the married ones had young children and only 9 per cent of all
men had a disrupted home life. Disburbed home life appears
to be of greater importance to the females than to the males.
However, looked at the other way round, the majority of both
men and women attempting suicide did not come from a disrupted
home. Clearly if break up of the home or the parental home
plays a part in the aetiology of attempted suicide it is not
a major factor. It is a matter of great importance that such
a high percentage of the women taking an overdose of drugs
will take the risk of leaving young children motherless.

The importance of attempted suicide as a medical illness
of young adults is shown more clearly by the percentage that
such individuals are of all medical admissions in their age
group. This is shown in Fig.12.4 for those aged 20-29 years.
Relatively early in the decade there was a sharp rise in this

TABLE 12.3

Analysis of attempted suicide patients in the borough of Cambridge for 1969

		Females	Males
Married	Total	62	23
Divorced, separated or widowed		13	6
From broken parental home		7	0
		20	6
With children 15 years or younger		33	11
As percentage of married		53	48
Single	Total	36	46
From broken parental home		1	0
With children 15 years or younger		2	0
Total married and single		98	69
Total both sexes		167	

percentage among the female patients; the numbers reached 50 per cent by 1964 and have remained at approximately that level while the total medical admissions for women in their twenties have risen from 83 in 1964 to 163 in 1970.

The situation in the males is similar, but delayed for several years compared to the females. The sharp rise in the percentage of medical admissions made up of attempted suicides in the males in their twenties came in 1967 (Fig.12.4) and remained close to 45 per cent in the later years of the decade. In both sexes in their twenties, attempted suicide is now the commonest medical illness requiring admission to hospital. Whatever the factors were that brought about this fairly sudden change in our society, they appear to have influenced the females some years before the males and to a greater extent. The previous

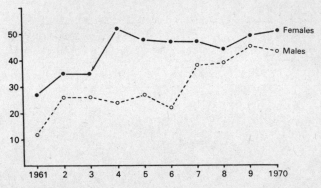

Fig.12.4 Admissions for attempted suicide in the age group 20-29 years in each year as a percentage of all medical admissions in that age group.

data which showed that a disturbed home life affected females more than males might indicate that females may in general be more upset by factors influencing their sense of security. If this is true, the males seem to become similarly upset at a later date.

DEATHS FROM SUICIDE

It has been said that deaths from suicide are commoner among students (Stengel 1964). It might be thought, therefore, that in a university town like Cambridge the numbers of attempted suicides might be increased above the average for non-university towns, by the presence of the students. An analysis of the data for the Borough of Cambridge for the age group 15-24 years and for the years 1966-9 inclusive is given in Table 12.4. It is apparent that in both males and females for the borough as a whole the attempted suicide rate is appreciably greater than it is for the University students alone. As a result the rate amongst males in the age group 15-24 years who are not University students is 3 times the rate among students at the University The difference is not so striking among the females, but it must be remembered that the non-University female group includes nurses, physiotherapists, and students being trained for teaching.

One of the most striking changes in attempted suicide during the decade occurred in the teenage males. In the early 1960s the

TABLE 12.4

Mean attempted suicide rate per 1000 per year in the 15-24 years age group in 1966-9 (Cambridge borough)

	Mean population		Attempted suicides per 1000	
	Males	Females	Males	Females
Cambridge Borough	13 800	8600	2.20	3.32
University students	9065	1130	1.21	2.67
Cambridge non-University	4735	7470	4.01	3.48

numbers each year were very small (see Fig.12.9). From 1965 there was a relatively sharp rise reaching a peak in 1967 and falling back slightly the following year. In the later part of the decade the numbers remained about four times what they were in the early 1960s. This change in the middle 1960s coincides with a number of other measures indicating a rapid rise in social unrest at this time. (These factors are compared and discussed later.)

Deaths from suicide have been falling steadily in this country since 1964, although the death rate from suicide in the 15-24 years age group continued to rise. There is, of course, appreciable variation in what is called suicide by different coroners. In Table 12.5 is shown the number of 'suicides' of all ages and both sexes, as assessed by a study of the pathologist's report, for the Cambridge area, from 1961 to 1970. The fall in numbers occurred only after 1967. While the deaths from suicide rose by a factor of 1.7 from 1961 to 1967, the year of their peak, the attempted suicides rose by a factor of 2.7. This is because the greatest fall in the death rate from suicide has been in the older age groups where the rates are still highest, whereas the attempted suicides have risen most in the younger age groups.

In contrast to the deaths from suicide in the older age groups, the attempted suicides which were not fatal in people in these age groups were low (see Fig.12.3). The numbers of patients attempting suicide each year in the Cambridge area in the age

TABLE 12.5

Yearly deaths from suicide in the Cambridge area

1961	1962	1963	1964	1965	1966	1967	1968	1969	1970
27	34	34	38	39	42	46	30	27	23

group 50 years and older are shown in Fig.12.5. There has been surprisingly little change throughout the decade. Whatever it is that has affected the younger age groups, the older individuals seem to have been little affected by it.

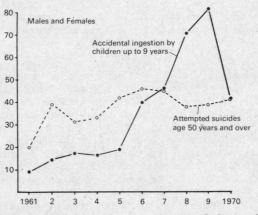

Fig.12.5 The admissions for overdoses of drugs in the Cambridge area for 1961 to 1970

ACCIDENTAL POISONING IN CHILDREN

The data presented so far have concentrated on the individuals who purposely took an overdose of drugs. Accidental drug overdose is not a matter of great significance in adults. However, it is of interest in young children. The data shown for children 0-9 years in Fig.12.5, in fact represent children of under 5 except in one case. They are predominantly children 2, 3, and 4 years of age. In each year there were many

more male children involved than female, except in the years
1966 and 1968. This is assumed to reflect the fact that young
male children are more venturesome and perhaps more likely to
eat tablets when they find them. The remarkable fact shown by
this graph is the dramatic increase in the number of children
involved from 1965 onwards until 1969. Clearly the children
take no purposeful part in this activity in that they are
unaware of the nature of the tablets. The figures do not
represent any change in admitting policy because they include
all children brought up to admissions after swallowing tablets,
regardless of whether they were admitted or not. They cannot
reflect the quantity of tablets dispensed at any one time since
for children of this age it would make no difference whether
it was one week's supply or one month's supply or more. The
change must reflect the chances of the children finding the
tablets at home. Since it seems highly unlikely that the
parents suddenly became very careless with tablets, it seems
most probable that there was an increased chance of young
children finding tablets in the house from 1965 onwards. This
is supported by the data for total numbers of prescriptions
dispensed each year in England and Wales and shown in Fig.12.6.
Since this shows the rise from the middle 1960s in total
prescriptions, it does not indicate the change in prescriptions
for parents with young children. The peak in the year 1967 is
of particular interest, as we shall discuss later.

These data on accidental poisoning of young children support
the view that in the homes of the parents of very young children
there was a sharp rise in the availability of tablets in the
latter half of the 1960s. The parents of these young children
are themselves likely to be young adults, probably mainly in
their twenties or early thirties. When this is considered together with the data on the age distribution of those purposely
taking an overdose of drugs it appears that during the 1960s
there was a considerable rise in the number of young people
going to doctors with complaints which led the doctors to
prescribe drugs for them. This led to the increased availability
of drugs to be found and swallowed by the young children or,
in some cases, to be used by the young adults to attempt suicide.
Most of the people taking an overdose of drugs use legally
prescribed ones. They may not have been prescribed for the
person who takes the overdose but are likely to have been
prescribed for someone living in the same house.

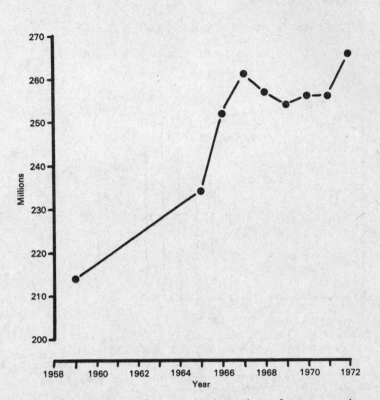

Fig.12.6 The number of prescriptions issued per year in England and Wales in millions. (Data from Health and Personal Social Services Statistics for England (1973).

ALCOHOLISM

Persons purposely taking an overdose of drugs frequently take them with alcohol. The study by Professor Wilson and his colleagues in Glasgow (Patel *et al.*, 1972) showed very clearly how high the incidence was of alcoholics among those taking a drug overdose. Nevertheless the peak age group was still in the twenties. It may be a reflection of the changes in society that such a percentage of young adults should already be using large quantities of alcohol. It is impossible to obtain any accurate statistics on the numbers of people taking alcohol to excess. However, some indication of the extent of alcohol

consumption by young adults may be obtained from the statistics of motoring offences. The Christian Economic and Social Research Foundation in their twentieth report (1973) published the percentage of drivers proceeded against for driving under the influence of alcohol who were under the age of 30. The data are shown in Fig.12.7. They assumed that

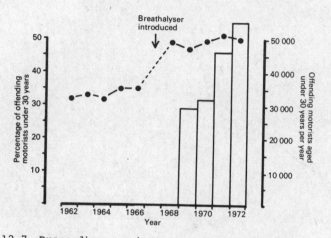

Fig.12.7 Proceedings against motorists for offences to do with drink or drugs for the years 1969-72: shown by histograms and right-hand scale. Left-hand scale in percentages. Data from the *Twentieth Annual Report on drink offences*, Christian Economic and Social Research Foundation (1973).

the change after 1967 was because of the introduction of the breathalyser test. Why should that affect people under the age of 30 more than those over the age of 30? Presumably it means that more people under the age of 30 will take the risk than people in the older age groups. The similarity in the age groups involved and the timing of the change with those of other factors shown in Fig.12.7 might lead one to think that the increased incidence of young drivers under the influence of alcohol could also be a reflection of the social unrest which increased sharply before the middle 1960s.

Not only drivers have been using alcohol in greater amounts. Pedestrians have also shown an increased incidence of offences for drunkenness since the middle 1960s (Fig.12.8). The numbers had been falling steadily in the early part of the decade but from 1967 onwards they have risen again and have steadily continued to do so. (Christian Economic and Social Research Foundation, twentieth report, 1973).

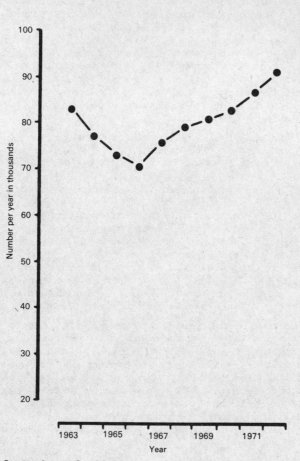

Fig.12.8 Number of offences of drunkenness per year for England and Wales for the years 1963-72. (Data from the *Twentieth Annual Report on drink offences,* Christian Economic and Social Research Foundation (1973).

DRUG OFFENCES

It may well be that the greater use of alcohol today is related to the greater desire or need for drugs. The number of prescriptions for drugs issued each year (Fig.12.6)

is likely to be influenced by many factors. One of these
would be the discovery of drugs to treat diseases which
previously were untreated. The discovery and development
of antibiotics was clearly an example of this. However, the
rise in numbers of offences of drunkenness (Fig.12.8) coincides
very closely with the more rapid rise in the numbers of
prescriptions issued from the middle 1960s. The data of numbers
of young children brought to hospital in the Cambridge area
with accidental ingestion of drugs (Fig.12.5) indicate the
increased incidence of availability of drugs in households of
young parents. This may correlate with the increased percentage
of individuals under 30 years old who were found guilty of
driving under the influence of alcohol.

The extent of the use of illegally obtained drugs can only
be surmised but the data on drug offenders in Mid-Anglia (kindly
provided by Mr.F.Drayton Porter, Chief Constable for Mid-Anglia,
Fig.12.9) show that this phenomenon is essentially one which
came to the fore in the middle 1960s. The variation in numbers
shown in Fig.12.9 is of great interest. They rose sharply in
1966 and 1967 and fell to about one-third of that number in
1968, subsequently to rise again. Anyone who was familiar with
the drug scene in 1967 was aware that it was rapidly getting
out of control. In those days anyone who wished could buy
heroin in Piccadilly Circus at a pound for a grain (enough for
six average 'jacks'). This was because of the overprescription
by a very small number of doctors, for self-declared heroin
addicts. They then sold the excess beyond their needs.

The disturbance among young people in the year 1967 was very
great. It was difficult for teenagers to go to any social
gathering without there being an appreciable body of drug-takers
there. Even so most drug-offenders were apprehended for possess-
ing or using marijuana or hashish. Why, one may ask, was there
a sharp fall in offenders in 1968? It was early in that year
that an Order became effective under the Act passed at the end
of 1967 which made the prescription of heroin for a known
addict illegal by any doctor unless he were specially licensed
so to do.

The remarkable thing is that heroin limitation had an effect
on the whole drug scene even though most drug offenders were not
using it. The disturbance among late teenagers and those in their
early twenties is reflected by two facts. One is that drug
offenders are mostly young people as shown by the age incidence
in Fig.12.10. The mean age for each year since 1966 has
remained at about 20 years of age. The critical age group 15-24
years contains 92 per cent of all drug offenders for the years
1966-71. The drastic limitation in availability of heroin had
a much more widespread effect than might have been predicted.
Drug taking of all sorts decreased in Mid-Anglia largely because

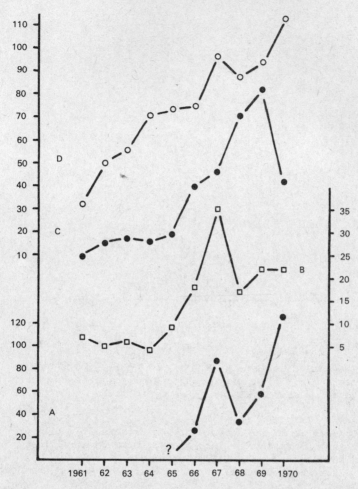

Fig.12.9 A. Lower left scale. Number of drug offenders in Mid-Anglia per year. (Data kindly supplied by Mr.F.Drayton Porter, Chief Constable for Mid-Anglia!)   B. Scale on right. Numbers of teenagers admitted to Addenbroke's Hospital each year for attempted suicide.   C. Upper left scale. Numbers of children 0–9 years old brought up to Addenbrooke's Hospital each year because of accidental ingestion of drugs.   D. Upper left scale. Incidence of attempted suicide per 100 000 population in Cambridge area for the years 1961–1970.

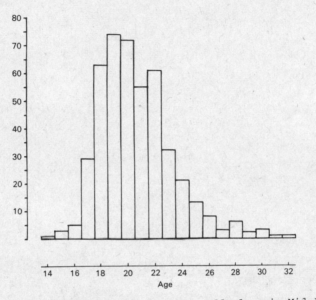

Fig.12.10.   Age distribution of drug offenders in Mid-Anglia
for the years 1966-71 inclusive. (Data kindly supplied by Mr.F.
Drayton Porter, Chief Constable for Mid-Anglia.)

the disturbance among the late teenagers decreased markedly in
1968.   The second fact indicating the disturbance among young
people is shown by the figures for attempted suicide by
teenagers over these critical years (Fig.12.9). As the incidence
of drug taking rose in 1966 and 1967 so attempted suicide by
these young people also rose, even though most of the cases
in Cambridge were not themselves drug-abusers, nor were illegal
drugs, like amphetamine, used to any great extent in the drug
overdose cases. The fall in numbers of teenagers attempting
suicide in 1968 is a reflection of the lessening of the sense
of unrest and disturbance in society at that time. Even the
total numbers of attempted suicides (all ages) decreased in
1968 (see Table 12.3), as did the total number of prescriptions
for all drugs (Fig.12.6).

It is of interest to note that the numbers of people known
nationally to be taking heroin or methadone did not begin
to fall off until a year or so after 1968.   Similarly, as an

indication of unrest among young people in society, the world-wide student unrest had its peak in 1967 and 1968. Two years later newspapers in this country were asking the question, 'Where are all the student rebels?' The reasons for this, however, are not directly related to the use of illegal drugs which clearly continued at a high rate outside this country.

The rise in drug offenders in Mid-Anglia in 1971 and 1972 does not reflect an increase in drug usage alone but a change of policy by the police. A very intense campaign was started in 1971 and has since been maintained. The lesson from the limitation of availability of heroin, methadone, and cocaine, is that widespread availability of drugs may help to increase the social unrest among the young but a clampdown by the authorities is ineffective if other socially disturbing factors are moving in the opposite direction.

SELF-STARVATION AMENORRHOEA

In severe dieting, menstruation is quickly stopped because of the failure of ovulation. The exact mechanism by which this is brought about is unknown. In the most advanced form this is known as anorexia nervosa. It used to be regarded as a fairly rare conditon, but in the last 10-15 years it has become relatively common. This self-starvation syndrome almost always occurs in females (99 per cent), whereas drug-offenders are mostly male (92 per cent). A small percentage of the girls were genuinely overweight when they started dieting to a more reasonable weight but then, as several of them have said, 'the diet took over and I could no longer determine what I ate.' In this state they become obsessed with the idea of losing weight. Their mental image of their body size becomes distorted and they imagine themselves much larger and fatter than they are (Slade and Russell 1973). Frequently, they have no sense of hunger, and they hold their views so strongly that they will go to any lengths to avoid being made to consume food. They dispose of food in a variety of ways when eating is supervised, and when made to eat they may vomit shortly afterwards. It becomes quite impossible to reason with them, because, although they may see the sense of what is said to them, they are quite unable to carry it out.

There have been many theories over the years to explain this curious behaviour, but none previously would explain why the condition became more common in the 1960s. The age distribution of these young women at the onset of severe dieting is shown in Fig.12.11, which represents 76 out of 80 who presented in the years 1968-71: in 4 the age of onset could not be determined. It will be seen that 85 per cent of them were in the crucial

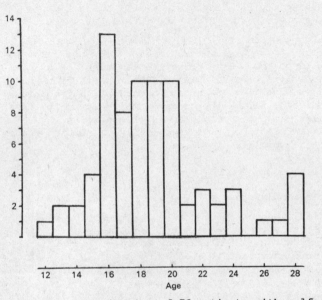

Fig.12.11. Age distribution of 76 patients with self-starvation
amenorrhoea (anorexia nervosa) who presented in 1968-71
(Mills *et al.* 1973.)

age range 15-24 years when crash dieting commenced. It has been
suggested that the 'Twiggy image' that was prevalent in the
late 1960s was responsible for this sudden popularity for slimness. Since many of these girls are extremely intelligent it
seems highly improbable that they would blindly follow that
particular girl. Although dieting for slimness is very fashionable
in teenage girls, by far the majority give it up after a week
or so. Those going on are to some extent self-selected in that
they are the more determined and driving ones who can continue
until hunger abates.

However, an analysis of what the girls and young women were
doing at the time of starting dieting was very revealing (Mills
et al. 1973) (see Fig.12.12). In 75 per cent of cases they
started intense dieting in the year in which they were working
for a public examination (CSE, GCE, nursing, or college or
University examination). A small number had developed anorexia
nervosa before the year in which they would take a major examination

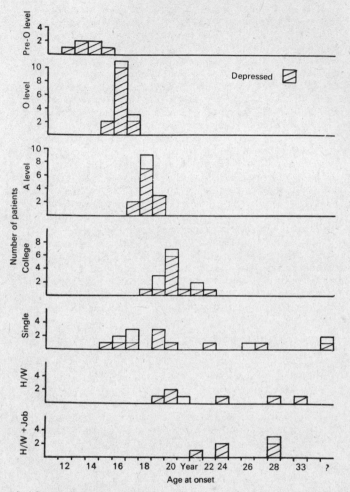

Fig.12.12 The frequency distribution of the age at the onset of severe dieting in girls at school before the year in which they would sit the GCE examination at O level: those in the year in which they were to sit the GCE at O level or at A level; young women at a college or university; single women not involved in academic work; housewives who were not doing an additional job and those who were. The cross-hatched blocks represent individuals who had features of depression at the time they were first seen (Mills *et al.* 1973.)

and they had mostly changed schools or lost time because of
illness. This very high correlation with academic pressure
was somewhat surprising. It does not mean that working for
an examination was the only factor involved, but it suggests
it was a most important one. This is supported by the fact
that the peaks at 16 and 18 years, which correspond to the
usual ages of taking GCE and O and A levels, are separated by
a trough at the age of 17. Very few cases of anorexia nervosa
started at the age of 17 Of the patients were not engaged in
academic pursuits, despite the fact that by 1971 only 18 per
cent of girls were continuing in an educational establishment
at this age (Social Trends 1972). The fact that Cambridge is
a university town should not distort the statistics for the
ages below that of university entrance. The peak at the age
of 18 for those who started crash dieting while working for GCE
at A level is drawn from a population which on average was
only 18 per cent of that which was at risk up to the age of
compulsory education. This suggests that the incidence of
crash dieting while working for GCE at A level is appreciably
higher than that among girls working for GCE at O level. Of
course, Cambridge University might well select out those girls
who would work particularly hard for university entrance, and
they might be prone to developing anorexia nervosa, but this
would still imply that academic pressure was an important
precipitating factor.

Of 626 patients with menstrual disturbance presenting at our
endocrine clinic in 7 years, 21 per cent were suffering from
total amenorrhoea which had been precipitated by crash dieting.
This is now the second commonest cause of menstrual disturbance
in young women and the major cause of amenorrhoea lasting more
than a year. In 30 per cent of the patients depression was
considered to have played a part in the menstrual disturbance;
some of these had anorexia nervosa and some had other primary
conditions, mostly the polycystic ovary syndrome. Our earlier
data showed that 50 per cent or more of women with menstrual
disturbance had polycystic ovaries (Mills *et al*. 1971), and our
most recent data still support this view (Mills *et al*. 1973).
At the time we considered that the high incidence of ovarian
enlargement in depressed women represented the overlap of two
common conditions, but data are now accumulating to suggest that
the strain and depression may precede the menstrual disturbance.

AGE DISTRIBUTION OF PSYCHIATRIC PATIENTS

The incidence of depression among the general population is
unknown. There have been a variety of theories to explain the
onset of depression, but none is satisfactory unless it relates
to what is happening in present-day society. It is clear that

an appreciable number of patients who attempt suicide were
depressed at the time of taking the overdose of drugs. Very few
still feel suicidal when questioned after the event. The final
incident which triggers off taking of an overdose is frequently
a relatively trivial event when looked at in isolation, but a
more detailed study of the patient's preceding life frequently
reveals a variety of stresses and strains that many of us would
find difficult to cope with. We have been struck by the
similarity of our studies in patients who have risked suicide
with those of Brown and his colleagues in depressed patients
(Brown *et al*. 1973). They found that the frequency of threatening life events in the 6 months prior to the onset of depression
was very much higher than in their matched control group. This
raises the question of whether a series of challenges or a
prolonged severe challenge taxes the ability to cope with the
problems. Such a concept has to be seen in the context of
social conditions because, for instance, a prolonged illness
for a man in a position which ensures full salary for some
months may impose little strain on him and his family. The same
illness in a man further down the socio-economic scale may lead to
a sharp fall in income, possibly difficulty in paying rent,
possibly debts because of commitments, perhaps loss of his job,
and under some circumstances perhaps even loss of his home.
The commitments entered into tend to rise as our society becomes
more affluent. Many people now regard a car, television set,
washing machine, record player etc. as essentials of life.

Some of these people who have problems may be referred as
psychiatric outpatients before they have got to the point of
attempting suicide. Over the last 10-15 years the age distribution
of patients referred to a psychiatrist has progressively changed.
In Fig.12.13 is shown the percentage of all new patients seen at
psychiatric outpatients in Cambridge who were in the age group
15-24 years (these data were kindly supplied by the late Dr.
Malcolm Heron.) This age group comprised about 20 per cent of
all new patients in 1957 but now represents 50 per cent of all the
new patients. It seems doubtful that the lessened resistance of
patients nowadays to agree to be sent to a psychiatrist should
make such a very large difference in the age distribution of the
patients attending psychiatric outpatients. It seems more likely
that this represents further evidence that the young people in
the age group 15-24 years are feeling and manifesting much more
disturbance in our society at the beginning of the seventies than
they were 10 years before.

The Samaritans (a voluntary organization which helps people
contemplating suicide) also have reported a rise in the incidence
of young children seeking their help. Their complaint is
frequently that they can no longer tolerate the strife and rows
between the parents.

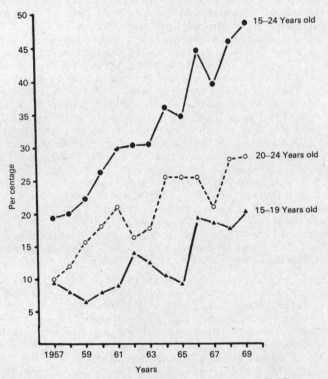

Fig.12.13 The new patients in the age groups 15-19 years,
20-24 years, and 15-24 years presenting at the Psychiatric
Outpatients of Addenbrooke's Hospital, Cambridge as a
percentage of all new psychiatric patients in each year.
(Data kindly provided by Dr.Malcolm Heron.)

THE PERMISSIVE SOCIETY

Changes in social *mores* took place particularly rapidly in the
years of the middle 1960s. It was then that Mary Quant declared
that she would design a dress that no one over 30 would dare
to wear: the mini-skirt war had begun. There was a much
freer discussion in magazines and newspapers and finally on
radio and television of the changing sexual attitudes and customs.
The impression was certainly produced that a higher percentage

of unmarried young people were engaging in sexual intercourse.
This impression was probably wrong, as judged by our data
showing that only 30 per cent of unmarried women under 21
had had intercourse. However, the impression was probably used
extensively by young men to indicate to young women that there
was something wrong with them if they refused. One result of
this increase in sexual activity in the latter half of the
1960s was the sharp rise in the numbers of new cases of
gonorrhoea reported each year in young people under the age of
25 years (Fig.12.14). The numbers rose sharply in both males

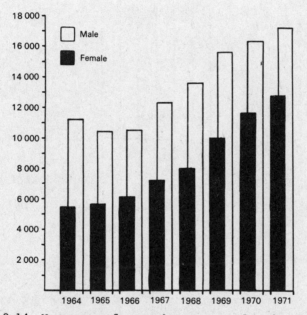

Fig.12.14 New cases of gonorrhoea reported each year aged up
to 24 years in England and Wales.

and females. Whereas in 1964 and 1965 the female new cases were
half the number of male ones, by the early 1970s the female
new cases were more than 70 per cent as high as the new male
cases.

Along with this there was a 50 per cent rise in the rates of
pregnancies conceived outside marriage in girls aged 15-19 years
of age: from 24 to 37 per 1000 unmarried females. In this age

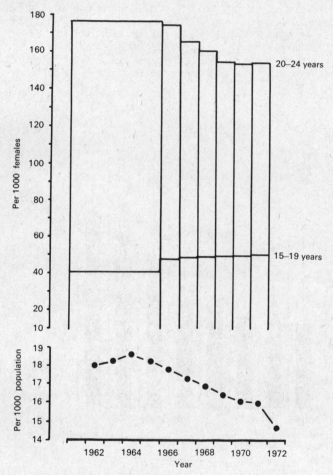

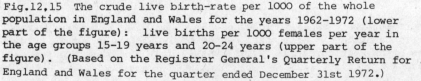

Fig.12.15 The crude live birth-rate per 1000 of the whole population in England and Wales for the years 1962-1972 (lower part of the figure): live births per 1000 females per year in the age groups 15-19 years and 20-24 years (upper part of the figure). (Based on the Registrar General's Quarterly Return for England and Wales for the quarter ended December 31st 1972.)

group 70 per cent of the births were conceived before marriage.

The change in sexual *mores* and in girls' dress imposed a strain both on the girls themselves and on their parents. For 2 or 3 years the battle was waged and increased the social disturbance in young people. At length most parents came to accept a lot of the changes in dress and sexual activity as normal. The teenagers who grew up under the changed conditions accepted them as normal without the parental battle. This is probably what happened with the student rebels: once they had fought for changes and increased student representation on committees, those that followed had no battle and appeared to be non-rebellious.

The change in sexual activity was only slightly reflected in the live birth-rates to females aged 15-19 years (which went up slightly in the middle 1960s) and to those 20-24 years (which steadily fell from 1965 onwards). The whole population birth rate has been falling in England and Wales since 1964, several years before the Abortion Act came in in 1968 (Fig.12.15). Indeed this Act had little effect on the crude live birth-rate figures, which fell steadily from 1964 to 1971. It is perhaps surprising that with the evidence of increased sexual activity from the middle 1960s the birth-rate both for all ages and for those 20-24 years old fell at the same time. The increased use of oral contraceptives might explain these facts but they might equally reflect a genuine fall in fertility rates.

DISCUSSION

Two things in these studies stand out strikingly. One is that the age group 15-24 years of age recurs repeatedly in various forms of social discontent. The peak age for attempted suicide is in this age group and the group may contain a lot of alcoholics. There has been a rise in the percentage of drivers under 30 who are charged with driving under the influence of alcohol. The majority of drug offenders are in this critical age group, and girls who go in for crash dieting and stop their menstrual periods are mostly in the age group 15-24 years. Finally the fact that 50 per cent of new psychiatric patients in the Cambridge area are now in this age group confirms the view that considerable disturbance occurs in these young people in our society.

The second important point is the increased incidence of so many of these factors during the 1960s and especially the sudden rise in the middle 1960s. Attempted suicide in local areas and nationally appears to have risen much more sharply during the 1960s than during the 1950s (Figs.12.1 and Table 12.1). Among the teenage males there was a sharp rise in

numbers of the cases of attempted suicide in the middle
1960s, at the same time as the rise in drug offenders in Mid-
Anglia, and an increase in the accidental ingestion of
tablets by young children in the homes of their young parents.
There was also a sharp rise in the total numbers of prescriptions
issued, which no doubt reflects the greater chance of the young
children finding drugs at home.

It appears, therefore, that society in general and the younger
adults in particular were obtaining and using drugs of all
sorts, legal and illegal and including alcohol, on a much larger
scale from the middle 1960s onwards. The question that should be
asked is, 'What events in society were responsible for these
relatively dramatic changes?' Was the development of the so-
called permissive society the cause of the troubles or a
reflection of internal changes in society? We suspect that in
part it was the latter but as it developed it certainly added
to the strains on young people. These were due partly to
battles with parents and authority but also to the fact that,
as the changes developed, the young people had many more
decisions to make, such as, whether to have intercourse, what
time to go home, whether to use illegal drugs, etc.

Rising affluence itself brings problems. The availability
of machines to lessen work or to improve the utilization of
leisure, such as cars, washing machines, television sets, record
players, transistor radios, etc. provides a stimulus to those
who do not possess them to strive to obtain them. The principle
of relative deprivation is a very powerful one if you are the
only person in a community without some of these modern
consumer goods. More wives now go out to work, more men
take second jobs to earn the money for such goods. As both
get more tired, more friction develops in homes, and this leads
teenagers to sense the strain and insecurity. This is frequently
an important factor in their attempts at suicide or in their
contacting the Samaritans.

Competition for a share of affluence is not only intranational
but also international and leads to demands for increased
efficiency and productivity which impose still further strains
on workers. The increased frequency of strikes in the last
decade has been clear evidence of the underlying unrest and
frustration.

Research is urgently needed to assess and define the factors
in modern society which appear to be imposing an increasing
and intolerable strain on the relatively young age group of
15-24 years. This group is at the peak of many parameters of
social disturbance but as the peaks get higher the spread over
into younger and older age groups becomes more apparent.
We are no longer surprised when 11-12 year-olds present with

self-imposed starvation or attempted suicide. The speed with which the young, upon whom the next generation depends, are being caught up in social disturbance is so fast that steps will have to be taken very soon if we are to be able to reverse this trend. Who would deny that the rising incidence of alcoholism, attempted suicide, drug-abuse, self-starvation, etc. reflects a retrogression in society? Only a greater understanding of their causation will enable us to tackle the problem of the reversal of this process.

REFERENCES

BROWN, C.W., HARRIS, T.O. and PETO, J. (1973) Life events and psychiatric disorders. Part 2: nature of causal link. *Psychol. Med*. 2, 159-76.

EVANS, J.G. (1967) Deliberate self-poisoning in the Oxford area. *Brit. J. prev.soc.Med*. 21, 97-107.

GRAHAM, J.D.P. and HITCHENS, R.A.N. (1967) Acute poisoning and its prevention. *Br.J.prev.soc.Med*. 21, 108-114.

GREER, S. and GUNN, J.C. (1966) Attempted suicide from intact and broken parental homes. *Br. med.J*. ii, 1355-57.

Hospital treatment of acute poisoning (1968) HMSO, London.

MATTHEW, H. and LAWSON, A.A.H. (1967) *Treatment of common acute poisonings*. Livingstone, Edinburgh and London.

MILLS, I.H., WILSON, R.J., TAYLOR, R.E. and DAVISON, S.H.H. (1971) *The investigation of patients with menstrual disturbance and the response to treatment with clomiphene*. Pfizer Medical Monographs 6, Edinburgh University Press.

MILLS, I.H., WILSON, R.J., EDEN, M.A.M., and LINES, J.G. (1973) Endocrine and social factors in self-starvation amenorrhoea. In: *Symposium - Anorexia nervosa and obesity*. Publication No.42, Royal College of Physicians of Edinburgh.

PATEL, A.R., ROY, M. and WILSON, G.M. (1972) Self-poisoning and alcohol. *Lancet ii*, 1099-102.

SLADE, P.D. and RUSSELL, G.F.M. (1973) Awareness of body dimensions in anorexia nervosa: cross-sectional and longitudinal studies. *Psychol.Med.3*, 188-99.

Social Trends No.3   (1972) HMSO, London.

STENGEL, E.   (1964)   *Suicide and attempted suicide.*   Pelican Books, London.

Twentieth Annual Report on Drink Offences (1973)   Christian Economic and Social Research Foundation, 12 Caxton Street, London.

13 Biochemical responses to environmental stress

Malcolm Carruthers

Since Claude Bernard postulated that the integrity, and
hence continued health, of the organism depended on its ability
to regulate the internal environment, the major part of medical
and physiological research has been directed towards studying
the physical factors which can disturb its homeostatic mechanisms.
The idea that emotional factors can cause alteration in the
internal environment that could lead to physical disease may have
been felt to be true, but was neither extensively investigated
nor acted upon. The main reason for this was that, while the art
of medicine will allow for emotional factors in the causation and
treatment of physical disease, the science of medicine demands
measurement of the physical results of these factors. The development of sensitive and reliable methods of measuring blood
catecholamines, together with more portable recorders of physiological events, has made possible more objective measurement of
human responses to stress and the biochemical changes which
accompany them.

ANXIETY, AGGRESSION, AND CATECHOLAMINES

The passive emotion of fear predominantly increases blood-
adrenaline levels, and the more active emotion of aggression,
even when subdued as in frustration, causes more noradrenaline to
be secreted (Longson and Christy 1964; von Euler 1964). The
increasing tendency to aggression in modern societies has been
deftly outlined by Desmond Morris in *The Naked Ape* and *The Human
Zoo*. This aggression finds one of its most blatant expressions,
except in times of war, in driving. Here the individual not
only has his status and territory to protect but also his prowess
to prove. It has been shown (Bellet *et al.* 1969) that ordinary driving
increases catecholamine secretion rates by 80-100 per cent and
racing driving by up to 1000 per cent (Taggart *et al.*1969), most
of the increase being in noradrenaline. Similar increases

† My thanks are due to Dr.Peter Taggart with whom practically
all the clinical work has been done. Dr.Walter Somerville
has given continued guidance and encouragement throughout.
At the Middlesex Hospital, Professor R.H.S. Thompson helped
to initiate these projects. In their continuation at the
Institute of Ophthalmology, Professor Norman Ashton has been
unfailingly helpful. Financial support was provided by the
Medical Research Council, the Sports Council, the British Heart
Foundation and CIBA-Geigy Ltd.

in catecholamines secretion were found in airline pilots
(Ministry of Defence 1969) where the rise was largely
proportional to the work-load, and hence the responsibility
of flying the aircraft.

CATECHOLAMINES AND FREE FATTY ACIDS

Adrenaline and noradrenaline both cause a rise in blood
free fatty acids (FFA) by lipolysis of triglyceride in adipose
tissue. The increase provoked by noradrenaline is greater
and more prolonged than that due to adrenaline (Wenke 1966),
and can be up to 400 per cent. Obese people, who have higher
resting levels of FFA, tend to show notably sustained
increases (Dole 1956), as do the physically less fit
(Johnson *et al.* 1969). Similar factors apply with cigarette-
smoking, where catecholamines, especially noradrenaline, are
secreted, causing rises in FFA of up to 80 per cent (Murchison
and Fife 1966). With all these stimuli the elevation is
accompanied by an increase in platelet aggregation. The
association of smoking with aortic (Sackett *et al.* 1968) and
coronary (Auerbach *et al.* 1965) atherosclerosis is well known
and is accompanied by a 200-300 per cent greater incidence
of ischaemic heart disease in heavy smokers.

FREE FATTY ACIDS AND ENDOGENOUS TRIGLYCERIDE

Following publication of the equivocal results of various
dietary studies and cholesterol-lowering regimens applied to
at-risk groups (MRC 1968; Oglesby *et al.* 1968), hope of finding
a single exogenous constituent responsible for atherosclerosis
is fading. Indeed, the finding that an increase in pre-β
triglyceride is one of the common lipid abnormalities in
coronary-artery disease (Albrink and Man 1959) has begun to
focus more attention on endogenous alterations in lipid metabolism. Also the composition of fibrous plaques in the aorta
resembles that of plasma-triglyceride, while their cholesterol
esters are so grossly different from those in the plasma that they
are almost certainly synthesized *in situ* (Smith *et al.* 1968).

In the absence of immediate metabolic requirements, circulating
FFAs are converted to triglyercide by the liver. The conversion
is accelerated by high glucose levels. The newly formed triglyceride is not normally stored in the liver but is recirculated
as pre-β-lipoprotein. After severe stress, even individuals
who have been fasting show a marked lipaemia due to the rapid
synthesis of endogenous triglyceride. Deposition of triglyceride
in vessel walls has been shown to be enhanced by both high FFA
levels (Rutstein *et al.* 1969) and insulin (Stout and Vallance-
Owen 1969).

AGGRESSION AND ATHEROGENESIS

The strong association between the active aggressive Type A behaviour pattern and atheromatous processes affecting the heart (Friedman *et al*. 1968; Morris and Gardner 1969) has been described but not explained. On the basis of the evidence cited above and the close correlation between the factors causing raised free fatty acid levels and those associated with an increased incidence of ischaemic heart disease (Truett *et al*. 1967; Morris *et al*. 1966), we shall consider in this explanation.

Under the stresses of modern urban living, a large proportion of the population maintains high levels of catecholamines, especially noradrenaline, for the greater part of the day. This results in mobilization of free fatty acids in amounts greatly in excess of the oxidative needs of the tissues of sedentary workers on high-carbohydrate diets. The levels of FFAs are increased, and maintained over longer periods, by obesity and lack of exercise. The excess FFAs may take one of two metabolic pathways. First, they could be directly taken up by arterial walls, possibly aided by increased hydrostatic pressure and endothelial damage in hypertension. In arterial walls, in the presence of high glucose levels, they are rapidly converted to triglyceride. Secondly, they could be converted to endogenous triglyceride in the liver, and, under the action of the raised cortisol levels found in stress (Selye 1971) and raised insulin levels accompanying obesity, be deposited in the arterial walls, causing atheroma. Finally, having induced atheromatous narrowing of the coronary arteries, the free fatty acids may well initiate the final thrombotic episode by their effects on platelet adhesiveness and myocardial contractility (Kurien and Oliver 1966; Oliver *et al*. 1968). On admission to hospital a further iatrogenic increase in free fatty acids is caused both by giving heparin (Rutstein *et al*. 1969) and noradrenaline and by intensive cardiac monitoring. The aim of this chapter is to study this hypothesis by describing some experiments in which the catecholamine and lipid responses of humans to a wide variety of environmental stresses have been studied.

AGGRESSION

To illustrate the suggested chain of biochemical events which occur when aggression is the predominant emotion (Fig.13.1) the stress reactions of racing drivers, traffic drivers, and public speakers were studied. Modification of these responses by β-blockade was also investigated in these groups, both to provide additional evidence for this theory and to explore a potential remedy for some of its effects.

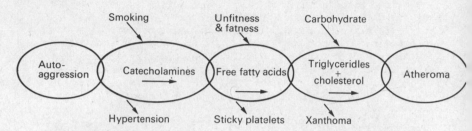

Fig.13.1   *The Central Dogma*. The suggested chain of
events linking aggression and atheroma.

In 1967 Dr.Peter Taggart, himself an international-class
racing driver, reported the preliminary results of radioelectrocardiographic studies made on the drivers in competitive circuit
races (Taggart and Gibbons 1967). Three healthy experienced
racing drivers showed during these events an increase in the
heart rate to between 190 and 205 beats per minute. The rate
was recorded at 150-180 in the 15 minutes before the race,
and at the signal indicating 2 minutes before the start a rate
in excess of 180 was usual. This increased up to 200-205 at the
start, and was usually maintained near this level throughout the
event.

As well as suggesting an extremely high level of sympathetic
activity, extension of these (Taggart *et al*. 1969) and other
studies (Frost *et al*. 1951; Walker *et al*., 1969) indicated
that racing driving might be the ideal test-bed for investigating
acute aggressive emotion. Dr.Taggart also observed, during
these earlier studies, that the drivers' plasma samples, although
clear before the race, often became markedly lipaemic after it.
As the majority of drivers voluntarily fast for several hours,
or even overnight, before racing, it appeared probable that the
lipaemia resulted from increased synthesis of endogenous triglyceride induced by the emotional stress of racing driving.
The catecholamine and lipid responses of a group of these drivers
were therefore investigated to establish the biochemical
mechanism giving rise to this secondary hyperlipidaemia.

Results of experiments on racing drivers

One, two, or three plasma samples were taken from each of 16
drivers during the 3-hour period following a race. Two drivers
were studied repeatedly throughout the season. The majority of
events were of international status, taking place in England,
Germany, Italy, Spain, and Belgium; the remainder were Club

events, and the drivers had the appropriate range of experience
and ability. Their ages ranged from 22 to 39 years. All were
apparently healthy and of average build.

Blood (20 ml) was drawn rapidly from an antecubital vein –
with the driver still seated in his car for the immediately
pre-race or post-race samples, or while he was seated in some
convenient situation such as the first-aid post for the later
samples.

All drivers had been fasting and abstained from alcohol. The
biochemical methods of measuring plasma catecholamines
(Carruthers *et al.* 1970) and free fatty acids (Carruthers and
Young 1973) are reported elsewhere, and the electrocardiographic
methods were those of Taggart *et al.* 1973.

The results are shown in Fig.13.2. As would be expected from
the stresses involved in these intensely competitive events,
total catecholamine levels were greatly raised at the time of
the race, although in the samples taken after 15 minutes,
considerably lower values were obtained. The high levels were
almost entirely due to noradrenaline, although there was also
some elevation of adrenaline.

FFA levels were high both before and immediately after the
race. Samples taken after one hour or later showed lower values,
approaching normal resting levels. Triglyceride levels were
slightly raised immediately after the race, peak values being
obtained after one hour. Cholesterol levels did not alter
through the period studied.

A strong positive correlation was present between total
catecholamine levels below 2 µg per litre and free fatty acids.
If catecholamine levels above 2 µg per litre were included, the
correlation was poor (Fig.13.3). A strong negative correlation
was present between FFA levels and triglyceride levels
(Fig.13.4).

The results suggest a linear relationship between the rapid
rise in FFA and noradrenaline levels until an FFA plateau
is reached with catecholamine levels of about 2 µg per litre.
Above that level, no consistent rise occurs (Fig.13.3). Previous
studies demonstrating this relationship have been carried out
either with small doses of exogenous catecholamines (Jurand
and Oliver 1970), or with the relatively low levels of endogenous
catecholamines reached following acute myocardial infarction
(McDonald *et al.* 1969; Nelson 1970). Also, the rise in triglyceride levels is inversely related to FFA levels, suggesting
interconversion. The endogenous origin of the triglyceride was
also demonstrated by the electrophoretic patterns, which showed
transition from an FFA band in the albumin region immediately
after the race to an increase in the pre- -triglyceride, which
was maximal an hour later.

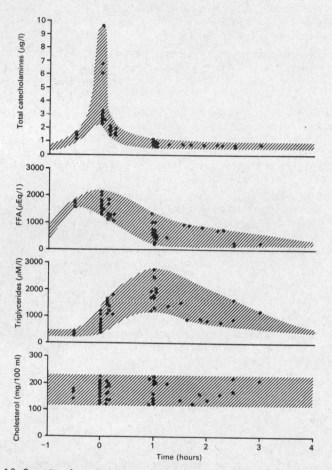

Fig.13.2   *Racing drivers*.   Plasma catecholamines, free fatty
acid, triglyceride, and cholesterol levels before and at
varying intervals after the end of races.   They are plotted
against a common time axis, demonstrating their temporal inter-
relationships.   The ranges of each are represented by the shaded
areas.

Although a great deal of important work has already been done
on stress-induced hyperlipidaemia (Carlson *et al*. 1972), the
emotional factor usually receives scanty attention when the types
of hyperlipidaemia thought to be associated with atherosclerosis
are considered.   The study indicated, however, that a maximal
lipid response may be triggered by relatively low plasma-catechola-
mine levels.   It has been shown since (Taggart and Carruthers 1972)

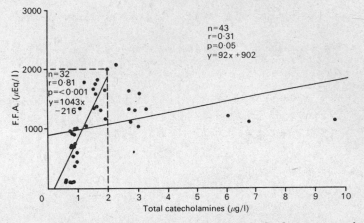

Fig. 13.3 *Racing drivers*. Relationship of plasma catecholamine
and free fatty acid levels analysed for catecholamine values below
2µg per litre (within interrupted lines) and for all values.

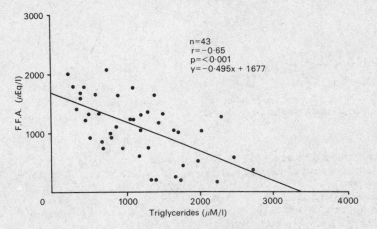

Fig. 13.4 *Racing drivers*. The negative correlation between
plasma free fatty acid and triglyceride levels.

that β-blockade can lessen the tachycardia, and prevent rises
in lipids and glucose in this extremely stressful situation.

Results of experiments on traffic drivers

Eight drivers, six of whom were members of the Institute
of Advanced Motorists, were studied on a total of twelve
occasions. In view of the extensive ECG studies previously
performed by Taggart *et al.* (1968, 1969) and Bellet (1968), it

was decided not to include this method of investigation in these tests.

After fasting overnight, the subject was bled at home and the plasma samples separated. He then drove his own car through morning rush-hour traffic of approximately similar density for half an hour. Immediately after pulling up while the subject was still in the driving seat, a further blood sample was taken for lipid and catecholamine analysis.

These results are shown in Fig.13.5.

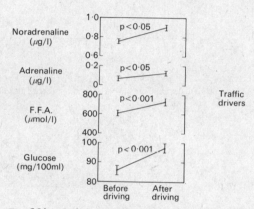

Fig.13.5   *Traffic drivers.* Plasma catecholamines, free fatty acid, and glucose levels before and after a half-hour drive in traffic.

From the limited number of drivers tested, it appears that the metabolic results of driving in traffic are similar in type, if not in scale, to those seen in racing drivers. The rise in noradrenaline previously reported in studies carried out on urine by Bellet *et al.* (1969) tends to confirm the impression frequently voiced by psychologists that motoring brings out the aggressive element in man's nature. One reason for the small rise in noradrenaline could have been that the subjects were experienced motorists on their best behaviour.

In general, the study proved too laborious and time-consuming to enable conclusive results to be obtained. A modified experimental design, using urinary rather than plasma catecholamines and investigation of alterations in the response to this important everyday stress by β-blockade, are suggested as extensions of this pilot study.

Results of experiments on public speakers

As medical knowledge is largely imparted verbally, many doctors have a wide personal experience of the stress of public speaking. The most common sequence of sensations experienced by a speaker is a steady increase in anxiety for some minutes or even hours before speaking. In the more nervous it may be accompanied by palpitations and dryness of the lips and mouth leading to hoarseness, and only partially relieved by the water traditionally provided for this purpose. Fear that the speaker, as well as his buccal secretions, will 'dry up' is the main dread of those unaccustomed to public speaking, and even of some of those that are.

Therefore, depending upon the personality of the speaker, his experience, the subject of the talk, and the likely or actual reaction of the audience, this situation represents a challenge of variable intensity. To stand up to speak requires a determined effort for the majority of people, although if the talk proceeds well a certain degree of elation may ensue as he 'makes his points' at the expense of his mute, seated, captive audience. As in many other situations, a mood of anxiety and uncertainty is often succeeded by one of defiance and even anger if he is interrupted during the talk, or he feels his views are not being well received. It is the com-bination of aggression and anxiety, experienced by many people in the groups most at risk from coronary heart disease, which suggested this topic for investigation, as being more representative of the type of emotional stress present in modern urban life.

A wide range of speakers, addressing audiences of greatly differing sizes, were studied. These included medical students and housemen giving factual case histories to small groups of their colleagues, experienced lecturers talking to more critical audiences of up to several hundred people, and television performers appearing 'live' before an estimated ten million viewers.

Of the 30 subjects, seven had suffered myocardial infarcts 6 months to 10 years previously. To investigate the potential benefit of β-blockade under these conditions, 15 of the subjects, including all the post-infarction cases, were given a variable single oral dose of oxprenolol (Trasicor) half to one hour before speaking.

Continuous electrocardiographic recordings were obtained before, during, and after the speeches. In the majority of cases the C and M radioelectrocardiograph, linked to a UHER tape recorder, as in the racing-driver study, was used for this purpose. Later in the study the less fallible and cumbersome Vingmed 'Recard' system was used. Except for the subjects on

television, who made it one of the features of their programme, none was allowed to reveal that they were being monitored lest the confession should alter their responses. Similarly, the pre- and post-speech blood samples were taken in another room without the knowledge of the audience.

The reactions of the individual subjects, regardless of experience, were found to be so varied that only those of the blocked and unblocked groups will be considered separately. The mean maximum heart-rate in the normal unblocked subjects was 151 beats per minute (range 125-180), usually reaching a peak within a few seconds of the start of the speech and being maintained at only a slightly lower level for most of its duration. The rapidity of this response was clearly seen in the television reporters, whose heart rates were being recorded on cardiotachometers attached to the oscilloscopes displaying their electrocardiograms. Transient peaks were reached within 10-15 seconds of the television camera 'cutting' to them. Although considerable variation of heart-rate occurred due to sinus arrhythmia, this initial marked acceleration often occurred during the rapid inspiration preceding an opening sentence, and was not repeated in the succeeding slow breaths accompanying speaking.

Rates of up to 180 beats per minute were also reached by many of the 15 speakers, the mean maximum being 140 (standard error 4.29), studied separately when they were on placebo tablets, and ectopic beats were occasionally observed. However, in those subjects in whom they did occur, they tended to be prolific and often multifocal. Additional evidence of high levels of circulating adrenaline was provided even in the healthy subjects by the characteristic sloping ST-T depression referred to in the section on anxiety, as in the J-E wave (Taggart, Carruthers, and Somerville 1973). In six out of seven post-coronary subjects, ischaemic-like changes appeared on the electrocardiogram while they were speaking, and one of these experienced angina. Such changes were present in three of these before speaking, but in six subjects the ST configuration worsened during their talk.

After taking an average of 20 mg of the β-blocking drug, the mean maximum heart-rate was 82 (standard error 2.80) ($p < 0.001$) and no ectopic beats were seen. None of the post-coronary group showed any worsening in relation to their resting pre-speech electrocardiogram, or developed angina while speaking, after taking these small single doses of β-blockers.

Total catecholamine levels were raised in both groups before and after speaking, although the increase was not as great in the blocked group. The noradrenaline rose in both blocked and unblocked groups, while adrenaline remained the same in the latter and decreased slightly in the former (Fig.13.6). Free fatty acids rose in the unblocked group, and fell from a signifi-

cantly lower pre-speech level in the blocked group (Fig.13.6).
Triglycerides rose slightly from 197 mg per 100 ml to 208 mg per
100 ml in the unblocked group, and fell from 131 mg per 100 ml
to 114 mg per 100 ml in the blocked group, with no significant
alterations in cholesterol in either group.

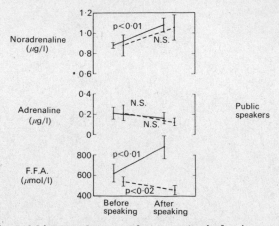

Fig.13.6 *Public speakers.* Plasma catecholamines and free
fatty acids in 15 subjects before and after speaking, when
taking placebo tablets (——) and oxprenolol (----)

The increase in endogenous triglyceride synthesis occurring
in some of the former group was clearly visible in the pre-β
region on celluose acetate lipoprotein electrophoresis (Fig.13.7)
The most marked exception was the one female speaker in the
unblocked group whose free fatty acids rose from 560 to 640
μEq per litre, but triglyceride fell from 102 to 83 mg per 100
ml, with no alteration of the lipid pattern on electrophoresis.
This may reflect the more rapid metabolism of free fatty acids
to ketone bodies in the female (Jenkins, Welbom, and Goff, 1970)
which could be a valuable protective mechanism against ischaemic
heart disease in pre-menopausal women.

Public speaking appeared to be a moderately intense emotional
stress for most people, although this was seldom evident from
their calm exterior. Although anxiety was the predominant
emotion leading up to the event, this merged with a more confident aggressive mood as the talk progressed. The biochemical
changes accompanying this mood-swing were a slight decrease in
adrenaline accompanied by an increase in noradrenaline. This
was reflected in the electrocardiographic changes which were
similar to those described by Lepeschkin *et al.* (1960) during
infusions of both amines in healthy subjects. The thermogenic

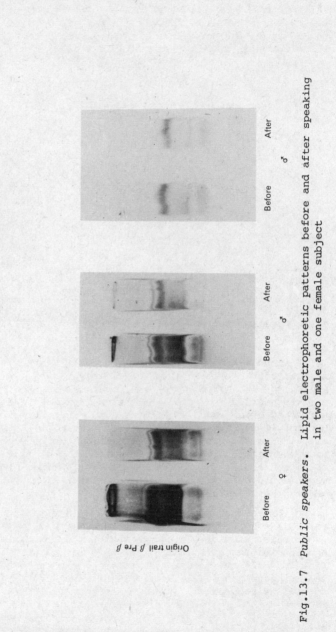

Origin trail β Pre β

Before   After   Before   After   Before   After

♀   ♂   ♂

Fig. 13.7 *Public speakers.* Lipid electrophoretic patterns before and after speaking in two male and one female subject

action of noradrenaline in promoting the release and oxidation
of free fatty acids may explain the description of a heated
argument (Carruthers *et al.* 1973). This study confirms the
marked tachycardia reported by Ira *et al.* (1963) as occurring
even in experienced medical speakers.

The effectiveness of β-blocking drugs in preventing the
electrocardiographic changes due to adrenaline (Suzman 1971;
Jackson 1971), and the increases in free fatty acids and
triglycerides brought about by noradrenaline, were just as
marked as in what, for some people, is an everyday situation,
as in racing drivers. Several of the speakers noticed a
lessening of the apprehension they normally experienced
before the event when taking the drug. This may have been due
to interruption of the self-perpetuating action of anxiety,
postulated by Breggin (1964), as was demonstrated in stutterers
taking diazepam by Leanderson and Levi (1967). In no case was
there any perceptible impairment of performance, and in some
more anxious individuals it may have been improved in that they
felt and appeared less flustered and spoke more slowly and
distinctly. It could be claimed that β-blockers can pace both
the heart and the speech.

ANXIETY

In many respects the effects of anxiety are both more distressing and more obvious than those of aggression. Anxiety
and associated uncertainty often precede almost any form of
emotional stress, and the symptomatology of 'panic in the
breast', pallor, perspiration, pilo-erection, and pupillary and
palpebral dilation are more dramatic than the slight flush of
anger. Similarly, the extract of the adrenal medulla, known
as 'adrenin' (Cannon 1929), with which most of the early studies
on the biochemistry of stress were carried out, is likely to have
contained considerably more adrenaline than noradrenaline, both
because of its greater stability and its higher concentration
in the gland. Thus the adrenaline/noradrenaline ratio in the
preparation originally available was 4:1, about the same as in
the human adrenal gland. Further, the tachycardia and
glycosuria which adrenaline causes, were more easily demonstrated
than the increases in blood pressure and plasma lipids produced
by noradrenaline, so that the former became the hallmarks of
sympathetic action.

Only with the isolation of the two hormonal components of
adrenin, and the development of methods for their separate
estimation, did the biochemical differentiation of anxiety from
aggression become possible. Even then the situation investigated
tended to be of mixed emotional content rather than ones of
pure anxiety, and increases in the rate of secretion of both
adrenaline and noradrenaline were reported. Also the studies

were mainly based on urinary catecholamine measurements over
periods of an hour or more during which time the subject could
have undergone several changes of mood. It therefore appeared
that the biochemical changes associated with anxiety could best
be characterized from plasma samples taken during periods of
acute anxiety, as occurred in parachute-jumping and rock-climbing,
as well as the previously reported studies on airline passengers
(Carruthers, Taggart and Somerville 1973) and subjects with
dental phobia (Edmondson, Roscoe and Vickers 1972).

Results of experiments on parachutists

Twenty-five young, healthy parachutists were studied during a
total of 30 jumps. Their degree of experience varied widely,
from the inexperienced doing their first jump (A) and
moderately experienced 'free-fallers' (B) to the Parachute
Regiments' 'Nomad' sky-diving team (C).

All the subjects were fasting before dives, which was found to
be no great hardship, particularly for the inexperienced group.
Plasma samples were taken in eight cases immediately prior to
the ascent.   Using the 'Recard' system, electrocardiographic
recordings were obtained with the subject in several different
positions, including prone and while hanging upright in a
training harness, to allow for postural variations during the
descent. The subject then switched the EGC recorder on
approximately 5 minutes before jumping and left it on during
the descent, landing, and for several minutes afterwards, to
obtain a full record and 'recovery' tracing.

A further blood sample was taken as soon as the subject could
be reached, which was usually within a minute for the more
accurate, experienced parachutists, but was sometimes up to 2
or 3 minutes if the less experienced fell wide of the mark.
Samples were separated immediately, using a centrifuge powered
by a portable generator, and placed in vacuum jars containing
solid carbon dioxide or water-ice, as appropriate.

The major interest of this study lay in the electrocardiographic
rather than the biochemical, changes. The most marked feature
of the tracings was the extremely high heart-rate, commonly
in the region of between 180 and 200 beats per minute. This
usually returned to normal within 2 minutes of landing, demonstrating the rapidity of decay of adrenaline and the difficulties
of obtaining a truly representative plasma sample. The most
rapid deceleration of heart-rate, from 200 to 50 beats per
minute within a minute, was seen in one subject who fractured
his ankle on landing.

In addition, in the majority of subjects the recordings taken
before and after the descents (Fig.13.8) showed the characteristic

Subject No.1

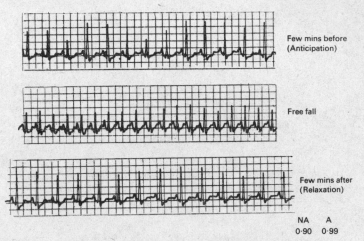

Few mins before
(Anticipation)

Free fall

Few mins after
(Relaxation)

NA   A
0·90   0·99

Fig.13.8   *Parachutists*.   Tracing from a 'Vingmed Recard'
ECG recorder, before, during, and after jumping, in an
inexperienced subject.

ST-T depression which, together with the transitional stages
of the J-E wave, is suggestive of the action of high
circulating adrenaline levels on the heart (Taggart *et al.*
1973).   These changes were not present when the same subjects
exercised to a similar heart-rate, and were therefore unlikely
to be produced by the tachycardia alone.   They can be prevented
by giving β-blocking drugs (Jackson 1971), aiding the important
differentiation to be made between anxiety and cardiac ischaemia.

The biochemical results showed large rises in adrenaline and
glucose (Fig.13.9), with no change in lipid levels.   ,

One of the major practical and ethical problems in the
investigation of anxiety in healthy volunteers is the means of
inducing a sufficiently intense response to produce clearly
defined changes in the variables being measured within a safe and
acceptable experimental design.   At the same time, as far as
possible other emotions, such as anger and aversion, together
with physical exertion, have to be excluded.   For these reasons

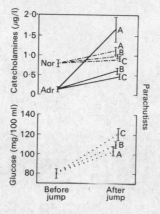

Fig.13.9.   *Parachutists.*   Plasma catecholamines and glucose levels before and after jumping in nine inexperienced (A), twelve moderately experienced (B) and five experienced (C) parachutists.

the extreme situation of parachute jumping forms an ideal setting for the study of intense anxiety in a fairly pure form associated with little physical exertion.

In previous studies, Von Euler and Londberg (1954) demonstrated increased urinary adrenaline, and Basowitz et al. (1955) impaired performance of psychological tests in men undergoing parachute training.   Increases in heart-rate up to 180 beats per minute during parachute descents were reported by Shane and Slinde (1968), but the radioelectrocardiographic tracings were not suitable for demonstrating the marked ST depression and other changes seen in this study.   As would be expected, the transitory rise in plasma adrenaline, even when measured after a few minutes delay, is proportionally greater than that measured in urine, which represents the average secretion rate over an extended period of time.   As suggested by Frankenhaeuser's (1971) work, the adrenaline response decreased with increased parachuting experience.   The poor correlations between adrenaline levels and rises in blood-sugar and heart-rate again emphasized the individuality of sympathetic responses.

Results of experiments on climbers

Eleven male climbers whose mean age was 31 years (range 22-48) were studied while scaling the limestone escarpment known as Bowles Rocks near Tunbridge Wells. Although not of great height, the ascents were reasonably anxiety-provoking, even for these experienced climbers using ropes, because of the steepness of the rock face which had been recently moistened and rendered slippery by rain.

On a single blind basis, the fasting subjects were given placebo tablets an hour before their first climb, and 40 mg of oxprenolol (Trasicor) an hour before the second. Blood samples were taken before the climb, and within a minute of finishing. The electro-cardiogram was continuously recorded throughout the climb by means of the 'Recard' tape-recorder system. Each climb lasted about 15 minutes, and consisted of several ascents, descents, and traverses.

With oxprenolol the maximum heart-rate during the climb decreased from a mean of 166 beats per minute to a mean level of 120 beats per minute. Alterations in the configuration of the ST segment, similar to those observed in the parachutists, were abolished, by this β-blocking compound. The drug also halved the rise in plasma adrenaline. No change was found in plasma noradrenaline, suggest-ing that the physical exertion involved was one of mild intensity, and that most of the increase in heart-rate was due to the anxiety induced by the climb.

No change in free fatty acids, triglycerides, or glucose was observed in either group, although a slight increase in cholest-erol occurred in the unblocked climbers, as with other exercising groups described elsewhere (Carruthers and Murray 1976). No change of mood or agility was noticed in those taking oxprenolol.

The reduction in pulse-rate produced by β-blockade in this situation was not as marked as that occurring under conditions of intense emotion but little exertion, like racing drivers (mean decrease 169 to 102 beats per minute) and public speakers (140 to 82 beats per minute). This supports previous claims that tachycardia due to emotional stress is predominantly mediated by β-receptors, and hence is suppressed by β-blocking compounds, while that due to physical exertion mainly results from other physiological effects and is consequently less affected (Imhof and Brunner 1970). Using the same oral dose of oxprenolol, Imhof and Brunner obtained closely similar results in ski-jumpers. The tachycardia associated with the ascent to the starting plat-form was reduced from 130 to 115 beats per minute, while the maximum heart-rate, which occurred 15 seconds after landing, was reduced from 150 to 100 beats per minute.

In the biochemical characterization of anxiety, three main approaches have previously been used (Breggin 1964). First,

comparisons were made between both the physiological and
psychological responses to injected adrenaline and noradrenaline
in healthy subjects and patients with a variety of mental disorders. In 1919 Tompkins *et al*. showed that the impure adrenal
extract could cause anxiety in previously conditioned or 'neurotic'
subjects. Since then a large number of studies, using the pure
hormones, have demonstrated that the ability of physiological
doses of adrenaline to provoke the signs and symptoms of anxiety
is heavily dependent on environmental cues and the previous
conditioning of the subject.   It was also found that while small,
intermittent doses of adrenaline produced the sympathetic
effects of 'arousal' in healthy subjects, large sustained dosage
produced parasympathomimetic effects of 'fatigue', especially
in neurotic subjects, possibly through a feedback action of
adrenaline on the hypothalamic trophotropic functions (Rothballer
1959). Thus, even more than most drugs, adrenaline actions appear
to be dependent on the dosage, on the subject, and on conditions
of administration.

A second group of experiments involved the measurement of urinary
catecholamine excretion, together with other physiological
parameters in normal subjects and patients with neuroses, anxiety
states or paranoia. In general, the findings in these studies
agree with those reported by Funkenstein (1956) of increased
adrenaline excretion in anxious, depressed patients, and
increased noradrenaline excretion in angry, paranoid patients.

The third group of experiments involves the investigation of
subjects experiencing anxiety-provoking situations. The wide
variety of situations studied is indicated by the reviews of
Martin (1961) and Levi (1969).   In general they support the
early work done by Ax (1953). Within a contrived laboratory
situation he demonstrated that the physiological response to
anxiety was similar to that of injected adrenaline, while with
anger the response more closely resembled that produced by
noradrenaline and adrenaline together, with the former hormone
predominating.   There were higher intercorrelations in the
physiological variables studied in anger, indicating greater
physiological integration.   Conversely, between-subject variance
was greater than within-subject variance, especially in anxiety,
suggesting 'uniqueness in physiological expression of emotion'.
Although the majority of studies of urinary catecholamines in
these two types of emotional stress support this physiological
evidence (Levi 1969), they also reflect a similar high degree
of individuality in biochemical responses in different people.

The studies reported here reinforce the association between
the emotion of anxiety, the secretion of adrenaline, and the
consequent rise in pulse-rate and plasma glucose. They also
suggest that the increase in plasma adrenaline up to 10 times
greater than that of the tranquil person may form a chemical
basis for the suggestion made by James in 1890 that anxiety

symptoms can reinforce anxiety.

Thus the acute anxiety reaction could be self-perpetuating, a spiralling sequence of anxiety, adrenaline secretion, and learnt sympathomimetic symptoms perpetuating the anxiety. An important action of β-blocking compounds in relieving anxiety might be to interrupt this cycle. Such a mechanism would explain the beneficial effects obtained with a low dosage of β-blocking drugs in anxiety states (Turner *et al*. 1965; Granville-Grossman and Turner 1966) and in cardiac disorders related to anxiety (Bester-man and Friedlander 1965). This is consistent with the lesser increase and smaller· rises in adrenaline secretion seen in the blocked airline passengers and climbers. It contrasts with the failure of sedatives such as diazepam to reduce adrenaline levels or heart-rate in phobic dental patients (Edmondson and Roscoe 1972) or of amytal to decrease the sinus tachycardia of patients with anxiety states (Turner *et al*. 1965). For these reasons, as well as their lack of side effects such as depression and impairment of concentration, β-blocking drugs may be more beneficial than sedatives in the treatment of anxiety.

The absence of effects of plasma noradrenaline or lipid levels in situations purely evoking anxiety, shown in these and previous studies of dentistry (Edmondson and Roscoe 1972) and air-line passengers (Carruthers, Taggart, and Somerville, 1973), suggests that anxiety is unlikely to be the form of emotional stress implicated in the long-term causation of atheromatous arterial disease. This coincides with the clinical finding (Friedman and Roseman 1959) that it is usually not the anxious, 'always-ill' people who suffer most from coronary thrombosis, but the aggressive, tough, driving, high denial, never-ill ones.

AN ANALYSIS OF THE EFFECTS OF URBAN SOCIETY ON HUMAN BIOCHEMISTRY

Writing about the causation of atheroma and hypertension in 1911, Cannon and De La Paz stated, 'The temptation is strong to suggest that some phases of these pathologic states are associated with the strenuous and exciting character of modern life acting through the adrenal glands. This suggestion, however, must be put to experimental tests.' Experimental tests on humans have helped us to obtain more direct evidence on the failure of biochemically primitive man to adapt to modern urban life.

Both retrospective and prospective psycho-social studies are consistent in suggesting that coronary heart disease is strongly associated with the aggressive, competitive, driving type of behaviour pattern. Investigations of situations where this emotion had been predominant have shown that subjects have a marked increase in plasma noradrenaline levels, with a smaller and

more variable increase in plasma adrenaline. These noradrenaline
increases were linked to the duration of the emotion which
prompted them. They were, however, accompanied by rises in free
fatty acids and more sustained elevations of endogenous triglyceride. Apart from the immediate social dangers of this
emotion, the physical hazards of elevated blood-pressure and
lipid levels are considered to be major causative factors in
atheroma formation.

The stimulant action of aggressive emotion was clearly
recognized a hundred years ago by Darwin when he wrote, 'As
a proof of the exciting nature of anger, that a man when excessively jaded will sometimes invent imaginary offences and put
himself into a passion, unconsciously, for the sake of
reinvigorating himself.' That high circulating levels of
noradrenaline can elevate the mood and lessen the sensations
of discomfort and fatigue has been demonstrated recently
(Frankenhaeuser 1971). In this respect it may be considered
as a self-administered drug of addiction. Dependency on this
drug is carefully fostered in Western society, largely for
commercial reasons. Its increased secretion during smoking
could explain particularly the attraction of this habit
(Carruthers 1976). Similarly, the amount of money people are
willing to spend on motoring, and the risks they are willing
to take, suggests deeper motivation than the need for a
convenient means of transport. Competition of all forms is
encouraged by business to make the employee more productive at
work, and by advertising to promote the sale of consumer goods.
The other component of the agressive Type A behaviour pattern,
- time and deadline consciousness - can also be stimulated
in modern society by frequent time checks on the radio and
television and by putting clocks in offices and all public
places. It is especially effective when used synergistically
with motoring, as considerable excitement with presumably a
high noradrenaline content) can be generated by trying to
beat self-imposed lap records (Carruthers 1974).

Anxiety, is found, by contrast, to be accompanied by
increased adrenaline secretion, with little or no increase
and sometimes even a decrease in noradrenaline. Although no
alterations in plasma lipid levels are produced by this form
of emotional stress, the responses which did occur might be
considered to have short-term dangers for the subject with
coronary heart disease. These responses are increased oxygen
consumption in a rapidly beating heart and the action of
adrenaline in provoking arrhythmias and possibly increasing
the coagulability of the blood. However, relatively few
people enjoy being anxious, so this hormone seems potentially
both less addictive and less harmful.

Short-term studies of some of the automatically mediated
responses to stress require confirmation by longer-term
investigation of catecholamine excretion and lipid levels in

relation to behaviour patterns and prevalence of coronary
heart disease. Work along these lines has been in progress for
nearly 10 years in the Western Collaborative Group Study
(Rosenman *et al.* 1970), and has indicated that people showing
the type A behaviour pattern exhibit marked biochemical differences
from people showing the type B pattern. The former have higher
catecholamine excretion rates, free fatty acids, triglycerides,
and cholesterol. They also have a far greater incidence of
coronary thrombosis than the other group. Such biochemical
distinctions between high- and low- risk groups appear worthy
of further exploration in this country.

Serial lipid estimations in the same subjects over a period
of years, as well as showing the seasonal alternations, have
indicated that wide fluctuations in cholesterol and triglyceride
levels occur for several months before coronary thrombosis in
the large majority of cases (Groover *et al.* 1960). It is
suggested that one of the most potentially profitable, and yet
so far more underdeveloped areas of biochemical screening,
is that of lipid profiling (Carruthers, 1973; Carruthers and
Taggart 1974). Such screening has so far tended to exclude
tests which cannot be fully automated and has not been completely
satisfactory.

It is in the prevention and treatment of coronary thrombosis
that the theory that emotional stress is a major factor most
needs to be put to the test. There is a scope here for
health education, particularly in individuals who have survived
a warning coronary attack (Nixon 1972) and who wish to avoid a
further, fatal attack. An explanation to the patient of the
ways in which the pattern of living can affect the plasma fat
pattern, together with help in reappraising the patient's life
style to eliminate some areas of conflict and habits such as
smoking, may be of considerable preventative value.

More encouraging, and often more acceptable, is the possibility
of balancing a high level of emotional activity with a moderate
level of physical activity. The Medical Research Council trial of
'exercise therapy' (Carruthers, Nixon and Murray 1975) suggests
that two or three brief but intensive periods of exercise each
week can be of considerable benefit both in healthy and coronary
subjects, by increasing general physical and mental well-being,
increasing cardiovascular function, and reducing plasma fat
levels. Similar non-competitive forms of whole-body, isotonic
exercise should be investigated for this purpose and facilities
provided. Swimming appears to be one such form of exercise,
providing the effort is gradually increased and it is not
carried out in cold water.

A further possibility for those who are unable or unwilling
to modify their life style, or take exercise, is the use of
β-blocking drugs. This could either be intermittent, to cover

brief periods of stress, or as a regular preventive measure.
Several primary and secondary prevention trials using these
compounds are in progress, and early results are encouraging
(Lambert 1974).

One of the most unexpected facts to emerge from a recent
study was that church-going halved the incidence of coronary
thrombosis. This unexplained finding could be taken to
indicate that the avoidance, or perhaps the confession, of sins
likely to provoke emotional stress may be of considerable
importance in the prevention of coronary-artery disease. The
hypothesis investigated here suggests that, in modern urban
life, wrath, reinforced by sloth and gluttony, is the deadliest
of the seven sins.

REFERENCES

ALBRINK, M.J. and MAN, E.B. (1959) Serum triglycerides in
coronary artery disease.   *Arch.int. Med.* 103, 4-8.

AUERBACH, O., HAMMOND, E.C. and GARFINKEL, L. (1965). Smoking
in relation to atherosclerosis of coronary arteries. *New
England J. Med.* 273, 775-79.

AX, A.F. (1953)*. The physiological differentiation between
fear and anger in humans.   *Psychosom. Med.* 15, 433-442.

BASOWITZ, H., PERSKY, H., KORCHIN, S.J., and GRINKER, R.R.
(1955). *Anxiety and stress.*   McGraw-Hill, New York.

BELLET, S., ROMAN, L., KOSTIS, J. and SLATER, A. (1968)
Continuous electrocardiographic monitoring during automobile
driving: Studies in normal subjects and patients with
coronary disease.* *Am.J.Cardiol.* 22, 856-62.

BELLET, S., ROMAN, L. and KOSTIS, J. (1969) The effect of
automobile driving on catecholamine and adrenocortical excretion.
Am.J.Cardiol. 24, 365-8.

BESTERMAN, E.M.M. and FRIEDLANDER, D.H. (1965) Clinical
experience with propanolol. *Postgrad.Med.J.* 41, 256-35.

BREGGIN, P.R. (1964) The psychophysiology of anxiety: With
a review of the literature concerning adrenaline. *J.nerv.
mental Dis.* 139, 558-568.

CANNON, W.B. (1929) *Bodily changes in pain, hunger, fear and
rage* (2nd ed.) D.Appleton, New York.

CANNON, W.B. and DE LA PAZ, D. (1911) The stimulation of adrenal secretion by emotional excitement. *J.Am. med.Ass.* 56, 742-44.

CARLSON, L.A., LEVI, L. and ORO, L. (1972) Stress or induced changes in plasma lipids and urinary excretion of catecholamines, and their modification, by nicotinic acid. *Acta med. Scand. Suppl.* 258.

CARRUTHERS, M. (1973) Maintaining the cardiovascular fitness of pilots, *Lancet,* 1, 1048.

CARRUTHERS, M. (1976) Modification of the noradrenaline related effects of smoking by beta-blockade, *Psychol. Med.* 6, 251-6.

CARRUTHERS, M. (1974) *The Western Way of Death*, Davis-Poynter, London.

CARRUTHERS, M. and MURRAY, A. (1976) F/40. *Fitness on 40 minutes a week.* Future Books, London.

CARRUTHERS, M. NIXON, P.G. and MURRAY, A. (1975) Safe sport, *Lancet,* 1, 447.

CARRUTHERS, M. and TAGGART, P. (1973) Vagotonicity of violence: Biochemical and cardiac responses to violent films and television programmes. *Brit.med. J.,* 3, 384-89.

CARRUTHERS, M. and TAGGART, P. (1974) Paleocardiology and neocardiology. *Am.Heart J.,* 88, 1-6.

CARRUTHERS, M., TAGGART, P., CONWAY, N., BATES, D. and SOMERVILLE, W. (1970) Validity of plasma catecholamine esternations. *Lancet.* 2, 62-7.

CARRUTHERS, M. TAGGART, P., and SOMERVILLE, W. (1973). Some effects of beta-blockade on the lipid response to certain acute emotions. In CIBA Symposium *New perspectives in β-blockade,* eds. R.K.Pondel and S.H.Taylor, pp.307-311.

CARRUTHERS, M., TAGGART, P., SALPEKAR, P.D., and GATT, J.A. (1975) Some metabolic effects of beta-blockade on temperature regulation and in the presence of trauma. CIBA-GEIGY Symposium on beta-blockers, *Present status and future prospects,* pp.248-56.

CARRUTHERS, M. and YOUNG, D.A.B. (1973) Free fatty acid estimation by a semi-automated fluorimetric method. *Clin. Chim.Acta,* 49, 341-48.

DARWIN, (1872)   *The expression of the emotions in man and animals*. John Murray, London.

DOLE, V.P. (1956)   A relation between non-esterified fatty acids in plasma and the metabolism of glucose. *J.clin. Invest*. 35, 150–154.

EDMONDSON, H.D., ROSCOE, B., and VICKERS, M.D. (1972) Biochemical evidence for anxiety in dental patients. *Brit.med. J.* 4, 7–9.

EULER, U.S. von (1964)   Quantitation of stress by catecholamine analysis. *Clin.Pharmacol. Therap*. 5, 398–404.

EULER, U.S., and LUNDBERG, U. (1954)   Effect of flying on the epiephrine excretion in Air Force Personnel. *J.app.Physiol*. 6 551–5.

FRANKENHAEUSER, M. (1971)   Experimental approaches to the study of human behaviour as related to neuroendocrine functions. In *Society, stress and disease*, (ed.L.Levi) Oxford University Press, p.22.

FRIEDMAN, M. and ROSENMAN, R.H. (1959)   Association of specific overt behaviour pattern with blood and cardiovascular findings. *J.Am.med. Ass*. 169, 1286–96.

FRIEDMAN, M., ROSEMAN, R.H., STRAUS, R., WURM, M. and KOSITCHER, R. (1968)   The relationship of behaviour pattern A to the state of the coronary vasculature. *Am.J.Med*. 44, 525–37.

FROST, J.W., DRYER, R.L. and KOHLSTADT, K.G. (1951)   Stress studies on auto race drivers. *J.Lab.clin.Med*. 38, 523–25.

FUNKENSTEIN, D.H. (1956)   Nor-epinephrine-like and epinephrine-like substances in relation to human behaviour. *J.nerv.mental Dis*. 124, 58–65.

GRANVILLE-GROSSMAN, K.L. and TURNER, P. (1966)   The effect of propanolol on anxiety. *Lancet*, 2, 788–90.

GROOVER, M.E. Jr., JERNIGAN, J.A., and MARTIN, C.D. (1960) Variations in serum lipid concentration and clinical coronary disease. *Am.J.med.Sci*. 239, 133–9.

IMHOF, P. and BRUNNER, H. (1970)   The treatment of functional heart disorders with beta-adrenergic blocking agents. *Postgrad. med.J*. 46, Suppl.22, 96–9.

IRA, G.H. Jr., WHALEN, R.E. and BOGDONOFF, M.D. (1963). Heart rate changes in physicians during daily "stressful" tasks. *J.psychosom, Res.* 7, 147-150.

JACKSON, W.B. (1971) The use of propranolol in ECG diagnosis. *N.Z. med. J.* 73, 65-68.

JAMES, W. (1890) *Principles of psychology.* Holt, New York.

JENKINS, D.J.A., WELBOM, T.A., and GOFF, D.V. (1970) Free fatty acids, β-hydroxybutyrate, and ischaemic heart disease. *Lancet,* 865-66.

JOHNSON, R.H., WALTON, J.L., KREBS, H.A., and WILLIAMSON, D.H. (1969) Metabolic fuels during and after severe exercise in athletes and non-athletes. *Lancet* 2, 452-5.

JURAND, J. and OLIVER, M.F. (1970) Effects of acute myocardial infarction and of noradrenaline infusion on fatty acid composition of serum lipids. *Atherosclerosis, 11,* 157-70.

KURIEN, V.A. and OLIVER, M.F. (1966) Serum FFA after acute myocardial infarction and cerebral vascular occlusion. *Lancet* 2, 122-7.

LAMBERT, D.M.D. (1974) Hypertension and myocardial infarction. *Lancet, 2,* 685.

LEANDERSON, R. and LEVI, L. (1966) A new approach to the experimental study of stuttering and stress. *Acta Otolaryng. Suppl.* 224, 311.

LEPESCHKIN, E., MARCHET, H., SCHRODER, G., WAGNER, R.P., De PAUL SILVA and RAAB, W. (1960) Effects of epinephrine and nor-epinephrine on the ECG of 100 normal subjects. *Am.J. Cardiol.* 5, 594-603.

LEVI, L. (1969) Neuro-endocrinology of anxiety. *Brit. J.Psychiat.* Special publ. No.3.

LONGSON, D. and CHRISTY, N.P. (1964) In *Biochemical disorders in human disease,* (ed. R.H.S. Thompson and E.J.King, p.398, Oxford University Press, London.

MARTIN, B. (1961) The assessment of anxiety by physiological behaviour measures. *Psychological Bull. 58,* 234-55.

McDONALD, L., BAKER, C., BRAY, C., McDONALD, A. and RESTIEAUX, N. (1969) Plasma catecholamines after cardiac infarction. *Lancet,* 2, 1021-3.

MEDICAL RESEARCH COUNCIL (1968)   *Lancet 2*, 693.

MINISTRY OF DEFENCE (1969). Flying personnel Research Committee, Report No.1240.

MORRIS, J.N., KAGAN, A., PATTISON, D.C., GARDNER, M.J., and RAFFLE, P.A.B. (1966) Incidence and prediction of ischaemic heart disease in London busmen. *Lancet 2*, 553-9.

MORRIS, J.N. and GARDNER, M.J. (1969) Epidemiology of ischaemic heart disease. *Am.J.med Symp on atherosclerosis, 46*, 674-83.

MURCHISON, L.E. and FYFE, T. (1966) Effects of cigarette smoking on serum-lipids, blood glucose and platelet adhesiveness. *Lancet, 2*, 182.

NELSON, P.G. (1972) Recovery from coronary illness. *Rehabilitation 81*, 23-27.

NIXON, P.G., BETHEL, H., and GRABAU, W. (1975) British Pilot Study of exercise therapy: Patients with cardiovascular disease. *Brit.med.J.* (in press)

OGLESBY, P., MacMILLAN, A., McKEAN, H. and PARK, H. (1968). Sucrose intake and coronary heart disease. *Lancet, 2*, 1049-51.

OLIVER, M.F., KURIEN, V.A. and GREENWOOD, T.W. (1968) Relation between serum free fatty acids and arrhythmias and death after acute myocardial infarction. *Lancet, 1*, 710-14.

ROSENMAN, R.H., FRIEDMAN, M., STRAUS, R., JENKINS, C.D., ZYZANSKI, S.J. and WURM, M. (1970). Coronary heart disease in the Western Collaborative Group Study. A follow-up experience of 4½ years. *J.chron.Dis. 23*, 179-90.

ROTHBALLER, A.B. (1959) The effect of catecholamines on the central nervous system. *Pharmacol. Rev. 11*, 494-547

RUTSTEIN, D.D., CASTELLI, W.P. and NICKERSON, R.J. (1969). Heparin and human lipid metabolism. *Lancet 1*, 1003-8.

SACKETT, D.L., GIBSON, R.W., BROSS, I.D.J. and PICKREN ,J.W. (1968). Relation between aortic atherosclerosis and the use of cigarettes and alcohol.   *New.Eng.J.Med. 279.* 1413-20.

SELYE, H. (1971) The evolution of the stress concept - Stress and cardiovascular disease, In *Society, stress and disease,* ed. L.Levi. Oxford University Press.

SHANE, W.P. and SLINDE, K.E. (1968) Continuous ECG recording during free-fall parachuting. *Aerosp. Med. 39*, 597-603.

SMITH, E.B., SLATER, R.S., and CHU, P.K. (1968) The lipids in raised fatty and fibrous lesions in human aorta. *J.Atheroscler. Res.* 8 399-419.

STOUT, R.W. and VALLANCE-OWEN, J. (1969) Insulin and atheroma. *Lancet*, 1, 1078-80.

SUZMAN, M.M. (1971) Effect of β-blockade on the anxiety of electrocardiogram. *Postgrad. med. J.* 47, suppl. 104.

TAGGART, P. and GIBBONS, D. (1967) Motor-car driving and the heart rate. *Br.med.J.* 1, 411-12.

TAGGART, P. and GIBBONS, D. (1968). Some cardiovascular responses to driving. *Br.med.J.* 2, 1043-44.

TAGGART, P. and CARRUTHERS, M. (1972) Suppression by oxprenolol of adrenergic response to stress.   *Lancet*, 2, 256-8.

TAGGART, P., CARRUTHERS, M. and SOMERVILLE, W. (1973). Electrocardiogram, plasma catecholamines and lipids, and their modification by oxprenolol when speaking before an audience.   *Lancet* 2, 341-6.

TOMPKINS, E.H., STURGIS, C.C. and WEAM, J.T. (1919). Studies in epinephrine II, *A.M.A. Archs. Int.Med.* 24, 247-53.

TRUETT, J., CORNFIELD, J. and KANNEL, W.A. (1967). A multivariate analysis of the risk of coronary heart disease in Fremingham. *J. Chron.Dis.* 20, 511-24.

TURNER, P., GRANVILLE-GROSSMAN, K.L. and SMART, J.V. (1965). Effect of adrenergic receptor blockade on the tachycardia of thyrotoxicosis and anxiety state.   *Lancet 2*, 1316-18.

WALKER, J.L., COLLINS, V.P. and McTAGGART, W.G. (1969) Measurement of sympathetic neurohormones in the plasma of racing-car drivers. *Aerosp. Med.* 40, 140-1.

WENKE, M. (1966) Effects of catecholamines on lipid mobilization. *Adv. lipid Res.* (eds. R.Paoletti and D,Kritchevsky) 4, 69.

14 Environment and performance

D. E. Broadbent

Designing buildings to provide optimum comfort in an urban environment - where we may all suffer unduly from the effects of heat, light, and noise - has been discussed in Chapter 5. This chapter is concerned with how one decides what environmental conditions adversely affect our working performance.

All the experiments which will be discussed in this chapter employed the same investigative technique; each required human beings to perform some task in normal conditions on one occasion and to perform the same task in some unusual environment on another occasion. The speed or accuracy of the two performances was then compared.

The technique has obvious limitations: it leaves us ignorant of the feelings or preferences of the people studied, or of any changes in them which are not revealed by their degree of success in achieving some goal. For instance, we know nothing about their irritability in social situations or the effects of their environment on their physical or mental health. It also has to be admitted that many of the conditions which have been studied are rather extreme by comparison with those met in domestic life, even in urban environments; they are often more typical of conditions in industry or the armed forces. If we are thinking of the quality of life as a whole, rather than merely of the efficient performance of work in an urban environment, then there is more to be studied than these experiments can reveal. Nevertheless, the technique is a very powerful one. Because of the objectivity of measuring speed and accuracy at work, we can reveal changes in human beings, produced by their environment, which are hard to show by other means. Therefore we can draw conclusions about the relationship between people and their surroundings which have far wider implications than might at first be apparent.

EFFECTS ON PERFORMANCE FROM SINGLE ENVIRONMENTAL CONDITIONS

The first point which had to be established was that human beings really are less efficient when they work in heat, noise, abnormal air pressures, and so on. Although many people will confidently assume that this is so, others will equally confidently say that a man can perfectly well maintain normal efficiency when he is, for example, hot, however unpleasant he may feel. Even recordings of industrial output are somewhat suspect, because of the well-known phenomenon that workers respond favourably to a sign of human concern and interest on the part of management, and therefore may quite well show higher output in places where the

management has been concerned to try and make conditions pleasant, without any direct genuine effect of the environment on the functioning of the man. Admittedly, the relationships between accidents and temperature (shown by Vernon (1918) and accidents and noise (Kerr 1950; Raytheon 1972) are harder to explain in this way, since it hardly seems plausible that a man would have an accident to spite the management! Nevertheless, accidents are affected by all kinds of irrelevant factors, and laboratory experiments are therefore valuable as confirming evidence.

In fact, laboratory performance has been shown to get worse when people are exposed to vibration, weightlessness, acceleration, high or low pressure air, excessive physical effort, and other such stresses. We need not consider them all here: a convenient introduction to most of the factors which will depress performance has been provided by Poulton (1970). For present purposes, most of the points of interest can be shown by discussing only the effects of heat, noise, and sleeplessness. These three factors have been studied particularly intensively, and they illustrate points which apply to other conditions as well.

Each of these conditions has been shown to reduce efficiency. Each of them, furthermore, has its effect only when the change from normal conditions exceeds some limit. In each case, the borderline between conditions which will impair performance and those which will not is rather blurred, and depends on other circumstances. The degree of humidity alters the effect of temperature, the spectrum alters the effect of noise, and the time of day at which sleep is taken alters the amount of it which is necessary for unimpaired performance. However, quite clear deterioration in performance can be seen with an effective temperature of 33 °C, with a noise level of 100 dB of white noise, and with the complete loss of one night's sleep. In general the results to be mentioned here are obtained with these levels.

Another feature which all these stresses have in common is that their effects increase with time. This shows most clearly in the case of noise and sleeplessness. In each of those, the first 5 minutes of work in an experiment may actually be better in the unusual conditions than it is in normal ones. Only after 10-15 minutes of work does the sleepless man, or the one in noisy conditions, begin to show his inefficiency (Broadbent 1953; Wilkinson 1961). In the case of heat, most of the experiments show an effect as soon as the task commences; but this does not quite mean what it seems to mean. Experimenters with heat usually place their victims in the hot room for some time before they start taking measurements of performance. This is because a man brought into a hot room from normal conditions gains heat from his surroundings, and it takes a time before the whole system settles down to a steady equilibrium. Experimenters tend to allow this

process to be complete before starting to take readings; whereas
in the case of other stressful conditions, they often start
taking their readings straight away. In fact, however, it has
been shown by Wing (1965) that the reported effects on efficiency
depend both on the temperature to which the man is exposed and
on the length of time for which he has been exposed to it.
Inefficiency appears at a lower temperature when the exposure
time is longer. In fact, one observes clearer and more
consistent effects of heat if one looks at performance in
relation to the actual temperature of the body rather than the
temperature of the surroundings (Wilkinson, Fox, Goldsmith,
Hampton, and Lewis 1964). Thus the effects of heat, like those
of sleeplessness and noise, actually require prolonged exposure
to the situation rather than appearing immediately. It can be
added that Hartley (1974a) has confirmed, in the case of noise,
that it is the exposure to the noise rather than to the work which
really matters. He showed that the efficiency of people
working in noise was affected if they had been sitting in the
noise for 20 minutes reading rather than working. Thus the
effects of all these conditions seem to build up as time goes
on.

Tasks suitable for environmental experiments

This point leads on to the question of the nature of the tasks
which are used to measure performance. Some tasks are extremely
resistant to reflecting the ambient environmental conditions,
and their performance varies very little even when the man performing them is acutely uncomfortable. Others are highly
sensitive to environment, and will show impairment of performance
very readily indeed. The effects of high temperature are fairly
easy to detect, and have been shown on a number of tasks;
those of loss of sleep are rather more difficult, and some tasks
show very little effect even when the subject has gone 60 hours
without sleep (Wilkinson 1964). The effects of noise are even
more difficult to demonstrate, and very many tasks have been
studied in a noisy environment with no detectable change in
efficiency. However, tasks which display the effects of noise
are likely also to show those of the loss of sleep and even more
of heat.

These sensitive tests are long, boring, and yet require
continuous attention. They also tend to be tests in which one
measures not so much the average state of the man but the extent
to which he has any momentary fluctuations of efficiency. For
example, one should not look for any change due to an abnormal
environment in a test of prepared reaction time: that is, a
test in which a man is warned that he is about to receive a
reaction signal and can pull himself together to a state of
maximum alertness and press a key as soon as he sees the

reaction signal. If such a measurement shows a drop in efficiency, the man must be in a very bad way indeed! Only a little more sensitive are tests such as conventional intelligence tests, in which a series of problems are presented and the man works in his own time, the score being the number achieved in a prolonged period. Any momentary wanderings of attention or mental blocks can then be compensated by faster work, and the test itself is to some extent intriguing and stimulating.

A much more sensitive type of test is the 'vigilance task', in which the man has to keep watch for half an hour or more in search of a very faint signal, which can always be seen if it is presented at a known time, but which in the test arrives without any warning. Such a task goes on for a long time, provides no excitement, and will also catch momentary inefficiency, without allowing any chance for harder work in the intervals. It does have the disadvantage, however, of providing only a limited amount of data from each experiment.

As a result, one of the most widely used techniques is a test of serial reaction, often called the five-choice test. In this, people are faced by five lights and five contacts, and at the start of the test one of the lights is illuminated. The person being tested touches a corresponding contact, whereupon the light goes out and another light comes on. They touch the contact corresponding to that, and the process is repeated. This task can go on indefinitely, although it is usually used for a standard period of half an hour or so, and it has the enormous advantage that one can measure the average rate of work, pick up any mistakes, and also detect any increases in variability, such as occasional slow reactions. One or other of these measures is usually sensitive to any particular stress, if there is any test at all which shows reduced efficiency under that stress. As a result, this task has become almost a standard method of measuring performance.

From the various experiments that have been conducted on isolated stresses, therefore, we can conclude that people do work less efficiently in unpleasant conditions. But they do not break down altogether, and to that extent results justify the scepticism of those who point to the adequate efficiency of sailors or factory workers in extreme heat or noise. The effects of unpleasant environments build up over time, and show themselves as erratic performance rather than necessarily as changes in the average level sustained.

DIFFERENCES AND INTERACTIONS BETWEEN TYPES OF ENVIRONMENTAL CONDITIONS

Perhaps the best way of introducing the next stage in the

problem is to emphasize that, although the five-choice test is
very sensitive to unusual environments, it is not always the same
score on the test which changes. As a general rule, but with
certain special exceptions, noise tends to increase errors and
sleeplessness to increase the number of occasions when a
correct reaction occurs but does so very slowly. In the
traditional phrasing, sleeplessness makes it more likely that
we shall leave undone those things which we ought to have done,
while noise makes it more likely that we shall do those things
which we ought not to have done. The effects of loss of sleep
are to produce inertia and underactivity, while those of noise
are to produce excessive incorrect activity.

This observation is a pointer to the processes that are going
on inside a man when he is exposed to either of these conditions.
We can look further by considering what happens if we increase
the incentives which a man has to work well in one of these
experiments.   This complication of the conditions has to be
introduced, not for theoretical reasons, but because of its
practical importance. It could well be argued that people in
real situations care much more about their work than they
do in experiments, and it could be argued therefore that
results from a laboratory were of no importance. There are
various ways of increasing incentives to people in the
laboratory, and several of them have been used. One particularly
common technique is to give the man regular information during
his work about his score and the way it is changing, and after
each trial to display publicly his score and those of the other
subjects so that each can compare himself with the others. This
produces a substantial improvement in performance under normal
conditions. If the same kind of incentive is supplied when
working in high temperatures, there is again an improvement.
People who think that the factory worker's concern for his pay
packet might be important in determining performance even in
heat are therefore right; but the key point is that the improvement under hot conditions is the same size as the improvement
at normal temperatures. Although the well-motivated man works
better in heat than the badly motivated man, he would work even
better if he were cool. The laboratory experiments therefore do
have some meaning for real life (Mackworth 1950).

The cases of sleeplessness and noise are rather different.
In the case of sleeplessness, the ill effects are actually
cancelled in some experiments by high incentive: the well-
motivated man does as well when sleepless as he does under normal
circumstances (Wilkinson 1961). It is the badly motivated
man who shows a big deterioration in efficiency when he has
gone without a night's sleep. If our practical situation is
that of a man fighting for his life, therefore, perhaps
laboratory experiments on sleeplessness are rather less relevant
than those on heat; although of course really prolonged sleep-

lessness will sooner or later overcome even the highest
possible incentives.

Noise, however, works on performance in just the opposite
way. The man who is well motivated does worse in noise
than in quiet, whereas the man who is badly motivated shows
less deterioration or even an improvement when he is put into a
noisy environment (Wilkinson 1963).

In other words, the conditions which make the effects of sleeplessness worse tend to make those of noise less. It is not only
incentive conditions which do this; if we vary the rate at
which a task presents signals, we find that a low rate of
signalling makes the task more sensitive to sleeplessness, but
a high rate of signalling makes it more sensitive to noise
(Corcoran 1963; Broadbent and Gregory 1965). In general, the
stimulating and exciting condition seems to make the task more
vulnerable to noise, while the relaxing and unstimulating
condition makes it more vulnerable to sleeplessness. Perhaps
the most revealing experiment is to keep a man without sleep
for a night and then make him work in loud noise. To some
extent, the two stresses cancel out. Sleeplessness impairs
performance less if a man is working in noise (Wilkinson 1963):
or to put it another way, a man who is sleepy may be less
efficient in quiet than in noise, whereas a man who is wide
awake is worse in noise than in quiet.

The obvious conclusion from these results is that the various
aspects of an environment do not all have separate effects
but rather produce an impact on the person's general state. Some
conditions push in one direction and some in another; those
which push in the same direction reinforce each other's effects
and are antagonistic to the effects of conditions in the other
group. The word used for this general state is 'arousal', but
we could equally well talk of it as 'excitability' or
'reactivity'. Putting all the results together, we can argue
that noise, or a high rate of signals from the task, or a high
state of incentive all tend to increase arousal, while sleeplessness decreases it. We then argue that the best efficiency
of work occurs when the man is in a moderate state of arousal.
He can be too sleepy, or too excitable, and as a result a
combination of sleeplessness, poor motivation, and an undemanding
task will produce inefficiency; while poor work may also
result from noise, high motivation, and a highly demanding
task.

But this picture is really too simple. For example, we have
already seen that, on average, heat does not increase or
decrease the effect of incentive. Similarly, on average, it
does not increase or decrease the effects of sleeplessness or
of noise. But this is true only of experiments in which the
environmental temperature is raised without attempts to control

the actual body temperature precisely. As we have already
seen, it is the latter rather than the former which is the
most precise measurement of what is happening to the subject,
and Poulton (1970) points out that a small rise in body
temperature seems to slow down responses as if it lowered
arousal, while a slightly larger rise in body temperature
speeds them up, equivalent to an increase in arousal. Anybody who has sat in a gently warm committee room after a
sleepless night will doubt whether temperature really has no
connection with the problems of sleeplessness, but a fiery
heat is the opposite to a gentle comforting warmth. As a
result, the fact that heat seems not to alter the effects of
incentives, noise, or sleeplessness may simply be due to
different individuals being affected in different ways.

A yet more drastic complication in assessing the results of
these experiments lies in the effects of alcohol; the
effect on performance of alcohol intake is *increased* by
incentives and, at least in some cases, may oppose the effects
of sleeplessness. Both these results would suggest that
alcohol intake increases arousal, which is, on other grounds,
most unlikely. More plausibly, the alcohol is impairing some
control process which holds down the effects of changes in
arousal. There is a certain amount of tentative evidence in
favour of such a view (Broadbent, 1971).

Although a simple picture of environmental influences causing
rises and falls in arousal may be inadequate, there does seem
to be truth in the idea of a general state of arousal, modified
by the environment and showing itself in the way a person
performs tasks. There have been two recent and particularly
convincing demonstrations of this, both involving the use of
noise. The first was an important series of results obtained
by Glass and Singer (1972), who showed that performance was
affected not only when the person was in a noisy environment
but that it was also affected if a task was performed *after*
the noise had been removed. Hartley (1974*a*) showed a similar
effect, using the five-choice task mentioned earlier; and
it seems quite clear, therefore, that exposure to noise alters
the state of a person so that his subsequent behaviour is
different even when the noise is removed. There could scarcely
be a more convincing demonstration that noise has its effect
not by distraction or by masking faint sounds in the environment
but rather by altering the state of the subject who is exposed
to it, by increasing his excitability or arousal.

THE DISADVANTAGES OF A HIGH STATE OF AROUSAL

The broad structure of the results we have considered thus
far is easy to accept; but there is one major problem. It

is easy to see why work is inefficient when a man is sleepy,
unmotivated, and generally unreactive. It is even easier to see
why the effects of this drowsiness should appear first in the
occasional slow reaction or moment of inattention, which itself
jerks the man awake again and perhaps produces a spurt of faster
work to compensate. Why, however, should a high state of
arousal or reactivity be a bad thing? Surely the faster the
nervous system reacts, the better? The answer lies in the fact
that a man in any real situation is not presented with just one
stimulus but with many; he does not simply see a lamp light up
in a blank wall and press a key, but has a complex panel full
of instruments to watch, or a number of nuances to hear in the
voices of a group of people, or some other complex array of
stimuli. Bursill (1958) used an ingenious laboratory situation
to study the effects of high temperatures on the distribution
of attention between several stimuli in this way; and this
technique was developed and extended by Hockey (1970) using a
noisy environment. The basis of the technique is to give the
man a central task, such as following an oscillating pointer
by moving a lever which controls another pointer, and attempting to keep one on top of the other. While this task is being
performed, there are a number of faint lights around the field
of view, and the man has to report any which are lit up.
Some are quite close to the moving pointers, and others well
away, so that one can only see them out of the corner of one's
eye. Bursill found that reactions by the subject to these
'peripheral' lights were more sensitive to the effects of heat
than those to the central lights. Hockey found a similar
result with reactions in a noisy environment. This might mean
that there is some complicated, but essentially rather
unimportant, change in the sensitivity of different parts of
the retina of the eye. However, Hockey showed by a number of
other experiments that this was not the explanation. The
reason why men in a noisy environment neglect the peripheral
lights is that they think those lights are less likely to
deliver signals. People do in any case tend to look more
frequently at places where they expect information to appear,
so the effect of the noise seems to be to disturb the distribution
of attention, by exaggerating concentration on those parts of
the surroundings which would get most attention in any case.

Another example of the same type of thing is reported briefly
by Broadbent (1971). In this experiment a clearly-visible
common word in black was flashed on a screen together with a
less clearly-visible rare word in red. Some people were asked
to read out the black word, and some the red word, and the
duration of the flash was increased until they could just do so.
In noise, the easily visible word was seen at just about the
same duration of flash as it was in a quiet environment; but
the more difficult word needed a considerably longer duration of

flash in the noisy situation. In control experiments, the words were presented one at a time without any competition from another word. In that case, the reading of the harder word showed no greater effect due to noise than the easier word. It is the selection of one set of stimuli and the suppression of another which is impaired by noise.

We can see that an increased responsiveness to dominant stimuli will help performance if the task requires attention to those stimuli, but will hinder it if at this moment the dominant stimulus is one which is intruding. The mechanism is shown particularly well by a test used by Glass and Singer (1972) and also by Hartley (1974b). This is the 'Stroop test', in which a man is asked to look at a list of printed names of colours. Each name is printed in a different coloured ink, and the ink in which a given name is printed does not have the colour to which that name is appropriate. Thus the word 'blue' is printed in red ink, and so on. The task the person has to perform is to call out as rapidly as possible the names of the colours of the *inks* ignoring the words which they form. Naturally, this task takes considerably longer than naming a series of blobs of coloured ink, or reading a series of printed names, because the printed name keeps interfering with the naming of the ink. This task of selection and suppression is impaired by noise, and indeed, as Glass and Singer show, continues to be impaired when the noise has ceased. The state of high arousal seems, once again, to be one which gives undue prominence to the momentarily dominant stimulus.

It is easiest to experiment on the process of selecting one stimulus from amongst several presented externally; but the same mechanism may also apply to the selection of one item from amongst many in the person's memory. Experiments, by Hörmann and Osterkamp (1966) and by Hamilton, Hockey, and Quinn (1972) suggest that the organization of memory also is disturbed by noise. That is, when noise is present a series of learned items are less likely to be reproduced in clusters of similar meaning. This effect is still not well understood, but suggests that disruption due to high arousal goes further than merely an effect on perception.

CONCLUSIONS

Adverse environmental conditions outside the normal range do make it harder for people to carry out tasks. People are not merely annoyed or irritated by difficult surroundings, but less well able to get things done in such situations. Indeed, sometimes their performance is impaired when they have no feeling of annoyance from a particular adverse condition, and may even believe it has no effect on their work. The decline

in efficiency is, at least in part, not due to the specific effects of each stress, but to changes in the general state of alertness of the subject, which may be either too high or too low for efficiency. When alertness is too high, the effects appear in the selective functions, which pick out certain stimuli for attention from the surroundings. Further-more, this state of excessive arousal can persist after the person leaves the environment which has caused it.

Anything beyond this must at this stage be speculation. However, there are certain obvious gaps in knowledge which deserve further investigation. For example, if somebody were repeatedly exposed to an excessively arousing environment, would the effects become chronic? We have no warrant for saying that they would, since the experiments of Hartley and of Glass and Singer show a carry-over only of a matter of minutes. On the other hand, one of the persistent grumbles of those engaged in stress experiments during the day is of their lowered tolerance of minor domestic irritations in the evenings after the experiments; and Jansen (1959) reported that family disturbances were more frequent in steelworkers exposed to loud noise at their work than in those who were not. It would perhaps be plausible to suggest that attention only to the immediate negative aspects of some social situation, neglecting longer-term and restraining features, might well be a function analogous to looking at the central lights of Hockey's task experiment and neglecting peripheral ones. However, Jansen's result may be explained in other ways, for example, with reference to class biases in selection of people for particular jobs. Nevertheless, the possible chronic effects of over-stimulating and arousing environments is a worrying one, and, in these days when many urban environments come in this category, it deserves further examination.

REFERENCES

BROADBENT, D.E. (1953) Noise, paced performance and vigilance tasks. *Br.J.Psychol.* 44, 295-303.

BROADBENT, D.E. (1971) *Decision and stress.* Academic Press, London.

BROADBENT, D.E. and GREGORY, M. (1965) Effects of noise and of signal rate upon vigilance analysed by means of decision theory. *Hum.Fact.* 7, 155-62.

BURSILL, A.E. (1958) The restriction of peripheral vision during exposure to hot and humid conditions. *Q.Jl.exp. Psychol.* 10, 113-29.

CORCORAN, D.W.J.   (1963)   Doubling the rate of signal presentation in a vigilance task during sleep deprivation.   *J.appl.Psychol.* 47, 412-15.

GLASS, D.C. and SINGER, J.E. (1972)   *Urban stress.* Academic Press, London and New York.

HAMILTON, P., HOCKEY, G.R.J., and QUINN, J.G. (1972)   Information selection, arousal and memory.   *Br.J.Psychol.* 63, 181-9.

HARTLEY, L.R., (1974a)   Effect of prior noise or prior performance on serial reaction.   *J. exp. Psychol.* 101, 255-61.

HARTLEY, L.R. (1974b)   Similar and opposing effects of noise on performance. *Proceedings of the International Congress on Noise as a Public Health Problem.* U.S. Environmental Protection Agency.

HOCKEY, G.R.J. (1970)   Signal probability and spatial location as possible bases for increased selectivity in noise.   *Q.J. exp. Psychol. 22,* 37-42.

HÖRMANN, H. and OSTERKAMP, V. (1966)   Uber den Einfluss von kontinuierlichem lärm auf die Organisation von Gedachtnisinhalten. *Z.exp angew.Psychol.* ₁3, 31-8.

JANSEN, G. (1959)   Vegetative functional disturbance caused by noise.   *Archiv.Gewerbepath. Gewerbehyg.* 17, 238-61.

KERR, W.A. (1950)   Accident proneness of factory departments. *J.appl.Psychol.* 34, 167-70.

MACKWORTH, N.H. (1950)   *Researches in the measurement of human performance,* M.R.C. Special Report, No.268, HMSO, London.

POULTON, E.C. (1970)   *Environment and human efficiency.* Thomas Springfield, Illinois.

RAYTHEON SERVICE COMPANY (1972)   *Industrial noise and worker medical, absence, and accident records,* Contract HSM 099-71-6 Burlington, Massachussetts.

VERNON, H.M. (1918)   *An investigation of the factors concerned in the causation of industrial accidents.* Health of Munition Workers Committee Memo, No.21, Cd.9046, HMSO, London.

WILKINSON, R.T. (1961)   Interaction of lack of sleep with knowledge of results, repeated testing and individual differences. *J.exp.Psychol.* 62, 263-71.

WILKINSON, R.T. (1963)   Interaction of noise with knowledge of results and sleep deprivation, *J.exp.Psychol.* 66, 332-7.

WILKINSON, R.T. (1964) Effects of up to sixty hours sleep
deprivation on different types of work. *Ergonomics* 7, 175-86.

WILKINSON, R.T., FOX, R.H., GOLDSMITH, R., HAMPTON, I.F.G., and
LEWIS, H.E. (1964) Psychological and physiological responses
to raised body temperature. *J.appl. Physiol.* 19, 287-91.

WING, J.F. (1965) Upper thermal tolerance limits for unimpaired
mental performance, *Aerosp.Med.* 36, 960-4.

15 The psychology of urban life

C. I. Howarth

Does city life of necessity affect behaviour or mental health?
Can the answers to this question be used to improve the quality
of life in our cities?   Both of these questions are difficult to
answer because cities and city lives are so varied and complex.
We need to decide which are the most important characteristics
of city life and to disentangle a great deal of conflicting and
uncertain evidence. But despite the difficulty of the exercise,
it is important to attempt it. In the past, urban life was an
option, which many people could choose or reject. Now, for most
of us, it is inescapable. The difference between city life, as it
is now, and rural life, as it was in the comparatively recent
past, seems to be increasing. It follows that we must not only
adapt to our cities as they are now but must prepare our children
for the very different cities of the future, which we are at
this moment creating.

In the following pages I shall argue that the complexity of
the problem is a result of the complexity of man's response
to his environment. We adapt culturally as well as individually,
and the basis of cultural adaptation is social interaction,
particularly that between adults and children. City life is
most hazardous when it degrades the quality of that interaction.

TYPES OF EVIDENCE AVAILABLE

Evidence concerning the psychological consequences of city life
comes from many different sources and is of varied quality.
Immediate effects of the environment on stable well-practised
behaviour, such as driving to work (see Chapter 13), are relatively
easy to study.   The results are seldom surprising, but are
frequently ignored. The attitudes of people to their surroundings
are also easy to study but characteristically unstable.   They are
important but are not very closely related to the physical nature
of the environment. Perhaps the most important consequences of city
life are its long-term effects on social relationships or mental
health. These can be most important when they extend across
generations, but such very long-term effects are also the most
difficult to study.

Immediate effects on stable behaviour

Simple, well-practised behaviour, in a familiar and voluntarily
endured environment, tends to be more stable than complex,

unpractised behaviour in novel and perhaps feared or resented
surroundings. Unstable behaviour is necessarily difficult to
study, and environmental effects on it are only meaningful in
the long term. However, when behaviour is stable it can easily
be studied in more than one way. Observational studies may
describe differences in behaviour in different environments,
urban and rural, primitive and civilized, middle-class or working-
class, old town or new town. In some cases the observation
may be made before and after some change in the environment,
which can be accidental, planned or experimental. Laboratory
studies can, with much greater freedom, observe the relationship between the artificially manipulated environment of the
laboratory and a laboratory analogue of the behaviour which
has been observed in the real-life conditions. If people
voluntarily accept the conditions in which they are working
and if the behaviour being studied is stable, then similar
results may be obtained from all three types of work. This
sort of stability is found in studies of sensory acuity, of
skill in simple motor tasks, and in standardized tests of
intellectual performance, such as intelligence tests.
Laboratory studies have concentrated on the effects of
relatively easily manipulated environmental stresses such
as heat, noise, lack of sleep, and information overload on
these types of behaviour. Chapter 14 reviewed these studies.
To a gratifying degree they can be related to real-life
problems and used to alleviate them.

Ergonomists, occupational psychologists, and other psychologists
have studied the effects of the layout of work space on simple
and well-practised skills. It is found that the ease with which
controls can be operated depends upon the extent to which they
are tailored to meet a man's anatomical characteristics. Controls
must be in easy reach, in a logical sequence, and the man should
be comfortable. We know that accidents can be reduced by improving the design of instruments in factories and of road signs
on city streets. The relationship between the display and the
controls should be clear and conform to the man's expectation.
The expectations are sometimes dignified by the jargon term of
'population stereotypes'. Studies of this kind produce very
similar results in the laboratory and in field trials (Murrell
1965). These studies have led to improved design of work place
and of road systems, they have increased productivity, and by
reducing accidents have saved lives. In many respects the
results of these studies seem so obvious that similar improvements
ought to have been obtained by the application of common sense.
Unfortunately, designers and engineers tend to overestimate the
adaptability of the people who must operate machines and move
about in cities. In many instances this does not matter, but in
moments of stress, when critical decisions must be taken quickly,

anything less than the optimum conditions may be disastrous.
For example, it has been demonstrated repeatedly that when the
layout of a system is changed, people will very quickly learn to
operate the new one. But in moments of stress they will revert
to earlier habits and behave as if they were still dealing
with the old system. For this reason the clutch, brake, and
accelerator pedals are similarly placed on all cars. But horns,
indicators, and gears still vary from car to car, and road
signs and markings continue to be changed with alarming frequency.

Studies of accidents to child pedestrians have shown the
extraordinarily high risk which young children run when they
attempt to cross city roads. Many attempts have been made to
reduce this risk by exhortation and training. The recently
introduced 'Green Cross Code' and its associated campaign, may
have reduced accidents by as much as 6 per cent, but the effects
of such campaigns tend to be transient. Here again much more
could be achieved by changing the environment. In this case
what is needed is physically to separate pedestrians and motor
vehicles. Unfortunately, this solution would now be prohibitively
expensive.

Attitudes to the environment

The stable behaviour considered in the previous section is
particularly easy to observe and to assess. Most behaviour at
work or in the home is more complex, and more difficult to
describe or quantify. In such cases it is much easier simply
to ask people what they think about their environment, whether
they like it, whether they feel comfortable in it, and whether
it helps or hinders their performance at work or play. A number
of studies have demonstrated a slight correlation between
favourable attitudes and other things such as working efficiency
or mental health. This provides additional justification for
studying peoples' attitudes to their surroundings.

Craik (1969) has summarized a great deal of the evidence about
peoples' aesthetic responses to the environment, but it is so
variable that no simple description of it is possible. Langdon
(1966 *a,b*) discusses studies of how people assess the comfort and
convenience of different office layouts, and the effects of
lighting, noise level, and the provision of windows; again the
results are extremely variable. This is very disappointing and
suggests that attitudes are being affected by other than environmental variables. Fortunately we now know a great deal about
these additional variables.

In many cases people overestimate the attractiveness and convenience of a familiar environment. Most conceptions of the ideal
environment have an obvious historical origin. There are aesthetic

'population stereotypes' as well as practical ones. So if
people move to a new situation they may not like it simply
because it is new and they have not got used to it. This
reaction may be reinforced by genuine difficulties as in the case
of the new housing estates to which people are moved after slum
clearance (Young and Willmott 1962).

However, we cannot be sure that all change will be disliked.
People will respond favourably when their new surroundings really
are better than the old. If they believe the change is for their
benefit, they may even react more favourably than the real change
warrants. In the well-known 'Hawthorne' experiment (Roethlisberger
and Dickson 1939) it was found that each of a series of changes in
working conditions was liked and each one produced an increase in
production, even the final change, which returned conditions to
what they were at the beginning of the experiment. In the 'Hawthorne' experiment, the changes were imposed by a benevolent
management. If the attitude to the management had been different,
it is likely that the reaction would have been different. Also
the changes required no effort on the part of the workers. Festinger (1957) and Aronson (1972) have shown that in some cases
we value change because of the amount of effort we have put into
it, or because of what we have given up to achieve it. The
importance of these social factors in determining attitudes accounts
for the lack of any simple relationship between environment and
attitudes.

There is a similar variability in the relationship between life-
style and environment. People use different strategies to cope
with similar problems. Some may react to stress by withdrawing
from social contact, others may throw themselves into feverish
social activity.

The long-term effects of the environment

One suspects that the most important effects of the urban environment may occur over a relatively long time span. People do not
immediately have nervous breakdowns when they go to live in a city
nor do they immediately turn to crime. Nevertheless, in certain
parts of our cities, mental health is relatively poor and crime
rates high. In the centre of most large cities are people living
in conditions which, to most of us, appear appalling and which
are associated with delinquency, mental disorder, and poor
occupational status. This association may be due to the migration
of relatively unsuccessful people, under economic pressure, to
the less desirable places to live. Nevertheless, the poor environment may accentuate such peoples' difficulties and may have an even
greater effect on their children. The children of the poor find it
very difficult to escape from poverty; this phenomenon is called
the 'cycle of deprivation'. It is a common aim of programmes of

urban renewal, of compensatory education, and of the social
services to break this cycle. The difficulties which these
programmes encounter suggest that the people responsible for
them do not fully understand the nature of the problem.

Poor environment is not of itself a sufficient explanation,
since the poor of today are better fed, better housed, and
better educated than the majority of the population in earlier
times. Hence the relative ineffectiveness of higher social
security payments, slum clearance, and compensatory education.
Poverty is a relative thing. As society gets richer so do
the poor, but their relative status is unchanged. In our society
the relatively poor tend to be demoralized, but there is no
reason to think this is inevitable. To understand the nature
of the demoralization we need to look at the problem more
analytically.

Two types of explanation are offered for the 'cycle of
deprivation': those based on heredity and those based on the
environment. There is some evidence that hereditary factors
affect intelligence and that lack of intelligence is associated
with poverty.   Hence the unintelligent are likely to be poor,
and their unintelligent children are also likely to be poor.
However, this cannot account for all, and perhaps not even for
the major part of, the 'cycle of deprivation'. Intelligence
is also influenced by the environment in which a child is
reared. Educational and professional attainment are even more
obviously related to the child's early experience. The child
born and raised in a slum is now thought to receive less intellectual
stimulation than the middle-class child living in more pleasant
surroundings and educated in a modern suburban school. The
influence of environment on personality may be even greater
than its influence on intelligence.

The 'cycle of deprivation' might be broken either by selective
breeding, which in a free society means by the provision of
free contraception and abortion on demand, or by environmental
engineering. We do not know enough about either method to be
confident of the results it would achieve, and we need to know
very much more about environmental effects on children in order
to make environmental engineering more effective than it has been
so far.

Studies of the long-term effects of the environment may be cross-
sectional or longitudinal. Cross-sectional studies have revealed
the association between the inner-city environment and mental
disorder, delinquency, and poor professional status, but they
do not clearly establish any causal relationship. Longitudinal
studies of child-rearing, such as that carried out by Douglas
(1964), and the Newsons (Newson and Newson 1964, 1968) provide
rather better information, showing in still greater detail the
association between family circumstances and the development of

children. But even these finely described longitudinal studies
do not provide unequivocal evidence of causal relationship.
Only intervention studies could do that, and unfortunately
most of these have been relatively unsuccessful.

THE RELEVANT VARIABLES

One of the major difficulties in studying the psychological
effects of urbanization is the very large number of ways in
which urban and rural life differ. Another is the complexity
of these differences. In this section I shall simply discuss
some of the variables which have been considered most important.

High density dwellings and traffic are the most obvious
physical characteristics of cities. These tend to be associated
with simple physical consequences such as noise and fumes.
They may also result in frequent and various social contacts
and in complex and changing economic organization. Any or all
of these may be stressful singly or in combination. However, it
is difficult to get simple or complete knowledge of their
effects because of the variety of human adaptations to them.

Complexity and variety of physical stimuli

The urban environment is often considered more varied, and
hence more stimulating, than the rural environment. If we are
more stimulated by man and his artifacts than by nature, then
this may be true, although it is not true in any objectively
measurable physical sense. Indeed, most of our artifacts have
the purpose of controlling nature and making it more predictable.
A city may be the more noisy than the country, but its noise
is frequently less complex, and in a technical sense contains
less information than the quieter sounds of the country.
Similarly, it has been suggested that the urban environment is
more challenging and presents more problems than does life in
the country. If this is so, it is by accident, since cities
are to a large extent designed to protect us from the challenges
inherent in a struggle against nature. However, there is some
direct evidence that the 'greater pace of urban life' is a
reality, since Berkowitz (quoted by Millgram 1970) has found that
people walk faster in cities than in small towns, while Lowin,
Mottes, Sander and Bernstein (1971) have shown that the speed
of transactions, such as buying cigarettes is also faster in the
city.

It seems likely that urban life is both stimulating and boring,
challenging and degrading, but for different people and at
different times, depending on the way of life they adopt

and what they consider important.

Noxious stimuli

Some of the physical stimuli we encounter in cities are not just complex but positively harmful. Noise, fumes and smoke are perhaps the ones we worry about most. The noise may be generated by traffic, by near neighbours, by industry, or by crowds such as those at football matches or coming out of schools or pubs. Since the introduction of smokeless zones, traffic fumes, including those from aircraft, are perhaps the most important of the many types of airborne pollution. Atmospheric lead, sulphur dioxide, oxides of nitrogen, and various by-products of industrial processes are also present in greater amounts in cities.

The physical effects of these noxious stimuli are fairly well understood. Noise can cause deafness. Fumes can cause respiratory disease. But the psychological effects of these stimuli are much more complex. Noise usually reduces the efficiency with which we perform difficult mental tasks. But if we are short of sleep and performing a relatively easy routine task, the noise may actually improve performance (see Chapter 14). The noise of the city interact with other stresses, and its long-term effects are very poorly understood. However, many people adapt remarkably well to noisy environments and may even choose to take their pleasures in situations in which their hearing may be at risk (Lipscomb 1969, Wood and Lipscomb 1972).

Responses to other noxious stimuli may also be more dependent on the attitude people have towards them than on their physical characteristics or their known physiological effects. We know that smogs and fogs are injurious to health, yet many people do themselves much more harm by smoking and may choose to spend an evening in the smoky atmosphere of a party, which is worse than any smog. On the other hand, fumes from a new factory may seem so unpleasant that in addition to any physiological damage they may do, they may cause people subjected to them to become seriously anxious or depressed.

Variety and stability of human contacts

If one chooses to do so, one can make a very large variety of human contacts within a city simply because of the proximity of so many people. One might expect city dwellers to develop greater understanding and wider sympathies as a result. While there is some evidence that city dwellers do have greater sympathy for different kinds of people, most of the evidence goes the other way. For example, people in cities are less likely to help strangers in trouble (Altman, Levine, Nadien and

Villena 1970). One explanation for this is that in crowded
conditions we protect ourselves from excessive intrusion by
erecting conventional but invisible barriers around ourselves,
which make us less approachable (Fast 1970). One very clear
example of this is the great difficulty we have in talking to
strangers crushed against us in a 'tube' train. A similar but
more mundane explanation is the need to protect oneself against
the possible delinquency of city dwellers (Altman *et al.* did
their experiments in New York). Yet another possible explanation
is that when others are around we hope that they will offer help
and so relieve us of the burden. Darley and Latane (1968) have
shown experimentally, in natural and artificial situations,
that people are less likely to communicate with strangers when
there are other people present. So, paradoxically, people in
cities may so restrict their contacts with other people that
they have less contact than they might have had if they lived
in a less crowded environment. To some extent this explains
how loneliness can be a problem in cities (Reiseman 1950).
Furthermore, the city increases the ease with which we can
restrict our human contacts to people of our own kind. In cities
very specialized subcultures develop whose sympathies and
experience can be much more limited than those of the country
dweller.

In cities above a certain size, the inhabitants may spend an
inordinate amount of time travelling. This is not entirely
a function of size, since it depends also on the relative
positions of work, housing and services. It has, for example,
been pointed out that almost all the inhabitants of Los Angeles
could walk to work if they could be persuaded to exchange
houses. Whatever the reason, commuting time is stressful and
unrewarding. It has been argued that we have over-reacted to
increased speed of travel by travelling, unnecessarily, greater
distances and that, as a result, the quality of life has been
impoverished. Jane Jacobs (1962), in a penetrating analysis
of the quality of city life, has reached very similar conclusions.
The richness and stimulation of city life may easily disappear
if the scale is too large.

Perhaps the most important effect of the complexity and
mobility of city life is the disruption of social relationships
which can occur. The separation of generations and the break
up of old friendships are a result of the greater frequency
with which people now change houses and jobs. In turn this may
be reducing the amount of contact which children have with adults.
This is accentuated by the use of nursery schools and baby-
minders to enable mothers to work. Katherine Nelson (1973)
has shown that verbal ability is higher among children who
interact regularly with a large number of adults rather
than with their peers. It is likely that other things besides
language need to be learnt from adults. In attempting to improve

the quality of children's lives by providing play schools,
ordinary schools, youth clubs and discotheques, we may actively
hinder this.   It is not surprising that a youth culture has
developed with its corollary of the 'generation gap'.

Crowding

Perhaps the most obvious feature of urban life is the increased
density of the population. Experiments on animals (for example,
Calhoun 1962) have shown that abnormal behaviour develops above a
certain density. The abnormal behaviour may be related to the
disruption of normal territorial behaviour. Ardrey (1966) has
argued that in man, as in animals, there is an innate tendency to
regard an area of space as one's own and to react aggressively
towards intruders.   Hall (1963) and Sommer (1969) have
described some important uses of space in human interactions
but these are not necessarily simple territorial behaviour.
The space people put between themselves is characteristic of how
they regard each other. The closer people are, the greater the
intimacy of their relationship. But there are very big cultural
and national differences which make it unlikely that these
relationships are instinctive. For example, an Arab apparently
chasing a European around the room in slow motion is simply
misunderstanding the European's idea of what is the appropriate
distance for that kind of conversation.

Density of population can be measured in a number of ways.
Jalle, Cove, and McPherson (1972) have looked at the relationship
between indices of social disorganization and four different
measures of density. They found that the incidence of children
in care and of aggressive acts were most closely related to
density measured in terms of persons per room. Psychiatric
disorders correlated most highly with the number of persons per
housing unit. These measures do not differentiate between urban and
rural conditions. A large number of people per room or per
housing unit implies large households and small houses and is
characteristic of poverty. Other, more obviously urban measures,
such as number of housing units per structure and number of
structures per hectare, were not so obviously related to social
disorganization.

Crowding is not an uncomplicated stress of urban life. It is
confounded with many other variables, notably poverty. As in the
case of noise, people may seek crowded conditions on special
occasions. It is probably most stressful when it is unavoidable.

Rate of change

Jane Jacobs (1969) has argued that, at its best, city life can
provide ideal conditions for technological and cultural change.

She even argues that neolithic agriculture must have been developed in paleolithic trading centres in which, as in modern cities, merchants specialized in trading different kinds of goods such as stone implements, grain or live animals. Under these conditions, natural hybrids would occur under the eyes of people experienced in assessing the quality of grain, fruit and animals. Similarly, she argues that the rapid technical advances which led to the industrial revolution occurred because of the proximity in cities of the craftsmen, manufacturers, financiers and traders, whose co-operation was essential. In more recent times we have attempted to foster creativity by putting together diverse collections of talents in universities, research institutes and industrial laboratories, but these are more specialized, and to that extent more limited than the collection of talents available in some rich urban communities such as Birmingham and New York in the mid-nineteenth century and in some cities at the present time. However, the activities of planners have tended to segregate the talents and needs which stimulated each other in the past. Also, successful innovations may destroy the conditions in which they grew. The successful firm expands and moves away from the area where, as one of many small firms, it could call on the expertise of others. The successful political movement sets up its own organization, its own offices, and withdraws from the society which gave it birth. The conditions for successful innovation may be destroyed by failure as well as by success. In some old industrial towns of the north of England, in the stagnant market towns of rural England, in the depressed central areas of large cities, and in some of the cities of the developing world, failure can lead to excessive conservatism or apathy.

Rate of change is not a regular characteristic of city life, but when it is, it can accentuate the effects of the variables already discussed. Physical stimuli and social contacts are all more stimulating and more disturbing when they are new. Conservatism is yet another strategy for protecting ourselves from excessive stimulation. However, there is strong evidence that change, of itself, is important. Holmes and Rahe (1967) and Ruben, Gunderson and Arthur (1971) have shown a close correlation between 'life events' and susceptibility to physical and mental illness. Whether the events are happy ones, like marriage or promotion, or unhappy ones, such as losing one's job or a bereavement, an excess of them makes us more likely to be ill.

Diet

Although there is no evidence that diet is now very different

in the city compared with the country (see Chapter 7) there
have, in the past, been very big changes in diet, paralleling,
and partly a consequence of, the increase in urban living.
There is very little evidence that our present diet has much
effect on behaviour or on mental health. There was a big
improvement in physical health, particularly of children, in
England during the Second World War. This was believed to be
due to improvements in diet produced by rationing, the banning
of white flour, and the increased availability of nutritional
advice. However, this improvement in physical health was
not obviously associated with any improvement in mental health.
There was a reduction in the number of suicides, but that is a
common phenomenon in wartime.

This generally reassuring picture is somewhat disturbed by
the activities of a movement known as 'Orthomolecular Psychiatry'
(Hawkins and Pauling 1973). Pauling is well known for his
unorthodox views about the dietary optimum of vitamin C. He
has now taken up the equally unorthodox theory that schizophrenia
(and other forms of mental disturbance) is associated with a need
for vitamin B_3 (niacin) and perhaps for other vitamins and
nutrients (Hoffer and Osmond 1960; Hoffer 1962). This theory
received no support from orthodox psychiatry or orthodox nutrition,
and it has been severely attacked on scientific grounds (for
example Oken 1968). There is a great deal of evidence that
behavioural abnormalities can be produced by dietary deficiencies
(for example pellagra and scurvy both produce mental disturbance
as well as bodily changes. What is disputed is the possibility
that dietary deficiency is sufficiently widespread in the developed
countries of the world to explain more than a small proportion of
mental disorder. It is also disputed that simple dietary supple-
ments can 'cure' well-defined mental disorders such as schizophrenia.

However, Pauling and the orthomolecular psychiatrists do have
some interesting and important points to make. They argue that
dietary requirements vary so much between individuals that diets
known to be adequate for most people will inevitably be deficient
for some. An equally important argument is that most dietary
requirements are determined by the amount needed to prevent the
development of a gross physical disorder, such as scurvy or
pellagra. The brain may have a higher requirement for a nutrient,
either because the brain cells use more of it or because it has
difficulty crossing the blood-brain barrier. Pauling (1968) has
also argued that the optimal amount of a dietary factor is likely
to be considerably higher than the minimum requirement. In view of
these powerful *a priori* arguments it is a pity there has been
so little replication of the work of the orthomolecular psychiatrists.
Until these ideas have been better tested, we run the risk of
confusing effects of diet with the effects of other stresses.

Competition and insecurity

It is often claimed that city life provokes anxiety either because people in cities are more obviously in competition with each other ('the rat race'), or because modern life is more dangerous due to the possibility of nuclear war or of unforeseen pollution, or simply traffic accidents. It is very unlikely that these claims are justified. Modern life, including city life, is more co-operative and less competitive than at any time in the past. Social Security, the National Health Service and the social services all ensure this. Modern life is also less dangerous than at any time in the past, as is revealed by changed life expectancies, and the much less severe consequences of professional failure. Moreover, the most dangerous occupations are mining, agriculture and fishing, which are not related to city life or a product of a modern life style.

It seems likely that the complexities and stresses previously discussed are inappropriately described in terms of the 'rat race' and the 'insecurity' of city life. The work on the effects of 'life events', as previously referred to, shows that our conception of what is stressful needs to be revised.

This survey of the relevant variables reveals that the effects of the urban environment on behaviour are very complex and to a large extent affected by our attitudes to it and by the strategies we adopt to cope with it.

THEORETICAL VIEWPOINTS

So far the effects of the environment have been considered at a rather superficial and atheoretical level. Some of the difficulties encountered may be due to this, and a coherent theory of the relationship between man and his environment is clearly desirable. Unfortunately, we do not yet have any theory which is sufficiently well articulated to help us to judge the rather conflicting evidence. Nevertheless, there are two theoretical viewpoints which might eventually prove useful in evaluating the quality of life which is possible in different environments.

The psychological impact of urban life cannot be considered in isolation. It must be studied in a social, economic, and a medical context, since these affect the way people behave and the way they see themselves. But by studying the way individuals behave in different environments we may hope to explain or amplify the work of others on the pathology of organizations or of individuals.

Psychologists tend to ask two quite clear-cut questions about the way an individual adapts to his world. The first is,

'Are we fitted by evolution to thrive in this environment?'
The second is, 'Can people be taught how to thrive?'   The first
question is challenging and potentially important, but has not
so far proved very useful. The second question is the focus
of a great deal of research, some of which may prove to be
very useful indeed.

The evolutionary viewpoint

Like other biologists, we assume that man's hereditary
character is determined by evolution and that our genetic capacity
is an adaptation to an environment which no longer exists.
In the relatively short period during which civilization has
developed, there has not been time for such a slow-breeding
species to adapt genetically to the new conditions. One might
therefore expect some degree of mismatch between our present
way of life and our genetic predispositions. It is tempting
to attribute many of our current difficulties to a life style,
which is, in that sense, unnatural and to attempt to alleviate
some of the 'stresses of modern life' by seeking ways of life
which are not physiologically and behaviourally too different
from the life of primitive man.

Unfortunately there is little direct evidence for any mismatch
between our genetic natures and our way of life or, if there is,
that it creates any difficulty for us. We have very little
idea of the conditions in which primitive man evolved. Various
authors, including Lorenz (1966), Ardrey (1966) Morris (1967),
Tiger (1970), and Elaine Morgan (1972) have presented fascinating
but conflicting accounts of the evolution of man. The archaeo-
logical evidence cannot confirm or deny their speculations about
the evolution of behaviour or about the relationship between
primitive nature and modern environments. Our way of life is
also evolving, and its evolution may always be consistent (more
or less) with our animal natures. Furthermore, as man seems to
have a greater capacity to learn than any other animal, it is
possible that, even if our present environment is unnatural,
we can easily learn to be 'at home' in it.

However, there is strong evidence that our learning ability
is itself based on some specific and possibly innate patterns
of behaviour, so that there is considerable interaction between
the evolutionary viewpoint and the developmental viewpoint which
seeks to understand man in terms of ontogeny rather than
phylogeny.

The development viewpoint

Whether phylogeny or ontogeny is considered the more important
in determining man's nature depends on the view one takes of

human potential. Various *'tabula rasa'* theories of development imply that we may be capable of adapting to almost any physically viable environment, provided we are appropriately reared. This view is most closely associated with behaviourism of the extreme kind exemplified by Watson and Skinner. But even if our adaptability is limited by a heavy load of evolutionarily determined instincts, it is still important for us to rear and educate our children in a way which fits them for adult life. Although psychologists do not have any strong theories about the nature of a healthy society or a 'natural' way of life, they do believe that children can, and should, be helped to develop a happy and co-operative personality together with a creative problem-solving intelligence.

A very great deal of learning takes place in the first few months of life. Indeed, learning to talk is such an impressive achievement that some linguists and psycholinguists (for example, Chomsky 1965) have argued that much of our knowledge of language must be innate. Piaget (1952) argues, on the contrary, that in learning to handle his body in space and time and by learning to interact with other people, the child is already learning something about the structure of language even before he can speak. Recent studies of mother-child interactions have made it even easier to understand how babies learn so much in such a short time. Mothers and other adults seem to be very good at teaching things to small babies, who in turn seem to be ideal pupils. Their early social behaviour rewards adults in a way which increases the effectiveness of their teaching. So even if very little of language is innate, the basis of the mother-child interaction almost certainly is. Its function is to facilitate the social, emotional and intellectual development of the child. If children are put into environments which prevent these innate behaviours from having the desired effect, then the children may develop poorly. There is evidence that this can happen in institutions such as orphanages (Tizard and Tizard 1972). It may also be part of the explanation of the 'cycle of deprivation'.

When children go to school, instruction becomes more formal. There is evidence that formal instruction may improve children's ability to solve abstract problems as well as provide them with specific knowledge (Cole, Gay, Glick and Sharp 1971). The most effective strategies for formal instruction are beginning to be better understood (for example, Bruner 1971; Skinner 1968; Wood and Middleton 1975), although we do not know how they interact with informal strategies such as those used by parents.

Intelligence is enormously affected by experience, which ideally should be varied, interesting and appropriate to the child's

level of development, and should be provided in a highly verbal
and literate context (Hunt 1962). We also know that personality
is equally affected by experience, particularly early in life
(for example Shaffer 1973). Ideally children should have stable
and affectionate relationships with adults and opportunity to
learn to live with their peers. The effect of these many
different aspects of the early environment on intellectual and
social development is far from being fully understood. However,
there is no doubt that these things are important, and probably
more important than poverty and poor housing in producing the
'cycle of deprivation'. If they are not taken into account our
remedies may make the situation worse.

CONCLUSION

Despite its deficiencies, the available evidence seems to
justify the following conclusions.

1. That the psychological differences between different
urban environments and between urban and rural life depend most
upon people's attitudes and life styles and cannot be simply
related to the physical environment.

2. That despite this, when behaviour is of a simple and
stable type, and when the people concerned subject themselves
voluntarily to simple changes in their physical environment,
very clear relationships are found which can affect such
phenomena as productivity or accidents.

3. That the effects of the environment on attitudes and
mental health are much more variable and are largely determined
by the social context.

4. That the long-term effects of environment, such as the
'cycle of deprivation', are even more difficult to assess and
require a more sophisticated theoretical analysis.

5. That it is impossible to describe a natural environment
for man, in contrast to which city life may be considered
unnatural.

6. That the most subtle and perhaps the most far-reaching
consequences of the urban environment occur when it affects
the nature of social interactions and social learning.

REFERENCES

ALTMAN, LEVINE, NADIEN (1970) quoted by Oates, J. (1974)
People in Cities, The Open University Press.

ARDREY, R. (1966)   *The territorial imperative,*   Collins,
London.

ARONSON, E.   (1972)   *The social animal,*   Freeman, San Francisco.

BRUNER, J.S. (1971).   *The relevance of education,*   W.W.Norton,
New York.

CALHOUN, J.B. (1962)   Population density and social pathology,
Scient. Am. 206,   139-46.

CHOMSKY, N. (1965)   *Some aspects of the theory of syntax,*
MIT Press, Cambridge, Massachussetts.

COLE, M., GAY, J., GLOCK, J.A. and SHARP, D.W.   (1971)
The cultural context of learning and thinking,   Tavistock-
Methuen, London.

CRAIK, K.H. (1970)   Environmental psychology,   *New Dir.
Psychol.* 4, 3-121.

DARLEY, J.M. and LATANE, B.   (1968) Bystander intervention
in emergencies: diffusion of responsibility,   *J. person.
soc. Psychol. 8,* 377-83.

DOUGLAS, J.W.B.   (1964)   *The home and the school,* MacGibbon
and Kee, London.

FAST, J., (1970)   *Body language,* Souvenir Press, London.

FESTINGER, L. (1957) *A theory of cognitive dissonance,*
Row, Peterson, Evanston, Illinois.

HALL, E.T. (1963)   *The hidden dimension,* Doubleday,
Garden City, New York.

HAWKINS, D. and PAULING, L. (1973) *Orthomolecular psychiatry,*
Freeman, San Francisco.

HOFFER, A.   (1962) *Niacin therapy in psychiatry,* Thomas
Springfield, Illinois.

HOFFER, A. and OSMOND, H.   (1960) *The chemical basis of clinical
psychiatry,* Thomas, Springfield, Illinois.

HOLMES, T.H. and RAHE, R.H. (1967) The social readjustment rating scale. *J.Physchosom.res*. 11, 213.

HUNT, J. McV. (1962) *Intelligence and experience*, Ronald Press, New York.

JACOBS, J. (1962) *The death and life of great American cities*, Pelican, London.

JACOBS, J. (1969) *The economy of cities*, Cape, London.

JALLE, O.R. COVE, W.R., and McPHERSON, D. (1972) Population density and pathology: what are the relations for man? *Science, N. Y*. 176, 23-30.

LANGDON, F.J. (1966a) Modern offices: a user survey. *National Building Studies Research Paper*, No.41, HMSO, London.

LANGDON, F.J. (1966b) The social and physical environment: a social scientists view. *R.Inst. Br.Arch*. 73, 460-4.

LIPSCOMB, D.M. (1969) Ear damage from exposure to rock and roll music. *Archs. Otol*. 90, 29-39.

LORENZ, K. (1966) *On aggression*, Methuen, London.

LOWIN, L., MOTTES, J.H. SANDER, B.E. and BERNSTEIN, M. (1971) The face of life and sensitivity to time in urban settings. *J.Soc.Psychol. 83*, 247-55.

MILLGRAM, S. (1970) The experience of living in cities. *Science*, 167, 1461-8.

MORGAN, E. (1972) *The descent of woman*, Souvenir Press, London.

MORRIS, D. (1967) *The naked ape: a zoologists study of the human animal*, Cape, London.

MURRELL,H. (1965) *Ergonomics*, Chapman and Hall, London.

NELSON, K. (1973) Structure and strategy in learning to talk, *Mongr.soc.Res.Child.Dev*. 37, No.4.

NEWSON, J. and NEWSON, E. (1964) *Infant care in an urban community*, Allen and Unwin, London.

NEWSON, J. and NEWSON, E. (1968) *Four years old in an urban community*, Allen and Unwin, London.

OKEN, D. (1968) A reply to Pauling, *Science, N.Y.* 160, 1181.

PAULING, L. (1968) Orthomolecular psychiatry, *Science N.Y.* 160, 265.

PIAGET, J. (1952) *The origins of intelligence in children.* International Universities Press, New York.

REISEMAN, D. (1950) *The lonely crowd,* Anchor Books, Garden City, New York.

ROETHLISBERGER, F.J. and DICKSON, W.J. (1939) *Management and the worker,* Harvard University Press.

RUBEN, R.T., GUNDERSON, E.K.E. and ARTHUR, R.G. (1971) Life stress and illness patterns in the US Navy V. Prior life change and illness onset in a battleship crew. *J.Psychosom Res.* 15, 89.

SCHAFFER, H.R. (1973) *The growth of sociability,* Penguin Books, Harmondsworth.

SKINNER, B.F. (1968) *The technology of teaching,* Appleton Century Crofts, New York.

SOMMER, R. (1969) *Personal space: the behavioural basis of design,* Prentice Hall, New York.

TIGER, L. (1970) *Men in groups,* Nelson, New York.

TIZARD, J. and TIZARD, B. (1972) The institution as an environment for development. In *The integration of the child into a social world* (ed. M.P.Richards) Cambridge University Press.

WOOD, D.J. and MIDDLETON, D. (1975) A study of assisted problem solving, *Br.J.Psycol* (In Press).

WOOD, D.J. and LIPSCOMB, D.M. (1972) Maximum available sound pressure levels from stereocomponents. *J.acoust. Soc.Am.* 52, 484-7.

YOUNG, M. and WILLMOTT, P. (1962) *Family and kinship in east London,* Routledge Kegan Paul, London.

16 Mental health in urban environments

J. K. Wing

Both components in the title of this chapter can mean all things to all men. Much of the conflict and confusion in current statements about the influence of modern urban life-styles on individual psychological functioning arises from a failure to agree upon terms. The problems involved in defining what is specifically *'urban'* are explored in other parts of this book. *'Mental health'* is an even more difficult concept, which includes at least four overlapping levels of definition. At one extreme there are the severe *'mental illnesses'*; recognizable psychological syndromes concerning which some more or less plausible theory of somatic aetiology, pathology, biochemistry, or treatment can be put forward. The most obvious examples are the symptomatic psychoses (delusional or hallucinatory syndromes due to alcohol or drug intoxication, epilepsy, brain tumour, etc.), the dementias, and the various conditions accompanied by severe intellectual retardation, such as Down's disease (mongolism) or various biochemical defects. This group also includes the so-called 'functional' psychoses and neuroses such as schizophrenia, early childhood autism, mania, obsessional neuroses, and severe depressive disorders and anxiety states. The psychological syndromes by which these conditions are recognized can be delineated with a good deal of precision and reliability if sufficient trouble is taken to use agreed definitions of symptoms, to standardize methods of interview, and to apply predetermined rules of classification (Wing, Cooper, and Sartorius 1974; L.Wing 1976). Disease theories of these conditions have only been partially validated so far, but a fairly strong case can be made for many of them. These severe mental illnesses give rise to such serious problems, either during the acute attack or because of the residual chronic disabilities, that the individuals suffering from them are likely to be referred to specialist social and medical services. During the course of a given year, just under 2 per cent of the population of countries with well-developed services are in touch with a psychiatrist. This is as true of Hawaii or Aberdeen as it is of Baltimore or London (Bahn *et al.* 1966; L.Wing *et al.* 1967; Wing and Bransby 1970). Obviously not everyone referred to hospital is suffering from a severe mental illness, nor does everyone with such a condition get referred. However, the statistics of referral to outpatient clinics and admission to hospital do provide a useful source of epidemiological information and much of our present knowledge about the social factors involved is derived

in this way.

A more complete picture can be obtained from studies of samples of the general population, or of the clientele of general practitioners, and it then becomes apparent that very substantial proportions of the population have some kind of psychological problem, though not usually amounting to severe mental illness in the sense described above. In the first instance we can consider the problems of those who themselves feel that they are not mentally healthy but complain of what might be called *'mental ill-health'*: worry, tension, irritability, depression, or anxiety. Estimates vary from 10 per cent to 25 per cent of the population, depending on the criteria used and on the assessment of severity of any accompanying social disability (Hare and Shaw 1965; Shepherd *et al.* 1966; Srole *et al.* 1962; Taylor and Chave 1964).

In addition to this large group, there is another proportion of the population who do not necessarily complain of their own mental suffering but whose socially deviant behaviour leads other people to be concerned about them. Conditions coming under this heading of *'social deviance'* include the conduct disorders of childhood and adolescence, delinquency, crime, alcohol or drug dependence, destitution, violence, destructivenss, and attempted suicide. Although deviance which is defined in purely social terms should not be regarded as in itself evidence of psychological disturbance, many of the individuals are clearly not functioning at their psychological optimum, and many of them do actually complain of mental ill-health. The three groups of conditions (mental illness, mental ill-health, and social deviance) overlap a good deal, and many authors writing on the psychological problems of life in large cities have been tempted to lump them all together as though there were some unitary 'mental malaise' which was athe alternative to 'mental health'. Indeed many modern writiers specifically reject any attempt to isolate for study some particular psychological abnormality with a restricted definition such as schizophrenia, just as they do such socially defined conditions as delinquency, because they feel that a positivist approach diverts attention from more fundamental social problems. The theoretical alternatives put forward vary from neo-Marxist to ultra-right-wing, but what all modesl have in common is the use of a historical (or historicist) method of analysis and a tendency to regard psychological and social problems of all kinds as epiphenomena floating and social problems of all kinds as epiphenomena floating on the surfaceof one or another kind of struggle for power, whether within family, class or nation.

Whether one starts from some deliberately restricted problem, as West (1973) did in his study of delinquency, or from a political critique of the society which makes the laws defining delinquency (as did West's critic in the *Times Literary Supplement* of 1st

March 1974), the aim is ultimately the same: to discover means
of diminishing disabilities and enhancing assets. However, the
theorists who see psychological disorders only in political
terms rarely bring forward empirical evidence in support;
indeed it is often part of their thesis that empirical evidence
is valueless. It is certainly true that the methodological
problems are formidable and the opportunities for experimental
hypothesis testing limited but there is nevertheless a body
of work worth considering.

Before undertaking a brief review of this work it is necessary
to mention the attempts that have been made to define mental
health, not in terms of the absence of mental illness or even
of mental ill-health but in terms of positive criteria.
Jahoda (1958) has summarized these. The difficulty is that to
specify any particular combination of traits such as intelligence,
independence, creativity, social consciousness, self-control
or self-fulfilment, as desirable, depends upon the operation of
subjective value systems which, in some countries, are reinforced
by government fiat or by religious ideology, and in others follow
the dictates of the market or the media or local fashion or
social class. Health, in fact, is a social concept (Lewis 1953).
Any attempt to define characteristics of urban life which will
enhance 'positive mental health' is therefore likely to turn out
to be a statement about the author's own values. On the whole
it is better to state these clearly for what they are, rather than
to give them an appearance of authenticity by appealing to a
supposedly objective concept of mental health. When Frankenberg
(1966) states, 'I would rather enough cubic feet of housing space
and an efficient milkman than three acres of land and a cow',
the element of value is openly avowed and there is no need to say
that one system is 'healthier' than the other. The same is true
of terms like 'morale', since morale may be high in a communal
gang or in a warship at sea without any assumption being made
that these forms of social organization should form a model for
the rest of society.

MENTAL ILLNESS AND MENTAL HANDICAP

Schizophrenia will be used as an example of a severe mental
illness that has been studied in some detail in epidemiological
surveys in order to discover social causes. The problems
involved in definition have been explored in two recent multi-
national studies. There is a central syndrome on which
psychiatrists everywhere are agreed and which accounts for about
two-thirds of the cases diagnosed. Surrounding this central
syndrome there are others which are less homogeneous but which
can be reliably recognized. In addition, in certain countries
(notably the United States and the Soviet Union) there is a

tendency to give a further range of conditions the same label, although elsewhere they would not be regarded as schizophrenic in nature (Cooper *et al.* 1972; WHO 1973).

Faris and Dunham (1939) found that there were higher rates of first admission to hospital with schizophrenia from the central areas of Chicago than from the suburban and commuter areas further out and concluded that poverty and social isolation were responsible. However, these characteristics of cities do not necessarily go together. In places where they can be separated geographically, as in Bristol (Hare 1956) or London (Stein 1957; Wing and Hailey 1972), it is found that social isolation (characterized by a high proportion of lodging-houses, a substantial movement into and out of the area, a high divorce rate, etc.) is the important factor, not poverty. The same is true of suicide rates (Sainsbury 1955). Hare (1956) also showed that schizophrenic patients had often moved into the socially isolated areas quite recently before admission. Dunham (1965), in a study of Detroit, came to the conclusion that migration into the isolated areas was the main reason for the concentration of schizophrenic people there.

On the whole, there is little evidence that schizophrenia is less frequent in rural areas, although first admission rates seem to be higher in large American towns than in small ones. Two surveys of rural areas that led to unusual prevalence rates were carried out by Böök (1953) and Eaton and Weil (1955). Eaton and Weil studied an Anabaptist sect, the Hutterites, who lived in small closely knit farming communities in Northern America Property was owned in common and everyday life was simple, austere, well regulated, and pious. There appeared to be a rather low prevalence of schizophrenia. Böök, on the other hand, carried out his survey in the north of Sweden, where the climate was severe and many of the population lived isolated lives under very primitive conditions. He found the expectation of schizoprhenia to be 3 times as high as in other Scandinavian studies.

These results might be interpreted in various ways to indicate the effect of genetic or socio-cultural influences. However, it is necessary to be sure that comparable techniques of population screening and diagnosis were used before looking for other types of explanation. It is quite likely that Böök's case-finding techniques were more thorough and that there was a smaller out-migration of affected individuals from the North Swedish area. It is impossible to compare the diagnostic processes used in the two surveys, although variation in these can account for large differences in frequency counts. Murphy (1968) did not find that first admission rates for schizophrenia from the Hutterite communities in Canada's prairie provinces were significantly below average.

Analyses which link other social factors such as emigration
(Ødegaard 1932), marital status (Ødegaard 1946), education
(Noreik and Ødegaard 1966), and occupational class (Goldberg
and Morrison 1963), to schizophrenia similarly seem not to
be directly causal. Kohn (1972) still considers that there is
evidence in the social-class data, but it is doubtful whether
he has made his case (Mechanic 1972). This is not to say that
the social environment is unimportant in schizophrenia. On
the contary, there is good evidence that personal relationships
are very important (Brown, Birley, and Wing, 1972), that the
quality of the hospital milieu can be crucial (Wing and Brown
1970), and that schizophrenic patients are more vulnerable
than most people to everyday social stresses (Brown and Birley
1970). However, none of this evidence so far implicates
specifically urban environments or styles of living. There
is not even any evidence that schizophrenia has increased in
frequency during the period since massive industrialization
began (Goldhamer and Marshall 1953), although the data are not
good enough to be certain. Since reasonably good record-keeping
began on a national level in this country, there has been no
change in the first admission rate for schizophrenia, which has
been remarkably stable; between 15 and 20 per 100 000 per
year since 1949.   The rate for Wales is approximately the same
as that for England.

Although equivalent rates are not available for completely
non-urban areas, a nine-nation study carried out under the
auspices of the World Health Organization which included urban
centres in Colombia, India, Nigeria, and Taiwan, indicated that
typical cases of the major 'functional' psychoses -
schizophrenia, mania, and depressive psychosis - diagnosed on
the basis of standard techniques, could be found in each area
(WHO 1973; Wing, Cooper, and Sartorius 1974).

'MENTAL ILL-HEALTH'

Most investigators studying the 'mental-health' problems of
general populations have used empirically derived check-lists
of 'symptoms' such as anxiety, depression, worrying, and
irritability, and have interpreted the score to indicate the
level of what might be called 'mental ill-health'. General
practioners' diagnoses, which have also been used, are often
largely symptomatic and equivalent to check-list scores.
Although crude and undiscriminating, such methods do have a
certain clinical face-validity. Shepherd *et al.*, (1966)
emphasize the sheer size of the 'morbidity' measured in this
way: 'Of some 15 000 patients at risk during a 12-month period,
just over 2000, or approximately 14 per cent, consulted
their doctor at least once for a condition diagnosed as largely

or entirely psychiatric in nature.' Studies by Hare and Shaw (1965), Srole *et al.*, (1962) and Taylor and Chave (1964) indicated that about a quarter of the adult urban population were quite severely disabled by such conditions in London and New York. On the other hand, the proportion found by Hagnell (1966) in rural Sweden, by Leighton *et al.* (1963b) in rural Canada and by Leighton *et al.* (1963) in rural Nigeria was very little different. There is no evidence here of a 'stress' effect of modern urban life although its is true that factors which might differentiate urban from rural styles of living (Wirth 1938) were not closely measured. Leighton (1959) has argued that social disorganization is an important factor and that this may affect rural as well as urban communities. Patient consulting rates per 1 000 population in 106 general practices in England and Wales did not show any marked rural-urban differences so far as psychoneurotic disorders were concerned (Logan and Cushion 1958). On the whole, however, the more skilled workers had higher rates and farmers had lowest rates. Shepherd *et al.* (1966) found no association with occupation.

A review of work concerned with housing environments (Wing 1974) came to the conclusion that there was evidence that living in tall apartment blocks tended to decrease social interaction between neighbours and had a deleterious effect on children, particularly of pre-school age. However, a number of individuals living in any kind of housing environment will express considerable dissatisfaction, though the reason given will vary according to the setting. The most dissatisfied people tend to have the most neurotic symptoms. A recent longitudinal study of the problems of people approaching retirement age suggested a similar conclusion; a proportion had adverse reactions whether or not they had retired from work, though for different reasons in each case (Streib 1974).

Nevertheless, when studies of groups of individuals are undertaken in order to discover what types of stress have recently been present, there is quite good evidence that 'mental ill-health' does result (Dohrenwend and Dohrenwend 1974). Bereavement is an obvious example (Parkes 1964). Brown and others have shown that threatening 'life events' lead to 'neurotic' reactions, particularly in the absence of supportive personal relationships (Brown and Birley 1970; Brown, Bhrolchain, and Harris, 1974; Brown *et al.* 1973; Cooper and Sylph 1973). Thus if, instead of studying one particular 'stress', such as housing relocation (Fried 1964; Wilner *et al.* 1962) or retirement (Streib 1974) or aircraft noise (Gattoni and Tarnopolsky 1973), *all* the various types of adverse social factor are studied together, it becomes possible to pick out the vulnerable individuals. Whether there are more of these in the town than in the country and,

more specifically, whether urban life actually produces them
is not yet clear. To the extent that it does, the common
factor may be disruptive childhood experiences, as we shall
see in the next section.

SOCIAL DEVIANCE

Many of the wide range of conditions arbitrarily included
under the heading of social deviance can be fairly definitely
related to aspects of the social environment in which the
individuals are living. Children's disorders may be taken
as an example. Rutter (1973) described the results of a survey
of 10-year-old children carried out in the Isle of Wight and
in an Inner London suburb. The London children showed nearly
twice as much 'behavioural deviance' as measured by a teacher's
questionnaire (19.1 per cent compared with 10.6 per cent). Both
'neurotic symptoms' and 'conduct disorder' followed this trend,
as did educational attainment, for example, specific reading
retardation. Basically, the disturbed children in both areas
came from unhappy, disruptive, quarrelsome homes, but these
were commoner in London. There was evidence that some schools
were more associated with disturbance than others, as Power,
Benn, and Morris (1972) have shown for delinquency, though West
considered that this was due to selective intake. West (1973)
found five background factors of particular importance for
delinquency: low family income, large family size, parental
criminality, low intelligence, and poor parental behaviour.
Earlier ecological analyses, showing that delinquency occurred
particularly in areas of high unemployment, overcrowding, poor
housing and few amenities (Shaw and Mackay 1942; Wallis and
Maliphant 1967), were thus confirmed.

Vandalism has also been associated with certain urban environments, for example high-rise housing blocks, possibly because
of the fact that tenants cannot develop any sense of individual
proprietorship for communal spaces such as corridors, stairs,
courts, and gardens, and therefore do not help to control
destructive behaviour (Newman 1974). Robins (1970, 1973)
pointed out that neurotic symptoms in childhood and adolescence
are usually of short duration and do not usually predict mental
disturbance in later life. Deviant behaviour, however, has
a more serious prognosis since, 'in a large minority of cases
it presages life-long problems with the law, inability to earn
a living, defective interpersonal relationships, and severe
personal distress. In fact, if one could successfully treat
the anti-social behaviour of childhood, the problems of adult
crime, alcoholism, divorce and chronic unemployment might be
vastly diminished.'

Accounts of the spread of drug dependence among young people
(D'Alarcon and Rathod 1968) suggest the importance of 'social
networks', defined by Mitchell (1969) as a set of linkages among
a defined group of people which help to explain their social
behaviour. Kreitman, Smith, and Tan (1969) have used a similar
concept to help explain attempted suicide. It is clear that
certain children are very much more likely than others to
start smoking and drinking early (Bynner 1968; Davies and Stacey
1973), to take drugs (Wiener 1970), to be aggressive, to drop
out of school, and to become delinquent (West 1973). These
tendencies are much enhanced if a subculture is formed which
reinforces deviant behaviour by attaching high value to it.
A geographical area in which poverty and family instability are
endemic provides an environment in which such a culture can
become established over a long period of time so that its values
come to be tolerated even by those who do not share them.

Clearly there will also be selective in- and out-migration.
This is most obvious in the case of destitution (Tidmarsh and
Wood 1972). Among the clientele of the Reception Centres in
the large conurbations is a disproportionate number of men who
originally came from areas of high unemployment (particularly
in unskilled occupations) and poor housing (particularly for
single people). These men migrated to the cities in their
early twenties, but managed to support themselves for a while
in marginal employment (kitchen porters, building labourers,
etc.) before becoming destitute. Many take to alcohol as a
kind of narcotic to deaden the pains of living. The age of
this first migration is now dropping and the length of time
taken to reach destitution seems to be getting shorter. Other
people, usually in an older age-group, have become destitute
because of physical or mental handicap. (Schizophrenia is
quite common among Reception Centre populations, but there is no
evidence that it is caused by the way of life - rather the
opposite.) The city areas where many destitute people live
(often very stable lives, in the sense that their daily
routine may vary little over the course of many years), tend
to be both poor and socially isolated and rates of mental
illness, mental ill-health, and social deviance are *all* high.

CONCLUSIONS

The association of severe mental illness with various indices
of urban life is mainly explicable on grounds of selection
rather than stress, and even lesser degrees of mental ill-health,
although common and likely to be reactive to factors in an
individual's social environment, do not seem to be caused by
features which are specifically urban. Predisposing factors,
including genetic constitution, physical ill-health, previous

experience of adversity, the absence of supportive personal
relationships, and lack of intellectual, vocational, and
social skills, are often crucial, both in precipitating and
in maintaining illness or ill-health. On the other hand,
in the case of behaviour labelled as socially deviant, social
factors are often predominant.   The three main groups of
macrosocial factors implicated are those associated with
social isolation, with poverty, and with social networks which
positively maintain the undesirable behaviour. Combinations
of these factors may be found at one extreme of the urban-
rural continuum, but, taken singly, they may occur in any
geographical area, urban or rural. This conclusion is likely
to be even more evident if social deviance is taken to include
'middle-class delinquencies'. Social deviance, in any case,
is not a good index of mental ill-health or mental illness,
although the people concerned are certainly at higher risk.
To equate the activities of 'urban guerillas' or teenage
gangs at football matches with manifestations of 'sickness'
is to lose all hope of understanding them. As for 'mental
health', we have seen that it is a social concept. It is
open to argument whether delinquency is a 'healthy' or an
'unhealthy' phenomenon in terms of the future of our society.
It is not for any particular professional groups to pose as
impartial arbiters on such questions.

We should not even expect social improvements, for example,
the reduction of poverty, unemployment, and homelessness,
necessarily to decrease the prevalence of severe mental
illness or even that of worry, depression, or anxiety. Human
beings adjust their levels of expectation to their immediate
environment. The fact that they are not depressed or dissatisfied does *not* mean that nothing need be done. As can be seen
in families containing a severely handicapped and difficult
child, or in other extreme situations which might be regarded
as intolerable by most people, it quite often happens that the
people involved live lives which they themselves find
satisfactory.

So far, there is rather little evidence that social changes
affect the prevalence of deviant behaviour. Kreitman, Smith,
and Tan (1969) found that people who made suicidal attempts
in Edinburgh were selectively drawn from, and shared in, local
subcultures in which self-poisoning or self-injury was a common
means of dealing with crisis situations. Kreitman (1973)
argues that 'only a major change in the whole fabric of society,
or at least in the relevant subcultures, is likely to make any
appreciable difference to the currently very high rates of
parasuicide.' One even wonders whether major changes might not
make matters worse. It has been suggested that counselling
services, such as the Samaritans, can effectively reduce this
rate, but the evidence is not yet compelling. Even from the

point of view of *secondary* prevention, that is, prevention
of a second attempt once the first has been made, current
work is not optimistic.

West (1973) pointed out at the end of his study of delinquency that 'the translation of research findings into social
action is a task that investigators are apt to find repugnant.'
Since young recidivist delinquents come from disturbed home
backgrounds and themselves tend to perpetuate the same
problems in the next generation, successful intervention at
any point within the cycle should have beneficial results.
However, like Krietman, West is pessimistic, not only as to
the results of intervention through helping agencies (he
points out that society is prepared to spend far more on medical
than on social crises) but also about the likely outcome of
social methods of primary prevention. What techniques of
providing adequate parental role models would be most successful
and economical when the potential clients are reluctant to
accept help or even to see the necessity for it? Influences
outside the home tend to confirm the delinquent behaviour
rather than to discourage it. Schools are unable to counter
this process. Lee Robins (1973) is doubtful about the
efficacy of group treatment, psychotherapy, or educational
remedies. She does not consider that even highly-structured
educational innovations of the Head Start type, which provide
for 4-year-old low-income children in the United States the
kind of nursery school enrichment that many middle-class children
receive in private schools, have proved their value in the long
run, although there is often an immediate improvement in
intellectual performance. New experiments are needed to
discover whether other methods of intervention, which attempt
to utilize the motivation of young people themselves, are
effective. Schemes in which selected offenders are trained to
help others, or in which young people are encouraged to set
up their own commercial enterprises, or in which social action
on behalf of underprivileged groups is undertaken, may also
offer opportunities for effective counselling.

In summary, there is no evidence that specifically urban
styles of life lead to severe mental illnesses such as
schizophrenia, although socially isolated city areas may attract
people who are predisposed to develop such illnesses. Lesser
degrees of mental ill-health are very common, and often
reactive to stresses in the social environment, but it seems
that such stresses may occur as frequently in rural life as in
towns. People defined as socially deviant are at particular
risk of developing adverse psychological reactions and there
do seem to be important environmental factors which, in certain
combinations, are commoner in towns. So far, preventive
techniques, whether social or psychological, have not been shown
to be effective. Action to prevent poverty or social isolation

or to improve the quality of family relationships has to be taken on the basis of general social values rather than because it has been demonstrated to reduce the incidence or prevalence of mental ill-health.

REFERENCES

BAHN, A.K., GARDNER, E.A., ALLTOP, L., KNATTERUD, G.L. and SOLOMON, M. (1966) Comparative study of rates of admission and prevalence for psychiatric facilities in four registered areas. *Am. J.publ. Hlth*, 56, 2033.

BÖÖK, J.A. (1953) A genetic and neuropsychiatric investigation of a North-Swedish population, *Acta genet. Stat.Med.* 4, 1-100.

BROWN, G.W., BHROLCHAIN, M., and HARRIS, T. (1975) *Social class and psychiatric disturbance among women in an urban population.* Sociology 9, 225-54.

BROWN, G.W. and BIRLEY, J.L.T. (1970) Social precipitants of severe psychiatric disorders. In *Psychiatric Epidemiology* (Eds.E.H.Hare, and J.K.Wing) Oxford University Press, London.

BROWN, G.W., BIRLEY, J.L.T. and WING, J.K. (1972) Influence of family life on the course of schizophrenic disorders: a replication. *Brit.J.Psychiat.* 121, 241-58.

BROWN, G.W., SKLAIR, F., HARRIS, T., and BIRLEY, J.L.T. (1973) Life events and psychiatric disorders: some methodological issues. *Psychol. Med.* 3, 74-87.

BYNNER, J.M. (1968)   *The young smoker,* HMSO, London.

COOPER, J.E., KENDELL, R.E., GURLAND, B.J., SHARPE, L., COPELAND, J.R.M. and SIMON, R. (1972), *Psychiatric diagnosis in New York and London.*   Maudsley Monograph No.20, Oxford University Press, London.

COOPER, A.B. and SYLPH, J. (1973) Life events and the onset of neurotic illness: an investigation in general practice. *Psychol. Med.* 3, 421-35.

D'ALARCON, R. and RATHOD, M.K. (1968) Prevalence and early detection of heroin abuse. *Br.med.J.* 2, 549-53.

DAVIES, J. and STACEY, B. (1973)   *Teenagers and alcohol.* HMSO, London.

DOHRENWEND, B.S. and DOHRENWEND, B.P. (eds.) (1974) *Stressful life events, their nature and effects.* Wiley, New York.

DUNHAM, H.W. (1965) *Community and schizophrenia: An epidemiological analysis.* Wayne State University Press, Detroit.

EATON, J.W. and WEIL, R.J. (1955) *Culture and mental disorders,* The Free Press, Glencoe, Illinois.

FARIS, R.E.L. and DUNHAM, H.W. (1939) *Mental disorders in urban areas,* Hafner, Chicago.

FRANKENBURG, R. (1966) *Communities in Britain,* Penguin Books, Harmondsworth.

FRIED, M. (1964) Effects of change on mental health. *Am.J. Orthopsychiat.* 34, 3.

GATTONI, F. and TARNOPOLSKY, A. (1973) Aircraft noise and psychiatric morbidity. *Psychol. Med.* 3, 516-20.

GOLDBERG, E.M. and MORRISON, S.L. (1963) Schizophrenia and social class, *Br.J.Psychiat.* 109, 785-802.

GOLDHAMER, H. and MARSHALL, A.W. (1953) *Psychosis and civilisation: two studies in the frequency of mental disease.* The Free Press, Glencoe, Illinois.

HAGNELL, O. (1966) *A prospective study of the incidence of mental disorder,* Berlingska, Lund.

HARE, E.H. (1956) Mental illness and social conditions in Bristol. *J.ment. Sci.* 102, 349-357.

HARE, E.H. and SHAW, G.K. (1965) *Mental health on a new housing estate,* Oxford University Press, London.

JAHODA, M. (1958) *Current concepts of positive mental health.* Basic Books, New York.

KOHN, M. (1972) Class, family and schizophrenia, *Soc.Forces,* 50, 295-313.

KREITMAN, N. (1973) The prevention of suicidal behaviour. In: *Roots of evaluation,* (eds. J.K.Wing, and H.Hafner) Oxford University Press, London.

KREITMAN, N., SMITH, P., and TAN, E.S. (1969) Attempted suicide in social networks, *Br.J.prev.soc.Med.* 23, 116-23.

LEIGHTON, A. (1959) *My name is legion,* Basic Books, New York.

LEIGHTON, A.H., LAMBO, T.A., HUGHES, C.C., LEIGHTON, D.C.,
MURPHY, J.M. and MACKLIN, D.B. (1963a) *Psychiatric disorder
among the Yoruba,* Cornell University Press, New York.

LEIGHTON, D.C., HARDING, J.S., MACKLIN, D.B., MACMILLAN, A.M.,
and LEIGHTON, A.H. (1963b) *The character of danger: psychiatric
symptoms in selected communities.* Basic Books, New York.

LEWIS, A. (1953) Health as a social concept. *Br.J.Sociol.* 4,
109-24.

LOGAN, W.P.D. and CUSHION, A.A. (1958). *Morbidity statistics
from general practice.* Studies in Medical and Population
Subjects, No.14. HMSO, London.

MECHANIC, D. (1972) Social class and schizophrenia: some
requirements for a plausible theory of social influence.
Soc.Forces, 50, 305-9.

MITCHELL, J.C. (1969) Urbanization, detribalization,
stabilisation and urban commitment in Southern Africa, In
Urbanism, urbanization and change. (eds. P.Meadows, and
E.H.Mizrudie), Addison-Wesley, London.

MURPHY, H.B.M. (1968) Cultural factors in the genesis of
schizophrenia. *The transmission of schizophrenia,* (eds.
D.Rosenthal and S.S.Katz) Pergamon Press, New York.

NEWMAN, O. (1974) *Defensible space,* Architectural Press,
London.

NOREIK, K. and ØDEGAARD, Ø. (1966) Psychoses in Norwegians
with a background of higher education. *Br.J.Psychiat.*
112, 43-55.

ØDEGAARD, Ø (1932) Emigration and insanity: a study of
mental disease among Norwegian born population in Minnesota.
Acta psychiat.neurol, scand. Suppl.4.

ØDEGAARD, Ø. (1946) Marriage and mental disease: A study
in social psychopathology. *J.ment.Sci.* 92, 35-59.

PARKES, C.M. (1964) Recent bereavement as a cause of illness.
Br.J.Psychiat. 110, 465.

POWER, M.J., BENN, R.T. and MORRIS, J.N. (1972) Neighbourhood,
school and juveniles before the courts, *Br.J.Criminol.* 12,
111-32.

PRINGLE, K.L.M. (1965) *Deprivation and education,* Longmans,
London.

ROBINS, L.N. (1970) Follow-up studies investigating childhood disorders. In: *Psychiatric epidemiology,* (eds. E.H.Hare, and J.K.Wing) Oxford University Press, London.

ROBINS, L.N. (1973) Evaluation of psychiatric services for children in the United States. In *Roots of evaluation* (Eds. J.K.Wing and H.Hafner) Oxford University Press, London.

RUTTER, M. (1973) Why are London children so disturbed? *Proc. R.Soc.Med.* 66, 1221-5.

SAINSBURY, P. (1955). *Suicide in London*: an ecological study Chapman and Hall, London.

SHAW, C.R. and MacKAY, H.D. (1942) *Juvenile delinquency in urban areas,* University of Chicago Press, Chicago.

SHEPHERD, M., COOPER, B., BROWN, A.C., and KALTON, G.W. (1966) *Psychiatric illness in general practice,* Oxford University Press, London.

SROLE, L., LANGNER, T.S., MICHAEL, S.T., OPLER, M.K,, and RENNIE, T.A.C. (1962) *Mental health in the Metropolis: The midtown Manhattan study.* McGraw-Hill, New York.

STEIN, L. (1957) "Social class" gradient in schizophrenia. *Br.J. prev.soc. Med.11,* 181-95.

STREIB, G. (1975) In *Life history research in psychopathology,* Volume 4 (eds. R.D.Wirt, G.Winokur, and M.Roff) University of Minnesota Press, Minneapolis.

TAYLOR, S. and CHAVE, S. (1964) *Mental health and environment,* Longmans, London.

TIDMARSH, D. and WOOD, S. (1972) Psychiatric aspects of destitution. In *Evaluating a community psychiatric service.* (eds J.K.Wing and A.H.Hailey), Oxford University Press, London.

WALLIS, C.P. and MALIPHANT, R. (1967) Delinquent areas in the county of London: ecological factors. *Br.J.Criminol.* 7, 250-84.

WEST, D.J. (1973) *Who becomes delinquent?* Heineman, London.

WIENER, R.S.P. (1970) *Drugs and school children.* Longmans, London.

WILNER, D.M., PRICE, W.R., PINKERTON, T.C. and TAYBACK, M.(1962)

The Housing environment and family life. John Hopkins Press, Baltimore.

WING, J.K. (1974) Housing environments and mental health. In *Population and its problems* (ed. H.B.Parry) Clarendon Press, Oxford.

WING, J.K. and BRANSBY, R. (eds.) (197) *Psychiatric case registers.* Department of Health Statistical Report, Series No.8 HMSO, London.

WING,J.K. and BROWN, G.W. (1970) *Institutionalism and schizophrenia.* Cambridge University Press, London.

WING, J.K., COOPER, J.E. and SARTORIUS, N. (1974) *The description and classification of psychiatric symptoms: an instruction manual for the PSE and Catego system.* Cambridge University Press, London.

WING, J.K. and BRANSBY, R. (eds.) (1970) *Psychiatric case a community Psychiatric service: the Camberwell Register 1964-71.* Oxford University Press, London.

WING, L. (1976) *Early childhood autism.* Second edition. Pergamon: London.

WING, L., WING, J.K., HAILEY, A., BAHN, A.K., SMITH, H.E. and BALDWIN, J.A. (1967). The use of psychiatric services in three urban areas: an international case register study. *Soc.Psychiat.* 2, 158.

WIRTH, L. (1938) Urbanism as a way of life. *Am.J.Sociol.,* 44, 1-24.

WORLD HEALTH ORGANIZATION (1973) *International pilot study of schizophrenia.* WHO, Geneva.

17 Genetic aspects of human biology in urban–rural comparisons

John B. Gibson

The title of this book and the theme of many of its chapters imply that to some extent a particular range of environmental variables can be recognized in urban areas which differ qualitatively and quantitatively from those to which people are exposed in non-urban areas. Although it is recognized that most of the environmental variables will form a continuum between urban and non-urban areas and that no individuals will live their lives exposed exclusively to any single set of environmental variables, the central theme of this book is whether or not mean differences between these environments are associated with biological differences between people. Included with this are questions about whether groupings of individuals based on social or geographical criteria have any biological significance and if biological differences are found between the groups, whether they are the result of differing environmental experience of the groups, or due to other mechanisms promoting biological diversity within the population of any particular area.

In seeking answers to these questions it must be remembered that biological comparisons between any groups of individuals include not only differences that arise because the environments differ but also differences arising from genetic variety between the two groups which may not be related to the immediate environments to which the groups are exposed. I am not concerned here with attempting to characterize any environments or to defend an urban-rural dichotomy, but rather with illustrating the relevance of genetic factors to all studies directed towards making meaningful biological comparisons between identified groups.

Although there is a paucity of data on the nature and extent of biological variation within and between populations in industrial societies, a general but highly significant finding in human biology is that whenever a biological character has been investigated, considerable variation between individuals of the same age and sex has been found. The majority of the variation, whether it be in biochemical, physiological, or psychological characters, is not directly pathological and is usually regarded by biologists as being normal, but some of the variation is associated with disease. There are likely to be genetic components of the variation and genetic factors determining the capacities of individuals to adapt to particular environments or to maintain homeostasis in adverse environments.

Genetics is a science which can explain differences between individuals or between the means of some variable in separable groups of individuals, and in the present context two key questions can be formulated which genetic analyses would attempt to answer. (a) What proportion of the total phenotypic variance for each biological parameter we are interested in is genetically determined? (b) Does some of the difference in the mean values of biological variables between identified groups have a genetic component? It is axiomatic that the answers to such questions also reveal the environmental components of the biological variation although this important point is often overlooked.

Genetic aspects of the biological variation relevant to the theme of this book fall into five general sections. First, one needs to enquire into the extent of genetic variation in terms of the protein products of structural genes, regardless of their phenotypic effects, to provide some guide to the underlying level of genetic heterogeneity in the population. Second, the incidence and prevalence of genetically determined diseases should be assessed, even though there is no precise information on the mode of inheritance or the mechanisms of the genes involved. This section should include discussion of the getic components of biological variables that to varying extents are implicated in disease and the problems of the genetic analysis of such variables are illustrated by reference to studies on coronary heart disease.

Thirdly, evidence for geographical heterogeneity of genetic variation ought to be considered, as should, fourthly, the ways in which genetic convergence and divergence might occur. Lastly, but perhaps the crux of the whole problem, the limitations to the genetic comparisons of populations need to be discussed.

All of these topics involve theoretical and practical problems which in some cases are the subject of controversy in the interpretation of genetic studies in any organism. However primarily because man is not an experimentally convenient organism, genetic analyses in human populations are beset with additional difficulties and pose what appear to be unsurmountable problems. Nevertheless, in some areas of population genetics man is a convenient and well-studied organism, and in these areas genetic studies have been particularly rewarding in elucidating biological phenomena.

GENETIC VARIATION IN HUMAN POPULATIONS

The presence of genetic variation in any population is most readily demonstrated when individual phenotypes associated with allelic variation at a specific gene locus can be identified. McKusick (1971) catalogued what is often referred to as man's mutational repertoire, listing 574 phenotypes for which the mode of inheritance is certain and determined by single genes located on the sex chromosomes or autosomes. In addition he

noted 568 autosomal dominants, 418 autosomal recessives, and 64 sex-linked genes where there was strong evidence for the mode of inheritance indicated. This catalogue includes the polymorphic genes as well as those which are rare and determine specific diseases. Excluded are those phenotypes for which the genetic determination is obscure. Studies on red and white blood cell antigens (Race and Sanger 1968; Van Rood, Eernisse, and Van Leeuwen 1958), serum proteins, and genetically determined electrophoretic enzyme variants (Giblett 1969) have shown that in human populations (Lewontin 1967; Harris 1970), in common with those of most other organisms, on average about 30 per cent of the gene loci are polymorphic such that for these loci the rarest allele appears to be maintained at a higher frequency than would be expected on mutation - selection balance. These results suggest that the average level of heterozyogsity per individual is between 6 per cent and 16 per cent. Yet these estimates of genetic heterogeneity in the population are likely to represent a lower limit, for techniques presently available for detecting genetic variants of enzymes depend heavily on the amino-acid substitutions having effects on the charge of the protein molecule. Evidence is accumulating that within and between electrophoretic enzyme variants there is variation due to genetically determined alterations to the proteins which do not affect the electrophoretic mobility (Harris 1966; Gibson and Miklovich 1972; Bernstein, Throckmorton, and Hubby 1973).

Controversy about the maintenance of these levels of polymorphisms in populations has polarized into two schools of thought (Harris 1971) one interpreting the data as indicating the operation of natural selection whilst the other, whose proponents display enviable mathematical ingenuity, claims that alternative forms of alleles are neutral in their effects and that their respective frequencies in populations are essentially due to chance processes. Indeed it has proved extremely difficult to detect natural selection operating in human populations, apart from the well-known examples of blood-group incompatibilities, some haemoglobin pathologies (Allison 1964) and birth weight (Karn and Penrose 1952).

As it is not yet clear to what extent these polymorphic loci represent random samples of all variable genetic loci it is emphasized that extrapolations from the level of heterozygosity based on electrophoretic studies to levels of heterozygosity for other genetic systems must be made with caution.

The variation in many biological characters in human populations is continuous and only rarely have specific genes been identified. Techniques for the genetic analysis of continuous variables have been developed from the theoretical base provided by Fisher (1918), who showed that it was possible to derive measures of the resemblance

between relatives for polygenic characters, as the proportion of
genes in common was predictable for various degrees of relationship.
These biometrical techniques aim to partition the variation, first
into the generic and environmental components, and then to subdivide
the genetic component into that resulting from differences between
homozygotes and that resulting from specific effects of various
alleles in heterozygotes (Mather and Jinks 1971). The interpretations
of. such analyses applied to human material is fraught with difficulties,
for cultural and biological inheritance cannot always be separated
and may have similar effects. Children in a sibship might resemble
their parents because, for one reason or another, they share
similar environments or because they have most of their genes
in common with their parents. Resolution of these factors, which
may or may not be operating in the same direction for any particular character, is hardly ever possible, and familial predisposition by itself is open to a variety of interpretations
(Edwards 1968).

Theoretically, the genetic and environmental components of the
phenotypic variance can be partitioned by the use of twin studies,
but such studies have only rarely been carried out with the
most appropriate design. The technique requires comparison of
sets of monozygotic twins reared together with sets reared
apart, as well as control studies on age - and sex-matched
sets of dizygotic twins. As parental behaviour towards twins
can vary with the parents' belief of zygosity it would ideally
be necessary to take this into account in any comparisons. The
fact that it is possible for monozygotic twins to be discordant,
perhaps due to cytoplasmic factors (Darlington 1970), and that
the similarities and differences of the environment of a twin
pair cannot be measured, adds further to the difficulties in interpreting data from twin studies. Nevertheless, twin studies
have demonstrated higher rates of concordance in monozygotic
than in dizyogtic twins for many morphological, physiological,
biochemical, and psychometric continuous variables in human
populations (Table 17.1), indicating the presence of genetic
factors.

Casting a benevolent eye on all of these problems of the
interpretation of data on the genetic analysis of continuous
variables, it can be said that, in general, whenever adequate
studies. have been undertaken the evidence suggests that
genetic factors are implicated in most biological continuous
variables in human populations. This is not surprising for no
two individuals, apart from some monozygotic twins, will be
genetically identical.

TABLE 17.1

*Concordance in pairs of monozygotic and dizygotic twins (sample
sizes in parenthesis*

	Per cent concordance	
	Monozygotic	Dizygotic
Blood pressure	63 (62)	36 (80)
Pulse rate	56 (84)	34 (67)
Electrocardiogram	59 (39)	24 (25)
Electroencephalogram	70 (34)	30 (29)
Form of thorax	65 (64)	19 (49)
Form of diaphragm	64 (64)	21 (49)
Form of heart	60 (64)	14 (49)
Form of stomach	32 (24)	5 (19)
Beginning of sitting up	82 (63)	76 (59)
Beginning of walking	68 (136)	31 (128)
Smoking habit	91 (34)	65 (43)
Alcohol drinking	100 (34)	86 (43)
Blood-sugar concentration	33 (30)	9 (32)
Vaccination reaction	75 (25)	25 (22)
Phagocytic action	78 (42)	58 (25)

From Stern (1973) and other sources.

GENETIC FACTORS IN DISEASE

The biological variables that are of obvious relevance in
comparisons between people living in different environments
are those associated with the patterns of disease occurring
in the two groups so that genetic variation in susceptibility
to disease is of the utmost significance.

It has been estimated that at least 4 per cent of all live
births have a genetically determined condition which will
require medical treatment at some stage during the individual's
lifetime. Indeed Stevenson (1959) found in Ireland that 26
per cent of all institutional beds, 6 per cent of all consultations with general practitioners, and 8 per cent of those
with specialists were for patients with genetically determined
diseases. In general, the prevalance of genetic diseases of
various categories amongst admissions to paediatric hospitals
is higher than for adults and higher percentages of genetic
diseases among the causes of death have been reported in studies
in children's hospitals. Day and Holmes (1973) analysed the
primary and secondary diagnoses in 800 medical records of

paediatric and adult inpatients and outpatients at the Massa-
chusetts General Hospital. Their data indicate that 17 per cent
of paediatric inpatients and 9 per cent of paediatric outpatients
had primary diagnoses in which genetic factors were implicated.

Nevertheless, it must be stressed that most diseases with a simple
genetic component in which a single identified recessive or
dominant gene is involved are rare (Table 17.2). Some mild
single-gene-determined conditions may have much higher frequencies
in the population, but it has been argued that the serious
single-gene-determined conditions with incidences higher than
1 in 1000 are those where there is heterozygote advantage
(Carter 1969), although clear evidence for such examples, apart

TABLE 17.2

*Birth frequencies of some identified genetically determined
conditions*

	Condition	Mode of inheritance	Incidence per 1000 live births
Nervous system	Huntington's chorea	Dominant	0.10
	Myotonic dystrophy	Dominant	0.02
	Neurofibromatosis	Dominant	0.30
	Tuberose sclerosis	Dominant	0.02
	Neurogenic muscular atrophy	Recessive	0.15
Skeleton	Classical achondroplasia	Dominant	0.02
	Marfaris syndrome	Dominant	0.02
Intestines	Multiple polyps of colon	Dominant	0.12
Endocrine glands	Adrenal hyperplasia	Recessive	0.05

From Carter 1973

from sickle cell anaemia, is generally lacking. The commonest
serious single-gene-determined disorder in Great Britain appears
to be cystic fibrosis of the pancreas, which is reported to
have a population incidence of the order of 1 in 2000.
Chromosomal abnormalities are also rare, for in reviewing the
available data for adults in this country, Court-Brown and
Smith (1969) reported a frequency of autosomal structural
heterozygosity in somatic cells of 0.3 per cent. Sex-

chromosome abnormalities have a frequency of about 0.24 per cent among live births (Jacobs 1969), but it has been estimated that 25-40 per cent or more of all aborted foetuses expelled spontaneously are chromosomally abnormal.

Some tumors are determined by rare single genes, for example, the recessive gene for xeroderma pigmentosum leads to tumors of the skin and the dominant gene for polypersis often leads to cancer of the colon. Tumors of the retina are caused by the dominant gene for retinoblastoma and single-gene-determined tumors of the pituitary, parathyroids, adrenals, and Islets of Langerhans in the pancreas have been recognized. Predisposition to most tumors of various kinds does not have a simple genetic basis and environmental factors are involved, although concordance in monozygotic twins for the site of cancer is high, so that genetic factors are clearly indicated.

For the vast majority of diseases the evidence suggests that any genetic component is multifactorial, and individual genes have not been identified. Thus similar techniques to those required for detecting genetic components in normal variation must be used, but there are additional problems for there may be characteristic ages of onset hindering comparisons over two generations.

Most common diseases show some evidence of a degree of genetic determination, as the incidence amongst relatives is higher than in the general population, and Clarke (1964) has reviewed the type of information that is useful in deciding whether or not there is an inherited component to a disease.

As with normal variation, twin studies provide the least ambiguous evidence for genetic components of non-communicable diseases and in general concordance is higher for monozygotic than for dizygotic twin pairs (Table 17.3).

Carter (1969) has discussed the evidence for genetic factors in ischaemic heart disease, rheumatoid arthritis, and diabetes mellitus where in each there appears to be incomplete inheritance with a number of genes involved.

Similarly data on the major psychoses suggest the presence of complex genetic factors, and Slater and Cowie (1971) conclude that 'there is a strong case for accepting a genetical contribution to nearly all forms of psychiatric disorder'. Diagnosed schizophrenics, although perhaps concealing a variety of disorders with varying manifestations, have a frequency of about 1 per cent in the adult population. Although it is generally accepted that there is a genetic component in schizophrenia there is considerable controversy about the nature of that component; some favour a single dominant gene with limited penetrance, whilst others seek explanations for lack of penetrance in the possibility that a large number of genes, each of small

effect, are involved. It is unlikely that this controversy can be resolved without some clearer indication of the heterogeneity of diagnoses, and/or a biochemical indicator of the presence of a relevant set of behavioural symptoms.

Further evidence for genetic factors in the aetiology of many diseases comes from studies of associations between polymorphic markers on the one hand, and particular diseases and continuous variables on the other.

Reports of such associations are legion, but in the vast majority of cases subsequent studies have failed to provide support for any generality. Blood-group studies have been carried out in

TABLE 17.3

Concordance in twins for a number of different diseases

Disease	Per cent concordance	
	Monozygote	Dizygote
Arterial hypertension	25 (80)	6.6 (212)
Bronchial asthma	47 (64)	24 (192)
Cancer at same site	6.8 (207)	2.6 (767)
Cancer at any site	15.9 (207)	12.9 (212)
Club foot	32 (40)	3 (134)
Death from acute infection	7.9 (127)	8.8 (454)
Diabetes mellitus	84 (63)	37 (70)
Epilepsy	37 (27)	10 (100)
Manic-depressive psychosis	67 (15)	5 (40)
Mental deficiency	67 (18)	0 (49)
Measles	95 (189)	87 (146)
Paralytic poliomyelitis	36 (14)	6 (33)
Rheumatic fever	20.2 (148)	6.1 (428)
Rheumatoid arthritis	34 (47)	7.1 (141)
Rickets	88 (60)	22 (74)
Scarlet fever	64 (31)	47 (30)
Schizophrenia	69 (174)	11 (296)

From: Cavalli-Sforza and Bodmer (1971), Lerner (1968), and Stern (1973).

relation to the effect of cigarette smoking on lung cancer, and Cohen and Thomas (1962) reported an excess of group B among non-smokers and occasional smokers compared to a deficiency of B among heavy smokers. As there is no evidence for a deficiency

of B among those with carcinoma of the bronchus (McConnel, Clarke, and Downton, 1954) it has been suggested (Clarke 1964) that group-B individuals are likely to develop the cancer even though they are not heavy smokers.

Recently, Kellerman, Shaw and Luyten-Kellerman (1973) have obtained evidence suggesting that individuals homozygous for a genetically determined low activity variant of the enzyme aryl hydrocarbon hydroxylase are less likely to develop lung cancer than those homozygous for an alternative allele. It is not yet clear how the heterozygotes compare to the homozygotes, but work such as this holds out hope that some apparently polygenic characteris may turn out to be due to segregation at a single locus.

It is interesting that of the diseases associated with the ABO blood groups almost all are disorders of the gastro-intestinal tract or its appendages, and these probably provide the firmest examples of associations. People of blood group O are about 40 per cent more liable to duodenal ulcer than those of groups A, B, or AB and non-secretors are about 50 per cent more liable than secretors. There is evidence (Hanley 1964) that group O is associated with a larger average gastric acid and secretory cell mass than is group A, but these differences are not so apparent in comparisons of secretors and non-secretors. It may well be that the blood group O and non-secretor genes predispose to duodenal ulcer in different ways, and Clarke (1964) has lucidly reviewed these aspects in which immunological, hormonal and psychological factors are implicated in the aetiology of the disease.

The interpretation of associations is fraught with difficulties for they might arise through pleiotropic effects of the identified gene or through linkage disequilibrium involving genetically linked or unlinked genes. Distinction between these alternative hypotheses can only hope to be made through family studies and even then large carefully-controlled samples are required. Nevertheless, if a particular association is found to occur in most populations studied, it is good evidence for pleiotropy and directs biochemical research to investigate the effects of segregation at a specific gene locus permitting a direct attack on the biological variation associated with a particular disease.

GENETIC ASPECTS IN THE AETIOLOGY OF CORONARY DISEASE

Whilst it is impossible in the space available to review the literature on the genetic aspects of common diseases, the difficulties inherent in genetic analysis of any incompletely inherited disease can be illustrated by attempts to unravel the relative genetic and environmental components of coronary heart

disease.

The aetiology of heart disease is complex, with evidence suggesting that individuals with elevated levels of serum cholesterol, blood pressure, above average body weights, and electrocardiogram abnormalities appear particularly at risk in developing the disease (Keys, Taylor, Blackburn, Brozek, Anderson, and Simonson 1963; Paul, Lepper, Phelan, Dupertuis, MacMillan, McKean, and Park 1963; Chapman and Massey 1964; Gerler, White, Cody, and Whiter 1964; Kannel, Drawber, Friedman, Glennon and McNamara 1964; Kiessling, Schaaf, and Lyle 1964; Epstein, 1965; Gramer, Paulin, and Werko 1966; Seltzer 1966; Stamler, Berkson, Lindberg, Hall, Miller, Majonnier, Levinson, Cohen and Young 1966). In addition, associations between the incidence of the disease and particular patterns of behaviour have been reported (Ostfeld, Lebouits and Shekelle 1964; Jenkins, Rosenman, and Friedman, 1966, 1967, 1968; Zyzanski and Jenkins 1970). For each of these identified biological factors there is evidence for environmental influences, and in general it appears that the risk of developing the disease increases with the number of risk factors present.

Any of the biological factors could be affected by a variety of separate but interacting physiological and biochemical processes, such that the observed phenotypes represent the manifold effects of a variety of mechanisms each of which is likely to have a genetic component.

The biometrical approach to the genetic analysis of any of the biological factors implicated in coronary heart disease requires comparison of two generations of related individuals or twin studies. If the biological parameters are age related informative comparisons of the two generations will not always be possible, but further difficulties arise because the individuals to be compared may or may not share the same environments; indeed it is highly unlikely that the environments of any two individuals would ever be identical. Thus it is not surprising that the biometrical approach to any of the variables considered to be risk factors has produced equivocal results. Schaefer, Drachman, Steinberg, and Adlersberg (1953) found that the frequency of hypercholesterolaemia among the sibs and children of people with hypercholesterolaemia was higher than in an unselected sample and tentatively interpreted their results on the basis of the segregation of a single dominant gene with incomplete penetrance. Further studies (Schaefer, Adlersberg, and Steinberg 1958) revealed significant correlation coefficients for serum cholesterol only between blood relatives and not between husbands and wives. It was argued that as all members of families tend to share similar meals and a common environment the data suggested the presence of a genetic component although the inheritance did not follow a simple pattern. Consonant

results were obtained in studies of an Anabaptist religious isolate (Steinberg 1963) where people live communally, eat all meals together, and are offered the same food, although of course not everyone consumes the same quantity or components of the offered food.

In another attempt to control for familial eating patterns, studies in Israeli kibbutzim, where the parents and their offspring lived in different environments but ate in communal dining rooms, showed no evidence for associations in serum cholesterol levels between the two generations (Brunner, Altman, Rosner, Bearman, and Lewin 1971).

Even when significant correlations for serum cholesterol levels between generations have been observed the values for the father-daughter pairs are often higher than for father-son pairs (Schaeffer, Adlersberg and Steinberg 1958). Deutscher, Epstein and Kjelsberg (1966) reported an association between a child's level of cholesterol, systolic blood pressure, blood glucose, and parental risk of death from coronary heart disease, and again the association was more marked for mother-daughter, mother-son, and father-daughter than for father-son pairs. Investigation of the clustering in families of risk factors in a sample of fathers and their children revealed higher aggregations among father-daughter pairs than among father-son pairs (Thomas 1958; Deutscher, Epstein and Keller 1969; Feldman, Ibrahim, and Sultz 1973). These asymmetrical associations have usually been interpreted as evidence for some environmental factors differentially affecting members of family units such that daughters appear to be better indicators of their fathers' predispositions to the disease than are sons.

But such data can also be explained by a sex-linked mode of inheritance in which father-daughter and mother-daughter correlations are expected to be higher than for father-son — as the X chromosome in sons is derived from their mothers. Of course, any of the biochemical or physiological components of cholesterol metabolism could be sex-linked, but whether or not a sex-linked mode of inheritance would be detected depends on the relative contribution of that component to the total phenotypic variance in serum cholesterol levels. It is argued (Chapter 13) that serum cholesterol levels may be affected by the catecholamines, and at least in mice there is evidence for genetic variation in the activity of enzymes involved in the synthesis of catecholamines (Kessler, Ciaranello, Shire, and Bachas 1972). Thus with such a complex character as serum cholesterol levels the genetic analysis is confused by the multiplicity of ways in which a particular level of serum cholesterol can be produced. Recently it has been shown in cultured fibroblasts that the primary genetic abnormality in familial hypercholesterolaemia involves a deficiency in a cell surface

receptor for low-density lipoprotein (Brown and Goldstein 1974).

There is no less controversy concerning the extent and nature
of a genetic component of essential hypertension, where again
ambiguous data can be interpreted in a variety of ways. Platt
(1959) compared systolic blood-pressures of 252 siblings aged 45-60
- and of hypertensives aged 45-60 and obtained a bimodal distribution
which he interpreted as evidence for the segregation of a dominant
gene(s). However, Miall and Oldham (1963) found that the degree
of association between arterial blood-pressure of propositi and
their close relatives did not vary with the blood-pressure of
the propositi. Although Morrison and Morris (1959) also
obtained a normal distribution of blood-pressures in 302 symptom-
less London busmen they found that, whereas the blood pressure of
those busmen whose parents had lived to 65 or over formed a
normal distribution the remainder, who had a parent dead in middle
age, showed a bimodal distribution of systolic blood-pressure.
It has been pointed out (Keen and Rose 1959) that as those who
die in middle age include those who die of causes other than
hypertension, the finding of a familial resemblance in blood-
pressure tells us nothing of its relation to heart disease. A
further point which these data illustrate is that the form of the
distribution of phenotypes can be very misleading, as a normal
distribution could arise from segregation at a single genetic
locus if the environmental variance is significant. The form of
the distribution will often fit a variety of very different genetic
hypotheses, and we can draw no conclusions about the number or
nature of the genetic factors involved.

Extensive twin studies would perhaps resolve these problems,
for in a small sample of monozygous twin pairs Platt (1963)
reported complete concordance for severe essential hypertension,
and re-analysis of Miall and Oldham's (1963) data (Cavalli-Sforza
and Bodmer 1971) suggests that the variation in systolic blood-
pressure could be explained on the basis of a few genes with
dominance.

As far as I know there has been no attempt to investigate
familial resemblance in the behaviour patterns classified into
'Type A' (with high levels of competitiveness and time urgency)
and 'Type B' (with low levels), although there is evidence for
genetic components of other personality variables. It is however,
very likely that 'Type A' and 'Type B' behaviour are each
compounded by a number of variables some of which may be separable
by factor analysis, and hence it is likely that the genetics will
not be simple.

In summary it appears that there is controversial evidence for
both genetic and environmental components in the variance of some
of the biological risk factors involved in coronary heart disease,
but it is not yet possible either to quantify the relative
contributions of the genetic or environmental components or to

specify with any precision the modes of inheritance involved.

GEOGRAPHICAL HETEROGENEITY IN GENETIC FACTORS

Apart from a few notable exceptions there is a paucity of data on the distribution of genetic variation within the British Isles. Such data as do exist are inevitably limited to genes which can be identified so that the frequencies of different genotypes associated with segregation at a single genetic locus can be ascertained and gene frequencies calculated. In particular, the records of the National Blood Transfusion Service have provided detailed information on the distribution of the ABO blood groups, which has been extensively analysed and discussed, particularly by Mourant (1954) and Kopec (1970). Kopec attempted to draw geographical divisions that were internally homogeneous for ABO blood-group frequencies and significantly different to the frequencies in adjoining areas. Her results demonstrate extensive heterogeneity, with the frequency of blood group A increasing from north to south and from west to east, although the highest frequency of A is reached in the northern part of East Anglia. There are a number of important exceptions to this general pattern, with Glasgow and Lanarkshire having a lower frequency of A than the rest of Scotland.

Data on the geographical distribution of the frequencies of other blood group systems and genetically determined protein variants is, with certain exceptions such as phenylketonuria, patchy, for in general it has been obtained in intensive but geographically limited population surveys. Thus apart from Ireland (Sunderland, Tills, Bouloux, and Doyl 1973) we know little of the distribution of enzyme polymorphisms in the British Isles.

Nevertheless, many studies have revealed considerable geographical heterogeneity within relatively small areas. In their survey of eight Oxfordshire villages encompassed by an area of seven square miles, Harrison, Hiorns, and Gibson (unpublished) found significant differences in the frequencies of some genes both between villages and between the locally and non-locally born individuals. Other studies have produced similar results indicating considerable geographic variation in the frequencies of identified genes. Such differences have sometimes been taken into account in attempts to compare population groups for patterns of morbidity, as there is evidence for associations between some of the polymorphic markers and specific diseases. It is noteworthy that the north-south cline in the frequency of blood group A parallels to an intriguing extent a similar cline in morbidity although the mapped distribution of stomach cancer (see Chapter 10) differs in many significant respects to the relative A/O distribution.

When we turn to consider possible spatial genetic heterogeneity in the diseases or biological characters with incomplete inheritance we must admit that we have no way of identifying individual genes and counting their numbers in different areas. The biometrical tools for partitioning the genetic and environmental components of continuous variables in human populations do not provide a means of estimating genetic heterogeneity between different parts of the demographic population. Estimates of heritabilities obtained in one population sample cannot be compared in any meaningful way with those obtained in other samples in different environments (see below). And, as I emphasized above, we have no warrant for extrapolating from the frequencies of polymorphic genes to provide estimates of allelic variety of other loci which may be concerned with the variation in the relevant biological characters. Thus, although the Oxfordshire study also provided evidence of spatial heterogeneity in a number of biological variables with significant heritabilities, the authors were unable to partition the genetic and environmental components of the spatial heterogeneity.

Similarly the striking heterogeneity in the geographical distribution of congenital neural-tube malformations such as spina bifida cystica and anencephaly, which show an apparent south-east/north-west cline in Great Britain (Carter 1973), cannot be taken to represent a cline in gene frequency.

At best, there are some indirect methods which might be inform-ative, such as studies of those individuals who share a surname, and these have revealed associations with patterns of disease (Pinsent 1969) and might suggest that, as similar surnames indicate individuals who have through their ancestry shared to some extent a common gene pool, patterns of the frequencies of particular surnames might be used to indicate genetic similarities.

Thus for incompletely inherited continuous variables we have no direct evidence of spatial genetic heterogeneity in the population, although it would be highly surprising if it did not exist.

FACTORS PROMOTING GENETIC CONVERGENCE OR DIVERGENCE OF POPULATIONS

Geographical heterogeneity in the distribution of genetic factors in the population is open to a variety of interpretations that fall into three general categories. First, the accumulation of sampling fluctuations that have occurred generation after generation gives rise to random genetic drift such that part of a population may come to differ markedly in gene frequency from other parts of the population. Second, differences in the environment between parts of the population will bring about different forms of selection in different geographical areas, and, third, historical events (for example, both peaceful and aggressive migration) can produce

genetic heterogeneity of populations.

Effects of migration are usually invoked to explain a substantial part of the geographic variation in ABO blood-group frequencies in the British Isles, and Roberts (1973) has reviewed the possible effects on the genetic structure arising from movements of people into and within Great Britain. It is likely that random genetic drift and differential selection are also involved but evidence for these is difficult to obtain

The genetic interpretation of population structure necessitates information on population sizes, mobility, and patterns of mating. Meaningful comparisons between groups of individuals require knowledge of the extent to which the groups share a common gene pool via their patterns of mating, for this indicates the degree of genetic isolation between the groups.

Organisms are not randomly distributed geographically, and human settlements in particular occur as a patchwork of clusters of different areas and population densities separated by a variety of physical and in some cases social features. Migration occurs between these clusters, but the separation tends to give rise to a degree of reproductive isolation, with endogamy being more frequent than exogamy. Thus data derived from the 1960 Gallup Poll covering 3000 informants in England and Wales revealed that more than 70 per cent of all marriages were between people living in the same Local Authority areas (Coleman, 1973), and Thompson (Chapter 3) has described the complex patterns of migration that are at present discernable in the British Isles. The genetic population is extremely difficult to define, as any pair of individuals might well have ancestry in slightly different populations to any other pair. In the present context we are concerned with examining whether the populations of urban areas might share in different gene pools to those of the surrounding rural areas.

Rates of exogamy have increased over the last century with the development of transport systems facilitating movement of people between different geographic regions. These changes are evident in data derived from parish records of Otmoor. a rural area some 9 miles from Oxford, where in the period 1837-1900, 65 per cent of marriages were endogamous compared to 41 per cent in the period 1901-70 (Harrison, Hiorns, and Küche-mann 1971). The proportion of endogamous marriages contracted within the Otmoor parishes as a whole have been compared to those in the whole of Oxford City, and the data show that in both the rural and urban areas endogamy has decreased with time, but that there has always been a higher proportion of endogamous marriages in Oxford City (Küchemann, Hiorns, Harrison, and

Carrivick 1974). This result is not surprising, as rates of
endogamy increase with population size; villages and towns
with less than 10 000 inhabitants have an average rate of about
50 per cent endogamous marriages, whereas in towns of up to
25 000 inhabitants it is about 65 per cent, and 80 per cent in
towns over 50 000 inhabitants.

Exogamous marriage distances are also positively correlated with
population size, although this general trend conceals interesting
and divergent patterns. The proportion of marriage distances
below 5 miles decreases from 70 per cent in villages to 50 per
cent in places up to 100 000 population. For towns above 100 000
population the proportion of marriages within 5 miles is less than
30 per cent, but a similar proportion are over 20 miles, with a
median distance of about 13 miles (Coleman 1973). Such data can
be used to estimate the size of the breeding population in a
particular area. For example, in Ann Arbor, Michigan, the mean
distance from birthplace to marriage was found to be 110
miles, and this radius encompassed a population of 6.8 million,
providing a breeding unit of some 0.83 million (Spuhler 1961).

Patterns of marriage distance are not inconsistent with
geographical central place theory, which analyses the economic and
social influences of towns over a radiating area. This concept
has its biological and sociological counterpart in the view of
human populations as a series of overlapping neighbourhoods,
within each of which local knowledge and daily mobility habits
affect the variety of social contacts and hence the choice of
mate.

Other models based on principles of diffusion and gravitational
attraction have had some success in summarizing human mobility
(Cavalli-Sforza 1958) following Wright's (1943, 1951) pioneering
studies aimed at understanding the genetic consequences of the
geographical movements of people.

The quintessence of this approach is embodied in the
coefficient of kinship defined as the probability that at any
particular genetic locus two individuals will have a gene in common,
identical by descent (Malecot 1966). Given the distribution of
phenotypes and birthplaces over a region the coefficient of kinship
can be used to predict the spatial variation for comparison with
that observed, and using this approach Azevedo, Morton, Miki, and
Yee (1969) and Morton, Yasuda, Miki, and Yee (1968) have obtained
good agreement between observed and expected patterns in studies
in Brazil and Switzerland. Where the actual exchanges between all
geographic parts of a population are known over a period of time
models exist which predict the rate at which relatedness between
populations develops (Hiorns, Harrison, Boyce and Küchemann 1969)
and take account of differences in population size between the
clusters and incorporate stochastic elements (Bodmer and Cavalli-
Sforza 1968; Smith 1969). The relative advantages and limitations

of these various models have been discussed by Harrison and
Boyce (1972), but it needs to be stressed that all of the
models assume that the migration is not selective for any
character and that natural selection is not differentially
adjusting the frequencies of particular phenotypes in different
clusters, and hence that migration is tending to promote
homogeneity.

Although natural selection is difficult to detect we do know
that migration is often non-random and can give rise to
genetic divergence within a population. For example, Pinto-
Cistemas, Salinas, Campusano, Figueroa, and Lazo (1971) reported
that migrants from rural areas into the city of Valparaiso in
Chile had a higher blood-group O frequency than the recipient
population and that the frequency of O was highest amongst those
city dwellers with the fewest city-born parents and grandparents.
They also noted that socio-economic status of the migrants was
higher than for the non-migrants.

Indeed socio-economic stratification within the demographic
population can give rise to a degree of genetic isolation, for
the social heterogeneity is accompanied by positive assortative
mating for social class. The genetic effects of assortative
marriages are particularly important at the present time when
differential fertility based on socio-economic variables is
declining. Character-specific positive assortative mating
tends to maintain genetic variance in the population but without
changing gene frequencies (Crow and Felsenstein 1968). There
is ample evidence for differences in the incidence of certain
diseases and in the means of some behavioural and physical
characters (Davie, Butler, and Goldstein 1972) amongst parents
and their children between the socio-economic groups. A
proportion of the variance in some of these characters has a
genetic component and the socio-economic classes reflect
many environmental influences on psychological and physical
development.

Day and Holmes (1973) have reported some interesting data
(Table 17.4) on the primary diagnoses of paediatric inpatients
in which there is a higher proportion of 'environmental'
conditions in the lower than in the upper socio-economic
group. These data are difficult to interpret without more
detailed information on the patients and hospital catchment
areas, but they do suggest that analyses of hospital admission
records in this way might throw some light on the relationships
between social stratification in the population and genetic
heterogeneity.

Intergenerational social mobility will tend to promote genetic
homogeneity in the social classes if the migration is random
with respect to any of the characters with significant heritability.

TABLE 17.4

Frequencies of primary diagnoses of paediatric inpatients

Socio-economic status	N	Genetic	Probably genetic	Developmental	Environmental	Unknown
Upper	95	0.19	0.06	0.43	0.28	0.03
Middle	54	0.17	0.06	0.22	0.46	0.09
Lower	51	0.14	-	0.04	0.79	0.04

Both 'developmental' and 'environmental' categories are likely to include conditions with a genetic component. Dr.Day informs me that the high frequency of 'developmental' conditions is probably a reflection of the particular interests of the pediatric surgeons in the hospital.

From Day and Holmes 1973.

However, selective migration will have the opposite effect
(Gibson 1973) and tend to maintain or create genetic heterogeneity between social groups. We have evidence that intergenerational social mobility is selective for some behavioural
characters such as IQ (Gibson 1970; Gibson and Mascie-Taylor
1973) and Moran (1965) have argued that the higher frequency
of diagnosed schizophrenics in manual occupational groups
(Hare 1962) is due to the nature and treatment of the illness
fostering downward social mobility. Hiorns, Harrison, and
Küchemann (1973) have evidence that there has been less social
mobility in the rural area of Otmoor than in the neighbouring
city of Oxford, and it may well be that differences between
rural and urban areas in rates of mobility over time and in
the extent to which the mobility is selective have important
genetic consequences for the populations. There are, however,
few data on the distribution of major genetic markers between
the socio-economic groups in any area, and although we might
expect genetic differences in some continuous variables, we
have no means of quantifying the relative genetic and environmental
components of social class differences.

GENETIC COMPARISON OF POPULATIONS

The preceding discussion has attempted to show that there is
likely to be genetic heterogeneity within the demographic
population of the British Isles for some of the relevant
biological variables that need to be taken into account in any
urban-rural comparisons. We now need to consider to what extent
this genetic heterogeneity will affect the interpretation of
differences in the means of some variables in two or more
identified groups.

Clearly when the individual can be his own control in
investigations of the physiological or biochemical changes
accompanying a change in environment, genetic factors are relevant
only in so far as different individuals may show different
responses. But the presence of genetic heterogeneity in the
population will not confuse the interpretation of the responses
of individuals.

Where individual genes can be recognized, and hence counted
in two or more groups of individuals, direct comparisons of
gene frequencies can be made and are open to interpretation in
relation to any of the mechanisms promoting genetic divergence
or convergence in populations. There are no apt examples of such
gene frequency differences between human populations living in
rural and urban environments in the British Isles. In some of
the regions where malaria is endemic sickle-cell anaemia
provides an illustration of different environments adjusting
gene frequencies. Lehmann and Roper (1966) reported lower

frequencies of the sickle-cell gene in urban areas of Uganda
compared to the neighbouring rural areas. As the sickle-cell
heterozygotes are at a selective advantage in malarial regions,
these observations can be explained by the lower prevalence
of malaria, and perhaps better health services, in urban areas,
such that the fitness of the sickle-cell gene is lower in urban
than in rural areas.

With incompletely inherited variables the problems of population
comparisons seem intractable for group differences will be
correlated with environmental differences, and we cannot extra-
polate from estimates of within-group heritability to between-
group differences. At least in theory these problems can be
tackled by 'transplant' experiments (Thoday and Gibson 1970),
where random samples of individuals in each of the groups to be
compared are 'transplanted' to all of the other groups, and indeed
the conundrum can be solved by this technique in experimental
organisms. But there are always practical difficulties of
determining whether the 'transplanted' individuals are a random
sample of the group from which they came, and these difficulties
are particularly trying in human population.

Thoday (1969) critically discussed the limitations to the
genetic comparison of populations and suggested a technique by
which it should be possible to ascertain whether any two
populations differ in genes or gene frequencies affecting some
continuous variable. He makes the important point, however,
that 'evidence that two populations, living in different environments, differ genetically is in no sense evidence that the
difference between their means has a genetic component' (Thoday
1969). Thus for the present, we have no way of answering the
question whether there is a genetic component of group differences
in any incompletely inherited variables, and this must also mean
that we cannot say whether there is any environmental component.
Unfortunately some of the major questions prompted by urban-rural
comparisons of biological variables have for the present no
precise answers.

CONCLUSIONS

The main conclusion to be drawn from this outline of the
relevance of genetic factors to human urban biology is that
identification of some of the relevant genes concerned with
continuous variables and diseases would be extremely valuable
in any future research aimed at urban-rural comparisons.

The genetic analysis of continuous variables in human
populations has not progressed beyond partitioning the phenotypic variance into genetic and environmental components and noting
associations between certain traits and major genes. Whilst
the biometrical approach has been successful in showing that the

variance in many biochemical, physiological, and psychometric
traits has a significant genetic component and provides a more
complete analysis of phenotypic variance (Mather and Jinks 1971)
it cannot lead to the identification of individual genes.
Indeed, it has often been assumed that the effects of individual
polygenes would be so small relative to other sources of variation
that it is impossible to locate them in the genome and that a
large number would be segregating for any one trait. These assumptions have inhibited research for they implied that the intractable
problems must make it impossible to take the genetic analysis to
a level where the developmental or biochemical effects of some
of the component genes might be studied.

Results from different experimental approaches have recently
revealed that these assumptions were unduly pessimistic. Thoday
(1961) developed in experimental organisms techniques by which
effective factors can be identified, located, and shown to account
for a substantial proportion of the genetic variance of a quantitative character, and this technique has proved successful in a
variety of organisms as a powerful tool for dissecting the genetic
and phenotypic components of continuous variables (Spickett 1963;
Spickett, Shire and Stewart, 1967). Consonant results have been a
obtained by Spencer, Hopkinson, Harris (1964) Harris (1966), and
Eze, Tweedie, Bullen, Wren, and Evans (1974) in investigations of
enzyme activities in electrophoretic enzyme variants, for they have
shown that about 60 per cent of the phenotypic variance in human
red-blood-cell acid phosphatase activity is accounted for by
segregation of three alleles at a single structural gene locus.
In addition, and of prime importance, recent work suggests that
susceptibility to lung cancer might be determined by the
segregation at a single gene locus of variants of aryl hydrocarbon hydroxylase (Kellerman, Shaw and Luyten-Kellerman 1973).

Once the possibility is recognized that a proportion, sometimes
a substantial proportion, of the genetic variance in continuous
variables in human populations may be due to segregation at a
few loci with relatively large effects, an experimental approach
can be formulated. The location of polygenes technique makes use
of marker genes which are now available in human populations
primarily in the form of polymorphisms with alleles at intermediate frequencies, although the techniques must be modified for
human materials, where neither environments nor matings can be
controlled. Towards this approach Haldane (1963) and Thoday
(1967) advocated studies combining investigations of continuous
variables and polymorphic markers to search for associations.
Associations of this kind are open to a variety of interpretations
because they might be a consequence of the structure of the
populations studied and may not involve any linkage between the
marker genes and genes affecting the continuous variable.
Alternatively, the associations might be due to pleiotropic

effects of the marker genes or to linkage disequilibrium of
linked genes. Distinction between these alternative explanations could only hope to be made through family studies.
Penrose (1934 and 1938), Thoday (1967), Jayakar (1970), and
Haseman and Elston (1972) have suggested methods by which
studies of segregating marker genes can be used to investigate
linkage between continuous variables and marker loci. In
particular, Thoday outlined an analysis combining segregation
of marker genes and measurements on continuous variables in
families in which both parents were heterozygous for a marker
locus, whilst Haseman and Elston's technique makes use of all
types of mating with respect to a single marker locus and
requires data on both parents and at least two sibs. Inevitably there is uncertainty (Elston 1973; Renwick 1973;
Robertson 1973) about the sample sizes required for such
studies because these will vary with gene frequency, and with
the proportion of variance accounted for by the linked polygenic
locus (loci).

It should soon be possible to critically investigate these and
other techniques in human populations, for De Fries, Vandenberg,
McClearn, Kuse, Wilson, Ashton and Johnson (1974) and Gibson,
Harrison, Clarke, and Hiorns (1974) have described preliminary
results obtained in studies where family data is being collected
on a variety of psychometric and biochemical continuous variables
together with major genetic markers.

If successful in detecting linkages, this kind of work could
have immense significance for the study of quantitative variation
in human populations as it will open the possibility of detailed
biochemical and physiological investigations of identified loci
segregating in particular families and affecting the important
biological variables that need to be taken into account in
attempts to make meaningful urban-rural comparisons. Without
such information we are left in the position of only being able
to describe differences without assigning to either environmental
or genetic factors a quantitative component.

REFERENCES

ALLISON, A.C. (1964) Polymorphism and natural selection in human
populations, *Cold Spring Harb.Symp.Quant.Biol.* 29, 137-49.

AZEVEDO, E., MORTON, N.E., MIKI, C. and YEE, S. (1969). Distance
and kinship in north-eastern Brazil. *Am.J.hum.Genet.* 21, 1-22.

BERNSTEIN, S.C., THROCKMORTON, L.H., and HUBBY, J.L. (1973).
Still more genetic variability in natural populations. *Proc.
Nat.Acad.Sci.* U.S.A. 70, 3928-31.

BODMER, W.F. and CAVELLI-SFORZA, L.L. (1968)   A migration matrix model for the study of random genetic drift. *Genetics*, 59, 565-92.

BROWN, M.S. and GOLDSTEIN, J.L. (1974)   Expression of the familial hypercholesterolemia gene in heterozygotes: mechanism for a dominant disorder in Man. *Science, N.Y.*, 185, 61-3.

BRUNNER? D., ALTMAN, S., ROSNER, L., BEARMAN, J.E. and LEWIN, S. (1971). Heredity, environment, serum lipoproteins and serum uric acid: a study in a community without familial eating patterns. *J.chron.Dis.* 23, 763-73.

CARTER, C.O. (1969)   Genetics of common disorders. *Br.med.Bull.* 25, 52-7.

CARTER, C.O. (1973)   Nature and distribution of genetic abnormalities *J.biosoc. Sci.* 5, 261-72.

CAVALLI-SFORZA, L.L. (1958)   Some data on the genetic structure of human populations. *Proc. 10th Int.Cong.Genet.* I, 389-407.

CAVALLI-SFORZA, L.L. and BODMER, W.F. (1971)   *The genetics of human populations.* Freeman, San Francisco.

CHAPMAN, J.M. and MASSEY, F.J., Jr. (1964)   The interrelationship of serum cholesterol hypertension, body weight and risk of coronary disease: results of the first ten years, follow up in the Los Angeles heart study. *J.chron. Dis.* 17, 933-49.

CLARKE, C.A. (1964)   *Genetics for the clinician*, (2nd ed.) Blackwell, Oxford.

COHEN, B.H., and THOMAS, C.B. (1962)   Comparison of smokers and non-smokers. II. The distribution of ABO and Rh(D) blood groups. *Bull. Johns Hopkins Hosp.* 110,1.

COLEMAN, D.A. (1973)   Marriage movement in British cities. In *Genetic variation in Britain* (eds. D.F.Roberts and E.Sunderland) Taylor and Francis, London.

COURT-BROWN, W.M. and SMITH, P.G. (1969). Human population cytogenetics. *Br.med.Bull,* 25, 74-80.

CRAMER, K., PAULIN, S., and WERKO, L. (1966). Coronary angiographic findings in correlation with age, body weight, blood pressure, serum lipids, and smoking habits. *Circulation* 33, 888-900.

CROW, J.F. and FELSENSTEIN, J. (1968)   The effect of assortative mating on the genetic constitution of a population. *Eugen.Quart.* 15, 83.

DARLINGTON, C.D. (1970) Twin biology. *Heredity,* 25, 655-7.

DAVIE, R., BUTLER, M. and GOLDSTEIN, R. (1972) *From birth to seven,* Longmans, London.

DAY, N., and HOLMES, L.B. (1973) The incidence of genetic disease in a University Hospital Population. *Am.J.Hum.Genet.* 25, 237-46.

DE FRIES, J.C., VANDENBERG, S.G., McCLEARN, G.E., KUSE, A.R., WILSON, J.R., ASHTON, G.S., and JOHNSON, R.C. (1974) Near identity of cognitive structure in two ethnic groups. *Science N.Y.*, 183, 338-9.

DEUTSCHER, S., EPSTEIN, F.H., and KJELSBERG, M.O. (1966) Familial aggregation of factors associated with coronary heart disease. *Circulation* 33, 911-24.

DEUTSCHER, S., EPSTEIN, F.H., and KELLER, J.B. (1969). Relationship between familial aggregation of coronary heart disease and risk factors in the general population. *Am.J. Epidem.* 89, 510-20.

EDWARDS, J.H. (1960) Familial predisposition in man. *Br.med. Bull,* 25, 58-64.

ELSTON, R.C. (1972) Reply to "Message from a referee on the Elston method". *Behav. Genet.* 3, 319-20.

EPSTEIN, F.H. (1965) The epidemiology of coronary heart disease: a review. *J.chron.Dis.* 18, 735-74.

EZE, L.C., TWEEDIE, M.C.K., BULLEN, M.F., WREN, P.J.J., and EVANS, D.A.P. (1974) Quantitative genetics of human red cell acid phosphatase. *Ann.Hum.Genet.Lond.* 37, 333-40.

FELDMAN, J.G., IBRAHIM, M.A. and SULTZ, H.A. (1973). Differential filial aggregation of coronary risk factors. *Human Biol.* 45, 541-52.

FISHER, R.A. (1918) The correlation between relatives on the supposition of Mendelian inheritance. *Trans.R.Soc. (Edin.)* 52, 399-433.

GERTLER, M.M., WHITE, P.D., CODY, L.D., and WHITER, H.H. (1964) Coronary heart disease: a prospective study. *Am.J.med.Sci.* 248, 377-98.

GIBLETT, E.R. (1969) *Genetic markers in human blood,* Oxford and Edinburgh, Blackwell.

GIBSON, J.B. (1970) Biological aspects of a high socio-economic group, I. I.Q. education and social mobility. *J.biosoc. Sci.* 2, 1-16.

GIBSON, J.R. (1973) Social mobility and the genetic structure of populations, *J.biosoc. Sci.* 5, 251-9.

GIBSON, J.B. and MIKLOVICH, R. (1972) Modes of variation in alcohol dehydrogenase. *Experientia*, 29, 975-6.

GIBSON, J.B. and MASCIE-TAYLOR, C.G.N. (1973) Biological aspects of a high socio-economic group. II. I.Q. components and social mobility. *J.biosoc.Sci.* 5, 17-30.

GIBSON, J.B., HARRISON, G.A., CLARKE, V.A., and HIORNS, R.W. (1974) I.Q. and ABO Blood groups, *Nature, Lond.* 246, 498-500.

HALDANE, J.B.S. (1963) In *The genetics of migrant and isolate populations.* (ed. E.Goldschmidt). Discussant, 43. William and Wilkins, London.

HANLEY, W.B. (1964) Heredity aspects of duodenal ulceration: serum-pepsinogen level in relation to ABO blood groups and salivary ABH secretory status. *Br.med.J.* i, 936-40.

HARE, E.H. (1962) The distribution of mental illness in the community. In *Aspects of psychiatric research* (eds. D.Richter, J.M.Tanner, Lord Taylor, and O.L.Zangwill). Oxford University Press, London.

HASEMAN, J.K. and ELSTON, R.C. (1972) The investigation of linkage between a quantitative trait and a marker locus. *Behav.Genet.* 2, 3-19.

HARRIS, H. (1960) Enzyme polymorphisms in man. *Proc.R.Soc.B.* 164, 298-310.

HARRIS, H. (1970) *The principles of human biochemical genetics.* North Holland, Amsterdam.

HARRIS, H. (1971) Polymorphism and protein evolution. The neutral mutation-random drift hypothesis. *J.med.Genet.* 8, 444-52.

HARRISON, G.A., HIORNS, R.W. and KUCHEMANN, C.F. (1971) Social class and marriage patterns in some Oxfordshire populations. *J.biosoc. Sci.* 3, 1-12.

HARRISON, G.A. and BCYCE, A.J. (1972) Migration, exchange and the genetic structure of populations. In: *The structure of human populations,* (Ed. G.A.Harrison and A.J.Boyce), Clarendon Press, Oxford.

HIORNS, R.W., HARRISON, G.A., BOYCE, A.J. and KUCHEMANN, C.F. (1969). A mathematical analysis of the effects of movement on the relatedness between populations. *An.hum.Genet*. 32, 237-50.

HIORNS, R.W., HARRISON, G.A. and KUCHEMANN, C.F. (1973). Factors affecting the genetic structure of populations: an urban rural contrast in Britain. In: *Genetic variation in Britain* (ed. D.F.Roberts and E.Sunderland) Taylor and Francis. London.

JACOBS, P.A. (1969) Structural abnormalities of the sex chromosomes. *Br.med.Bull*, 25, 94-8.

JAYAKAR, S.D. (1970) On the detection and estimation of linkage between a locus influencing a quantitative character and a marker locus. *Biometrics*, 26, 451-64.

JENKINS, C.D., ROSENHAM, R.H., and FRIEDMAN, M. (19-6). Components of the coronary-prone behaviour pattern: their relation to silent myocardial infarction and blood lipids. *J.chorn.Dis*. 19, 599-609.

JENKINS, C.F., ROSENHAM, R.H., and FRIEDMAN, M. (1967). Development of an objective psychological test for the deter-mination of the coronary-prone behaviour patterns in employed man.   *J.chron. Dis*. 20, 371-9.

JENKINS, S.D., ROSENHAM, R.H. and FRIEDMAN, M. (1968) Replicability of rating the coronary-prone behaviour pattern. *Br.J.prev.soc.Med*. 22, 16-22.

KANNEL, W.B., DAWBER, T.R., FRIEDMAN, G.D., GLENNON, W.E. and McNAMARA, P.M. (1964) Risk factors in coronary heart disease: an evaluation of several serum lipids as predictors of coronary heart disease. *Ann. intern. Med*. 61, 888-9.

KARN, M.N. and PENROSE L.S. (1952) Birth survival and gestation time in relation to maternal age, parity and infant survival. *Ann.Eugen*. 16, 147-64.

KEEN, H. and ROSE, G. (1959) The nature of essential hypertension. *Lancet* ii, 1028-9.

KELLERMAN, E., SHAW, C.R. and LUYTEN-KELLERMAN, (1973) Aryl hydrocarbon hydroxylase inducibility and bronchogenic cancer, *New Engl.J.Med*. 289, 934-7.

KESLER, S., CIARANELLO, R.D., SHIRE, J.G.M. and BARCHAS, J.D. (1972) Genetic variation in activity of enzymes involved in synthesis of catecholamines. *Proc.Nat.Acad.Sci. U.S.A*. 69, 2448-50.

KEYS, A., TAYLOR, H.L., BLACKBURN, H., BROZEK, J., ANDERSON, J.T. and SIMONSON, E. (1963) Coronary heart disease among Minnesota business and professional men followed fifteen years. *Circulation* 28, 381-95.

KIESSLING, C.E., SCHAAF, R.S. and LYLE, A.M. (1964). A study of T wave changes in electrocardiograms of normal individuals. *Am.J.Cardiol*. 13, 598-602.

KOPEC, A.C. (1970) *The distribution of the blood groups in the United Kingdom*. Oxford University Press, London.

KUCHEMANN, C.F., HIORNS, R.W., HARRISON, G.A. and CARRIVICK, P.J. (1974) Social class and marital distance in Oxford city. *A.Hum.Biol*. 1, 13-27.

LEHMANN, L.T. and ROPER, A.B. (1966) The maintenance of different sickling rates in similar populations. *J.Physiol*. 133, 15-16.

LERNER, I.M. (1968) *Heredity evolution and society*, Freeman, San Francisco.

LEWONTIN, R.C. (1967) An estimate of the average heterozygosity in man. *Am.J.Hum.Genet*. 19, 681-58.

MALECOT, G. (1966) Identical loci and relationship. In: *Proc. V Symp.mathematical statistics and probability, Berkeley* (eds. L.Lecam and J.Neyman) Vol. 4, 317-32.

MATHER, K. and JINKS, J.L. (1971) *Biometrical genetics: the study of continuous variation* (2nd ed.). Chapman and Hall, London.

McCONNELL, R.B., CLARKE, C.A., and DOWNTON, F. (1954). Blood groups in carcinoma of the lung. *Br.med.J*. ii, 323.

McKUSICK, V.A. (1971) *Mendelian inheritance in man*. Johns Hopkins, Baltimore.

MIALL, W.E. and OLDHAM, P.D. (1963). The heredity factor in arterial blood pressure. *Br.med.J*. 1, 75-80.

MORAN, P.A.P. (1965) Class migration and the schizophrenic polymorphism. *A. Hum.Genet*. 28, 261-68.

MORRISON, S.L. and MORRIS, J.N. (1959) Epidemiological observations on high blood pressure without evident cause. *Lancet*, ii, 864-70.

MORTON,N.E., YASUDA, N., MIKI, C. and YEE, S. (1968).
Population structure of the ABO blood groups in Switzerland.
A.Hum.Genet. 20, 420-29.

MOURANT, A.E. (1954) *The distribution of the human blood groups.*
Blackwell, Oxford.

OSTFELD, A.M., LEBOUITS, B.Z. and SHEKELLE, R.B. (1964) A
prospective study of the relationship between personality and
coronary heart disease. *J.chron.Dis.* 17, 265-276.

PAUL, O., LEPPER, M.L., PHELAN, W.H., DUPERTUIS, C.W., McMILLAN, A.
McKEAN, H., and PARK, H. (1963) A longitudinal study of
coronary heart disease. *Circulation* 28, 20-31.

PENROSE, L.S., (1934) The detection of autosomal linkage in
data which consist of pairs of brothers and sisters of
unspecified parentage. *An.Eugen.* 6, 133-8.

PENROSE, L.S. (1938) Genetic linkage in graded human characters.
An.Eugen. 8, 233-8.

PINSENT, R.J.F.H. (1969) A transatlantic morbidity study.
J.coll.gen. Prac. 18, 137-47.

PINTO-CISTERMAS, J., SALINAS, C., CAMPUSANO, C., FIGUEROA, H.
and LAZO, B. (1971) Preliminary migration data on a population
of Valparaiso, Chile, *Soc.Biol.* 18, 305-10.

PLATT, R. (1959) The nature of essential hypertension.
Lancet i, 55-7.

PLATT, R. (1963) Heredity in hypertension, *Lancet* i, 899-904.

RACE, R.R. and SANGER, R. (1968) *Blood groups in man*, F.A.Davis,
Philadelphia.

RENWICK, J.H. (1973) Message from a referee on the Elston
method, *Behav.Genet.* 3,317-8.

ROBERTS, D.F. (1973)   The origins of genetic variation in Britain.
In: *Genetic variation in Britain* (ed. D.F.Roberts and E.
Sunderland) Taylor and Francis, London.

ROBERTSON, A. (1973) Linkage between marker loci and those
affecting a quantitative trait. *Behav. Genet.* 3, 389-91.

SCHAEFER, L.E., DRACHMAN, S.R., STEINBERG, A.G. and
ADLESBERG, D. (1953) Genetic studies on hypercholesteremia,
frequency in a hospital population and in families of hyper-
cholesteremic index patients. *Am.Heart.J.* 46, 99-116.

SCHAEFER, L.E., ADLERSBERG, D. and STEINBERG, A.G. (1958)
Heredity, environment and serum cholesterol: a study of
201 healthy families. *Circulation* 17, 537-42.

SELTZER, C.C. (1966) Some re-evaluation of the build and
blood pressure study, 1959 as related to ponderal index, soma-
totype, and mortality, *New Enq.J.of Med*. 274, 254-9.

SLATER, E. and COWIE, V. (1971) *The genetics of mental
disorders*. Oxford University Press, London.

SMITH, C.A.B. (1969) Local fluctuations in gene frequencies.
A.Hum.Genet. 32, 251-60.

SPENCER, N., HOPKINSON, C.A., and HARRIS, H. (1964)
Quantitative differences and gene dosage in the human red
cell acid phosphatase polymorphism. *Nature Lond*. 201, 299-300.

SPICKETT, S.G. (1963) Genetic and developmental studies of
a quantitative character. *Nature, Lond*. 199, 870-3.

SPICKETT, S.G., SHIRE, J.G. and STEWART, J. (1967) Genetic
variation in adrenal and renal structure and function.
Mem.Soc.Endoc. 15, 271.

SPUHLER, J.N. (1961) Migration into the human breeding
population of Ann Arbor, Michigan, 1900-1950. *Hum.Biol*. 33,
223-5.

STAMLER, J., BERKSON, D.M., LINDBERG, H.A., HALL, V.,
MILLER, W., MOJONNIER, L., LEVINSON, M., COHEN, D.B. and
YOUNG, Q.D. (1966) *Coronary risk factors: their impact and
their therapy in the prevention of coronary heart disease*.
Med.Clinics North America.

STEINBERG, A.G. (1963) Dependence of the phenotype on
environment and heredity. In: *The genetics of migrant
and isolate populations,* (ed. E.Goldschmidt).

STERN, C. (1973) *Principles of human genetics* (3rd ed.)
Freeman, San Francisco.

STEVENSON, A.C. (1959) The load of hereditary defects in
human populations. *Radiat.Res*. 1, suppl. 306-25.

SUNDERLAND, E., TILLS, D., BOULOUX, C. and DOYL, J. (1973)
Genetic studies in Ireland. In: *Genetic Variation in Britain*
(ed. D.F.Roberts and E.Sunderland) Taylor and Francis,
London.

THODAY, J.M. (1961) Location of polygenes. *Nature, Lond*. 191, 368-70.

THODAY, J.M. (1967) New insights into continuous variation, In. *Proc. 3rd Int. Cong.Hum.Genet*. (ed. J.F.Crow and J.V.Neel) pp.339-50. John Hopkins Press, Baltimore.

THODAY, J.M. (1969) Limitations to the genetic comparison of populations. *J.biosoc.Sci*. Suppl. 1, 3-14.

THODAY, J.M. and GIBSON, J.B. (1970) Environmental and genetical contributions to class difference: a model experiment. *Science, N.Y*. 167, 990.

THOMAS, C.B. (1958) Familial and epidemiological aspects of coronary disease and hypertension. *J.chron. Dis*. 7, 198-208.

Van ROOD, J.J., EERNISSE, J.G. and Van LEEUWEN, A. (1958) Leukocyte antibodies in sera from pregnant women. *Nature, Lond*. 181, 1735-6.

WRIGHT, S. (1943) Isolation by distance. *Genetics*, 28, 114-38.

WRIGHT, S. (1951) The genetical structure of populations. *Ann.Eugen*. 15, 323-54.

ZYZANSKI, S.J. and JENKINS, C.D. (1970) Basic dimensions within the coronary prone behaviour pattern. *J.chron. Dis*. 22, 781-95.

18 Urban images

Ruth Glass

WHAT IS 'URBAN'?

The question - what is 'urban'? - crops up persistently in
some form or other. But it usually remains unanswered - not
surprisingly so since it is unanswerable. (Regrettably, however,
this elementary difficulty is only rarely acknowledged.) The
adjective 'urban' is merely a term of convenience - of dubious
convenience; it does not refer to a universal, clearly
identifiable category of settlements, institutions or conditions.
It is merely a semantic device, or rather a semantic smoke-
screen, for lumping together quite disparate phenomena, thus
endowing them with a spurious likeness, which then tends to
be taken for granted without further scrutiny. So we get a
classic example of a circular definition. Essentially it boils
down to this: 'urban is urban'. (Or: 'urban is the opposite
of rural'.) And that might well be the end of the matter, but
for the fact that in this way the urban tag also become all
things to all men - a handy peg for airing their grievances,
their fears, and occasionally their hopes; a signal for
parading their hobby horses; altogether, a subject for emotive
soliloquies rather than for reasoned discussion.

CENSUS DEFINITIONS

It is only when the circular definition of the adjective 'urban'
is quite overt - as it is in censuses and other statistical
sources - that it begins to have a tangible, if limited, meaning.
In most censuses, the sole or main criterion which distinguishes
an urban from a rural area is its administrative status. A
'locality' (itself a vague entity, with arbitrary boundaries)
is called 'urban' if it is classified as such for administrative
purposes - regardless of its looks, density, the extent of its
built-up area; and irrespective of whether agriculture is still
a significant part of its economy or not. [1] As the administrative definitions of urban localities vary from country to
country, and over time, cross-national or temporal comparisons
of urban versus rural statistics have to be taken with substantial
grains of salt. [2] But at least when we look at such statistics
in any one country, at any one period, we do know what we can, or
cannot, read into the figures.

Fortunately, moreover, the statistical information is usually
more detailed - not simply aggregated in opposite urban-rural
columns. In most census reports urban localities are grouped
according to their population size; and administrative or

geographical sub-divisions of large cities are distinguished.
Such categorization, too, is rather crude (localities in the same
population size bracket, for instance, may be quite dissimilar
in all other respects). *[3]* Nevertheless, even the rough data
for the various size classes, or parts, of towns and cities do
indicate that both inter-urban and intra-urban differences -
in terms of vital rates, demographic, socio-economic and housing
indices, etc. - are as strong as, if not stronger than, those
between urban and rural areas. And this is so, for varied reasons,
in most areas of the world - not only, as one would anyhow expect,
in this country, which has by now been predominantly urban (in
administrative and occupational terms) for a whole century. (A
mere 22 per cent of the total population of Great Britain live
in rural areas; and an even smaller fraction - 3 per cent - of
the total labour force is engaged in agriculture.)

COLLOQUIAL TERMS

In common parlance, the existence of dissimilar urban settlements
is certainly acknowledged. The growing list of nouns for diverse
types and zones - towns, cities, capitals, metropolitan areas,
conurbations; central areas, West Ends, East Ends, suburbia,
ex-urbia, and so on - this list itself refutes the notion that
all such localities belong to the same species. Similarly, the
prevalent identification of particular place names with
particular forms of habitat and society reflects a detailed, and
indeed a remarkably accurate, perception of urban diversity.
Most large cities have clearly distinct quarters (such as Mayfair,
Hampstead, Bloomsbury, Soho, Notting Hill, Stepney and many more
in London) whose names alone convey an instant picture of life
styles - at once both a geographical and a social placing.

And, however reluctantly, sooner or later in academic discussions,
too, we have to revert to colloquial commonsense when we consider
subjects with an urban label. To begin with, it is usually helpful
to revise the vocabulary so as to avoid being hooked by a deceptive-
ly monolithic singular, such as '*the* urban society' or '*the* urban
environment'. The plural versions - urban societies or environments - though still rather vague, are more realistic.

SPECIFIC URBAN CHARACTERISTICS

But is it really true that the term 'urban' defies definition?
Is there not, after all, a family of urban settlements, large and
small, in all parts of the world? Are our images of particular
features which distinguish urban from rural localities merely a
snare and an illusion?

Yes and No. The term 'urban' is not subject to a universal
definition, although - or indeed just because - certain kinds of
urban settlement, especially large cities, evidently possess
specific socio-physical features which put them into a category
of their own. But - and this is the cautionary note - the accent
is decidedly on 'specific'. This has to be stressed not only
because of the strong individuality of towns and cities, even of
those in the same size classes, in the same country, at the same
period. [4]   More important still is the fact that none of the
miscellaneous criteria which might be used to distinguish urban
from rural settlements - such as population clustering, density
level, extent and pattern of the built-up area, institutional
equipment, economic and cultural functions, territorial mobility,
intricate social organization - is an absolute one. All these
criteria are relative - dependent upon the historical, geographical
and social setting in which they occur, and in which they are seen.
For example, there is no given population size or density which
turns a village into a town, or a town into a city (other than by
administrative decree). In a country or region where rural
habitations are scattered, every nucleated settlement, however
small, which would elsewhere be called a village, would be called
a town. And in the context of other settlement patterns, too,
distinctions between large villages and small towns are blurred -
so much so that the notion of the 'urban-rural continuum' has
had to be devised to rationalize the difficulty.

No doubt, it is easier to identify large cities. Indeed, our
images of 'urban' characteristics, in general, tend to be
synonymous with 'big city' characteristics, in particular. (And
they are therefore so problem-loaded.) Notions of urbanity are
focused on the assumed and observed features of specific dominant
cities within the horizon of actual or derived experience. Yet
again there is no fixed definition. The recognition of a big city
is not based on its actual population or area size, but on its
comparative size - in relation to other urban settlements, and
to the population scale of the region or country as a whole, at a
particular point in time. Thus, for instance, in 1871, the old
London of that date (covering the previous London County Council
area), which then had 3¼ million people, seemed to be just as
large as the new London did in 1971, when it had over 7½ millions
(in the expanded Greater London Council area). For at both dates,
London (within its old and new administrative area) had the same
share - around 14 per cent - of the total population of England
and Wales; and there was no other rival in sight. [5]

Moreover, both in 1871 and 1971 there were several Londons. This
is the rub: measurements of urban population and area size (and
thus also of densities) are not only relative, determined by their
context, they are also highly elastic within a given context -
dependent in London as in most other great cities upon the drawing
of discretionary or subjective boundary lines. [6]   (Hence the

perennial political and academic demarcation disputes.) And the
ambiguities of urban accounting are more noticeable still wherever
there is a coalescing of settlements which have been nominally
separate (as in the West Midlands and other British conurbations),
or a ribbon of contiguous localities along a coastal belt (as on
the west coast of the United States and in the Indian State of
Kerala). We can visualize, and classify, such ribbons of built-
up areas either as a series of villages, towns and suburbs - or,
just as well, as one large city region. There are all sorts of
notional permutations in the definition of urban entities.

Nor can we rely on any fixed images of the urban townscape
and of its equipment. Presumably, if we were dropped out of the
sky, without warning, into the centre of a great European city,
we would realize at once that we have arrived in such a place,
even if we could not name it, and if it were quite unknown to us.
(And this would be so also in some cities on other continents.)
But the recognition of the type of landing place would not be
equally swift in all parts of the world - not, for instance, in
Los Angeles or Johannesburg; in Accra or Ibadan; not even in
Calcutta or Madras. (Some cities have no central area with the
appropriate functions and layout on the European model. Others,
though evidently large and crowded with an impressive assortment
of people and traffic, are shabbily furnished: they do not
possess the visual decorum, the gloss and shop window sophistication,
or the material equipment, which we would expect in a great
metropolitan centre, as distinct from a provincial one.)

INCONSISTENT URBAN FEATURES

Naturally, images of urban attributes vary from culture to
culture, and over time. They tend to be ethnocentric, non-
comparative and unhistorical - indeed, paradoxically, urban
images are usually rather parochial. The city (in the abstract)
is thought of as something new, a product of recent history;
for better and for worse both representing and promoting
'modernization' (however defined). [7] And it is also assumed,
implicitly, that urbanity is a neatly packaged product - that
there are tidy combinations of characteristics which set off
cities from towns, or urban from rural settlements.

In the real world, however, this is not so. The various
characteristics which are supposed to denote urbanity - physical,
economic, social, cultural - are not consistently related, nor
do they necessarily coincide. Some towns and cities (including
national or provincial capitals) look and function like a loose
confederation of suburbs without a common core. Some are
administrative, commercial or industrial centres, but cultural
non-entities. Some lack the social heterogeneity, which is
usua-ly regarded as an essential attribute of urbanity; one

industry, one class, or even one set of age groups is predominant (for instance, elderly people in retirement towns;
young families in new towns).

Most important, the territorial definition of urbanity has
become rather weak. In this country, as in other parts of
Europe, North America and further afield, populations which are
urban in occupational and cultural terms, live in settlements
with pseudo-rural or genuinely rural physical features. [8]
Vice versa, major cities in the Third World have distinct rural
enclaves, dependent upon small scale animal husbandry or related
rural occupations. And these cities also contain itinerant
villages, peopled by migrants who move back and forth between
rural and urban places. Altogether, for various reasons, the
urban economy and culture is no longer synonymous with urban
location.

NO SEPARATE URBAN UNIVERSE

It follows that there is no such thing as a separate urban
universe with exclusive characteristics. 'Urban' features are
derived from, and pervade, the whole society, in all its diverse
locations. Towns and cities do not have a monopoly of social
inequalities, of poverty or wealth, congestion or spaciousness,
tension or relaxation, of regressive or progressive tendencies.
Such phenomena are not confined to towns and cities, although
they might well be more clustered and visible in some urban areas
than elsewhere because of the mere fact of population selection
and aggregation in these places.

But then again, such selection and aggregation, too, are
subject to general social trends, not to indigenous urban conditions
per se. True, once established, the pattern of urban grouping
and concentration adds a new dimension, and can have a momentum
of its own - though of varied kinds and with varied consequences,
depending upon its context and scale. (We would hardly expect,
for example, identical responses from the populations of
equivalent blighted areas in Belfast and Birmingham; or for that
matter even from the same Belfast locality before and during the
turbulent period.)

The whole question of urban characteristics is, and has to remain,
a hen and egg problem: it cannot be encapsulated in a straight-
forward cause and effect sequence. Therefore, whether one likes it
or not, one has to get used to the idea that the urban scene as
such, within its nominal boundaries, does not provide much scope
for environmental or social engineering. (For instance: we might
make plans for towns and cities in the fond belief that they are
discrete entities, capable of controlling their own affairs.
And yet no city, however massive - other than possibly a city

state - could be transformed within, and by itself, alone.)

ENVIRONMENTAL ENGINEERING

The fuzziness of urban definitions is sufficiently obvious to
be taken for granted. And so is the consequent unreliability of
the urban variable as a factor of differentiation between population characteristics and conditions. Nevertheless, a reminder,
however pedantic, that these definitions are rather brittle is
perhaps not out of place when we discuss urban environments
(plural or singular). For somehow or other, as soon as the
password 'environment' is mentioned (which is even more catching
with the urban prefix), the opposite assumption still creeps in -
the idea that urbanity has a firm territorial basis, with common
features and definite limits that can be precisely defined.
And this, in turn, is tied up with a mechanistic notion of the
effects of environment upon the state, physical, mental and
social, of its inhabitants.

It is a notion which comes in two versions - black and white.
Nowadays, it is usually the black pessimistic version which is
publicized, prompted by dire analogies drawn from the pathological
behaviour of the more disagreeable animal species. (Rats and
the rat race make good copy.)   In the nineteenth century, too,
similar doomwatch warnings were not uncommon (as a reaction to
Britain's rapid urbanization during that period). Even so, at
that time, environmental engineering also seemed to offer much
hope - an enviably positive view, perhaps best summed up by Sir
Benjamin Ward Richardson in his Utopia, *Hygeia - a City of Health*
(1876):

> 'Mr.Chadwick has many times told us that he could build a city
> that would give any stated mortality, from fifty, or any
> number more, to five or perhaps some number less, in the
> thousand annually. I believe Mr.Chadwick to be correct to the
> letter in this statement, and for that reason I have projected
> a city that shall show the lowest mortality.'

Richardson stressed that this was not a mere dream. 'The
details of the city exist. They have been worked out by those
pioneers of sanitary science.' [9]

And pioneers they were, achieving a great advance in public
health, not least by virtue of their trust in human capacity.
It is sad that we can no longer quite so readily share Richardson's
certainty that 'utopia itself is but another word for time'.

SOCIETY AND HABITAT

The sanitary reformers were so successful because their approach
was not wholly mechanistic. (Their notion of environmental

engineering was a rather flexible socio-physical one.)   They
did not think of the urban environment as a separate thing - as
a kind of ready-made physical container for urban society. *[10]*

There is an affinity, therefore, between the concepts of the
nineteenth century innovators of public health schemes and those
of subsequent literature of urban sociology - more affinity than
there is between the latter and some contemporary schools of
environmentalists. *[11]*   Although the sociological literature
does not present a united front - there are several urban
sociologies, some of which lean towards social engineering - it
has on the whole, explicitly or implicitly, a common notion of
environment, which differs from that in various other disciplines.
The concept of urban environment in this literature is, in a
sense, indivisible: it has no strictly demarcated boundaries -
temporal, physical or social. Nor has it any discrete components,
physical or social. It is one in which physical features are
inseparable from social organization, and therefore from the
historical, economic and cultural factors which influence such
organization.

Such a concept is no more than common sense. It merely serves
to remind us that the influence of habitat upon society cannot be
a unilateral process: it is not really quite so inexorable and
diabolical (or for that matter so easily ascertainable) as it is
often believed to be. And our attention is therefore directed to
the great variety of interactions between urban societies and their
'built environments' - indeed their artifacts, which are never
quite finished nor immutable, and which have not been magically
endowed with an independent, absolute power beyond the reach of
social control. *[12]*

We would thus expect to find, and do find, that the resemblance
between certain kinds of habitat is often more apparent than real:
environments which might look alike at first sight are quite
differently perceived and utilized by their inhabitants, and
thereby modified. This happens not only when there is a succes-
sion of occupants with contrasting socio-demographic characteristics (for instance, when a neighbourhood is socially upgraded
or downgraded); or when the original inhabitants are exposed
to a crisis which leads to a drastic change in their interrelations
(as in times of war, civil war, communal tension, or economic
depression). Similar differences in the use and shaping of
environments behind apparently matched facades in places A, B
and C occur also, no less strikingly, when the occupants, though
equivalent in economic and demographic status, differ in their
capacity for social organization.

This is illustrated, especially, when we compare the most
deprived urban slums in various parts of the world, or even in
different parts of a city. In one shanty town, the shacks made
of cardboard, mud, bits of wood and corrugated iron, pushed

closely together along narrow, unpaved lanes with choked
gutters, form in some miraculous way a lively, coherent
settlement. The shacks are repaired; wherever possible, the
exterior is white-washed or decorated with paintings. Inside
the hovels that serve as homes - often no more than 6 or 8 feet
tall and square - there is usually some ornament (a religious
picture, a plastic vase, a brass vessel, or even a transistor
radio). There is no lack of vitality among the children who
run around. Intense crowding, and the acute shortage of water
and sanitation, have been met by a remarkable resourcefulness -
a tightly organized, interdependent system of survival. Somehow
or other, despite the non-existence of latrines, human waste is
carted off; orderly queues form at the few standpipes, open
for a few hours a day; not a drop of water is wasted. The whole
place is governed by self-imposed rules of social conduct -
primarily by the law of give and take. [13]

By contrast, some other shanty town, near or far - with the
same kind of shacks, with the same poverty, congestion, water and
sanitation famine - is a scene of chaos, friction, filth and
desolation. Social disorganization is evident. The prevailing
mood is one of lethargy, interrupted by bouts of mutual
aggression [14]

ENVIRONMENTAL MODELS

One need not wait, however, to go to areas of extreme
deprivation (or to those at the opposite end of the scale which
co-exist in the same cities) to recognize that environmental
determinism, whether pure or diluted, does not make much sense.
We can see examples of the great variety of socio-physical
interactions all around us. They contradict the assumption
which nevertheless dies hard - that there are universal laws
in urban environments (or, for that matter, universal criteria
of urbanity). Nor would it be realistic to think of the built
environment as an assembly of separate parts - structures,
equipment, roads, traffic, open sites, sound, atmosphere, and so
on - parts that could be manufactured separately, and whose
respective effects on individuals and groups could be separately
ascertained and quantified. Apart from the elementary provision
of water, sanitation and some form of shelter in many 'developing'
cities which still lack such basic necessities, and of energy
supply, clean air and road safety in 'developed' cities, there
are scarcely any environmental components which, by themselves,
could be expected to have predictable influences on human health
or behaviour. (For instance, there is no reason to assume, or any
evidence to show, that given levels of population density *per se*,
or, as is often believed, a progression from low to high densities -
irrespective of the location, design and population composition
of areas with such densities - lead to increasing specific stress

symptoms. [15]   And again, it is implausible that any one
factor - such as crowding, noise, commuting - is the dominant
one in producing malaise.) [16]   But even if such propositions
were tenable, they would still be inoperative: it cannot really
be assumed that particular environmental parts could, or would,
be manipulated on their own, out of context, apart from all the
other socio-physical variables involved [17]

By and large, therefore, the probability that environmental
components, singly or jointly, have systematic additive effects
seems to be low.   Even their combined operations are liable to
be erratic.   The idea that it might be possible to identify the
precise level of urban environmental 'malnutrition' - a critical
aggregate of deficiencies which would tip the scale - is not a
promising one.   Similarly, it would be rather futile to try to
put all the pieces together so as to build not only a cautionary
model, but also an ideal model, of a total urban environment -
the best one, irrespective of period, situation and society.

EMPIRICAL SNAGS

Of course, there is no harm in trying to construct models,
so long as it is clearly recognized, and fully admitted, that
their empirical content is bound to be very thin. Propositions
about the mechanics of environmental cause and effect sequences,
in general (as distinct from some highly specific cases) cannot
be empirically tested - even if it would seem to be worth while
to do so.   They are destined to remain in the sphere of conjecture.

We might recall a few of the obvious snags which would arise
in a study intended to identify, or to disentangle, packages of
urban environmental stress factors - snags that would hamper even
a modest or pilot enquiry, for instance, confined to urban areas
in this country, at a given period.   (On this scale, the problem
of the relativity of environmental deficiencies would not be
as great as it would be for the design of broader, comparative
investigations.)

First, what exactly would be the pertinent 'urban environment'
for such an enquiry?   In a society such as ours, the majority
of the population experience different environments - at home, at
school or at work, for leisure;   and in each case both internal
and external environments - in their daily round, and certainly
during their lifetime.   And what about the highly mobile groups
which move frequently from one home or work place to another?
Would one then have to grade people according to the number of
environments in which they circulate?   Would one have to construct
different multiple environmental frames for different groups?   And
how could this be done?   (How could one weigh up the relative
importance of a person's various environments - urban and rural;

suburb and factory; Glasgow and Oxford, Manchester and New York,
etc? Which dominates or offsets the other?   This would clearly
not be dependent simply on the actual amount of time spent in
each during a given period.) It seems a daunting task. Even so,
the idea has to be ruled out that the sole or main relevant environmental category for such an enquiry would be that of people's
residential places at any one point of time.

Second, what would be the territorial unit for sampling - whole
towns or cities, or matching comparable districts within towns and
cities? The latter solution presupposes very detailed knowledge
of intra-urban differentiation throughout the whole country -
knowledge which we do not have at present, and which would have
to be obtained through a large scale study in its own right. And
yet the first solution - that whole towns or cities should be the
sampling units - would be still less satisfactory for our hypothetical enquiry. This solution would be based on a false assumption - namely that the resident population of a given city share a
common environment; and that therefore city location as such
(whether, say, in London, Liverpool or Leeds) is a genuine first
step in environmental classification. [18] In fact, cities are
rarely single entities: most of them are plural cities, containing quite different environments, even with distinct differences in climate. [19]

Third, how could the influence of particular urban environments,
or of their components, be isolated and tested in practice (whether
or not this seems possible in theory)? And how could this lead to
viable generalizations? Environmental (including micro-climatological) differences within cities are closely involved with socio-
economic differences - and not only in terms of a simple grading,
such as bad, middling, and good environments, occupied by low,
middle and upper social ranks, respectively. There is a kind of
population sieve : 'selected' groups, distinguished from one
another by multivariate characteristics (age, sex ratios, household size and type, tenure, housing conditions, occupation, origin,
mobility, etc.) live in specific localities (which also often
have mixed physical features); and members of these groups move
along circumscribed routes when their circumstances change.
(Social mobility, upwards or downwards, is usually accompanied
by equivalent territorial mobility.)   Increasingly, there is a
sorting-out in these respects in British cities. On the ground,
it would therefore hardly be possible to find truly matching
population groups in contrasting environments (that is, matching
groups in terms of the socio-demographic characteristics indicated),
or to find people who move from one place to a dissimilar type of
district while all their other conditions remain equal. None of
this is of much help for chasing propositions about environmental
determinants *per se*. [20]

ENVIRONMENTAL STANDARDS

Scepticism about notions of urban environmental mechanics,
and their empirical base, can hardly be avoided. But what
follows? Does it lead to a complacent or defeatist conclusion?
Does it mean that we need not attend to material improvements,
and can rely instead on the capacity of human beings to find a
modus vivendi even in the most miserable circumstances? Certainly
not. [21] Or does this scepticism imply that it is idle to
propose environmental standards, and unnecessary to test their
usefulness (in so far as this can be done)? Not at all - though
it is preferable to develop standards jointly rather than singly.
(There has been too much separatism in the advocacy of environmental causes, and too little concern for the interlocking of
socio-physical features.)

Environmental standards are essential, although they cannot
be rigid or absolute. Indeed, if they were, we would go backwards.
Environmental yardsticks have a socio-historical derivation and
validity: they are subject to changing expectations of environmental conditions; and they can, in turn, help to spread such
expectations, which are not synchronized even in any one society,
at any one moment of time. This process of changing, usually
rising, expectations is linked to a successive redefinition and
reassessment of risks - not necessarily quantifiable or vital
risks (of morbidity or mortality) but also, and indeed mainly,
risks of inequity (to use a shorthand term). In our society,
environmental norms are still, in principle, designed more often
for the purpose of lessening disparities than as direct preventive
measures against specified risks, in the sense that a shortfall -
a slight reduction of domestic space standards, for example -
could be proved to be harmful as such. Anyhow, such a reduction
would be unacceptable since it would be regarded as an anachronism.

So it is not a calculation of absolute risks that is involved,
but a gradual recognition of the changing tolerance - usually of
an increasing intolerance - for certain kinds and probabilities
of risks or disadvantages. (For instance, a given level of smoke
pollution in London, which would have been regarded as insignifi-
cant in the 1950s, would no longer be so regarded in the 1970s).
Altogether, therefore, in a society such as ours, environmental
standards are not dependent upon, nor do they need to be justified
by, a precise empirical verification of the risks which would be
incurred if they were reduced or ignored.

VALUE JUDGEMENTS

This empirical laxity should not be deplored: it is, in a
way, a by-product of 'development' - of a state of comparative
plenty. In periods and situations of extreme hardship and
scarcity, long-term or short-term, explicit rational choices

have to be made (at least in theory). But in such circumstances, the alternatives are so restricted, and expectations are so arrested or reduced, that there is not much scope for choice - in terms of a given value system. (To give a crude, not entirely fictional example: if, as a result of some natural or man-made disaster, a section of the British population were deprived of food and water, the provision of these necessities for them would have first priority, as a matter of course - so long as our prevalent value code remains intact. But in terms of some other codes, past and present, such deprivation would hardly be noticed: it would be regarded with indifference, or even with satisfaction. There are systems in which the neglect, or extermination, of vulnerable population groups is stipulated as a desirable objective.)

Perhaps we take our value code, and its pervasiveness - in any one city, in this society and beyond - too much for granted. It is certainly an integral part, if usually a tacit and rather incoherent one, of the development of environmental norms. Therefore, although we need not be intimidated by the lack of empirical rigour in definitions of standards, it is useful to keep it in mind. The criteria by which environmental conditions are assessed, and their categorization in policies or studies on these aspects, however carefully devised, are bound to contain substantial subjective elements, including inexplicit and divergent value judgements. It is well worth while to try to bring them to the surface.

HUMAN RESOURCES

The socio-physical concept of urban environments which has been indicated involves a re-examination of values, not least of value judgements about urbanity itself. One way of doing this might be to turn around the questions that are usually asked about urban conditions and their consequences.

We tend to look for causal relations or associations between specific environmental deficiencies (or 'pressures') and stress symptoms, individual or social. And that can be done in two ways either (as is indeed often necessary) by working backwards, so to speak, from cases with stress symptoms to an explanation of their conditions, or by a grand design of 'mapping' the whole universe of environmental situations so as to identify critical features, and then to follow up their effects. But the latter procedure is an endless one, quite apart from the inherent difficulty of establishing objective criteria for such an assessment, which has been mentioned. There are no environments, rich or poor, which are perfect, and no social situations which are free from stresses and strains.

An alternative approach can be suggested: to take as a starting point the notable resilience of social groups in dealing with stress factors, rather than the identification of these

factors as such. Comparative observations, historical and
contemporary, show how varied the apparent consequences of
environmental deficiencies are - even the effects of, and
responses to, the most dire deprivation. They provide a catalogue of remarkable human ingenuity and versatility in
utilizing inhuman environments. Even when men are, apparently,
prisoners of their environment, they still manage to retain some
trace of mastery over their environment.

When then are the elements in the make-up of social groups
which help to explain the varied degrees and modes of resilience?
A systematic concern with such positive questions is long overdue,
certainly in the sociological literature.

We cannot be sure that it would be possible to draw any viable
generalizations from such exploratory, comparative studies.
But there is one general result which would emerge - a more
thorough documentation, and through it a sharper awareness of
the tremendous waste of human capacity. And surely this is the
first step in any discussion on 'men in urban environments'?
Without it, we are liable to be bogged down; inhibited by
minor worries; diverted from the main theme - the great potential
that undoubtedly exists for the mobilization of human resources.

NOTES

[1] In the British census, the definition of urban areas has
    been strictly an administrative one. In some censuses,
    however, as in that of India, various additional criteria
    have been introduced - such as a minimum population size; a
    minimum proportion engaged in non-agricultural occupations;
    and/or the stipulation that an 'urban' place should have
    'pronounced urban characteristics'. Such attempts to give
    more meaning to the urban census definition in fact tend to
    give it less by introducing subjective, non-verifiable
    criteria; and thus making the definition even more circular.
    They also diminish comparability, and necessitate a re-
    classification of borderline 'towns' from one census to the
    next. A simple administrative definition, by itself, is
    therefore preferable. However, when (as has happened in
    some countries) rural areas are arbitarily promoted to the
    administrative status of towns, or are annexed by towns and
    cities for political reasons, the result is 'artificial
    urbanization', in statistical terms, which also complicates
    comparative assessments.

[2] This difficulty especially hampers comparative analyses
    of trends of urban growth and urbanization - that is, of the
    absolute or proportionate increase (or decrease) of the urban
    population in a given country or region. There is the

further problem that such trends are by no means uniform
in all parts of a city or metropolitan region. For many
decades, there has been generally in Western countries a
decline of the inner cities, while the population of suburbs
has been growing - actually, or artificially through the
annexation of rural areas. But even suburban population
growth has now generally been halted or even reversed.
Similar contradictory trends have started in many large
cities of developing countries. However, now as before,
such contradictions tend to be obscured because attention
is focused on average population changes for whole cities
or metropolitan areas, rather than on the changes in their
constituent parts. Hence the genesis of, and indeed
fixation on, mis-leading concepts and policies. Indeed,
persistent alarm calls about 'exploding cities', in turn,
divert attention from the actual movements which occur.
(See also note 8.)

[3] It is of course possible to use census and supplementary
data for a multivariate classification of towns and cities,
as was done by C.A.Moser and Wolf Scott in *British Towns -
a statistical study of their social and economic differences*,
Centre for Urban Studies, Report No.2, 1961.

[4] We all know that, for instance, Bolton and Bournemouth, though
both with populations of some 153 000 in 1971, or again
Oxford and Oldham both in the 105 000 to 108 000 population
bracket, have quite different personalities.

[5] Actually, in the context of the 1870s, London, though then
smaller in area, was seen as an even greater city than it
seems to be nowadays, on the contemporary scale. The earlier
image was influenced by London's rapid absolute and proportionate population growth during the preceding period: from just
under a million in 1801 to well over three million in 1871;
and thus from 10.6 to 14.4 per cent of the population of England and Wales during those seven decades. Moreover, by
the 1870s, London's territorial expansion, its development
as 'Greater London', had started, although at the same time
its relative population growth - its share of the total
national population - began to be stabilized; and there was
subsequently an absolute population decline - first of inner
London (since 1901); and then of Greater London (since 1961).
The London example thus illustrates various aspects of
'urban relativity', such as the ambiguities in the notions
of urban size and growth, and also the conceptual confusion
between the increase of the urban population and the expansion
of the urban territory, which has bedevilled urban policies,
and especially London policies. Attempts to curb London's

population growth - which were until very recently the key-
note of all London plans since the 1940s, and which continued
long after this growth had evidently already stopped - have
contributed greatly to a large expansion of London's area,
an exceptionally large one by comparison with some other major
cities in the world. (From 1871 to 1971, there has been a
more than five-fold expansion of London's territory - from the
area of the old to that of the new Greater London - versus a
just over two-fold population increase, as shown by the figures
in the text. One would expect some disparity - a territorial
expansion which is greater than population growth - as a
result of increasing space demands following from rising
space standards and technological changes. However, the
London disparity in this respect seems to be particularly
large.)

[6] The only exceptions are cities on island or peninsular sites,
or others with clearly marked geographical boundaries.
Otherwise, there is no foolproof method for an objective
demarcation of urban boundaries. The method of defining
city boundaries through a delineation of the various spheres
of influence of a city - journeys to work, journeys for
shopping, entertainment, use of services, etc. - is not fully
satisfactory since these spheres diverge, and also shift
constantly. The boundaries of Greater London, for example,
as defined in 1963, were by then already out of date.

[7] The city is thought of, especially, as a product of
industrialization. And this largely explains why urban
images were, and still are, so fearful, tied up with reactions
to the rapid industrialization and urbanization during the
nineteenth century. Memories of that period are not yet ex-
tinct - neither those of the apprehension with which the
potential 'mighty energies' of the growing urban industrial
working class, that new 'all-powerful explosive', was then
regarded; nor the memories of the harsh industrial discipline, of the squalid working and living conditions,
imposed during that period. More recent images of 'problem
cities' in an advanced phase of industrialization - sharply
divided, conflict-ridden, chaotic, controlled by remote
political and technological machines - reinforce the previous
anxieties.

[8] One of the first, if not the first, writer who recognized
this trend of 'urban diffusion' with remarkable foresight
was H.G.Wells in his *Anticipations of the reactions of
mechanical and scientific progress upon human life and
thought,* 1901 (revised edition 1914). He was practically the
only one of his contemporaries who read the signs (including

contemporary census figures) correctly; who distinguished
the contradictory changes of population decline in inner
cities, especially inner London, and suburban population
growth; and who therefore did not subscribe to the *idée fixe*
of the 'exploding city'. He saw that 'these great cities are
no permanent maelstroms'. It took over 70 years until the
trends which Wells had anticipated were eventually, and still
not wholeheartedly, taken into account in official planning
schemes. His forecast was that the antithesis between town
and country would cease: 'old town' and 'city' will be in
truth terms as obsolete as 'mail coach'.' Towns and cities
would be transformed into 'urban regions'. 'The boundary lines
will altogether disappear ... There will be horticulture and
agriculture going on within the 'urban regions', and 'urbanity'
without them'. And he realized, too, that 'it will not be a
regular diffusion ... but a process of throwing out the 'homes',
and of segregating various types of people'. (*op.cit.*)
pp.44,55, 60, 61, 64.)

[9] *Hygeia* is the published version of an address, which Richardson gave to the Health Section of the Social Science Congress
at Brighton in 1875. 'Depicting nothing whatever but what is
at this present moment easily possible, I shall strive to bring
into ready and agreeable view a community not abundantly
favoured by natural resources, which, under the direction of
the scientific knowledge acquired in the past two generations,
has attained a vitality not perfectly natural, but approaching to that standard.' (op.cit., p.18; quotations in text,
pp.17, 18 and 47.)

[10] For instance, Richardson's model city was primarily dependent
not upon its physical features, but upon its social
institutions. His main device for achieving the 'lowest
mortality' - a device which he thought could well be introduced in then existing cities - was a thorough and detailed
system of vital registration, and of constant health, food
and sanitary inspection.

[11] While this affinity of concepts may be incidental, the development of urban sociology, and in particular of the social
investigations of the late nineteenth and early twentieth
centuries, certainly owes a good deal to the empirical work
of the sanitary reformers. It was their zeal for fact-
finding, as well as the forcefulness and indeed the passion
with which they presented their reports and advocated their
causes, which undoubtedly set an example for subsequent
social enquiries; and thus contributed to a pragmatic
tradition in urban social studies which has not yet quite
vanished.

[12] Of course, social control over the environment is not, and
cannot be, confined to direct control, exercised by the
inhabitants themselves. And it is true that there are cases,
actual and hypothetical - extreme cases of environmental
devastation (Hiroshima and Nagasaki after the bomb) - when
social control is destroyed or powerless. But even then,
so long as any chance of social organization is left, the
built, or rather the shattered, environment will again lose
its primacy: it will once again become an artifact to be
readapted and rebuilt.

[13] Usually, in the type of 'organized' slum here indicated, it is
not the accumulation of filth (though by no means negligible)
which is noticeable at first sight, but the fact that there
is not much more of it, as would seem to be inevitable in such
conditions. 'And it is the people's reserves of energy and
their determination - to keep themselves and the place
together; to avoid constant quarrels with their neighbours
in such congested quarters - which are astounding. (See also
note 21.)

[14] The signs of such differences in social organization, or
disorganization, are consistent, and rather obvious to
anyone who is not blinkered, and who is prepared to look for
them. And it can also be assumed that the factors which would
explain these differences (such as factors under the headings
of economic relationships and cultural predisposition) are not
capricious: they can be broadly outlined, though they still
need to be systematically investigated.

[15] In any case, propositions about the possible health or
behavioural consequences of given population densities do
not make much sense - not least because the density
calculations themselves are bound to be imprecise,
equivocal and fragmentary. They produce variable results,
depending upon the units, scale and area boundary adopted for
measurement. (A simple distinction between gross and net
densities, for instance, will not suffice: there are different ways of calculating both.) Moreover, population density,
however measured, is only one aspect of space allocation:
building and circulation densities, for instance, as well
as the pattern of land use, are no less pertinent. Yet even
if precise multiple environmental indices could be, and
were, constructed - taking into account all aspects of space
distribution, including location, scale and design - one
would still find that the relation between the compound
environmental variable and individual or social malaise is
a very tenuous one. It is not the environment as such, but
its occupancy and use (by whom and how it is used) that

provide the clue. (For example, criticism of high-rise blocks is usually misdirected. It is not these structures *per se* that should be held responsible for causing stress, but the housing management that has put families with young children into such places - the very population groups for whom a bare high-rise environment is plainly unsuitable.)

[16] Nor would it be more helpful to widen the repertoire, and to single out for attention notional stress factors which are regarded as social or cultural phenomena, such as 'competition', a currently popular villain of the piece. The reservations which apply to attempts to isolate physical environmental components, and their cause and effect sequences, apply no less strongly to similar ambitions to hive off even more nebulous cultural components.

[17] This is not to say that specialization in various fields of environmental design and management (transport, housing, building techniques, etc.) is useless. However, the growth of such specialization, as well as the division of labour in dealing with environmental matters, which exists in legislation and in government departments, central and local, is rather deceptive. None of these disciplines or agencies can properly function on its own. Essentially, socio-environmental design and control are indivisible.

[18] This solution would be unsatisfactory for the hypothetical enquiry mentioned - so long as it is considered in practical terms, recognizing the limits of survey scale and procedure. However, in principle, the solution would be acceptable *if* it were proposed to use very large (40 to 100 per cent) samples, and huge questionnaires. On that basis, one would probably obtain a sufficient volume of data to establish a detailed socio-environmental classification, and to allocate the sampled population within each city according to the groups to which they belong. But in practice this would hardly be a feasible project.

[19] Micro-climatological differences within cities are more noticeable still in tropical than in temperate zones. And in many tropical, ex-colonial cities, there is an even closer, and much harsher, association between environmental and social grading than in Western cities: the poor have the worst climate (in the swamps); the rich have the best (on hill tops or along the coast).

[20] In this context, it should also be remembered that it is even more difficult to follow up people who move from comparatively good to bad environments than those who move in

the opposite direction. Nor have we had as yet, fortunately,
a suitable experimental situation in this country - such as
a compulsory mass migration and resettlement in specified
enclosed places - which might make it possible to observe
the effects of a controlled environment on both like and
unlike population groups. The actual pattern produced by
the socio-environmental population sifting which occurs in
our society scarcely provides any scope for such observations.
However, this sifting happens to be rather convenient for the
design of other kinds of enquiry - for that of social
investigations concerned with the multivariate influences and
cumulative benefits or hardships to which population groups
are exposed.

[21] This point must be stressed. For once in a while, whenever it
is noticed that squalid surroundings do not necessarily
contain (or produce) squalid people, when it is once again
discovered (or presented as a new discovery) that the poor
are human, their resilience tends to be taken as an alibi
for a re-affirmation of the *status quo*. It is then argued,
implicitly or explicitly: after all, as the inhabitants of
slums and shanty towns (or the pavement dwellers) get on quite
well, and seem to be quite happy, they can (or should) remain
as, and where, they are. And quite often the argument goes
even further, along 'preserve the noble savage' lines: it
is claimed that it would be harmful to the social organization
and cultural identity of these slum dwellers if they were
not left to their own devices, undisturbed in their squalor.
Needless to say that my conclusion is the very opposite:
the existence of so much mis-spent human energy and talent
points to a great opportunity, and indeed imposes an
obligation, to liberate the 'wasted' peoples from the
oppressive material degradation in which they live.